***He worshipped a god whose fiery maw belched flame and smoke and spewed the molten ore that built nations.* Once this god was named Baal. Franz Stoessel called him Success.**

The great blast furnaces of Pennsylvania's steel mills are the backdrop for a cast of unforgettable Caldwell characters.

Emmi, an idealist who fled Prussian Germany, who grew to hate and fear her only son Franz.

Ernestine, fragile, childlike, pampered daughter of a mill owner, whose blind adoration for Franz threatened to destroy her.

Baldur, Ernestine's crippled brother, silently and hopelessly in love with Irmgard.

Irmgard, who loved her cousin Franz with all her woman's heart and body . . . and despised him with all the passion of her invincible spirit.

"The lofty peaks of best-sellerdom are traditionally difficult to scale. . . . But there are three American novelists who have climbed to the top not once or twice but over and over again. In so doing they have established themselves as an elite among U.S. fiction writers. . . . All three are women: Edna Ferber, Frances Parkinson Keyes and Taylor Caldwell."

Life Magazine

Novels by Taylor Caldwell
in Pyramid editions

TIME NO LONGER
LET LOVE COME LAST
THE EARTH IS THE LORD'S
THERE WAS A TIME
THE BALANCE WHEEL
THE STRONG CITY
THE EAGLES GATHER
THE TURNBULLS
MELISSA
THE WIDE HOUSE
DYNASTY OF DEATH
THE DEVIL'S ADVOCATE

Taylor Caldwell

THE STRONG CITY

PYRAMID BOOKS ▲ NEW YORK

TO
MY BROTHER
with affection

THE STRONG CITY

A PYRAMID BOOK

Published by arrangement with Charles Scribner's Sons

Pyramid edition published March 1963
Fourteenth printing, May 1977

Printed in the United States of America

Pyramid Books are published by Pyramid Publications (Harcourt Brace Jovanovich, Inc.). Its trademarks, consisting of the word "Pyramid" and the portrayal of a pyramid, are registered in the United States Patent Office.

PYRAMID PUBLICATIONS
(Harcourt Brace Jovanovich, Inc.)
757 Third Avenue, New York, N.Y. 10017

FOREWORD

I wish at this time to acknowledge the kind and courteous assistance given me by the officials of the Bethlehem Steel Company of Lackawanna, N. Y., in acquiring the industrial background of this book. At all times they extended patient help to me, and gave me many suggestions. If I have made mistakes, they are my own.

While I was being conducted through the Lackawanna Plant, it was brought forcibly to my attention that great changes have taken place in America in labor-relations during the past few decades, and that there has been an awakening of a social conscience among the more powerful industrialists. I am sure that the Bethlehem Steel Company has played its tremendous part in this awakening.

TAYLOR CALDWELL

CHAPTER 1

THE GRAY November day was gritty with fog and coal dust. A visible ash floated through the dry dead air darkening what little light the morning gave like a palpable mist. The ash crunched under foot; it swirled against the walls of buildings and besmirched them still more, if possible. Every window was coated with it. Every door was streaked with it. Now that it was half-past six, and the dawn barely begun, a forest of chimneys, a veritable jungle of chimneys, vomited forth dark-brown, dark-gray and black volcanoes, which were absorbed into the permanent ash-mist of the city, increasing it, enhancing its body. The city heaved a subterranean groan, almost inaudible. It was morning. Behind a thousand, thousand walls the people were stirring, glancing heavily through the smeared windows, feeling a greater heaviness in their hearts as they faced the long, somber and oppressive day.

Those who were rich merely opened a jaundiced eye, shivered at the contemplation of the morning, and turned over in soft silken beds. Sleep was an escape. Those who were intelligent reflected that life had again demonstrated that the Chinese were quite correct in saying that most men's lives were lived in a state of quiet desperation. Those who were not rich, but merely middle-class, grumbled discontentedly, and pondered on whether the bacon would be burned this morning and execrated an overburdened maid-of-all-work for her languor or stupidity. And those who were poor and hopeless, and generally reputed not to be able to think at all, looked at the morning with the blind dull eyes of cattle, and felt, rather than reflected, that they were lumbering about in some vague, nightmarish pit of subexistence where even pain, however enormous, was a dim, all-pervading fog.

The mighty steel mills lined the border of the river, lead-colored, streaked with repulsive purple, green or blue in the sickly, underworld light. It was only half-past six, but the mills were muttering on a rising crescendo. The workmen were coming in, heavy-footed as yoked animals, their heads bent forward, their bodies shivering in thin patched clothing. They had only one desire: to be warm.

Mulberry Street was only one street in the city, but it was typical. It was a short street, begining in a confusion of cross streets, and ending abruptly against the blank brick wall of a paper-factory. Along the west side of the street there rose a three-story, thirty-family brick tenement, once terra-cotta colored, but now gray with coal-dust. The monotonous bay-windows were pewter-colored rectangles, behind which could be discerned the ghostly glimmer of dirty curtains. Three brown stone steps led down from every doorway to the street. Here the perpetual ash formed a thick layer on each step. Each bay-window indicated a five-room flat. Somewhere behind the shallow lugubrious windows a yellow gas-light burned, the light in a kitchen where the men were preparing to leave for work The acrid odor of fresh smoke smoldered through Mulberry Street. It was beginning to drizzle. The tenement house front became blistered with quick-silver drops of moisture, which ran down the windows and doors, and writhed in thin snake-like trickles over the brown stone steps.

Mulberry Street was paved with cobblestones, each one glistening with a livid light in the morning. Down this street, at intervals, clattered the brewers' wagons, laden, the horses, wet of rump and flank, bending heavily against the load. Now the sky lightened rather than brightened, and swollen with quicksilver-colored clouds, seemed hardly to clear the roof-tops.

A long, dull and doleful lament suddenly travelled the short length of Mulberry Street, accompanied by an equally sudden darkening of the sky, and a muted thunder. The lament pervaded the dank atmosphere, shaking it. The tenement and the cottages trembled, and the earth quivered underfoot. Behind the tenement was the long oozing slope of a muddy hill, littered with the household excreta of the dwellers, and at the foot of the hill a long train was passing, emitting its lament. Sparks and smoke blew from the engine, which was followed by an endless stream of cars, in furious flight. Once the train had passed, the quiet but faintly quaking rails gleamed in the morning's half-light. But the smoke continued to rise in dark choking billows, and obscured the dirty back windows of the tenement with another layer of soot. Mulberry Street crouched once more under the drizzle and the clouds.

One of the grimy doors opened, and a young man emerged into the rain. He stood on the hollowed brown stone steps and glanced critically at the sky. Shabby and frayed though he was, like the other dwellers, the folds of his face and hands grimy in spite of hard washings, he seemed like a stranger to the street and the city. Perhaps it was his bearing, which was almost jaunty and contemptuous. Perhaps it was because he was not bent, and did not shuffle or hang his head. He merely stood on the steps, surveyed the sky and the street with a curious detachment. And as he did this, he chewed contentedly on an apple. His worn workman's cap, brown and shapeless, was pushed far back on his head, showing his rough thick yellow hair, upon which the rain was dripping. In one hand he held his workman's dinner pail, covered with a white cloth whose edges were visible under the lid.

He chewed noisily. He detached one finger from the apple and reflectively scratched his ear. He beat one foot against the wet step as though in time to some internally hummed chorus. The foot splashed in the shallow pool of water which had gathered in the hollow step. His eye, surveying the street, was not bitter. It was just contemptuous. Swallowing the last bite of his apple, he hummed aloud in a deep and sonorous baritone. Now the humming emerged into fragmentary words, Franz Schubert's "Aufenthalt." His eye, sardonic and glinting, and intensely blue, continued to wander with heightened realization over the street as he sang. The strong and melancholy strain of the song, the passionate words, seemed to spring from some wry amusement in the young man. He kept his voice low, but the melancholy grandeur of the song took on a savagery and a faint fury from the very quality of his voice, and had there been a single listener to hear, though he might not have understood the German words, he would have understood instantly the import of the singer and the phrases he sang, and the meaning of his glance at the sky and the street. The nostalgic sadness of Schubert's love for his home became, in the voice of Franz Stoessel, ironic ridicule and a masochist's brutal self-disdain.

He stopped singing, but the unpleasant glimmer of a smile replaced the song. He leapt down the two remaining steps and began to walk quickly, but without haste, swinging his pail. He threw the core of his apple into a puddle, watched the breaking swirls for a moment, and walked a little quicker. His step was not a shuffle; he kept his head high with arrogance. But there was waiting patience in his arrogance, and no discontent, and still no bitterness. However, his three years in the mills had not been without effect upon him. His jocular walk was more than a little self-conscious and deliberately determined. The muscles of his shoulders and arms bulged from labor, but they did not weigh him down. He swung his arms lightly. He stepped high and firmly. As he walked down other streets, each more dreary and desolate than the last, his look became more and more rigidly detached and repudiating.

He stopped at a miserable little shop, skulking between a tailor's wan establishment and a grocery store. He bought a package of tobacco and filled his pipe. The tiny shrivelled old man behind the counter took his time about changing the silver piece Franz had given him. Franz had brought a breath of courage and non-surrender into the dark and fetid interior of the shop. The old man liked him, but his grin and his gestures were condescending, as they were always condescending to the "foreigners" who worked in the mills.

"Very bad morning, Franz," he said. He had been a bookkeeper, until his sight had failed. He was always careful to pronounce the endings of his words. It was his piteous belief that "real Americans" and superior people always pronounced the endings, thus distinguishing themselves from their inferiors.

Franz nodded. He sucked experimentally on his pipe. A cloud of good smoke emerged from his big mouth. He shot a critical but furtive glance at the old man.

"My mother gave me two slices of cheese cake for my lunch," he said. "She was pleased to hear you liked it. So, there is one for you."

He busied himself with his pail, which he had set on the splintered counter.

"That's very nice of her," said the old man, with condescending pleasantness. But a little wetness appeared at the corner of his sunken mouth. The shop was dark, lighted only by a swaying oil lamp hanging from the distempered peeling ceiling. The old man's hands grasped the edge of the counter as though he rigidly controlled them, but the big knuckles trembled a little. "Very nice," he repeated, in a dwindled voice, staring avidly at the pail. The tip of his tongue licked at the corners of his mouth.

Franz removed the snowy cloth and disclosed within a small covered dish of pigs' knuckles and sauerkraut, a half sausage, some rye bread, an apple and the two slices of creamy-gold cheese cake, tenderly cradled in a flakey pastry. Franz hesitated. He looked shrewdly at the old man, who had forgotten him, and whose whole poignant attention was fixed on the lunch. He was like some old emaciated bird hovering passionately over food after a starving winter. There was something horrible in his fixed ecstasy and tenseness. No one, thought Franz, should have come to the pass when the contemplation of even the simplest food could arouse him to such indecent rapture. It was especially indecent in the old, and shameful.

He frowned, and said, in his thickly accented and guttural voice: "My mother. How she is lavish with the food! No man could eat all this. Be my friend, and take a part of it. This sausage. Half of this bread. This apple. I do not like apples.

And this cake. If you do not take it, I shall have to throw it away, and it is a sin. No?"

With a painful effort, the old man removed his famished gaze from the pail. Again, he smiled condescendingly, and with indulgence. "My dear boy, how could I take your food? You work hard in the mills, I know. But then, if you really insist——"

Franz smiled grimly to himself. He placed the cloth fastidiously on the counter. These Americans! And soap was so cheap and plentiful. He put half his lunch on the cloth. He put the top back on his pail. The old man cocked his head whimsically and tried to survey the food with indulgent indifference. "I've had a big breakfast, too," he remarked, with affectionate self-reproach.

Franz made no comment. He nodded curtly, sucked on his pipe, and left the store. But he glanced back through the mired window. The old man had ravenously attacked the food. He was thrusting huge portions of the bread in his mouth. He crouched over his counter gluttonously. Franz's big heavy mouth twisted contemptuously. What an excellent philanthropist am I! he thought to himself, ironically. I am not really so good. But it does something really exceptional to me to give away food in this prosperous America! And to these superior Americans.

He reflected that his meal would be small. Nevertheless, the sardonic amusement in him was more valuable than food. It strengthened his fierce resistance to circumstance. Too much credit, he thought, has been bestowed on the giver. It would be harder to let the old Schweinskopf starve, and not nearly so pleasant. He hummed loudly to himself as he went down the street.

The streets were now filled with hurrying, shambling workmen going to the mills for the seven o'clock shift. They walked without conversation, without smiles, without glances beyond their feet. The desperate, piteous, contemptible laborers of the mills! Shabby, shivering, wet and hopeless, with dull fixed eyes, they aroused in Franz, not pity, but hatred. He deserted them for a roundabout way, which took longer.

He passed down a shut and squalid street composed of thin red-brick houses with shuttered windows. The street slept in its squalor of rain and soot, silence and furtiveness. Franz looked about him with interest. He jingled the change in his pockets. In five months, he reflected, he had not been able to afford a woman on this street. But in four more weeks it could be managed. That had been a pretty girl, that Hungarian, with the starved white face and gaunt eyes. She had coughed excessively. No doubt she was tubercular. In Germany, she would have been sent to a great clean white hospital, where, without cost, she would have been treated. He could not forget the girl. Probably she was now dead, poor creature. It was good. Human derelicts have no right to live. Those without resistance have no right in a world that demands resistance at every hour. His mother called it courage. But he knew better: it was resistance, and had nothing to do with any quality of the soul. Rather, it was compounded of contempt and anger, and a great disgust for the rest of humanity.

It was nearly seven. He began to walk faster. He had a long rapid stride, for his legs were strong and clean. He had come to a good middle-class neighborhood, two miles from his own home. The small houses were fresh and prim, the shutters white and green against the red brick. His walk quickened. More streets, each more prosperous than the last. And finally, a broad quiet avenue whose lawns, even in November, were wet and dimly green. Bare brown trees formed the skeleton of a nave that was all green shadow and religious silence in the summer. Beyond the lawns were houses of gray stone and red stone, pillared, pilastered, corniced and fretted. Behind really enormous polished windows he could see the silken shadow of curtains, the curve of rich velvets. Here and there was the golden glow of a lamp. Housemen, in the rain, were cleaning broad stone steps. Some were scouring horse-blocks. Franz stopped, as he stopped almost every morning, before a particularly huge red-stone mansion. The stone was the color of old dim morocco leather, and here the windows were twelve and fourteen feet high, and at least six feet wide. The house was full of porticoes, surrounded by pillars of smooth red stone. He saw gigantic carved doors and grille-work. An immense carriage-drive curved to the stables in the rear, and a driveway on the opposite side of the house led to gardens and conservatories. The air here was fresh and without corruption. He knew that in the multitude of chambers upstairs slept those who drew their profits from his own mill, the Schmidt Steel Company.

Here lived his employer, who had never dreamt of his existence. Hans Joachim Schmidt, his fine wife from Philadelphia, his invalid son, Baldur, and his daughter, Ernestine. Franz knew all about them. He made it his business to know. From a thousand obscure sources he knew that Schmidt had come from Bavaria, and had worked in the very mill he now owned, as a "puddler." He had married the aristocratic Frances Bradhurst. Of this marriage had come the invalid son, and the frail dark unhandsome daughter, now nearly thirty, and still unmarried. Derelicts, thought Franz, thinking of Mrs. Schmidt, her son and her daughter. Sad that such a one as

Hans Joachim Schmidt, of good German peasant stock, could have found no better culmination for his life of terrible effort Franz had seen him at a distance, a short, immensely fat man, resembling a stout bellicose pig disgruntled and soured in the midst of a luxurious sty.

Franz, who loved line and grandeur and simplicity, knew that this house was hideous, for all its grandeur and monstrous size. It expressed all the ugliness and wealth of Schmidt's life, all his power and his lack of taste. But it also expressed solidity and strength. Franz had caught glimpses of great gloomy rooms and ceilings twenty feet high. He had seen strings of shining carriages bowling up that driveway. He had seen a multitude of servants.

Suddenly, he heard a shrill, far wailing, and knew it was the seven o'clock whistle. He would be late. Cursing to himself, he turned and ran down the avenue. Leaving Pinehurst Road, where Schmidt lived, he ran furiously down several adjacent streets and hailed a horse-car, which came lumbering and weaving down its rails. He caught the car, swung himself up the steps, and paid his five cents. Five cents. He would not be able to afford his daily beer, now. But he was satisfied. He found a seat between two drowsing charwomen. He was content, as he was always content after seeing the mighty hideous house on Pinehurst Road. His resistance became stronger. He smiled to himself.

It was nearly half-past seven before he reached the mills. There they stood, gigantic, clouded with smoke, behind a wire barricade. Their thunder shook the wet air. Fire belched from their chimneys. Heaps of slag littered the gray, cinder-strewn grounds. The atmosphere was filled with acrid stench and cinders.

A new day had begun. He went into the mills.

CHAPTER 2

Hans Joachim Schmidt could not rid himself of his habit of early rising though he was now a man of wealth and substance. At six o'clock in the morning he was awake, no matter how late he had retired the night before. Achingly awake he was, red-rimmed of eye, inexecrable of temper, with a dull pounding behind his pink-skinned forehead and yellow-gray eyebrows. His belly was enormous. He always had the sensation that he had to lift his flesh from the bed as a man lifts a heavy extraneous load. His height was not more than five feet five inches, yet he weighed nearly two hundred pounds. His short legs were like barrels holding up the round dome of his body. He had apparently no neck. His round mighty head seemed set squarely on massive shoulders. His great face was square, the color of the inside of a pinkish saffron melon. His short broad noise was snoutlike, the nostrils flared and visible like holes in the center of his countenance, thus making his upper lip extraordinarily long. His mouth was thick and pink and swollen, brutelike and gross. Under those gray-yellow eyebrows he had tiny vivid blue eyes, like illuminated glass. They belied his general grossness with their fierce intensity and fixed glare. Over a damp ruddy forehead, perpetually wrinkling and frowning, stood the short coarse bristles of his hair, yellowish-gray like his eyebrows. Through these bristles could be seen his rosy polished skull, always damp like his brow, and shining. His ears were pieces of reddish flesh, crumpled against the sides of his porcine skull. His excessive pride lay in his tiny plump hands overgrown with curling blond hair.

He liked cold baths with plenty of soap and rough towels. His weight shook the thick polished floor of his gigantic bedroom as he traversed it on the way to his bathroom, icy-cold this early winter morning. The floor of the bathroom was paved with blocks of white marble, and the mahogany doors were set with mirrors. He ran cold water from the silver faucets, climbed weightily into the marble tub, and slowly sat down, grunting. The water eddied and foamed round his reddening flesh. He splashed it vigorously over his body. His skin was white as milk until the water flushed it with renewed circulation. He began to feel better, the ache subsiding behind his eyes. Covered with lather, he began to sing, hoarsely. It was a German song, a peasant song, of plows and fields and blue morning skies. Like most German lieder, it was melancholy, yet strong with gloomy grandeur. He forgot where he was. He saw his native Bavaria, dark and gloomy like the song, courageous and stormy and barbarous. It was his favorite saying that the Germans had escaped Roman civilization, had been unbefouled by the Renaissance, had retained their barbarian soul. Odin and Thor still lived in them, swinging sword and thunderous hammer. They had never emerged into reality. The black forests of legend were still filled with the Nordic gods, and lived close to the very breath of all true Germans.

He would often say that Luther had not merely liberated the German spirit from the fetid clutch of Romanism: he had really liberated it from the clammy, sickly effluvium of Christianity, so alien to that spirit.

He, Hans Joachim Schmidt, had married his aristocratic Frances. He had become an American industrialist. He had conformed to many American customs. But his resistance was powerful against all these circumstances. When he was alone, he was a German once more, washing more than his body free from alien corruptions. His overwhelming romanticism returned like a flood of healing water, rising up in him, an irresistible fountain. His blue eyes became jets of light. Even his grossness became strength and dignity.

He dried himself vigorously, and returned to his cold bedroom, a veritable vault in the morning's half-light. He would have no rugs. His huge four-poster mahogany bed stood in the center of the gleaming floor. It was a German bed, white and broad, heaped with thick pillows and puffy silken quilts. Curtains of old tapestry hung at the vast windows. He pulled them aside and stared gloomily at the gray day. He began to dress, taking a fresh suit from the towering mahogany wardrobe, and fresh underclothes and shirt and collar and cravat from the giant dresser. He would have no valet. He had fought out this battle with Frances years ago. He wanted no lackeys about him, he said. But the real reason was his unconquerable shyness and fastidious modesty, which would allow no other creature to see his nakedness. It was not that he was ashamed of his body. But he had an innate dignity, as well as shyness and modesty. He thought that unashamed nudity was a mark of Latin corruption, of abandonment of all self-respect and pride. Even his wife had never seen his nakedness.

In spite of his fat, he gave an impression of geometrical squareness. He wore black broadcloth almost exclusively, which he believed minimized his bulk. His linen shirt was glossy and stiff, as was his collar. He tied and folded his black silk cravat neatly. His little hands were dexterous and swift as a woman's. He had a small stiff blond mustache, which he waxed. He carefully brushed his bristling hair with a silver brush. He flicked open his great square of a linen handkerchief and sprinkled a few drops of Eau de Cologne upon it. The odor of lemon verbena filled the cold darkness of the bedroom. Then, creaking and starched, he allowed himself an approving glance in the mirror. Across his enormous black waistcoat hung the thick golden chain of his watch. On his cuffs glittered golden links. As a final touch he thrust a diamond pin into the depths of his cravat. He was ready for his breakfast. It was barely seven o'clock.

Carefully affixing his pince-nez on his porcine nose, he opened the door of his bedroom. The great hall outside was quiet and dark, the night-light still burning at the end of the corridor. The sleeping quarters of the family were on the third floor. On the fourth floor slept the servants. He walked down the carpeted hall to the stairway. From the enormous first floor a tremendous circular stairway of marble and mahogany coiled upwards to the fourth floor. Leaning over the banister, he could look down the well to the first floor, and up, to the fourth. He never tired of the pleasantly giddy sensation this survey gave him. A man could plunge straight down, he thought, with never a hindrance, to the bottom of that circular well. The German soul, always so furtively enamored of suicidal death, was titillated. It was not thought, but emotion, which made him go through this morning ritual of contemplating swift extinction. Nor did the emotion depress him. Strangely, it lightened him, put him into a more agreeable humor.

He went downstairs, a small fat bulky figure on those vast marble steps, moving with ponderous dignity and sureness. On the second floor landing there was a huge window of stained glass. He liked to pause and gaze at its gloomy somberness, its squares of dull green, purple, crimson and blue. When he was certain that no one observed him, he would stand on tiptoe and look through a few of the lower squares. He could see a bare tree, the sky, the neighboring lawns and a section of the quiet street below. But when he looked through a blue square, the view became nightmarish, spectral, a scene on the moon, where dreadful phantoms lurked just out of sight, but waiting. He would change to a crimson square, and the very same scene became a vision of the uttermost depths of smoldering hell, a stormy frozenness, a wild and savage cavern. Pleased, he would look through a purple section, and the scene became that of a land under graves, eternally dead and filled with amethystine mist. He would hum again, mystically soothed, the sullen capricious spirit under his flesh refreshed by its momentary escape into fantasy.

He was no egotist. He did not hug the thought to himself that no one ever suspected what lived within the folds of his gross body. Nor did he ever wonder what really lived within the bodies of others. That was because he was brutally selfish, and in spite of his romanticism, not possessed of considerable impersonal imagination. His sentimentality was for himself, but it was a clean, childlike sentimentality, without noxiousness.

The dining-room was fully forty feet long, and high in proportion, with a curved and frescoed ceiling. The walls were panelled in black walnut. Within the black marble fireplace smoldered a dim crimson fire which hardly relieved the chill of the room. The furniture, too, was of black walnut, high, ponderous, intricately carved, and upholstered in red plush. The gigantic sideboard was a-glimmer with ancient silver, polished and twisted. Above it, the mirror reflected ghostly shadows. From the ceiling hung a cluster of crystal gaslights, faintly burning. The mammoth china closet threw back darker shadows from its glass doors. The big long table was covered with a thin lace cloth, and here, in ceremony, was laid out his breakfast, a gross breakfast. For it was composed of thick hot pork sausages, eggs and pancakes, jams and popovers, cream and coffee.

The room, chill, splendid and gloomy, was weighted with silence. For the mistress and the son and daughter were still asleep in their beds. The butler came on slippered feet through the swinging door from the pantry, and drew out the master's chair. Hans sat down, growled a good-morning, and opened his napkin. His feet did not quite touch the floor, so a red velvet hassock had been discreetly placed there for them. He scowled at the sausages, suspicious that they were not at the right degree of heat. He cut off a large morsel and put it into his mouth. Still scowling, he chewed on it belligerently, while the tall gaunt butler waited with apprehension. It was nothing new for Hans to thrust the plate violently from him, bellowing, when the food did not please him, spilling the contents all over the table. But this morning the sausages were exactly to his taste. The scowl lightened. He grunted something grudgingly, and the butler relaxed with a faint sigh. In silence, and with deftness, he presided over the table. The only sound in the room, now, was the gross, loud, smacking sounds of mastication. The gaslights flickered. There were faint hollow echoes from all over the house. A subdued clinking came from the kitchen. All at once the wind rose and lashed half-frozen rain against the dull windows, which reached almost halfway to the ceiling.

"A bad morning, sir," ventured the butler, timidly.

Hans growled something, sullenly. His guttural voice was usually half incomprehensible to the English servant at the best of times. But the man had trained himself to listen for intonations rather than actual words. He was even more relieved. From the porcine growling he had discerned agreement with his remark.

Hans finished his breakfast with three mighty cups of good coffee. Then, and then only, did he open the newspaper near his plate. The butler lit his cigar which he had merely thrust into his mouth, waiting for the service. The man cleared the table, leaving only the final cup of coffee. He was halfway to the door when Hans exploded with a violent curse, almost causing the man to drop the silver tray in terror. He glanced with affright over his shoulder. But Hans was not looking at him. He was glaring at the paper. The butler fled in complete disorder, sweating.

What had aroused Hans's rage was the statement of a certain Senator that Hans's local competitor, the Brixton Steel Company, should be given the right to manufacture steel rails for the opening territories in the west. Hans knew Senator William Endicott, and hated that thin English face with the fine distinguished features and cold expression. When the Senator had let it be known that he was to visit Nazareth, Hans, without much delicacy, had extended an invitation to him to be his house guest. But the Senator had not even deigned to reply to the invitation. He had gone to George Brixton's home, instead. Mr. Brixton had invited nearly all of Nazareth's leading industrialists and best society to a dinner in honor of his guest, but he had not invited Hans and his wife. The double slight had infuriated Hans to the point of apoplexy. He had cursed with such violence that Frances had become really ill on top of her usual invalidism.

So, this, then, was what Endicott had been conspiring. Hans filled the morgue-like dining-room with volleys and thunders of foul German profanity. His hoarse gutturals bounded back from wall and ceiling. He flung the paper from him. He reached down from his chair and ground it under his polished boot. He spat at it, again and again. His face was bright purple. His voice rose to a scream. In the kitchen, the servants huddled together, whispering, their eyes glaring in terror at the pantry door.

After some time the uproar subsided. The butler tiptoed to the door and opened it an inch. The room was empty. He crept to the table and glanced through the velvet draperies that outlined the arch. He could see beyond the hall into the library. There Hans was stamping back and forth before the fire, his hands under his coat-tails, the cigar smoking like a volcano in his mouth. The butler could see the huge purplish face, the fat, boar-like figure. He shook his head, sighing.

He started, and again fled. Hans was crossing into the hall again. Whenever he was enraged, he took out his fury upon his family. Normally, he was totally indifferent to their absence from the breakfast table. He was not particularly fond of any of them except his daughter; in fact, he despised his wife and hated his son, and was glad of their customary absence. But he had to have victims. Now, shouting his curses upon them for a lazy, worthless congregation of imbeciles, he stamped violently upon the stairs to their sleeping quarters. The bristles on his head stood upright, like a pig's in a rage; his blue eyes shot out red light. His face was inflamed and congested. His shouts trailed after him in diminishing violence. The servants in the kitchen could hear his furious pounding on his wife's door.

CHAPTER 3

FRANCES BRADHURST SCHMIDT aroused herself out of her warm silken cave of a bed like a sick dark thin cat. Her room, all quilted satin French luxury, gilt, mirrors, eighteenth-century portraits of gay powdered gentlemen and ladies, perfume, ruffled satin draperies, plushy rugs and pale ornate furniture, was a strange setting for this meagre and feverish woman with her ailing flesh and sunken invalid's eyes. She was an alien in this lushness. Her body was shrunken and gaunt, and hardly made a rise under the puffy embroidered quilts. A fire burned night and day in its yellow-marble fireplace, for she was always cold and shivering and sniffling.

Rudely startled from uneasy slumber by her husband's bellowings, she sat upright on her gleaming pillows, pushing back her black, gray-streaked hair. She blinked her slightly bleared eyes. Her dry mouth opened on a muffled sound of terror. She fumbled on her bed-table, and lit one of the candles in the elaborate silver-gilt candelabrum. Then she drew the quilts up to her chin and called faintly: "Yes? Hans?"

He flung open the door. His snout of a nose wrinkled as usual as the odors of the room assailed it: stale perfume, closeness, and the sickly sweet effluvium of a chamber in which an invalid had slept all night with closed windows. He looked across the littered waste of thick purplish rugs to the bed, and grunted his disgust. In the aura of yellow candelight he glared at his wife with inimical rage and hatred. He could see her thin huddled shoulders behind the quilts, her long sallow face with its jutting cheekbones, her great dark eyes ringed and swollen. But her terror satisfied him even through his rage.

Shouting incoherently, he rushed at the windows. He tore

aside the golden and mauve draperies. The stream of gray light flowed in. He flung open a window, and the cold damp air swirled into the room. The fire crackled and smoked. Then he turned back to his wife, breathing violently, glaring at her with red eyes of fury.

"Seven o'clock, and you lie there and stink!" he shouted. When in a fit of madness like this his guttural accents thickened to the point of unintelligibility. "Seven o'clock, already, and there you lie! I eat my breakfast alone. I live alone. And the day goes on. A wife haf I! A wife!"

She gazed at him, petrified, frantically speechless. Once, early in their married life, he had struck her heavily. He had never done that again. But she still experienced that horror, that terror of death, whenever he was like this, after more than thirty years. She was convinced that she would die if he ever hit her again, die, not of the blow, but of that horror, that loathesome blackness. It was not death that she feared so much as the spiritual disintegration which would precede it.

He stamped to the bed, and she watched him come, her eyes growing larger and larger, and now brilliant with her awful attempts to keep down the drowning clutch on her throat. He stood at her feet, letting her see his disgust and detestation, his repudiation of her as a woman and a wife. She hardly breathed. But under the silken shroud of her nightgown her heart quivered and beat. She could not take her gaze from him. That gaze was like two frail arms extended to ward off a blow, to prevent it. If she looked away for an instant, she was certain that he would attack her.

"A wife!" he repeated, and then deliberately spat sideways on the rug. The nostrils in her long thin nose, bony and aristocratic, trembled. "Haf I a wife? Haf I ever had a wife? No! By Gott, no! I haf had a meowing cat. A sick scrawny cat! What a wife for a man like Hans Schmidt!"

Again her mouth opened, and emitted a piteous sound like a sigh. She shivered. The open window made the room cold. The draperies blew inward. She could see the tops of the empty trees, the wind-lashed rain. The candle flickered. Her face was ghastly, and slightly damp, and she had a look of death.

The door of her dressing room opened and her stout German maid entered. Matilda was a huge woman of thirty-five, buxom, phlegmatic, rosy and strong, with a mass of light-brown hair under her cap. Frances felt rather than saw her enter, and still without removing her eyes from her husband she cried out thinly: "Matilda!"

"Yes, ma'am," said Matilda. The maid stared for an instant like an ox at Hans. "Good morning, sir," she said amiably, as though his visit were customary, and his rage nonexistent. She stirred up the fire. Her buttocks, large and glossy, were outlined under her voluminous black silk skirts, as she poked at the fire. She passed Hans with a respectfully bent head, and drew the velvet curtains a little closer about the windows, which she closed. She moved surely and quietly, for all her bulk. Her round pink face was expressionless, yet pleasantly preoccupied. The huddled woman on the bed, the raucously breathing fat man at the foot of that bed, watched her with a kind of hypnotism. Frances's dry withered lips moved in a soundless prayer that Matilda would not leave the room. Hans was fascinated by this healthiness and placidity and sweet-smelling freshness. His rage began to abate. He loved health and robustness, and Matilda had these in earthy measure. To him, she resembled the cows he had once driven to pasture, sleek, handsome because they were strong and without sickness, serving a simple good purpose, and filling an ordained place in an orderly universe. It was true that she was overly stout, her black seams straining, her bosom like a pillow, her face that of a peasant, without great intelligence or much understanding. But all these things only added to her completeness and rightness.

Hans spoke to her in his native tongue: "I have not seen you before. When did you come?"

She turned to him quietly, but, being well-trained, and a German woman, she did not look at him directly. "I have been here two weeks, mein herr. I came from Saxony six months ago."

"Ah," he grunted. He plucked at the wax ends of his mustache. His belly swelled. But he was more pleased than ever. He forgot the sick woman on the bed, who had borne him two children. And Frances watched him. Slowly, the pain and terror abated in her heart. She gave a slow sad sigh. But she could not yet relax, though all the frail muscles in her body cried out against their own tenseness. She was afraid to lie down again, lest his rage rise against her once more. So she sat there, the quilts up to her chin, fright still brilliant in her sick eyes. She prayed that he would go now, and leave her to the peace of her medicines and her fire, and the strong ministering hands of Matilda. Coldness still lay like a sheath of ice over her thin legs and arms.

Hans, musing pleasantly on Matilda, continued to watch the maid with her competent hands and swift sure movements. Ah, what a woman! He had forgotten, in America, that there were such women. His mother had been such a one, and his sisters. They had smelled so of clean earth, wind, bread and milk. They had had hands like these, big and red and scoured of nail. They had worked hard, and long, in the fields and the house, among many clean children, yet they had had this freshness, this utter cleanliness. A frown suddenly appeared on his face as he remembered Frances's friends. They were not women! Perfumed, curled, whining, clad in silks and furs and velvet bonnets, with thin white faces and sick avid eyes, stepping from carriage to threshold and from threshold to carriage, shivering! He could hear their voices, high and faint and affected, and always with that undertone of delicate complaint. They were not women, with their muffs and gloves and lace handkerchiefs. They had no bodies, only bones covered by sick decaying flesh; for all the perfumed soaps, they were unclean. They were insults to warm luxurious nature. Yet, he had slept with such a one as these, and an outraged rigor stiffened his fat body, as though he had touched pollution. He felt corrupted in his flesh, befouled.

He mused upon Matilda. She would be good in a man's bed, sweet and strong and docile. A man would be reminded of hay and sunshine and distant cow-bells, and peace and tranquillity. He could wash himself in this fountain of fresh water, and the pollution would be gone from him. He was filled with a deep angry melancholy, a nostalgia, not of the spirit, but of the flesh. All his emotions came from his flesh, and never from his mind. All his frequent psychic disturbances, all his rages and hungers and ruthlessnesses, arose from no deep subconscious core of the mind, but from his body. Now he lusted for Matilda, not with a sensual lust, but with a mournfulness of deprived flesh, a really physical hunger.

Still musing upon her, and hungering, he did not hear his wife's bedroom door open, and was not aware of his son, Baldur, until he heard his low sweet voice anxiously asking Frances if she were well. He had, he said, heard a commotion, and thought perhaps she had been taken ill again. Frances, with renewed fright, was unable to speak. She merely thrust her thin hot trembling hand out to him, as though she were drowning. She knew how Hans hated his son.

At the sound of that detested voice, all Hans's fury returned, but renewed now by his impotent outrage against a fate which had deprived him of healthiness. He could never look upon his son without repudiation and loathing, as though Baldur's very existence was an insult to him, an insult which nothing in the world could remove, except death. He had longed for Baldur's death since the latter's birth, longed for it until it had become an almost irresistible urging to personal action. When the child had sickened frequently, he had felt that this will for his son's death had brought about the illnesses, and he had concentrated upon it fiercely, again not with his mind, but with all the force of his powerful flesh. He never saw Baldur without remembering that horrible hour of his birth, when the doctor had sadly told him of the club feet, the bent back. Dreadful operation after operation had taken place, thereafter, all through Baldur's childhood. Hans had not had any hope that the operations would cure the piteous defects, but some atavistic savagery in him had been satisfied because of the boy's suffering. And, too, he had hoped each time that Baldur would not survive the ordeals.

Frances, in her hours of greatest anguish brought upon her by her husband, yet consoled herself with the memory of his frantic insistence upon Baldur's operations. Surely, she would tell herself feverishly, Hans must really love the child, or he would not have spent so much money upon him and wasted so much of his time. She never suspected the real reason. But Baldur was not seven years old when he realized what lay behind that seeming absorption in his operations. He had been a silent preoccupied child, without physical fear for all his torments. He, of everyone in the household, was not afraid of Hans. He knew him completely. He was ironically amused by him, and out of each pit of pain succeeding the operations he would emerge with grim resolution to survive in order to thwart his father. That was his revenge upon him: his survival. He had not been horrified by what his sharp perceptions had revealed to him. Some preternatural intuition was in him, which enabled him to see behind words and actions and understand the source from which they had come. Because of this, rather than his disabilities, had come his love of solitude, his aversion for his kind, and yet, his enormous compassion for everything that existed.

The ghastly, unspeakable struggle between father and son had gone on all these twenty-seven years, and each knew that the other was aware of his motives. Baldur did not hate his father. He regarded him as a natural phenomenon, to be studied and observed in a spirit of detachment, and even amusement, and with much irony. At the time of his last operation, which was some twelve years before, and at which time Baldur had almost died, the boy had opened his eyes to fix them upon his father's savage and hopeful face. Then he had smiled, triumphantly, from out his torture, and Hans knew. The knowledge had momentarily shamed him and cowed him. For long months he had avoided seeing his son. He had been almost appalled at what he had seen in Baldur's eyes. But it had not lessened his hatred. It had not decreased his will that Baldur must die. He had been only embarrassed that Baldur had seen him fully, as though he had come upon him when he was naked. In fact, his hatred gained in virulence from that day on, and the silent hidden struggle became more intense. Hans felt that his son was ridiculing him, defying him.

Baldur, at twenty-seven, was no taller than a twelve-year-old boy, and very slight of frame. This was because his spine was curved and humped. His body was frail, almost tenuous, in its delicate and wraith-like quality. His hands were small, girlish and very fine. In this, he resembled his father. Moreover, he had inherited Hans's fairness of skin, hair and eyes, and largeness of head. This head was incongruous on the small body and twisted shoulders, for it had a heroic quality and pride and dignity. But it was his face that attracted fascinated attention. It was a face of beauty, quietness and intelligence, an almost angelic face, belied, at times, by the ironic gleam in the blue eyes and a faintly bitter smile. He was like a splendid statue that some mad sculptor, upon its completion, had struck violently with a heavy hammer, destroying its height and beauty and strength, and leaving a ruin with only the face untouched. The statue was misshapen and crumpled, crushed together out of all semblance to humanity, but the face had remained, conquering and triumphant, its splendor intact, its spirit enhanced. This Hans could not forgive. If his son had been an idiot, as he often openly declared he was, he could have forgiven him easily. But one could not ignore a man's soul in that ruined body, particularly when that soul understood, defied and laughed.

It was not until Baldur's birth that Hans learned that his wife's dead brother and one of her uncles had been born so. Thus, she too shared in his hatred for her son. He implied that in some way this degradation was her fault, that she had wronged him beyond forgiveness.

Years had not dulled the activity of his detestation. So, when he heard Baldur's voice, a thick jet of crimson blood seemed to spout up into his brain. He turned savagely upon his son, who was standing beside his mother, holding her hand tightly and warmly. Hans's blood-shot eyes became more suffused; his face purpled. But Baldur regarded him serenely, faintly smiling, as beautiful as a ruined angel.

"So!" shouted Hans. "You are up! Is it not too early in the morning for my fine gentleman?"

"No," replied Baldur, softly. "I usually get up at six."

Hans's fury increased to a murderous pitch. "So, you get up at six, already! That is good, very good. And what do you do with all the long day after six o'clock, you important gentleman?"

Baldur laughed gently. "Oh, many things, father. I read. I walk. I go with mother on her visits. I read again. I paint a little. And I think. Did you ever think, father? It is very entertaining, sometimes."

His voice was as beautiful as his face, soft and melodious, with an undertone of quiet mirth. A girl's voice, Hans had once called it in black contempt. Now the mirth, unafraid, and with a timbre in it of bored disdain. was very evident in that voice. Hans's fists clenched; his heart rolled over in his barrel-chest, thickly, sickeningly. Had he been able to kill, as he desired, he would have obtained enormous relief. And Baldur watched him almost musingly. still holding his mother's hand. Within his large blue eyes there was a strange spark. Hans had seen it only once or twice, and that in the last few months. He could not understand it. But for some reason it startled him, made his peasant's soul vaguely uneasy, chilled his fury.

"Think!" he bellowed, hoarsely, retreating a little. "What can you think, you idiot? Whole men don't think. They act, and work."

Baldur said nothing. He still smiled and regarded his father intently.

There was a little silence. Matilda was laying out her mistress's morning garments. She went to the door and accepted the breakfast tray which a maid had brought. She closed the door and brought the tray to the bedside table, smiling comfortably. "A little early, ma'am, but they must have known you were awake." She plumped up Frances's pillows, and then brought her a thick woolen shawl to put over her shoulders. Hans watched her. Again. that sad nostalgia of the flesh assailed him. and he forgot both his wife and his son.

He turned abruptly and stamped from the room. When he had gone. Frances began to weep. silently. the tears streaming down her cheeks. Baldur wiped her eyes with his own handkerchief. tenderly. "There. there, mother, you mustn't let him frighten you like that, the red-faced Dutchman! He loves to frighten you. He gets a perverse satisfacton from seeing your fright. Why do you humor him like that?"

She leaned her head against her son's chest and wept without restraint. "Oh, Baldur, my darling," she murmured. Matilda watched them for a furtive moment or two with a stolid expression, without compassion, but with something of curiosity and contempt.

Alone in the wide silent hall outside, Hans stood without moving for some time. He felt violently ill. He wiped his wet forehead. He was trembling. He was used to these fits of illness, after rage and hatred. He fumbled in his vest pocket and drew out a vial his physician had given him. He put a small pellet in his mouth and sucked it. It had a stinging, acrid taste, but it made his heart slow down just when it seemed that its pressure must burst every artery in his shaking body. He leaned against the low mahogany balustrade and stared somberly down the wide circular well of the staircase. As ever, its mysterious suggestion soothed and quieted him. Now he could breathe without pain and constriction. He glanced with last loathing at his wife's door and went down the hall. At another door he hesitated, then knocked gently.

There was no reply. He turned the handle, and entered his daughter's bedroom.

CHAPTER 4

IT WAS a relief to Hans, as always, to smell the odor of Ernestine's room. Like himself, she loved freshness and the odor of lemon verbena cologne. Though the air was warm, it was clean, and pervaded with that cologne, like a breath from a citrus grove. She, too, liked somber dark furniture and austerity and dark polished floors. But all this was enlivened by touches of pure blue and gold and scarlet, for Ernestine Schmidt had a gentle yet profound taste. She loved the breadth of sky, uncluttered, and her golden silk curtains were swept back from the enormous windows so that she could see the heavens in a broad sweep above her.

She did not hear him come in. She was sitting, dressed in a broad sill, her chin in her hand. The gray light of the morncrimson peignoir, by one of the windows, her elbow on the ing streamed over and past her. She was a small slight figure sitting there, somehow pathetic and very quiet, gazing down into the street. The vastness of the room and the windows made her seem even smaller than usual, even more defenseless. Her feet barely touched the floor as she sat in her large chair. Dark curls clustered at the nape of her thin childish neck. She was bent forward a little, as though something in the street had attracted her intense attention, and Hans could see the outline of her delicate thin shoulders. For some reason the line of her shoulders and throat always caught his breath with a sensation of sadness and tender protectiveness.

She was so fragile, so little, so defenseless, for all her twenty-eight years, and so immature and unformed.

He contemplated her for a moment, then it occurred to him that she was not moving, hardly breathing. Her tenseness seemed to increase. He tiptoed towards her, craning his neck curiously. Even when he stood behind her, she did not hear him nor was aware of him. He looked through the window, which dripped with long ribbons of pale water. He looked down to the street, past the lawns and the black empty trees, glistening in the leaden light. Then he saw what had riveted Ernestine's attention. A tall young man in workman's clothing and cap was standing on the sidewalk, staring fixedly at the house. It was evident that he had not seen Ernestine; his eye kept wandering slowly but thoughtfully over the house, as though it interested him in itself. The rain and the wind did not appear to disturb him. His cap was thrust back on his head, and Hans could see his thick yellow hair and rectangular face.

Hans squinted, the better to see. He liked what he saw, sourly. The young man was broad and strong and held himself well in his shabby shapeless clothing. Moreover, he did not have the workman's sullen posture and bent shoulders. The light was not good, but Hans had an impression of strong hard features and cold blue eyes. As the young man studied the house, he kept swinging his dinner pail idly as though in time to some inner marching song.

The seven o'clock whistle wailed through the rainy silence of the street. The young man started, then turned and broke into a dog-trot. He disappeared down the street, and was out of sight.

"Who is that man?" asked Hans, truculently.

Ernestine started violently. "Papa!" she cried faintly, her hand flying to her throat. She turned to him, frightened, and quite pale. She looked guilty and flustered.

"There, I frightened you," he said, with rough contrition. He bent and kissed her cheek. "Do not be frightened, liebchen. It is natural for a maiden to look at a man. Do you know him?" He was pleased that his secluded daughter had finally shown interest in a man, even if that man was only a workman. He had been much worried about her, for the prospect of heirs of her body had been fading steadily for ten years. Moreover, he had the German's aversion for a sterile woman.

"No, papa, I don't know him," she murmured. She gazed up at him with her great gray eyes, so luminous and untouched. She kissed his hand, which lay on her shoulder. She smiled, and then rubbed her thin colorless cheek against the hand she had kissed. A thrill of grieved tenderness ran over

Hans's gross body, and he blinked his eyes sternly. "But every morning, almost, he stops in front of the house and looks at it, like that, for minutes together. He never sees me. But I often watch for him." A febrile flush crept up to her forehead, then receded.

"But he's only a workman, probably one of the men in my mill," protested Hans, without much severity.

"But—but he looks so nice," stammered Ernestine, flushing again. "So—so clean. So strong. And so confident," she added, wistfully.

"A German boy, probably," said Hans, but his voice was abstracted. He regarded his daughter with a deep thoughtfulness, and renewed hope. He always thought of her as a child, for she was so small, so unformed. Many thought Ernestine colorless and drab, a fleshless wraith of a woman, with quite a resemblance to her mother. But Hans thought that she had a strange beauty, delicate and shy, and in this he was quite right. The fragile porcelain-like bones of her small thin face had an aristocratic fineness under her smooth pale flesh and skin. Her nose was little and very straight, with flared nervous nostrils. Her mouth was a child's mouth, faintly colored and innocent and melancholy, but with something of Baldur's sweetness and steadfastness in its expression. But it was her eyes that touched him the most deeply, for they were overlarge for that little face and sensitive features. Gray, black-lashed, shining with an inner radiance, they were filled with shy pure light and gentleness. It was these eyes which had embarrassed suitors attracted by the wealth of the Schmidts, and had driven them away. Only a man who loved her could bear that shining translucence and innocent purity, and no man had as yet loved Ernestine. This was because she had no social graces, in spite of the best schools and earnest teachers. Among strangers she was unbearably frightened and shy and wretched, and always found a corner to hide in at balls and other social events. When approached, she literally fled, confused and completely terrified.

She knew that her father urgently wished her to marry, for he had been outright in his demands, and even coarse when alarmed enough at the prospect of her never marrying. But though she frequently forced herself to speak to young men, her terrified smile, her blushes, her extreme nervousness and open terror, alarmed any prospects and sent them scurrying away. All this increased her fear. Therefore, more and more, as the years passed, she secluded herself and could only be compelled to go out and "look for a husband" when her father had become more than ordinarily exigent. On these occasions, it was more anxiety to please him and keep his love, than fear, which drove her to accept invitations. For she loved him with an aching passion and devotion, and lived only for his tenderness and affection. He had never had to strike her in all her life. Her desire to please him had always actuated her every word and deed. In her heart, she believed her failure with men was due to extreme ugliness and lack of charm and desirability.

H[illegible]s, with that intuition of his flesh, knew her terror of strangers. This was odd, for he had never feared anyone in his life. Nevertheless, he knew her fear as well as though he experienced it himself. Sometimes, watching her taut fear and her desperate little smiles, he would sigh and tell himself that he could not bear to drive her so, and that even if she did not marry it would not be so bad. This way he would always have her, the only dear thing in his life.

But lately his anxiety had returned, and with it, his exigency. He knew that he had a failing heart. What would become of Ernestine then, caught between an invalid brother and a whining fool of a mother? She must marry! Some man must take his place and protect her, and love her. But who? Her male contemporaries were already married. There remained only middle-aged bachelors, whom he rightfully distrusted, and widowers with children. Ernestine was too frail to take on the duties of another woman, and care for a brood of obstreperous brats.

Too, he remembered a certain day when Ernestine was ten years old, and her mother had timidly broached the subject of a boarding-school. He could not forget that day, for Ernestine had run to him, screaming. She had clutched him with her little white hands; she had burrowed her head into his body. She had trembled so that he thought she would die on the spot. "Don't send me away from you, Papa! No, Papa! I'm a good girl, Papa! I'll always do what you say. But don't send me away from you; I'll really die! Really, I will!"

He had not sent her away, of course. He had picked her up in his arms and had carried her to a chair. He had rocked her, murmuring soothing words, and finally had hummed old German lieder to her until she had become quiet and still. She had fallen asleep, worn out with the extremity of her terror and grief. He had sat for a long time, looking down at that exhausted, worn little face with the long wet lashes. And he had forgotten everything else, and felt that he had held the whole world in his arms, and nothing else had mattered.

In later years he suspected that Ernestine's aversion for strangers was due to her never-dying fear that she, by becoming attached to another, might have to leave her father. At first, this had increased his tenderness and love for her.

But now he was growing old, and had a bad heart, and would have to leave her.

Who would know his little Ernestine, and how to treat her? Who would protect her, and understand that fragile timidity?

But there were some things that he did not know about Ernestine. He thought that she was as indifferent to her mother as he was. It is true she was quite indifferent at times, but in the last few years she had begun to pity her mother, and understand her, and even to feel for her a sad affection. Moreover, she loved Baldur, her brother. But from her earliest childhood she had hidden this love from Hans, knowing how he hated Baldur. However, life for Baldur might have been much harder had it not been for this hidden love of Ernestine's. It was Ernestine who timidly intervened when Han's wrath and hatred had reached its highest peaks. Her intervention, even when she had been a child, was adroit, so subtle, that Hans never suspected it. He thought that he had just frightened the child with his furies, and made her ill with his violences. She was such a little sparrow, he would say to himself, fondly, and he ought to be ashamed of himself for alarming her so. Moreover, she had such a tender little heart, and could suffer nothing to be hurt, not even Baldur. And so, to please that sensitivity to pain, he allowed Baldur to study painting, and live a life of secluded study and quietness which would otherwise have been denied to the unfortunate boy. Ernestine had kept her secret from Hans, knowing that any peace or tranquillity falling to Baldur depended on her keeping this secret.

Hans never had that sick plunging pain in his heart without thinking first of his daughter, rather than of himself. Time was short. He must do something. Sometimes, thinking of this, his whole fat body would burst out into a flood of cold sweat. He must do something for her. He could not leave her unprotected in a world full of sharks and monsters. For Hans had no illusions about the world of men. He knew too much about it, and hated it with a sullen and vicious hatred.

Now, as he stood beside her, looking down at her deeply, he felt a sudden surge of hope. Ernestine had looked at a man with interest and without fear, even though he was only a workman. Hans had no false snobberies. He was totally free of the caste-love of the plebeian. It was enough for him if Ernestine married a clean and healthy man, with intelligence and courage, no matter if he came from the fields or the slums. Such a man would beget strong children. He suspected, with a peasant's dull suspicion, that the elegant young men, sons of Frances's aristocratic friends, would not be begetters of such children. More likely, they would beget creatures like Baldur.

"You do not know this young man, this workman, liebchen?" he asked, again, his thick blond brows drawing together, not with anger, but with concentration.

"No, Papa. I've told you." She colored again, with distress. Her father must think her very forward, she thought, and very unladylike. She made a movement to rise, but his urgent heavy hand pressed her back into her chair.

"You like his looks, eh?"

She dropped her eyes. "How can I tell?" she murmured. "I've never been close to him. But he stops so often. I've been watching him for months."

"Maybe he is a thief?"

Her eyes flew up, alarmed and indignant. "Oh, Papa, how can you say that? Thieves don't stand and look at a house, openly, day after day. And—and he seems so nice. Sometimes, when Gillespie comes out to see if the maids are washing the windows properly, this young man speaks to him, and they have quite a conversation together. I can't hear what they say——"

Hans was even more hopeful. If his butler, that Englishman, knew who the young man was, the matter could easily be settled.

"How'd you like to meet him, Ernestine?"

Again her painful blush ran over her pale face, and she shrank. "Oh, no, Papa! That would be terrible, truly. Why—why should he want to know me? Why, he wouldn't even look at me!"

Hans was silent. He stared at her with increasing thoughtfulness. He saw her piteous desire, and her fear that the stranger would repudiate her, or despise her. "Don't be a fool, child," he said at last, in his rough guttural voice. "Remember who you are. Well, well, if you are so frightened, you little rabbit, we won't speak of it again."

He frowned, drew out his watch, and cursed. He replaced it. He bent and kissed his daughter's cheek and patted her shoulder. He smiled a smug and secret smile. When he left the room he almost pranced, and hummed under his breath.

He emerged into the corridor with a better humor than he had felt for many a day. Matilda was passing down the hallway with Frances's tray. She dropped her eyes respectfully when she approached Hans, but a faint secret smirk touched her lips. Hans planted himself in her path, and she was obliged to halt.

"Your mistress is feeling better, eh?" he asked, beaming up at her from his short height.

She was surprised, but inclined her head.

"That is good. The women in the morning—hah!" he shook his head. He moved aside and allowed her to pass. His eye fixed itself with pleasure at a spot on her person just below the discreet bunching of her black dress which was a servant's modest attempt at the fashionable bustle. The spot was voluptuous and gleaming. His tongue touched the corners of his mouth and his neck swelled. Then he descended the stairway, humming aloud:

"Ach du lieber Augustine!"

He forgot to look down the well as usual. The morning, begun so inauspiciously, was beginning to take on the look of a happy and expectant day. He totally forgot Baldur. He never remembered Baldur, unless he was enraged about something.

Once downstairs, he went into the library, then into one of the great drawing-rooms, looking for Gillespie, the butler. He finally found him. The butler was severely and primly upbraiding a maid for some delinquency, and then, happening to glance up, he saw Hans in the doorway. He lost color. He stammered last instructions, and came towards his master, bending his head with anxious inquiry, remembering the fury of only an hour ago.

But when he came close to Hans, he saw that the formidable old man was actually smiling. It was a ferocious kind of a smile, but, thank God! it was really a smile. Gillespie was surprised, but thankful, and then he was amazed, for Hans was beckoning to him with an almost jocular air. Bemused, he followed Hans into the privacy of the library.

Once there, Hans attempted to assume a stern expression. He stood before the fire, with his back to it, his thumbs in his armpits.

"Who is that young feller who stops outside the house nearly every day? Eh? Do you know him?"

Gillespie started with renewed fright. He wet his drying lips, and made a drowning motion with his hands.

"Mr. Schmidt, sir! I—I am sorry. He is just some lad from the mills. Very pleasant-spoken, rather. Not a bad sort. Just a working-man, but with good manners. I have seen him for a long time, but he spoke to me recently. A—a foreigner of some kind, judging by his accent. I—believe me, sir, I don't encourage that sort of familiarity from persons of his class—but there seemed no harm—" He gulped. "I'll see to it, sir, that he does no more loitering—" The unhappy man's voice trailed away, stifled with fear, and the certainty that he would now be discharged.

But Hans was contemplating him thoughtfully. "What is

his name? Where does he come from? Where does he work?"

The butler struggled to regain his fainting voice. He was visibly palsied, and the color of raw dough.

"I know him only by the name of Franz. He told me his whole name, but—it was a foreign name. I don't remember it. And I believe he works in your mill, sir."

His frantic mind darted about, despairingly. It was so hard to find work in these days—he had been in America six months before he had gotten this post. And now a confounded swine of a German was going to lose it for him, and he would be adrift. His despair made him cry out: "I assure you, sir, it won't happen again! There'll be no more loitering on the premises!"

But Hans was merely gazing at him mildly, though his butler's distress gave him the sadist's thrill of pleasure.

"Stop jabbering, and answer my questions. What does he talk to you about?"

Gillespie gulped, wringing his hands until it seemed that he would pull the flesh from his bones. "Nothing—of consequence, Mr. Schmidt, sir. He is pleasant-spoken, and respectful. Just passes the time of day."

"But why does he stop at this particular house, and stare like that?"

Gillespie shook his head mutely. He said thinly: "He—admired it, he said."

Hans was pleased. He shot a furtive look about his enormous gloomy library with a smug satisfaction. But he scowled. "Oh, he did, did he? That's very kind of him. The impudence! What did he say, eh?"

Gillespie was so sure that he was to be discharged that he decided that nothing mattered. He bent his head and almost whispered: "He told me it was the finest example of ugliness he had ever seen, sir. He said—that there was something grand in complete ugliness."

Hans shouted, furiously, turning crimson. He stamped his feet, lifting each one and setting it down so violently that the crystal pendants on the lamps quivered and rattled. "The Schwein!" he exclaimed. "I'll go out there myself some morning and teach him a lesson!"

"Yes, sir," murmured Gilespie, completely undone now. "Shall I—shall I go now, sir?"

Hans glared at him, enraged. "Go? No, I'm not finished, yet." He paused. Slowly the crimson receded from his fat face. He began to smile again. "The man's not a fool, eh? You wouldn't call him a fool, would you?"

Gillespie took renewed hope. He looked up. "No, Mr. Schmidt! No!" He became feverishly animated. "I'd say he was a very respectable young person, for his class. And not at all impudent, or dangerous. He—carries a dinner pail, and seems hardworking and diligent."

"And he works in my mill?"

"Yes, sir."

"Hm." Hans began to pace slowly up and down the room. Gillespie watched him.

"I'll see he does no more loitering, Mr. Schmidt," he promised.

Hans stopped and stared at him inimically over his shoulder.

"You'll do nothing of the kind, you fool! Let him look. Why not?" He began to grin. "And now, get me my coat and hat, and call the carriage. I'm late enough already."

CHAPTER 5

THE LIGHT, though it quickened, did not become warmer. Rather, it grayed and sharpened, like the reflection from cold steel.

Baldur Schmidt flung wide the curtains from the great windows, and looked with dissatisfaction at the sky. There was no sign of clearing. The rain and the wind strengthened, and now there were flakes of vagrant white mixed with the rain. He stood for a long time, gazing out at the street and the sky, musing. Even in repose, and in solitude, there was no bitterness, no wryness, in his expression. Rather, it was contemplative, but not serene. It was even severe about the eyes and the extraordinarily pure forehead. His head was more than ever like that of a heroic statue's. All bodily activity was suspended in him in his contemplation, but there was something about him which suggested tremendous inner movement.

His room was large and plain and quiet, without one discordant object. It was lined with books. Here and there on a pedestal were the marble busts of Beethoven and Goethe, Schiller and Lessing, and, not incongruous in that noble array, was a bust of Abraham Lincoln. The busts were no more still than he, and between them and himself there was a curious lofty resemblance. In a distant corner was a more than life-size marble statue of a winged archangel, so beautiful, so strong and so powerful, that it seemed visibly alive and vibrant with passion. The figure stood in an attitude of profound prayer, but it was not the mealy-mouthed and sanctimonious posture of the conventional angel. The hands were lifted a little, palm up, and the head was arched proudly and thrown back, so that the eyes appeared to importune God without fear or sentimentality, but only with prideful reverence and urgency. It was not the usual sexless angel: it had the body of a strong and virile man, vivid with tremendous life and force, which would excite love not only in God but in women. The face was the face of an extremely handsome man, but not effeminate. Rather, it was somber and a little hard, with arrogant eyes and a heavy gloomy mouth. In looking at that body and that face, those half-folded wings and the lifted posture, one thought of the old Biblical legend which, in Genesis, sang of the splendid hour when "the sons of God came in unto the daughters of men," and "there were giants in those days."

Half in light, half in shadow, it lived and appeared to move with passionate breath. Clad in a beautifully carved robe, it was clasped at the waist by a broad belt, in which was thrust a long two-edged sword. Baldur Schmidt had bought the statue from a sculptor in New York who had confessed that he had carved no statue before this, and would carve no more. It was a vision that had been with him since childhood, and he had no wish to profane it with lesser work. He had studied his art only to give this one supreme vision objectivity.

Baldur's tastes were of the simplest. There were no gimcracks on the black marble mantelpiece, under which burned a quiet scarlet fire. His bed was neat and narrow, and covered with dark-red velvet. His tables were heaped with books, and in another corner was a small piano upon which he played frequently and softly. His chairs were small and straight, without softness or luxury, and the high ceiling was lost in shadow and darkness.

He left the window, finally, and went to the fire. He stirred it up. Lances of crimson flame leapt over the walls and the bare polished floor. He looked over his crooked shoulder at the busts and the statues. They semed, in that firelight, to be carved out of snow and fire, and the angel shook on his low pedestal. Baldur smiled his strange and secret smile. He was comforted, as always, by the coming to life of his friends, his companions in mysterious silence.

Someone knocked gently on his door. "Come in," he called. The door opened and Ernestine entered, smiling timidly.

"Good morning, Tina," he said, with fondness. "The light is very bad today. But I'll see what I can do."

On coming into this room, Ernestine's glance was always first on the angel. It never failed to make her heart tremble with ecstasy and fear. Now she looked at her brother and smiled uncertainly.

"If the light is so bad," she began.

"No, no, dear. Sit down in your usual place at the window." He regarded her with indulgent affection. She was a year older than he, but he always thought of her as much younger. He watched her walk across the wide floor with grace and shy lightness. She wore a bustled dress of dark blue velvet, and there was a fine string of rosy pearls about her childish throat. Her dark curling hair was swept back from her pale temples and lay in a knot of curls on the nape of her neck. She sat down in a chair by one of the windows, and half her grave colorless face was in shadow and the other in pallid light. But her gray eyes were radiant with inner lucidity.

Baldur talked of quiet inconsequential things as he prepared his paints. He was painting a miniature of his sister, which was to be her gift to her father for Christmas. She listened to her brother, smiled a little, and hardly answered. She was used to Baldur's gentle monologues, little of which she understood.

"On a day like this," he was saying, "one should not work. It's a day for contemplation and memory. But memories of what? Not of one's life, surely. There are very few memories of conscious existence which are worth thinking of. But memories of the mind—perhaps. Memories of old life, sensations—turn your head a little this way, Tina. That is right. The light's very bad. I don't think I'll be able to do much today, unfortunately."

He sat before her, his ruined body perched on a high stool, his brush in his hand. He peered at her intently. His brush moved delicately. Then he peered again, and paused.

"What's the matter, Tina?" he asked, anxiously.

She was surprised. "Nothing. Why?"

"I thought you looked a little feverish. There, turn your head a little, more this way. Are you sure you are well? There's quite a color on your cheeks."

Yes, he was sure of it. Over Ernestine's pallor was a faint rosy patina, just visible, but giving her face a freshness and roundness he had never seen before. He studied her thoughtfully.

"You look as though you've fallen in love," he said, lightly.

Ernestine's eye flew swiftly to the angel before she could

control herself. She was extremely embarrassed, then, and bent her head. She laughed a little. "I've been sitting for hours in front of the fire," she answered. "My face is hot." She paused. "Baldur, do you suppose any one ever looked like that angel?"

He turned his head and reflectively regarded the statue. "The sculptor had a model, no doubt. But sculptors always glorify the model in their work." He was silent a moment. "However, I'm sure there must be millions who look like that. Thousands, anyway. Not that I've ever seen one, though." His lip curled wryly. "For instance, you don't think Father, or I, look like that, do you?"

But her eyes gazed at him seriously. "Sometimes, Baldur, I think you look like that statue. Not that your features are so big or hard. But there's something—"

He inclined his head indulgently. "Thank you, Tina. But I'm afraid you're prejudiced in my favor. Lift your chin a little. That's better." He frowned at the miniature, then, with a sigh, put aside his brush. "It's no use. The light gets worse every minute."

Ernestine left the chair and went to the fire, where she rubbed her small dry hands. Baldur watched her acutely. She was quiet and colorless as ever, but he thought he detected a secretive excitement in her. He spoke to her. She did not answer. She was absorbed in some wistful, restless dream.

"I hope," he thought, sadly, "that it's someone decent. Poor little Tina."

When she had gone, he tried to sit down and read. But nothing interested him. He tried to play some selections on his piano. The sound was mournful and hollow. Nothing satisfied or quieted him. He walked restlessly about his room. Everything was silent, except for the rush of the wind and the lashing of the rain. He stopped at last before the statue, and stood there for a long time, gazing up at the lifted and arrogant face.

And then his vague and poignant, yet unaccustomed, melancholy passed away, and with it, this restlessness. His old calm returned, serene and silent as a winter sunset, which promised nothing and hoped for nothing.

When he had been younger, the years of his great pain and suffering had also been years of joy and inner excitement. He had believed himself endowed with some immortal gift. Crippled and in torment though he was, he had gone to New York, to get expert criticism of his writing, music and painting. He had come back, spent and broken and mute with a still and desperate muteness. He had discovered that he had little gifts, the dilettante's gifts, pleasant and pretty. Only in his music was there a promise, but even there it was insufficient. All the beauty, fire and splendor of his mind and spirit were doomed forever to be pent up behind the hand of mediocrity. Painfully, at times, they could emerge in a faint cry, a line of loveliness, a gleam of color. But the skill was not in his hand, for there was an eternal formlessness in his spirit. He did not know that it is only the vision which is mortal which can be adequately expressed. Art must be made of clay, as well as flame, to be able to emerge in a magnificent form. There was no clay in him, and so his hand was bewildered and uncertain, thwarted by the intangibilities in his mind. Divinity, at the last, can only be expressed in silence.

He had been twenty, then, and he had come home determined not to live any longer. There was nothing for which he could live, only pain and hatred and despair. Then there had been that morning when he had left his bedroom just before dawn and had painfully climbed to the fourth floor.

He was never able to forget that dreadful climbing, and could never remember where the anguish was greater, in his mind or his body. He lost orientation. He was not climbing up marble steps in a ghostly dawn-light, with the intense yet echoing silence all about him. He was climbing up clouds, seeking oblivion and death. Then he had reached the top, and was leaning over the balustrade, looking down into the dark and diminishing well, whose bottom was only a pit of darkness.

He leaned there for a long time. It seemed eternity to him, with emptiness open before him and darkness all about him.

And then, as he waited, a curious calm and serenity came over him, as he looked down into death. It was a calm and serenity without words or fully developed thoughts. He could not explain it; he could only experience it. His pain lifted, and he grew old and quiet. There was no comfort in him, no expectation. Merely a cessation of suffering and a rising of peace.

It was nearly an hour later that he crept down to his room and went to his bed. There, he slept profoundly. When he awoke, the calm was still with him, the serenity unshakable. He had looked into the nothingness of death, and he had come back. Nothing, thereafter, could move or disturb him much. He had taken on invulnerability.

His pain of body did not decrease with the years. But his pain of mind had gone forever. Everything that happened to him became small and without meaning in the gray light of his experience. He was protected from emotion. He could go about his music, his writing and his painting without ambition or heart-burning. They were like small gardens he was cultivating in quiet peace.

It was only on rare occasions, like today, when the old restlessness plagued him. But soon he could smile at it, and turn away from it, as from an old but wearisome acquaintance.

He slept deeply and unmovingly, sometimes with the help of drugs to relieve his physical pain, but mostly because of the tranquil immobility of his mind. When he had been younger, he had not slept, and had lived only in misery, because of desire. Now he was purged of all desire. If this were death in life, as he sometimes suspected, he was grateful, and set up fresh psychological defenses against the uneasy gnawing of desire. Not to desire anything at all! It was to live in a glass bell, seeing everything, but always insulated against raw attack, suffering, clamor and fury. If, as he sometimes ruefully told himself, he contemplated his navel, there was a certain stability in his navel, at least, and certainly a great deal less danger than in the world beyond it. Moreover, there were many more things less pleasant to contemplate.

And so, insulated against desire and emotion as he was, he could observe the little world about him with superficial detachment, and a steadily lessening sense of participation. He could look at his father, knowing him completely, but entirely indifferent both to his abuse and his hatred. Sometimes, he was even slightly amused, but it was an amusement languid with boredom. He was sorry for his mother, but it was a sorrow without indignation or pain. He was quite fond of her, but here again emotion was not involved in his fondness. Until very recently, he had been fond of Ernestine in the same way. It was only in the last few days that a faint stinging sliver had pierced his consciousness when he saw her, or thought of her. It took considerable effort on his part to repress these stingings, and sometimes he felt fear. Consequently, he tried to see as little of her as possible.

He had no friends at all. He lived his long days and dreamless nights in a state of suspension. Sometimes he wondered why he bothered to live. But then, it was more of an effort to die than to live, and he had looked at death once, and remembered.

If he truly loved anything, it was his statue of the praying angel. He began to identify himself with it; it was an extension of himself. It was only marble, but he gave it his own soul. He did not realize this consciously, and was not to realize this for some time still in the future. But in some hardly conscious way he thought of the angel's body as his own, and thought that the soul of the angel was in himself. Only once had this grotesque idea risen to the surface of his conscious mind, and though he had laughed suddenly and indulgently at it, its influence remained with him.

In a lesser way, he also identified himself with the noble busts of the heroes, musicians and poets in his room. They were in truth his friends. He needed no others. They were part of him, and he was part of them.

After his long contemplation of the angel, he moved away serenely, limping slowly and unsurely. He paused to look at the miniature he was painting of Ernestine. He was surprised as he looked at it, and lifted it to the light to study it more closely. Yes, he had caught her pathetic shyness and simplicity, and with it, a certain delicate grace of expression. A psyche-like expression, he thought, pleased. He had no delusions that Ernestine possessed any brilliancy of intellect or any subtleties. But he knew there was a clearness in her, a purity, which was infinitely touching.

He put down the miniature, sighing. The stinging sliver stung his numb flesh again, and the restlessness returned.

CHAPTER 6

THERE IS nothing so desolate as rain and wind in a strange land, thought Emmi Stoessel, nothing which can strike so formidably and mournfully on the mind and the heart. She paused to look through the streaked window as she lifted the coffee-pot. There was nothing much to see through this window except the narrow chasm of the "court" between the long and gloomy apartments on Mulberry Street. The opposite brick wall ran with mingled soot and rain, and what little light crept down the five-story well was dim and gray. She was like a prisoner, gazing despairingly at the walls of her prison.

The kitchen of the apartment was large, clean and as bright as the flickering gas jets could make it. She had the Teutonic woman's instinctive love for order and cleanliness, and the bare boards of the floor were scrubbed to a golden yellow, as was the wooden table on which she had set breakfast. Even the chairs were scrubbed to that smooth hue, and the sink-boards. She, herself, had papered the walls with gay red roses, and had hung flowered cheap curtains at the window. It was her own hands which had braided and made the small round rag-rugs scattered on the floor, and even the wooden cupboards above the black-iron sink. She had learned to work very hard in America, she, Emmi Hoffstedter whose father had been an army officer in Bavaria, and herself a schoolmistress.

With a sternly repressed sigh, she went to the table and poured the coffee into two thick white mugs. A smell of hot baking bread came from the black, cast iron coal range whose huge bulk was the largest thing in the room. She then went to the bare wooden stairway at the end of the kitchen and called urgently: "Egon, you must hurry. It is late, almost seven." Her strong, rather harsh voice, was commanding. She listened for the reply which came, eager, gentle, placating, and then went back to the stove to replace the pot and to look into the oven, where fresh hot twists of bread had turned brown. She removed the tray and examined the bread carefully. But all this was with an air of abstraction. She was frowning. She frowned so often that two deep clefts had formed between her brows, giving her an impatient, and even angry, expression.

While she waited for her husband, she again stared through the window at the wall of the court, and the clefts deepened between her eyes.

She was a very tall woman in her late forties, hard and angular of frame. Her shoulders were as broad as a man's, and there were no softnesses, no curves, on her spare long bones. Though it was so early in the morning, she wore her best black bombazine dress, as spare as herself, and with not even a suggestion of a bustle upon it. Over this dress she had tied a long crisp white apron, and the large bow of it added an incongruously feminine touch to her grenadier's figure. The round white lace collar, so high about her corded throat, was fastened with a beautiful brooch of gold filigree and pearls, but even these failed to soften the lines of her strong harsh chin and jutting cheekbones.

Strength was in the bones of her long rectangular face, pale and almost bleached in color. Her mouth was firm, rigid and uncompromising, a thin wide streak without rosiness or gentleness. Above this mouth was her finely shaped large nose, high-bridged and almost fleshless. Beneath thick light-brown frowning brows were her eyes, like direct blue lightning. Her light-brown hair, masses of it, was braided sternly and piled in a thick crown on the top of her almost arrogant head. She was a handsome and masculine woman, for all her spareness and rigidity and lack of softnesses and grace. She might command little love, but she would always command fear and respect, for there was no craftiness in her severe expression, no deviousness, no falseness. Moreover, there was a compactness and directness about her, not only in her movements, but in the swift hard glances of her small eyes and the set of her pale lips. One knew that here was a woman of great honor, power and pride, even though it was easy to guess that she knew no subtleties, no lavish gentlenesses, and no compromise. What she saw, she saw clearly and straightly, with bitter strength and hardness, and with extraordinary intelligence, and integrity.

Her hands, long and as large as a man's, were scrubbed and reddened and chapped, hands made for work and accomplishment. But they were not a peasant's hands. The fingers were well shaped and aristocratic, for all the marks of hard work. Her son, Franz, was a younger and masculine replica of her, at least physically. Mentally, she would think with bitterness and weary contempt, they had no common meeting-ground of minds. That was the most painful fact in her existence, and one to which her uncompromising nature was never reconciled.

She had endured everything for the sake of Franz. Her whole life had been lived for one purpose, since his birth. But everything had been useless, all her sacrifices and her pain, her hopes and her work, her dreams and her passions. No matter what she did, at any time, during all her waking hours, she thought of little except all this. And even at night, she dreamt of it, she awoke, aching spiritually with an almost unbearable agony.

What did it matter what one suffered if the suffering were justified? she would often think. No matter what anguish one bore, no matter what torment and frustration and passing despair, it was as nothing if what one worked for was accomplished. But to endure all this, and then to be thwarted at the last, and to see the work of years wasted and lost—this was the most dreadful thing of all, and not to be forgiven. She felt that Franz had mortally injured her, because her life, in him, had been without accomplishment. He had made a mockery of her years of work and sacrifice and pain. He had made them as nothing.

Even as she waited for her husband, Egon, she thought of this, and the clefts between her brows became even deeper, and the lines of her mouth were both cruel and embittered. She stood in rigid silence before the stove, not moving, hardly breathing, but there emanated from her rays of anger, rage and despair, and heavy grief.

Franz had once said to her, with amusement: "It is not inner righteousness which makes you so uncompromising and obstinate, mother. It is just your damned Prussianism." He had said much worse things to her, but though she forgot these, she never forgot nor forgave this remark. The reference to "Prussianism" was the great insult, for to her it seemed that Prussianism was the most frightful manifestation of Bismarck's new Germany, and the thing from which she and her husband had fled with loathing and hatred. It was the supreme motivation which had impelled her into exile, and had changed her life. She had been born in Bavaria of a Bavarian mother and a Prussian father. She had hated her father from the earliest childhood. To her, he was a combination of everything she detested: cruelty, harsh discipline, lack of kindness and affection, and inhuman implacability. Her mother, whom she had loved passionately, had died in the atmosphere he had created. Two things, therefore, prevented her from forgiving Franz: her own hatred of everything which her father represented, and a subconscious but horrified suspicion that she resembled her father in many ways. Sometimes, when glancing in the mirror, she saw the vague shadow of her father's features in her own. This caused her to avoid mirrors. Therefore, she was most outspoken in her denunciations of "vanity" and "self-love," and often declared that female decadence had begun on the day when mirrors were invented. There was only one mirror in the whole dreary flat on Mulberry Street, and that was in the dark bathroom behind the kitchen, where her husband and son shaved. When cleaning that bathroom, she would avert her eyes, in order to avoid glancing at her reflection. She felt a glow of righteousness in this, and often spoke of her lack of personal conceit and vanity. And in her, always, lurked the repressed fear that she was much like her father.

She heard her husband's soft uncertain steps on the stairs. She returned to the table and stood near it, like a soldier preparing for duty. Egon Stoessel emerged into the warm kitchen, shivering, and trying to hide his discomfort, as always, with a gentle and placating smile. He was a frail small man, some inches shorter than his wife, with the scholar's long pale face and short-sighted eyes. On his long nose he wore pince-nez with a black neat ribbon. Behind the pince-nez his eyes, soft brown and timid yet curiously courageous, looked out with sadness and gentleness. He, too, had been a teacher, and this was evident in a certain preciseness in all his movements, and a certain spinsterlike care in enunciation and inflection of speech. His mouth, faintly tremulous, and always eager to smile, was a woman's mouth, tender and deprecating. He might not inspire respect in the more robust, but he almost always inspired affection, for he was timid kindness itself. Unobtrusive, vacillating, hesitant and unopinionated though he was, his wife adored him with a cold stern adoration. She also ruled him with the same sternness, and frightened him almost continually.

He was partially bald, and neatly combed his thin strands of light brown hair over his knotty skull. His large cartilaginous ears gave his head a pathetic appearance of alarm, for they distended themselves from his head in an attitude of flight. Thin, bent, defensive, with delicate veined hands, he wore neat but shiny black broadcloth, and white stiff shirts. His black cravat was neatly folded about his scrawny neck. The gold watchchain which hung from his vest seemed too heavy for that fragile body. He was a bookkeeper in Hans Schmidt's factory offices. He rarely talked to his fellow clerks, and then only in the softest, gentlest voice in which the guttural German accent was, incredibly, made musical. He worked diligently and accurately, and was much esteemed by his office superiors. He had never confessed this to Emmi, but his whole being yearned only for peace and quietness, and rustic obscurity. Many years ago, Emmi had believed he had had as violent a hatred and scorn of Prussianism as she had, but though he was horrified at everything Prussian, and shrank from it, wounded and distraught, he did not hate it, or scorn it. To him, it was a manifestation as dreadful as storm and natural fury, and he wanted only to hide from it and forget it. Emmi's active struggle against it, and her violent denunciations of it, distressed him almost as much as did the thing which caused them. He might have made a compromise with it, in his little Bavarian village and in his little Bavarian school, by the simple method of ignoring its existence among his books and manuscripts. But he had come to America with his wife and his child, for it was more arduous to oppose Emmi than to accede to her.

Emmi had begun to suspect this very shortly after their arrival in America, which she had eloquently called "the new world where all justice and liberty and beauty are capable of fulfilment." But she would not allow herself to suspect it openly. Therefore, she became more rigid and uncompromising in her hatred, and more voluble. Nevertheless, she turned her hopes from Egon to Franz, and in that lay her final disillusionment and despair. She had loved her native land with all the passion of the Teuton, but she had willingly sacrificed all this to come to an alien land and live among an alien people, whom she was never able to understand or truly love. To find that this sacrifice had been in vain, and had been made a mockery, was an agony too great to be borne. At least, she had her cold but fiery rage to sustain her in her homesickness and misery. Egon had not even this. He was too gentle and kind ever to speak of his aching nostalgia, and his bewilderment, and Emmi often spoke scornfully of his "placidity" and lack of aggressiveness and conviction, and remarked acidly that he would be at home anywhere, provided he had his books. Once she had told herself that her husband was made of the stuff of serfs, but she quelled this thought loyally. It was just that he was so meek and so sweet-tempered, she had said to herself, sternly. He could not really hate anyone. She did not know that his inner torments were greater than her own, and his inner longings for his native land much more poignant and terrible. Had she known, she would have been incredulous, and more than a little aghast. She felt that in herself, and only in herself, the icy flame burned high and indomitably, and only she suffered the constant gnawing anguish of nostalgia.

When Egon sat down at the breakfast table, she gave him her usual sharp probing look. She loved him with all her heart and soul, and this morning's inspection was to reassure herself that he did not seem more fragile than usual, and that his color had not changed a little for the worse. But the soot, the dampness, the cold, and the drabness of this now hated city, had indeed lessened his vitality. He suffered much from respiratory illnesses, and always had a stifled morning cough. Moreover, he was always cold. Emmi kept the kitchen steaming for his benefit, and saw that he wore the thickest underwear, while she, herself, knitted him heavy woolen socks. Looking at him this morning, she thought with despair: There is no hope no matter where I turn. Everything that we have endured has come to nothing.

But her despair, this morning, was a little lighter than usual. She waited on her husband, insisting that he drink his hot milk and eat another of her fresh hot rolls. She forced him to eat his eggs, and he did so, though choking, for he knew that if he did not his wife would worry about him the rest of the day. Her gestures, her manners, her words, as she waited on him, were peremptory and disciplinary, but a vague softness lightened her face and made her hands almost gentle.

He held the thick white mug of milk to his lips in his blue-veined hands, and smiled at her fondly. He spoke to her in their native language:

"And did you sleep well last night, my love?"

"Yes, yes!" she replied impatiently, scrutinizing him again. Was it only her imagination, or was he even thinner than he had been a month ago? "I always sleep well. And you, Egon?"

He nodded, and sipped his milk. He never told his wife that he often wept at night, and that he slept very little. He would cover his pillow near his eyes with his handkerchief, in order that she might see no stain in the morning where his tears had dropped. Such tears, without bitterness, tears from his heart when he thought of Germany. He would sometimes awaken from his light sleep to find that he was weeping.

He put down the mug and fought his nausea meekly. He smiled brightly at Emmi, and the sudden radiance of that sweet smile unnerved her, as it always did. "But Franz—he was a little late this morning, was he not?"

"Yes. He was helping me to prepare the spare bedroom for Irmgard." She turned away abruptly, and stared through the rain-lashed window.

"She will arrive at ten, Emmi?" He sighed. "I hope she will like America."

Emmi did not turn from the window. "At least, America is not Prussia!" she exclaimed in a loud harsh voice.

"No," he agreed, almost inaudibly, "it is not Prussia."

Emmi brought him his worn heavy greatcoat and an umbrella. She helped him into his outer garment, and the outline of his thin bent shoulder-blades gave her a pang, as always. He was so meek, so sweet, so good, so gentle; she thought fiercely. "Irmgard is a sensible girl," she said, roughly. "She will not inconvenience us."

"I am not afraid of that," he said, quickly, pulling his woolen gloves over his hands. He smiled again at his wife. "It will be good to see another young face in the house." He had such a tenderness for the young that his eyes moistened. And then, knowing the secret places in his wife's heart, he added: "I hope very much that Franz will like her."

The coming of Irmgard Hoeller was the last assault of Emmi upon Franz, and was so desperately close to her desires that she could not bear to speak of it. She said, as she fastened the buttons on the greatcoat: "I remember her only as a baby. A very pretty child, as you remember. But my brother-in-law wrote me, before he died, that Irmgard was a splendid girl. Of course, that might be because he wished me to give her a home, and wanted to prejudice me in her favor. However, we shall see. She is not afraid of work, he said. I am afraid we shall have to prove that," she added grimly. She straightened up, a little flushed. "My sister was a weakling," she remarked.

Egon said nothing. He had loved Hertha, the sister of Emmi. But Hertha had not loved him, and had married Emil Hoeller instead. So, he had turned to Emmi, who at least reminded him of Hertha. He had a deep affection for Emmi now, though he had been more afraid of her in the beginning. Literally, she had married him rather than the other way about. When Hertha had died, at the time when Emil had been imprisoned for his revolutionary activities, Egon had suffered torments of silent grief and desolation. But this was something else that Emmi had never known. Thinking of Irmgard now, he wondered eagerly if she had become like her mother, the gentle, sweet-mouthed Hertha.

"We must make her happy," he said, as he went towards the door, already shivering in anticipation of the storm outside.

"Happy!" cried Emmi, loudly. "Who has the right to be happy in such a world!"

She followed him to the door, and waited until his bent form was out of sight before she closed it. She closed that door with tenderness, as one might close the bedroom door of a beloved but ailing child.

She allowed herself no time for thought and conjecture. She busied herself swiftly and in an orderly fashion in the kitchen, her grenadier's body moving in disciplined motions, without waste. She turned off the gas, leaving the kitchen in semi-darkness, rippling with rain-shadows, for she was very economical.

The kitchen restored to order, she opened the door upon a long dark hall, chill and gloomy. This hall led to the "parlor" of the flat. Emmi had furnished it with second-hand walnut and horsehair furniture, hideous bulking articles without beauty or comfort. The room was dark, like every other room in the miserable tenement, and coffin-shaped, with two long thin windows looking out upon the desolate court. Here, too, the air was that of some underground arctic tomb. A large square of turkey-red thin carpet lay upon the floor, and the boards bordering it had been polished to a deep blackish lustre by Emmi's stern hands. Upon this carpet lurked the monstrous horsehair furniture, like squat and sullen animals, a sofa and two chairs, and in the center of the room, a heavy round black walnut table with brass feet which Emmi had brought from Germany. She had hung stiff coarse lace curtains at the windows, rigid with starch and white as snow. The austerity of her nature was evident in the absence of all ornaments and knick-knacks and cushions. Everything was stiff and dead and bitterly cold. There was a black wood fireplace in the room, near a corner, but no fire burned there. Instead, black and icy, stood a tall circular coal stove with a fretted nickel top. A fire was always laid there, but rarely lit, the Stoessels preferring the more cheerful atmosphere of the kitchen. Over the fireplace hung a single picture, Emmi's treasure, a remarkably fine engraving of Goethe. Emmi knew everything about her beloved hero, including his scorn of the common people. As she had never considered herself as belonging to that class, she, in spite of her passionately democratic theories, felt no offense. Heaped on the table were piles of finely bound books, in German. These, however, did nothing to dispel the funereal darkness and chill and bleakness of the room.

Emmi moved rapidly about the room, wiping off the daily film of coal dust which gathered there despite the closed windows. This done, she went into the "front" parlor, a room which her economy had heretofore left unfurnished and closed off. But now this room, with the bay window fronting the bedraggled street and facing the blackened cottages on the other side, had been quickly converted into a bedroom for Irmgard Hoeller. A small rag rug lay on the thin long expanse of the polished floor. Emmi had bought a second-hand white iron bed, and it stood in the center of the room, narrow and white, hard and chaste, with pillow-shams and a thick cotton spread. There was a blackwood wardrobe there, also, a table, a rocking-chair, and a commode. Emmi surveyed it with satisfaction. It was a nun's room, without warmth or comfort, but achingly clean. She dusted the room, walked about it, restlessly, peered through the curtains without knowing what she did. But again, her look lightened.

In the rear, off the kitchen, was Franz's bedroom. A feature of these tenements was that there was a sort of garret room leading up from the kitchen, also in the rear. This was the room where Emmi and her husband slept. Only the first-floor flats had this room. Emmi could never have accustomed herself to sleep on the same floor with her kitchen and her son.

It was now eight o'clock, and the tenement was in order. The rain had increased, splashing desolately against the windows. Emmi mounted to her tiny bare room, removed her apron, patted her hair. Then she put on her tight broadcloth jacket and tied on her bonnet. She put on black cotton gloves, and then went downstairs briskly, her heavy broadcloth skirts trailing behind. She picked up her umbrella and marched to the door.

The rain and wind assaulted her. But she did not mind this. She walked rapidly and firmly down the mournful street to another flat in the building. There she briskly pulled the bell and waited. She was on her way to do her usual morning duties.

CHAPTER 7

THE HORSE-CAR went no farther than the gates of the mills. Emmi descended, holding her skirts high in her lean, black-gloved hand. A high, barbed-wire fence guarded the grounds of the mill, and there were iron gates at intervals, and watchmen in little wooden shacks. Emmi looked at the mill with gloomy distaste. The rain was heavier than ever, and the wind violent. Against a boiling gaseous sky of gray clouds the towering chimneys of the mills shot forth scarlet and fitful lightning, and masses of black smoke starred with red sparks. From the mills themselves came a prolonged confused roar. The blasted grounds surrounding the mills were heaped with slag and cinders, and busy with workmen wheeling barrows or driving cars with straining horses.

Before one of the gates there was quite a small crowd of workmen, their shabby clothing sodden from the rain, their caps pulled down over pale and anxious faces. They were engaged in arguing with the watchmen, who held clubs ready and talked bullyingly through the iron gates. Emmi approached the outskirts of the crowd and listened to the pleading of a leader.

"But, there weren't no call to shut us out, without notice. Here we come this mornin', and you won't let us in——"

A watchman shouted brutally: "Ain't I been tellin' you you was laid off? What more do you want?"

"But Saturday——"

"Today's Monday. Lots of things happened over Sunday." Another watchman added: "Want me to call the company police?"

Emmi touched a young workman on his arm. He turned a dazed discouraged face upon her, then tugged at his cap. "What is the matter?" she asked.

"Well, ma'am, seems like there's a lay-off, unexpected." He had an English voice and a deprecating English manner.

Emmi became alarmed. Franz had said nothing of a contemplated lay-off.

"But why is there a lay-off, young man?"

"Oh, some feller said there was some trouble in the mill. Some orders cancelled. I don't know, ma'am."

"I got six kids. They'll starve!" cried a workman to the watchman, in a frantic voice. The watchman shrugged, surlily.

"Is that my fault? What do you fellers have all those kids for, anyway? It ain't none of my trouble."

The men broke into a confused babble of voices, despairing, pleading, puzzled and bewildered. Here and there there was an angry voice, raised in furious protest. The watchmen glanced uneasily towards an approaching guard with a shotgun.

Emmi's dry cheek flushed. She bit her lip and turned away. Her heart beat heavily, with a deep, inward pain. The dark wet morning was all the darker and more desolate for her. Her face took on an expression of baffled anger and passionate indignation. Moreover, she felt twinges of anxiety for Franz. Of course, he was a foreman now, after three years in the mills, and he might not be laid off. Then this selfish thought disappeared, and the pain returned.

The station was three streets away, and by the time Emmi arrived at the miserable wooden building her skirts were wet and dabbled with mud. The station was situated in the midst of a laborer's slum, and was as ramshackle and soot-stained and broken as any other building in the vicinity. The long lines of rails leading up to it gleamed wetly in the gray light. A few engines puffed on sidings, and the streams of freight-cars on other sidings dripped with water. The air was full of grit and smoke, and clangorous with bells. Emmi entered the station, which was heated by a black, pot-bellied stove, and littered with broken benches, upon which sat ragged women and children with bundles. A large oil-lantern swung from the ceiling. It was five minutes to ten, and the train from New York was on time, the ticket-seller informed Emmi.

She walked restlessly up and down on the filthy floor, which was stained with tobacco juice. She lifted her skirts, and kept her head bent as though she could not bear to look at the wretched humanity in the station. Her face became more gloomy with every moment. Then she looked about her, as though she were a newcomer, full of new and sickened impressions. What would Irmgard think of all this, Irmgard who no doubt had young dreams of America? Never had she seen such poverty and dirt, Emmi was sure of that, remembering the clean bare stations of Germany. It was a sad day to arrive, and a sad day for Irmgard.

The train from New York approached up the rails, its wheels screaming and its bell thundering. It was a long train, the first few coaches black with soot, the coaches of the well-to-do large and much cleaner. Emmi went out upon the unsheltered platform and lifted her umbrella. Crowds descended the high steps clumsily. She watched every woman with great intensity. Which was Irmgard? Emmi was jostled by the crowds, but she held her place firmly, watching every face.

Then she started. It might have been her own sister, Hertha, who was descending the steps, clutching a raffia suitcase and a large bundle wrapped in black cloth. Hertha in her youth, vital, quiet, calm, in her old-fashioned cloth bonnet and bulky woolen skirt and jacket. But this was a taller Hertha, Emmi saw, and a much more beautiful one, and surer, and not so sweet of face or gentle of manner. Emmi could not move for some moments. Emotion held her rigid and immovable. Her vision clouded, and she blinked fiercely.

The girl, once on the platform, looked about her without bewilderment. She set down her suitcase, and put her bundle upon it, oblivious of the rain. She straightened her bonnet, and patted her jacket, shaking off some of the soot on her shoulders. There was no expression of confusion, disillusionment or fear on her face, only a great calmness and composure. Emmi, recovering herself, moved forward, and began to speak in German:

"Irmgard? I am your aunt Emmi."

The girl smiled, and the smile was like a flash of light. Emmi was tall, but the girl was taller. She bent her head and touched Emmi's cheek with cool fresh lips. Her ungloved hand, in Emmi's, was firm and young and very strong. Emmi's depression lifted. "Let us go in, out of the rain," she said, almost gayly. She took the black bundle, though the girl murmured in protest, and marched away into the station. Then Irmgard followed, carrying her weighted suitcase.

"I have no carriage," said Emmi with a wry twisted smile. "We must walk to the horse-car."

The girl smiled again. Emmi saw that one of her characteristics was her silence, illuminated by that gleaming smile. In the swaying light of the lantern, the girl's beauty seemed to increase, until it filled all the noisy gritty room. Her hair, under the bonnet, was as smooth as golden satin, and as heavy, twisted in a knot on the nape of an incredibly white neck. Her face was large and oval, and without color except that in her big exquisitely shaped mouth. Under bronze lashes were a pair of strange eyes, brilliantly green. She had the profile of a classic Grecian statue, and indeed, in her beautiful Junoesque figure, there was the quality of sculpture, which not even the homemade and bulky clothing could hide. Emmi had hoped that the girl would be comely. Her most optimistic hopes, however, had not prepared her for this. Her heart lightened still more, and she was filled with affection.

"Child!" she sighed. "I hope you are not too disappointed."

"I am never disappointed in anything," replied Irmgard, in a low deep voice.

"You are very like your mother," said Emmi, gazing at her sadly.

The girl was silent, and only smiled again. She gave an impression of profound spiritual strength and tremendous calm, without inflexibility. Yet, there was nothing bovine in her composure, nothing static. She was one who accepted everything, Emmi thought, without rebellion or despair. But for all the girl's silences, Emmi suspected there were depths which very few would be permitted to know.

Emmi lifted the bundle again. "We must go," she said, briskly. "You must be tired, after a night on that dirty train."

They went out into the sooty rain. Their feet splashed into puddles. Irmgard glanced about her, at the slums, the mills in the distance, and the bowed women creeping along the sidewalk.

"This is probably much different from what you expected," said Emmi, hoping the girl was not too discouraged.

"I never expect anything," replied Irmgard, and smiled once more.

Is she stupid? thought Emmi, for a quick moment. But surely the daughter of Hertha and Emil Hoeller could not possibly be stupid! She was so involved in her thoughts that she did not speak to the girl on the car, and only sat beside her, staring straight ahead. The passengers on the car, awakened from their lethargy by the sight of such spectacular beauty, gazed at Irmgard with expressions of sullen astonishment. If the girl were aware of the attention she attracted, she gave no sign of it. She sat upright, and quietly, her hands in her lap. Emmi studied those hands, large, well-shaped, chapped, but of fine formation. Serenity and stillness flowed out of Irmgard, like a calm light.

When they were finally walking up Mulberry Street, Emmi said:

"You will find America much different from Germany. This is a strange and hopeless land, Irmgard."

The girl did not reply. Emmi was yet to learn that the hard rigidity about her mouth was not customary, but was an evidence of tremendous self-control. She must learn to be more communicative, thought Emmi. But she is probably feeling very strange just now, and overwhelmed.

Emmi opened her flat door, and they entered into the clean dim chill of Irmgard's bedroom. The girl looked about her briefly. The hard lines about her lips softened. "You must unpack immediately," said Emmi, "and change. Then, come into the kitchen, in the rear, where it is warm. I must prepare my dinner."

She went away, closing the door after her. She mounted to her room and removed her jacket, stole and bonnet. She was surprised to find that her hands were trembling a little, and curious excitement thrilling in her blood. She thought of Franz, and how astonished he would be at seeing such loveliness and strangeness. She descended to the kitchen again. It was odd that the loneliness of the flat had gone already, and it seemed filled with comfort. Emmi peeled some potatoes, and prepared some cheap lamb for the stew kettle. But her thoughts were occupied with that bare bedroom in the front of the flat.

The door opened and the girl, dressed in an obviously new black gown, entered. The dress was old-fashioned, without taste, and clumsy. It was evidently her best. She came into the kitchen with a slow quiet step, full of dignity and composure. Emmi had laid out a place on the table, which she had covered with a clean white cloth.

"There is some hot coffee for you, my dear, and some fresh rolls and jam. You must be hungry."

The girl, not speaking, sat down. She looked about the kitchen with her long slow gaze. Without her misshapen bonnet, she was more handsome than ever, and her golden head more regal. She was only nineteen, but seemed much older. She ate obediently, and with appetite. Emmi busied herself about the stove for long silent minutes. There were so many things she wished to say, so many questions to ask. But that silence held her back, like an upheld hand.

Finally, however, she said: "You must not expect much of America, Irmgard. What we heard in Germany about this country is only lies. There may be beautiful places here, but I have not seen them yet. I have seen only dirtiness, ugliness and hopelessness. All this is for the poor. There is no dignity here. In Germany, even the poor have dignity, even the poorest peasant. But unless one is rich in America, there is only shamefulness and weariness."

The girl, having finished her small meal, rose and went to the kitchen window. She had not spoken since she had entered the room. She stood, and looked through the streaming window at the grimy wall of the court opposite.

Emmi, at the stove, paused, and looked at that young and vital figure. She spoke again, in a loud harsh voice of bitterness:

"Do you understand, Irmgard? There is no spring here."

Irmgard turned and looked at her aunt with those brilliant green eyes. "No spring?" she murmured. And then Emmi knew she understood.

"No springtime of hope, Irmgard. It is always winter. A new land, without spring. A land of promise and strength and newness, which was blasted in midwinter, and went no further. Noise and confusion, and much running about, and fever, and no brightness. I have seen other cities in this state, and they are all the same. There is a sickness in them all, and a sick madness. A money madness."

She paused, then went on in a lower, but an even more bitter voice: "When we came here, I thought: It is a new land, and all the hopes of men are here, all the hopes which were killed in Europe. Here, anything can happen, everything brave and glorious and free, and good. I have found it different, Irmgard. I have found that men came from Europe, but brought their illness in a worse form with them."

Her long pale face contorted in a sudden spasm, as though she could not control her years of grief and despair, and acrid disappointment.

"It was not money I wanted, Irmgard. I wanted a chance to live in a land where all things are born, and great things accomplished. Where all the dreams of noble men could come true, and live. Perhaps those who made this country thought so, too. But it is all a lie." She added: "I left the sickness which was the new Germany, and the cruelty, and the misery and oppression. I found them here. They were even worse in America, for they were dirty, and men were even more corrupt."

Irmgard had been listening intently, her eyes fixed on Emmi's working face. Emmi then turned abruptly to her stove. "But what can one do?" she muttered. There was a salty burning at the corners of her lids.

"And Uncle Egon? And Franz? They find it so, also?" asked Irmgard.

Emmi bent her head over her kettle. "Egon never speaks," she said in a stifled voice. "He is a bookkeeper in the same mill where Franz works. Franz—well, you will hear Franz, himself. He is a foreman in the mills, and doing well. We have twenty-eight dollars a week, and I save much of that. That is all one can do—save a little, grimly. Beyond the money, there is nothing. We all work very hard."

"And I shall work, too," said Irmgard. "I am not afraid of work. Will you let me help you, now?"

Emmi turned from the stove. She paused. Irmgard smiled at her, and the smile was so sweet, so understanding, so gentle, that Emmi could not speak.

CHAPTER 8

EGON STOESSEL worked only until half-past five. He arrived home at about six o'clock. But long before that time Emmi was at the front windows, peering carefully through the lace curtains. By six o'clock she was usually in a nervous state of apprehension. Egon had been careless, as usual, and was crushed under the hoofs or wheels of the horse-cars. He had fallen, and injured his skull. He had got lost. He was ill. She alternated between her stove and the windows, her face dully flushed, her eyes sharp with fear. Irmgard, setting the table, watched her with sympathy, listened to her mutters about Egon's carelessness and absentmindedness. As time passed Emmi became more and more irascible, and railed against her husband, telling Irmgard, in a high stifled voice, about the time that Egon had forgotten to leave his desk; the time he had forgotten his overcoat and had walked home in the cold rain, subsequently developing a bronchial trouble which had never left him; or another occasion when he had "taken a walk" after his work and did not arirve home until eight o'clock, seemingly much bewildered because it was so late.

"What can one do with such a man!" she cried, with a manner that implied that Egon exasperated her to the point of active dislike and fury. But Irmgard saw the passionate love and fear in Emmi's pale blue eyes. "It is not yet six o'clock," she said soothingly. Emmi stared at the kitchen clock angrily.

She went to the window again. Egon was coming up the street under his umbrella, walking with his slow uncertain step, his head bent. A pang went through Emmi, as she watched him come. The street-lamps had been lighted. Their yellowish flickering light wavered over the wet and glistening street. Egon bent before the wind, struggling against its force. Across the street, lamps had been lit in the miserable cottages, but these lights merely enhanced the gloomy desolation of the whole scene. Now hail was mingled with the wind and rain, and just as Egon entered his flat, the fusillades of ice-bullets rattled against the windows.

"Where have you been? You are wet to the skin. You are so careless, Egon!" upbraided Emmi, helping her husband with his coat, hat and umbrella. But though her voice was loud and impatient, her face was suddenly beautiful with tenderness. She bent her head and kissed his damp sunken cheek. He smiled at her. He was dimly excited. "Irmgard?" he murmured, rubbing his cold thin hands together.

"She is here." Emmi took his hand, as though he was a child, and led him into the warm kitchen.

Irmgard stood up, as the two entered. Egon stopped in the doorway, his smile fading as though he were greatly shocked. He stared at the tall girl for a long moment. Hertha! said his heart, fainting in him.

"Your Uncle Egon, my child," said Emmi, briskly. The girl curtseyed, then came forward to kiss the old man. He looked up into her beautiful face, and then he thought to himself: It is Hertha's face, and her body, but it is not truly Hertha. He had turned quite pale, but he smiled again.

"I hope you will be happy, liebchen," he said. "It is a strange country. But you have come to those who love you."

He held her hand between both of his tremulous palms, and gazed at her with sad earnestness. Hertha had been so modest, so gentle, so tender, blushing at a word with inarticulate shyness. But he doubted that this girl would blush much, that she would ever be shy or distracted. There was Emmi's inflexible strength in her, and a still, immovable power. Her beauty was cold, almost static, like that of the moon. He saw her vivid green eyes, so at variance with her large calm features. Those eyes had fire, but as he looked at them, he saw it was an icy fire.

He sat down in a wooden rocking-chair near the stove, and Emmi brought him his slippers. She removed his wet boots, scolding under her breath, and put his slippers on his tired feet. She brought him a glass of hot milk, which he obediently drank. As he did so, he watched Irmgard as she helped Emmi, noticed her sure firm movements. The curve of her shoulders and long back was amazingly lovely, but without fragility. He glanced quickly and with a question at his wife, and her answering look satisfied him. A faint thrill of excitement ran along his nerves. "Franz will soon be home," he said.

"Franz!" muttered Emmi, in a dissatisfied tone.

While they waited for Franz, Egon asked Irmgard timidly about Germany. "Has it changed much, in the last ten years?" he asked.

"I saw little change, Uncle Egon," answered the girl, respectfully. "But then, there is very little change in villages. My father taught his school, and I managed the farm. It was very quiet." Egon liked the low deep voice, though it was not Hertha's voice.

"It seems strange that such a one as Emil could have settled down to teaching school," said Emmi, with a snort. "I remember him. He burned. He was like a torch. I admired him very much. He would have come to America, after he came out of prison, had it not been for his child, you, Irmgard. He seemed much subdued, like a banked fire. Did he become entirely a petty bourgeoise, Irmgard?"

Irmgard smiled. "No. He still believed in mankind, Aunt Emmi."

Emmi, who was scrutinizing the stew, turned with a sudden sharpness to her niece, and frowned. "You speak as though you were amused," she said. "And cynical."

The girl saw that her aunt was both annoyed and suspicious, and curiously startled.

"No," she replied, and that was all. But the frown remained between Emmi's brows. She appeared to have been taken aback. Egon looked from one woman to the other with apprehension.

"We must have some music after supper," he said, helplessly. "Did you bring your violin, child?"

"Yes, I have it. I have not played much, lately, Uncle Egon."

He brightened. "Ah, you must make Franz play. He does it so beautifully."

"You know very well that Franz has not played for months and months, Egon," said Emmi, in a hard voice. Egon sighed, said nothing, sipped his milk.

An odd constraint filled the warm lighted kitchen. Something had gone wrong, reflected Egon. But what was it? Had he said something wrong? He was always offending Emmi, his poor Emmi. That was probably because he was very stupid. His gentle face became humble and distressed. He removed his glasses and polished them on his clean white handkerchief. His weak eyes blinked in the strong light, and were moist, as though full of tears. Irmgard went about her work as calmly and quietly as ever, seeming to know exactly what to do.

Egon made another attempt. "I have always wanted a farm," he said timidly. "I can never reconcile myself to living in a city."

"But not in America!" exclaimed Emmi. "Oh, never in America! When Franz marries, and is settled, we might return to Germany, and see what we can do." Her voice had repudiation in it, and resistance, and bitter defeat. Irmgard lifted her head slowly and gazed intently at her aunt's flushed profile.

"You would return to Germany, Aunt Emmi?" she asked. "My father said you would never return."

The flush deepened roughly on Emmi's lean cheeks, and the bitter lines became sharper about her lips. "I never thought to return. It was the last thing I desired. I turned my back upon Germany, forever. I had a dream of America—" She straightened up, and turned away from both the old man and the girl, and her tone became lower, and a trifle hoarse. "There is no dream. The only thing I wish to do, perhaps very soon, is to go home, and forget I ever had a dream, or a hope." She pressed her clenched hands savagely on the window-sill and stared at the blackness outside. "I was a fool," she said, huskily.

There was no sound in the kitchen, except Egon's sigh of distress. Then Irmgard said softly: "There never was, and never will be, a Utopia, Aunt Emmi. We must live as we find life, and human beings. But with the stuff we have, we can approach our hopes."

Emmi did not answer for a long time. She did not seem to have heard the girl. Finally she turned and regarded Irmgard strangely. She was very pale. If she meant to speak, she was prevented from doing so by the arrival of Franz.

Franz came in, laughing to himself. He had completely forgotten that his cousin was to arrive today. His strong fair face, all squarenesses and angles, was flushed and damp with rain and wind. The shoulders of his shabby gray coat were black with moisture, and he took off his cap and shook it, shedding sprays of water. His thick yellow hair rose like a crest from his forehead, and under it, his blue eyes glittered in the gaslight. There was an exuberant Norseman quality about him, suggestive of seas and forests and long open plains, a quality of vital and savage energy and strength. But his mother, as always, saw that though he laughed his mouth was long and brutal, and the same brutality was in the square wide line of his jawbones and the breadth of his nose.

"A bad evening, Mama, Papa," he said, still laughing at some inner joke. He kissed his parents lightly. Irmgard stood in the pantry door, still unnoticed.

Emmi had turned her dry colorless cheek to her son to receive his kiss. Now she said severely: "Franz, your cousin, Irmgard Hoeller."

Franz turned with a startled air of remembrance, and saw Irmgard, quietly watching him from the door. His eye ran over her quickly. He saw that she was almost as tall as himself, and he was much taller than average. His first thought was: A handsome cow. A stupid, handsome cow. He did not like tall fair women, and this was perhaps rooted in the antagonism between himself and his mother. He preferred delicate fragile women, small and dark. A level flash of hostility darted between himself and Irmgard. Very stupid, he thought again, and smiled.

He greeted her courteously enough in German, and in a low indifferent voice she answered. She moved to the table in her bulky shapeless clothing, and laid fresh silver upon its whiteness. She could manage a plow like a man, Franz's contemptuous thoughts continued, and he saw her hands and felt distaste. Bigness in women revolted him. This was no dainty piece of woman-flesh, but a girl who could run a farm with Teutonic thoroughness and hot health and strength. He stared covertly at her broad shoulders, but was pleased by the slenderness of her waist, so compact and fluid.

Emmi had been watching the girl and the young man with passionate attention. She saw Irmgard's indifference and her son's contemptuous hostility. Anger and furious disappointment seized her. In essentials, her nature was so like Franz's that she could almost always guess or feel his thoughts.

"We must make Irmgard as happy as possible in this strange country," she said, in her loud hectoring voice, as though it were a command.

"Most certainly," replied Franz politely. He hung up his coat and cap, and rubbed his hands over the red lids of the fuming stove. He glanced over his shoulder at his father. "You did not get wet, Papa?" he asked, with affection.

"No, my son, not very much," answered Egon, smiling with love. "But your own boots are very damp. Do you not think it best to change them?"

Franz glanced indifferently at his boots. "I think not." He sat down at the table and looked with pleasure at the food. He broke off a huge piece of bread and buttered it lavishly. His inner joke absorbed him again.

"I think there is going to be a strike," he said, chuckling.

Emmi, who had been waiting upon him, paused, a dish in her hands and alarm in her face. "A strike! Why should there be a strike, Franz?"

He shrugged. "Business is very bad. We had to shut down three more furnaces today. Several orders have been cancelled, the superintendent told me. There has been a big uproar, because the last shipments were porous. Our way of making moulds is at fault. There is a fortune waiting for a man who can make dependable moulds. So far, we have not found it. Now, we have many shipments back on our hands, fine enough on the surface, but full of air-holes in the center, brittle and worthless. That is something we must always expect, in some quantities. But unfortunately, the entire shipments were in that condition. This is a very bad thing for the Schmidt Steel Company, for our waste has heretofore always been small. Our reputation has already suffered. So—they have had to lay off many more men, and must reduce the wages of those who have been retained."

Emmi's disappointment was swallowed up in her apprehension. "You will be laid off, Franz?"

He gave her a smiling, cunning look. "Not yet, at least, Mama. You need not fear too much for the bankbooks."

She flushed with anger and embarrassment, but before she could reply, Egon said, distressedly: "I knew of this some days ago. But I did not know it was so bad."

"It is very bad," said Franz, tranquilly.

Emmi exclaimed: "You do not seem too anxious, Franz! Times are very poor. What will you do if you are laid off?"

He looked at her, narrowing his smiling eyes. "I have said, Mama, that there is no danger, just yet."

This important matter settled, Emmi could momentarily forget personal matters. She inhaled a deep breath of relief. Then she frowned. "This morning, I saw the workmen at the gates of the mills. They had been locked out. It was very terrible. Their faces——"

"Starving is not very pleasant, I agree," said Franz, devouring his food.

"You can say that so indifferently!" cried Emmi, passion thick in her voice, the crimson deep in her flat cheeks. Irmgard, washing some dishes at the sink, became alert, and listened with intentness. From her aunt's tone, and her cousin's light laugh, she guessed that some deep implication lay beneath them, and that some sore and oozing animosity of long standing was implicit between the woman and her son. Their words were like sparks shooting upward from a hidden and smoldering fire.

Franz looked at his mother with an air of amiable patience. "Now, Mama, must we quarrel again about the same old thing?"

Emmi thumped a plate down upon the table. Her worn hands were trembling. Her corded throat throbbed. She gathered her breath for a reply, but Franz gave his cousin a smiling glance over his shoulder.

"It is an old story, between mama and me," he said, lightly including her in the conversation.

Irmgard had been cutting the cheese cake at the sink. She now looked at him, in silence. The gaslight shone in her eyes, and he was suddenly startled at their clear and brilliant greenness, so comprehending, so intense. So taken aback was he at their singular beauty, glowing out at him from between their thick bronze lashes, that he hardly heard his mother's hurried, passionate words, so filled with rage, breathlessness and incoherence:

"You do not care, Franz! It is nothing to you if other men starve. It is always yourself, only, always! Those men's faces—! And their wives and children. It is wrong, terrible. This ought not to exist in a country so rich, so abundant. There should be no starvation, no terror of unemployment. The selfishness of those responsible——"

"I am not responsible," said Franz, still smiling slightly. But his eyelids flickered as though he were controlling himself. He looked at Irmgard again, in order to see her eyes. But her white lids obscured them as she wiped dishes, and he saw only her calm profile. "What can I do, Mama?"

Emmi's nostrils distended with her furious breath. She ignored her husband's alarmed, deprecatory touch on her arm.

"What can you do? I do not know. It is your attitude, so unconcerned, so indifferent, so selfish, so callous! And your attitude is the attitude of those responsible for all this misery. It is the attitude which needs changing——"

"You wish me to project thought-waves?" asked Franz, in a maddeningly amused voice. He had been over this so many times with his mother. "I do not believe in thought-waves, Mama. I am only a foreman in the mills. I am just to my men, if they are just with me. I do my daily work. I am nothing at all, remember, but a foreman in the mills. The decisions come from some one else. I get my wages—I do my work. That is my only concern, and must be my only concern."

Feeling, even under her fury, the logic of this argument, but her fury increasing because of her impotence against it, Emmi turned violently to her niece:

"You see, Irmgard! This is America, where men starve among riches, and children go sick and hungry among luxury. If a man is injured, he is thrown out, to die or beg. You have not seen America, Irmgard! But you will see it, and you will hate it as I do."

And then Irmgard knew that it was indeed Franz's attitude which so filled his mother with despair, grief and distraction. It was this attitude which lay at the roots of their mutual antagonism, and deeper than the roots was Emmi's uncompromising integrity, idealism, and the sacrifices she had made. Her heart lay there, and her son was poisoning it. The girl glanced at her aunt with compassion, but said nothing.

It was this silence of hers which began to intrigue Franz. He had expected that his cousin would be a garrulous, simple girl, full of Teutonic simplicity and ingenuousness. He had thought of her as a peasant, remembering that she had been attending the small farm practically single-handed, while her formerly vitriolic father had covered his revolutionary fires with the text-books of village children. Her silence might be stupidity, but Franz, who was very astute, began to suspect that it was not stupidity. His interest quickened. He drank his hot coffee, but he watched her closely, becoming more and more pleased with her profile and the slenderness of her waist. Now he saw that she was beautiful, and waited impatiently for the clear lucidity of her eyes to look at him again.

"Freya," he said aloud. His mother had begun another tumbling and chaotic series of denunciations, and Egon was sunken over his coffee in silent despondency. The steam of the coffee had blurred his glasses; his thin narrow head was bent as though he had fallen into some mournful trance. He knew that it was useless to interfere between Emmi and his son, and he could only endure the unpleasantness with inner quakings. So neither he nor Emmi heard Franz's casual word. Franz, watching Irmgard, wondered if she had heard. But Irmgard showed no sign that she had. She would not know what it meant, anyway, thought Franz, and was slightly disappointed. After all, her schooling must have been narrow. Unless her father, once renowned for his scholarly background, might have instructed her.

"There is no hope for the poor in America!" Emmi was crying, wringing her hands in her apron, her face burning and her pale eyes flashing. "The most miserable peasant in Germany is happier than the workmen here. It is an illusion, a lie, that there is liberty, freedom, happiness and comfort in America. These are only for the rich——"

Franz regarded her with calm. "That has always been so, everywhere in the world, Mama, as I have told you so many times. But you are always chasing moonbeams and dreams. What do you expect of America?"

"I expect that she live up to some of her lies," said Emmi.

Franz shrugged. "What nation ever did? We must accept things as they are. The incompetent and the weak must die. I have not done badly. I shall do better. Because I am strong. Do you think America should be an asylum for the unfit and the worthless, the inadequate and the useless? Why? Is this a hospital, a haven, a sanctuary? Even America must deal with the stuff of men, and if the stuff is feeble and rotten, then it must be destroyed. That is the law of nature. Even the dreamers in America must eventually be confronted by that law, and bow to it.

"I am a foreman in the mills. Some day, I shall be more than that. I shall see to it that I am. I was an immigrant, too, with only a little knowledge of English. Yet, I have risen higher than native Americans, and other immigrants. What I have done, they can do. If they cannot do it, they must be content with the bones and the crusts thrown to them. America is not static. She is in a state of flux. The strong will rise to the surface. The weak will fall to the bottom. I did not make this law. It has existed since the first man breathed."

"You have risen because you are ruthless!" cried Emmi.

Franz shrugged again. "Ruthless! Dreamers always call strong men ruthless. It is their pet word for the will-to-power and the will-to-survive." He laughed shortly. "If it were not for the 'ruthless' the weak would not eat even what they have to eat. We build the walls that shelter them, and make the bread which keeps them alive. Men are not born equal. It is no fault of mine that I was born stronger than many others, and that the majority of men are weak and rotten. I live according to laws laid down before I was born."

"Have you ever heard of mercy?" asked Emmi in a choked voice.

"Mercy," repeated Franz, in a contemplative voice, as though he had not heard this a thousand weary times before. "What has mercy got to do with law?"

He pushed back his chair, and smiled kindly at his mother, whose eyes were filled with desperate tears. "We shall have a fire in the parlor tonight, Mama? To welcome Irmgard?"

He got up. He passed close to Irmgard. He hesitated. It seemed to him that some powerful and irresistible current passed from her body to his, though her back was to him. He saw the fine golden hairs on her white neck, and the living whiteness of her flesh. Then he left the room, humming under his breath.

Egon again put his hand on his wife's arm. "Emmi, do not be so distressed. Franz is only teasing you. Why do you quarrel so with him?"

She made a movement as though to throw off his hand. But when she looked down at his gentle tired face, her own features worked. She sat down in Franz's chair, and said harshly to her niece: "Irmgard. We must eat our dinner." Her neck still throbbed; the burning color was still high on her dry cheekbones. Her whole posture was one of futile misery and grief.

Irmgard sat down near Egon. Her tranquillity was infuriating to Emmi. "What do you think of my son?" she asked bitterly.

Irmgard lifted her eyes and smiled, not at Emmi, but at Egon, and he smiled back, touched at so much beauty.

"He can be disagreeable," said Irmgard, as though with amusement.

CHAPTER 9

THE "PARLOR" was chill, dark and dank. Franz built a fire in the stove, and lit the streaming gaslights. His father entered the room, uncertainly. Egon did not like the room with its narrow gloomy slits of windows and cold stark walls. He preferred the kitchen. He still wore his broadcloth coat, and his neatly folded cravat and black-ribboned spectacles, and his bent frail figure gave him a scholarly air. He seated himself timidly as near to the crackling stove as possible and rubbed his hands, shivering.

"It will soon be warm, Papa," said Franz, moving restlessly up and down the room, his hands in his pockets. He was incongruous in that room, with his big body and limbs, his yellow hair and large and somewhat brutal face. Egon thought of the young Prussian officers he had seen, marching and helmeted, and he felt the same shrinking from his son that he had felt for them. Franz was a stranger to him, though there was a fondness between them. When Emmi talked of the things of the mind, there was a harsh aggressiveness in her, as though she were using her knowledge as bludgeons. Franz would then pretend a prodigious stupidity, in order to harass and infuriate her. But he never pretended to his father. He always listened with great alertness, and answered astutely. This was the point of contact between them. But still, they were strangers, this elderly scholar and the Prussian son.

Egon's escape from a painful world was in revery. His reveries were always gentle, filled with the green mist of remembered trees and tranquil hills. They were always more real to him than the unreality of this dreadful America, with its noise and soot and clamor, its stretching of clanking limbs, its shaking of its enormous steel head. America had never been more than a troubled nightmare to him, though he had lived here for fourteen years. He felt that his body was one shrinking fiber, a thin root, forced to seek its sustenance in a cindered yard. He forced himself to endure, for his wife's sake, but it was the enduring of pain of a man partially under an anesthetic. His real life was in his reveries, where he saw the faces he had known under quiet skies, and heard the distant cow-bells on the quiet hills. Even the men in his office were shadows in a dark dream.

Franz heard his father's sighing. But he was accustomed to that, though the sound always touched him. Stranger though he was to his father, he knew his thoughts, as one knows a familiar voice.

Emmi had not yet come in. She was still busy in the kitchen, while Irmgard was helping her. Egon glanced sideways at the door, and murmured:

"Franz, you should not tease your mother. She has a lot to bear. But you are always tormenting her. It is not good, or kind."

Franz laughed shortly. "Mama and I understand each other," he said, with lightness. He, too, looked at the door, and frowned impatiently.

Egon sighed again. "Did you have a hard day at the mills, my son?"

Franz lifted his brows. "We are slow, today. Very slow. We have been getting slower for the past two years. Unless something is done, the mills are finished. They have been going down steadily. You know that, Papa."

"Yes, I know."

Franz stopped his pacing and stood before the stove, frowning somberly.

"I might have to leave. It is no use staying with a sinking ship. Yet, I should not like to leave. My plans are all there."

Egon glanced up in gentle surprise. "Your plans? What plans?"

Franz shrugged. "How do I know? But something keeps me there."

"Loyalty, perhaps? Liking for your work?" Egon was softly surprised that these two virtues existed in his son.

But Franz burst into a loud laugh. He looked at his father as a man might look at a child. "Loyalty! For what? For an old fat man bursting at the seams with richness? No. Loyalty to myself. There is something in that mill for me. There are other mills. Once I even thought of going to Windsor, and getting work in the Sessions Steel Company. But for a man with a future like mine, it is better to be in a dying company. That does not sound sensible, but I feel it is. For, if I rescue it, it is mine."

Despite his unworldliness, Egon smiled involuntarily. He

felt tender towards his son, who, for all his large manhood, was apparently unsophisticated. "But, Franz, you are only a small foreman in the mills. How can it ever be 'yours'?"

But Franz was silent. A shrewd hard look settled on his face. He hummed a little to himself, and, opening the stove door, critically examined the dull red coals within. He poked them vigorously.

He said finally: "Schmidt knows he is failing. He rarely comes into the mills. But today he came in, with the superintendent fawning like a dog on his heels. Stamping and grunting like a short fat pig, and shouting and swearing." He laughed again, shortly. "The two of them came up to the hearth where my men were working, and the superintendent said something to him. He looked at me, and glared. He said: 'Is your name Franz? Franz what?' If he thought to intimidate me with his glaring, he was mistaken. I told him my name. His German is very bad; it is evident he was a peasant, in Bavaria. He seemed suspicious of me, and just rocked on his heels, glowering, and asking questions. Where was I born? What were my people? How long had I been in America? I was careful to answer him in my best manner in order to convince him that I was not a peasant, as he was."

Egon was alarmed. "I hope you were not disrespectful, Franz? You are always so flippant."

Franz smiled. "One must never be subservient to peasants, Papa. They become increasingly arrogant. I was respectful to him as my employer, but I let him know that my class was superior. At times, he had difficulty in understanding me. His vocabulary in English is much better, but in German, he speaks in the peasant's idioms and coarsenesses."

"You angered him, Franz?" cried Egon, thoroughly dismayed.

"No, on the contrary, he seemed pleased. You should have seen the superintendent, that Saxon swine! He gaped like a fish. He could not understand his master's condescension. As for my men, they were paralyzed. When Schmidt speaks, the whole mill sinks into comparative silence."

"I think he was very amiable, to stop and speak to his workmen," suggested Egon, despondently. He was certain that Franz had angered the mighty Schmidt. He, himself, had seen his employer only once, and then at a distance. Egon, in spite of what he was, had the German's innate terror and awe of a superior. He could hardly believe that the great man had really stopped to exchange pleasantries with an obscure foreman in his mills. He was bewildered. He moistened his dry and sunken mouth. "I hope you were not disrespectful," he whispered hopelessly. But he was increasingly bewildered.

Great men do not condescend even to recognize the existence of their servants. He remembered the days of his army service, and shivered again.

"I do not understand it," he said aloud, and helplessly. "Why should he speak to you, Franz? It is not natural."

"Perhaps he was impressed with my beauty," replied his son, laughing.

The door opened, and Franz glanced eagerly in its direction. But it was only Emmi, untying her apron. Her face was still hard and grim as she looked about her. But she merely said that Irmgard had insisted upon finishing by herself.

She added, turning to Franz: "I presume you are pleased with yourself in displaying your disrespect for your mother, and your coarseness, to your cousin?"

Egon sighed miserably. He had never accustomed himself to the bickering between his wife and his son. "Now, Emmi," he murmured, depressed.

But Franz smiled good-humoredly. "I was not disrespectful. Sit here, Mama. It is the only warm spot in this cave."

Emmi sat down, stiffly, on a chair far from the one Franz had indicated.

"I am ashamed of you," she said, bitterly.

"That is nothing new, Mama." Franz's voice was light. He knew why his mother had brought Irmgard here, and was highly amused. "You did nothing to impress her that I would be a desirable husband, did you?"

Emmi flushed. Her pale eyes sparkled with fury. She looked at Franz, who was grinning down at her. "No! Why should I? She is far too good for you."

Franz glanced again at the door, and dropped his voice. He became serious.

"But what are we to do with her? You do not need help in the house. She must go out into service, of course."

"Ha! You are afraid her presence will be expensive here?"

But Franz answered coolly: "Yes, that is true. After all, we must consider the money."

"It is always 'money' with you!" exclaimed Emmi, angrily.

"And with you, dear Mama," said Franz, in that same cool and insistent voice. "When have you been lavish with money?"

"Now, Franz, that is very disrespectful," said Egon, sadly. "You must not talk so to your mother."

Emmi turned to her husband almost savagely. "It is your fault, Egon! When I wished to thrash him when he was a child, you always interfered. This, then, is your doing."

"I detest brutality," said Egon, faintly, and paling. "I loathe violence. Have we not had enough of it, in Germany?"

"Mama still has the soul of a Prussian," remarked Franz, smiling.

He knew how this infuriated her. He was accustomed to her furious words in reply, and her incoherent denunciations. But he did not know how overwrought she was tonight, and so, he was not prepared for her leaping to her feet and striking him violently across his mouth. Her action was instinctive, and so was his grasping of her wrist, and his thrusting of her backwards. She was almost as tall as he, and mother and son, so alike in feature, in build and in coloring, glared malignantly at each other above their hands. An aura of violence quivered about them, like a red and fuming light. Their identical eyes glowed with hatred. They did not move or speak, only stood there, Emmi's wrist still in Franz's crushing grip. They were like two statues, held in turbulent immobility. Two drops of blood appeared on Franz's lower lip. But their eyes grappled together like assailants. They looked deeply into each other, the savage man and the equally savage woman.

Egon was so horrified, so sickened, that he rose to his feet, and had to grasp a chair to keep from falling. "Lieber Gott!" he cried, faintly.

After a long and horrible moment or two, Franz flung his mother's hand from him, with a gesture of contempt.

"Do not do that again," he said, in a low slow voice. "Never again."

Egon rubbed his hands, and almost wept. Emmi had fallen back. She still looked at her son, her eyes strained and distended, and filled with that red light. And he gazed back at her. In that moment, they both knew, something had happened between them which would never be healed, and never forgiven, even in death.

"This should never have happened," whispered Egon, closing his eyes.

Franz turned away. He wiped his mouth. "It was not my doing," he said, but his voice was hard as ice.

There was no sound now in the kitchen. Franz suspected that Irmgard had heard the blow and the words which followed. So, when after a short but terrible interlude the door opened, he turned to it, curiously and watchfully. Irmgard entered. If she had heard, she revealed nothing. Her face, her manner, her movements, were full of dignity and great calmness.

Emmi sat down near her husband, in silence. But he saw that tremors were shaking her lean body as though she were suffering from a chill. He was amazed at her composure, and understood what control lay behind it, for her face was ghastly.

"Come in, child," she said, in a quiet voice. "It will soon be warm in here."

Irmgard advanced into the room, and Franz, forgetting his mother, watched her come. Freya, he thought again, fascinated by that large beauty under the flickering gas-jets. She made the narrow coffin-like room, with its dismal furniture, shrink away into nothingness, as though it was ashamed of its meanness and ugliness. Yet, Franz thought, it was not only her physical beauty which did this. It was some heroic quality in herself, which rayed outward from her flesh. In her was the strength of impregnable hills and ramparts, the strength of vast landscapes.

She looked at Franz impersonally, and he wondered if she had heard what had taken place in this room. He thought she looked at him as a painted portrait might look. She then bent towards Emmi with a slight smile, and also smiled at Egon. She sat down tranquilly, every movement full of composed splendor.

"Is there something else I can do?" she asked.

"No, my dear." Emmi's harsh voice trembled. She laid her rough hand for a moment on the girl's hand. Egon smiled at her tremulously, though he was still quivering visibly. If the hot smell of violence was still in the room, the girl did not seem aware of it. Her profile, turned to Franz, was serene.

He moved nearer to her, standing by the stove, and looking down at her quizzically.

"And what do you think you will be able to do in America, cousin?" he asked.

She looked at him, her brilliant green eyes unmoved and impersonal. "I shall work, certainly. That is why I have come. Tomorrow, I shall look for work."

Franz bit his lip. Had she heard everything that had been said in this room?

"There is no hurry, Irmgard," said Emmi. "I am lonely in the day. You shall keep me company."

Irmgard smiled at her affectionately. "That is very kind of you, aunt. But I am accustomed to work. I cannot live on your generosity. I never intended it."

Egon interposed in his gentle eager voice: "But you have worked so hard all your life, liebchen. You must rest a little. We want you, and we love you. This is your home, also."

Irmgard regarded him with quiet tenderness. "If you wish it to be my home, then it is my home, Uncle Egon. But that does not absolve me from working. I could not be happy in idleness." She lifted her hands and looked at them. "I am accustomed to work," she repeated.

There was silence in the room. Franz said to himself: Does

she really think, or is all this, her body and her tranquillity, only the evidence of deep stupidity, a peasant's stupidity? He could not like her. He was irritated by her, and troubled. He thought again: A handsome cow. He repeated it to himself, viciously: A handsome cow. He looked up, to see that Irmgard was regarding him steadfastly. A flash of something deeply inimical passed between them, and his gorge rose. Truly a peasant, with peasant eyes!

He knew now that she disliked him, felt only cold hostility for him, even contempt.

It was Egon who broke the silence. "You will not find America like Germany, child," he said, sadly, his faded eyes looking inward.

"I did not expect to find it so," replied Irmgard, in her deep voice. "But, I must live. I must compromise with, and accept, my new life. I knew things would be strange, and different. But what of it? It would be foolish of me to be discontented."

"And you do not regret leaving Germany?" asked Emmi, aggressively.

She turned her head to her aunt slowly. "Regret? It is silly to regret necessity. It is a waste of time."

The peasant's philosophy, thought Franz. He put fresh coal upon the fire in the stove. Pastures are always pastures, to cattle, he reflected, no matter if they are strange pastures.

He turned to his father, contemptuously dismissing the two women.

"Have they laid off any men in the office?"

Emmi, despite her rage and her bitterness and humiliation, immediately became interested, and looked at her husband anxiously.

"Two or three clerks, I believe," replied Egon, despondently.

"Bookkeepers?" asked Emmi, leaning towards her husband.

"Not yet, Emmi. But one never knows where the blow will fall next."

Emmi was gravely alarmed. If the mills shut down, and Franz and Egon were dismissed, her last solace would be gone. The bankbooks would cease to grow. Her alarm increased.

"What is wrong? Can nothing be done to save the mills?"

No one answered her. She momentarily forgot her fury against her son, and turned to him impatiently. "Times are not bad. What is the matter with the mills?"

He answered her indifferently, but looked at his father: "Schmidt has not kept up with new inventions. He makes steel in the same old way. He knows nothing. What was good twenty years ago is good enough for him now. Or, perhaps it is not his fault. The newer methods are taken by the larger and newer mills. But even the newer mills have not solved the problems of the mould. Even they must count on waste and inadequacies."

Irmgard turned her head slowly to her cousin and regarded him with her odd steadfast look. The red reflection of the burning fire in the stove, coming through the isinglass windows, carved her face in scarlet light and shadow. He thought that she had the aspect of a remote and placid statue.

"You are very interested in the mills? You love your work?"

He laughed. "No. I am not interested in the way you mean, nor do I like it. But it is the thing I began, and the thing I now understand. I want only one thing from it, only one thing from the sweat and labor."

"Yes? And what is that?"

"Money."

They looked at each other in another sudden silence. Franz could not read those calm features, which he now decided had no expression at all.

Emmi, whose deep and long-seated disappointment in her son could not keep her quiet even after her humiliation, exclaimed: "It is always money, with Franz! He cares for nothing else."

He gazed at her for a long moment, coldly. "And, in America, what else is there but money?"

But Emmi did not answer him. She turned to her niece. She was highly excited, and the rough color scarred her flat cheeks. Her eyes jumped in their sockets. She laughed with peculiar hysteria.

"You see, Irmgard? In Europe, men are not so concerned with money. They regard family, learning, accomplishments, honors, as much more important. The mere man with much money is despised—"

"That is your fantasy," interjected Franz. But his mother ignored him. Her smile was taut and wild as she continued to say to Irmgard:

"But in America, the people have no family background, no learning, no accomplishments, and no great honors. Therefore, they solace themselves with getting money, whether they earn it or steal it."

Franz interrupted her again, looking at his cousin, whose expression was inscrutable:

"My mother puts it too baldly. It is not money for money's sake, that Americans desire. The money means power to them. They are not a military nation, and so do not get power by conquest. They do not rely on a dead past to give them honors, and their accomplishments are purely industrial. But they share with all of us the desire for power. Money in America is power. Without that power, your hypothetical family, accomplishments and honors mean nothing at all. Perhaps it is wrong. But it is a fact, and I have always believed in accepting facts and dealing with them on their own terms."

Emmi still looked at her niece with that wild and piteous smile:

"You see? There is nothing here, but this struggle for money. If you have it, you live. If you do not have it, you die. How can one endure in such an atmosphere, where learning and dignity are despised because they do not create money? Worse even than that, is the condition of the working people in America. You have not yet seen, Irmgard! But I shall take you among our neighbors, and it will sicken you. I have seen such things!"

Irmgard smiled at her aunt with grave sympathy.

But Franz said, with smiling contempt: "My dear mother believes that the industrialists should have a tender regard for their workmen, that they should pay them what she calls 'adequate' wages, though what adequate wages are she is not too certain, herself. She believes that there should be some sort of insurance for unemployment, sickness and accident. A paternalistic form of life, with each employer anxiously coddling his employees. She will not see that industry is the same as any other barter. Do we expect our shop-keepers, who give us goods for money, to demand that we pay their doctors' bills and protect them from bad times? Men barter their time for money. Those who buy their labor have no more responsibility for them. If a man is unable to sell his labor, it is unfortunate. But it is no one's fault. That is realistic."

Emmi turned to him with savage fury. "Men are more than goods, and barter. I have tried to teach you that. To put them in the same class with goods is immoral. There are intangible things to be considered: conduct, humanity, mercy, justice and decency. Are men bales of cotton and machinery and goods? To think so is barbarism. To think so is cruelty, and chaos."

Franz turned away, making a contemptuous mouth. He glanced at his cousin fleetingly, as though to say: "You see how absurd she is."

Irmgard looked at her hands and said quietly: "I have always found life cruel. I have tried to find out why it should be so, but still I do not know." Then she lifted her head with a quick movement, and said to Franz:

"Why do you want money so?"

The green flash of her eyes startled him, and again he was

confused and uncertain about her. This made his flippancy, when he answered, more obvious than ever:

"Why? I have told you: it means power. And I want power because it will protect me from other men. I have no illusions about mankind. It is everything that is foul and contemptible, mean and vulgar, vicious and degenerate. Only money can protect one against his fellow men."

Emmi regarded her niece significantly, but Irmgard, to her sadness, saw that the older woman's eyes were filled with burning tears.

Emmi said, in a shaking voice: "You see that my son believes nothing of what I have tried to teach him, and for which I made such sacrifices. A man who despises others is a suspicious character, himself."

Irmgard hesitated, then she said very quietly: "In many ways, I must agree with Franz. People are hateful and treacherous, selfish and greedy. They prefer lies to truth, and cruelty to kindness. I have often wondered why God endured the world to exist. It is full of wickedness and enemies. No man ever lived who had a friend. I have seen nothing but slyness and avarice, betrayal and lies. My father used to say that this is because existence has compelled men to be so, and circumstance. I do not believe it. Men make circumstance. The world is what it is because men wish it to be so, and prefer it that way."

Her beautiful face darkened. A pinched and shadowy look appeared about her nostrils and her large mouth. Her green eyes sparkled with anger and contempt.

Emmi was so taken aback by these strange words that she could say nothing. The silence was broken by Franz's sudden hard laugh.

He left the room and went into the kitchen. When he had gone, Irmgard put her hand on her aunt's arm, almost urgently, and tried to see that pale averted face.

"Do not think I approve of cruelty and selfishness. I do not. But, who can change them? They exist. We can do nothing."

But Emmi's arm was stiff and unresponsive under that warm hand. She kept her face averted, as though she repudiated this girl from whom she had hoped so much. Irmgard, distressed, turned to Egon, and said: "Uncle. What do you think?"

The old man lifted his head and regarded her with intense sadness.

He said: "I have lived a long time, liebchen, and I have not yet found life endurable."

After awhile Franz returned to the room with a pitcher of beer and some glasses. He poured the foaming liquid, and offered it to his mother and his father. Egon accepted, but Emmi, who loved beer, refused, not in words, but in the turning aside of her head. Irmgard took a glass and held it in her hands, as though she were unconscious of having it.

Franz drank deeply. He stood near the stove, tall, broad, smiling derisively. He looked at Irmgard:

"Unser Amerika!" he said.

Emmi sat like an image of grief, her indomitable shoulders bent, her head fallen on her meagre chest.

CHAPTER 10

FRANZ SAT alone, smoking a last pipe. His parents had gone to bed. Irmgard had retired to her room. The stove had lost its earlier cherry-colored belly, and the room was becoming cold. Before she had left, Emmi had prudently turned out all the gas jets but one, but this filled the room with vague uncertain shadows. The rain had stopped, but the wind rattled the narrow slices of windows. It had begun to snow fitfully. Franz was encased in the silence of the sleeping flat, the sleeping street. Even when a passing train, behind the building, howled like a lonely wolf, the sound seemed to infuse itself into the silence rather than invade it.

Franz propped his feet on the ledge of the stove and tilted back his chair. He glanced about the room impassively, though he hated its ugliness and starkness. The horsehair seats gleamed darkly in the gaslight. The portraits on the walls were blurs. He rubbed his cold feet against the stove and was rewarded only by a faint warmth. The gaslight hissed. From somewhere came a child's dim sharp cry, and then silence again. Hail was mingling with the first snow, and its rattling against the windows increased the desolation of the night.

When he glanced idly at his watch, Franz saw that it was well past midnight. But he was not sleepy. He often sat alone, thinking, the pipe in his mouth and a glass of beer at his elbow. He would rock slowly back and forth on his straight chair, thinking a thousand thoughts. He preferred his own company, and one of his characteristics was an intense love of solitude. He remembered what Heine had said, that every German has the mind of a philosopher and the soul of a soldier. He knew he was no philosopher, and decidedly no soldier. Nevertheless, he was a solitary. He was contemplative, rather than philosophical. He amused himself with no abstracts. He dealt with facts, and all the ramifications of facts. Sometimes, when he was alone, he read intensely. He liked Nietzsche, though he laughed at his tormented and impotent will-to-power. It was the impotence which amused him, rather than the philosophy. He had long ago come to the conclusion that the passionate devotees of power were all eunuchs. He wanted power for himself. As an abstract he did not adore it, as Nietzsche adored it. It was a personal thing, for him. But for Nietzsche, it was the adoration of the hero, the superman. Franz knew there were no supermen. There were only men who wanted personal power, and were able to obtain it, and men who lusted for power, and could never obtain it. The impulse toward power smoldered in every man. There were only a few who knew how to get it. The rest merely adored.

He got up and took his mother's precious volume of Schiller's poems from the table. He lit another gas jet, and idled through the pages. He was much obsessed by poetry. It was like looking into a fantastic world where real truths were born for projection into the world of reality. The womb of the unreal created the real—but Schiller could not fascinate him tonight. A curious restlessness crept along his nerves. He lifted his head and listened. His eyes glanced at Irmgard's door. He put aside the book.

The restlessness increased. He thought of his mother. He was fond of her, though she annoyed and amused him. He knew what she wanted of him. He was incapable of fulfilling her wants, and from childhood he had resented her urging hands upon him. He had an instinctive knowledge of the world of men, and his mother seemed to him to be foolish. So he had taken to tormenting her. He did not acknowledge to himself that his pleasure in tormenting her had its roots in cruelty. Had he acknowledged this, he would have been more pleased than embarrassed. For, above all things, he despised humanity.

Nevertheless, he wished that he had not participated in that shameful scene with her. Some latent German respect for parents still endured in him. But, he thought, she is such a fool. She has always been a fool. Those who dream of distorting men out of their natural shape are always fools. Jesus had tried it, and had received proper justice. Hundreds of other teachers and philosophers had tried it. The kindest thing that men had done to them was to forget them.

He forgot Emmi. He looked at Irmgard's door again, and

frowned. She puzzled him, and vaguely excited him. Such immobility was not natural in one so young. He never allowed anything to puzzle or disturb him. The fact that Irmgard had done so increased his first hostility towards her.

He scratched his head. He yawned. The yawn was deliberate, in order to dismiss his thoughts of Irmgard. But he could not forget her pale hair and pale face, and the green eyes like jewels. He thought of his mother's not too subtle desire for a marriage between her son and her niece. He grinned involuntarily. It was now easily to be seen that she had imagined that Irmgard would bring with her some of the Social Democratic theories which had afflicted her father. Emmi, in other words, had brought up reinforcements. The German in her would not admit final defeat. Hell, what did she want with him! Yet, he could feel some compassion for her, for he understood her shrewdly. What must life be like, when one was tormented by fantasy and fanaticism? And helplessness?

He stood up, and stretched. The restlessness tingled all through his big body. He knew he would not be able to sleep. Angry irritation prickled his flesh. This was the first time that any woman had been able to do this to him. He had no time for women, except for a casual woman occasionally. Irmgard's face rose up before him, and the angry prickling increased.

He looked at her door, closed and final. There was only silence behind it. Suddenly, she took on the aspect of an enigma. He laughed at himself, shortly. This country girl, with the peasant's hands and the peasant's passivity! He was not much moved by beauty, and Irmgard did not appeal to him particularly. It was that infernal passivity of hers, he thought. He could not believe that anything very profound lived behind it. But at least the wench, not having anything to say, knew how to keep quiet. That was a rare thing in a woman.

It was nearly one o'clock, and he was wasting time thinking about her. He emptied his pipe in the stove, and pushed back his chair. He would go to bed. He turned out the light.

Then, to his own stupefaction, he found himself knocking gently on her door.

When he became aware of what he had done, he stepped back, hastily. His first impulse was to run, an ignominious act. But he forced himself to wait, grimly. Of course, the girl was placidly asleep. He waited for a few moments, and then turned away with relief, contemptuous of himself.

Just then the door opened silently, and Irmgard stood there, in the light of the gas jets. She wore a coarse crimson woolen robe, closely wrapped about her. Her hair hung over her shoulders in thick shining braids. She looked at Franz silently, but now he saw that her pallor was accentuated by faint streaks of red under her eyes. So, she has been crying, he thought. He felt a twinge of sympathy, but was also obscurely annoyed and affronted. Then, there was something after all, beneath that passivity. The realization irritated him.

He smiled casually. "Were you asleep? I hope I did not awaken you. I thought, if you were not asleep, we could talk for a few minutes."

She closed the door behind her. She walked to the stove as though she did not see him, and stood there, her back to him. "Will you sit down?" he asked, indicating the chair he had vacated. She sat down. She folded her hands on her knee. But still, she did not see him. She was like an automaton. He stood behind her, and saw the heroic modelling of her head, and the glistening of her pale hair. He pulled up another chair and sat near her. He spoke again, in a low voice:

"This is all so strange to you, Irmgard, is it not? But the strangeness will pass, and everything will be all right."

She did not answer. But she turned her face to him. Her green eyes were very still, and her lips moved as though she tried to speak. They looked at each other, and could not look away. He felt as though two strong hands held his head and forced him to look at his cousin.

"Do you speak English?" he asked, at last. He was a little shaken. For a moment he had experienced an almost irresistible desire to take her hand.

"Yes," she said. "My father taught me. It is enough. It is correct, but slow. That ought to be sufficient."

He paused. Her shoulders were full and strong under the frayed robe. He saw the high pointed mounds of her breast, and the slope of her large arms. That curious tingling along his nerves quickened into a gathering fever. And she looked back at him quietly. What she thought he did not know. But he saw that her nostril widened, and the quiet lines of her large mouth became rigid.

"You are thinking that my conduct to my mother was inexcusable," he said. He waited. She still regarded him with her strange eyes, but said nothing. He leaned back in his chair, and assumed a rueful expression.

"My mother does not understand America. She never will. She imagined that, being a new land, it would be full of new hopes and new dreams. A sort of bright vision emerging from the darkness of Europe. She believed that we should find here everything that was beautiful, significant and immortal in Europe, combined with the splendor of complete realization, growth and culmination, with something of German overtones. She expected to find the leisure and tranquillity and Gemütlichkeit of old Germany, too, a federation of mankind overlaid with peace and friendliness. And much talk and philosophy. A nation where everything was in the glorious process of becoming, and where everyone dined out under awnings and discussed Heine."

He paused. Irmgard still did not speak. But her eye-sockets
awnings and discussed Heine."

He tried to laugh. "Perhaps that is not a complete picture. She knew how America was expanding and growing. She expected to find a tumult of work here, a kind of heaven where everyone was working for the common welfare and common good. Work. She has always worshiped work, even for its own sake. She thought she would find her work here, and that I would advance it. You can see how foolish she was. And—this is where she ended." He made a sweeping gesture about the room, which seemed also to include the flat, the street, and all of America.

Irmgard's lips had fallen apart. They were very pale. But she still listened in silence.

"My mother had read a lot about America," he went on. "She knew its philosophers, its statesmen, its heroes. The only sad thing is that she believed them. She did not want to come here for money. She hated what Germany had become. I think, yes, I truly think, that had we settled in a hut somewhere, she would not have minded even if we had eaten only once a day, provided that she could have had the company of large-minded poets, philosophers and political geniuses about her. Provided she could have had a part in the growth of America towards those immense ideals which she believed existed here." And he laughed again, his short, unamused laugh.

"She is the worst kind of egotist," he said.

Then Irmgard spoke, and her voice quivered tensely: "And you do not see how piteous that is?"

He was taken aback. He had been talking to her, believing that she did not understand anything of what he had been saying. It had been enough for him to see her. He stared at her blankly.

"Piteous? Yes, I suppose it is." But he was hardly conscious of what he had been saying.

She looked at him for a long time. And now he saw that he had been wrong. This was no stupid peasant girl, with the passivity of a summer landscape within her. How could he have thought that the daughter of Emil Hoeller could have been stupid? It is I who am stupid, he thought. But the thought brought no consolation to him, but only a great irritability and an obscure anger against her.

He looked away from her face, to her hands. He was surprised to see that they were clenched, as though she were experiencing some passionate emotion.

"It is not her dreams which are so bad," she said, still in a low voice. "It is your attitude towards them."

"And what is your attitude?" he asked. His eyes wandered from her chin down the length of her large white throat.

"I understand what she has wanted, though I knew America was not so," she replied. "I know that the world is all alike, wherever you go. I do not know how I know this. Everything is the same. One must understand it, and accept it."

Again, there was a silence between them. The room was very cold and dark, in spite of the hissing gas jets. The wind had come up again, rattling the windows with fury. It seemed to Franz that he could hear his heart beating loudly in the stillness, and that the only reality was this girl with the green eyes and Roman body. Every inch of his flesh was alive with this reality. Suddenly he wanted to touch her, to hold her, and the desire was like a fire in him.

"You do not like me, do you, Irmgard?" he asked, very softly, leaning towards her.

She regarded him straightly. Her expression was unmoved. Then she stood up. "No," she answered. "I do not like you. Good night."

She stood up, and left the room. Her door closed silently behind her.

She was gone. The chill of the room came through Franz's garments. But he sat still and stared at her door. It seemed to him that he stared for hours.

When he finally went to bed, stiff with cold, he could not sleep. He knew only one thing: he hated this girl.

CHAPTER 11

Years later, it was frequently written that Franz Stoessel had often said that steel had been his very life, that from the first moment he had entered the great cavern of the Schmidt Steel Company in Nazareth, Pennsylvania, he had known that this was to be part of himself. This was probably a sentimental lie, or one of Franz's innumerable cynical hypocrisies. Other men might utter expected hypocrisies without wincing, feeling themselves amiable and good-natured in doing so. Worse, they very often came to believe in their hypocrisies. Franz was frequently a hypocrite, for he was both expedient and realistic, and if hypocrisy was necessary to his advancement, then he surpassed rivals in the art of lying. But he never ceased to be amused at it. He had long ago come to the conclusion that men hated truth, hated directness and sincerity, and that they preferred lies. They gave honors and riches to men who lied, and power. Therefore, from the first, he gave them what they wanted. This filled him with disgust, but also with that never-ending amusement and wry contempt. And so clever was he that they never suspected the sincerity of his insincerities. He was all things to all men, and so he was trusted. Better still, he prospered.

No one, not even Hans Schmidt, ever suspected that Franz neither liked nor hated the mills, that had chance thrown him into another industry his attitude towards it would have been exactly the attitude he had for this. It was only a means to an end. He never revolted against chance or circumstance. He merely used them. But devotion to the mills was expected of him, and he gave them outward service if nothing else.

Nor was he ever fascinated, even from the first, by the immense murky gloom of the mills, lit by the red fires, and smothered in smoke and heat. He looked without much interest at the half-naked men guiding the mighty kettles of liquid metal which blazed like the sun. He felt the promise in the mills, the promise for himself. That was all. He did not feel that here were men who were doing something, creating rails and locomotives. If he saw, in this inferno of Vulcan, deafening and gigantic, hoarse with voices and the hiss of molten metal as it ran into the moulds, the drama of a young and growing industry, he saw it only in relation to himself. The clanging and the cries, the groan of cranes, the acrid smell of acids, the thin gray coiling smoke, the enormous hammering, filled him with excitement. But it was the excitement of his own promise. It is true he began to live only for the hours he spent there, grimy, naked to the waist, sweating and straining; it is true that the uproar and the thunder were a tremendous symphony in his ears. But still, it was only because he felt that his own promise was being forged in these mills. The clamor seemed to him only to be a terrible and godlike prelude to something greater for himself.

At home, he was morose, preoccupied, determined. He brought strange books home, which he had borrowed from the local library. He read the history of steel. Had he been thrown into a mining community, he would have studied mining with equal absorption. He read everything he could find on chemistry, the vast juggling of opening resources, the terrific tide of mechanics which was rising in the new world. His mind became a file in which he laid away small items that he subconsciously knew were vital. He read and filed with grim purpose for himself, and not for love. At times, when he was tired, he even hated the mills.

He had worked here for five years, starting as a puddler. He became a moulder. Then, because he was able to wring the last drop of sweat from his unfortunate co-workers, he was made a foreman. He was held in approving esteem by his immediate superiors, because his "gang" could be made to produce more than any other. He was relentless, ruthless, implacable. His men hated him, but so far they were still too helpless, too wretched, too cowed, to lift their hands against him. But he knew, as he walked through the mills and saw the black-faced and sweating men with their sullen and desperate faces, that a danger lived here, stronger than steel and more terrible than armies. The mills were not only forging steel, he thought. They were forging terror. This did not disturb him. He felt in himself a power stronger than the power of these men. They hated him, but he hated them more, with a purity of hatred undisturbed by consideration of family or fear of hunger. They hated him for his oppression of them. He hated them for what they were. All this life, this hatred of his kind was the whip which gave him power over them, a psychological power against which they were almost always impotent. He had long ago stumbled on the frightful truth that to subjugate men, and rule them, it was necessary only to hate them.

So far, there had been no strikes in this mill. But he knew they were coming. They had occurred elsewhere, with bloodshed and death and disorganization. He read the newspapers thoroughly. He found, or thought he had found, the solution to this problem, which was growing more acute every year.

The laborers worked twelve hours a day, six days a week. He also worked these hours and these days. But he had his own promise to sustain him. They had no promise. He never felt compassion for them. He could look without emotion on an injured or dying workman, even though aware that starvation faced his family. He was not concerned with sentimentality. His smiling hatred was too strong for that. Never, at any time, did he regard his men as being of the same flesh and stuff as himself. If they had been, he reasoned, they would have had his own promise in themselves. Not having this promise, they were unworthy of life. They lived only for service. When they could not perform this service, their reason for living had been removed. They had no right to live.

However, he made friends with his fellow foremen, and in particular, with a young Englishman by the name of Tom Harrow. He was hardly less friendly with another foreman, a "hunky," who was a giant of a man, like a gorilla. At one time Franz had worked under Jan Kozak, and it was from him that he had learned moulding. Franz had the instinct of being able to seek out those who could be of benefit to him. Tom Harrow was no benefit, but he was Franz's recreation, for the Englishman had a wise obscene humor and a never-ending good-nature. He was both ignorant and clever, philosophical and vulgar, shrewd and dirty. Franz enjoyed his company, for he liked to laugh, provided it did not interfere with more important things.

From the very first, Franz had begun to look about among his fellow workers for one or two who could advance his purpose. He had been discouraged. Some of the men had come originally from the small farming communities around Nazareth. Many had been imported from the enormous mills in other towns in Pennsylvania, enticed by a promise of higher wages. But the majority had been brought by the shipload from Middle Europe and the Slav countries. There were Prussians and Bavarians, Serbs, Poles, Hungarians, Magyars, Austrians and Bulgars. Franz, looking at them quickly, knew them for what they were. Only Jan Kozak attracted him. When he had been assigned to Jan's moulding "gang," he knew that this man could be his teacher. Jan was arrogant in his new power, and he had an abiding hatred for Germans, and a passionate aversion. But very shortly, he was pleased by Franz's deference, docility, and eagerness to learn and work. He began to teach the young man all he knew, letting him accompany him about the mill during the noon period, explaining everything in his halting dialect, going to unusual lengths and heights in behalf of this appreciative novice. Jan, ignorant and illiterate, nevertheless had a vague but gigantic realization of the coming power of steel, and its majesty. He had found only loneliness and dissatisfaction in the brooding stolidity of his other men. With Franz's advent had come contentment, justification.

Jan had a brother, Boze, and a sister-in-law and a swarm of little nephews and nieces in Nazareth. Boze was part of his "gang," a dull heavy peasant with the body and neck of a wrestler. He had none of his brother's intelligence. Jan had brought him and his family to America, but had only contempt for him. He did not hear the Thor-like symphony which Jan heard in the mills.

Jan had a lonely secret, and it was not long before he mysteriously hinted of it to Franz. But he no more than hinted. Moreover, he was not certain of it, and he waited with all the patient, ox-like waiting of a peasant.

One night he led Franz back into the mill, with many mysterious noddings, long after the men had gone. He pointed to the heap of ruined moulds in a corner of the mill.

"See 'em?" he muttered. "Gone. Lost. Lots of money lost. The moulds done that. It gets worse. I've got a new way. Any old fool would make good moulds, no mistakes, with the way I got. Make twice—three times—many more moulds, in one hour than does now. See? And cheap, too, twice cheap."

Franz had nodded thoughtfully. He displayed interest, but not too much, for Jan had begun to watch him with his tiny cunning eyes. Later, without speaking of the moulds again, he injected raw flattery into his sincere appreciation of Jan Kozak. He waited upon him, served him, added a flare of conscious hypocrisy to his respect. And the simple peasant became more and more delighted with him. It was partly on his recommendation that Franz was made a foreman.

Even after that, on the scent of the secret, Franz maintained the highest intimacy with Kozak. The three men, Tom Harrow, Franz and Kozak, ate their noon meal together. After hours of work, Franz intensely enjoyed Harrow. Moreover, the intimacy of the meal increased the friendliness between himself and Jan Kozak. Franz's instinct for life, the realist's instinct, impelled him to retain those two, the one to refresh him, the other to benefit him more solidly. He was one of those men, whose number is larger than is generally suspected, who build their lives on the lives of others, and who, at the last, gain the fame of having accomplished their success single-handed. Always, he was able to use others. Never, at any time, was he original. He well knew his lack of originality, and was completely aware that only by utilizing others, making use of their brains and their work, could he attain a personal power.

He told himself, coldly, that he hated waste. Without men like himself in the world, the marvelous inventions of many men would never come to light. It took more than originality and genius to gain the world's ear and the world's adulation. It needed men like himself, to exploit the originality and genius.

Had he been less of a realist than he was, he might have deluded himself that his capacities were as great as any other man's. In the end, he would have been defeated by his limitations, and would have spent the rest of his life in bitter envy, and would have concluded that some mysterious combination of men and fate had crushed him, and not his own lack. In such futility, he thought, are nourished the seeds of great revolutions. Only in revolutions can mediocre men temporarily attain the heights which their own nature had denied them.

Not hoping, therefore, for any revolution which might, in its roiling, swirl him upward for an evanescent moment, he set about methodically to gain what he wished by making use of greater wits than his own. At one time he had considered organizing a labor union in the mills. He had considered this long and coolly. Then he had discarded it. Perhaps, after long and dangerous and exhausting work, he might raise himself to power on this high step. But the time was not yet ripe for strong labor unions, and he disliked hardship, danger and strife as being too time-wasting. He knew that the day of labor unions, strong and powerful, was approaching. But he could not wait for that day.

Knowing that his instincts were predatory only, he calmly set himself to utilizing them, discarding anything immediately that did not feed them.

"I have the true German personality," he said once, to his mother. "I have the ability of utilizing the inventions and the brains of others, without possessing those qualities. That, in itself, is genius." When Emmi had angrily pointed out what she considered original genius in many Germans, he had merely laughed and ruthlessly torn away this gossamer of illusion. Wagner? A half-Jew, by all accounts. Beethoven, partly Belgian. And many others.

The highest attainment of nature, he said, was the combining in one man the genius for utilization, and originality. As for himself, if he had the choice of one of these, he would choose the genius for utilization. In that, as in other things, he demonstrated his powerful life-instinct.

When the noon whistle blew, he would wipe his hands on pieces of waste, pick up his dinner pail, and make his way through the shouting and hurrying men to a certain far corner of the mill, where there was comparative quiet. Here, on a pile of discarded and broken moulds, Tom Harrow and Jan Kozak would be waiting for him. He would climb up beside them, grinning, his sweat- and dirt-begrimed face cheerful under his light yellow hair, his blue eyes incongruous in the stained dark flesh. Tom always greeted him with a slap on the back, and an obscene remark. But Jan's heavy peasant face lighted with simple affection.

This noon was the same as usual. Franz made his way through the throngs of released men, under the immense cavernous roof of the mill. Sheets of red lightning glimmered into the semi-darkness from the open hearths. Voices and hammer-blows echoed in the noon-day lull. Cranesmen sat in their cages, sang, yelled, and ate. The dusk floated with soot and particles of ore. It was a pit under the earth where demons worked, and now, momentarily rested. The floor gritted under Franz's boots. As he walked, groups of men sullenly stepped away from his path, for he was generally hated by all except his two friends. He saw Slav faces, German faces, Hungarian, Polish, Negro and American faces. But he saw no friendliness. Race was swallowed up in animosity. However, this did not concern him.

He reached the pile of moulds, where Tom and Jan were already devouring their meal. Tom shouted, upon sighting him: "Well, here's the Dutch bastard at last! Found a girl in the washroom, Franz?" But Jan smiled with shy broadness, and made a place for his friend.

They usually exchanged portions of their lunch. Jan had some excellent sausage today, Franz had some Bismarck herring, and Tom's wife had given him three apple tarts mixed with raisins. They ate voraciously for several minutes, without speaking. Their half-naked bodies were glistening with sweat, mixed with grime. From their high perch they could look down at the teeming floor of the mill. There was no light in the mill except that sullen scarlet flare from the hearths.

Tom Harrow, like many Englishmen, was short, stocky and broad. He was in his early thirties. He was also very dark, almost Gaelic in complexion, with a long horse-like face ending in a sharp projecting chin, which gave him a Punch-and-Judy look, further enhanced by a long curving hook of a nose which, when he smiled, appeared to touch his short upper lip. Sometimes Franz called him, "that English Jew," but Tom was pure Cockney, born within sound of the Bow Bells. His eyes, very close together on each side of his high-bridged Hebraic nose, were tiny, sharp, black, and eternally restless, always glinting with sardonic humor and shrewdness. These, combined with the chin, the thick mass of black curling hair surging upwards from a narrow brow, the nose, and a wide crooked mouth always grinning or twisting, increased his Punch-and-Judy look to a remarkable degree. Unlike most Englishmen, he was not stolid. He crackled with energy, strength and vitality. Though hardly literate, he was nevertheless extremely intelligent and clever, and though his conversation was liberally profane and dirty, it was also pungent and original. He had three children, all little girls, of whom he was extremely fond, a fact which he could not conceal for all his frank remarks about them. "I picked the wrong sow," he would say, an observation which seemed to be disrespectful to a little Englishwoman who was all cleanliness and bustle, but was really his way of expressing his pride in her.

"Hell," he would say, "I'm an Englishman, and all that. But I'm a chap as always thinks other chaps've got a right to live, too." He would turn to Franz and poke him painfully in the ribs. "That's where me and you is different, bo."

"A man must earn the right to live," Franz would amiably answer, in his slow, careful, correct English.

"How're they goin' to do that, with such chaps as you on their backs?" Tom would ask, without rancor. He liked Franz very much, and disagreed with him always. But during disagreements, he could always laugh. But Franz could not laugh at those times. A curious blank look would come over his face, and an implacable stare would enter his eyes.

When they had finished their meal today, Tom said to Franz: "Well, 'Andsome 'Arry, anythin' new?"

"No. Except that I had orders to lay off three more men. What about you, Tom?"

A quiet sullenness darkened Tom's already dark features, but this strangely did not detract from his Puckish look.

"Three, too. Hell, it's enough to make a chap puke." He leaned his elbows on his knees, rested his chin in his hands, and somberly regarded the mill. "Wot're we goin' to do? Whole blasted place will be closin' down next, what with the rotten moulds, and the orders bein' cancelled."

Jan, licking from his fingers the last residue of the tarts, smiled secretly. "Maybe things not so bad. Maybe I got an idea to make better moulds." His smile became shy and sly, yet apologetic.

Franz said nothing, but Tom turned quickly. "Eh? Wot's that? Better moulds?" His tiny bright eyes narrowed as he studied the Hungarian's broad peasant countenance. "Blimey, I bet you have! So that's wot you've been doin' after hours!" He paused, bit his lip, and his expression became shrewder than ever. He glanced quickly at Franz, who was apparently unconcerned and indifferent. "Well, now, Jan, you just keep it to yourself. Make money on it, yourself. Thieves around, y'know."

"I watch thieves," replied Jan placidly. "I no tell anyone, yet."

"I've told him to hold his tongue, myself," remarked Franz.

Tom's narrow long face twisted together shrewdly. "Aye, I bet you have!" Despite his affection, he had no illusions about Franz Stoessel, and his quick wits were already at work. He put his hand on Jan's broad brown shoulders.

"Don't trust a bloody soul, Jan. Not me, not 'Andsome

'Arry here. Nobody. Hold your blasted tongue. Then maybe me and Franz and the rest of us chaps'll be workin' for you some day, instead of that stinkin' Dutchman, Schmidt." He scratched his nose reflectively, his eye on Franz. "Rather'd work for you, Jan, even if you're a Hunky. You're a man, not a swine, and that's somethin'."

Franz smiled, and said nothing.

"I trust nobody," insisted Jan, shyly, beaming upon the Englishman.

Tom waved his hand largely. "When you got it all settled in your mind, Jan, get a lawyer chap."

He immediately returned to his morose contemplation of the mill. "They've sacked a third of the men already," he said. "There ought to be some way— There is." He regarded Franz directly. "Provided we can get all the men and the foremen together. Still objectin', Franz?"

Franz shrugged. "I've told you, Tom: I don't approve of unions, and strikes. What do you expect to get when Schmidt isn't making any profits? You can't get blood out of a turnip, to quote your own expression."

Tom surveyed him with slow, irate humor. "There you are, again! I've told you a hundred times. If we got a union, we get dues, and we keep the men when they ain't workin', or when they get hurt. That's one side of it. That's what I was talkin' about, now. Look what Schmidt does: when things get better, he hires men again. But does he hire the old chaps? No, not if he can get cheaper labor. It don't matter if a man's worked for him for ten years. He gets rushed with orders, and down go wages, so he can pile up more swag. We got no protection. That's why I say, why don't you join us?"

"Look here, Tom, I've told you a dozen times. I don't want any trouble. I have my own plans. Do I get laid off very often? No. Nor do you, nor Jan. We're competent. The others aren't competent. They're cattle. They must suffer the troubles of cattle. Unions are only exploitations of employers, because they take no account of competence or ability. Unions abrogate the right of employers to hire the best, or the cheapest, and run their organizations they way they wish to run them. That is a fundamental liberty of everyone. You ought to be the last to argue against it, you, with your shoutings for personal liberty all the time!"

"Ain't the men got any liberty, or rights?" demanded Tom.

Franz raised his eyebrows. "I told you before, a man must earn them, not have them given to him," he answered, with exaggerated weariness.

But Tom was angry. "Who gave any one man the right to say what other men've got the right to live?" he shouted. "Did

God Almighty say to some chaps: 'Here, you, you be the judge. You tell Me wot chaps can live, and wot chaps must starve to death. You're brighter than I am."

"Well, if you're goin' to bring theology into this—" smiled Franz.

"Wot?" Tom was puzzled. "Wot's theology?"

"What you are saying. Never mind. It isn't important. But a countryman of yours, Darwin, speaks very highly of the struggle for existence, and the law of the survival of the fittest."

"Never heard of him," said Tom promptly. "Bet he's got a bloody mill like this. But it comes down to this: every man's the same as any other. He's got a heart and a brain, and he feels the same things——"

Franz lifted a hand, and over the subdued muttering of the idling mills, he chanted; paraphrasing a little:

"Hath not a man eyes? Hath not a man hands, organs, dimensions, senses, affections, passions? Fed with the same food, hurt with the same weapons, subject to the same diseases, healed by the same means, warmed and cooled by the same winter and summer, as others are? If you prick us, do we not bleed? If you tickle us, do we not laugh? If you poison us, do we not die? And if you wrong us, shall we not revenge?"

"Wot's that bloody poetry?" demanded Tom with suspicion, while Jan stared, uncomprehendingly.

Franz laughed. "Just Shakespeare. Did you ever hear of him? He's also a countryman of yours, Tom."

"Oh, him," said Tom, with an air of erudition. "Wot's a Dutchman like you got to do with that chap? He's ours, not yours. Besides, where'd you learn poetry, anyway?"

"I told you, Tom: I went to school for four years, in England, before we come to America. And my father was a schoolmaster. And I'd like to tell you this: a ten-year-old German boy knows more about Shakespeare than your graduates of your damned public schools. Germans, even the poorest, have a high regard for scholarship. You English haven't."

"Wot's all that got to do with unions?" said Tom, annoyed.

"Nothing. Nothing at all."

There was a little silence. Franz was unconcerned, but Tom glowered at his profile, feeling in some mysterious way that he was at a loss.

"You're a rum one," he said, in a surly voice. "Foreman in Schmidt's piddlin' mill, and quotin' poetry. I'll never understand you foreigners."

"But you've just said that all men are alike," laughed Franz.

"You grant the equality of men, but you shout about your being an Englishman! You're inconsistent, Tom. Now, I don't grant the equality of men, but I'm not concerned with race at all. There's no such thing. You say you are an Englishman, but you're a mixture of Swede, Norwegian, ancient Briton, French and even Dutch, not to mention your largest racial origin, which is Angle and Saxon, Teutonic races——"

"Don't call me a damn Dutchman!" said Tom irate.

Franz laughed again. But his eyes did not laugh. He stood up. The whistle was blowing again. He looked down at the glowering Tom with an air of good humor.

"But seriously, Tom, I want to warn you. It won't be long until the big men hear about your union activities, and your going about among the men trying to get them to join your miserable little union."

"They won't hear about it, yet, if someone doesn't tell them," said Tom, with a hard upward look at his friend. His eyes were sharp black balls in their glistening whites. He was not amused, now. His expression was grim and murderous.

"Just hold your tongue, and don't talk so much," said Franz, amiably. He hesitated. Jan had only caught a portion of this extraordinary conversation, but Franz did not trust what he had caught. He dared not leave him with the aroused Englishman. "Come on, Jan, your men are already at the furnaces."

"Clever, ain't you?" grunted Tom, with a sneer.

Jan obediently and heavily got up and prepared to follow Franz, who was waiting for him at the foot of the mould pile.

"Don't trust any bloody chap, least not our Dutch friend, here!" shouted Tom, over the renewed roaring of the mills.

"I no trust anybody," responded Jan, with a wave of his hand. He lumberingly followed Franz, and after a morose moment or two of reflection, Tom climbed down and went to his own furnaces. Once there, his curses were more ferocious than usual, but under them he was thinking rapidly.

CHAPTER 12

"ALL MEN are as good as I am, but I am an Englishman," thought Franz, wryly, thinking of Tom Harrow. A German was more consistent. He said: No man is as good as I am, and I am a German. Franz was not confused by such inconsistency as Tom Harrow's. He was only amused by it. The inconsistencies and stupidities of mankind, its meannesses, brutalities, treacheries, falsenesses and dirtinesses always amused him. A man with less hatred for his species might have been angered or saddened. But Franz was firmly convinced that both reformers and exploiters have their roots in the same hatred, and either might have been the other with equal single-mindedness.

At three o'clock, during a lull, he went to Tom and borrowed some pipe tobacco. His own pouch was full, though he pretended he had no more. It was part of his plan not to allow animosities to come between him and those who might serve him. Tom gave him his own pouch and watched him tranquilly fill his pipe. The Englishman's eyes were hard and suspicious, though he smiled slightly.

"No hard feelin's?" he asked at last.

Franz raised his eyebrows. "What for?"

"Come off! Don't be so blasted innercent. My pa used to say that Germans and elephants never forget."

"Your pa didn't like Germans, evidently. What would you have done at Waterloo, anyway, without us? We've been good friends of England, and always will be."

"You're talkin' through your bally head. You've got the wind up since Bismarck, that old boar. We'll have to knock the stuffin's out of you yet, mark my words."

"I'm not interested in politics, Tom. I'll soon be an American citizen. Here's your pouch. Going off on time tonight. We'll walk home together."

Tom nodded curtly, and turned back to his work. But he watched Franz out of the corner of his eye. He saw Franz pass Jan Kozak, with only a casual nod. He's got somethin' on his mind, thought Tom. Blimey, we've got to get him to join the union. We don't dare leave him out.

At four o'clock, the man in charge of all the moulding tapped Franz upon the shoulder. Fritz Dethloff, from Prussia, had no liking for Franz, in whom he recognized a nature similar to his. He was suspicious of his fellow-German for this same reason. Nevertheless, he expressed the utmost friendliness for Franz, and often stopped to talk to him about other matters not connected with the work. Had there arisen an opportunity to do Franz a mischief, he would have seized it gladly.

He was holding a small black book in his hand. A big bald man in his forties, with a scrubbed round face and pursy lips and little brown eyes, he always had an air of jovial good-fellowship, which deceived everyone but Franz. He held a pencil poised over the book, and blinked amicably at the younger man over his glasses.

He spoke in German: "I wish to ask you a few questions, Franz. Have you a moment or two to spare?"

Franz nodded. His first thought was that he was to be ordered to lay off more men, and he was annoyed. "What is wrong? I cannot operate with less men, Fritz. Or, have the last moulds been rejected?"

"No, no! Nothing is wrong. This noise: let us find a quiet corner."

Franz wiped his hands, and accompanied his superior to a corner of the mill where a furnace was idling. Once there, Dethloff said nothing for a moment or two, but merely stood, blinked at Franz thoughtfully. He still smiled, but his small eyes were intent and suspicious.

"It is the Superintendent, Franz. He wishes me to ask you a few questions." He paused.

He was relieved at Franz's genuine surprise. His job, to him, was like a bone to a dog. Let it be threatened, and he would be ruthless and murderous. The Superintendent's questions had aroused his blackest suspicions that Franz had found favor. If this was so, either of two things might happen: Franz might be elevated to a position equal to his own, or might be scheduled to replace him. The latter had filled him with corrosive anxiety. He regretted the first, but it was not as bad as the second. He had done nothing to recommend Franz for anything, and had deprecated him on all occasions. He had even gone so far, on numerous occasions, as to credit Tom or Jan with work done by Franz's men. He thought he had done some excellent work against this ambitious countryman of his, and was just faintly uneasy. He, therefore, beamed with the utmost affection upon Franz, and offered him a cigar.

Franz accepted. He detested Dethloff, and knew everything about him. But, as Germans, they must stand together against the other hordes. Franz had already concluded that it was better to have this enemy an amiable one than an openly antagonistic one.

"Just a few questions, Franz. I do not know the purpose of them, but perhaps they are preparing some inventory of the men. You are not married, nor contemplating marriage?"

"No."

"You are twenty-four years old, ja? And your place of birth? Thank you. Your parents, and their position in the Fatherland?" He wrote busily. He then put away his pencil, and frowned and smiled in quick succession. "Such foolish questions! Have you any idea what they might mean, Franz? They have never been asked before of the men."

"I have no idea." There was a genuine note in his denial, and Dethloff was satisfied. "Have they been asking these questions of others?"

"Nein. That is what has puzzled me. Even I have not been asked." He grinned jovially. "Have you been in trouble with the police?"

Franz laughed, shaking his head. Dethloff clapped him upon the shoulder, and Franz returned to his work, dismissing the puzzle.

But the questions had set him to thinking. He was twenty-four. In six years, he would be on the verge of middle-age. What had he done, so far? Nothing. A mere foreman in the mills, for a few dollars. Unless opportunity arose very shortly, to exploit Jan Kozak, he would be exactly where he was now at the end of those six years. A sensation of restless hurry assailed him, and a dull anger. He had been set back in his plans, through Tom Harrow's warning tongue. The work of months had been lost by that warning to Jan Kozak. He would have to begin again, that painful winning of the Hungarian's confidence.

Then he cursed himself for a fool. Jan, like Tom, was involved with the furtive, underground union. He had only to join it, himself. He was about to go to Tom with a confession of capitulation, when the paymaster's assistant came through the mill, to give their envelopes to the foremen.

Franz opened his envelope, and automatically counted his money. He knew what it should contain. Then he stiffened. There was six dollars more than the usual amount. Incredulous, he counted again. A mistake, no doubt, or a trap. He gave a few orders to his men, then went to the paymaster's little office just off the mill. Franz and the paymaster were not good friends. But now, to his surprise, the man greeted him cordially, and laughed a little.

"Like your raise, Franz?"

"So, it was a raise. Why, Mr. Thomas, when the mill is laying off men?"

The paymaster wagged his head. "Are you going to quarrel with me about the money? Well, if you don't want it, give it here," and he extended his hand with a knowing wink.

"Did Dethloff recommend me for this raise?" asked Franz, incredulously.

The paymaster looked mysterious. "I don't know who recommended you, Franz. But the order came through from the Superintendent an hour ago. But you are a bright fellow: you might know it wasn't through Dethloff's influence." And he laughed, slyly.

"But Dethloff was asking me a few personal questions an hour or so ago——"

The paymaster's face wrinkled with sudden interest. "Yes? I believe I saw him talking to you. He came back with your answers, I suppose, and went into the Superintendent's offices. Right after that, the Super's clerk came in with an order to give you a raise. That's all I know."

"Does Dethloff know about this?"

The paymaster grinned. "I don't know. But he seemed mighty anxious. He wanted to know if you had had a cut, and I let him believe you had. He seemed pretty happy, then. Don't tell him different. He might have a stroke."

Franz went back to his work, thoughtful. He could not understand this. He was now receiving three dollars a week more than Tom Harrow, who had been in the mills for ten years, and was acknowledged to do the best work. It was extraordinary. He thought nothing more surprising could occur that day. But it did, shortly before six o'clock.

At that time he was ordered to appear before the Superintendent, himself. Hastily washing, he went to the offices. These offices were not connected with the body of the mills, and he had to cross a muddy, cinder-infested stretch of ground to a smaller building. Here, the Superintendent and all the clerks occupied some five rooms. In one of them, Egon Stoessel had his desk. The Superintendent's private office had a carpet, a mahogany desk, panelled walls, a hot red fire, and clean broad windows. At the far end of the room was a door on which, in gilt letters, was inscribed the noble word: President.

The Superintendent, "the Saxon swine," as Franz called him, looked at the young man shrewdly. He, himself, was a small spare man of middle age, with smooth ashen hair, ashen face, and pale hard eyes. Like many Saxons, he despised the Prussian, and his practiced eye had long recognized the Prussian in Franz Stoessel. In Franz, he saw everything which the Saxon, always a man of smooth diplomacy, thought and peace, and courteous craft, hated instinctively. In that square high-colored face, the strong jaw and the short, wide-nostrilled nose, he saw the Uhlan. It was long a belief among Saxons that the Prussians were not pure Germans, a belief now reluctantly admitted by the younger scientists, since Bismarck. The long-suspected Slav blood of the Prussians revealed itself, in Franz's face, in the wide splayed cheekbones, the slightly tilted corners of his eyes, and his expression, at once immobile and alert and brutal. Mr. Heinrich knew that that bland and open stare, so prepossessing to the uninitiated, covered implacability and ruthlessness. He thought to himself: "Animal!" He looked with aversion at Franz's big quiet mouth, and saw, or thought he saw, the taint of Slav blood in its jutting fleshiness. Nor was he moved to admiration, for all Franz's large splendor of body and strong muscles. Even his blondness, he thought, was the strong spectacular blondness of the Slav, and had no relationship to the paler blondness of the true German.

Nevertheless, being crafty and astute, he concealed his aversion and dislike. He smiled. His voice was soft and ingratiating, but after a furtive look at the President's door, he raised that voice as though he suspected a listener.

He spoke in German, the softer and more musical German of the Saxon:

"You are pleased with your increase, Stoessel?"

"Yes, Mr. Dietrich. And very grateful."

Dietrich smiled agreeably. He looked down at the papers on his desk.

"Do you think you are qualified to assist Dethloff, or even take his place?"

Franz was astounded. His bland stare was genuine now. Then he asked bluntly: "Why?"

Dietrich laughed gently. "That is a curious question. 'Why?' Perhaps we think you competent."

Franz was silent. His face had flushed deeply. He leaned back in the chair he had taken without invitation. He studied the Superintendent with his hard "Prussian" eyes. His thoughts were quick, and his heart was beating heavily. He had no illusions about himself. He knew he was no better than Tom Harrow. He reviewed his own lack of originality, and even when he admitted that he had power over his men, that power was small and would go almost unnoticed in a mill of this size.

There was something else, here. His thoughts were concerned with that.

The Superintendent broke the silence. He still did not look at Franz. "We think you competent," he said. "However, it has not been settled yet."

Franz continued to think. If he accepted this most astounding offer, he would be far removed from Jan Kozak. He would never come into possession of the secret. Therefore, he must decline this offer, and remain with Jan until he had gotten the secret, whereupon he would then be in a position to strike for a much larger prize than this which was being offered him. Or, he must accept, taking a gamble that the "secret" was worthless. It was a hard choice. If he refused now, and found that Jan had nothing valuable, he might never recover the ground lost. Opportunity, he had observed, was skittish.

"Well?" asked Dietrich, impatiently.

Franz examined his fingernails. The gesture seemed nonchalant, but his mind was seething. Finally, he lifted his eyes and looked at Dietrich straightly.

"Who would not be delighted by this offer?" he said, making his voice low and troubled. "But how do I know I am competent, myself? Suppose I suggest this, Mr. Dietrich: Let me remain where I am for another four weeks. There are some matters I do not know. I want to know many more things about the work, in order that I will be adequate to the new position. I—I am working on an idea for a new mould, which will revolutionize our present system. I cannot do it unless I am right there, at the furnaces. It may come to nothing. If it does, then I have not lost much. If it is valuable, then we shall all gain."

Dietrich was jolted out of his smiling indifference. He stared at Franz with open curiosity and intense interest. "Ja? This is very extraordinary. Can you tell me something about it?"

Franz assumed an expression of childlike slyness, and self-deprecatory modesty. "Not yet, Mr. Dietrich. As I have said, it may be worthless. It is purely in the experimental stage, at present."

Dietrich was excited. "You need more men, more materials, more help? We shall give them to you, gladly. The moulds—it is a serious matter, now."

"I would rather work by myself, Mr. Dietrich."

There was a silence in the office. The Superintendent drummed on the desk with his thin fingers. Then, at last, he smiled.

"Shall we, then, say that you may remain where you are for another month? Then, we shall see about the moulds. At any rate, the position will still be open to you."

Franz inclined his head in grave thanks, and rose.

"One moment, Stoessel. You speak High Dutch. You were not a peasant in the old country?"

"No, my parents taught school in Bavaria. I also speak French. We lived in France for two years. Thereafter, for four years, we lived in England, before coming to America."

"Extraordinary! Ja, I can see you are an unusual man, Stoessel. But why did your parents go to France, then to England, before coming here?"

Franz smiled with faint derision. He thought of Emmi's frantic and heart-breaking pilgrimage to equality, fraternity and liberty, a crusade to the non-existent. But he said: "My parents could not make up their minds."

He had hardly left the office when Hans Schmidt explosively opened his door and charged into the Superintendent's office. He was scarlet, sweating and beaming, as though he had heard something of astonishing import and good news.

"Well!" he exclaimed. "It is good, nein? We have a man, here! What do you think of him, Dietrich? Do I understand men, or do I not?"

The Superintendent hesitated. He knew that any dissent would inflame Schmidt against him. He could not understand Schmidt's unusual interest in a mere workman in his mills. But Dietrich had gotten his present position not by opposition, but by assent, shrewd and subtle assent. So he smiled, as though unwilling to admit that Schmidt's judgment had been better than his.

"I am surprised, sir. But now I am convinced that you are right."

"Right? I am always right, Dietrich! You are pig-headed. I have always said so. Well! Let it be. We shall hear from this man again, shall we not?"

"I am certain of it."

When he was alone, Dietrich frowned and bit his lip, thinking. He was more bewildered than ever. He did nothing, however, until Hans called for his carriage, and was driven away. The November twilight had settled down over the mills and the city, and fog and smoke mingled in an acrid pall over everything. Then he sent for Dethloff.

"This man—Franz Stoessel," he began, abruptly. "What do you know of him?"

Dethloff brightened with malice. "Just a Dutchman. I never liked him, Mr. Dietrich. The men hate him. He drives them. A good workman, but nothing extraordinary. Are we to lay him off?"

"Nein!" said the Superintendent, testily. He stared at Dethloff thoughtfully. "The Old Man is interested in him. Why, I do not know. There is no answer to his whims. But you will be especially pleasant to this Stoessel. You will give him any assistance he desires. Is that understood?"

Dethloff was alarmed. "Can we not undermine him to——?"

"Not if you value your job," said Dietrich, grimly.

CHAPTER 13

BEFORE LEAVING that night, Jan Kozak, with many innocent and mysterious gestures, told his friend, Franz Stoessel, that he was going to remain. He implied that he was to do some important testing that evening, and Franz was welcome to watch the results. But Franz shrewdly refused. He was tired. Earlier, he would have excitedly accepted the invitation. But he knew that suspicion of him had been ably instilled in the big Hungarian by Tom Harrow. When he saw the uncertain and thoughtful look in Jan's eyes, he congratulated himself upon a very subtle move.

He joined Tom Harrow, who was shrugging himself into his patched overcoat. Tom and his family lived on a small street off Mulberry Street, and the two young men frequently walked home together.

"Jan not comin'?" asked Tom, seeing his friend alone.

"No. He wants to work on his experiment."

Tom's eyelids narrowed, and he smiled. "The more I see of you, Fritzie, the more I think you're a bloody clever chap. Now, I'm not a chap as doesn't like cleverness in others. But there's such a thing as bein' too clever."

"I'm not the least clever," replied Franz, smiling in reply. He picked up Tom's cap from a small heap of slag and gave it to him.

Tom laughed sourly. "My old woman used to say: 'Keep your eye peeled for a chap as says he ain't clever. He'll steal the pennies from a dead man's eyes.' " He put on his cap, and regarded Franz thoughtfully. "I like you, though," he added.

They went out. Near the gates of the mills they purchased newspapers. The election was finally settled, announced the papers. James A. Garfield was now the twentieth President of the United States. Ominous prophesies were uttered by the more Tory newspapers about the probable results of this election.

"He's a good man," said Tom, angrily. "He don't believe in murderin' strikers. The big industrialists and the mine owners and the railroads'll have to watch themselves now."

He went on to say that the Knights of Labor now numbered some two hundred thousand. "They can't keep us down," gloated Tom, striking the newspaper with his clenched fist. "They can't keep us down!"

The yellow street-lamps shone on his dark ugly face with its sparkling eyes. A fanatical light gleamed on his features.

Franz yawned. "I'm not interested in anything but keeping my job and getting my wages," he replied, indulgently. A mist was drizzling through the murky air. He put up his coat collar and thrust his hands in his pockets.

"Wouldn't you like a livin' wage?" demanded Tom, irately.

"When I earn it yes."

Tom swore contemptuously. "You Dutchmen 'aven't any guts," he said, with disgust. "Well, wait until you're sacked, or laid off. You'll sing another tune."

"So far as I can see, the unions have caused nothing but bloodshed and confusion," remarked Franz, indifferently.

"That's because we're just organizin'. Everythin' good's got to be fought for. If you'd just attend one meetin'."

"All right, then, I'll attend," said Franz, with an air of weary and good-tempered capitulation. He gave Tom the impression that the latter's repeated arguments had finally broken down his resistance. "When is the next meetin'?"

"Tomorrow night." Tom was delighted. He clapped his friend on the shoulder. "We'll make a good Knight of you yet!"

"I'm not promising anything, remember," warned Franz. "But I suppose this is the only way I can get you to stop nagging me."

Tom was elated at finally breaking down Franz's stubborn resistance. Franz smiled to himself ironically in the darkness.

Tom's home was a poor but neat little cottage, which his wife, Dolly, made as gay and homelike as she could on eighteen dollars a week, with the handicap of three small girls. The cottage had four tight little rooms, warm, gay, overcrowded, and brilliantly clean. The house was like herself, diminutive, tidy, fresh and gallant, and full of briskness. Franz frequently stopped in on the way home, for a cup of tea, and to play with the children, of whom he was genuinely fond.

He stopped in tonight, and Dolly greeted him with her

never-failing pleasure and gaiety. She was a tiny woman, with a bird-like bosom and bird-like movements. Her light brown hair was always elaborately waved, and her round dimpled face and merry eyes were pretty and sparkling. She loved fashion, and in a poor and pathetic imitation, followed it with grave religiousness. She made her own clothing, and her children's. Tonight, she wore a dress of crimson cloth, well-fitted, if of poor quality, and enormously bustled, looped and draped. Her little girls, Mary, Polly and Pansy, were neat and clean, their dark hair curled into careful cockscrews, white starched pinafores over their neat plaid dresses. The kettle was steaming on the stove. A fire was lighted in the little "parlor," and every table was heaped with gimcracks and covered with embroidered cloths. Franz liked this house, so different from his own. Despite its poverty, it was cosy and heart-warming, and full of laughter. Dolly fancied herself quite a lady, and was always simpering, coy, smiling and flirtatious.

She was very glad to see Franz, whose splendor of body and general appearance always excited her. Moreover, his fondness for her children had convinced her that he was a very fine young man, indeed.

"I've brought 'Andsome 'ome for a cup of tea," announced Tom, kissing his wife, and then kissing the three prim little girls.

"And glad I am you did!" responded Dolly, smirking gaily at Franz. She bustled to the stove, and sent the older girl, Mary, to put out another cup. She hung up the young men's coats, after vigorously shaking them free of drops of water.

Franz sat down, and warmed his hands at the cheery fire. Mary came to him shyly. She was his favorite, a dark sober little girl with tinkling and reluctant laughter. She had Tom's eyes and coloring. But she was very pretty, in an elfish way, and much older than her ten years. She allowed herself to be lifted to Franz's knee, and the other little girls came up, jealously, to stand at his side. Polly and Pansy were twins, with round, fresh-colored faces and their mother's dark blue eyes. They did not like Mary, and were consolidated against her, for instinctively, despite their brief six years, they knew she was different, and a stranger. They adored Franz, and could not understand his preference for Mary. So Polly surreptitiously pinched her sister, and Pansy thrust a furtive finger-nail into the girl's leg. Mary winced, but proudly refused to cry out, or protest. Franz saw the little play, and frowned menacingly at the twins.

"Now then, you're being naughty, aren't you?" he asked. "That's no way to get what you want."

"How do you get what you want, Uncle Franz?" asked

Pansy, pertly, and not at all abashed at the discovery of her meanness.

"By being nice, and pleasant, and agreeable," replied Franz, smiling involuntarily.

"Like Uncle Franz," interjected Tom, sardonically. "Always keeps smilin' and smirkin' like a bloody puppet, and the world'll fill your paws."

Franz laughed without offense. But Dolly, pretending to be shocked at Tom's "swearin'," reprimanded him. "The children!" she exclaimed. She cut some bread very thin and buttered it lavishly. She opened a pot of damson jam with a flourish. Franz could smell the supper cooking: a thick rich oxtail soup. Dolly put a clean white cloth on a corner of the table, and set out the cups and saucers in a neat row. Even the children had their cups. Dolly poured the black steaming tea, and liberally added sugar to the cups, and pushed a pitcher of milk in Franz's direction. Her pretty twinkling face beamed upon him slyly.

"I saw your Ma, today, Franz. And a young lady was with her. Your cousin, your Ma says. Ooh, what a beauty!"

Her gay Cockney voice rose in an arch of cunning laughter.

Tom was interested. "Oh, that lass you told me about, eh? So, she's here."

"And such a face, and such a color!" exclaimed Dolly, peeping knowingly over the rim of her cup at Franz. "We'll be havin' a weddin' soon, mark my words!"

Franz smiled, and drank a little tea before answering. Then he put his hand over Dolly's tiny, work-reddened fingers.

"You know I'm true to you, Dolly," he said. "I can't look at any other woman."

Dolly laughed gaily. "Laws, what a tongue you've got, Franz! You make my heart flutter. And don't you be holdin' my hand. Tom won't like it."

Tom smiled at her affectionately. He was very proud of her prettiness and vivacity. The twins sat on his knees, and Mary still was perched on Franz's knee.

"Don't let me catch you two kissin' behind doors," he said, frowning darkly. "A man's got some rights."

He turned to Franz. "The lass'll be goin' into service, I'm thinkin'?"

"Probably." Franz produced a small silver piece for Mary, who took it with heightened color and shining eyes. She held it in her little hand, and glowed upon him with deep love.

"Buy yourself some candy," he suggested.

"No. Bank," said Dolly, briskly rising quickly like a bird and taking down a plaster pig from the mantelpiece. "Come along, Mary, put it in." The twins watched with deep envy and resentment.

"Let the child have it for herself," urged Franz, seeing the light fading on the girl's face.

Tom shook his head, dourly. "No, thank you. She must learn to save. One of these days we'll have to break the kids' banks for bread, if times don't improve. Come along, Mary, do as your Ma tells you."

Mary, with tears on her quiet lashes, dropped the coin into the pig. The twins chortled maliciously. Franz kissed the child's cheek.

"Never mind, Mary. Tell me what you want for your birthday, next week, and I'll bring it to you, even if it's the Tower of London."

She smiled with dark excitement, though her eyes were still wet. But before she could reply, her mother said reprovingly: "Now, Franz, you'll spoil the girl."

Franz continued to look into the child's eyes. "A doll? A new dress? A little locket? Or a purse, or some handkerchiefs?"

"A doll," she whispered. The tiny purple veins in her pale temples fluttered. Her face shone again. "A doll, with yellow curls, like yours, Uncle Franz."

He hugged her to him. Like most Germans, he had a deep and genuine affection for children. "A doll it is, with yellow curls. And don't let those Vandal sisters of yours get at it, either."

The twins were more envious than ever. They climbed down from their father's knees, and clamored about Franz. "It's our birthday in June!" they shouted. "We want dolls, too, bigger dolls than Mary's!"

"Didn't you hear your Uncle Franz say as that was no way to get what you want—screamin' and demandin'?" asked Tom, with heavy sarcasm.

When Franz went out again into the raining night, he felt that he had left warmth, gaiety and joy behind him.

He could so control his mind that he had not given Irmgard Hoeller a thought during the day. Now, as he approached his dreary home, he thought of her with sudden excitement and a curious anger. He saw her beautiful calm face and green eyes. He heard her slow quiet voice. He ran up the gritty stairs at 18 Mulberry Street, and flung open the door.

After Tom's home, this flat was incomparably dim, cold and somber. No fire was lit in the parlor stove. He went into the kitchen. Emmi and Irmgard were setting the table. Egon was reading near the stove, so close to it indeed that the chill air smelled with a faint scorching. He looked over his glasses at Franz and smiled his usual sweet shy smile. But Emmi gave him a brief nod, and Irmgard merely glanced at him impersonally. Franz kissed his father's cheek. He omitted this usual greeting for Emmi. But he smiled at his cousin, trying to catch her eye.

"What have you been doing today, cousin?" he asked, genially, moving to the stove and putting himself in her way so that she would have to look at him. Her pale cheek colored unwillingly. She looked at him steadfastly, and the green eyes were cold with dislike.

"I have gotten a position," she said. She bent over the stove and examined the contents of a pot. He saw her high full bosom pressing against the tightness of her black basque. He saw the smoothness of her white throat and the curve of her chin.

"A position! So soon! Where?"

The girl did not answer. But Emmi, standing in the center of the kitchen with an iron spoon in her hand, made grim reply.

"Maid to a lady. She begins tomorrow. It is for a Mrs. Schmidt. The wife of the owner of the mills. The housekeeper left today, and Mrs. Schmidt's maid is to take her place. Irmgard is to attend Mrs. Schmidt."

Franz stared. Then he burst out into his loud, unmirthful laughter.

CHAPTER 14

EMMI'S SAVAGE disappointment in her niece, Irmgard, had somewhat abated by morning. Her own integrity and singleness of mind had recognized similar qualities in the girl, and for these, she could forgive much. To her, Franz's mind was a devious labyrinth, full of malicious enemies and obscure dangers. She did not know that the completely amoral mind was in reality as simple as her own. She would never know that the truly complicated mind was that mind continually assaulted by self-interest and a larger and more impersonal nobility. The only difference between herself and Franz was that Franz was at peace, and full of content. To the end of her life, her own simplicity was constantly at war with reality, and so she suffered eternally. But Franz was adjusted to reality, and had long ago accepted it, and so he was torn by no agony such as hers.

Once he said to her, with that smiling malice she found so intolerable: "You will not realize that you and I have the same type of mind. The only difference lies in our eyes. You could easily be me, and I could easily be you. Only our susceptibilities are different." Some deep subconscious acknowledgment of this truth had merely served to increase her passionate antagonism to him.

"You believe," he said, "that all men are your brothers. I believe that no one is my brother. Our beliefs, perhaps, are both excessive. So, even in our excesses, we are identical."

"You will not face facts," they both said to each other, Emmi with bitter anger, and Franz with amusement.

She would never know that in truth her mind was as amoral as Franz's. The truly moral mind accepted evil and vileness. She never accepted them. She was as intolerant of human nastinesses as Franz was intolerant of what he called sentimentality. He believed in the right of using his fellow men, and was ruthless in this. Emmi believed in the duty of assisting her fellow men, and was just as ruthless. She undertook to guide Irmgard's life as ruthlessly as Franz contemplated using it.

So, the next morning she said to Irmgard: "You insist upon securing work? Then, I will go with you, and you cannot accept anything of which I do not approve."

Irmgard thought: My life is my own. But she merely smiled and said nothing, proving that her mind was not as simple as Emmi's.

Emmi had wished her to remain in the flat on Mulberry Street indefinitely, secretly hoping that Franz would be brought under the influence of both Irmgard's beauty and her honesty. But Irmgard had gently insisted that she would be no burden, and had already decided that she must earn her own living. "Otherwise," she said, "I should not have come to America."

Emmi, in principle, approved of such Teutonic independence and pride. Moreover, there was always the question of expense——

She took Irmgard to an employment office which dealt with domestic servants. Being healthy of spirit, she did not deplore that the daughter of German bourgeoisie and small landowners should have to seek her living as a servant. She, herself, had been brought up in the sound German tradition that honest work of any kind was not degrading. The degradation lay in the mind of the individual. Irmgard would be no less proud and self-respecting in menial work than if she had been a school-mistress. One accepted what circumstance had placed in one's hands to do, and one did it well and with lofty pride.

The employment office was a dingy room in a line of grimy mercantile buildings. A severe middle-aged woman presided over it. Accustomed to the sight of many raw peasants seeking work in the houses of the rich, she was startled by Irmgard's noble bearing and excessive beauty, and was inclined to be antagonistic. Moreover, she was surprised at the girl's command of English, slow and careful though it was. However, Irmgard had little chance to talk. Emmi did most of the talking, with a prim hard arrogance which affronted the woman.

"My niece speaks French, as well as English," she said. "I think she would make an excellent governess."

The woman smiled contemptuously. "I have no such positions. My calls are for cooks, housemaids and personal maids." She eyed Irmgard hostilely over her blinking glasses. "My clients do not care for German cooking, though many of them are Germans. Moreover, this young—lady, is too large to be a housemaid. My clients prefer small girls. And as for her being a personal maid—" she smiled again, "I am afraid that mistresses do not like girls who are too good-looking. They have to watch their husbands, you know."

Emmi rose, tall, lean and harsh in her bonnet and jacket and muff. "Then, you have nothing?" She turned to Irmgard and said: "Come."

"You are too hasty," said the woman, frowning. She looked at Irmgard. "Can you massage?"

Irmgard thought of the weary years in which she had faithfully massaged her suffering father's body, which had been afflicted with rheumatism since his prison days. She answered quietly: "Yes."

The woman rustled some papers. "I have a call here for a strong girl to be the personal maid of a lady who suffers with rheumatic pains, and is very delicate. Massage is a requirement. She also wishes some one with a gentle voice and nice manners. In short, a girl who knows her place."

Irmgard's lovely calm face flushed. She stood beside Emmi, in her old country garments, her hands folded before her. "I know my place," she said, and her voice became strained, as though she were choking.

The woman was pleased by these signs of discomfiture. "The young female chosen must be very exceptional." She bridled. "Not so long ago I sent her a German girl, Matilda, who was so adequate that she has become the housekeeper in the lady's mansion. It is a very distinguished household—one of our best families. The name is Schmidt. Mr. Schmidt is the owner of the Schmidt Steel Company. You can see that only a very capable and well-bred young person would be accepted there. One with excellent manners and a good address."

She wrote busily on a card. "The remuneration is twenty dollars a month, which is very, very good. But Mrs. Schmidt is noted for her kindness and generosity. You will also have a room of your own, and will be on call twenty-four hours a day. Alternate Thursday afternoons are yours, and one Sunday in four. Very, very generous. I have heard that Mrs. Schmidt is very considerate with her servants, and not at all over-bearing. You will, in a way, be her companion, too."

She gave Irmgard the card, and the two women left the office.

It had begun to sleet. Emmi put up her big black umbrella, and took Irmgard's arm. "It is not far," she said, economically, "and we need not take the cars."

They walked fast through the gritty and murky streets. Emmi stared grimly ahead, silently and witheringly answering the employment-office female in her mind. Her features worked with her blasting emotions. She breathed stormily. She almost forgot the girl with her, and so did not see the sad mournfulness of Irmgard's expression, the sudden drooping of her shoulders. But this passed, and Irmgard lifted her head and walked firmly and proudly. A look of resolution appeared about her mouth, and a gleam of steadfastness in her brilliant green eyes. She put aside all sorrowful and depressing thoughts with a distinct effort of her will. She expected nothing of life, and would not go down under its assaults.

"On your Thursdays and Sundays, you will come to us," said Emmi, at last, having demolished the employment lady in her mind.

Irmgard smiled, without replying.

"You must not be lonely," said Emmi, severely.

"I have never been lonely," replied Irmgard, lifting her skirts over a puddle.

Emmi grunted. "That is just the arrogance of the young, who feel so self-sufficient. Of course you will be lonely! But you must learn to control your feelings."

Irmgard smiled again, involuntarily. She knew by now that Emmi never controlled herself. She also knew that those who talked constantly of certain virtues never possessed them.

"I always control myself," she said, equably.

Emmi gave her a sharp look, but Irmgard's face was serene and unreadable. In fact, the slight skirmish between them had raised the girl's spirits. A faint depression, like a dimple, appeared near one lip, and her eyes sparkled.

"It will be all strange, and perhaps intolerable, to you for a while, this stranger's house in a strange country," said Emmi, with severity. "But you must not allow yourself to become depressed, or hopeless. You must reconcile yourself to situations and circumstances, and be courageous."

But you, thought Irmgard, with compassion, have never reconciled yourself. However, she merely inclined her head. Emmi, after delivering herself of these high sentiments, felt sternly exalted, and marched quicker, became more erect, stared sternly before her. She seemed to derive some inner stiffening for herself in her remarks to her niece. Like many people, she could obtain personal virtue in advising others.

"You must never allow yourself to weaken," added Emmi, feeling strong and formidable.

"No, Aunt Emmi," replied Irmgard, meekly, understanding the other with a sudden surge of sadness, comprehending her weaknesses.

Emmi continued to march. Her black skirts swirled about her buttoned boots, like the cloak of a general. Her features became rigid. Her eyes flashed. Bugles seemed to accompany her. Her own heaviness of heart had vanished. She felt invincible. Irmgard, watching her, smiled sorrowfully. She walked a little behind, for Emmi's sharp elbows poked her uncomfortably, and consequently the girl was more than a little damp when they approached the Schmidt mansion.

Emmi had already begun to march up to the front entrance, when Irmgard caught her arm. "No, dear aunt. The servants' entrance."

Emmi stopped, and glared. Then, flinging up her bonnetted head again, she led the way to the rear. They were admitted by the butler, who was surprised to see this grenadier of a middle-aged woman and so beautiful a young lady. Irmgard silently presented the card, which the butler carried away.

The two women stood in a small dark entry before the back stairway. Emmi was breathing audibly again. She said: "You must never forget your manners, Irmgard, no matter the provocation. You must be submissive and obedient and silent. I hope you understand. You must not disgrace me."

"No," said the girl, softly.

The butler returned and said that Mrs. Schmidt would see the applicant.

He led the way to the stairway. At the foot, Irmgard touched her aunt gently, and her eyes were pleading. "Aunt Emmi, I must go alone."

Emmi was outraged. She stood at the foot of the stairway,

one foot planted on the first step. "Nonsense!" she said, loudly. "You are a raw girl. I must see the lady myself, and judge whether this is a proper place for you."

They spoke in German. The English butler paused halfway up the steps and looked down at them impatiently.

"Moreover," Emmi went on, "you do not know what to say. You will make no impression. I must talk for you."

"No," said Irmgard, softly but firmly.

The green eyes looked into the violent blue eyes. Emmi flushed a dark crimson. Her lean features, so dry and sharp, worked. This was intolerable!

"I insist," she said, more loudly than ever. "You will not get the position without me."

"I must learn to stand alone," said Irmgard. She stood on the step and regarded her aunt with quiet resolution.

Her words softened Emmi, made her irresolute. After all, she had been urging this very resolution upon the girl!

"I am much offended," she said, but she removed her foot from the step, and assumed an injured expression.

"But, you would want me to do this alone, would you not?" urged Irmgard, shrewdly. "You would not want the lady to believe I am a weakling, who must be talked for, and explained?"

"If the young person will accompany me," said the butler, stiffly.

Emmi drew a deep breath, and thrust her hands stiffly into her muff.

"Go then, and do not blame me," she said.

She looked up into that young face, so pale, so smiling, so gentle, and a hand seemed to squeeze her lonely and desolate heart. She tried not to smile in return, and moved away, abruptly, taking a severe place near the door. Irmgard was overwhelmed with compassion, as she regarded that lean and lonely figure, so defenseless, and so assailed. Then, firming her lips, she went up the stairway in the butler's wake.

Irmgard's impression was that this house, for all its splendor, was a dark, gloomy and dreary place, with its great echoing rooms and dim furniture, with its intense laden silence and dusky shadows. When she reached the second floor, and passed the mighty well of the curving staircase, she had a sudden impression of complete horror. She saw the light that came through the stained window on the landing, and it absurdly frightened her with its ghostly tints. There was a smell in this house, a hushed rank smell which was compounded of all the emotions of this dreadful place, and which she could not define. But her animal instinct sent a prickling along her spine. She could not go on for a moment or two.

Her legs were trembling under her long thick garments. Her breath seemed stopped in her throat. She looked about her wildly, and to her quickened imagination, every shut door along the great corridor seemed to harbor a terror and a threat, and a thick and sickening danger.

She was alone. The butler had opened a door and had disappeared within it, thinking her at his heels. She was sweating slightly. Her whole skin was alive with a dull fear. There was no sound, only that dreadful waiting hush, broken only by distant booming echoes, as though the house stirred in itself. Her feet were sunken in the thick carpet. She smelled again that rank and choking smell. She looked over her shoulder in fright, saw the long spectral corridor behind her, and before her. She was seized with a nameless desire for complete flight. The darkness of the house loomed all about her, like gloomy chaos.

She actually took a step, when she heard a faint but lovely sound. Some one was playing softly on a piano behind one of the doors, a phrase or two of Chopin, infinitely melancholy and infinitely grand, like a divine meditation. The heavy echoes of the house became stilled. The music flowed over them, like a flood of soft light. It was the grave voice of a friend, calling to her. She stood and listened. Chords rose and broke against the dark walls and the high lost ceilings, in radiant but mournful spray. Tears rose to Irmgard's eyes, and her lips shook. A strange emotion struck her heart, almost like the passionate convulsion of love. Never had she felt so lonely, nor so at peace.

The butler reappeared. "If you will come this way," he said, reprovingly, seeing her standing there in utter immobility in that immense and dusky hall.

She went towards him. She was no longer afraid. She was sure, in some foolish way, that the person who was playing that music had known she was there, and had spoken to her. She was not alone.

CHAPTER 15

WHEN IRMGARD entered the gloomy, fetid and luxurious room of Mrs. Hans Schmidt, she was so far composed that she could see everything in one quick glance.

She saw an abnormally thin dark woman with a sick face lying on a crimson velvet chaise-longue, her feet covered by a shawl. A white shawl was also about her compressed shoulders, above which her face was a death's-head of suffering. Her black hair, heavily streaked with white, was curled, frizzed and banged, and pinned at the back in a heavy chignon. Near her, on a stool, and leaning forward the better to see by one dim lamp, was a young woman, sewing quietly and steadily. It was evident that she was the daughter of the older woman, for there was a marked resemblance between them, though the younger woman had a still and innocent sweetness of expression, and some pale and fragile prettiness. She wore a gray velvet dress, elaborately looped, draped and bustled, with a fringe of white lace at her throat, caught with a gold and diamond pin. Her thick dark hair was, like her mother's, banged and frizzed and tortured, but it shone with a black lustre like satin. Near them, uncompromising, buxom and arrogant, stood another woman, fair, belligerent of expression, in a black silk dress covered by a black silk apron. At her belt was fastened a large bunch of keys. Her hands were folded primly on her abdomen, and as Irmgard entered, she looked at her hostilely, and with impudent appraisal. What she saw appeared to infuriate her, and she took a step towards the girl. The other women looked up, and seemed surprised and taken aback by Irmgard's heroic appearance.

"You are the girl who is come for the position?" asked the buxom woman, in a strongly accented and goading voice.

"Come in, my dear," said the sick lady on the chaise-longue. She smiled gently, and half extended an emaciated hand. The buxom woman, evidently an upper servant or housekeeper, glared at Irmgard.

Irmgard quietly advanced into the room, full of strong

serenity. She curtseyed with some awkwardness, and without a word, gave the sick lady her card, which the butler had returned to her. Mrs. Schmidt held the card in her faintly tremulous hands, but continued to regard Irmgard seriously.

The buxom woman suddenly began to speak to Irmgard with great rapidity, in German.

"You are a German? A raw girl, no doubt. What do you know of what is required here?"

Her tone was bullying, and a little frightened. She covered her fear with bluster. Irmgard listened to the inflections and the words, and had difficulty in understanding. The woman spoke in Low Dutch, and a slight contempt stirred behind Irmgard's calm green eyes.

"Yes. I am from Bavaria," she replied, politely. "I am not raw. I have taken care of invalids. My father was an invalid. I think I am competent."

The younger woman, who understood Irmgard's cultured German perfectly, though only partially able to follow Matilda's uncouth accents, smiled at the girl.

"I am sure you are competent," she said, with great soft kindness. "My mother is not well. I think you would serve her excellently."

Matilda glowered. She turned to Mrs. Schmidt and said loudly: "I know these girls from the Old Country! Girls like these, too. They think they are better than others. They know nothing." She swung upon Irmgard again. Her heavy face was crimson with hatred, and her pale blue eyes squinted.

"You will not do," she said, with fury. "You will please go."

Mrs. Schmidt shrank, and pulled the shawl closer about her shoulders. She wet her dry and broken lips. It was evident that she had no courage to resist any one. But the young woman rose with a sudden quiet authority, and looked at the housekeeper.

"My mother is the best judge of who is competent to attend her, Matilda," she said, and under her soft voice there was a sharp edge of steel. She bent over Mrs. Schmidt. "Are you willing to try Irmgard, Mother?"

Mrs. Schmidt's upward look at her daughter was full of helpless and silent fear. Her lips moved, but no sound came from them. Ernestine smiled, touched her mother's cheek, and looked at Irmgard.

"It's all right," she said, gently. "We will try you, Irmgard."

But Matilda shouted violently, clenching her big fat hands, and regarding Ernestine with murderous fury: "Your father, the master, Miss Ernestine, told me I should care for things.

I know what is best for your mother. This girl is not what is needed——"

Ernestine gazed at her thoughtfully. Her small face paled, but her dark eyes were filled with unusual lightnings. Her soft pink lips curled with scorn and anger, and complete comprehension.

"Matilda, you have received your morning orders from Mrs. Schmidt. If she has nothing more to say to you, please leave at once."

She was a small and delicate creature in her gray velvet, and she looked like a child beside the large stout German woman. But Irmgard saw that she was suddenly all tempered strength in this emergency. She and Matilda locked wills, and it was Matilda, at the last, who turned away, muttering savagely. She stamped to the door, opened it furiously, and then shut it behind her with a thunderous bang, which echoed all through the house.

Ernestine, smiling to herself as though somewhat surprised and more than a little triumphant, sat down on her stool again near her mother. "I must really speak to Papa about her," she said. "She has become impossible lately. And since he made her housekeeper, she believes she owns us body and soul."

Mrs. Schmidt spoke in her tremulous, dying voice, with great and nervous haste: "No, my dear! Don't speak to him. You know how highly he regards Matilda! It will do no good. And—and," and she wet her lips and her thin face flushed as though with inner shame and despair, "it will—do no one—any good, if Matilda is seriously annoyed. Perhaps it would have been best——"

"Nonsense," said Ernestine, with firm gentleness. She lifted her eyes and smiled at Irmgard. "You are just the person to take care of mother. I know. She needs some one like you. You will take the position?"

"Ernestine," protested Mrs. Schmidt feebly, inordinately frightened again.

Irmgard hesitated. Her quick mind had grasped many things. She certainly did not wish to intrude herself into so unpleasant a household, where everything she had seen and heard confirmed her first repulsion. She had recognized Mrs. Schmidt as a great lady, though a weakling. She knew she lived in some mysterious state of chronic terror. The girl glanced quickly about the great, ill-smelling room, overburdened with its scent of sickness, cologne and danger. It was a horrible place, a horrible household! Her nostrils quivered, and her lips opened and flattened with aversion. And then she looked at Ernestine, and saw that the girl had a strange intent expression, full of silent pleading.

"Yes," she said at last, in her slow meticulous English, "if you wish." A slow warmth gathered about her chilled heart, and the two young women smiled at each other, as though they had concluded a bargain between them.

Mrs. Schmidt drew a long quivering breath of exhaustion and resignation. Then she smiled her sad, uncertain smile. Irmgard noticed that her sunken eyes were never still, but flickered and roved about like those of a hunted animal. Moreover, she had a habit of constantly moistening her cracked lips. Her facial muscles jerked and leaped, even when in repose. But her smile was sweet.

"I hope you will be happy, my dear, with me," she said, apologetically. "I—I am not very well, as you can see. There are very few days when I can rise at all. You will find me quite a burden, I am afraid."

Irmgard felt a deep pang of pity. "I will do my best, madam," she said, very gravely.

Then Ernestine laughed a little. "You mustn't be afraid of Matilda. She is only our housekeeper. But like so many—I mean, women of her kind, she is inclined to take her duties too seriously. She has only been housekeeper for a few days, and I think it has gone to her head. You mustn't mind her. She is really excellent——"

"Oh, very excellent!" said Mrs. Schmidt eagerly, and her eyes flickered about the room again, as though she were speaking for the benefit of a hostile and violent listener, of whom she was completely terrified.

Ernestine rose. "Perhaps Irmgard would like to see her room, and hear about her duties," she said. She led the way to a room off Mrs. Schmidt's apartments, and Irmgard was pleased by the neat austerity of her new bedroom. Ernestine explained everything in a low economical voice, but all the time her shy and friendly eyes were fixed on Irmgard's face. She said suddenly, in a tone of sorrowful but smiling envy: "You are so pretty!" And colored at the involuntary words.

"Thank you, Miss Ernestine," answered Irmgard, without smiling, but with a glance that softened the brilliance of her eyes.

Ernestine sighed, and continued to gaze at the other woman. "You remind me of some one," she said, almost inaudibly. "I can't remember—" She colored again. "Your face—the way you stand, and turn your head. It is very strange."

There was a silence in the small closed room. Ernestine had lit a lamp on the table. It shone on the two young faces.

"How old are you, Irmgard?"

"I am almost twenty, fräulein."

"So young! I am eight years older than you."

Irmgard was surprised. She had thought Ernestine the same age as herself, for the other girl was so small, so immature of body and face.

"I'll be so glad to have you here!" exclaimed Ernestine, naïvely. Irmgard saw that her naïveté was one of her more outstanding characteristics, a naïveté that was so childlike that it could come only from a simple heart and mind unaccustomed to more sophisticated usages. "Mother needs some one like you, so healthy and calm." She hesitated. "You must not let Matilda annoy you. She—she is really a detestable person, but—but my father likes her very much, and believes her exceptionally competent. I am afraid she will try you very much, but I think you can manage her. Don't let her bully you. If you are too respectful to her, she will hate you, and make your life miserable." She twisted her small hands, and the color quite left her face. "She makes mother's life miserable. Part of your work will be to protect my mother against her."

She put her hand pleadingly on Irmgard's large arm. "I can trust you? You will protect my mother?"

Again, Irmgard was aware of unclean things under the surface, and she regretted her decision to remain here. She wanted no part in this ominous household. But while she hesitated again, she could not resist Ernestine's small pleading face and wretched eyes.

"I will do my best, fräulein," she said.

Ernestine averted her head. "Thank you," she whispered. There was another silence. Irmgard saw that Ernestine's cheek was pale, and even a little shrunken. She seemed to be struggling in herself, trying to speak, and then to prevent herself from speaking.

Then she took courage, and looked at Irmgard directly:

"You—you may think us an odd household, Irmgard. Mother is an invalid, and then there is my—brother. He is a cripple, and not able to go about very much." She paused. "Then—my father. He is really a very good man, but with rather abrupt manners. Some people do not always understand him. But believe me, he is so good!" Her eyes pleaded abjectly with Irmgard.

"If you say he is good, then I am certain he is, fräulein," said Irmgard, becoming more and more convinced that she ought not to stay here, but unable to see how she could extricate herself.

Ernestine sighed. She forced herself to smile, and the smile, to Irmgard, was pathetic. "That is all, then. You can come tomorrow?"

"Yes."

"We live a very quiet life," said Ernestine, leading the way to the door. Irmgard saw that she seemed to float, so light was her step, so effortless the motions of her tiny body. "You will not work too hard."

When she reentered the large bedroom, Irmgard saw that a stranger was there, with Mrs. Schmidt. She was so startled at the sight of him, that she recoiled a step. She saw a cripple almost half her size, with a beautiful and splendid head. He looked up at her as she stood in the doorway, and an expression of profound astonishment, and even awe, came over his colorless but arresting face. He was standing beside Mrs. Schmidt, and holding her hand in both of his. Now, he dropped the hand he held, and continued to stare as at an astonishing vision.

Ernestine flitted to him and kissed him. "This is Irmgard Hoeller, Mama's new maid, Baldur," she said.

He recovered himself, and gave her a smile of infinite sweetness.

Ernestine said, turning to Irmgard: "This is my brother, Mr. Schmidt, Irmgard."

Irmgard curtseyed awkwardly. The gesture was evidently a new one with her. Her clear green eyes gazed at him straightly, and what she saw went to her heart. She knew instantly that he had been the unseen player of that lovely and mysterious music which had so strengthened and reassured her. "It will not be so hard, with him in this house," she thought.

Ernestine remarked briskly to her mother that she had explained the duties to Irmgard. Fortified now by the presence of both her children, Mrs. Schmidt seemed more composed. "It will be so nice to have another young person in the house," she said. She took her daughter's hand. "And so nice for Ernestine. I am afraid she is very lonely, sometimes."

Irmgard had a quick thought that all this was very strange. She was being accepted as a young friend and a companion by these miserable people, and not as a servant. They looked at her with simple openness, and seemed to draw from her some strength and hope. She felt these virtues flow out from her to them, and for the first time she was glad that she was to remain.

She left, rather than was dismissed. She went silently down the rear stairs towards the lower landing. Then she stopped, startled. A door on the second landing opened, and Matilda stood there, breathing heavily, her face congested.

"You will not be here long," she said viciously, and nodded with menacing satisfaction.

Irmgard regarded her scornfully. She lifted her heavy skirts deliberately, and passed Matilda without speaking. Just as she did so, she heard Matilda mutter a foul epithet in German. Irmgard descended the steps without hurry, and without giving any indication that she had heard. But her face was white, and her forehead was damp. The passionate temper beneath her calm exterior was aroused. She had to control herself, to keep herself from going back and striking that florid peasant face.

Emmi was waiting impatiently. She watched Irmgard descending the steps.

"So?" she demanded.

"I have the position," answered Irmgard quietly. "Shall we go now?"

But Emmi looked shrewdly at the girl. "You are ill," she said, uncertainly. "I do not know if you should come here. What has happened?"

"Nothing," said Irmgard. She opened the door and went out into the cold rawness of the November day. She stood on the step and breathed deeply, as though she could not get enough of the clean air.

CHAPTER 16

FRANZ LAY and listened restlessly to the dull night sounds, as he tried to sleep. He heard the dolorous wailing of the trains passing at the foot of the slope at the rear of the flats. It was raining furiously, and he could hear the cataracts of water rushing down the sooty windows. Faintly, he could also hear Emmi's muffled snoring, and the lighter sounds of his father's slumber. A cat screamed in the darkness. Hollow footsteps went slowly by on the street.

His mind felt hot and in a turmoil. He relived the scenes with the Superintendent and with Dethloff. More and more, he was convinced that much lay behind them which was incomprehensible. He did not flatter himself that these men had discovered hidden genius in him. In dull times he was the first foreman to be laid off. It is true that he could drive his men competently, but there were other foremen who could do as much. Moreover, he knew he was no favorite with Dethloff and the Superintendent. He knew they hated him, especially the "Saxon Schweinehund." So, what lay behind all this? Realist as he was, he shrewdly conjectured that they, too, were being caught up into something which infuriated them. He recalled, suddenly, the questions of Hans Schmidt, and he sat up in bed, thinking rapidly. But Schmidt had not seemed unduly impressed by him, and his questioning had been sharp and contemptuous. However, that was one possibility. But why? It was well known that Schmidt never interfered with the decisions of his Superintendent, and, knowing himself, Franz dismissed as ludicrous the idea that the Superintendent had eagerly recommended him.

There was no answer to the puzzle. He could only wait and see. He lay down again and sternly closed his eyes.

And then he knew that his intense thoughts were deliberately induced in order to shut out all thought of his cousin, Irmgard. Now that he had dismissed them, Irmgard came back into his mind with vivid force, and he stared into the darkness, his eyelids smarting with strain. His flesh felt hot and dry, as with fever, and he was aware of every inch of it, as though it ached. He sat up again in his bed, cursing audibly, hating himself for his own fever and his own inability to control himself. He looked at the door. It seemed to pulse in the dark, as though some one waited and breathed behind it. He would not allow himself to think objectively. For such objectivity brought her face before him, painted in bright colors on a black background.

He was surprised and enraged to find himself pulling his worn robe over his night clothing, and thrusting his feet into his icy boots. He seemed to be moving under some mysterious compulsion. He opened the door. The kitchen was still warm. He stood by the stove, irresolute, wondering angrily at himself. A stupid girl, a big peasant girl! He felt no real urge for her, and her beauty had not excited him, he told himself. It was the beauty of immense and impersonal landscapes, which a man might admire, but would certainly not want to embrace! When he thought of her, an intense annoyance rose up in him, and a sort of dull anger. He had even felt a desire, more than once, to slap that pale calmness into red-printed discomfiture and fear. She was a block of ice, with fixed green eyes. He had never permitted himself to be emotionally disturbed by anyone before. But she disturbed him, and wherever he turned his restless inner eye, she was there, unmoved, inexorable, not to be avoided. He could not understand himself! He could not understand his emotions, his urges, his angers, and his hatred. For by now he was certain that he hated her intensely. The admission humiliated him as much as a confession of passion would have humiliated him. No human being, he had long ago told himself, should ever be allowed to intrude into his mind either by the door of love, anger or hatred. The man involved in emotions, either joyous or tumultuous, was a man crippled. He had not allowed himself to hate real enemies, nor to waste time in plotting revenge. Yet, here was a stupid heavy girl, of no consequence and no visible brilliance, standing before him with compelling force, and gripping his thoughts strongly in both her large hands!

Why? he fumed to himself, disgusted. He could recall nothing she had ever said. Yet, he heard her voice echoing in him like a wind. He could see again her pale bright hair, and the delicate curls on her neck. Her presence was so vivid that he turned around sharply in the darkness, almost expecting to see her in the flesh.

He was more surprised and enraged than ever when he found himself in the dark chill parlor, whose blackness was lighted only by the feeble glow of a street-lamp penetrating into the court. Then his heart seemed to move and lift in his chest. He saw a thin pencil of lamplight under Irmgard's door. He held his breath and listened. He heard faint sounds behind the door, the swish of garments. No doubt the girl was packing her clothing, for she was to leave early in the morning.

He watched the pencil of light. All at once it was blotted out, as she apparently stood between the lamp and the door. He heard her sigh, a deep and clearly audible sigh. To his dull amazement, his heart beat painfully, and the fever in his flesh increased to a thrilling fire. He moved silently to the door. He put his hand on the wood. He knew that she stood only a few inches away from him, separated from him only by the flimsy wood. The door seemed alive under his hot hand. It appeared to pulse, like a sheath of flesh. His ears rang with loud noises, and he heard a deep far thudding which he knew was his heart. He had the strange impression that something of his inexplicable passion had communicated itself to the girl behind the door, that she had been caught by it as though in a trap, and that she was helplessly palpitating. He knew he had made no sound, yet he was mysteriously sure she felt his presence, and that she was holding her breath. She was not moving. He could feel her behind the door, and knew that she was staring at it. They stood, less than a foot apart, and the door was only a more intense path of communication between them. It vibrated between them like a struck gong, involving them in waves of electric sound.

It seemed to him that timeless eons passed. He could not think. His hand was still on the door. Now he could hear her breathing, and the sound was fast and agitated. He pressed his own lips tightly together, and breathed lightly. His hand on the door appeared to have established some electric contact, and he could not move. His will was powerless in its surging waves. He was not a man any longer. He was only a swirling mass of impulses, a vortex of fiery sparks which struck through the wood of the door into the body of the girl beyond. As steel is drawn irresistibly to a magnet, so he felt that she was being drawn to him, that the very door would dissolve in its resistless energy, and they would cleave together with sudden violence, their own wills dissipated, their own desires annihilated in a single destructive flame.

As though her own emotions had become too fierce, the girl suddenly flung the door open and confronted him. They looked at each other in a ringing silence. The dim lamp behind her threw her into relief, and made a halo about her majestic head. He could barely see her face, but he knew it was white and tense and rigid.

Then she said, in a low voice: "What is it you want?"

You, he said silently. The passionate word seemed to have struck the air like a violent sound, and to have come from him involuntarily. He was so appalled at it that he could do nothing but stare at her, paralyzed, as if he had admitted something of terrible implication for himself.

He heard himself saying: "May I come in for a moment?"

She hesitated. The air between them was charged with shock. And then he knew that she was trying to deny him something of much more importance than mere entry into her room.

"Just a moment," he urged, smiling.

Her hand was on the door. She looked at him with white gravity. The lamplight lay on his face, and she saw the strong rectangular planes of his features, sharp as though drawn with a charcoal pencil. Some mysterious force sprang at her from his body, enclosed her in a capsule of paralysis. It was more to escape this force than to assent to his request that she fell back from the doorway.

He stepped inside the room and closed the door quickly behind him. A deep flush ran over the girl's cheeks. She continued to move away from him. He looked about the room, smiling casually, seeing her half-packed boxes on the narrow white bed, and the chair.

"I will not see you tomorrow," he said. "So I came to say goodbye tonight."

The walls of the room enclosed strong but unseen charges. Irmgard's eyelids flickered, as if with sudden and primitive terror. But she looked at him, fascinated, her lips slightly fallen apart. Her hands were clasped tightly together. Franz stared at her. He saw her open fear of him, and the emotion which prompted it. He was excited, as a beast of prey is excited, at the scent of fear from the hunted. He was filled with exultation. He moved towards her. He was now so close to her that he could see the faint throbbing in her temples, and the gleam of her teeth between her parted lips. She was deathly pale again.

But, she was stronger than he thought. At the moment he put out his hands to take her, she stepped back again. She leaned against the bed. Her eyes repudiated him through her fear.

"Goodbye," she said, almost inaudibly.

Frustrated, and both angered and amused, he exclaimed softly: "Why do you dislike me, Irmgard?"

She exhaled loudly. "I do not know," she said. And then she turned quickly from him, and picked up a shawl, folded it, and laid it in her box. Her hands shook visibly. But her movements were sure. Her back was to him, and he saw her erect firm shoulders and the slender stem of her compact waist. He was seized with a primitive and overpowering hunger for her, which drove out all logic and all sanity, and which was all the more intense because of his real hatred for her, a hatred which rose from the acknowledgment that she could do this to him.

"You will come here often, to visit us?"

She did not answer. He repeated the question, in a louder voice. Then she glanced at him fearfully over her shoulder. "Hush! Your mother will hear. She will not understand why you are in my room at this hour."

"Then, you must be polite enough to answer me."

She flung aside the garment she had picked up, and faced him with great agitation. Her eyes flashed like ice which had been struck by an arctic sun. "I did not ask you to come here, and annoy me! I need not answer you! Please go. I am tired, and I must get up very early."

Her voice was thick and stifled, as though she was trying to control some inner torment. He looked at her, pleased and surprised. He had not thought this calm and stolid girl capable of such visible and frantic emotion, which was all out of proportion both to his words and his mere presence in her room.

He pretended contrition. "I am sorry, then, that I have intruded upon you, if you are so tired. But I am more sorry to see that you dislike me so. What have I done to you? We agree upon many things. Last night you hurt my mother because you agreed with me. Is it impossible for us to be friends?"

"Impossible!" she cried, and shrank back from him, putting the narrow bed between them.

"Why?" he asked, softly and reasonably.

She was silent. She averted her head. He saw the white straining tendons in her throat. Her hands were pressed flat to the wall behind her.

"What have I done?" he urged, even more softly.

Her lips moved, and she whispered: "It is not what you have done. It is what you are." But still she kept her tense profile to him.

He laughed gently. He took a furtive step or two towards her, so that his knees pressed against the bed.

"And what am I?"

She turned her face to him, and he was surprised and amused to see it so extravagantly tragic. This expression gave her a younger, weaker, more vulnerable look, like that of a harried child.

"You have no heart," she said, through shaking lips. "You are only a machine. You are not even wicked. You—you are just empty. I am not afraid of wicked people, or malicious people. Sometimes I find things in them to like. But I cannot like empty people. They—they do not even live!" Now, there was a real horror in her eyes, and this took him aback. "You are like a nightmare!" she exclaimed, and her voice was suddenly loud and clear. "You have no human thoughts. You are not human at all! You move like a man, and speak like a man, and smile like one. But you are not really alive!"

To his concern, Franz heard a cessation in his mother's snoring, a peevish murmur, and the creak of a bed. Irmgard had not heard it. She was now completely overwrought, and breathing stormily. She opened her mouth to speak again, but in a second he had run around the bed, seized her, and put his hand over her mouth. Over the edge of his hand her emerald eyes extended, dilated, with complete terror and rage. She clutched his wrist to thrust away his hand, but it was too powerful. He looked into her eyes, and his own were hard and gleaming.

"Be quiet!" he whispered. "My mother has heard you!"

They stood in rigid silence, listening intently. Irmgard ceased her struggling. Her eyes did not leave his, but a dim film came over them and her lids drooped. His arm was about her, crushing her to him. Her flesh was soft but firm, and a faint fresh scent came from her body, warm and maddening. The girl did not move. She was faint, and she felt as though she were floating in dreamlike waters. She leaned against him, and suddenly closed her eyes. She was conscious of nothing except her heart, which seemed like a molten ball of fire, sending streams of heated blood throughout all her veins. She had never experienced anything like this, and it was so profound, so terrible, that she could not resist it. A scarlet light glowed against her closed lids.

Emmi had apparently fallen asleep again. Franz heard the renewed rhythm of her snoring. Then he looked down at the girl in his arms. Her head lay on his shoulder. A soft rosy light covered her face, and her lips pulsed with scarlet. He bent his head and kissed her mouth with a kind of ferocity, again and again. His ferocity was not satiated by the touch of her soft lips. It mounted to fury, tumultuous and shaking. Her hair loosened, and a coil fell on her shoulders. He bent her backwards, and now she tried to escape him, struggling and thrusting, turning her head from side to side. There was something terrible in this silent struggle between them, for neither dared make a sound. A sick shame overwhelmed the girl. All the color was gone from her face. She tried to kick him, but her long heavy garments and his very nearness prevented this. Her breast strained against his chest, repudiating him with mingled terror and humiliation.

He finally released her, laughing under his breath. She fell back from him, against the wall. She regarded him with wild hatred.

"Go away!" she cried, her hands fumbling at her hair and garments. "Go away, or I shall call your mother!"

He hesitated. His face was deeply congested. "Irmgard," he began.

But she had recovered herself. "Go away!" she cried again.

There was now a definite creaking and grumbling upstairs. Franz heard his mother shuffling for her slippers, and Egon's faint questioning voice. He looked at the girl, and his lips drew back from his teeth in a swift flash. She was looking at him as though he were a loathsome visitation. She was fully aroused, and was capable of anything. He saw that, and he smiled in reluctant admiration. He recognized such ruthlessness, and acknowledged it, sardonically.

He opened the door. Emmi was already feeling her way in the darkness down the kitchen steps. He closed the door behind him, and swiftly ran back to his room, just as Emmi opened the kitchen door. He flung himself onto his bed and pulled the quilts over him.

Emmi came into the kitchen, grumbling. "Who is there?" she called.

The wind answered her. Franz could feel her listening in

the darkness. Then, muttering angrily to herself, she went up the stairs again.

Franz lay tense for a long time. His flesh was hot and feverish, his head aching and humming.

Then he began to laugh silently to himself.

CHAPTER 17

HE CAME into the kitchen earlier than usual the next morning. He had not slept. For the first time in his life, truly violent emotion had come to him, and the unfamiliarity of it, and the profound mystery, had thrown him into a turmoil. Mere lust, which he could understand, appeared to have a small part in it. Irmgard was like some disease which had entered all his body and his blood, consuming them, changing them, and filling them with an abysmal fever and anguished ache. If this were hatred, he could not recognize it, not having hated anything or any one before, except impersonally. By the time the first dim light appeared at his small sooty window, he was certain it was hatred. Surely it was hatred which made him get up this early, and go out into the kitchen! He started a fire for his mother, which surprised her immensely, and softened some of the bitter ice in her heart.

"That is very kind of you, Franz," she said, grudgingly, but her eyes were gentler than usual.

"Nonsense," he replied, with his charming smile. "I should have done it oftener. I will do it every morning, after this."

He insisted upon helping her set the table, and this so bewildered her, and softened her, that she touched him awkwardly once or twice with her rough hand. Her affection was always reluctant and hard, and expressed itself usually in scolding and recrimination. But now she was so overcome that she could scarcely speak.

Egon came down, and was delighted to see the amity between his wife and son. Peace-loving and gentle and amiable, and hating nothing but disorder and loud voices, his tired strained face lighted, and he could even laugh softly at

Franz's awkward efforts to assist his mother. A good warmth, not only of the stove, filled the snug kitchen, though outside the November day was dull and heavy and lifeless.

It was now breakfast time, and still Irmgard had not appeared. Nor did Emmi remark on the fact. Franz waited, his fever mounting steadily. Finally he said, with an air of carelessness: "It is getting late. Where is my cousin?"

Emmi turned to him, surprised and pleased. "Did you not know? Irmgard was to leave before breakfast. A carriage was coming for her very early. She said she would not disturb us."

She stopped, and stared at her son with growing amazement. His face had paled excessively. Even his lips had paled, and an ashen grimness turned his expression dark. "So," he said, slowly, "she has gone."

Emmi felt her heart lift incredulously, and with sudden ecstasy.

"You like her, Irmgard?" she exclaimed. "Franz!"

But he turned away abruptly, and went into his bedroom for his coat and cap. Emmi turned excitedly to her husband. "Egon! It is happening as I dreamed! He loves Irmgard! Mein Gott, I can hardly believe it!"

Egon smiled with deep affection at his wife. He wanted her to be pleased and happy. And now her gaunt tight face was alight with joy. Tears filled his eyes.

"It is good, it is good," he said tranquilly, taking her tremulous hand and pressing it between his thin palms.

Franz came from his room. Emmi smiled at him with strange tenderness. "But your breakfast, Franz?"

"I am not hungry," he said, with absent gloom. He did not look at his parents. "It is an odd return for your kindness—she should not have left you so soon," he added, as though to himself.

"But, she will be here often, my son," said Emmi, with sly gentleness. Suddenly, her small blue eyes widened, and she colored. But before she could speak, Franz had snatched up his dinner pail and had gone. Emmi turned with renewed excitement to her husband. "I remember! They spoke to each other last night. I knew it. I came downstairs, but no one answered me when I called. I was certain I heard their voices, and they were speaking loudly, and quarrelsomely. A lovers' quarrel!" She clenched her hands together, and Egon was unbearably touched by the light and joy in her eyes.

"Then, it will come about as you wish, Liebchen," he said, happy only that she was happy. He took off his pince-nez and wiped the mist from them.

Emmi picked up a corner of her apron, and rubbed it over

her eyes. She smiled, and sighed, and smiled again. Her taut face was dissolved in her joy. "There will be grandchildren, Egon," she murmured, and looked at him softly.

In the meantime, Franz hurried along the street, which was already shrouded with a veil of mingled drizzle and soot. His shoulders were bent. He walked almost at a running pace, and there was a sickness in him, mingled with fury. His head ached savagely; his eyes were rimmed in dry lids of fire. He hated himself, and hated Irmgard more. He was infuriated that she had dared intrude upon him like this. He flung his head about as though to throw off an incubus. The drizzle freshed to a sharp rain, which ran over his face. He did not feel it. His knees felt weak and uncertain, and now his breath came thickly. He stopped at the corner of the street, and breathed deeply, shaking his head again and again. "Curse her," he said aloud, and then again, "curse her."

He was appalled at his own weakness. He had never experienced strong emotion before. It was his own nature, and his own plan, to keep from feeling strongly about any creature. He had only one purpose. It was now dangerously threatened. He was suddenly frightened, with a raw abysmal fright. If he were capable of such strong emotion, then he was not to be trusted. His whole life was menaced, because of an obdurate and insignificant girl. She had shown him how weak he was. And if it were true that he was so weak, could be assaulted so easily, then his life would be nothing but failure, and he would end up in impotence. His fright increased to a real and shaking terror. He loathed himself. I am not what I thought I was! he exclaimed, in open and horrified despair.

"You are empty," Irmgard had said. She had known! Only she could understand him. And with this thought came such a powerful yearning, such an anguished grief, that he was appalled, and stood in rigid immobility, staring blindly at the rain. For he realized for the first time that he was not really alone in the world. There was some one else—. Then it was possible for some one to understand him, and by that understanding not to decrease his stature. He could be stronger for such understanding, after all. For he realized, with a flash of light, that he had always been lonely. He had never known it before. It was this loneliness, now, which was consuming him, and not truly the realization that he was impotent and weak!

All at once his hatred for Irmgard vanished, and it was swallowed up in a great yearning for her. She had not weakened him. She had only made him realize that he was lonely. He had endured loneliness; he could endure it again, if necessary. But surely it was not necessary. Irmgard's understanding could really strengthen him. He remembered her face, when she was in his arms, and her passionate if momentary yielding. All his flesh suddenly burned, and he was filled with exultation. He laughed openly, loudly, and the workmen, passing him curiously, turned and stared as at a drunkard.

Someone took his arm. "Are you balmy, man?" said Tom Harrow's jocular voice. "I've been watchin' you, standin' here like a duck in the rain."

"I was waiting for you, Tom," replied Franz, with one of those smiles which Tom always darkly suspected but could never resist. Franz's face, during one of these smiles, took on an expression of amused candor and affection. "Blast me," Tom would grumble to his wife, "I never can figger out if the chap is a rascal or not, when he grins at me. But I've seen chaps as was villains with the faces of babbies, so that's no tellin'."

Dolly would assure him heatedly that Franz was all kindness and gaiety and loyalty. But Tom was never convinced. He was not convinced now. He had often suggested that he and Franz walk together to work in the morning, but it was the rare occasion when Franz consented. Tom subconsciously knew that Franz was a solitary, and his primitive but shrewd instinct guessed that the solitary was always an enemy to other men. But when they were together, the solitary was masked with humor and affection, apparently open-hearted and jovial. It was very puzzling.

"Dolly's made us pork pies again," said Tom, stopping for a moment in the shelter of a doorway to light his pipe. His convex shoulders were thin under the patched overcoat, and rain ran down his sharp beak of a nose.

"Excellent!" said Franz. "And I've some apple kuchen."

"And Mary gave me her apple for you," said Tom, smiling, as they went on together. "Her school apple. The lass fair adores you, Franz, though God knows why."

"She is a sweet child," responded Franz, and for a moment his eyes flickered.

They walked in silence for a few moments. Then Tom said: "You 'aven't forgot the meetin' tonight, in the Elks Hall?"

"No, no. I'll stop at your house for you."

"You'll learn something," said Tom, with enthusiasm. He talked of the projected strike. "If we can only get the Hunkies and Dutchmen together!" he exclaimed. "But those chaps as 'ave lived in countries without freedom and decency is 'ard to learn anythin'. You've got to keep after them. Education."

"And you are going to teach them?"

"Why not?" demanded Tom, belligerently. "I've got a

tongue in my head, ain't I? And I know what it's all about. Didn't my Pa get killed in a mine? Didn't three of us kids die of starvation, after that? Who's better than me to tell them foreigners a thing or two?"

The open hearths were already glowing like the sun when they arrived in the mills. Men stood on small platforms near the furnaces and shovelled coal into the molten mass below. The great cranes scurried under the roof, clanging their bells, the mighty kettles of liquid, brilliant metal swaying from hooks. The kettles poised over ingot moulds, and the metal ran out, the thin hissing cataract too bright for the eye, the clouds of steam rising in a pale pink mist which filled the mill with the shadows of hell.

Schmidt's mill was one of the few in the State which combined the manufacture of pig iron with the making of steel. It had been prophesied by his rivals that he was "biting off more than he could chew," by this. "The next thing you know," they said, contemptuously, "he'll be making his own coke, and mining his own coal." But Schmidt, as though appalled at his own audacity, went no further than this.

Tom and Franz proceeded through the mill, which was hardly more than a shed open to the bitter winds of winter, to the bessemer and crucible steel mills. Beyond were the blast furnaces, fired by charcoal, which were able to make fifty to one hundred tons a day, a record produced by Schmidt, and which, to date, had not been surpassed by any of his competitors.

Tom passed Jan Kozak, and touched him on the arm. "Remember? The meetin'," he said, and Jan nodded and smiled.

Franz's temper had not been improved by his sleepless night, and he drove his men viciously. Tom could hear him shouting above the growling roar of the mill. Once he sauntered over and looked curiously at his friend's pale and livid face and malignant eyes. "Easy there, easy there," he said. "It's easy for a chap to give a slip and pour you a bellyful of hot soup. You can drive 'em just so far, you know."

"Go back and mind your own business," responded Franz. He did not give Tom one of his customary smiles. In fact, his expression was both brutal and evil, and Tom was taken aback. "There, there," he said, nonplussed. "You've got the face of a devil, lad. Look there, at the chaps lookin' at you. They'd love to do you in."

Franz clenched his fist as though it held a whip. Tom stared at him, more and more astonished. But in himself he thought: I knew it all the time. He studied Franz with increasing thoughtfulness. Two of the open hearth doors were open;

dazzling golden-white light gushed out into the dark mill, and its incandescent reflection shone on Franz's face. His distended blue eyes, his strong Norseman's face with its hard jaw and arrogant nose, his big mouth with the lips drawn back so that his teeth glistened vividly, and his big, well-formed body, naked to the waist, but white as milk, were bathed in that sunlike molten glow. His attitude was that of a man half-crouched to spring, and this, combined with his face and his body, gave him an unearthly look, both savage and wild and violent. He did not turn to Tom. He was staring at his men as a trainer stares at untamed beasts. And the men, caught by his look, stood motionless, shielding their eyes from the glare near which they stood, and stared back at him.

"You're a one!" stammered Tom. A thrill of something like fear crept along his spine. He saw murder in the driven men's faces. But this is not what subtly frightened him. It was Franz who frightened him inordinately. The Englishman had known many men, and thought he would never be surprised by his kind again. But there was something in Franz which he had not encountered before in all his life, something not to be understood by him. He could understand all villainy, all treachery, all wickedness, and even all cruelty. But this look and attitude of Franz's, as though he were a visitation from another world and had not human quality, appalled and astounded him.

It was over in a moment or two. The men, finally cowed by Franz's face and eyes, bent their heads and resumed their work. They closed the furnace doors. Now they were in dusk again. Tom turned to Franz. His friend was regarding him smilingly. "Well, what is it?" he asked, amiably enough, wiping his damp foreheaad and upper lip.

"Nothing," said Tom. He regarded Franz in a curious silence. Then he added: "Mark my words, one of these days you're goin' to get a shovel in your back. Not 'arf!"

"Why? Because I've shown them who's master around here?" Franz put his hand on Tom's shoulder.

Tom did not smile in return. "You hate the chaps, don't you?"

"Hate them?" Franz was amused. "Probably."

Tom went back to his work without another word. But he was abstracted. What he had seen depressed him, though he could not understand his own depression. He was tough and hard and wiry, himself. He knew men thoroughly. But he did not know Franz. And not being able to know him, his old distrust and wariness became stronger. "A rum 'un," he said to himself.

One of his own men was a German, a hard-working simple

giant of a man with friendly shy manners and a tremendous capacity for work. After some hesitation, Tom approached him and addressed him with the name he used indiscriminately with all Germans: "Look here, Fritzie, you come from Dutchland, too. Ever see such chaps like Franz Stoessel there?"

The big giant leaned on his charcoal shovel and looked long and earnestly down the mill to Franz's furnaces. His broad flat face darkened, and he paused, as though apprehensive. "Ja. Some. In the Army. Prussians. That's why I come here." He smiled diffidently. "I come, or I kill, see?"

"What a country!" exclaimed Tom. He had a sudden wild vision of a race of men like Franz, overrunning the earth. Then he laughed at his own extravagance. "Go back to work, Fritzie," he said, shortly, but touched the man in a friendly fashion on the arm. However, he did not return to work for a few moments, himself. His long dark face wrinkled and twisted with his thoughts, and his tiny black eyes seemed to draw closer to the bridge of his enormous nose. He scratched his thick black curls thoughtfully.

But when Franz met him at the noon hour, nothing could have been more amiable than his face. He shared his lunch with his usual generosity, and Tom, who had been preparing devastating remarks, found nothing to say.

* * *

For a long time Tom Harrow and one or two other men like him had been trying to form a union among the men who worked in the Schmidt mills. At the first meeting in the Elks Hall, which had been held almost a year ago, only half a dozen had attended, and they had been frightened. But Tom persevered with British grimness. Tonight, more than two hundred men came.

Tom was gratified and stimulated. He had a rolling gait, which was exaggerated when he was uplifted or excited. He would then set his shoulders doggedly, and look about him with friendly belligerence. When he stood upon the rough platform at the head of the hall, his Punch-and-Judy aspect was more marked than ever. His dark ugly face with its protruding and elongated jaw was alight with bawdy humor, but with deep underlying determination. The fact that he knew that over half his audience was only indifferently gifted with an understanding of English did not depress him. Shrewd and primitively subtle as he was, he knew that emotion is the language all men understand, and that voice and gesture and attitude can move or inflame any man to the complete satisfaction of the manipulator. He had never heard that an orator needs only emotion, but he knew it.

A more sensitive man would have been afraid that his unprepossessing physical appearance would have acted in his disfavor with an audience, and being so preoccupied with his fears would have inspired hostility. For men are atavistic, and open fear, instead of arousing sympathy or compassion, merely inflames the instinctive desire of all men to kill. But Tom was never sensitive about his appearance, for he rarely thought about himself at all. He lived externally in all things, whether it was a particularly violent or beautiful day, or other men. He never felt himself an individual, distinct from other individuals. He was in them, and they were in him. Had he been twice as ugly, it would not have impressed him, for he never saw himself either objectively or subjectively. He was emotion, and part of all emotion. This sublime unconsciousness won him fascinated attention whenever he spoke or acted. For he seemed to others merely extensions of themselves.

The hall was incredibly dirty, narrow, small and drab, and was rented out on numerous occasions to all sorts of activities, with a delightful impartiality. Its tall slits of windows were opaque with dust. The ceiling was unfinished, and the bare beams hung with banners of spider webs and fragments of gay paper festooning. The floor was unbelievably dirty and gritty from constant tobacco spittings and mud. Gas jets appeared along the filthy plastered walls, and their thin hissing yellow flames threw murky shadows over the seated rows of laborers who had come to hear Tom Harrow. They sat in their thick workclothes, for the hall was not heated, and their mingled breath made a visible steam in it. This steam seemed the smoking result of the foul odors in the hall, odors compounded of sweat, grime, unwashed bodies, alcohol, tobacco, and the constant presence of the acids used in the mills. Every man either smoked or chewed, and spat with impartiality.

Tom stood on his platform, grinning. He looked down at the two hundred uneasy faces, dirty, stained, oxlike and brutish with privation and endless work. The stench did not disturb him, for he had no doubt that he stank likewise. He saw, not stolid and ignorant human beings, fit to arouse the contempt of thinking and more fastidious men, but creatures who suffered and were abused beyond endurance. They were his flesh, whether they were Magyar or Slav, German or American, white or black. From his body there poured out to them his own brotherhood and universality. They were not cattle. They were part of him and he was part of them. Nor did he feel any detachment or superiority. If he aroused them, it was because he himself was first aroused. He was full of angry compassion, for all his grin and his grotesque gestures. It was not that he was full of Messianic passion. He was merely boiling with an infuriated sense of outrage and injustice.

He saw Franz sitting calmly by the side of Jan Kozak. Franz was puffing on his pipe; his arms were folded upon his breast. Nothing could have been more attentive or impersonal than his attitude. But for some reason Tom's fury lost its usual objectivity, and strangely enough, became all the more powerful because of this.

He stamped his feet, waved his arms, and shouted. The deep roar of men's voices subsided. "If I'm bloody well goin' to shout my lungs out at you, I want you barstards to listen!" he screamed. "If you don't want to listen, you can come up here and talk, yourselves!" The voices sank into deep silence. "Now, then," resumed Tom, glaring about him. "Shut your traps and listen to a better man."

Laughter shook the hall. Even those who had hardly understood a word chuckled with approval, knowing what he had said.

Franz looked at the broad squat figure of his friend on the platform. He was somewhat surprised, and interested. In the yellowish and uncertain flare of the gaslights, Tom had taken on an appearance of resolute command and authority. Even while he grinned, as he was doing now, power, compact and aware, emanated from him. His ugly face and bent shoulders, his big arms swinging loosely at his sides, his thick short legs and massive chest, were arresting. The other men must have been impressed by this, for they looked at him in profound silence. Their dull faces begin to stir sluggishly, as though the submerged spirits had risen to the surface of calloused flesh.

Tom spoke, not loudly, but in a penetrating voice: "Now then, is there a blasted mother's son among you who knows why we're 'ere?"

The men murmured, and looked sheepishly at each other. Tom nodded grimly. "I see lots of faces as never came to meetin's before. You must've 'ad a reason." He pointed suddenly to some one in the audience. "You, Tomas. Why'd you come, eh?"

The men tittered, as schoolboys titter when one of their number is singled out for the unpleasant attentions of a teacher. Tomas, a huge lumbering Slovak with a red face and dirty hands, turned an excessively sanguine tint. Tom's voice prodded him to his feet, and he looked about him sheepishly, smirking. His companions roared their approval of his discomfiture, with all their childlike delight. He finally looked at Tom, with complete embarrassment.

"I think you get us more money," he mumbled, and sat down abruptly.

Tom waited until the thunder of applause and laughter subsided. His face was grim and sardonic. He put his arms akimbo. He nodded vigorously.

"So, you 'think I get us more money,'" he mocked, with elaborate derision. "That's all you mutton heads think of, eh? A few cents more an hour! Well, I might've known!"

The men chuckled uncomfortably, but with bewilderment.

Then Tom began to curse them, with mingled fury, compassion, understanding and tenderness, and even angry despair. A few cents more an hour! And suppose if by the grace of God they were able to get a few cents more: what then? A few coppers forced from "the bosses" would do no good. The hours and the working conditions would be the same. And if men all over America struck for a few more cents, then the cost of living would rise in proportion and all would be as it had been. Nothing would be gained.

Franz listened, leaning forward tensely, surprised at this shrewd logic, his respect for his friend rising. Only a few men understood the words, and could ponder on them abstractly. But the vast majority felt the logic emotionally, and understood that their simple request would not get at the heart of the problem which so bedevilled them.

"It is not the money, damn you!" shouted Tom, with obscene embellishments, and shaking both his fists furiously in the air. "It's the whole bloody system which 'as got to be changed! The whole bloody idea of the bosses that us chaps that work for 'em is cattle and dogs and swine! With no human rights. Oh yes, they'll throw us a few coppers extra to shut our mouths, if we yelp loud enough. But does that change anythin'? No! No! Will it change our hours, give us protection when we get nicked in their blasted mills? No! Will it protect us in lay-offs, and us with kids and wives as 'ave got to be fed and sheltered? Will it make the toffs realize that we've got human flesh, too, and we bleed like them when we get pinked? Will it make us men with men, arguin' on a decent man-to-man basis? No! No, you stuffed pigs' heads!"

He beat his chest with both his fists and glared savagely at the silent listeners below him.

"You got to get at the root of the stinkin' problem!" he shouted, with renewed passion. "The rotten thinkin' of the bosses! Until we change that, we'll get nowhere. And who's to blame for all this blasted mess? The bosses? Well, a little. But it's you men at the root of it—you who never thought of yourselves as men! And that's what I'm here for, shoutin' my lungs out at you—to make you think of yourselves as men."

The men listened, open-mouthed, in utter stupefaction. Then, one by one they looked at each other dumbly, like men awakening to an astounding truth. It is true, said each pair of simple peasant eyes—it is true, I never thought of myself as a man, with a man's rights and a man's desires. I was only a beast, working under the cracking of whips. But I am a man! The idea was so amazing, so profound, that they were filled with a passionate astonishment. Their own lives seemed to be laid out before them, from birth to death, a life in which they had never been men, but only laboring, suffering brutes, content if they were fed partially, content if they were allowed to live.

"It is our world, too!" screamed Tom, literally dancing up and down the platform. "Who said it was just their world? They did, and you agreed with them! Now, it's time for us to disagree. Is it going to be a struggle? Yes, a terrible struggle! But what in hell is worth anythin', if you don't struggle for it? What man got anythin', without fightin' for it? But ain't it worth fightin' for? Answer me, you chaps!"

They roared out at him, not obediently, but with spontaneous and indignant agreement. They were still in the throes of their tremendous and revealing astonishment. Some rose to their feet, and looked about at their fellows, their faces flushed, their fists doubled. And Tom looked down at them, smiling in grim satisfaction, and nodding.

Franz sat with folded arms. He looked only at Tom. A smooth sheath of flesh hid his thoughts. But he thought to himself: He is dangerous. Much more dangerous than the usual labor agitator.

A vast and sudden exhilaration filled the hall. Men muttered and gasped, breathed heavily, shifted on their wooden chairs. The dim gaslight showed scores of flashing eyes and working faces. Manhood stirred at last, violently, under the flesh of patient beasts.

Then one man shouted: "Mister, what we got to do?"

The men roared their eager agreement, and they stared at Tom avidly.

He smiled, satisfied. "We got to organize, first. Every last bloody mother's son of us. Not one here and there. But all of us."

He spoke for a long time, but no one became restive or bored. They listened to him urgently. He told them of the Knights of Labor, of the great labor wars that were taking place in the mines and the mills in other cities. He told them of the frightful vengeance of the industrialists, and the detectives that clubbed and killed men and women and children. He told them of bought courts and oppressions and pitched battles in open streets. He told them of children working in factories and mills.

"We're wakin' up!" he screamed. "All over America, we're wakin' up! Not altogether, not in a body, but in groups. America, that was meant for all men, as was built for all men, got in the hands of the bosses, who said it was meant just for them! And we was just created by Almighty God to help them get the fat of the land. 'No!' we say. 'We wasn't. We was created for ourselves, too. We was created to get some happiness out of livin'. We'll do our job and our duty. But we are men, too. The earth is ours, too. We want our rights.'" He paused, looked down at them with his black and glittering eyes. He smiled, and there was something terrible in his smile. "'Give us our rights, as men,' we say. 'For, if you don't, we'll take 'em. And you won't like what we'll do when we take 'em.'"

* * *

Franz and Tom walked home together. The night had cleared. Frost hung in the air, and the stars, above the drab rooftops, were clear and sharp.

"Well, I've done a good night's work," chuckled Tom, at last.

Franz said, with curiosity: "And you, Tom, what are you going to get out of all this?"

Tom looked at him with astonishment. "What am I goin' to get?"

Franz shrugged. "Come, now. You know what I mean. You've got a good tongue, Tom. You can do things with men. You know all this. What do you want?"

Tom stopped in the middle of the street. His homely face had paled, but his eyes sparkled dangerously at his friend. He spoke in a low voice:

"What d'ye think I'm after?"

Franz smiled frankly, though he was annoyed and uncomfortable.

"Oh, don't strike attitudes with me, Tom! You've got the beginning of a strong union, now, among the men, and it will get stronger, if nothing stops it. If nothing happens to you." He paused. "Tom, I know that no man does anything out of real altruism. I've lived long enough to know that. So, in your own words, I ask you: 'What are you after?'"

Tom was silent. He stared piercingly at his friend. His pale face became gray. But his eyes were pinpoints of concentration. He licked his lips. Moments passed, as they stood under a street lamp, looking at each other.

Then an expression of quiet savagery came over Tom's features. He took Franz's arm, and they resumed their walking. They did not speak. They came to Tom's house, and halted again. Then Tom looked at Franz, and there was a deadly gleam in his eyes.

"You'll keep your mouth shut," he said, and his words were not a question.

Franz nodded, smiling as though with amusement. He went on his way, alone. Tom watched him until he was out of sight. His heart was thudding wearily, and painfully.

"I should never have took him there," he thought. "A chap like that—he'll never understand."

In all his turbulent and precarious life, Tom had never experienced fear. Now he knew it, acrid and sick on his tongue. He did not fully understand what he feared. But depression lay heavily on him when he unlocked his door and entered his house.

Dolly was waiting for him. As usual, a kettle steamed, in anticipation, on the fire. "A cup of tea, lass!" cried Tom, kissing her. "God, I could do with a cup of tea, tonight!"

CHAPTER 18

IRMGARD DREW back the heavy draperies across the window of Mrs. Schmidt's bedroom, and looked out at the clear colorless December day. The rains had washed the sky and the earth, fading them but clarifying them also. But she did not see the long quiet street beneath her, nor the dun lawns and stark empty trees. She saw the hills and fields of her home, sleeping under a pale autumn sun. Her eyes dimmed with nostalgia; the hand on the draperies tightened as on an unbearable pang. She had been in America for eight weeks, and this was the first time that homesickness and grief had been allowed to race over her in dark waves. Expecting little of life, she had endured existence calmly. Never had she hoped for much, nor expected radiance at the next dawn. Consequently, her life had been filled with a monotonous peace, a sort of lofty and indifferent serenity. If pleasure had come—a beautiful day with the grass knee-high, and dusty, and humming with insects, or hot coffee on a cold night, or spring woods full of white spectral shadows and the scent of wet earth—then she had accepted it with a sudden faint thrilling of the heart which still could not disturb the deep unexpectant placidity beneath. If there was something static and lifeless, something without youth or joy, in all this, there had also been few shocks, few assaults on the spirit, and little sorrow.

Even when her father had died, she had not felt this sudden disintegration of self-control, this sudden torture that ran through her heart like a thin knife. Her cool mind was frightened at this, as at the betrayal of an ally. Once before, she had felt something keen and devastating and destructive in her flesh and her spirit, and that had been on the night when Franz had come to her room. She had been able to regain self-control almost immediately afterwards, but the wound quivered and ached for days afterwards. Then the pain had almost gone, to be renewed by nostalgia.

Mingled with her acute suffering was mortification, and fear. Her hand tightened on the draperies still more. Her body felt alternately cold and hot, as though it had been attacked by some physical illness. She gritted her teeth and her young smooth face became like carved stone.

Mrs. Schmidt stirred in the depths of her pillows, and half lifted her haggard head, with the gray-streaked dark hair dangling against her gaunt cheeks. She blinked her eyes in the wan bright light of the morning.

"What is the weather, Irmgard?" she asked, in her faint peevish voice.

"Very nice, Madam," replied Irmgard. The girl drew a deep breath, and turned with dignity from the window. "Perhaps we can ride today." She approached the bed, tall, serene, composed, her golden hair in braids about her head. Mrs. Schmidt watched her come, gratefully. Strength came to her from the touch of Irmgard's hands, peace with her slow reluctant smile, calm from her gentleness and placidity. Irmgard was able to make the stoniest pillow soft, and to ease the most vague, persistent pain in thin shriveled limbs.

"I do not think I am well enough to drive today," said Mrs. Schmidt, closing her eyes restfully while Irmgard brushed and braided her hair. Irmgard smiled slightly. She was accustomed to these complaints, and had learned not to heed them very much.

"Perhaps you will feel better after your coffee," she said, softly. She brought a bowl of warm water and a linen towel, and proceeded to wash the sick face and hands. "It is so beautiful a day. A drive will do you much good."

"I am sure I am not well enough," sighed Mrs. Schmidt.

"You did not sleep well?"

"Very poorly," replied Mrs. Schmidt, sighing again. Irmgard knew this was not true. She had given her mistress her hot milk the night before, and had slipped into her room several times in the darkness. Mrs. Schmidt had been sleeping like the proverbial baby. "Such dreams!" exclaimed the invalid, with a shiver.

This was now Irmgard's cue to ask soothingly about the dreams. But instead, with unusual briskness, she said: "Dreams. They are nonsense. There is only today. You look very well, Madam. Quite young and fresh."

At this startling remark, Mrs. Schmidt opened her eyes and stared in astonishment. Then a bitter smile touched her parched lips. "Young and fresh!" she murmured. Shadows made her sunken eyes dim, as though with memory. "They said I was a pretty girl," she whispered.

"Like Miss Ernestine," suggested Irmgard.

Mrs. Schmidt gave her a glance of fugitive pleasure. "Do you think Ernestine pretty? She believes she is very plain, and I can't interest her in fashion at all. If she would only take an interest! You would not believe it, Irmgard, but there have been so many young men, and she would not look at them! I have told her a woman must not be too particular, or she will end by being an old maid."

She regarded Irmgard suspiciously. "And Ernestine is really quite young yet." She paused, searching Irmgard's face for an expression of mockery. But Irmgard was regarding her with simple affirmation.

"Yes, very young," said the girl, almost sadly.

Sudden animation sent a dull flush over Mrs. Schmidt's features.

"Perhaps we can persuade Ernestine to go shopping with us today! It is really very nice outside. Do you think we can persuade her?"

"I am sure of it," said Irmgard.

Mrs. Schmidt patted her braided hair. She sat up without the aid of pillows. "Irmgard, before you go for my breakfast, will you give me those copies of *Harper's*? I should like to look at the winter fashions again. And will you ask Ernestine to come into my room, if she is ready?"

Irmgard smiled. "Most certainly." She gazed at Mrs. Schmidt with compassion and affection. The poor thin sick lady, with the deep graven lines of suffering on her face, and the parched lips! But now her eyes, really fine dark eyes, were sparkling, and if there was something feverish in her unusual animation, it gave some color to her ashen skin.

The girl left the room with her quick but silent tread, and Mrs. Schmidt watched her go. What a lovely thing, so majestic and serene! she thought, wistfully. Whatever would I do without her, now! She understands me so perfectly, and Ernestine seems to be happier since she came. But what if she marries, as she most probably will? How can we bear to part with her?

A consoling thought then occurred to her. Irmgard must marry some responsible and industrious person, sober and reliable. Perhaps, then, he could be employed by the Schmidts as a coachman or a butler, and she, Mrs. Schmidt, would not then lose her! Her face brightened at the thought, and she feverishly began to plan. Gillespie, the English butler! It is true he was a widower, and forty, but he was childless and responsible, and almost a gentleman. When questioned by Mrs. Schmidt as to his opinion of Irmgard, he had said reservedly, but with visible admiration, that she was "a very capable young person, who knows her place." Matilda, unfortunately, had been virulent in her opinion, but then, Matilda was probably jealous of so much beauty and reserve.

Mrs. Schmidt, then, with unusual excitement, began to plan Irmgard's wedding. A plain gray silk, not too elaborately looped, and draped. That would be unbefitting her station. But a silk of excellent quality, which could be purchased only in New York. She could then wear it on holidays, and at church. A gray velvet bonnet, decorous, with perhaps a bunch of violets on its narrow brim, and two violet ribbons to tie under that firm white chin. A gray wool jacket, and a mole stole. She, Mrs. Schmidt, had just the thing, locked away in her wardrobe, in camphor balls. It had been very expensive, and she had had it for years, but had hardly worn it. The bridal couple, of course, must have a brief honeymoon. She would see to that. Her present to Irmgard would be two hundred dollars. Of course, they would not spend it all. They would put most of it in the bank, as a nest egg. Naturally, too, there would be a trousseau, of good plain quality, a black broadcloth for winter, and perhaps a demure foulard for the spring. Petticoats and chemises of fine strong nainsook, with tatting edges. Mrs. Schmidt's excitement rose. Irmgard must be married by Mr. Wettlaufer in the First Lutheran Church, of course. That was in keeping. Mrs. Schmidt was an Episcopalian, herself, but her sense of propriety and fitness would not allow her to consider a wedding in her own elaborate church. Besides, almost all Germans were Lutherans, she thought vaguely. Except when they were Roman Catholics, which was pretty dreadful, she meditated. What had Hans once said? "A German Catholic is an insult to Luther."

She must have a talk with Gillespie. A little delicate hinting, perhaps——

Irmgard opened the bedroom door and came in with the breakfast tray. Two spots of color burned on her smooth cheeks, for she had had another encounter with Matilda. But her manner was still tranquil. She moved across the floor like a princess, in her old-fashoned black dress and white ruffled apron. She placed the tray on Mrs. Schmidt's knees, smiling. "There, a lovely egg, and very nice toast," she said, in her low, charmingly accented voice. "And such good coffee!"

Mrs. Schmidt watched her fondly as she prepared the egg and poured the coffee from its small silver pot. "My dear," she said, "have you thought of marrying?"

For an instant Irmgard's hands halted. But it was only an instant. She put sugar into the thin china cup, brimming now with clear dark liquid. "No, Madam," she said, quietly. "I have not thought of it."

"But a young woman like you, Irmgard! So beautiful, too. Ah, I am afraid that is too good to be true, and I am afraid I shall be losing you one of these days."

She studied that serene and perfect profile, that long white neck and beautiful breast.

Irmgard smiled again. "I shall remain with you, Madam, until you tell me to go," she said. "But you must eat the egg; it is cooling."

Mrs. Schmidt felt a thrill of happiness and satisfaction. She lifted a dark emaciated finger archly. "Then, we must get you a husband I can approve of. I shall not let you marry someone unworthy, Irmgard. Then, he must not take you from us. Someone, perhaps, who would be willing to work here, too——"

The girl was amused. She looked at Mrs. Schmidt and laughed a little. Then she said: "But your breakfast, Madam: it is spoiling."

Mrs. Schmidt pretended to stubbornness. "I shall eat nothing, Irmgard, until you promise not to leave me."

"I promise," answered Irmgard, lightly. "But I shall not keep the promise unless you agree to go for a drive today."

"Ah, you are so sweet, my dear."

The sick woman ate with unusual appetite. In the meantime, Irmgard busied herself about the great, dank, luxurious room. She opened a window surreptitiously. The clear cold air, so fresh and pure, invaded the chamber, driving from it all the fetid odors of the night. The draperies stirred in the slight wind. Sunshine lay on the broad mahogany sills. Morning stillness lay outside, broken only by the sound of a leisurely passing victoria. Irmgard saw the wheels twinkling in the sun, saw the light shimmer on the backs of two sleek gray horses. Two coachmen sat stiff and erect in the rear, in uniform. The driver was a fat old man, and in the carriage sat a fat old woman in sables, very straight and uncompromising.

"Do you like America, Irmgard?" asked Mrs. Schmidt from the bed. She was drinking her coffee thirstily.

Irmgard turned and inclined her head. "Everyone is kind to me," she said. If there was indifferent reserve in her voice, Mrs. Schmidt did not detect it.

"It must be strange to you, coming from Germany."

"But people are the same everywhere," said Irmgard.

"And you do not find America strange?"

Irmgard was silent. Strange! The curious immobility that lay over her senses prevented her, almost constantly, from feeling the impact of strangeness. Perhaps, she thought, there was a deadness in her, which precluded a response to unfamiliarity. Days, to her, were always the same, without color or vitality.

"I live as I can," she said.

Mrs. Schmidt found the remark very odd. But her tired mind always refused speculation. It exhausted her. She finished her coffee.

Ernestine came in, first peering archly around the door, and then tripping into the room with her shy gaiety.

"Good morning, Mama! Good morning, Irmgard! Such a nice day, after all that rain." She kissed her mother's thin cheek. "How well we are, this morning. Perhaps we can have a drive today?"

As if she too felt release from the long days of miserable weather, she had dressed herself in crisp red silk, looped with black velvet ribbon. She looked very pretty, her dark chignon breaking into little curls on her neck, and the dark fringed bangs giving sparkle to her innocent eyes. Her tiny immature figure was compact and neat, her small hands ringed, and there was a faint aura of rose perfume floating about her. Mrs. Schmidt regarded her with wistful love.

"Irmgard suggested a drive, too, my pet. And do you know, I almost feel inclined for it! I thought we might do some shopping," she added, uncertainly.

Ernestine gurgled. "Shopping! Excellent!" She clapped her little hands like a child. "I am in the mood for shopping. I hear that Mlle. LeClair has some lovely new bonnets, which they say just came from Paris. Probably from New York, instead, but perhaps quite nice."

Mrs. Schmidt was delighted. She could not remember Ernestine being so exuberant as this, so sparkling and happy, so young.

She, herself, had not been out of bed for days. But her illness was in her mind, not in her tortured body. Irmgard had long suspected this. She had also long suspected that in invalidism Mrs. Schmidt had found retreat from an intolerable world, and in that retreat, a slow, self-willed suicide. Now that she was suddenly happy, the almost strangled will-to-live sent her sluggish blood more quickly through her veins. She felt practically well, and eager again. And how long had it been since she had been eager!

"I feel so well," she said suddenly, and as though the words astounded and frightened her, her frail voice trembled, and her eyes filled with tears. Her expression became one of blank astonishment, as if she had heard another speak in her voice, and not herself.

"Of course!" cried Ernestine, clapping her hands again, and actually capering a little dance step on the thick rug. "I knew that Irmgard would do you so much good! She has been good for everyone. Even Baldur. Perhaps we can persuade him to drive with us, also, though it will not be so interesting, to a gentleman, to accompany ladies when they are shopping."

Her little dance had brought her to Irmgard. Impulsively, she rose on tiptoe and kissed Irmgard swiftly on the cheek. Irmgard started. Color ran over her face, and a great softness came into her eyes with her smile.

"It is you, who are so good to me," she said, falteringly.

"We love you so, Irmgard," exclaimed Ernestine, with a childlike lack of reserve, and with simple affection. "The house has been so different since you came."

"Indeed!" cried Mrs. Schmidt, pushing herself up from her pillows. "I have quite an appetite now. Ernestine, love, do come and look at *Harper's*. The most extraordinary styles this year. The bustle, it appears, is definitely passé. There is hardly a suggestion— And the boots! Really quite foolish."

Irmgard picked up the devastated breakfast tray and carried it out of the room, leaving the ladies to their absorbed and excited contemplation of the fashion magazines.

She liked this house now no better than she had liked it the first day. She still could not traverse the long lofty corridors, so gloomy and chill, without the original repulsion and depression. The sombre rooms, dim with sinister shadows, the whole air of sinister conspiracy and chronic fear which pervaded every corner, the atmosphere at once cold and repellent and dank, sometimes made her plan desperately for escape. There were very few visitors to this house. Mrs.

Schmidt's invalidism, Ernestine's shyness, Baldur's infirmity, and the crudeness and boorishness of Mr. Schmidt, were no assets to hospitality. Though Irmgard had been in this house for nearly two months, there had been no parties, no dinners, no gaieties. The inhabitants of the great mansion lived in isolation and semi-darkness, almost ostracism. Irmgard had seen the ballroom and the billiard room. In the former, the chandeliers were shrouded in muslin, as were the tiny gilt chairs. The windows were shuttered, and dust lay gritty on the polished floor. The billiard room tables were shrouded in covers. The vaulted library, the tremendous parlors, the desolate dining room, lay in dim silence, day after day. Ernestine had told Irmgard that the last ball had been held in this house nearly two years ago, the last dinner six months previous. Irmgard had discovered that the two women, and the son, hated this house, not actively, but passively, as prisoners hate a prison.

"If we could only have a small, bright, pretty house, in the suburbs, or the country!" Ernestine had sighed. "With big gardens, and clean air. But Papa loves this house. He built it. So, we say nothing. Even in the summer we remain here, though the weather at all times is very bad for Mama."

So Irmgard knew that there were no escapes to the seashore, to the mountains, to the fields. There was no normal life for these sad people, who lived in wretchedness and silence and deep loneliness. They were cut off from the warm world of men and laughter and eagerness as though they lived in a vast tomb, enduring a sort of semi-life without hope or gladness.

Even the servants in their quarters were overcome by the general gloom and dreariness. Mrs. Flaherty, the cook, declared that only the unusually high wages kept her in this house. She was very frank in confessing that on her days off, and sometimes at night, she "took to the bottle." "Shure, if I did not," she would say, "it's crazy as a loon I'd be." Gillespie, the butler, shared her loathing opinion of the house, but high wages was also the reason for his remaining. He was a very good friend of Mrs. Flaherty, who was a widow, and spent his hours off duty in her rooms, probably taking to the bottle also. The three chambermaids, dull Slovak girls, with little imagination, huddled together in their common bedroom, hardly talking above a whisper. But sometimes they would laugh or sing or dance, secure in the knowledge that they would not be heard under the roof. The two coachmen, and the three stable-boys, had their rooms above the stables. The lights in the mansion were usually off by ten o'clock, but

Irmgard, from her window, could see the happy lights burning above the stables far into the night.

Irmgard's constant duties kept her employed until bed time. However, she had already made friends of both Mrs. Flaherty and Gillespie, and sometimes she was able to escape for an hour, after Mrs. Schmidt was comfortably settled for the night, and at that time she would climb the narrow winding back stairway to Mrs. Flaherty's rooms. There she had some small escape in the company of the little fat Irish cook and the dignified Englishman.

From the smallest chambermaid to Gillespie, they all hated Matilda, who had a pleasant sitting room and bedroom and bath on the third floor. They whispered darkly together, and snickered, for they knew that "the master" was a frequent visitor to those rooms, and that the door was kept shut sometimes for hours after his entry. Had Matilda, however, been amiable and agreeable and kind, they would not have minded her unusual position in this household. But she was tyrannical and mean, arrogant and contemptuous, and so overbearing that Mrs. Flaherty often threatened to assault her with an iron saucepan. "A Prussian overseer," said Gillespie, with lofty disdain. His learning and worldliness inspired great admiration in Mrs. Flaherty, who knew nothing of Prussians, but who privately thought all Germans something apart from common humanity. Nor was the apartness complimentary in her opinion.

"Mark my words," Gillespie would say darkly, "we'll all have something to do with those chaps, yet."

This cheered Mrs. Flaherty, whose lively imagination waited impatiently for that day, when she would be able to batter Matilda with numerous iron saucepans to her heart's content, without fear of "the law." "Not that I'd kill the bitch," she would say, magnanimously, "but I'd lay her up, good and proper."

They soon learned that Matilda hated the new arrival, Irmgard, and this alone would have been sufficient to inspire a friendship for the girl. But she won friendship in her own right, also. She made Mrs. Flaherty reverse her former opinion that Germans were a race, or a species, apart, and Gillespie soon adored her with dignity. "A lady, and no mistake," he said, with a nod of his austere head. They loved her beauty and gentleness, her green eyes which could sparkle with quiet amusement, her considerate manners, and her great quiet patience.

They knew many things. They knew that Matilda worked unceasingly for the girl's dismissal. Once they had heard angry voices behind the housekeeper's door, and one of the voices was that of the master. The voices spoke in German, but Gillespie, lurking in the hall, heard Irmgard's name. They also knew that Miss Ernestine championed the girl, and opposed her father vigorously in her gentle way. They dared not express their hatred for Matilda openly, for fear of dismissal, but in a thousand small ways they let her know without uncertainty what they thought of her. She took her revenge on them more freely, because of her position. Irmgard, because she was so immured with Mrs. Schmidt, rarely crossed her path, but on the few occasions that she did so the housekeeper tormented her, abused her, and insulted her beyond endurance. "How the colleen can stand it, I don't know," Mrs. Flaherty would say. "But those quiet ones— One of these days the worm will turn."

Irmgard endured the abuse and the insults with silent dignity. She hardly seemed to listen. She went her way calmly, though sometimes her face would flush and the green eyes would flash with emerald fire. The other servants soon learned that Irmgard despised the housekeeper, and that it was contempt and self-respect which kept her silent and withdrawn in the face of reprimands and oppression. They admired her the more for this, but candidly did not understand.

They did not know that she loathed this house. They did not know that she remained in it because of Mrs. Schmidt, Ernestine and Baldur. Kind-hearted though Mrs. Flaherty was, this would not have interfered with her leaving, had it not been for the unusually good wages. "The mistress," she would say to Irmgard, "is a fool, and sickly, but she is a great lady, and no mistake. Miss Ernestine's a fool, too, but as innocent as a lamb. And Mr. Baldur is good and kind, though it gives me the shudders to look at him, for all he's got such a lovely face. As for the master, he's a fair one! Gillespie calls him a boar without hoofs." She giggled. "Though I'd not be surprised he had 'em. Better ask Matilda." So Irmgard soon learned that the servants all despised their mistresses and masters, some with pity, some with indifference. Therefore, had Irmgard told them that her great compassion and affection for the two desolate women and the crippled man kept her in that house, they would have stared, dumfounded and incredulous.

"The mistress can never keep a personal maid more than a few weeks," said Mrs. Flaherty. "So, you'll be leaving us soon, I suppose, Irmgard."

At this, Irmgard would only smile. As the weeks went on she became thinner and even more silent. She had never had much color, but her very pallor had been luminous with health. Now, she was only pale, and the splendid modelling of her face became sharper and more attenuated.

This morning, her first delight in the pale December sunshine began to fade, as she moved down the hall with Mrs. Schmidt's breakfast tray. No amount of sunshine without could penetrate into that lofty vast gloom, nor drive away its mustiness and chill. The distant windows were bright with light, but the light did not extend beyond the wide window-sills. The curving well of the staircase was splashed here and there with blue and crimson and yellow, as the sun struck against the stained glass window on the second landing. But all this only made the dark rooms darker and more funereal in comparison, more tomb-like.

She passed Baldur's door. It was open, and he stood near it. When he saw her, he smiled radiantly, so that his face had a light of its own.

"Come in, Irmgard," he said, standing aside.

She put the tray on a chair, and followed him to an easel.

He had been painting her at odd intervals, when she could be spared from ministering to his mother. The portrait was half-finished. He had painted her as she was, with no elaborate background or dress. The pure calmness of her face and eyes gazed out from the canvas with a remote nobility.

"The light is excellent this morning," he said. "Can you spare me a few minutes?"

He looked at her with that strange light on his face, and she looked down at him in a momentary silence.

"Mrs. Schmidt and Miss Ernestine wish to go for a drive," she said, smiling a little. "It is such a nice day. Perhaps you will go with us?"

He glanced through the window, restlessly. "Is it a nice day?" he murmured. He turned back to her. "This will only take a few moments, Irmgard."

She sat down, obediently, and he picked up his palette. He painted rapidly, in silence. As she sat, she looked at the great angel in the corner. Her lips tightened somewhat, because a faint pain contracted her heart. She had come to dislike the statue with an odd and passionate dislike. It reminded her too strongly of Franz, at once supplicating and arrogant and arresting. Yet, she could not look away from it. Now her lips drooped a little, mournfully. She started when Baldur spoke so gently and softly that she was hardly aware of his voice:

"You have changed, Irmgard. You don't look very well. You are confined so much."

She turned her green eyes to him. "I am perfectly well," she said.

He paused in his work and regarded her gravely. He seemed

about to speak, then apparently changed his mind. But he stood there before her in his ruined and tragic splendor. He often stood like this, motionless, gazing at her. At these times his eyes would seem to glow and enlarge, so that they poured light out over his face.

"But you are not happy?" he asked at last.

She did not reply. After a moment or two he went on painting. But she saw that his delicate hand trembled. He put aside his paints.

"That's all, Irmgard," he said, gently.

She stood up. He waited. They looked long and intently at each other.

"I shall tell your mother you will go with us?" she asked.

He did not answer at once, and then he said: "Do you want me to go, Irmgard?" His voice was hardly audible.

She was silent. His blue eyes still glowed with that inner radiance, but his face was very grave, and filled with a bitter appeal. She began to tremble a little. She half drew back when he took her hand, not hastily, but with the utmost gentleness. Now his expression became intense and despairing, and he looked up at her imploringly.

"Yes, I want you to go," she whispered. Pain flowed along her nerves. She could feel the smart of tears against her lashes. She tried to smile.

"You say that because you are kind," he said, but his thin hand tightened on hers. "It is because you are kind, Irmgard?"

She forced herself to smile. "I am not very kind," she replied.

He released her hand, but he held her by his look, so desperate and yearning.

"I will go," he said, quietly. His features became small and pinched. His lips parted as though he wanted to say things which must be left unspoken.

She picked up the tray and went out of the room. For a long time after she had gone he stood where she had left him, a mournful ruined figure held in sad and bitter reflection.

CHAPTER 19

MRS. SCHMIDT wished to ride in the brougham, but Irmgard gently insisted upon the victoria. "Such nice air and sunshine!" she said. "And soon, the winter will be here. We must cherish the sun."

So Mrs. Schmidt wrapped herself in a cape of sables. Above this mound of rich fur her face was wan and shrivelled, but still faintly lighted by a piteous eagerness. Irmgard brought her her best bonnet of brown velvet and dark plumes, and ordered hot bricks for her feet. "I am so excited!" she exclaimed, looking at Irmgard pathetically. Ernestine appeared in a black astrakhan jacket, but her small bonnet was gay with velvet flowers, and her face shone with delicate color and excitment. In an extravagant mood she had pinned two pink rosebuds on her astrakhan muff, and one near her throat. When Baldur came slowly downstairs, in his broadcloth cape with a fur collar, his broad shallow hat in his hand, he was smiling. The cape hung almost to his ankles, and he might have been a child in his father's garments had it not been for his large heroic features and melancholy blue eyes.

Before leaving, Irmgard wrote a hasty note to her aunt. "Again, dear Aunt Emmi, I must ask your pardon for not spending this Thursday afternoon with you. Mrs. Schmidt needs my services today. I am taking her for a drive. This is the first time she has been out of this distressing house since I came here. Nor, I regret, is Sunday possible, though it is my own Sunday. Please forgive me. My duties are very pressing."

She sealed the note, sighing tightly to herself. Her aunt, she knew, would be excessively annoyed and hurt. She must make a special effort to go to her on her next Thursday afternoon, leaving before Franz would return home. She thinks me ungrateful, thought the girl. But I must risk this. It is so terrible, though, that I cannot see Uncle Egon. She sent the note by one of the stable boys, and watched him go with sudden heavy depression.

They drove away in the pale cold sunlight, the scentless and sterile wind in their faces. The streets were quiet and filled with shadowless light. The wheels echoed on the pavements, and the hoofbeats were soporific in their rhythms. The coachman and footman, high on their perch above the women and Baldur, sat straight in their uniforms of plum and gold, and the whip flashed in the sun. Ernestine chattered breathlessly, looking about her with the wide bright eyes of a young girl, distended and brilliant. A fever seemed to be running in her body. Her lips turned a vivid red. She laughed almost incessantly, sometimes turning to kiss her mother's cheek impulsively, as though she could not contain her excitement, and sometimes leaning forward to press Irmgard's or Baldur's hand.

Baldur smiled sympathetically at his sister, delighted and surprised at her animation. He was filled with content. Irmgard sat beside him, quiet and dignified in her awkward black clothing, her hands in black cotton gloves. But he saw how the sun made a huge knot of smooth gold of the hair under the bonnet, and brought out sparkles of blue light in her green eyes. When he looked at her serene large profile, so classic in its repose and immobility, the chronic pain in his heart subsided, leaving only a dreamlike content behind. He had learned to live for the moment, to refuse to believe in the possibility of tomorrows. There was only this Now, heavy with peace and fulfilment. His head was on a level with her breast. For a single burning instant, which it took all his strength to quell, he had an almost irresistible desire to lay his head on that high and beautiful breast, and forget everything but ecstasy. But the instant passed. It left warmth in his flesh, and something like a still shining light in his mind. He had never known happiness. He did not recognize it when it came to him now. He had only one wish: that this drive might go on forever, that time might be suspended, that his thigh might continue to press against her thigh, and that night might never come.

They went through street after street of tall houses, silent in the sunshine beyond the green-streaked brown lawns. Here and there a nursemaid in a cloak wheeled a perambulator along the walks, or scolded a running child. Here and there a cart, loaded with vegetables, stopped along a curb, the horse nibbling at sparse blades of winter grass. Once they heard a faint far hammering, and sparrows fluttered and shrilled on the empty boughs of great trees. Once they caught the mournful churning of a hurdy-gurdy on some distant street. The air was full of sleepy echoes, blowing like faint breezes in the December light.

Irmgard watched Mrs. Schmidt closely. The poor lady lay huddled in her mound of sables, her thin feet pressed against the hot bricks, which were wrapped in a piece of red flannel. She spoke very little, but she looked at her children, at Irmgard, at the streets, with sick eyes once more bright with a spectral hope. Sometimes the hope was quenched in a shadowy fear. They had all left the house while Matilda had been marketing. What would she say when they returned? It was in vain that Mrs. Schmidt tried to force herself to remember that she was mistress of her great house, and Matilda only her housekeeper. But even in her weakness she dared not so humiliate herself as to confess that she was afraid of the buxom German woman. But Matilda can be such a drill sergeant, she thought, distressedly. And so unpleasant when crossed. No doubt she is activated by a deep regard for my health—she is so solicitious, and so stern with poor Irmgard, always suspecting her of neglecting her duty to me. But perhaps I am not so ill as Matilda thinks. I feel quite strong today——

Nevertheless, when thinking of Matilda, she shivered. She remembered how infuriated the woman had become yesterday when Irmgard had insisted on throwing open windows and drawing draperies in the afternoon, and had urged Mrs. Schmidt to rise from her bed, and, warmly wrapped, sit by a window. "You want to kill the lady?" Matilda had shouted, crimson with rage. She had slammed the windows, drawn the curtains so that the room was once again in semi-darkness and fetid. She had literally lifted Mrs. Schmidt from the chair and carried her back to her hot and uneasy bed. "The poor lady!" she had mourned, viciously. "Her head is heated. Her hands are like ice. You are a murderer!" she had screamed, turning violently upon Irmgard.

Irmgard had been silent during all this. But all at once she said something to Matilda in a low and rapid German which Mrs. Schmidt, with her faulty knowledge of the language, could not understand. But the effect was terrible. Matilda had straightened up. Her broad face had turned white as death, and her eyes had become malignant. She had tried to speak, but could not. After a few moments, she had left the room. Then Irmgard had asked Mrs. Schmidt if she would like to sit by the window again. But Mrs. Schmidt shrank back on her pillows with dread and fear, pleading weariness.

That night the other servants heard the furious controversy between Matilda and Mr. Schmidt as it rumbled through the doors of her apartment. They did not understand the words, but they gathered that Irmgard was again under fire.

Thinking of Matilda, Mrs. Schmidt gave Irmgard a sudden nervous smile.

"Matilda will be so annoyed, don't you think, my dear?"

she asked, unaware that she had broken into a running breathless rhapsody from Ernestine.

Irmgard returned the smile tranquilly. "I am afraid she pampers you too much, Madam," she replied. But the smile touched only her lips. Her eyes were hard and still as jade.

Ernestine had paused to listen. Her head was held like a bird's, poised and eager. She burst out: "That terrible creature! I have been trying to persuade Papa to let her go. She—she tyrannizes over us. When she first came to us she was as meek and sweet as butter. Now she is arrogant and mean, and frightening."

In quick terror Mrs. Schmidt exclaimed: "Oh, Ernestine, that is so uncharitable. She has our interest at heart. Your Papa says we are so undisciplined. Perhaps Matilda is good for us. The house runs so smoothly now. We must forgive her for much, for she is so devoted." She turned to Irmgard. "My dear child, what did you say to her yesterday, to disturb her so? I have been very curious."

Irmgard had said: "You wish to kill this woman. You think you will take her place. But first, you must step over me, and you shall never do that."

She looked at Mrs. Schmidt calmly. "I only said, Mrs. Schmidt, that I was your maid, and I knew what was best for you."

"How determined of you!" said Ernestine, with admiration and love.

But Baldur said, smiling: "Do we have to discuss that detestable female? I thought this was a drive for pleasure." His thigh pressed a little closer to Irmgard's. It seemed to him that a wave of warm strength flowed from her body to his. He looked at her lips. Did he imagine that they were a little paler?

Nazareth had only one long street of important shops, and these were only about a dozen in number. The street was really a "square," filled with trees, and in the center a fountain surrounded by Civil War heroes. On the east side of the square were the poultry and fish shops, the meat market and the grocery stores. At right angles was the street devoted to hardware and farm equipment, and facing it, opposite the square, also at right angles, were feed shops and furniture stores. On the west side of the square were the clothing shops, the boot shops, the millinery establishments. Only one of these shops was patronized by the more fashionable ladies of Nazareth, who preferred to do most of their shopping in Philadelphia or New York. This shop, Morgan's, was voted "extreme" by the middle-class ladies, so New Yorkish was its atmosphere and so gay and expensive its gowns and frocks and mantles and coats. Cheek by jowl with it was Mlle. Le Clair's, owned by Morgan's. Here the millinery was also too "extreme" for solid middle-class taste. But this did not prevent all the ladies, from the farmers' wives and daughters and up through the middle-class matrons to the very fashionable, from pausing for ecstatic half hours to gaze on the three or four distracting bonnets on display behind the broad plate-glass windows.

Mlle. Le Clair's was all gray plush and velvet and rich deep gold in décor. The three salesladies were clad in looped, braided and bustled gray satin, caught with yellow velvet ribbons, and they wore tiny Watteau hats all yellow velvet and vivid green throughout the day. They were charming girls, from Philadelphia, all blondes, with thin affected voices and very chic manners. The customers sat on gray velvet divans, and had bonnets presented to them with great gravity and reverence. The salesladies held large gold-framed mirrors. If the ladies wished to observe a complete ensemble, they were led to the opposite wall, which was lined with mirrors. Only one bonnet was brought to a customer at a time, and if rejected, was carefuly placed behind glass in the rear. Everything was hushed and devout within the salon. The salesladies were really young priestesses whose lives, apparently, were lived and breathed exclusively within those plushy purlieus.

Mlle. Le Clair was ostensibly French. She rarely emerged from the rear of the shop except when a very important customer entered. She was a tall thin woman of regal carriage and hectic color and Continental manners and exquisite accent. Always clad in severe black, she added éclat and awe to the shop. Her name was really Mamie Murphy, and she was a farmer's daughter, but her soul, she would say to herself, was French. Her heart was French. She was France itself. She knew only a dozen French words, which she used with such "la's!" and such gestures, such shruggings and winkings and jerkings of the head, such uplifted hands and rolling of the eyes, that the meagre words were quite adequate for the purpose of impressing the unsophisticated and guileless. A few of Nazareth's fashionable ladies wished to freshen their finishing-school French with the aid of Mlle. Le Clair, and were charmed by her vehement: "Non! Non! I am now Americaine! I am patriot! I no speak Français in America!" They thought this excessively "sweet" and touching, and bought extensively of this patriot, even curtailing their visits to the New York milliners.

Mlle Le Clair designed her own hats, and they were both astonishing and chic. On more than one occasion New York designers had copied them without reticence. Mlle. Le Clair loved hats, and seemed quite indifferent to gowns and other feminine paraphernalia. She wore no jewels or laces, and if she had changes of garments, they were not evident, for she invariably wore her regal and almost puritanical black. She did not really need to design bonnets for a living, for she was part owner of a very exclusive and flourishing brothel in Nazareth, and from this source came a greater part of her very substantial wealth. This brothel was also a house of assignation, and more than one discreet young maiden and matron made furtive arrangements in the quiet rear of the millinery shop. Mlle Le Clair had one true characteristic of the French, a passionate and parsimonious love of money, and she watched the market reports with the absorbed anxiety of a male broker, and was a shrewd gambler.

Moreover, she was always alert to the possibilities of new recruits among the maids who accompanied their mistresses to her millinery establishment. Therefore, when hastily called to the salon at the advent of the ladies of the Schmidt family, her hard black glance touched them swiftly, then fastened itself with a rapid fascination upon Irmgard. But this instantaneous appraisal was not obvious, and with obsequious murmurs and gestures, she gave all her flattering attention to Mrs. Schmidt and Ernestine.

After a murmurous inclination of her head to Baldur, and a purred "Monsieur," she led Mrs. Schmidt and Ernestine to a gray divan and beamed, and clasped her hands.

"Ah, you are so a stranger, Madam Schmidt! And Mademoiselle! But so delightful to look upon you again! I am what ze call, overcome. A bonnet for Mademoiselle? A bonnet for Madam? For the winter mode? For the early spring?"

Irmgard and Baldur sat side by side on another divan at a distance. Irmgard was both amused and enthralled and repelled by this woman, with her painted harpy's face and tiny black cruel eyes and elaborate coiffure. Her body was apparently fleshless, and composed solely of tendons and nerves and stringy muscles under the sweeping black silk. Her hands, brown and lean, fluttered in the air like predatory birds. On one bony finger she wore an enormous marquise diamond, her sole ornament. She smiled, twittered, exclaimed, and her eyes, malignant and obscene in their cunning, never smiled for a single moment.

She brought Mrs. Schmidt a bonnet of purple velvet trimmed with plumes of pale lavender tipped with the faintest rose, and floating with deeper mauve ribbons. She held it high in her hand, rapturously, her fleshless body curved sideways on its narrow waist, her head tilted. Her hair caught the sunlight, and one saw that its jet glossiness was obviously the work of a skilled cosmetician, for it had a purplish and metallic gleam. The sunlight also struck her cheek, showing its canvas coarseness, conspicuously veined and thickly crimsoned. Her painted lips grimaced in what she no doubt considered an ecstatic grin.

"When I created this so chic bonnet, Madam, I said to myself: 'It iss only for Madam Schmidt! No other lady is worthy of it, no, not even in New York!' "

Mrs. Schmidt murmured deprecatingly. Her sallow face puckered with humble anxiety. Timidly, she glanced at Ernestine for an opinion.

Ernestine clapped her small hands and bounced a little, so that her garments rustled gaily. "Do try it on, Mama! It is beautiful, just your style. There! Now tie those ribbons under your chin—so. It is lovely! It gives you such an air!" She looked eagerly at Baldur and Irmgard across the room. "Isn't it charming? Do say it is, for you know I am right."

Baldur spoke solemnly and consideringly, but with a wicked twinkle in his blue eyes: "Mademoiselle Le Clair, croyez-vous que le chapeau va bien à ma mère?"

Mademoiselle Le Clair's eyes flickered at him rapidly, and under the greasy crimson of her lined cheeks, a natural color ran congestedly. Then, coquettishly tossing her head, she raised a finger at him, and cried with great vivacity:

"Ah, Monsieur Schmidt, you are a naughty, naughty boy! I am Americaine! I speak English!"

"And quite well, no doubt," said Baldur, gravely, the twinkle deepening in his eyes. "Well, speak English, if you must. But please answer my question."

Now her eyes were malevolent, full of hatred. Never had Irmgard seen such eyes, and a finger of ice touched the nape of her neck, absurdly. Her elbow furtively nudged Baldur, a gesture which merely elicited a polite and innocent stare of surprise at her.

Feeling annoyed at the young man, and trying to control the corners of her lips which had a sudden tendency to turn upwards, Irmgard rose with dignity and approached Mrs. Schmidt and Ernestine, who were guilelessly puzzled. The girl looked down at Mrs. Schmidt, and thoughtfully considered the bonnet from all angles. Mademoiselle, understanding everything, smiled, grimaced, fluttered her hands, exclaimed, and all the time flickered her eyes at Irmgard with the most vicious enmity: "It is plain to see, my child, that you have ze most wonderful taste. Is not the bonnet charming on Madam?"

Irmgard studied the rich violet and mauve hues of the bonnet, which cast a sickly yellowish shadow over Mrs. Schmidt's already sallow complexion.

"The bonnet is beautiful," she admitted, doubtfully. "But the color—do you think it suitable, Mademoiselle?"

"Oh, Irmgard," said Ernestine, with playful impatience. "It is delightful. Look what it does for Mama's profile."

Mlle. Le Clair, in whose sunken temples bruised pulses were visibly beating, held the mirror for Mrs. Schmidt. The poor lady, completely confused and uncertain, looked at herself with great anxiety. "Perhaps Irmgard is right, Ernestine. The color is quite wrong—perhaps?" She sighed, however, and her eyes yearned.

Irmgard said quickly: "You like the bonnet, Mrs. Schmidt? Then, have it, please. One always looks well in something which one believes is flattering. It is the eye of the mind, and in some way, the belief of the wearer is communicated to the one who sees."

"Bravo!" said Baldur, ironically, from his divan, patting his hands delicately.

The four ladies ignored him ostentatiously. Mlle. Le Clair, Ernestine and Irmgard bent over Mrs. Schmidt with the utmost concentration, as though this were a momentous matter. And poor Mrs. Schmidt, who had not desired nor thought of a bonnet for years, looked at her image in the mirror with shy pleasure. Irmgard understood, now, that the color did not matter. The thing of importance was that desire had once more stirred feebly in that meek and harassed breast.

"I was wrong," she murmured. "The color is truly beautiful on you, Mrs. Schmidt. Please."

"You see, Mama," said Ernestine, happily.

Still Mrs. Schmidt hesitated, turning her head, craning her neck. Under that color, her throat was brown as earth, and dull orange shadows streaked the discolored areas under her eyes. Then, timorously, she glanced up into the young faces of her daughter and her maid.

"You are quite certain, children?"

Hearing that note in his mother's voice, Baldur no longer felt gaily sarcastic. He rose and came over to them, small and gnomelike under his long heavy cape. He was full of remorse.

"Mama, I agree with the girls. It looks very well on you." He put his hand on his mother's shoulder, and pressed it gently. "You are young and pretty again, as you were when I was a brat. You must have no other bonnet." He turned to Mlle. Le Clair, whose eyes flashed at him like the eyes of a hating rodent. "Please put it in its box, and we shall take it with us."

Mrs. Schmidt beamed at him with soft love and shy pleasure. "You truly like it, Baldur?"

Mlle. Le Clair, determined not to allow doubt to jeopardize

a sale, removed the bonnet from Mrs. Schmidt's head reverently, as one might remove a precious crown. She laid it in a nest of paper in a round black-satin box, flourishing her hands. Mrs. Schmidt watched the operation with the innocent and jealous eyes of a child.

"And now," she said, breathing deeply and audibly, "there must be a bonnet for Ernestine, Mademoiselle." It was evident that the pseudo-Frenchwoman intimated her, as all determined and inexorable people intimidated her. "Something young and pretty, perhaps."

"I have just the chapeau for Mademoiselle!" crooned the other. She put her head on the side, and surveyed Ernestine so critically that the girl blushed. "Ah," breathed Mademoiselle, rapturously, as though overcome. "I know! I know!"

She tactfully whisked the black satin box away with her, in order that during her absence no further and surreptitious tryings-on might ensue, with subsequent danger of final rejection. When she had disappeared behind the gray velvet curtains, a small hiatus resulted, and no one spoke. Then Ernestine said in a low voice:

"Baldur, whatever possessed you? You seemed to want to torment the poor woman."

But Baldur, unrepentant, and still intoxicated by the nearness of Irmgard, replied lightly: "My dear child, I hate only two things in this world: a brute and a hypocrite. And our Mademoiselle Le Clair, née Murphy, is both."

"But so insignificant, and unimportant, surely," said Ernestine, with a compassionate glance at the gray curtains.

Irmgard looked at the smiling Baldur directly, and tried to make her voice respectfuly reproving: "Perhaps Mr. Baldur does not realize that most of us must pretend a little. Otherwise, we could not endure ourselves, as we are in truth."

He turned to her, and all at once he saw nothing else but that grave and beautiful face with eyes the color of water reflecting the green of spring leaves:

"Irmgard, I know that only too well. Believe me." His voice was quiet, but filled with such intensity that her face saddened.

Mademoiselle emerged with a rustle from behind the curtains. By nature and profession, she saw everything, and she saw the faces of Irmgard and Baldur. Her eyes narrowed gloatingly, and her smile was arch and significant. In her hands she carried a gay little bonnet of soft blue silk flowering with yellow daisies and tea-roses, and dangling long blue satin ribbons. It was really a pretty thing, and everyone, including the thoughtful Baldur, admired it elaborately. Perched on Ernestine's small dark head, it gave vivacity and light to her heart-shaped face, in which her lips were suddenly blooming and her eyes sparkling.

"A coquette! You will break hearts, Ernestine," said Baldur, wishing to compensate for his unaccountable behavior over his mother's bonnet.

"My darling, it is lovely," said Mrs. Schmidt, and love, admiration and tenderness brought tears to her tired and sunken eyes. She clasped her thin dark hands, trying to control a heart-breaking emotion. Never had she seen Ernestine look so gay and young, so irresponsible and so unutterably dear.

"It is not too flighty?" asked Ernestine, with delight. She ran lightly to the mirrors on the opposite wall, and pirouetted and peered and almost danced.

"But you are a flighty female anyway," said Baldur, laughing, and wishing this were true. A pale sadness had settled over his joy and peace.

Mademoiselle said nothing. She merely stood in a transfixed attitude of complete fascination, shaking her head a little, as though the picture Ernestine made was unbelievable, even to her.

"Impossible," she sighed, almost inaudibly, but, of course, not quite so.

Ernestine looked at them with increasing and breathless delight, as a child might look who had been presented with an incredible and overwhelming gift. Her lips trembled and smiled; she blinked her eyes, speechless. She thought to herself: Perhaps, if he might see me like this—! Some morning, when he stands there—! Her color suddenly turned scarlet. It seemed that she might burst into tears.

"Please, do not remove it," said Irmgard, her heart aching. "It is too beautiful."

"Certainement!" cried Mademoiselle, deftly whisking Ernestine's old bonnet into another black-satin box. "That is so clevaire! Mademoiselle Schmidt must wear it in the carriage, exciting admiration of the dull people!"

"It might rain," demurred Ernestine, wistfully, but her shy eyes urging the others to disagree with her.

"Nonsense," said Baldur, sturdily. "Irmgard is right. It is a fine day. And you must give other people a treat, you know. Life is dull enough, God knows."

The sale consummated, Mrs. Schmidt still did not rise. She hesitated. She flushed a little. Then, awkwardly, she reached for Irmgard's hand and gazed up at her imploringly.

"My dear, you will not be offended with me? But it would give me such pleasure—" Her eyes begged humble forgiveness, but yearned upon the girl.

Ernestine came quickly to Irmgard's side. She laid her hand on her arm, silently, eagerly.

Irmgard said nothing. There was no false plebeian pride in her, and though she hesitated, it was not from offense, nor touchy fear of patronage. She knew indeed that the gift of a bonnet, to which she was completely indifferent, would give her employer and Ernestine an extreme pleasure which she had not the heart to refuse them.

Mademoiselle, understanding again, had swiftly left the salon. She came back instantly with a bonnet in a poke shape, of thick deep green velvet, simple but exquisite, tied with delicate velvet ribbons. There were no flowers on the bonnet. But its shape, its material and air were elegant and rich.

In a complete silence, she put it on Irmgard's pale golden head, and with the slow momentous gestures of a priestess, she tied the ribbons under Irmgard's white chin. The bonnet framed her still, beautiful face like a dark emerald halo, and brought out vivid clear green lights in her eyes. Ernestine exhaled a faint gasp, and clasped her hands tightly to her pounding breast. If I only looked like that! she thought, with intense admiration mixed with melancholy. But there was no envy in her, only a sad regret for herself. Mrs. Schmidt gazed at Irmgard speechlessly. Irmgard's old bonnet was black and shapeless, and had made her look older than she was. But this bonnet gave her youth and splendor and feminine loveliness, and a grace that was almost incredible.

Irmgard smiled at their awed delight in her. She glanced at Baldur, involuntarily. He was looking at her, and he was quite pale, not even smiling. A sudden fright touched her, a sudden sharp sorrow. She turned to Mrs. Schmidt too quickly.

"Thank you, Mrs. Schmidt," she said, simply. She had not even glanced at herself in the mirror which Mademoiselle was holding, and in which she had been trying to catch Irmgard's reflection.

Mrs. Schmidt stood up, feebly. Then, taking Irmgard's face between her two hot dry palms, she kissed her gently on the cheek.

Mademoiselle, smiling, looked only at Baldur, and there was an evil gloating in her eyes, and a thoughtful reflectiveness.

CHAPTER 20

THE SHORT DECEMBER twilight was clouding the air with a dim mist, and the street lamps were already beginning to stain that mist with diffused yellow moons, when the party returned home to the dreary mansion on Grove Street. But they were very gay, if tired, and striped boxes and parcels filled every available inch in the victoria. Pearly satin for Ernestine, black lengths of bright velvet for Mrs. Schmidt, and green foulard the color of the wide bonnet for Irmgard, not to mention tasselled boots and gloves for all, and lace-bordered handkerchiefs, and delightful perfumes, constituted the loot which Morgan's had yielded up to the bottomless purse of the Schmidt's. One of the footmen held three boxes alone, which he considered violated his dignity, for he sat on his high perch with a fierce and remote expression.

"Miss Zimmermann is really an excellent dressmaker, and I think it is an affectation for so many of the ladies to go to Philadelphia and New York for their gowns," said Ernestine, bouncing excitedly in her seat. She turned to her mother. "And now, Mama, we must really have a party!"

As Ernestine had never before in all her life suggested a party, Mrs. Schmidt was so overwhelmed that she could not speak. She could only smile tremulously, and press her daughter's hand, trying to catch her breath. After several long moments, she said: "My darling, would you like a Christmas Eve dinner? A few friends—if they have not forgotten us," she added, sadly.

Ernestine's eyes sparkled. "We could ask Mrs. Harcourt and Emily, and Mr. and Mrs. Burton, and Cecilia, and Mr. and Mrs. Uhl and the three girls, and their two brothers, and Dr. and Mrs. Bruning, and Fritz and Gretchen——"

"And my poor sister," suggested Mrs. Schmidt, timidly, thinking of her widowed sister in Philadelphia, whose only diversion since her husband's death had been her endless ailments. "And she would bring little Dickie, and Marcia." She looked at her daughter and son, with imploring hesitation.

"Of course, your Papa might not like it. He was never fond of Elizabeth."

Ernestine and Baldur had no liking for their dolorous Aunt Elizabeth, but they expressed dutiful enthusiasm. Mrs. Trenchard was immensely wealthy, but her children were insupportable, in the Schmidts' opinion.

Mrs. Schmidt and Ernestine then began an anxious discussion as to whether Miss Zimmermann and her assistants would be able to finish the gowns by Christmas. In the meantime, Baldur said nothing. He looked at Irmgard, shadowy now in the twilight.

Mrs. Schmidt, though she said nothing, was completely exhausted by the time the carriage reached home. She glanced up at the gloomy mansion, where not a window was lighted save for a dim spectral burning in the reception hall. Her spirits fell. She felt again the old helpless and dreamlike impotence she had always felt in that house, the old sensation that she did not really exist, but was some vague disembodied ghost lurking in her distant apartments.

However, they had no sooner entered the house, with the coachmen carrying the many parcels and boxes, when Matilda advanced towards them like a compact violence. A servant came in her wake, lighting the gas, and carrying a taper in her hand. Matilda stood before the returning culprits, breathing heavily and audibly. Her eyes flashed upon them for an instant, but all their malignancy, at the last, was only for Irmgard.

"So!" she cried, "the moment I am away, the mouse will play. It will take the poor sick lady out, to her death!"

Her big stout body, enclosed in its tight black silk, her large red face and fiery blue eyes, seemed to vibrate. Her big hands clenched and unclenched like claws.

"Matilda," began Mrs. Schmidt, shrinking. But Ernestine paled. Her small face became tight and grim.

"Matilda," she said, quietly, "this is no way for our housekeeper to talk. We owe you no explanation. You will please help Irmgard take mother to her rooms."

Irmgard, composed, glanced at Mrs. Schmidt. How much did the poor woman know? How was it possible for her to know nothing? Yet, the girl doubted the extent of Mrs. Schmidt's ignorance. She looked like death. Her sallow face withered and puckered. She dropped her muff; the sables sagged on her shrivelled body as though they would drag her to the floor.

Then Baldur spoke, firmly. "You will obey Miss Ernestine at once, Matilda."

Matilda turned on him as though she would strike him. Her

expression became one of coarse and brutal derision and contempt. But he fixed his calm blue eyes upon her, those eyes with the new deep spark of danger, and she subsided. She actually cringed, wetting her full red mouth.

"Mr. Baldur, your mother—she is a sick lady. A very sick lady. She should not stir from her bed."

"Are you, or are you not, going to obey Miss Ernestine?" he asked, inexorably.

She hesitated. Her large bosom heaved with violence, and her face became congested. Then she took Mrs. Schmidt by her trembling arm, and Irmgard took the poor woman's other arm. They helped her up the immense winding stairway, and slowly and painfully disappeared into the upper reaches.

Ernestine said, with shaking lips, to her brother: "That creature is impossible. I shall speak to father tonight, about her."

Without thinking, as he might have done after a moment's reflection, Baldur said cynically: "What good will that do? The Sultana will have the last word after all."

He was immediately alarmed and ashamed, for Ernestine looked at him, stricken, shame and grief and horror making her face vivid in the dim light.

"No," she said in a low voice, and then louder, as if in anguish: "No! No!" She wrung her hands in her gloves, and her pale mouth twisted.

"I am sorry," said Baldur, with gloom and embarrassment.

"Baldur, what shall we do?"

He shrugged, slipping the heavy cape from his deformed shoulders.

"She will try to get rid of Irmgard tonight. You are the only one who has influence with my father." He paused. "The trouble with all of us is that we have no courage, no fortitude. You might try them, Ernestine."

"But—Papa and Matilda," she whispered. Suddenly she was weeping. "Oh, I cannot bear it. I cannot bear it, Baldur! Mama——"

"I don't think she knows. Perhaps, there is nothing to know. Don't have the vapors, Tina," he added, gently. "You had better go to your room and lie down before dinner." His embarrassment increased before his sister. He had had no right, he reflected, to smudge that virginal innocence, no right to dull its bright shining purity. But he considered the modern denial of earthy facts sheer affectation and hypocrisy. How could a woman live to be Ernestine's age so utterly unconscious of sexual urgencies, and the dark subterranean flood, so primordial and exigent, beneath the niceties of an artificial life? Did no desire ever disturb the fragile flesh of his sister? Did no dusky heat ever possess that immature little body? He looked at her, tear-stained and disheveled in the sombre gaslight, weighted with rich concealing garments, and wondered, not now with embarrassment, but with intense interest.

He thought of his father, lusty, virile, strong with earth, not with his usual amused hatred, but with a sudden understanding and sympathy. How could such a one endure the life he led within these thick lightless walls, without madness, unless he had an escape into the body of such as Matilda, who was like the earth, also? His poor mother— What man could desire her now?

He put his arm about his sister, almost with impatience. "These things go on, Tina. You are not a child."

"But mama," she stammered, sobbing. "It is so dreadful for mama." She put her hands to her suddenly scarlet face. "She—she is his wife."

"No," he said through hard lips. "She was never really his wife. Just as we are not really his children. He was cheated, too. There. Do not be a fool, Tina. Go and wash your face." He added: "And you will be a greater fool, if you let it make any difference between you and father."

He pushed her gently towards the stairs. Then, when she had gone, still weeping, he stood beneath the flickering gaslights, thinking deeply.

What is to become of all of us? he thought. Is there nothing living for us in all the world? Must we continue this endurance, hardly half alive, like corpses growing slowly cold?

He was greatly perturbed. Not for years had he had thoughts like this. Not for years had life so impinged itself upon him, with its old torment and bitterness. He had thought he had quieted it all. For a long time he had lived in a lofty suspension of all exigent thought, a remote removal from all desire. What had happened to him? He looked at the empty staircase, and suddenly it seemed to him that Irmgard stood there, filling the dark chasm with light and glory.

But now the glory was made cold by the old catastrophic thoughts he had believed he had buried years ago. The glory was made cold by the threat of tomorrow, by time which clouded everything by its steaming breath. What of Irmgard, and tomorrow? Today, there had only been today, and joy and peace. But there was tomorrow, and its long spectral shadow was falling over Irmgard.

He went into the vast dark library, where only the street lamps threw any light. He sat down in an immense chair, and his feet swung above the floor. He closed his eyes, and again, he thought sharply and cruelly, and the thoughts were almost intolerable, like the thoughts of a man who is slowly emerging from a prolonged drinking bout where everything had been roseate, possible, suspended and warm.

He asked himself simple questions, and writhed under them: I am a cripple: how dare I think of myself as a man? How can I expect so young and beautiful a creature to look at me, and not think of me as an object for commiseration, but as a man? What have I to give her? Money? I know she cares nothing for that. I can't buy her. If I could buy her, I would not want her. She is intelligent and thoughtful, she has shown she likes my company. We speak without words. Is that enough for her?

His features worked in the darkness. In bed, would she be revolted by me? Would she see that under the ruin I am still a man, with a man's potentialities? Could she endure the thought of bearing me children who might be like me?

He thought of his twisted collapsed body lying beside hers, so smooth and strong and lovely, and even to him it seemed sacrilege. Nevertheless, the thought flooded all his flesh with fire, and a wild cry of bitter yearning rose from his heart, a longing like a devouring flame. I am a man! clamored his heart. Under all this, I am a man. I cannot be shut out of life, like this! I cannot go back to my life in death!

Someone had thrown open a door upon light and ecstasy, and he stood in his room of drugged softness and looked out. If he had ever known pain before, it was nothing like this pain now. Every nerve thrilled and wrenched with it, until it seemed to him that he must really die.

Perhaps one has only to will death, he said to himself. He knew, from his own experience, that very often men die or live by will alone. He had, perhaps, only to let go, to sink down, not to breathe, not to struggle.

And then he knew that he could not die. Not so long as Irmgard lived, could he die. Perhaps, after all, it was better to suffer like this, hopelessly and madly, than never to suffer at all.

The high hot tide of mingled suffering and joy swirled over him again, as he thought of Irmgard, her sympathy, her gentleness, her understanding and patience. He knew she was young. Yet, in spirit, she was not young. Under her serenity, her immobility, he felt a stern repression and iron self-control. He was overcome with compassion. My darling, he thought, but his lips moved with the words, I cannot give you a straight body or strong shoulders. But I can give you my soul. I can give you all my life. I can take from you the fear you will not acknowledge, the deep hidden fear of living, which might give you pain. I know all about this pain. I have had it, myself.

He must have slept, from sheer exhaustion of mind and body, for when he opened his eyes once more, he was surprised to see that a distant glass lamp, hung with glittering prisms, had been lit.

Darkness and fog hung outside. The promise of the December sunlight was gone. Rain washed and rattled against the black window-panes, which reflected the vast library, its massive sombre furniture lit only by that distant lamp. There was no sound but the rain, insistent and melancholy. Baldur lay deep in his plushy chair. Under the lamp, yards away, sat his father, doggedly reading his evening paper, a dull low red fire hissing and snarling beside him.

Had he noticed the small deformed figure in its chair? Baldur did not know. The chair was half-turned away, in semi-darkness. He looked at his father, saw the short fat figure in its black broadcloth, the belly distended, the thick thighs spreading on the cushions. The lamplight shone on his pinkish skull, showing through the bristling gray-yellow hairs. The paper partially hid his face, but Baldur saw half of it, sour, thickened and bellicose, the moist skin darkly flushed. The pince-nez hid the eyes, but the expression about them was frowning in chronic anger and concentration. At intervals he shook the paper with a loud crackling noise, as though it infuriated him dully. His watch-chain flashed in the lamplight, as did the diamond in the stickpin which indented his rich crimson cravat, and the diamond in the single ring on his small fat white hand.

Through his half-closed lids Baldur watched his father, his tormentor, his enemy. But now through his usual amused hatred ran a pale golden thread of compassion and understanding. The great dreary house, silent and sinister, loomed all about and above them, like the crushing weight of stones forming a mighty tomb. What joy had this little fighting man, so brutal and ruthless, in his failing beloved business, in his sick shrinking wife who rarely saw him, in his fragile repressed daughter without health of body or desire, in his deformed son who lived immured like a monk from all life and love? What joy he had was in the ignorant arms of a peasant woman, who could give him nothing but her clean flesh. He had no friends, no intimates, hardly any acquaintances. He lived, surrounded by gloom and emptiness, and enemies. Even his own were his enemies, even Ernestine who loved him. He had a joyless, cold and lightless life, this peasant who loved earth and health, strength and robust competition and struggle. He, no less than any other member of his family, was a prisoner. They submitted, silently. He roared at his walls, and impotently kicked his doors.

He should have a gay and vital mistress, thought Baldur. Some one of light and luxury, some one who could laugh and chide and dance, and amuse him. He did not have even this. His money had bought him nothing but frustration and despair. Whose was the fault? His own? Perhaps. But a man who is a victim of himself deserves no less pity than the man who is the victim of others. Perhaps he had brutalized all joy and love from his life. But it was he who sat among the ruins, hating and growling, and suffering.

Baldur, overcome with his compassion, and forcing himself to forget past torments, sat forward in his chair. "Good evening, father," he said, in his quiet and beautiful voice.

Hans did not look at him. He rattled the paper viciously. His thighs contracted, relaxed. He grunted. He continued to read. But the dark flush deepened on his face.

Baldur paused. What did one say to an enemy, who had done his best to destroy one, but whom one could only pity? For weeks, they had neither seen nor spoken to each other. Sometimes they had passed in halls, without a glance or a word.

"We all went driving today," said Baldur, looking for words.

This time not even a grunt answered him, but only the rain.

Baldur bit his lips. He pulled himself together. "I should like to go through the mills soon, father, if I might."

He was not prepared for what followed. Hans dropped the paper with a loud report like a pistol. He glared at his son, and all his hatred, his detestation, his savage disappointment, and his ridicule, blazed at Baldur through the pince-nez. And with it all was a complete and devastating amazement, as though a rabbit had spoken to him. The pink skull turned crimson; the fat brutal face swelled.

"You!" he cried, finally, in a loud and ferocious voice. "You!" he cried again, and in that voice was now a choking sound, as though the mind behind it seethed with the accumulation of years of frustration, despair and hatred.

Baldur was silent. He turned pale. His eyes widened in their sockets with a measureless pain. He pushed himself slowly from his chair. He stood before his father, small, misshapen, humped, impotent. Suddenly Hans burst into loud and brutelike laughter, his fat body shaking violently.

Baldur went from the room, walking with dignity and quietness. He ascended the stairway. His father's laughter followed him, like the cracking of whips, like the blows of a stick. But under the laughter he heard a lifetime of misery and hopelessness.

His hand slid along the mahogany banister, and the small palm was wet and shaking.

CHAPTER 21

GILLESPIE, THE ENGLISH butler, knocked discreetly on Irmgard's door. There were two doors to her room, one leading into Mrs. Schmidt's apartments, and the rear opening on the back servants' hall. It was this latter door upon which Gillespie knocked.

It was nine o'clock. Mrs. Schmidt was already asleep after her warm bath and hot milk, and Irmgard had been sitting under her quiet oil lamp, reading. She had brought little to America in the way of clothing or money, but she had brought all her father's books, four or five large boxes of them, the best of Goethe and Schiller, Heine and Lessing, with many German translations of Shakespeare, Hugo, Boswell, Dickens, Dumas, Voltaire, Emerson and Thoreau, and innumerable others. She had read them all, over and over, but she never tired of them. Of them all, Thoreau was her favorite. It was Thoreau she was reading now, infusing strength from him for herself.

At Gillespie's knock, she opened the door, and looked at his smiling and apologetic face in silence.

"The master would like to see you, Irmgard," he whispered cautiously. He coughed gently behind his hand. "In Matilda's apartments."

Irmgard said nothing, but her expression became strained and a little hard. She closed her door again, tiptoed into Mrs. Schmidt's chamber. That lady was sleeping peacefully, a look of complete relaxation on her worn dark face. Irmgard blew out the candles on the night-table, drew a blanket over her mistress' exposed arm. Then she went out into the great corridor. All color had gone from her face, even her lips.

As always, the vast house was silent. But as Irmgard went noiselessly down the corridor, Baldur began to play in his room. Irmgard paused by his door. She pressed her palm against the wood, and listened. A sound like mighty winds filled with echoes rose in the room beyond, blew through the door, filled the upper reaches of the house. Irmgard held her breath, listening.

When the wind of passionate music subsided, she went on. She mounted the stairs to Matilda's apartments, and knocked sharply on the door. Matilda herself opened it, fat, fair, gloating and triumphant in her black silk, the basque of which strained over her large breasts, the skirt looped and bustled and draped elaborately, the rustling skirt bordered with rows of silk braid. She was heavily scented. Her light hair was piled in coils and puffs and curls over her head, and in her ears were clusters of tiny pearls and filigree gold. About her neck hung a necklace of gold and small pearls, and chains dangled on her wrists. She was, now, no longer the soberly clad and efficient housekeeper.

She stood aside, and Irmgard entered the hot room. It was Matilda's parlor, crowded with furniture. A blazing fire burned high on the white-tiled hearth. In each of the four corners stood a huge vase, filled with peacock feathers and plumes. The mantel was draped in fringed red velvet, and upon it stood a gilt clock, several vases, and a number of Dresden figures. On the wall behind it, a large gilt-framed mirror reflected the light of a number of prism-hung lamps, each prism trembling slightly in the heat, and throwing back little slivers of radiance. There were a number of crowded tables about, covered with ball-fringed red velvet "throws," and heaped with numerous small ornaments. It was a hot, ugly and vulgar room, in the lamplight and firelight. In a crimson-plush chair near the fire sat Hans Schmidt. He still wore his black broadcloth. But he had removed his boots. His feet, in their black silk socks, were stretched to the leaping heat of the hearth. Near him, on another table, stood a silver tray with a silver coffee pot, "kuchen," and two cups and saucers. His fat thighs were liberally sprinkled with crumbs, and as Irmgard entered, he was wiping his pursy mouth with a white napkin.

Irmgard, immobile of face, stood in the center of the room, and then curtseyed briefly. Her hands were clasped before her. She waited. She had seen her master only a few times before, and had spoken to him only once. Matilda sat down, fat and triumphant and hating, in a chair on the other side of the fire. Irmgard was struck with the racial resemblance between these peasants, so strong and healthy and lusty. She had seen them often in the fields of home, bending over plows and planting seed. The thought of Mrs. Schmidt was incongruous, and she felt a sudden sympathy for Hans.

He was regarding her, not without good humor. He spoke to her in "low Dutch," the language of the peasant.

"So! You are the girl who is causing this household much trouble, eh?"

Irmgard replied quietly, trying to keep her words simple, in order not to arouse the peasant's instinctive antagonism against her class.

"I am sorry if I have caused trouble. I did not mean to, Mein Herr. If I did, it was without my knowledge."

Hans grunted. He picked a large luscious crumb from his knees and put it into his mouth. He rolled the crumb appreciatively on his tongue, and stared at Irmgard narrowly. He was delighted at her beauty. His tiny blue eyes wandered to her throat, to her breast and hips, then back to her mouth, where they remained, lecherously.

But now Matilda could not contain herself. She colored violently, and cried in a loud voice: "That is not true! You are a sneak, my girl. You disobeyed my orders behind my back, and took Frau Schmidt into the cold, after she has not been out of her bed for many days. If she had died, you would have been the murderer!" She beat her fat fists against her knees, and repeated: "Murderer!" Her eyes were full of fear and hatred.

"Quiet, woman," said Hans, in a still louder voice, turning savagely upon Matilda, and glaring at her with even more savagery. He looked at Irmgard again, and smiled, though his face was still congested and damp. "Speak, girl," he said. Matilda subsided, breathing hoarsely, rage darkening her features.

Irmgard's fingers pressed themselves tightly together. She looked directly at Hans. She had always accepted her beauty with indifference, and had never used it before. She saw she must use it now, and with self-loathing, she made herself smile radiantly, opening wide her strange green eyes so that the light of the lamps could shine in them.

"I never intended to disobey any orders, Mein Herr. But it was a nice day, and Mrs. Schmidt seemed so much better. I suggested a drive. She was eager for it. I consulted Miss Ernestine, and she believed her mother might benefit. That was all."

"You suggested a drive!" shrieked Matilda, half lifting her heavy buttocks from the chair, and glaring at Irmgard with concentrated ferocity. "You, knowing the poor lady's condition—you took her into the cold, after I had told you a thousand times that she must be protected from all air and chill!"

Irmgard turned slowly, and gazed at her fixedly. "It is not I who wishes Frau Schmidt's death," she said, very quietly.

Hans did not understand, nor hear, the significance under her words. He glowered at Matilda, who had subsided, her nostrils distended, her teeth glistening wetly between her full lips. She looked like a clean fat sow, with bared fangs, waiting, but fearing to attack.

"So," said Hans, slowly, to Irmgard, turning again to his pleased contemplation of her face and body. "You believed it would benefit your mistress? Then, perhaps, it was your judgment that was at fault, if your discretion was bad."

"She is sleeping peacefully, and well," said Irmgard, in a low voice. "Much better than any other night. The drive gave her great benefit. She is not such an invalid as one might believe. She needs encouragement to rise from her bed, and resume a normal life. I give her that encouragement. I am certain her physician would approve of this."

Hans smiled. "You are a bold piece," he said. "An obstinate hussy, like all the Dutch." His smile broadened to a grin. "You are obstinate," he repeated, as though he were complimenting her. "So. But you must admit that you disobeyed Matilda, who is in charge in this house."

Irmgard again smiled radiantly. Her jade-colored eyes softened deliberately as she gazed at the man. "But Frau Schmidt is still the mistress, is she not, Mein Herr?"

Matilda grunted coarsely. Hans' eyes shifted away from Irmgard. He thrust out his thick lips, and stared at the fire. "It is true," he muttered. "But Frau Schmidt's judgment is not always reliable. She is of a gentle nature. If you insisted, then she had no strength to resist you."

"There was no harm done," said Irmgard, very quietly. "But much good, instead. She is sleeping well."

"Obstinate," repeated Hans, smiling again. He paused. He twiddled his thumbs. "Nevertheless, the opinion is yours. Matilda differs. I am not the one to interfere with servants. Matilda is housekeeper in this house. It is she who gives the orders, and whose commands must be obeyed. I should not have interfered, now, allowing her to discharge you if she saw fit. But it seems that you have gained some influence over Frau Schmidt and over my daughter."

"A sneaking, contriving baggage!" cried Matilda.

"Hush," said Hans, sternly, flashing his eyes upon her. He looked at Irmgard, more mildly.

"I am a man of peace, my girl. Matilda tells me that you have repeatedly disobeyed her orders, and created confusion and annoyance in this house. This is bad for all. It undermines discipline. It cannot be endured. You are intelligent. You can see that. There must be order and discipline in any establishment. If one is allowed to disobey, then there is only anarchy."

Irmgard paled. She clenched her hands together, kept her

voice steady. "I am sorry if this is so. I shall endeavor to obey in the future." She was terribly frightened, and sickness struck at her heart. She thought of Mrs. Schmidt and Ernestine, and Baldur. She thought of the little peace and pleasure she had brought them. Only she stood between them and black wretchedness. She would promise anything, if she were allowed to remain and protect them!

Hans grunted. He tapped his knees thoughtfully. All at once he was ill at ease. Finally, he shook his head.

"Do not think I do not appreciate your kindness to Frau Schmidt. Fräulein Ernestine has spoken well of you, frequently. But this cannot go on, this hostility between my housekeeper, and you." He paused, and added, almost conciliatory: "Let us be sensible. You, yourself, cannot be happy in this atmosphere. But I am not insensible to what you have done. I intend to give you five hundred dollars and an excellent reference."

Irmgard was silent.

Just at this moment Gillespie, with his usual discretion, was knocking at Ernestine's door. She came and opened it, dressed in a ruffled white wrap.

Gillespie coughed. "Miss Ernestine, I thought you might like to know. Irmgard has been called to Matilda's rooms. You know that Matilda is very angry with the girl." He coughed a little. "The master is there, also."

Ernestine stood before him, her dark curls on her shoulders. Her little face paled, and her lips dried. Then a light of resolution flashed into her eyes, and her mouth tightened. She looked much like her father in that moment.

"Thank you, Gillespie," she said, very quietly. She closed the door behind her, and ran down the corridor. She disappeared up the stairway. Gillespie, smiling with smug satifaction, went down to the kitchen, where he and Mrs. Flaherty awaited new developments.

"Like a little white flame she was," he said to the cook, "running up the stairs. Not a sound out of her."

"It will take more than a little white flame to scorch that fat pork of a Matilda," said Mrs. Flaherty, grimly.

Hans was saying, almost with sympathy: "I am sorry, my girl. But there is nothing else to be done."

Irmgard turned to Matilda. "It is you who wishes me to go," she said, bitterly, "for your own evil reasons. I know them."

Matilda smiled widely, with malevolence. "You have heard the master. Go and pack your bags at once. You will not attend Frau Schmidt in the morning. I shall do that, until I can replace you."

The door opened. Ernestine ran into the room, curls and white draperies flying. She ran to Irmgard, and took her hand. She faced her father, who gaped in angry surprise. She did not look at Matilda, who rose and stood near the hearth, rage and hatred in her eyes.

"Papa!" cried Ernestine, vehemently, "what is this?"

"It is none of your affair," replied Hans, trying for his usual brutality. He glowered at his daughter, so small and childlike, so furious and aroused, and in spite of himself, he was delighted at such unusual spirit and passion. The child had changed; there was life in her, at last! His voice became mild, fond. "Go away, Ernestine. This is a matter between servants. You have nothing to do with this."

"Haven't I!" exclaimed Ernestine, furiously. "I have a great deal to do with this, and I won't stand by and see Irmgard abused, or dismissed." She swung like a small nemesis upon Matilda. "It is all you! You have always hated Irmgard, because she is young and pretty, and good, and you are afraid of her! It is you who should be dismissed. You have caused us a great deal of trouble. You are insolent and tyrannical. I have wanted to talk to my father about you before—"

"Ernestine!" roared Hans, half rising out of his chair.

She turned upon him, almost beside herself, and before that diminutive rage, he fell back, open-mouthed, but strangely and happily amazed.

"Papa! How you can listen to this—this woman, is beyond me! She hated Irmgard from the first. She has always persecuted her." Suddenly shame turned the girl's cheeks scarlet. She looked at her father, and tears of grief and humiliation filled her eyes. She began to stammer, in a choked voice. "I—I know you have always listened to Matilda, Papa. It—it is more than I can bear——"

He stared at her. And then, very slowly, he knew that she knew. His eyes dropped. He thrust out his lips. He was overcome with embarrassment, and pity, and a dull anger. Out of the corner of his eye he saw her shame and loathing, her wild misery and sorrow. It was unbearable. In all the world, he loved only this little daughter of his. Now, she was despising him. It would take little more on his part to make her hate him. His heart began to beat painfully. He was suddenly impersonally enraged, as though some one, but not himself, had tarnished her innocence and destroyed her virginal simplicity.

His rage turned upon Matilda, who had done this thing against him and his daughter. He hated her, savagely. He lifted his eyes, and they struck the woman like a whip. His face became crimson, swelled.

"Is it true then, that it is you, and you alone, who have looked for reasons to dismiss this girl?" he bellowed.

Matilda was stupidly aghast. Her mouth fell open. She stared, idiotically, at Hans.

Ernestine began to sob, aloud, as though her heart was breaking. She put her hands over her eyes, as if to shut out the sight of her father. Tears ran through her fingers. Hans could not bear it. He shot to his feet. He stood on the hearth, breathing stentoriously.

"Take Miss Tina to her room," he said to Irmgard. "Put her to bed. I will be in to see her, later."

He stared at Irmgard. His thick features worked. "Everything is as it was. If you wish to remain, do so."

He paused. His hands twitched. He wanted to put his arms about his child. He could not. He stood before her, humiliated, frightened, filled with remorse and yearning. His expression was very moving to Irmgard, so humble was it, so sad, so confused and wounded.

Irmgard took the weeping girl's hand. She bent and whispered in her ear, urgently: "Miss Ernestine, speak to your father."

Ernestine's hands dropped from her face, which was covered with tears. She tried to speak. Her voice choked. Then, followed by Irmgard, she went out of the room.

Hans stared after them. His face worked with his painful efforts to breathe and swallow. Matilda sat in silence, shrinking in her chair, forgotten.

CHAPTER 22

BALDUR HEARD the sound of muffled weeping trailing by his door, as he paused in his melancholy playing. He tiptoed to his door and opened it, just in time to see his sister, with Irmgard supporting her, disappear into her room. There was a sound in that weeping which frightened him, so desolate and abandoned was it. He waited a moment, then followed the two young women, and tapped softly on Ernestine's door.

Irmgard opened it, and when she saw him, she silently admitted him.

Ernestine had flung herself upon her bed, and lay there, sobbing, clutching the coverlet, her head buried in the pillows. He had seen her cry before, but never like this, as though her heart were breaking. His first thought was that his mother was dead. Black sparks suddenly flickered before his eyes. He ran awkwardly across the room, took his sister by the shoulders, and cried: "Ernestine! What is it? Is it mother——?"

When his sister did not answer, only weeping with increased desolation, he turned almost furiously to Irmgard.

"What is it? Are you both mute? Can't some one tell me?" His voice broke.

He saw that Irmgard's face was stern and pale, but full of pity.

"No, Mr. Baldur, it is not your mother." She paused. Now she flushed a little. "It is just that—that Mr. Schmidt wished to dismiss me. He called me into Matilda's apartments. Some one told Miss Ernestine about it——"

A strange look of blue fury blazed in Baldur's eyes. "Dismiss you, Irmgard? That is impossible! We shall not allow it!" His chest tightened with dread and a frantic fear.

Irmgard clasped her hands tightly together, and went on as though he had not interrupted: "Miss Ernestine came into that apartment. She—she accused Matilda, before Mr. Schmidt, of plotting against me." Her color deepened. "Mr. Schmidt was very kind. He understood. I am not to leave."

"Then why—," began Baldur, giving his sister's shaking body a puzzled glance. Then he knew. He hated himself for first instilling that unclean suspicion in his sister's mind. But what could one do? She would have to know. It was ridiculous, a woman of her age. But he remembered, then, that she had the mind and soul of a child.

He went back to his sister, and sat beside her on the bed, gently smoothing the disordered dark curls.

"Ernestine, you will make yourself ill. You are not a baby. There are some things which seem intolerable—in one's father. But they are really little things."

Ernestine suddenly paused in her weeping. She sat up so suddenly, and with such small violence, that, startled, Baldur recoiled. He looked at her face in amazement. It was almost purplish in its suffusion. Her teeth were bared. Her father's eyes looked at him, distended with fury, shame and grief.

"Baldur! How can you talk like this? This humiliation, this disgrace—mama—! Such a terrible, shameful thing to do this to mama, in her own house!" She beat her hands on the bed, in a frenzy, her little fists clenched. "It is unendurable! Disgraceful! Contemptible! Disgusting! I cannot bear it!"

Her curls lay disordered against her wet and swollen cheeks. Baldur was silent. His eyes studied her gravely, thoughtfully, as though he were seeing her for the first time. Irmgard brought a glass of water, but Ernestine thrust it aside fiercely. She was panting now. Her breast heaved. The process of becoming mature, thought Baldur, was very painful in those who had long passed childhood and early youth. Ernestine's eyes were horrified, but they were also enraged. She repudiated the hot wet hand of life, suddenly placed on her naked flesh. She denied it. She shuddered at it, feeling herself unclean, polluted.

"I shall tell him, tonight, when he comes in to see me, as he promised, that he must get rid of that—that creature! Tonight! He must send her away! I shall tell him——"

Baldur's hand reached out and seized her by the shoulder. His fingers pressed into it, painfully. But his voice was quiet.

"You will do no such thing. You little fool! You will say nothing to him."

His words, the tone of his voice, hard and contemptuous, never heard from him before, quieted Ernestine's hysteria as though he had thrown icy water over her. She crouched on her bed, glaring at him, her panting subdued to a faint whimpering. She was astounded. She kept blinking her eyes. Her mouth had fallen open, childishly, with her astonishment.

Baldur stood up. He began to pace the room, his head bent, his hands clasped behind his deformed back. He began to speak, but softly, as though thinking aloud.

"One must consider everything. One must go easily." He continued to pace. Ernestine watched him with a blank, almost idiotic expression of complete amazement. But Irmgard, understanding, stood back in the shadows, only her face illuminated by the tall candles on a table nearby.

Baldur turned to his sister, and his voice was low and bitter, if compassionate.

"Think," he said. He made a wide and desolate gesture with his arms. His face took on a look of deep sorrow. "Look at us. What has he got from us, from living? Mother? Let us be reasonable, if loving, about mother. I think she was like you, in the beginning, Tina. A silly, shrinking little thing, who would not admit that life existed. When she saw that it did, she ran away from it into terror and invalidism. Just as you probably will run away."

He lifted his hand. Ernestine had cried out, choked and gasping. But his gesture silenced her immediately.

"Look at us, Tina. Look at us frankly, and honestly. Look

at me. I am his son. He hoped for a son. Some one who would take his place, be a man beside him, inherit what he had built up, and created." He laughed, lightly, despairingly. "Look at me! What am I? Am I the son he wanted? Perhaps it is not my fault. But it is not his fault, either."

Irmgard's lips contracted with pain and compassion. But Baldur did not see her. He saw only his sister.

"Look at you, Tina," he resumed, a little more gently. "Are you the gay happy, lusty daughter he wanted? He has the peasant's gregariousness. He would like a house filled with young dancing people, with parties, with balls and laughter. He would like a healthy daughter, who could give him grandchildren. That is the German in him. But we are like our mother. We have no blood or guts." He saw Ernestine's delicate wincing at the word. "Guts," he repeated, inexorably. "Have you guts, Tina?"

"O Baldur, do not be disgusting," she said, sobbing again.

He smiled wryly. He shrugged. "You do not like the word? But it is true, we are gutless."

He paused, resumed his pacing once more.

"He has frightened us, you might say. He has terrified us, sending us shrinking into corners. He has made us so spineless that we have forgotten how to live. We have made a grave for ourselves, in this house. But we also tried to make a grave for him. He has strength and health enough, fortunately, not to lie in it. If he frightened us, it is our own fault. He hated us, because he knew we hated him. Or, perhaps, because he made us hate him."

He was silent, then spoke again, reflectively: "If a man hates, he becomes hated. But that does not eliminate his deep human desire to be loved. Hatred breeds hatred. Had we returned his frightened and disappointed hatred with love and understanding, he might have loved us in return. We had neither the courage nor the intelligence to know this. We might have consoled him. It is too late for me, and for mother. But it is not too late for you, Tina. It is not too late for you to make him happy, with your understanding and sympathy."

"Baldur!" she cried, feebly. "What are you asking me to do? To countenance that woman in this house?"

He made a despairing, a hopeless gesture, as though he thought it useless to speak again. Then, with determination, he sat down on the bed again and took his sister's hand. He held it tightly. He looked into her streaming eyes.

"Tina," he said, gently. "Listen to me. It is very important. When he comes to you, promising anything, if you will believe in him, and trust him again, you must say: 'I understand.

It is all right. I want you to be happy. I will be very unhappy if you send Matilda away. Let us not speak of it again.' "

She stared at him, blinking aghast. Then she said, not without some cruelty: "You can plead, so, for him, Baldur, remembering what he has done to you?"

He made a slight gesture, as though to fling her hand from him. Irmgard saw the gesture, and when she saw him restrain it, her heart swelled and her eyes filled with tears. She heard his voice, even more quiet than before:

"Do not be petty, Tina. Or stupid. This is no time for any of us to think of self, alone. We must understand. Tina, I shall hate you, really hate you, if you make him miserable. I shall feel guilty, too. You will make me miserable. I refuse to be any more miserable than I am now. If you induce him to send Matilda away, I shall go away. I promise you that you shall never see me again."

"Baldur!" she gasped, disbelieving.

He nodded his head, grimly. "I am quite serious, Tina. You shall not make him unhappy, again. Matilda must stay. And you must arouse yourself to be more what he would wish you to be. You must stop this devilish terrified seclusion of yours, your self-preoccupation. You must find a way out, for him, and for you. Never mind mother and me. You must not think of us again. We are already dead."

She cried again, but silently, pressing her small fingers to her eyes in a gesture of utter defeat and sadness.

He stood up, and turned to Irmgard. "You will help?" he asked, simply.

"Always," she replied, as simply, but her green eyes wet and shining. They looked at each other intensely.

As though they had consulted each other, they went out of the room silently, parting in the hall, too full of words spoken before Ernestine.

Ernestine sat where they had left her, rigid, staring blindly into the darkness, lit only by the candles on the table. She thought as she had never thought before. Sometimes a wave of crimson ran over her face, and she beat her fists again on the bed, vehemently. Then she would become quite still, her mouth drooping mournfully, and the tears would run over her face. A long time passed. She became more quiet. Her head fell on her breast, and a dry sob broke from her lips, a child's desolate sob. Then at last, she was completely quiet, and her expression become grave, heavy, thoughtful.

When she rose from her bed, a new maturity was on her pale face, a new resolution and womanliness. She bathed her eyes in cold water. She brushed and combed her disheveled hair. She returned to her bed, and picked up a book, holding it as though she were reading it. But it was upside down. She waited, her eyes still staring sightlessly, but with quietness and calm.

A timid knock sounded on her door. She called serenely: "Come in, Papa." The door opened slowly. Hans stood there, his short fat body not belligerent now, but flaccid, defeated, hopeless. His eyes surveyed her timidly, and he put his hand to his head and scratched it. It was that plebeian gesture which broke the last lingering resentment and hardness in her, and she smiled.

"Papa! I thonght you'd never come. I'm so sleepy, and I was just going to blow out the light."

Her voice, sweet, high, fluting, rippled with pretended sleepy laughter. He stared at her, dumfounded. He looked at her face, gay, childish, loving, and at her extended hand. If it trembled, he did not know it. Like a man walking in his sleep, he approached her, and with each step his dull expression lightened. He stood beside the bed, still incredulous, not daring to hope. She closed her eyes in her old childish gesture, screwing up the lids and pursing her mouth for his goodnight kiss.

She heard a sound break from him, a dim, heart-breaking sound. She felt his lips on hers. She thought: He has just kissed that abominable creature. But she sternly repressed her sudden wincing. She returned his kiss with passionate affection. The bed creaked; he was sitting beside her. He was putting his fat arm about her. She dropped her head on his shoulder. They sat like this for a long time, with no sound about them but the rain, and no light, but that of the flickering candles.

Then he said, hoarsely, haltingly: "Tina, my little pet, if—if Matilda annoys you, I shall send her away at once. We—we can get another housekeeper."

She lifted her head and stared at him with pretended astonishment.

"Papa! How silly! Matilda is an excellent woman, and our house has never been kept so well before! Of all things! It is true she never liked Irmgard, but that is settled now, thanks to you, darling Papa. I really shall not let Matilda go, even if you want her to!"

He looked down into her eyes. They were lucid, innocent, surprised, as always, and shining with a clear virginal light. He did not know what that acting was costing her. He was convinced that nothing had happened, that he had imagined everything. The indignation in her voice lifted the tightness from his chest. His pince-nez dropped from his nose, and lay on his chest. His belly heaved a little. His large gross face seemed to dissolve into helpless, humble lines of gladness and relief.

"Well," he grumbled, pretending reluctance. "She was very bad, tonight. She was impertinent. But, Tina, if you insist——"

"I do insist," she replied, vigorously, giving him a gay admonishing tap on the cheek. "I never heard anything so ridiculous!"

He regarded her with humble love. It was this expression which finally completed her melting, fused her new understanding into pity and clear pain. She flung her arms about him. She kissed him passionately, holding him tightly.

"Papa, papa!" she mourned. "I am afraid we have all been so horrid, so contemptible, to you!"

"No, no!" he exclaimed, holding her so strongly that her bones seemed to bend in his arms. "You are my liebchen, my little one, my dear little one, Tina!" He had relapsed into German, and the guttural voice was full of rough music. "Tina, Tina!" he crooned. "My little flower, my little star. My little happiness. There is no one like my Tina."

He pressed his lips to her forehead. She felt the prickling of his yellow mustache. The pain in her heart was a physical one now, and she sobbed and smiled at one and the same time.

"Papa," she said, softly, and with pretended reluctance. "Would you mind if I had a party? A party at Christmas? I should so like a party."

"A party!" he cried, waving his hand. "A thousand parties for my Tina!"

She lifted her head and gazed at him with simulated joy.

"Papa, I bought so many pretty gowns and hats and boots today! I shall show them to you tomorrow——"

"No, now!" he commanded, animation making him clumsier than ever. "I wish to see them, now!"

She leapt out of bed with a shy gay laugh. She ran to her wardrobe and began to pull the boxes from the depths. In a few minutes the bed was covered with glistening fabrics, the new bonnet, the new tasselled boots, the gloves and kerchiefs and reticules, and even the brave new silk stockings. Hans, blinking, smiling foolishly, lifted each article in his small fat hands, holding it up, loudly admiring it, stealing glances at his daughter's bright animated face, so girlish now, so happy, so flushed. She put on the bonnet at a coquettish angle, tying the ribbons beneath her chin, sparkling upon him. He was entranced. He smiled even more foolishly.

Then he pulled her to his knee, bonnet and all, and they sat among the shining litter. He began to stroke her hair.

"Tina," he began, haltingly, "that young man, who stares at the house— He works in the mills. I—I have investigated him. A fine feller. He will go a long way. I—would you mind if I invited him some evening, for dinner?"

She lay still in his arms, so still that he was suddenly frightened. Then he glanced down at her face. Her eyes were closed. Tears were running down her cheeks. But she was both flushed and smiling.

CHAPTER 23

IRMGARD SAT quietly near the window, holding a letter in her hand, but not reading it. She had read it several times. Each time that she had read it, she had been alternately angered and amused. But now she gave all her attention to the animated scene before her.

She was sitting in the sewing room, in the midst of a colorful confusion. Miss Zimmermann, the seamstress, and two of her assistants, were busily fitting Mrs. Schmidt and Ernestine. Lengths of shining cloth lay over everything. Ernestine stood on a stool, turning gravely and anxiously. The new gown was almost completed, and the seamstresses worked feverishly. The pearly satin Ernestine had chosen was comparatively simply made. The basque was decorated with a close row of tiny black velvet bows from neck to waist, and was topped with a short cape bordered with thin black lace. The skirt was looped and draped with large bows of black velet, and the bustle was topped by another bow. "Very chic," said Miss Zimmermann, proudly, sitting back on her heels and gazing upwards at her creation. "Very Parisenne."

But Irmgard looked at Ernestine's face, illuminated and alive, as though the girl had some secret and passionate excitement and joy within her. Her curls were untidy, her mouth as red as a moist rose. Her eyes shone and sparkled and danced. When she spoke, it was with little catches in her breath. Mrs. Schmidt sat nearby, shawled and smiling, her feet on a hassock, a copy of Harper's open on her knee. She could not look away from her daughter. She had had a fitting, herself, and was very tired. But her expression was serene and contented, and though illness still strongly marked her face, a faint glimmer of health rested in her eyes.

"Charming, Tina," she said, and sighed a little, and smiled.

"It is very lovely," said Irmgard, slowly.

Ernestine laughed. She pointed a small finger at Irmgard. "I was waiting for you to speak," she said. "You have been so absorbed in that letter of yours." She sparkled roguishly. "A beau, Irmgard? If you do not tell me about it, I shall really hate you!"

Irmgard glanced at her letter, folded it tightly, and put it in the pocket of her apron. "No beau," she said. It was time for Mrs. Schmidt's afternoon rest, and Irmgard conducted her to her room. Once there, Mrs. Schmidt turned to her with imploring anxiety: "Irmgard, are we very wicked, working on Sunday? Those three poor women—I feel I have done something very unchristian in asking them to come today. But it is so necessary, if the dresses are to be ready by Christmas——"

"I am sure you are not wicked," smiled Irmgard. "Besides, are you not paying them much extra? Money covers a multitude of sins."

Mrs. Schmidt regarded her with sad reproof. "Irmgard, my dear, aren't you a little cynical? And so young, too. I am afraid, though, that you are trying to salve my conscience. The Sabbath——"

"If they are not concerned, you ought not to be, Mrs. Schmidt."

"But I asked them," persisted the poor woman. She sat on the edge of her bed while Irmgard removed her boots. She wrung her hands anxiously. "I am afraid we have done so wrong. I feel quite sinful."

Irmgard felt some impatience, but when she glanced up and saw that thin troubled face, the impatience disappeared. "The Sabbath was made for man, and not man for the Sabbath," she said. "It is very important for Miss Ernestine that the gowns be finished. I am certain that God is not angry. Who could be angry with Miss Ernestine?"

The mother's face softened, melted. Tears rushed to her eyes, but she smiled through them. "I have never seen her so gay, so light-hearted, Irmgard. You have brought sunshine into this house, and health, and brightness. Ernestine is so changed, lately, I hardly know her. She is like a bride."

"She will be soon, I know," replied Irmgard, with warm conviction. Mrs. Schmidt looked at her intensely, and then bent forward with Ernestine's own impulsiveness, and kissed her cheek. "My dear," she murmured, and began to cry, helplessly, but not with pain.

Irmgard made her comfortable in bed. Another thought

made Mrs. Schmidt raise her head from the pillows. "I am so selfish!" she cried. "It is your Sunday, Irmgard. No, no, you must listen to me, my dear. I have taken all your Sundays——"

"I wished to stay in," said Irmgard, her lips tightening obstinately.

"But it is not good for you, child. Surely your aunt must want you to visit her. It is such a lovely day, almost like summer. Please me by going out today. If you would like the carriage, for a drive? But today must be your day, alone. I insist upon it. Do not worry about me. Ernestine is here, and will not be going out."

Irmgard drew the silken quilt up to her mistress' chin. She smiled gently. "If I change my mind, I shall go. But I shall return early."

She went into her own room and sat down. She drew the letter from her pocket. It had arrived yesterday. She reread it again, her lips twitching, her color heightened.

It was written in German, in a hard flowing script:

"My mother reproaches you constantly for your neglect of her, which gifts and letters cannot condone, nor make her forget. You have visited her once in almost two months, and then only for an hour. No doubt your new life and duties are engrossing. But have you remembered that we are the only ones of your blood in America, in the world? It is not a German spirit, which forgets these things."

"But you never remember," thought Irmgard, angrily.

She continued to read:

"If the weather is fine on Sunday, I shall be waiting for you at the corner of Howard Street. I shall begin to wait at two o'clock. If you are not there at three, I shall come to the house, and demand to see you. That will cause you embarrassment. I shall not care. I shall continue to embarrass you until I see you. Do you not owe some duty to your relatives?"

Irmgard glanced at the small gilt clock on her dresser. It was ten minutes to three. She had doubted, since receiving the letter, that Franz would really carry out his threat at three o'clock. But now, suddenly, she did not doubt. She stood up. She had only to request Gillespie to say she was not at home. That would settle everything. She took a step towards the door. Then she paused. This was insufferable. She would go, herself, to Franz, and request him not to annoy her again. She had no wish to see him. His letter was impudent. She would tell him so.

She did not analyze the reason for her sudden trembling, for the sudden acceleration of her heart. She glanced through the half-open window. It was one of those deceptive days so well known in Southern Pennsylvania, which occur in mid-winter, and which hold a false promise of the spring so long in the future. It was mild, almost balmy, this Sunday afternoon. The sun shone with a warmth that was heartening and exciting. A fresh spring-like wind blew, and sparrows chattered hopefully in the bare trees. A ruddy light lay on the corner of the roof which extended past Irmgard's window. It was that light on the dark slate which now so strangely excited Irmgard, so that her breath stopped in her throat. Not pausing now to analyze or dissect her emotions, which was her frequent peculiar pastime, she opened her wardrobe and drew out her new dark-green cloth dress. She fastened the basque with fingers that were cold-tipped and shaking. The black velvet buttons marched severely from neck to waist; about the throat there was a ruffle of delicate real lace, which Mrs. Schmidt had made, and which she had insisted upon Irmgard accepting. There was a jacket to match, which was trimmed with a strip of black astrakhan, also the gift of Mrs. Schmidt, as was the black astrakhan muff. Irmgard put on her new green bonnet and tied the ribbons under her chin. She looked at herself in the mirror, directly, appraisingly. Her smooth pale cheeks were now flushed with rose, and her green eyes sparkled with a new lustre. For one of the few times in her life she saw herself as a woman, studied the bands of pale gold that framed her face on the underside of the bonnet. There was one final hesitation, rueful and wry: Ernestine had given her a vial of sweet scent for her birthday. It was with a reckless gesture that she now opened the vial and touched her hair with the glass stopper, and her throat. She suddenly laughed, not without bitterness, but also with a catch in the laughter.

She went out of the house through the servants' entrance. Her knees were trembling, and a curious dreamlike quality began to pervade her, a sense of unreality which was heightened by the unseasonly warm sun and the cool scentless air. Several times, on her way to the corner of the street, she halted, telling herself that this was ridiculous, that she did not wish to see Franz Stoessel, that she ought to return to the house and give Gillespie the message. Her face was burning; her breath came fast; there was no sensation in her feet.

She reached the corner. The four streets stretched far away into the distance with herself like the spoke of a wheel. There was no one in sight, save three young children playing on a walk, and no sound but the wind and the sparrows. Irmgard stood there, looking in all directions. At a little distance stood a buggy, the horse idly nibbling at sparse blades of grass. But that was all. The Sunday quiet lay over the city, faintly echoing, and muted.

He is not here, he did not come after all, thought Irmgard. He has forgotten. He never meant to come.

A great coldness gathered in the region of her heart, and like veins of ice, crept through her body. The sun was no longer bright, the air no longer thrilling with excitement. She stood and waited. Her eyes dimmed. And then a strong and bitter anger and humiliation assailed her. She was some cheap serving girl, waiting for a man who would never come, standing there alone and exposed on the street! It was unendurable. She thought of Franz with hatred and rage. It would not be beyond him to stand in some distant hidden doorway, laughing at her, watching her mortification. She had the sudden impression of his eyes, and her heart began to throb strongly with a gathering fury.

I will walk on, she thought. But something held her, waiting. She waited for nearly ten minutes. A carriage rolled by, the occupants eyeing her with severe disapproval, this loitering servant girl exposing herself immodestly on the street.

At the end of the ten minutes tears of shame were thick in her eyes, and her face was scarlet. She heard the clock of a distant church-tower strike the half hour. Then, lifting her chin resolutely, her eyes blind with a furious hatred she had never felt before, she walked down the street. She reached the idling buggy, and was about to pass it when she heard a light voice calling her. She turned swiftly. Franz was sitting on the seat, the reins in his hand.

For one terrible instant it seemed to her that her very flesh dissolved in a fire of joy, that her heart stopped on one upward leap, that her blood murmured and sang. She could see nothing but his face, full of suppressed laughter, and his knowing blue eyes. She could not move, could hardly breathe.

The next instant, her rage returned. He had been waiting there, all this time, watching her, hidden, exulting and laughing over her. He had seen her looking up and down the streets, for long minutes, and only heaven knew what he had been reading in her changing expressions. Humiliation turned her as white as snow, now. She wanted nothing in the world but the ability to move on proudly, not speaking, not acknowledging him. She made a tremendous effort, and her legs obeyed her, carrying her on. Her breast felt tight and full of intolerable pain.

She heard him slap the reins on the horse's back, heard the wheels following her. The hack was abreast of her. Out of the corner of her stony eye she saw Franz leaning out.

"I shall follow you, you know, until you get in," he said, laughing.

She walked on, more and more rapidly. She would turn around the corner, and so come back to the Schmidt mansion, and then she would go in, still without speaking. The wheels and the hoofs followed her. It was intolerably ridiculous and mortifying. Franz was humming casually. He began to whistle, softly. She hated him more than ever.

"A nice day for a walk," he remarked from his high seat.

She looked ahead, savagely.

"Do not be a fool," he said, relapsing into German. "You know I shall follow you. If you return to that house, I shall still follow you. You would not like a scene?"

This so infuriated her that she turned, words seething to her lips. But he was looking at her with such good humor, such deep laughter, that she could not speak. She could only gasp, her eyes green fires in her white face. She believed him. He would do anything. Resistance on her part would only increase her humiliation. The thought of his forced entry into that house, with the subsequent confusion and explanations, could not be endured.

"Leave me alone!" she cried, clenching her hands in her muff.

He appeared greatly surprised. "Did you not come out to meet me?" he asked, innocently raising his brows.

"No!" she cried again, very loudly.

He stared. Then he burst into laughter.

"You are a bad liar," he said, at last, through his laughter. He pushed his low black bowler far back on his head. She saw that he was very well dressed, in an obviously new checked coat and dark blue trousers. He, too, had dressed in his best, to meet her, as she had dressed in her best, to meet him. The same thought seemed to occur to him. He studied her appraisingly, still laughing a little.

"Very handsome," he remarked. "Too handsome to waste on the street."

He sprang down lightly from the buggy, and ceremoniously bowed to her, pressing his hat to his heart with an exaggerated gesture.

"Gnädige frau," he murmured, "will you honor me by accompanying me for a drive?"

She was still trembling with anger. And then, in spite of herself, she could not restrain her sudden laughter. "You are such a fool," she said. The first joy came back, the first gladness at the sight of him. She thought to herself that she was the fool, letting him see her humiliation. She ought to have ignored the fact that he had kept her waiting; she ought not to have let him see her wounded anger. This had given him the advantage.

I will put him in his place, once and for all, she thought, not stopping to analyze her relief at her own decision. She gave him her hand, trying to sustain the mood of his ridiculous and exaggerated deference. He raised the hand to his lips. At his touch on her hand, a flame ran up her arm to her heart, then to all her body, a shameful flame that made her pulses pound. Preoccupied with its strangeness, its terror, its wanton abandon, she allowed him to help her up the high step to the narrow seat. A mist floated before her eyes. It seemed to her that the universe had stopped in its whirling, and that she stood at its core, panting and disheveled.

He climbed up beside her, took up the reins. He began to whistle again, softly. They rolled down the street, not speaking. Irmgard sat as far from her cousin as she could, primly, staring straight ahead, only her eyes revealing the emotions that tormented and frenzied her. She felt the sun striking on her cheek, and wondered vaguely why it was so hot and burning. She could hear the pounding of her heart, and was afraid that he might hear it, too.

To fill in a silence that was fast becoming too much for her, she asked coolly: "And how is my aunt, and my uncle?"

"Well, but wondering why you have neglected them," he replied. He was looking pleasantly at the black rump of the horse.

"I did not neglect them," she said slowly. "But Mrs. Schmidt is an invalid, and needed me."

He made no comment. The silence was thicker than ever between them. It was like a darkness in which she fumbled for words frantically. But none would come. She knew he knew why she had not visited the flat on Mulberry Street. Again, mortification struck at her. She was a fool. She ought to have gone to her aunt, frequently, thus proving to Franz that he had no power to disturb her. All my actions, she thought angrily, have only raised his own self-conceit, his own belief that he has some power over me.

"I shall visit Aunt Emmi on my next Thursday," she said, aloud, in a muffled voice.

He was still silent. She dared not look at him directly, but she looked at his hands, strong square brutal hands, from which prolonged scrubbing could not entirely eliminate the stains of his work. After the first glance, she tried to look away, but could not. The hands fascinated her, hypnotized her. She was aware again of the renewed acceleration of her blood, and of an unfamiliar but terrible yearning. Her eyelids stung as though with brine, and now all the joy was gone, leaving behind it only a passionate sense of sorrow and desolation.

They drove through the almost deserted streets in a silence which was as intimate as the touch of hands on naked flesh. They drove like this for over half an hour, until they reached the outskirts of the small city. The houses became fewer and fewer, and the short winter day inclined slowly toward the twilight. The wind was brisker, more chilly. Then they were driving rapidly over a country road, the horse's hoofs beating a rhythmic pattern against the still, cold silence. Once they heard the wail of a distant train. The empty trees were crowding about them, filled with shrilling sparrows, and the sun fell wanly through the black branches in a fret-work of pale light.

Now, not a house could be seen, though here and there, on the horizon seen occasionally through the trunks of the trees, a wisp of smoke unfurled itself against the dim blue sky. Irmgard felt a freshening wind against her cheeks, a wind that told her that the false promise of the false spring was passing, and winter coming. Her desolation increased. The winter without hope and without joy. A weight, as of cold iron, lay in her breast. It was too heavy for shivering, too profound to be analyzed.

Then Franz spoke, softly: "You do not look happy, my cousin."

"I am very happy," she said, trying to make her voice formal, but it shook in spite of her. She felt his eyes upon her, thoughtful, considering eyes.

"If that is happiness, then I have never seen misery," he said.

Her cheeks colored at this intimacy, this insolence. She lifted her chin proudly, not answering.

"I have often seen that house," he said, reflectively. "A catacomb. And the people in it are probably corpses, to correspond."

Her sadness was momentarily forgotten in her indignation. She turned to him fully. "That is not true. They are kind people, and very good to me."

"What!" he exclaimed cynically. "I have heard of them. An old daughter, and a crippled idiot son. It is the talk of the mills. And Schmidt's wife, they say, is a bed-ridden invalid, whom he never sees, probably with good reason."

It was not for a long time that she realized he was artfully drawing her out about the people in the mansion on Grove Street, and that his seemingly casual and indifferent questions were not to make conversation, but for a deep personal reason of his own. But today she mercifully did not know this, and only felt her indignation increasing.

"Miss Ernestime is not old. She seems very young, and sweet, and pretty. Her mother's invalidism has kept her confined a great deal, but things are becoming better. There is to be a party soon, and everyone is very happy. And Mr. Baldur is no idiot. It is true that he is a cripple, but he is a splendid gentleman. He plays beautifully, and paints. He has painted my portrait——"

She paused, for Franz's face was suddenly sharp and grim, his eyes boldly appraising as he stared at her.

"So," he said, slowly, in a hard voice, "the cripple is still a man, eh?"

Baldur's face suddenly flashed before Irmgard. She saw his blue eyes, so melancholy, so quiet, yet so alive, so full of what he dared not say to her. Again, sorrow struck at her, but not for herself. Franz saw the sadness about her mouth, the deep brooding tenderness in her eyes, a tenderness he had never suspected she could feel for anything. He could not understand the quick fury that seized him, the outrage which was like the result of a slap in the face. His hands tore brutally at the reins, the horse reared up. Irmgard was startled at this action, and looked at him.

"Your portrait!" he said, with ineffable contempt. "What will be next? Love-making? You, and that—that cripple?"

Irmgard could hardly believe she had heard these outrageous words. Her face took on such a blank expression that it was almost idiotic. Then, recovering herself, she cried out: "How dare you? Oh, how dare you!"

She thought he would laugh, that he would dismiss the subject with one of his airy, casual remarks and gestures. But he did not. He looked into her eyes, and his own were like slits of blue steel, and the contempt deepened on his face.

"You do not like it, eh? Well, I will tell you that I do not like the look of you, when I speak of him. I might say to you: 'How dare you?' And to him, also."

"You—you are contemptible!" she exclaimed, her cheeks bright red. Her breath came fast. "Take me back at once. If you do not turn about, I shall get out of this carriage at once, and walk home!"

He stared at her, and then, very slowly, the hard lines about his mouth relaxed, and his eyes began to smile.

"Forgive me," he said, his voice hypocritically contrite. "But I did not like the thought that my cousin might be involved with a cripple, even innocently. Perhaps it is the healthy German in me," he added, with an air of frankness. "You must forgive my candor. I was always candid."

"You were never candid in all your life!" she cried. "And I cannot forgive your unspeakable remarks about that poor gentleman." She was breathing fast. There was a disordered look about her, of mingled indignation and deep sorrow.

"I have asked your pardon," he reminded her tranquilly. "You are as hard as iron, Irmgard. And as ruthless. You see, I know all about you, too. But see, it is a pleasant day. Let us forget the words were ever spoken."

"I cannot forget," she said, and her voice broke. Nevertheless, she did not demand again that he turn the vehicle about, and take her home. He heard that break in her voice, and though he smiled deprecatingly, the fury still lurked in him, murderous and outraged.

"You are my cousin," he said gently. "You are alone in the world, a young female without protection except what we can give you. You must forgive me if I am so concerned with your welfare."

"You!" she said, scornfully, glancing at him with passionate disdain.

He laughed now, good-temperedly. "You do me an injustice," he said.

He looked about him. They were far out in the country. To the right, the bank of the road rose upward, steeply, rising to a small low hill. The hill was crowned by a country cemetery. Against that dim blue winter sky white crosses leaned in solitary silence, the spectral light glancing from pale granite slabs. Mingled with these mournful monuments were the skeletons of the winter trees. To the left of the road, the brown and silent countryside spread away to the shadowy purple distance. And over it all was that ghostly light of the winter, falling from the empty heavens. It might have been spring, but there was no sound of spring in the chill air, no awakening voices, no promise. It was the death of the year, the death of the earth, brown and sterile and done, held in a tomblike stillness, without echo.

Franz reined in the horse. Irmgard glanced about her. They were all alone, and not a house was visible. She looked up at the cemetery, and then down at the country to the left, so desolate, so abandoned. Franz had gotten out of the buggy, and was standing below her, extending his hand. She hesitated, then ignoring his hand, she lifted her long skirts and sprang out of the vehicle. Why had he brought her here, to this lonely and melancholy spot? But she was too proud, and still too angry, to ask him.

He said: "A little way down the road there is an inn, where we can have our supper. But the sun still shines a little, and there will be few days like this. I thought we might walk here for a while, and talk."

"I have nothing to say to you," she said, and knew at once that the words were childish.

She preceded him up the hill to the cemetery. At its rim was a white bench, drifted over with dead leaves. Franz swept the leaves away with his kerchief, and Irmgard sat down. He sat down beside her. He did not speak for a long time. They gazed over the country at their feet, in complete silence. Irmgard did not look at her cousin, but she was again hotly aware of his nearness, of his shoulder near her chin, so strong and hard. She had seen him in workclothes only, before, and they seemed more appropriate to her on this muscular body than in the new garments he was wearing now. The folded black cravat, so carefully arranged, was incongruous about that hard throat. He had taken off his black bowler, and it lay on his knees. She knew, without looking, that the silent wind was blowing through his yellow hair.

She was aware that he was watching her profile steadfastly and boldly. She feigned indifference, affecting to be absorbed in her contemplation of her surroundings. She knew, instantly, however, that he was moving closer to her, and that he was bending his head so that his breath was on her cheek.

"I have never had an opportunity to talk to you like this before," he was saying, in a quiet, intimate voice. "I have never asked you about your life in Germany. I knew about it only from what my mother told me."

"There is nothing to tell," she replied coldly, wishing with despair that she had the strength to move away from him, and struggling against the soft languor that was beginning to possess her.

"Nothing, Irmgard? But you must have had a hard life."

She was silent. She thought of the years on the little farm, and her father. She thought of the days of endless work and suffering and endurance, the frugal living, the hopeless months that went by, one by one, in a dark procession. But they had given her strength to endure all things. Life, she thought, could never really hurt her, never pierce through the wall of undesiring courage which she had raised stone by stone between her and its exigencies. She had lost, perhaps, the capacity for happiness or great ecstasy. But, perhaps, she had also lost the capacity to suffer.

"And your father," Franz was saying. "It must have been intolerable for you."

But her life with her father, she thought, had given her one thing: it had made her distrust all frenzy, all dark rapture, all vehemence and passion. She had seen to what despairing depths these things could hurl the human soul, and how futile they were, and how stupid. They had given her contempt and strong ridicule for them. Men like her father spent their lives in a wild dream, full of imagined glory and ecstasy. But at the end they were like blazing torches thrown, hissing, into a swamp, to sputter out impotently in the universal night. Men like her father were full of splendid and terrible hallucinations. They moved in a vision that never shone on land or sea. What good did they do? They were without reason, without thoughtfulness. They shone on dark hills, a will-of-the-wisp leading other men to death and ruin. She would not let herself think that they might be great bonfires, lighting the darkness, great living beacons dissipating the night. She had seen how her father had died, lonely and abandoned, derided and impotent. He had accomplished nothing. He had brought only sorrow and death to her mother, and had brought these things to himself. He had brought himself pain, years of torment which were the result of his years in prison.

Then she remembered the night he had died. There had been no one else there but herself. She had lit the solitary candle beside his bed, and had sat there, waiting, full of bitterness and sadness, yet resenting this emaciated man with the tortured face and the bright burning eyes. She had even felt a contempt for him, this man of flame and unreason. She had listened to his tormented breathing, his gasping for another breath, and then another. She had listened quietly, sitting beside him with folded hands, her young face cold and still. She knew he was dying. She felt no regret, no grief, but only a sense of waste.

All these years he had hardly noticed her in his frightful preoccupation with the rights of man and the glory shimmering on the horizon of the future. She was only a creature that tended the farm, and cooked the poor meals, and milked the cows and fed the few chickens. She was not his daughter, his flesh, to him. She was a shadow in the background, serving him, often rubbing his swollen limbs at night. He had not had the time, in his dreams, to think of her kindly, or to speak to her.

Tonight, he knew he was dying. For the first time, he was aware of his daughter. He looked at her near his bed, the light throwing dim shadows on her young and quiet face. This, then, was all he had to leave to the world, this woman, so cold and grave and indifferent. Nothing else, but this woman. All his manuscripts had been burned long ago. What he had written lately was nothing, only echoes. Only the dream had remained, the dream of peace and justice, of enlightenment and serenity, of a world of one brotherhood and one joy and one hope and one love. But with him, his dream would die. His old companions were either dead, or had become fat, or had long disappeared. If he had had a son, he might have handed the gilded manuscript on to him. But he had only this daughter.

The pangs of agony and death were nothing now compared with this thought. If the dream should lie moldering in his grave, then he had lived for nothing. He forced his eyes to see her more clearly; he forced himself not to die yet. Yet he was filled with the black coldness of an infinite despair.

"Liebchen," he croaked, in his dying voice.

He had never spoken this word to her before, and she was shatteringly touched, so touched that she began to weep, this young thing who had never known love or tenderness.

"Do not weep," he had whispered, painfully, and he had reached out and placed his cooling and skeleton-like hand on hers. "But listen to me, my child. I have so little time. I have not been a father to you. But there was no time!" he cried, brokenly. "Never time for the things I must do—never time enough."

She had felt, then, the first sorrow for him, the first heart-breaking knowledge of what his impotence had meant to him.

"Listen to me," he had panted. And he lifted his hand and pointed to the rows and rows of books which lined one side of the poor room. "There is everything I have believed, of goodness and peace and justice. They are all I have to leave you. Read them, many, many times, over and over. You are only a maiden. But you will have children. You will tell them of these things, my grandchildren." He looked at her piercingly, and for the last time the flame leapt upward into his dying eyes. "You will go to America. My grandchildren will be born there. In America, there is still hope for the world."

"I will go to America," she promised him, and was frightened. America! She had no desire to go to America. She had not thought of it before.

He had died soon after that. He had kissed her, she remembered, kissed her with lips like dry dead leaves. But to the last he had looked at her, with the flame in his eyes.

As she sat now beside Franz she suddenly laughed, with such bitterness that he became alert and deeply interested.

"Why do you laugh?" he asked.

"I am thinking of my father," she said.

He disliked her cold and acrid smile. "Why should he make you laugh?"

But she did not answer him. Then, finally, she said: "He

believed in so many foolish things. He was entirely without reason. He never knew reality."

Franz studied her keenly. Then he began to smile with contempt, thinking of the uncle he remembered from his childhood.

Franz said: "You are still young, Irmgard. You must forget your father. There is all your life before you. If you would only let yourself live, and enjoy living."

He added: "You are so stolid. There is no passion in you."

She turned fully to him now, smiling bitterly. "You know so many things which are not so. I am not passive, nor stolid, not dead. I could love life, and all the things of life with great zest. But because I see no opportunity for having any of this, I will not allow myself to groan over them, and be miserable."

He knew then that she had never spoken so to any one else in the world, had never revealed herself so, and he was taken aback with a kind of shame. She was so honest, so young. He had been invading her privacy only because of a perverse curiosity, and she had shown him herself, without reticence or duplicity.

"There is opportunity here for everything," he said, with lameness, still preoccupied with his sense of shame.

"Do you believe that—you?" she asked, looking at him with her cold green eyes which saw everything.

He laughed, as a shield against those eyes.

"With reservations. Opportunity is here for any man strong enough to take it. The weak, of course, never see opportunity."

"And you think you are strong enough to take it?"

Now he could speak with frankness. "Yes, I believe I am strong enough. I am making the effort." He clasped one knee with his hands, and looked away from her over the countryside. His whole big strong body expressed his inexorable confidence in himself. "I have no delusions about my capacities. I am intelligent. I understand men and life. I never waste time in any regrets because I am no genius. But I know how to get things from other men. I know how to exploit them for my own advantage. You think that wrong?" he asked, turning with a smile to her.

She was silent. He lit his pipe and smoked it tranquilly. He was thinking of many things, the things he had set in motion. He smiled to himself.

"What is it you want," she asked, after a little, with curiosity.

"Money. Not just a little, not just enough to be safe. That is the aspiration of small men, men who are contented with the leavings. I want millions. I want to make myself too strong for any other man to attack me successfully——"

She interrupted him, with a laugh of sheer gloating and triumph: "You are afraid!"

He glared at her, suddenly flushing.

"You are afraid of life!" she cried again, with a sort of amazement at her discovery, and a deep malice. "I would never have believed it, if you hadn't told me yourself!"

He could not endure her smiling contempt, her triumph. Yet he knew that she had spoken the truth. He hated her for this, hated her for revealing him to himself, to his own ignominy. Yet, in some obscure way, he knew that she disliked him less for this discovery, and even felt some compassion for him. It was the knowledge of this compassion which infuriated him. He could have struck her.

"It is more than that, but you would not know it," he said, through tight pale lips.

She looked at him for a long time. Then she said quietly: "Yes, I see there is more, more than the fear. There is hatred of all other men."

He could smile now. "Perhaps. What is there in other men to love? They are all beasts in the jungle. They are all animated by only one desire, to tear and rend other men and devour their bodies. Those who say this is not true are hypocrites. The first and only law of life is to devour or be devoured. This is not a new theory, invented by me. Clever men have realized this long before.

"I won't be devoured. To survive, I must devour. I shall do this."

"And take pleasure in the devouring," said Irmgard, with renewed contempt.

"It is the world's greatest pleasure," he assured her.

"And you think money will make you entirely safe, Franz? Nothing will reach you through it?"

"Nothing." There was so much confidence in his voice that she felt desolate again, and utterly alone. Her father had thought dreams would make him and the world safe. And she had been alone, alone like this.

"One must be realistic," Franz was saying. He laughed a little. "The old men of the Bible were realists, not dreamers. One of them said: 'He that is despised and hath a servant, is better than he that honoureth himself, and lacketh bread.' And another said: 'Wealth maketh many friends; but the poor is separated from his neighbor.' And how wise was the old man who said: 'All the brethren of the poor do hate him: how much more do his friends go far from him? He pursueth them with words, yet they are wanting to him.' And last, but certainly not least, to me: 'The rich man's wealth is his strong city——.' "

He spoke freely, not slowly, feeling his way, as he did with others. With this girl he could be himself, knowing that even if she despised him, she also understood him. When with her, it was like taking off clothes that bound, shoes that pinched, belts that inhibited. It was an unmasking, after which he was revealed, breathing easily. Even he could not completely understand why he felt so relieved. He had thought himself above the petty desires of other men, and the desire for confession and unburdening. He had not thought himself cramped and muzzled. But the ease that followed his frankness with his cousin, was the ease that followed the relaxing of muscles too tired, too tense, and too cramped. Even the unscrupulous, it seemed, needed a father confessor.

"But all this," said Irmgard, "comes to nothing in the end but that you are afraid."

He was not angry, now, but annoyed, though he flushed. "How you dwell on fear! But perhaps you are right. We all live in fear of something, and because we fear it, we hate it. Who is there without fear?"

Irmgard was about to say: "No one." But then she remembered her father. He had never been afraid! The thought was like a dazzling light suddenly come into a dark room. He had never been afraid. In all her life, she had known no other man who had never feared anything. He had suffered and endured all things, for a thing which was greater than himself. Men feared, for the things they wanted were only of their own stature, and they knew how readily they could be assailed and lost. But Emil Hoeller had loved and served something greater and stronger than himself, something he believed imperishable, and so he had been freed of all fear. Perfect love still overcame all things, but this love was not self-love, and it still cast out fear.

"I never understood my father before," she said, almost inaudibly.

"He was an idealist, and all idealists are fools," said Franz.

But Irmgard was lost in rapt contemplation of her father. Her eyes still looked at the cold and barren country, but she was seeing the vision her father had seen. It dazzled and stupefied her, filled her with awe and humility, and a fragile joy, touching and too beautiful for endurance. She did not believe the vision, but she saw it. He had believed, and though he had died for it, he had died, believing. How lovely to believe in that vision! Nothing, then, which life and circumstance might do, could create a lasting pain, a lasting despair, a lasting sorrow. It had been said that a people without vision must perish. But a man with a vision lived forever. His life was like a mirror which caught the sun and reflected it in the darkest and most hidden places, even into prison houses, even into the pits of hell.

Tears filled the girl's eyes, and they were tears for herself because she had no such vision. She looked at Franz, and it seemed to her that he was all barrenness, all sterility, all emptiness. She said as she had said that night a long time ago:

"You are empty."

It seemed to her a sad and frightful thing, this emptiness. She felt its own echoes in herself.

He stared at her young face, so pale and sorrowful. He looked at her lips and eyes. And he thought to himself: There is nobody in the world for me, but this girl. No matter what happens, she must belong to me. His expression became so gentle then, so kind, that she was startled and unbearably touched.

"Do not say such things to me, Irmgard," he said.

He did not touch her, but she felt as though he had put his arms about her. Her mouth trembled. She smiled a little, and again was inundated with joy.

"My father wanted me to come to America," she said, speaking automatically to hide her thoughts.

"He thought you might find his dream here?" asked Franz, and though his voice was cynical, it was still gentle. "It is good he never came here, himself. America is green fruit rotting on the bough before it ripens. It was born yesterday; it is dying today. Most nations pass from barbarism to civilization and maturity, evolving an art and a vision. But America is passing from barbarism into another kind of barbarism, like an ape dressing in men's clothes." He added: "It has no civilization, no art and no vision."

"If you think this, why do you stay here?" She was obscurely wounded and angry for her father's sake, for her father who had believed in the vision that might come true in America. She felt that in some way that dead face had been trampled upon by rude boots.

"Because America has what I want: the opportunity for strong men to attain anything they are strong enough to attain. It is the biggest jungle that the world has ever known."

"And you think you are strong?"

She stood up, now. The memory of her father's face was like a spear in her side.

"Yes," he said, quietly, standing beside her. "I am strong."

They went down the hill again. Soon they were driving down the road in a sudden twilight that was blue and cold, and infinitely mournful.

There is no springtime here, Emmi had said. There is no springtime in this land.

But Emil Hoeller had believed there was a springtime in America.

CHAPTER 24

THEY DROVE along again, in renewed silence. Now the twilight had come, and the sky became a boiling mass of gray clouds, streaked with writhing black whips. The wind, held in check during the day by the sun, roared back upon the earth with a thousand dark voices. Once Franz got out of the livery hack to put up the side curtains. Though the rain had not yet come, the air was full of its scent. Within a few minutes it became very cold, so that Irmgard's feet began to ache.

"Do you not think we ought to turn back?" she asked, peering out into the darkness through the cracked ising-glass window in the curtain.

"No. We have only half a mile to go to the inn," he answered.

Because of the wind they could not even hear the horse, trotting anxiously in the sudden night. They could hear only that wind, increasing in strength. Then the rain came, loud, rattling, thundering on the roof of the buggy. The road had become rutty, and the light flimsy vehicle began to sway. Irmgard was thrown repeatedly upon Franz's shoulder, and at each impact a wave of mingled repulsion, terror and ecstasy rolled over her. She could not see him, but she heard his breath in the tiny cave of their rolling refuge. Once she thought: I would not care if this lasted forever. And was overcome with renewed terror and wondering disgust at herself. She could not understand the peace that came to her between the waves of the terror and amazement. Their bodies made a slight warmth in the darkness. Finally, because of the increased swaying of the hack, Franz put his arm about her. Her body stiffened momentarily, then relaxed. She closed her eyes, listening to the wind and rain outside, and Franz's quiet breathing.

A light flickered now in the distance. They arrived at the inn. Irmgard was surprised to see that the earth was running with livid water. The trees that surrounded the inn bent almost double before the gale. It stopped the girl's breath, and she was obliged to clutch her skirts and her bonnet. Her hair was torn loose about her face, which immediately became drenched with rain. Laughing, they ran together to the inn, after hitching the cowering horse.

The inn was a small and shabby place, gritty and untidy. Irmgard, who had vaguely expected some replica of a clean, bright, warm German tavern, was much depressed. It was hardly more than an enlarged shack, and was used mostly by commercial travellers between Nazareth and Windsor. It was flimsily built of wood, which was left unfinished within, and roughly painted. Irmgard saw a large bar, very dirty, an open fire, and a few tables covered with turkey-red cloth. She had a glimpse of an impoverished "parlor" beyond, filled with wooden rocking chairs, two leather sofas and a tinny piano. One glass lamp burned dismally on a distant table, showing the distempered walls and the cold fireplace filled with ostrich feathers.

She wanted nothing so much as to leave. But the proprietor, a surprised big fat man in his shirt-sleeves and wearing an apron, came forward and led them to a table. He gaped frankly at Irmgard, and rubbed his dirty hands on his apron. He informed Franz that he had nothing to offer in the way of supper but some country ham, some eggs, coffee and bread. "I really do not want anything," said Irmgard, hurriedly. But Franz ignored her, and ordered.

No one else was in the tavern, apparently, but themselves. The dirty, unwashed and uncurtained windows ran with cataracts of water. Irmgard removed her bonnet and ruefully contemplated the spotted velvet. She smoothed her hair. Franz sat near her, and he smiled at her dismay.

"A nasty place," he said, but with no note of apology. "But it was recommended to me. I ought to have known better."

The proprietor affably brought them some beer. He spoke to them both, but stared insolently at Irmgard. "Bad night. Nobody with sense travelling much. Goin' to Windsor?"

"No," said Franz, shortly. The man wandered away. They sipped their beer. It was very bad, and with wry faces, they put down the glasses.

"Only in Germany have they the secret of making beer," said Franz.

For some obscure reason, his tone annoyed Irmgard. But she pressed her lips together. They were always quarrelling, it seemed. She lifted her eyes and looked at him, and their glances met and held. Irmgard laughed a little, to cover her sudden confusion.

"I have never been in an American inn before," she said.

Her face, recovering from the cold outside, was very flushed. In the dim mingling of lamplight and firelight, her eyes glittered with sparkling green lights. Franz smiled. "You have missed nothing," he said, somewhat absently.

Irmgard, drawing her eyes from his with an effort, looked about the room and shivered a little. The air was dusty and stagnant, and in spite of the fire, very cold. It was laden with the mingled odors of beer, kerosene and frying fat. She felt slightly sick.

"Americans have not learned to live," said Franz.

"They will, in time," she replied.

"No, I think not. There is something missing in them. What the Germans would call a 'soul.' Perhaps they will become more garish, more elaborate, more luxurious, but they still will not have a soul. I have felt it. I know. Perhaps it is because so many millions of the soulless and the rootless have come to America, carrying their empty drabness with them. They are a race of plebeians, or perhaps it would be best to say that they are a mingling of all plebeian races."

"Including, then, we Germans," said Irmgard, tartly. "Do not forget there are many, many thousands of us here, too."

Franz smiled. "Perhaps there is something in America which kills the souls of men, and makes them either cattle or machines."

"You ought, indeed, to go back to the Fatherland, then," said Irmgard, with increasing tartness. "A man of your sensibilities should not stay in America."

The proprietor, hearing a foreign tongue, was disappointed. This couple was so unusual, so handsome, so well-dressed, that he had thought them a grand lady and gentleman. Now, it appeared, they were only "foreigners." He brought the ham and eggs to them with considerable disgruntled condescension, and said: "Guess you better pay now."

Franz lifted his light blue eyes and held the man as one transfixed.

"I shall pay when I am ready," he said, quietly.

"Rules," muttered the man, disconcerted, but angered.

"I shall pay when I am ready," repeated Franz. They stared at each other in a momentary silence, and then the man, quailed by the other's eyes, wandered away, muttering. He barricaded himself behind his bar, and looked at Irmgard with knowing insolence. Damn' foreigners! America should get shut of them. If he had his way he'd pile them all on boats and ship 'em all back where they belonged. It was gettin' so a decent American got shoved around too much, in his own country. Uppity, they was, the swine.

The ham was salty, the eggs hard-rimmed, smelling of burned grease. Irmgard tried to eat, but the food was insufferable. She drank a little of the black coffee, and gave it up. Franz sampled the food, frowning. "They spoil the simplest things," he muttered. He struck his knife loudly on his plate, and the proprietor, after a prolonged wait, sauntered to the table. "What's the matter?" he demanded belligerently, but avoiding Franz's eyes.

"This food—it is rotten," Franz replied. "Have you nothing better?"

"What's the matter with it?"

"It's rotten, I said. The lady cannot eat it. If you have nothing better, bring us some milk and some bread and butter."

"Choicy, ain't you?" muttered the man. "Good American food not nice enough for you?"

"No, it is not," said Franz, coolly. He put his hands on the table, as if to rise with one spring. The man saw the gesture, and hastily carried the plates away.

"You are brutal," remarked Irmgard.

"I know when to be brutal, and when to be amiable," replied Franz, laughing. "I believe that is the secret of success. Am I not remarkable? I have discovered a fine formula."

"If he put us out, your formula would be no good." But she smiled in return.

"But instead, he will bring us something fit to eat. Perhaps."

He lit his pipe while they waited for the bread and milk. The fire flickered and snarled. The lanterns which hung from the wooden ceiling swayed in a draft of wind. The storm outside was increasing in violence. The dismal chill of the place sank deeper into Irmgard's bones, but she felt this only abstractedly, for Franz sat near her. A light fever was running through her, like an intoxication.

"If there were enough of us Germans in America, we might be able to accomplish something, bring some solidity and richness to American life," said Franz, contemplatively. "We might bring some gemütlichkeit."

Irmgard stared at him with sudden steadfastness, and it seemed to her that she saw him so clearly that it was not to be borne.

"But you care nothing for gemütlichkeit, Franz," she said quietly. "You are an alien to it. You have no real place, either in America or Germany. You are a stranger in both countries." Her eyes widened with a kind of surprised discovery.

"An alien everywhere. And I feel that there are many men like you, who have no country anywhere in the world. It is all just your hunting ground. And—and I feel you are a danger to the people wherever you live."

She added, almost to herself: "It is not a matter of race. Men like you have no race."

She thought he would be angry, with that quick brutal anger of his. But instead, he began to smile with complete enjoyment, as though she had said something both remarkably funny and remarkably true.

He leaned towards her, and put his hand over her cold fingers.

"I like you, my cousin. That is because you know all about me. It is such a relief not having to be a hypocrite."

She remembered something Baldur had said, about hating brutes and hypocrites.

"You are both a brute and a hypocrite!" she cried, involuntarily. She tried to draw away her hand, but he held it tightly. He still smiled. She was lost in the blue smiling blaze of his eyes, in which she saw something both evil and implacable.

"But you have no desire to change me?"

"None." She finally wrenched her hand away. Her fingers stung.

He leaned back contentedly in his chair, smoking, still smiling. "That is such a relief. You are not like my mother, who tries to change everyone. But you are no Prussian, such as she is."

The proprietor brought some thick coarse bread and a pitcher of milk, which he thumped down before them. He was now so angry that he would have liked a fight. He saw Irmgard's perturbaton, and shot a sidelong glance at Franz. "Anythin' wrong, lady?" he asked.

"There is nothing wrong. Go away at once," said Franz, sharply, again putting his hands on the table, and half rising.

"Say, who you think you're talkin' to?"

"You. Get away."

"Franz!" protested Irmgard.

But the two men's eyes were locked again. It was the proprietor who finally looked away. He lumbered back to his bar. "God damn' bohunk!" he said, aloud.

Having conquered him, Franz ignored him. He returned his attention to Irmgard. She was white with indignation. He poured a glass of milk for her, and then for himself. He spoke, tranquilly: "No, you are not like my mother. You are a realist. Knowing all about me, you still like me."

Irmgard was silent. She drank her milk, but her sickness increased.

They ate without speaking for a few minutes, under the glare of the proprietor. Then Franz said reflectively: "Yes, we Germans might do a lot for America. But there is one difficulty. Bismarck knew it when asked what was the most important political fact in the world today. He said: 'America speaks English.' "

An unaccountable tiredness was stealing over Irmgard. All at once she cared for nothing. Her depression was like dust in her mouth and a weight on her heart. She said mechanically: "That may be so. But Americans are not a race. They are only a people. Perhaps in that there is enormous hope for the future."

She stood up. "Shall we go, now?"

They could hear the thundering of the storm, which was increasing. Franz walked calmly to the bar, and laid down a bill. "Ninety-five cents," said the proprietor.

"For what? Two glasses of milk and a slice of bread? Not more than twenty-five cents. You owe me seventy-five."

"You had ham and eggs! And coffee, too!" shouted the proprietor.

"We couldn't eat that hog-swill, and you know it," said Franz, softly. He drummed on the bar with his fingers, and looked at the man. "Seventy-five cents, please."

Irmgard stood near the door, overcome with mortification and uneasiness. She saw the proprietor reach under the bar for something, and cried out. Franz's hand shot out, fastened itself about the man's wrist, wrenched it upwards. He was holding a short thick club. He tore the club from the man's hand and flung it far across the room. Then he twisted the other's hand savagely. "Seventy-five cents," he repeated, still softly.

The man was completely cowed, now. He had felt that great and unexpected strength. He had seen the capacity for murder in Franz's eyes. He whimpered, rubbed his sprained wrist. He flung seventy-five cents upon the bar. Franz picked it up amiably, and said: "Good night."

He went to the door and took Irmgard's rigid arm. He opened the door, and they stepped out onto the flat unsheltered porch. The wind and rain tore at them, howling. The light of the tavern shone out fitfully onto the river-like earth. Then Franz cursed aloud. The horse and hack had gone. He ran down into the mud and the water, stumbling, and tried to see up the black and swimming road. The horse, terrified, had broken loose from the hitching post, and was no doubt miles away, heading for the stables.

Franz ran back to the porch, and thrust Irmgard back into the tavern. He spoke in a low rapid voice near the door: "The horse has gone."

Irmgard cried out again. Franz stood near her, biting his lip. "We cannot walk through that storm. We should lose our way. There is a flood outside. It is ten miles to town."

"What's the matter?" asked the proprietor from behind his bar, grinning evilly. He had seen the horse and buggy tear loose not ten minutes before, when he had glanced through the window.

Franz looked at him thoughtfully. He had nothing to gain, now, by being brutal and arrogant. He walked to the bar. "Have you a horse and buggy to lend us?" he asked.

"Nary a one," gloated the man. "I ain't a rich feller. Can't get rich on twenty-five cents."

Franz clenched his fists, but spoke quietly: "My buggy has gone. The horse got away. Is there any way we can get back to town?"

"Well, sir, the milk carts go by here at five in the morning," said the proprietor, happily. He wiped the bar with a rag, with meticulous care.

Franz paused. He looked at Irmgard, pale and shivering near the door.

"I must go home, tonight," she said, through quivering lips.

The proprietor glanced airily through the window. "Beginnin' to sleet, too," he said, thoughtfully. "Folks out on a night like this, walking ten miles knee-deep in water and mud, 'ud come down with lung fever, likely as not." He added: "If they didn't end up in Blindman's Creek, a piece up the road, or get lost in the fields." He sighed, deeply. "A lady'd never make it—ten miles to town. Freeze to death. It'll be snowin' hard in an hour."

Franz was silent. He drummed on the bar. The back of his neck slowly turned red. Then he looked thoughtfully at the proprietor, who grinned.

"Five dollars for the night, for the two of you. Paid in advance," he said. "Got two nice rooms, connecting, upstairs. Milk carts go by at five in the mornin'."

Franz glanced at the sign over the bar. "Accommodations—one dollar per night," it read. The proprietor saw the glance, and grinned again.

"Five dollars to you," he exulted, wiping the bar again. "I'll throw in breakfast, free. Cheap at the price," and he winked.

Franz knew when he was beaten. He laughed a little, and turned back to Irmgard, who was shivering violently, pressed against the door. He felt some regret for her. She watched him approach, and her eyes widened, and she pressed still closer to the door.

"You see how it is, Irmgard," he said gently. "We cannot go out. We must remain here till morning."

"That is impossible!" she exclaimed, passionately. "I must go home! I promised. If you do not come with me, I shall go alone."

"Do not be a fool," he said, reasonably. "You will never reach town. It is ten miles, and it is beginning to snow. You do not even know the way."

"I cannot stay here," she said. Her lips were as white as her face. But she looked steadfastly at Franz.

He shrugged. "Well, I am not such a fool as to go with you. I never cared for gallantry. If you must go, you must go. I shall stay here till morning."

Irmgard wrenched open the door. She looked out at the wild black night. In the light of the lamps, she saw the new swirling flakes of snow, and felt the wind lash her with whips of iron. She closed the door again, whiter than ever.

Franz turned to the proprietor. "All right, then. Show us the rooms."

"Five dollars, in advance," said the man, smiling sweetly.

Franz laid five dollars on the bar, and the man, with great amiability, pocketed it, and came from behind the bar, warily keeping a distance between himself and the other. "If the lady and gentleman will follow me——"

He led them up a bare steep flight of stairs, ricketty and dark, carrying a lantern before them. Irmgard, holding up her skirts, ignored Franz's offered hand. They followed the proprietor down a narrow black hall, from the distempered walls of which strips of paper were peeling. It was as cold as the grave here. The proprietor flung open a door, and they entered a bitterly chill chamber, dank and dusty. Irmgard saw a white iron bed, a commode, a chair, and a strip of ragged carpet. There was also an empty fireplace, filled with dead white ashes. He opened a door off this room and revealed a smaller chamber, without a fireplace, and as poorly furnished as the larger room.

"Lovely rooms," said the proprietor, rubbing his hands. "I call this the bridal suite."

"I call it a pig-pen," said Franz. "Can't we have a fire here?"

"Of course, of course! But that will cost you a dollar extra."

For one moment, the frightened girl thought Franz would leap on the other man. But he evidently thought better of it. He produced another dollar.

"I do not need a fire!" cried the girl, miserably.

"But I do." Franz's voice was quiet and deadly. "I am cold to the heart."

"Nothin' like a fire for cheeriness on a night like this," said the proprietor, picking up the coal scuttle. "I'll have a fire for the lady in a jiffy."

He scurried out of the room. "Schweinkopf," said Franz, reflectively, but without rancor. He began to laugh, almost with appreciation. He turned to Irmgard, who was standing rigidly in the center of the room. The lantern, placed on the table, showed her despairing face.

"What shall I tell Mrs. Schmidt tomorrow?" she asked, wretchedly. "How can I ever face any one again, after spending the night here, with you, alone?"

"You are afraid you are being compromised?" he said, amused. "No one need know. Tell her you spent the night with your aunt. It is a wild night. She will understand that you could not return."

"Lies come so easily to you," she said, bitterly.

He shrugged, with impatience. "Do not be a fool."

The man returned with fuel for the fire. Franz sat on the bed, but Irmgard would not sit down. She stood, tall and rigid, her hands in her muff, her bonnet still on her head. They watched him make the fire. Soon it was spluttering and burning. The proprietor lit the oil lamp near the bed, lifted his lantern. He saluted Franz derisively. "Happy dreams," he said, with a lecherous wink. And went out, closing the door behind him, giving Irmgard a last hungry look.

Franz stood up. "I do not trust the pig." He locked the door. He turned to the girl. "Let me take off your jacket. And remove your hat. You might as well be comfortable, now that we are staying."

She resisted him for an instant, then hopelessly let him remove her damp jacket. She took off her bonnet. Her face was young and distraught between its bands of pale yellow hair. She wrung her hands.

"This is very terrible. I shall never be able to face any one again—" She looked at him despairingly. "What will your mother say?"

"Nothing," he answered, tranquilly. "I am often away at night."

She stared at him, then suddenly flushed a dark hot red, with mingled shame and embarrassment. He returned her stare with a bland expression, and she dropped her eyes. She sat down stiffly in the chair near the fire. He saw that she was trembling a little. He went into the next room and brought out a chair for himself, and sat near her. She was amazed to hear him begin to laugh.

"That rascal! But he had me. I admire him for that, anyway."

"It is not amusing," she said, with anger. She looked at the sagging bed, and shuddered. "Nothing will induce me to lie on—that. I shall sit here until morning."

Franz glanced idly at his watch. "It is only eight o'clock. You will be very uncomfortable in that chair all night. You can lie on top of the bed, and I will cover you with my coat, if, as you suspect, the bed is dirty."

She was suddenly touched at this generosity. "But what will you do, Franz? I, at least, have a fire in here, but your room will be very cold."

"I am not so fastidious as you, child." He looked at her, his blue eyes smiling. "But if you feel charitable, I will lie down before this fire, and sleep."

"That is impossible," she said, coloring again.

"You women," he said, with affectionate derision. "You must be proper, even if no one sees you. How will it be compromising you more for me to sleep before your fire than to sleep in a connecting room?"

She was silent. She felt foolish. But her heart had begun to beat with sickening strength and rapidity. All at once she could not endure his nearness, in this silent mean room, with the storm shrieking and thundering outside. She knew he was watching her. She felt his eyes on her profile, and she knew those eyes had become, in an instant, the eyes of a ferocious and hungry enemy, still lurking in ambush, but waiting. She bent her head. The fire warmed her feet, and the heat of it seemed to rise through all her flesh. Terror began to drum in her pulses. She clenched her hands so tightly that the nails wounded her palms.

She felt him draw closer to her. "I may sleep before the fire?" he asked, very softly.

She shrank away. "Yes. Of course."

Her terror rose fiercely. She tried to calm it. This was not a strange man, locked alone with her in a desolate room. It was her cousin, Franz. Almost her brother. His mother and hers had been sisters. He was almost her brother! She was a fool. She was making a small matter a thing of importance.

She forced a smile to her stiff lips. She turned her head and looked at him. And then she saw this was not her cousin, almost her brother. It was a stranger, rapacious, congested of face, red and savage of eye. He did not touch her. But he looked at her, and it was this look, intent, predatory, lustful and implacable, which fired her terror to new heights.

I must talk. I must talk, constantly, she thought with frantic fear. A long slow trembling ran over her entire body.

"It will be dreadful if Mrs. Schmidt sends the carriage after me," she said, and her voice was muffled.

"Is she likely to do that? Are you not entitled to the night, also?"

His voice was calm. She did not look at him again. She must have imagined that look, she thought. If it had really existed, his voice could not have been so calm, almost so indifferent.

She tried to reply as indifferently: "She knew I was anxious to return." Then, full realization came to her, and she exclaimed: "If she sent the carriage after me, I can never return to that house! And your mother—! She will know we are together!"

"Not necessarily," reasoned Franz. "I did not tell her I was to see you. If the carriage came for you, no doubt she will be worried. Have you made no friends? Can you not say you stayed with them for the night?"

"No, I have no friends." She wrung her hands. "This is so dreadful."

"Then, we must hope that the carriage was not sent. I hardly think it would be. Mrs. Schmidt thought you were going to my mother."

She tried to fix her mind on that hope. But she could not. The sense of his nearness was like a devouring fire. Her muscles were tense, with the resistance to that fire. She saw his knees, and his strong hands on them, and had to close her eyes against the shameful pang which seemed to open in her heart like a great rose of desire. She fought against it. Her limbs relaxed, and quivered.

She knew he had lit his pipe, for she smelled the smoke. He was leaning forward now, staring thoughtfully at the fire. He appeared to be preoccupied with new thoughts, and she drew an audible breath that was almost a sigh of passionate relief.

She said, faintly: "And how are you doing at the mills, Franz?"

He glanced at her with a surprised smile. "I was just thinking of them, Irmgard. I was thinking of tomorrow. For tomorrow I shall become assistant to the superintendent." Now his smile was inward, exultant.

"Is it so?" she exclaimed. "That is good, for you, and very flattering."

"But not enough," he replied. "Not half enough. I have many more plans." He paused. "Have you mentioned to Herr Schmidt that you have a cousin in his mills?"

"No," she said, surprised. "I have talked little with him. It had not occurred to me."

He pressed the smouldering tobacco in his pipe with his thumb. He said, not looking at her: "Then, you will please me by never telling him. Not that it is important, but sometimes it is not liked, for relatives to be employed so."

In her innocence, she did not suspect the real reason for his request.

"I shall say nothing," she said.

Franz got up to poke the fire. The red light shot up, vividly. She saw his face, strong, brutal yet full of vitality and power, and again terror took hold of her with wrenching hands. And yet, there was something intoxicating in that terror, something which made her nerves throb, something which made a frightful roaring in her ears.

He sat down again. He did not look at her. He spoke casually:

"And the daughter—Fraülein Schmidt. She is her father's favorite?"

"I believe she is all he loves on earth," she said simply. All at once, she felt embarrassed. "I do not like to speak of my employers. I feel it is disloyal, and disrespectful. Do we need to speak of them?"

He answered with an impersonal and disarming smile, tinged with affection:

"I wished only to know if the situation was a happy one for you."

She looked at him directly, the terror waning. "I do not believe you," she said, quietly. "Those words are hypocritical."

He laughed, but with assumed surprise. "What a cynic you are, Irmgard! You believe nothing but evil of me."

"What else is there to believe?" she said, almost inaudibly, and with sadness.

There was a silence. She bent her head and gazed at the fire, and he studied her profile, his face wrinkling with his thoughts. He said at last: "I am not evil. I am not good. I am only natural. Why do you not believe that of me? Why do you not realize that you and I are alike, beyond good or evil?"

She did not answer. The slow long rigor was creeping over her limbs again. He studied his pipe intently, turning it about in his fingers.

"Shall I tell you about myself, Irmgard? When I was a child I heard nothing but noble sentiments. If I wished to give an unscrupulous ruler a theory for building a race of unscrupulous machine-men, men without mercy or gentleness, I would tell him to allow children to hear nothing but lofty and noble sentiments all through their childhood. And then

I would tell him to let these children see the world as it is. That would be all.

"My mother and father were all nobility, and all foolishness. What they said came into violent conflict with the world as I began to see it. Then I knew they were fools. I was assaulted, defenseless, on all sides by a savage reality. I had no shield against it. I began to hate my parents, for having made me so vulnerable. I began to see that they ought to have armed me with adequate weapons against other men. They did not. I was full of wounds. I had to grow an armor, quickly, or I might have been utterly destroyed. I grew the armor. If it grew too thick and heavy, it was their fault, not mine.

"It is said that when a lobster is deprived of one of his claws he grows another, and this other is much heavier, much stronger and larger than the original. So, I grew claws. They were stronger and larger than they might have been if I had not had fools for parents."

Irmgard lifted her head and interrupted him with a scornful flash of her jade eyes. "It is so easy for one to blame one's parents! It is also very cowardly. Because one must learn to stand alone, and not to denounce others. I am afraid you are a coward. I knew it from the start. But why do you not have the courage to stand on your own feet, and accept your nature as your own responsibility? I believe you are a weakling because you could not adjust yourself, as others adjust themselves, to reality."

He looked at her without speaking. Green fire blazed from her pale face. Her disordered hair was bright gold in the firelight. A slow heavy flush rose over his own face, and it became secret. Then he said softly: "Why do you hate me, Irmgard?"

Angry words rushed to her lips, and then she could say nothing at all. Hate you? drummed her heart. Hate you?

He stood up, and began to walk slowly up and down the room. She could feel him pause occasionally, and look at her, but she did not turn.

"Why do you not let yourself be free, Irmgard? You have no emotion, and you will not think, because you are afraid. And you call me a coward! You are afraid of living, even though you have never lived."

She still gazed at the fire: "It is late," she said. "I think I shall lie down."

He stopped behind her. He put his palms to her cheeks. At his touch, renewed fire, roaring and trembling possessed her. She tried to struggle against them, but she could not move. But it seemed to her that her very flesh responded to his touch and ignited, as dry wood responds to flame. Tears filled her eyes, and something choked in her throat, as though all grief had concentrated in her, and all ecstasy. She felt him bend and press his mouth against her hair. A dreadful yearning came over her, and with it, a renewal of her grief.

"My dear, my darling," he whispered.

Now it appeared to her that all the strange things which possessed her suddenly roared up in her with passionate fury and overwhelming anger. "You do not mean that," she said, in a low breaking voice. "No one to you, ever, will be your dear or your darling, except yourself."

He sat down beside her, and took her hand, and she had to look at him. His expression was strange, and curiously gentle. He lifted her hand to his lips, and kissed it slowly and deeply. He looked into her eyes, still holding her hand.

"I loved you from the first moment I saw you. Believe me, Irmgard. It is true. If I never speak the truth again, I am speaking the truth now. Do not look away. Look at me, and you will see I am not lying."

She tried to gaze at him with a pale and scornful smile. But her smile faded. His blue eyes, always so hard and smiling, were gentle, piercing. He did not smile now. His expression was grave, almost sorrowful. He is acting, she thought. But she knew this was not true. Ecstasy flowed up and within her, like a golden tide. Truly, he loves me, she thought, with a kind of simple wonder. Truly, he loves me, as I love him.

The golden tide, flowing from her, seemed to stretch visibly before her eyes, spreading out over a dazzling landscape bright with joy and amazement. She sat and looked at it, overcome with astonishment, and with a joy so intense that it did not seem possible to bear it. Slow tears began to run over her white cheeks, and she smiled a little, like a child.

He held her hand tightly, and leaned towards her. "I thought I hated you, at first. You knew too much about me. And then I knew it was necessary for me to have some one who knew all about me. It is a strain, living alone, always acting. I do not need to act, with you. And I knew never in my life would I want anything as I want you."

Now, he will ask me to marry him, she thought, and a spasm of rapture ran through her. They would marry, and they would be together to the end of their lives, and they would understand each other. Nothing else would ever matter.

Her short dark life, the winter of her life, seemed to be breaking up all about her like black ice floes, and the living water welled and bubbled through them, bringing life and glory to the barrenness of her existence. She looked at him simply, the living water shining in her eyes, her lips parted and glowing.

And he knew what she was thinking, as he would always know. He bent his head, and ran his thumb gently over her hand. He could feel its trembling. For an instant shame filled him, and a strange kind of regret. Nothing would ever make him pause and look back, when he had once decided upon a thing. But he knew that the thing he could not look back upon lay behind him, and he would not look. For a few moments he did want to glance back. But the inexorable torrent of his nature soon overcame the weak desire, the human softening and yearning. He believed that a man could have all things, if he were strong enough.

Yet, he was stung with compassion for her. He had never felt compassion before, and he knew he might never feel it again. It was weakness, he told himself. If he were weak, now, he was ruined. A man could have all things, if he were not weak.

The design and pattern of his life was before him, laid out, waiting, by his will. Nothing must interfere with it, not even Irmgard. But he need not sacrifice his desire for her, even if she would not be allowed to interfere.

He took both her hands now, and kissed them fiercely, goaded by his compassion.

"I want nothing but you, my darling," he said, his lips against her fingers.

He has not said the words, but he means them, she thought. She had a swift vision of her aunt, who would be overcome with happiness. She smiled again, with childlike simplicity. She laughed a little, in a shaking voice.

"And I—I want nothing but you, Franz," she said, her words dropping into a whisper.

He was shaken by this virginal simplicity, this trust, this pure candor. He had never known a woman like this, he thought, with astonishment, and returning shame. To him, women were either prudes or wantons. The wantons were candid. He had never known a woman before who was not a wanton, but spoke openly, from the purity and sweetness of her heart. For an instant he thought: I must not touch her. I must go away, and never see her again. It would be a dreadful thing if I took her now.

He actually dropped her hands and stood up. She lifted her eyes and gazed at him, puzzled and surprised. She rose slowly and stood before him. His expression was earnest, even grave, and thoughtful. She waited. And then, simply, she put her arms out to him.

To his credit, he hesitated even then, though the dark color rose from his neck and washed over his face. It was more in compassion than desire that he took her hand and drew her gently to him. He put his arms about her, with an odd impulse to comfort her. She lifted her lips to his, and smiled, waiting, her eyes trembling with light.

He intended to kiss her, as a brother might do, and then put her from him. But when he did kiss her, everything was forgotten. The design of his life was washed away from his sight in a dark roaring of passion and desire. It was there, under the roaring, and his cold mind knew it, knew that nothing must interfere with it tomorrow. But there was this night——

She clung to him, and even then he was astonished at the power of her love. He felt the pressure of her firm young breasts, the warm clinging of her arms, the fire of her lips under his. He murmured something inarticulately, in a thick hoarse voice. She murmured in return, and he heard the beating of her violent heart against his.

Still holding her against him, so that they seemed one flesh, and one flame, his hand reached out and turned out the lamp.

Then there was only darkness, faintly lit by the red glimmering of the fire on the dirty hearth. There was only the wind and the rattling of the sleet against the windows. But once there was a woman's faint cry, filled with premonition, fear and dread, and then complete silence, except for the wind.

CHAPTER 25

It was the gray soiled light of dawn which finally awakened Irmgard. It crept through the dirty windows and lay on her face. She stared, confused, terrified, disoriented. She looked about her. Franz still slept at her side, his fingers entwined in her long yellow hair. Icy water appeared to creep over her body, and her limbs became rigid and very cold. What have I done? she thought. She felt Franz's warm breath against her throat, but it did not warm nor console her. She turned her head slightly and looked at his sleeping face. It was the face of a terrible stranger, who had destroyed her.

Painful, aching tears crowded her eyes, and self-hatred and shame made her heart beat sickeningly. In the gray light of the coming day she saw the drabness, the sordidness, of the room. The fire was white cold ashes on the hearth. The windows were streaked with dirt and water. The wind was louder, and the window-panes rattled desolately.

Gone was the night of ecstasy and joy, of passion and peace, of self-forgetfulness, rapture and fulfilment. Gone was the glory that had lifted the earth into radiant seas of blissful exhaustion. Gone was the sublime satisfaction and the mystery of love. There was left only this gray dead light, the dead ashes, the shame and the despair and the overwhelming dread, the miserable hidden room.

Irmgard had heard a discreet phrase from Mrs. Schmidt about girls "who forgot themselves." It had to do with a former servant, a slut who had to be spirited away one shameful night through a back door.

I "forgot myself," thought Irmgard, with self-loathing. She had forgotten herself, as completely as though she had been some scullery maid, and she had nothing left but this humiliation, this terror, this cold waking day. She dreaded Franz's awakening, dreaded the first recognizing glance. He must surely hate her, and scorn her now. That was the terror, which sent tears of ice down her cheeks and dripping into her heart. She no longer hated him; she hated only herself.

Some one knocked loudly on her door. She started violently, and answered in a faint voice. It was the proprietor, and he rattled the handle impotently. She crouched on the bed, wrapping her half-naked body in her arms.

"Milk cart goin' by here in less'n a hour,"-he said. "Better get ready, lady. Breakfast downstairs." She heard him tramp away, grumbling.

Franz had been disturbed by the knocking. He stirred, yawned, opened his eyes. He awoke without a start, and lay looking at her peacefully, as she sat beside him. Now, she could not meet his look; she folded her arms and her knees and bent her head upon them.

She felt him put his arm about her; she shrank away from him, cowering. Then, with an exclamation of annoyance, he pulled her hands from her face and taking her face in his palms, he made her look at him. But her lids dropped. From under them the tears dripped, one by one. She remembered nothing of the first joy she had ever known in her life, the first fulfilment, the first rapture. Under his kisses and embraces she had come alive, like a stagnant tree forever held in winter and feeling for the first time the warmth of the living sun. She only knew that she would gladly die now.

"Irmgard," he whispered. "You must look at me. My darling, what is the matter?"

She lifted her eyes, looked at him with new dread, expecting to see his derision and smiling contempt. But he was very grave and gentle and concerned. She suddenly forgot the shame and the fear, and remembered, with a warm rosy glow that spread over her cold flesh, the security and the peace, the ecstasy and wild happiness, which she had felt in his arms. With a loud sob, she relaxed against him, her hands clutching him, her lips against his throat. In that abandonment was a pathetic pleading, a passionate renewal of hope, a frantic trust. He held her to him, murmuring against her hair, kissing her cheek, her ear, her throat and her lips.

"Franz," she sobbed, "you must never, never leave me!"

He replied softly, but with a strange undertone in his voice: "Leave you, my darling, leave you? No, never. Never to the end of my life. Did you ever doubt it?"

Her weeping was more quiet. She pressed herself against him, as one who is cold presses towards a fire. He held her tightly, almost crushingly.

"Even if you wanted to leave me, I should not let you," he said, and his voice took on hardness. "Wherever you went, I should follow you, and make you come back to me. You belong to me. I knew that from the first."

She listened, and the joy came back, for she believed him. She knew he was not lying to her.

"I should die if you left me," she whispered.

"You shall not die, my dearest. You shall live. No matter what happens, you are mine."

She lifted her wet face, and smiled tremulously. He saw her moist green eyes, and the renewed life of her beautiful face. To cover some pang in himself, he kissed her again, and then again, with rising passion, ardor and love.

"And I thought I hated you!" she exclaimed, laughing a little. The sound was full of pathos to him. "I thought I hated you, all this time, all these weeks! But I really loved you. It is so strange."

It was all settled, then. They would be married almost at once. They would have a home together. A home with Franz! At this thought a prolonged thrilling ran along her nerves, and a drowning bliss.

She looked at him simply. "And I shall tell Aunt Emmi?" she asked.

He knew her thoughts. Pale lines etched themselves about his lips. He looked at the dirty window. Then he said: "Not yet, my sweet. There are some things— I must be sure I can take proper care of you. It will be only a little while. You can wait?"

A sick and horrible disappointment filled her. She looked

at him with a wild question in her eyes, and a terror. "Franz! We cannot wait. I could not bear waiting!"

He took her hands and held them tightly, fixing her with his blue hard look. "Irmgard, you must not be hysterical. I have told you that today, or tomorrow, I shall be assistant to the superintendent. That is a matter which must solidify. There must be some security. I—I cannot have you live as my parents live,—or others. I want only the best for you."

"And I want only you," she said brokenly, weeping again. "I am used to hardship and uncertainty. I am used to heavy work and sacrifice. These are nothing, if we are together. I know. I am not romantic; I have worked very hard."

He smiled, played with her hair. "But—I want the best for you. You must humor me. You trust me, my pretty one?"

After a moment, she answered, heart-brokenly: "What else can I do?"

He pressed his lips against her bare shoulder, and said: "I want everything for you. Comfort, security, safety, luxury, happiness. Money alone can buy these. I promise them to you. If I—took you away now, I would have nothing to give you. That would injure my self-respect permanently. It would all be drab and ugly. If we are to be happy, I must be free for a little longer. Then I shall know that I have you to work for, and that will be sufficient."

He lifted his head, and she saw that strange, hard, indomitable expression of his again. He did not see her. He was looking beyond her, grimly. She was ominously frightened again. She put her hand on his, and pleaded: "Franz."

He smiled then, with returning tenderness. "Remember, my darling, that I shall not allow you to leave me. That is not a promise. It is a threat."

She tried to laugh at such absurdity, but all at once he was not smiling. He was looking at her, for just an instant, with inexorable resolve, almost as though she were an enemy who was about to deprive him of everything he wanted.

He went into his own room, in which he had not slept, and she heard him washing in the cracked bowl. She hastily dressed, washed her own face, patted her hair and braided it as tightly as possible. In the cracked mirror she saw her pallor, the heaviness of her eyes. But there was something else there, of new softness, a bloom, a maturity and completeness. Happiness rose in her so passionately that she had to grip the corners of the commode to support herself. She trusted him. He had not lied to her. She had seen truth in him. She belonged to him, and he would never let her go.

The gray light was no longer ugly to her. It was a promise

of spring, of summer. It was the promise of America, full of strength and glory.

He returned to her, and for the last time, they embraced in silence, clinging to each other. Then, hand in hand, they went down the stairs together. The milk cart was at the door. It was too late for breakfast, but they hastily swallowed a cup of black steaming coffee. Franz glanced at his watch. It was a little after five. He frowned. He would be late, on this morning which was the most important morning in his life.

"How long will it take to drive us into town?" he asked the farmer. Behind him stood the proprietor, who had evidently had quite a conversation with the yokel before the guests had descended.

"Depends," drawled the other, with a shrewd look. "If I get two dollars, you get into town at eight o'clock. But if I get five, you get in at seven. Please yourself."

Franz counted his money, his lips tight and brutal with suppressed rage. But he never fought against the inevitable. He had six dollars. The night had been an expensive one. "All right, five dollars."

"In advance," said the farmer, holding out a calloused palm, and grinning briefly at the proprietor.

"No," said Franz, calmly, "not in advance. I shall give you two dollars now. When we reach town, you get the other three. It is up to you."

"No, sir, it's up to you. Five dollars, or eight o'clock."

Franz laid two dollars on the board seat beside the farmer. "It is up to you," he repeated. "You've got to chance getting the other three."

He turned to Irmgard, and helped her climb up on the seat beside the farmer. The man muttered and growled. Franz leapt up now, and seated himself beside Irmgard. "Let us go on," he said.

"I don't trust you foreigners," said the farmer, obstinately.

"Then we are even. I don't trust you either," said Franz, tranquilly.

The horses strained, and pulled away from the inn. It was very cold, in the early morning light. The sky was like dull pewter, heavy with clouds, and beneath it, the earth was rutted iron, veined with snow. The frozen trees they passed were freckled with white, and swayed dolorously in the edged wind. On each side of the pitted road the country stretched away, blank and dead, streaked with white tall dry grasses, whispering their litany of death, tufting the empty fields. Crows fluttered against the sky, like vultures, cawing. Nothing stirred, except for a few cows snuffling despondently at the tufts of grass.

Franz put his arm about Irmgard to protect her from the cold. She leaned against him. She was very tired. She fell asleep, her head on his shoulder. The springless cart, loaded with its milk cans, swayed and lurched over the black and narrow road. The wind blew strands of Irmgard's bright hair over her sleeping face, and Franz touched them gently with his finger. He saw nothing but her lips and her closed eyes, fringed with their bronze lashes. He held her closely yet tenderly, as he might have held a child. He said to himself: She shall never leave me. I will follow her to the ends of the earth.

He heard an approaching wagon, and hoofbeats. A strange closed black buggy passed him. On the seat sat a young bearded man with an ascetic face, grimly holding the reins. Beside him sat a plump, rosy young woman, beaming. The farmer touched his cap. "Mornin', Mr. Barbour," he said. The young man responded by a dignified bend of his head. The young woman dimpled. They went on.

The farmer, bearing no grudges, spoke. "That's Mr. Barbour. His dad's the richest man in the state. Maybe in the whole country. But he don't care about money, young Mr. Barbour. He married a nice Amish girl from hereabouts, and they live down the next road a piece. Good farm, too. One of the best in the country."

"The Amish—they are Germans, aren't they?" asked Franz, with a little curiosity.

The farmer scowled. "Yep, but we don't figure them as bein' foreigners. Nice folks. Mind their own business, and even though they got funny ways, we like 'em. Good, hard-workin', and no foolishness. Girls as pretty as pictures, even if they wear them funny bonnets, and marry their own kind. Best women folks in the state, they are, not always rushin' off to town and spendin' their men's money on fancy dresses and sinful boots with tassels on 'em. They just stay at home, and tend the cows and chickens, and the gardens, and their kids. And the men can make a miser'ble farm produce more than any two other men with better land. Very church-goin', too, allus singin' hymns and havin' prayer-meetin's."

"Barbour," said Franz, reflectively. "You don't mean Barbour-Bouchard, the munitions and steel people?"

"Yes, sir. That's them. But young Mr. Barbour won't have no truck with 'em. They say his old man's mean as hell. I wouldn't know. But everybody hereabouts likes young Mr. Barbour, even the Amish, though he ain't a German."

"He must be a fool," remarked Franz, looking back at the black buggy, now a smartly trotting speck in the distance.

"That's what you say," replied the farmer, sardonically. "But all folks ain't so crazy about money as some."

"Such as you," said Franz.

The farmer grinned. "Well, 'tain't my fault, exactly. Bill, back there's my cousin. He told me this mornin' you was a hard feller to get money out of, and you wouldn't pay your just bill for supper. Said I'd better get my money in advance." He glanced sideways at Irmgard. "Your wife's tired, ain't she? Prettiest girl I ever did see. Funny thing, she looks like you, more'n a little."

"She's my cousin," said Franz. He looked down at the sleeping girl thoughtfully, and then with increasing interest. Yes, there was a great resemblance to himself in her profile. The same calm withdrawal, the same implacability, the same shape of lip and nose, and the same curve of chin. His passion for her increased. The Narcissism which is in all men was unusually strong in him. This was a feminine reflection of himself, and with this thought his arm tightened strongly about her, as if with self-protection. We belong together, he thought. We were made for each other. We are really only one person. He added to himself, with a smile: And I am that person!

He was not weakened by his love for her, he thought. He was made stronger. Nothing would ever separate her from him. Even though he could never marry her. He had known that always. She should never get away from him, even though he could not, and would not, marry her. It was nonsense. He and Irmgard were above the mean little formalities of marriage. He would marry some day. Perhaps soon. That would have nothing to do with Irmgard and himself. He was confident that he would be able to overcome any last scruples she had, any reproaches, any silly hysterics. You shall never get away from me, he said to her silently, touching her forehead with his lips.

They were approaching the outskirts of Nazareth. The dismal little suburbs were already steaming with smoke, and a horse-car rattled down a street.

"How far do you go?" asked Franz.

"Got to let off this load at the station. Then I'll take you where you want to go. That's if I get my three more dollars now."

Franz laughed, and gave the farmer the balance of the money. A church bell in the distance tolled seven o'clock. He would not be very late, after all, though he would have no time to go home and change his clothes. He glanced down ruefully at his new suit and coat.

"Take me to the Schmidt mills, and then you can take the lady to her home," he said.

They stopped at the ricketty station, and men came out to

help with the unloading of the milk. Franz gently aroused Irmgard, and she sat up, staring and stupefied.

"We are here," he said. "Within half an hour, you'll be home."

They looked at each other in a smiling silence, Irmgard shy and speechless. Franz pressed her hands warmly in his. "Soon?" he whispered.

"I have no day off until after Christmas," she said, not smiling now, but looking at him with pathetic intensity.

"But Christmas Day? You will come to the flat, then?"

"Yes." Suddenly she was smiling again, clinging to his hands. "I will be there. Franz?"

"Yes, my darling?"

"You—you do not despise me?"

He said nothing, only gazed at her steadfastly, and she was satisfied, warmth stealing hotly over her cold and aching body. They held hands when the farmer climbed back upon the seat, and drove towards the mills. They did not speak, only smiled, when Franz was dropped off at the gates. The cart drove on. Irmgard looked back to wave, but Franz was already gone.

The farmer, alone with this pretty girl, made himself agreeable.

"Good-lookin' feller, yore husband, Missis. But harder'n nails." He chuckled. "I like a feller with git-up. Looks like you, too."

Irmgard was silent. The next immediate problem confronted her. This drab home-coming, furtive in the morning, her disheveled hair and stained face and crushed garments, excited her anxiety and embarrassment. She smoothed her hair with her chilled hands, rubbed her cheeks with her handkerchief, settled her bonnet. When the cart approached Grove Street, she flushed deeply, and began to tremble. Shame returned to her. She climbed down from the cart, and with bent head, hurried towards the Schmidt mansion. The blinds were still drawn, and nothing stirred. She silently let herself in the rear entrance, praying that she would encounter no one. The dark chill of the house smote her forcibly. It was like a catacomb, as Franz had said. She crept up the back stirway, having still encountered no servants, though she could hear Mrs. Flaherty and the maids in the distant kitchen, and Gillespie setting the table in the dining-room for Mr. Schmidt.

Thank God, she breathed. She opened the door of her room. It was quiet and still, waiting for her.

She stood in the center of the room, hardly breathing, looking about it. It was her refuge, her quietness, her sanctuary. Suddenly she began to cry, pressing her hands against her cheeks. She flung herself on the bed, and wept. Utter desolation came over her, utter abandonment. She buried her head in the clean white pillows, felt the softness of the quilts under her body. It was as she had left it. It had waited for her!

Finally, she rose, and feverishly stripped her clothing from her, until she was naked, and the discarded garments were a crushed heap about her. She washed in the cold water in the bowl. She dressed in her black cloth dress, fastened a clean white apron about her slender waist. She combed and brushed her hair, and coiled it neatly. She looked in the mirror, and saw her face, calm but flushed, her shining smooth hair. Then she tiptoed into Mrs. Schmidt's room. That lady was still sleeping peacefully. The room was dark. Irmgard softly opened a window a little, then drew the silken coverlet gently over one of Mrs. Schmidt's exposed arms. She finally touched a light to the fire laid on the hearth. Completing this, she stood for a moment, motionless, looking about her.

She would soon leave this house. She would be sorry, but the regret would only enhance her happiness. Perhaps Mrs. Schmidt would allow her to visit her, bringing Franz. But she would leave this house, with its sadness and gloom! She had found here the only friends she had ever known, the only tenderness and solicitude and consideration. But after all, this house was not a prison, in which captives were held in chains! Mrs. Schmidt, Ernestine and Baldur were free to come and go. Free to see her whenever they wished. They would not remain behind, peering through bars, watching her going wistfully. It was all nonsense. Part of the illusions of her tired but exalted mind.

And then she knew that something more terrible than prison gates held these people eternally in this house. It was themselves. They had only to push on the gates and they would open. They lacked the will to push. Or perhaps it was something much more subtle and frightful than lack of will.

Still musing wearily, she went downstairs for Mrs. Schmidt's breakfast tray. She liked the great airy kitchen, the only room in the house which sunshine penetrated fully and completely. She liked the polished red tiles of the floor, the long black range against the brick wall, fuming with warmth and comfort. She liked the gigantic cupboards with their glass windows, behind which she could see the orderly rows of dishes, platters and soup tureens. Along one side of the wall were ranged the copper cooking utensils, brilliantly polished, ranging from a pan barely large enough to cook an egg to a pot almost as big as a washtub. These utensils caught the sun, flashed it back into the room in blinding golden light. A huge window, reaching from blackened ceiling to the floor, looked out upon the vegetable gardens and the stables. On the window seat, Mrs. Flaherty kept a great many pots of parsley, marjoram, mint and chives, blooming bravely though winter locked the garden and the land outside.

Irmgard was annoyed to find Matilda busily preparing a tray in the kitchen, while Mrs. Flaherty stood behind her, arms akimbo, and a look of dislike on her round red face. Neither saw the girl entering the doorway. Mrs. Flaherty spoke tartly and fumingly:

"I tell you, Miss Matilda, the colleen will be here soon. She's got relatives in town, and stayed overnight for a change. She'll be here."

"A slut," said Matilda, in a tone of satisfaction. "I knew she was a slut. She will not return. It is only good riddance."

Irmgard halted, flushing deeply. But perhaps she was too sensitive. Perhaps Matilda was speaking of one of the chambermaids. She advanced into the kitchen. Mrs. Flaherty turned, and by her deeper color, and the triumphant glitter of her eyes, Irmgard knew that it was indeed herself of whom they had been speaking.

"Here she is!" exclaimed the cook. "Well, now, and where've you been keepin' yourself, Miss?"

Matilda turned abruptly. Her broad fair face darkened with hatred and disappointment. "Where has she been?" she demanded, sardonically. "Ask her! And the poor lady upstairs is awake, and crying for her breakfast, which has been neglected and forgotten!"

"That is a lie," said Irmgard quietly, her green eyes fixing the other coldly. "I have just left her. She is still asleep. I have lit her fire and prepared her bowl." She turned to Mrs. Flaherty. "I think a poached egg will be best for her when she awakens, please, and perhaps a thin strip or two of bacon. No coffee, but hot chocolate. She has slept so well. I do not wish to disturb her with coffee."

"I have her breakfast!" cried Matilda, seizing the tray and lifting it. She confronted Irmgard, holding the tray like a battering ram. "Out of my way, girl! I will attend Mrs. Schmidt this morning. She will be glad to hear that there is one in this house who does not neglect her!"

Irmgard did not move. She paled excessively. But her face became like stone. Matilda halted, nonplussed. To get by Irmgard she would have to use physical force. She was prepared to use it if necessary, when Mrs. Flaherty briskly stepped to Irmgard's side, eyed Matilda belligerently, and shouted:

"You'll not take that tray, you spalpeen! All that rubbish,

ham and fried eggs, and coffee black enough to shine boots with! Don't look at me like that," and she suddenly flourished a very competent-looking fist. "One word out of you and I'll wipe up the floor with ye! And you needn't think you can frighten the likes of me with your glowerin'. I'll be glad to be out of this house, in a minute. But you'll have a fine time gettin' another to take my place, that you will!"

Matilda literally swelled and puffed with rage. She looked ridiculous, standing there, tall, broad, stout, with the tray dangling in her hands, the plates slipping. She glared at Mrs. Flaherty as though she would annihilate her, but Mrs. Flaherty snorted contemptuously, put her hands on her hips, and tossed her head. Irmgard could not help smiling faintly. It was too absurd. But she did not move from her position.

Mrs. Flaherty's demonstration, however, did cow Matilda. She was not accustomed to, nor familiar with, alien and unpredictable anger. But with Irmgard, there was a kindred, even if a hating one. She regarded the girl with savage hatred, until her small blue eyes almost popped from her head. She began to lash her with a torrent of German.

"I saw you come in this morning, you slut! Creeping by the window, with your head bent, and your bonnet on the back of it. Creeping in like a thief, with the guilt on your face. Do you not know this is a respectable house——?"

"Nein," said Irmgard, very quietly, looking the woman in the eye, "I did not know."

Matilda uttered a brutal cry, took a step towards Irmgard. But her expression became at once congested and furtive, and full of murder. Mrs. Flaherty seized the opportunity then to wrench the tray from the other's hand, and to set it down with a loud bang on the wooden boards of the sink. Matilda, her hands freed, took a step towards Irmgard, clenching her fists. The color was dark red to the very edge of her fair curled hair. Irmgard did not retreat. It was not possible that they would strike each other! she thought, incredulously. But she was prepared.

"Slut! Trollop!" spat Matilda. The saliva fell in droplets on Irmgard's cheek. She wiped it away with loathing, but did not look away from this maddened creature, who was crying with greater fury: "I shall tell the master! He will have no creature like you in this house!"

"Why not?" asked Irmgard, calmly. "He has you."

Mrs. Flaherty turned on both of them, then. "You two!" she snorted. "Jabberin' like heathens. Why don't you talk English. Irmgard, it's part of your work to help prepare the missus's breakfast. God knows, I've got enough work of my own. Lively there, Miss!"

At this moment Gillespie came, his long pale face alight with expectation. He had heard the loud and angry voices, and he hoped for "a jolly good row." However, he had expected only Matilda and Mrs. Flaherty in the kitchen. When he saw Irmgard, so grim and white, so immovable, he was surprised. "Why!" he exclaimed, "I was told you had not come back all night, and that you would not return! I am happy to see you again, Irmgard."

She turned her head a little, and smiled at him. "I was with relatives," she said. "The storm, it was very bad. I could not come home. I am glad no carriage was sent for me, and no trouble caused by any one."

She waited. She concealed her burning anxiety. Gillespie regarded her with open admiration. He coughed. "It was suggested to send the carriage. I did so, myself, to Mrs. Schmidt. But she said that you were so tired, and it was too bad a night to send for you. I hope you had a pleasant visit with your relatives, your good aunt and uncle, Irmgard?"

"Yes," she said, "I—I had a very pleasant visit."

Gillespie ignored Matilda delicately. He regarded the white girl sympathetically, his light eyes warming with a new shyness and hope. Such a pretty thing, this girl, even if she was a German. And such a lady. One could see she was well-bred. He had been looking for a girl like this for years.

Mrs. Flaherty brought him to himself with a tart reminder that it was time to lay the silver for the master's breakfast. Irmgard went to the stove, to prepare Mrs. Schmidt's tray. As for Matilda, she might not have been present. They heard her high heels tapping on the stone floor, heard her slam the door violently behind her. Gillespie, in his journeying between the scullery and the dining-room, paused and touched the side of his nose with his finger. "Wind up," he said.

"A bad one," agreed Mrs. Flaherty, nodding her head vigorously. When Gillespie had again left the kitchen, she turned smartly upon Irmgard, and looked at her with kindly shrewdness. "Men are good in their place, my girl. But a woman's got to keep them there. Never let them get the upper hand. They'll leave you weepin' and wailin' in the chimney seat if you do."

Irmgard smiled a little, as she bent over the stove, and poked the red coals. The smile felt rigid and painful on her lips. "Yes," she said.

"A fine colleen like you!" said Mrs. Flaherty. "It's the pick of all of 'em you have! Take your time. And no foolishness."

Irmgard carried the tray upstairs. She had almost reached Mrs. Schmidt's door when a small spectral shadow loomed up suddenly before her in the thick dusk of the corridor. It was Baldur.

"Did I startle you, Irmgard?" he asked, gently.

"No, sir. I am afraid I was thinking of something else," she replied, her voice trembling.

There was a little silence, then, pulsing with unspoken things. Irmgard could see his large heroic face more clearly now. It was sad and brooding, heavy with melancholy. He was looking at her with an almost passionate intensity. And then, gravely inclining his head, he went on.

CHAPTER 26

BY THE TIME Franz Stoessel had reached the gates of the Schmidt Mills, everything else but the immediate present had been eliminated from his mind. He had folded, indexed, and filed everything extraneous away into neat drawers and pigeonholes for future reference. There was nothing now but the hour ahead, and the other hours, parading behind each other in military and correct formation, still faceless, but the sound of their marching footsteps becoming clearer in his ears. He had the methodical German mind, not the mechanical mind hinted by enemies of the German personality, but the sort which will take up but one thing at a time, finish it, put it away, and proceed to the next. Irmgard had left his thoughts as completely as though she had never existed. There was nothing but now. Not being possessed of intuition and inspiration, as he well knew, he studied each hour, each minute, each situation, minutely and carefully, extracting from it every small and large advantage. Let the brilliant, the inexact, the irrational and the inspirational fly vaguely and feverishly about: this was not for him. Without direction, without mathematical judiciousness, without methodical summing-up, he knew he was completely lost. "The genius can afford to bumble around, alighting on opportunity by sheer instinct and inspiration," he would think. "I am no genius. I can only see clearly, without too much imagination." Imagination, he thought, was a blazing light, which showed pits and chasms as well as glories and heights, and so frequently paralyzed its exalted possessor. Not being hampered so, what heights he saw, he saw coldly, saw the laborious steps needful to ascend to them. He had no wings. But he had a good pair of tireless and sturdy and ruthless feet. He saw no rainbows, heard no music, saw no golden arches and white colonnades. He saw no colors. But he saw the grim cold outlines of reality.

I am color-blind, he would think. But colors were distracting. He had sufficient imagination to know this. If a man saw no colors, and so had no exaltations, he saw all the traps and the mud. He saw he could make good use of the inspirational.

He now had Jan Kozak's secret. It had taken him months of flattery, of friendly approach, of lies and hypocrisies, of bland sympathy which was as cruel as death. The secret was disgustingly simple. Even I, he thought, might have thought of it. It was as simple as the larding of a pie-plate by a housewife, before she inserts the pastry, which can then be easily removed after baking. Jan had merely hit upon the idea of smearing the inside of moulds with tar, or pitch, which released the mould thereafter without breakage and spoilage. A simple thing! Yet, a thing of genius. This almost illiterate peasant had had inspiration. The inspirational, Franz reflected, were usually quite stupid, fit only to be prey for the clever and the predatory. Look at Brahms, for instance. He had attained fame by using Beethoven. His imitations were so clever that he had caught glory from a greater glory, and fools believed him as great as the genius he had so ruthlessly exploited. But sometimes imitation struck some spark in the imitator, and at rare intervals he had flashes of true inspiration, himself. Franz, after securing the secret from Jan, had had a few vague flashes, and egotistically wondered if he had needed but an impetus.

He had promised Jan everything. Promises, he knew, were a glittering coin. They tarnished quickly. When he had been a child he had covered coins of small denomination with gilt paper which his mother had used to decorate Christmas trees. They had taken on a spurious aspect of great worth and brilliance. But under the gilt, they had been practically worthless. Thus were promises. He had covered their intrinsic nothingness with shining cheap paper of lies and falsenesses. Jan had accepted them simply, believing them valuable, believing them good, believing that the dull clink he had heard was the ring of gold and silver.

The clever man, Franz would think, smiling, dispenses promises without restraint, and thus attains a reputation for generosity and integrity. Promises cost nothing. But they yielded power and prestige for the man ruthless and courageous enough to issue them. When the time came for reckoning, the deceived discovered the gilded and chipping paper. But he had accepted them. His was the fault. He had only his stupidity to blame. It was his eyesight, his knowledge, his trust, which had betrayed him, not the issuer of the dull copper coin.

Franz was now ready to accept the position mysteriously offered him by the Superintendent, Dietrich. He had taken a giant stride. He was prepared. He decided not to put on the extra pair of overalls which he kept at the mills. He would go direct to Dietrich. He had everything he needed.

He was crossing the mill where he worked, when he was hailed by Tom Harrow. He paused, frowning, then instinctively smiled his usual friendly and charming smile. He now had no further use for Tom, but it was his nature to greet every one with that bland frank smile, which meant nothing, and which deceived every one, even Tom at times. Besides, in his way, he really liked the Englishman.

Tom came hurrying, his long dark face wrinkling with gravity. He paused, stared at Franz's Sunday finery. "Eh! A toff! Think you can work like that?' He was momentarily distracted from his purpose, and grinned in surprise.

"I was out all night, and could not get home in time to change," said Franz, easily. He was annoyed. He had not wanted to encounter Tom, who must soon become his enemy. Tom was no use in the new order which he, Franz, contemplated in the mills. It was very bad, and he had a slight regret. But an agitator and a disturber had no place in the new order. Docility and obedience and fear must be the new whips. These necessary virtues of the poor, the impecunious and the helpless, were not the virtues of Tom Harrow. Franz suspected that Tom would never be helpless. He was a blazing torch which would soon burn down any structure. He must be put out. For an instant, Franz saw little Mary, his favorite and his pet. Well, he had some hundreds saved. He would send one hundred dollars anonymously to little Mary. But Tom would have to leave Nazareth. That was certain. He would have to be driven out of the town, where his dangerousness would no longer be a menace. He and his damned embryo union!

Tom grinned, and winked. "A lass, eh? A young chap can't have enough of a piece, can he? Mind, I'm not blamin' you. I was a corker once, myself. Until I met Dolly." He rubbed his long Punch-and-Judy chin, and frowned again. "Bosh Things in their place. I've got to talk to you."

Franz fumed internally. He felt something like hatred and disgust for Tom, but under it glowed his real liking for the man, like a live coal slowly choking to death under a heap of cold ashes. He kept the bland smile on his face.

"What is it, Tom? I'm late. I must get my overalls."

"I'm goin' into the bloomin' mill for the rest of the day, Fritzie. So I can't wait." He came closer to Franz. The roar and boom and clamor of the mills covered his low voice. His small black eyes pierced the blue opaque eyes so close to his. "We got a meetin' tonight."

"I thought it was next week?" Franz's smile became impatient. The idiot union, with its mumblings of a strike! He would attend to that, himself!

Tom shook his head. He came still closer. Now his face was hard and grim. "It's now or never. You never can tell with these foreign chaps. Like rabbits, they are. Got to get 'em in hand. I'm goin' to call the strike, tonight. Tomorrow," and he chuckled grimly, "these damn mills'll be closed tighter than a fist."

Franz's smile disappeared. He chewed his lip thoughtfully. Internally, he raged, and was filled with cold murder. He said: "Isn't that too sudden? Will the men follow?"

Tom nodded his head shortly, with a dark smile. "They will. They're keyed up to it. Next week will be too late. I know. I call the strike tonight."

Franz paused. He had his hands in the pockets of his checked coat. They clenched slowly and murderously. Tomorow, his first day as assistant to the superintendent! And a closed mill, silent and deserted. It was not to be borne.

"Can we talk?" he asked, quickly, looking about him.

"We can go into the —— house," said Tom.

Franz, with rare humor, thought this might be an appropriate place for discussion. But he said: "I know a better and quieter place, where there will not be so much coming and going. Wait for me a moment."

He waited until Tom had returned to his station, then quickly made his way to the Superintendent's office. Dietrich looked up with sly sharpness as Franz entered. But before he could speak, Franz said rapidly: "Herr Dietrich: I have only a moment or two. But this is very serious. Tom Harrow is calling a strike tonight——"

Dietrich's slyness disappeared into an expression of consternation and amazement. Franz lifted his hand with impatient authority, which made Dietrich draw his thin lips together in anger.

"Please let me finish, Herr Dietrich! I must find out the details. I have been spying on the men for some time. I did not speak of it to you, because matters had not come to a head." He paused. Schmidt's door was ajar. Franz saw one fat black arm, a hand, and a section of watch-chain through the slit. Hans, at his desk, was listening alertly. Franz knew this clearly.

"I joined the union," Franz went on. Dietrich leaned back in his chair, listening with his closed Saxon face, which Franz loathed. His hand played with the objects on his desk. His light blue eyes were glazed and expressionless. But there was a twitching around the pale tight mouth.

"I joined the union," Franz repeated. "I had to discover everything. You understand, Herr Dietrich? It was necessary. Tonight is extremely important. The strike must be prevented, in some way. Therefore, I must still be in the mills, today, in order not to excite suspicion. I must attend that meeting tonight."

Dietrich had not glanced behind him at the partly opened door. But he knew Schmidt was listening with rigid attention. He made himself smile briefly, with assumed approbation.

"You have been clever," he said, speaking in German, as Franz was speaking, but with the softer accent that Franz despised. "It is well, then. Do what you think best." He paused, and said, with a wry twist of his mouth: "I can see that you will be very valuable, here."

There was a scraping of a chair, a hoarse and infuriated grunt. Hans Schmidt, empurpled and swelling, appeared at his door. Dietrich rose. Franz stood at rigid attention, like a soldier, his face wearing that indescribable look of military expressionlessness which only a Teuton can adequately summon. Hans glared at him, from the doorway, his little blue eyes fiery and ferocious.

"A strike!" he exclaimed. "What is this nonsense?"

Franz did not reply. He left that to his superior officer, Dietrich. Dietrich explained softly, the wry twist still on his lips. "Herr Schmidt," he ended, respectfully, "I have reason to believe this report of—of Stoessel's. I have heard rumblings. I did not think it serious." He paused, and added sourly, with a keen respectful glance at Schmidt: "Stoessel is to be congratulated."

But Schmidt was momentarily obsessed with his rage and fury. His eyes took on more fierceness. They shot out red sparks. His blond-gray hair bristled on his pink skull like the bristles of a hog. He breathed heavily, and a film of sweat burst out over his fat broad face. He regarded Franz with savagery.

"It is not possible! A strike, now! Who put this nonsense among the men? Now, now when I have been able to secure a government contract right out from the hands of Sessions, in Windsor! My first good order in months! I will not stand it! It shall not happen!" He snorted, as though strangling. "There has never been a thought of a union in my mills! I will not have it! It must be stopped." He doubled up his small fat hands and waved them in the air with a gesture of smothering, hatred and madness.

"I shall stop it, Herr Schmidt," said Franz, softly.

The sound of that quiet firm voice halted Schmidt. Slowly, the thick purple tide began to recede from his face. He stared. He seemed to see Franz fully for the first time.

"How?" he asked, shortly.

"I will find a way," said Franz. "A day or two of disturbance. But there shall be a way. In the meantime, may I respectfully suggest that you send for a large force of detectives? There is an office in Windsor. The Barbour-Bouchard and Sessions interests use them frequently. Let them arrive, tonight, if possible. There is no time to waste."

There was a silence. Hans lifted his right hand and savagely chewed the nail of his index finger. Above his hand, his reddened and infuriated eyes had become calculating, and thoughtful, as they stared fixedly at Franz. Then, to Dietrich's surprise, the formidable fat little man began to smile. He dropped his hands, as though suddenly relaxing.

"I know you," he said to Franz, with a cunning intonation in his rough voice. "I trust you. I knew what you were, from the beginning." He turned to Dietrich, with brisk hard purpose. "A telegram immediately, to Windsor." He turned back to Franz, and smiled again. "I must have a word with you, before you leave tonight. In the meantime, return to the mills."

He said nothing else. He had attained power and wealth by not wasting time, by not asking involved and useless questions. His intuition precluded these. He knew whom to trust. He knew he could trust Franz. The Superintendent, who was cautious and slow, always, was bewildered, enraged, and astounded. He never did things without an immense amount of consultation and discussion. He had a high respect for red tape and judiciousness and consideration. He invariably suspected speed and lightning decisions. Yet these two men, Schmidt and the detestable Prussian with his Slavic eyes, wasted no time, but were almost indecently precipitous. It was ridiculous.

Nevertheless, concealing his anger and hatred, Dietrich said quietly: "The telegram shall go at once." He turned, frowning, to Franz. "Go, Stoessel. Why are you waiting?"

Franz bowed deeply, not to Dietrich, but to Schmidt, and left the office. Dietrich then said, biting down on the hatred within himself: "Herr Schmidt: this is all bewildering. Do you not think we should have questioned Stoessel more carefully? Have found out more?"

Hans grinned his mirthless and ferocious grin. "Dietrich, you are an excellent man. But you would strangle us in yards of tape and questioning. I know when to move fast, and when to move slowly." He prodded Dietrich with his stubby finger, right in the other's lean and shrinking belly. "That is why I am Schmidt, and you are only Dietrich."

He went back into his office. Though the thought of the strike roiled about his head like a black storm, he was still smiling. This Stoessel! One could trust the boar. Of course, only so far as his own interests were concerned. But when his interests were involved, one could depend completely on his loyalty and devotion. There was no hypocrisy in this. There was only realism. Schmidt smiled again, chuckled, rubbed his hands.

The blooming mill had not yet gone into operation. A few workmen were preparing the machinery. But this was all. It would take some hours yet.

Tom Harrow was waiting impatiently, pacing back and forth, his long gorilla arms behind him, his hands clasped together. When he saw Franz, he said, with garnishings of obscene profanity: "Where've you been? Think I got all day to be waitin' for a bloke like you?"

Franz smiled easily. But he did not meet those hard and honest eyes. He led the way to a row of empty casks and sat down upon them. Tom sat near him. A curious thing happened to Franz: an inexplicable cold thrill ran over his skin at the proximity of Tom Harrow, and a strange wavering sickness made his stomach feel empty and cramped. Something said to him: If it were not he! Then he had a plan, swift-born, which dissipated the sickness in a quite sentimental surge of hope.

"I have been thinking," he said, still not meeting his friend's probing eyes. "Is this strike not premature? Why not present demands, new demands, on the Company? Modified ones, of course. Something they can meet, and consider." He turned a candid smile upon Tom Harrow.

Tom's face had become quiet and ominous. He slowly brought out his pipe, stuffed it, lit it. Then he said, not looking at Franz: "You know we have made demands before. The barstards didn't even sniff at them. They'll do the same, now."

Franz spoke quickly, with an eagerness not usual with him:

"Look here, Tom, give me the demands. I'll take them to Dietrich, personally——"

Tom looked at him so oddly, that Franz was abruptly silent.

"Dietrich," murmured Tom, reflectively. "Wot've you got to do with Dietrich, the swine?"

Franz fixed his eyes on the near distance. "We are both Germans. We understand each other," he said.

Tom said nothing. Out of the corner of his eye, Franz saw the slow curling of Tom's smoke against the gray and empty gloom of the blooming mill. He said, trying to keep his voice normal and reasonable: "The Company has just gotten the first real contract in months, Tom. We—the men, need the work."

Tom said, in a peculiar still voice: "Every week, we've given 'em demands. The last demand was just Friday. They'd gotten the contract, then. They never answered." He suddenly beat his fist on his knees. "It's no use. I call the strike, tonight. If they've got sense, they'll settle with us now."

"Why not wait a week longer?" urged Franz. "A week until things get started well?"

"It will be too late," said Tom, loudly, harshly. "The chaps'll be workin' then, gettin' a little money. They'll be satisfied. You can't teach chaps like this anythin', I tell you. A little money, a little bread, keeps 'em satisfied. And then when the contract's done, wot've they got? Nothin'. They couldn't save a penny. They'll starve again." He paused. "You know this, Fritzie."

Franz did not speak. The lines about his mouth were white and grim.

Tom touched him on the arm. "You know this," he repeated, softly. "Don't you?" Then in a louder voice, "Aye, you know this."

Franz turned to him with a last eagerness, but when he saw Tom's eyes, his expression, he was silent.

Tom nodded. He smiled. His smile was black and bitter. "I might've known it," he said, as though to himself.

"Tom." Franz made a last effort. "Listen to me. Don't be a fool. I'll tell you something: don't ask me how I know, but it is the truth. Don't call this strike. And I can tell you that you won't suffer for it."

Tom did not move. He sat like a lump of dirty stone, his head bent, the strange smile on his broad thin mouth, his eyes fixed on the floor. Franz colored. For the first time, he felt shame, dark and overpowering self-contempt. All at once it seemed to him that he must do something to save his friend, to remove that look from his face. For in that look he saw not only understanding, but sad disillusion.

"Let's be reasonable," he said again, too quickly. "Who is going to suffer the most from this, Tom? Dolly, Mary, the twins. Do you think you have the right——"

Tom turned on him then, with such a blaze of black fury on his face that Franz recoiled. The Englishman's eyes were bits of burning coal.

"My kids! Dolly! God, you fool, do you think even they matter, now? Wot abaht all the other wives and kids? All over America? All over the bloody world? A man's got to start somewhere, even if it's in his own home!" His voice choked. "God, but I'm talking to a stone wall! You'll never understand."

"Do you have to be a damned Messiah, all by yourself?" said Franz, his strange and unaccustomed emotions sickening him still more. "Do you think these—these animals here would care what happened to your own family, or you? Why do you have to be such a fool?"

Tom stood up abruptly. His fists were clenched at his sides. He did not look at Franz. He looked into the distance. He began to speak, as if reviewing a long stream of faces and events that marched before him:

"When I talk to you like this, I know I'm spittin' my guts into the wind. I know you're a blasted Judas. But I've got to talk to you.

"Wot you were in Dutchland, I don't know. But I know what England's like. I know what America's like. I know what my old man and old woman were like.

"My old man." He laughed bleakly, but not with resentment, only with understanding. "He was a miner. Frightened of his shadow he was. There were six of us kids. Know wot he used to tell us: 'Lads, when you go out to a job, remember this: keep your heads down. Always keep your heads down.' "

Tom paused. Then he flung up his large curly head, and it was no longer grotesque and amusing. " 'Keep your heads down!' " he shouted. "Think of that, think wot it means? All the chaps everywhere, havin' to keep their bloody heads down! All the young lads, being told by their dads to keep their heads down! There you've got 'em now, all over the world, keepin' their heads down, the guts frightened out of 'em, like old nags with their ribs stickin' out of their skins. Starvin', afraid to open their mouths, workin' like dumb beasts, afraid to look up!"

He paused, breathing heavily. He ran his hands through his black curly poll with a distracted gesture. He stood over Franz.

"There it was. In our 'ome. The old man comin' in at night, all covered with coal dust, creepin' in. There was my old woman, cookin' some gruel in a pot. Three rooms we had, with a leakin' thatched roof. We never got away from the toffs! They were there, all the time, tellin' us to keep our heads down! The big owners. Eight of us in that house, keepin' our heads down, and our old man, sittin' there, eatin' his gruel and bread, and seein' that we did!

"He was a man once. My old woman told me. A big strappin' chap, with red cheeks. A country fellow, as was used to his two quarts of milk a day, and big hams, and butter. Then he got to work in the mines. I used to look at him. I couldn't believe my mother, lookin' at that shamblin' old nag, keepin' his head down. Six kids, and not enough to feed 'em on. And lay-offs, whenever the toffs thought the market was goin' down. Wot'd they care? We was only dogs, waitin' for bones."

He paused, choking. "I know wot cold is, and goin' without boots, and eatin' gruel when my guts were yellin' for meat and bread and potatoes." He was silent a moment. "My old man came to London, seekin' his fortune. He worked as a navvy, there. Married my old woman, takin' her from service. Then—six of us kids. He had to do somethin'. So, he got into the mines. I know wot it is," he said, inaudibly. "My three older brothers—nice lads. Went into the mills, after two years' schoolin'. Not more than twelve and thirteen, they were. The three of 'em died in three years, of lung-fever, from the dust. Coughed their lungs out, there in the house, with the roof leakin', and the old man mutterin': 'Keep your heads down.' " Tom laughed with a sudden wild bitterness. "They did! Six feet under!"

He beat his fists together. He seemed unconscious of the silent man near him. A long booming went through the mill.

"I used to see the toffs, sometimes. In their carriages. On their horses. Shiny boots and top hats, and white handkerchiefs held to their bloody noses, the barstards! I wanted to kill. Aye, I wanted to kill. I was ten then, and was in the mines."

He paused for a long time, as though his thoughts were too terrible for speech. Then he resumed in a muffled voice: "My old man died in the mines, with a hundred others. Wot happened to their women and kids? We got an order to leave, and six shillings. That's all. Three of us kids left. My old woman took us to London again, got jobs charrin'. I was twelve then, and there was a little sister, eight, and a baby, two. I took care of 'em, in a ratty garret. When it wasn't rainin', we ran the streets, barefoot, hungry, pickin' up crusts and bones in the alleys. Sometimes we slept in doorways, in the rain, and the bobbies would come along and belt us. The old woman 'ud be so tired she'd fall on the floor. She wasn't no older than Dolly, but her hair was white, like strings. I got odd jobs, washin' windows and puttin' up shutters and cleanin' privies. Sometimes I'd make a shillin' a week!" He laughed again, and the sound was terrible.

"Sometimes, on Sundays, the old woman'd take us for 'fresh air.' Three scrawny kids, famished, in broken boots, but washed clean. The old woman was good at washin' us, when she had time. She'd carry the babby in her arms, and we'd walk. In the Parks? In Kensington, where the kids of the toffs could look at the flowers? Christ, no! That wasn't for us. We was just cattle, from the slums. Hundreds, thousands, of us, walkin', in the precious damned sunshine even they couldn't take from us. We used to pass a house. It had high walls, and iron gates."

He stopped. He saw the ivy-covered wall, the mighty gates, the soft green lawns and flowers beyond, and the great house, brown and sun-softened in the distance.

"One Sunday, the rats was bad in the garret, and the sun was shinin', and the poor old woman took us out. We passed that house. It was summer. There was a lawn party. You could hear 'em laughin', and there was music, and fine ladies walkin' around with flounced silk dresses and little bonnets and lace parasols. Dainty as you please. And the toffs, with their top hats, and gold canes and silk weskits and big-skirted fawn coats. We could see it all through the gates. Nearby, there was a table, and a bloody bishop, or vicar, was sittin' there, with ladies, drinkin' tea and eatin', and the servants scurryin' around like sparrers. Oh, it was capital! All so nice and peaceful, and the fat bishop in his black, stuffin' his belly, and oglin' the pretty ladies! And the grass so green, and the music so nice!

"The old woman dragged along, her ragged skirts on the flags, holdin' my little sister, and my other sister trailin' along with me. We stopped at the gates. The old woman looked in. She held onto the iron railings, and she said: 'Oh, dear God, oh, dear God!' And there we stood, with the water runnin' out of our mouths."

He stopped again, breathing in a disordered fashion. Franz looked at the brick floor of the mill. His expression was inscrutable. But he thought: You fool, can you not see that you stood on one side, and they on the other, because they were superior to you? Born superior?

"We stood there," said Tom. "And then the servants saw us. One of 'em, a big chap in a flowered weskit, came up to the gates, and said: 'Be off with you. Be off!' And my old woman looked at him, and whimpered: 'My babbies are hungry. Just a few scraps, mister, for the love of God."

Tom began to pace again, as though he could not bear his memories. "She clung to that gate, and the tears runnin' down her cheeks, and us kids began to yell and scream. And the big chap, the navvy in the weskit, shoutin' at us to be off, us bloody beggars and scum. The blasted bishop heard us, and he put his hankie to his nose and looked at us as if we hurt his cursed eyes. Then he got up and led the pretty bitches away, and told the big chap as was shoutin' at us to call the bobbies."

Tom was breathing heavily. His little black eyes were red with rage and hatred, and filmed over with bitter memory. He looked at Franz, but did not see him. He saw his mother's face, and her gaunt torn hands clinging to the railings, pleading for food for her children. He saw her dirty skirts, and the whitened hair under her battered bonnet. He heard the cries of his little sisters. He beat his fists together, and his breath was hoarse with frightful emotion.

"Two bobbies came runnin', wavin' their sticks. They dragged Ma from the gates. They knocked the babby from her arms. She fought with them. I can see her yet. Us littls uns stood and screamed, and watched the old woman bein' clouted all over the blasted road. Then they threw her in the gutter, and went away, sayin' it was a warnin' to her, not to harass her betters. She didn't hear 'em; she lay in the gutter, with the blood arunnin' out of her mouth, and her eyes closed. God! God curse 'em!"

Franz examined his finger-nails. He said nothing. More and more men were coming into the mill, calling and clattering. Some were standing on platforms, shoveling coal and charcoal into the cold furnaces. But Tom was oblivious to everything except his aching, red-lit memories.

"I was only a lad," said Tom, in a low shaking voice. "But I made an oath, as was a man's oath. I would do some'at abaht all this, when I was a man. Even if I died for't, under the bobbies' sticks and boots. I never forgot. I got a job soon as a navvy, and helped the old woman. I began to think. The old woman knew! She was no fool, that one! She had been in service, in the big houses. She used to say to me: 'Lad, it's the toffs, the leddies and the lords, as is ruinin' England. There'll have to come a reckonin', mark my words.' I began to go around in all the slums, listenin' to the chaps. I used to listen to 'em, in Hyde Park, on Sunday. I read all the books I could borry or steal.

"And I found out the old woman was right as rain. It was the toffs, the fine folk, as was killin' England and the English people. I found out abaht the Napoleonic Wars, and how the royalty and the snobs was all for bowin' to Napoleon, if he'd promise 'em to help 'em to put the English in chains again, and put whips over 'em. But the English folk came awake, just in the nick of time, and the toffs hid in their big mansions and country estates, and shut their mouths. The English are a patient lot, as wants no quarrels and no cloutin's and no blood, but when they get the wind up, they kill better than others. It was the English people, the ones in the slums and the shops and the rented farms, as put Napoleon on St. Helena—not the toffs, who hate us. Then there was the Franco-Prussian war——"

Franz looked up alertly, his eyes narrowed and intent for the first time.

Tom nodded fiercely and bleakly. "There was the Frenchies, askin' the British for help. They said: 'Ye'll help us now, against the swine, or ye'll be fightin' her alone some day, and she'll tear your guts out.' But the toffs, would they help? Not them! They was afraid France was gettin' too strong. Besides, they 'adn't forgot that it was the Frenchies as had 'ad a Revolution puttin' the fear of God in all the toffs, all over the world, and wakin' the common people up. So—they let France be whipped by the Prussians."

"You mustn't forget that the English and the Germans are really the same people," said Franz, with a slight smile.

Tom shook his head grimly. "Not them! They's some'in in the English ain't in the Fritzies. There's a love o' liberty in the English, which naught can stamp out. But the Fritzies hate liberty. They want some'un as is strong enough to clout 'em about the head. That's what they love. But show an Englishman a whip and some chains, and he'll rip the throat out of ye.

"I read all I could abaht history, I tell you. I read as how the toffs wanted the Spanish to land and conquer the old country, and put them in Popery again. But there was the English, hatin' chains and slavery. And there was Good Queen Bess, as was a trollop after every Englishman's heart, hatin' the toffs who 'ad tried to kill her for puttin' that whore, Mary, on the headsman's block. So, it was Good Queen Bess, and the English yeomen, and the little shopkeepers, as kept Popery out of England, and kept liberty burnin' for all the world to see.

"And then there was America. Could the toffs get good Englishmen to fight good Englishmen in the Colonies? Be blasted if they could! No, they had to get their Fritzie King to hire the Hessians to come over here to fight Englishmen. Aye, it was the toffs, in their red officers' uniforms, as led the

Hessians against Englishmen in America, but the English folk knew a thing or two. It was the old fight again, betwixt the toffs and the people, as was bein' fought all over the world. They knew it was the same old fight—they knew it would go on, forever."

His passion was rising. His long Punch-and-Judy face burned with a wild and exultant fire. He stopped before Franz, and shook his fist in his face.

"And that's wot this strike is abaht, don't you see, you fool! It ain't just a strike, standin' out alone! It's the same old fight! Who's goin' to rule this world, as God made for all men? A few toffs on the top, or the people? Government by the people, or a State made up of lords and toffs and kings and military officers, enforcin' law with fists and whips and guns? The people or their natural enemies? Liberty or the knout? That's what the people 'ave got to decide every generation. And each time they win, they get stronger. Each time they lose, they put the chains on themselves. Each time they've got to decide to be men or to be slaves. It's up to them!

"Look at America. A new country, sworn to liberty and opportunity. Are the toffs lyin' quiet? Like hell they are! They'll never lie quiet until we put them under the ground, every generation, or shut their mouths. America was a land of independent chaps, until now. Now the toffs are beginnin' their dirty work again. There's big cities here now, and factories and mills, good forcin' ground for slavery. America's got to fight, every damn last one of us. Each fight we lose makes the next harder. Each time the toffs, as 'ates the people, get stronger. If America's got to be saved for the American people, it's got to win all the fights! As plain as the nose on your damned face, Fritzie!"

Franz smiled involuntarily. He knew that Tom had been speaking the most grave and passionate truth.

"Look here, Tom, let me speak for a moment. How do the 'toffs,' as you call them, get so strong? Because they happen to be born superior, and stronger. It's still the same old story of the race to the swift and the battle to the strong——"

Tom exploded into a string of obscenity. He was almost beside himself. "The race to the swift!" he shouted. "The people is the strongest, not the toffs! But the people are peace-lovin', and slow, and they believe lies, because they're simple and hate rows. The instinct of the people is always good, and ye're a fool if you don't know it! But they get lied to, and cheated, and the toffs hire the bloody vicars to help 'em. 'Be meek,' say the vicars, noddin' their silly heads. 'Be long-sufferin'. Your reward ain't here. It's in heaven. Suffer all things,' they says. It's a God-damned lie!" he shouted, with greater violence. "God didn't make men to suffer! He didn't make the earth for just a few! He made it for everybody, and there's enough on this earth to feed every man, and keep him sheltered. It's just the bloody toffs who want the whole cursed world! A world of slaves, to keep their beds soft and supplied with strumpets and whores, and their tables full of wines and rich food. Why? Because they hate the people. They know the people make laws to keep the toffs under control. So, they hate laws. *They* want to make the laws, so the people'll have nothin' to say, and keep their blasted heads down!"

His face was running with sweat. He shook his fists again. "They even try to get God Almighty to help 'em, the bloody pigs! They get the Church to wave the Cross at the people, tellin' them to be obedient to their masters! But they keep forgettin' that Jesus was a Man of the people, and hated the toffs. He was a chap as knew what the toffs was, that One! Jesus Christ, there's nothin' as they won't do, to keep the people down, the filthy pigs! Nothin they won't betray or bury. But the instinct of the people is always right, when they stop to think. It's the people as fights the fight for freedom, when they understand!"

Franz spoke reasonably and gently. "Look here, Tom, I want to tell you about myself. My people were poor in Germany. But I saw very clearly that the people deserve their own condition. A few of them can battle their way up out of the mob, and rise to the top. If the others don't they deserve what they suffer. They haven't the intelligence to rise."

"No!" exclaimed Tom, with increasing passion. "It's because they've been lied to, and they believe anythin'. They've been kept in ignorance. Let them see, and you'll see then how fast they'll rise! But you've got to show 'em. Ye've got to show 'em that when the toffs call 'em syndicalists and anarchists, they're just thinkin' of themselves."

Franz did not speak, but only smiled and shook his head.

Tom, exhausted, sat down near him, and wiped his face with his bare arms and wrists. He was panting a little. But the look of pale resolution was harder and grimmer on his face.

"That's why I'm callin' this strike. Look how the men've been starvin'. Livin' like rats. We've got to win this fight. It's only one skirmish in the Big Battle as is bein' fought all over the world, and will always be fought."

He turned suddenly to Franz, and said: "Ye're with us, Fritzie?" His eyes bored into the other's, with a cold and warning menace.

Franz shrugged. He stood up. "I gave my promise to you

some time ago. If you are bent on this strike, I can do nothing to stop you, I suppose. You are the leader."

But he did not look at Tom Harrow. He thought to himself: He has spoken the truth. I know it is the truth. That is why he must be stopped, no matter what it costs. We dare not let men like him open the people's eyes. His kind must be silenced all over the world. And all his liking for his friend was consumed in his hatred and fear.

Later, when he thought he was unobserved, he stole swiftly into the Superintendent's office and remained there over an hour.

CHAPTER 27

IT SEEMED to Franz that the murky lights in the hall were unbearably dazzling. But he knew this was his imagination. He knew it was some feverish blaze in himself which made Tom Harrow's long dark ugly face gleam and shimmer before him, as the Englishman stood on the platform and spoke to the assembled laborers below the platform. The hall was cold and damp, but thin threads of moisture ran down Franz's back, and there was a dull throbbing ache in his head.

A large burly man sat at Franz's right. He spoke out of the corner of his mouth to the younger man: "So, that's him, eh? Noisy bastard, ain't he? Well, we'll cook his goose, proper."

Franz answered, without turning his head: "Remember now, no roughness. That is agreed. You and Collins are just to knock him down and haul him off to the police-station. That was agreed, remember? He must not be hurt. Then, tomorrow, when the men come to the mills, prepared to strike, they will find their leader gone."

The burly man nodded. He smirked a little, flexed his beefy fists.

"That's our orders. We know 'em. A drunken fight, like. When he gets out, the men'll have cooled off, eh? You think so?"

"I know so."

Franz turned his head then, casually, and looked at the

other with his cold and merciless blue eyes. Before that look, the other winced a little.

"If you or Collins really hurt him, outside of mussing him up enough to book him for drunkenness, I'll attend to you, myself. You understand that? Please?"

John Brent nodded solemnly. His pale eye fixed itself on Tom Harrow with a malevolent expression. But the malevolence was for Franz, the "bohunk." Things had come to a pretty state when a foreigner like this could give orders, and look at a "real" American as though he was dirt.

Nearby sat Jan Kozak, almost directly behind Franz Stoessel. Franz had looked for the big Hungarian, but had not found him. Jan had entered late, and had taken his seat quietly. Franz, having failed to see him before, concluded that he had not come. For some reason, profound relief invaded him. But Jan had seen him. He leaned forward, to whisper some question to his "friend," but at that moment the stranger next to Franz leaned sideways and said: "How d'ye know he'll go along with you? He might change his mind."

"We always walk home together, after a meeting. Just follow us a little distance, until we come to a quiet place. When I think it safe, I'll drop my handkerchief. Then you can close in."

Jan Kozak caught the words, understood most of them, though they were said in a low voice, under cover of Tom Harrow's shouting, and the heavy breathing of the men. For Jan, accustomed to the roaring of the mills, had developed an acute "short" hearing for voices close to him. But his mind was slow. He decided not to speak to Franz just then, wondering stolidly about the identity of the stranger, whom he had never seen before. It was a full five minutes before that slow peasant mind, still dimly echoing with the puzzling words it had heard, came suddenly awake, and alert.

The big Hungarian sat up on his hard wooden seat, exhaling noisily, glaring at the back of Franz's large yellow head. His fists clenched on his knees. His teeth gleamed wolfishly between his hairy lips. He heard nothing more of what Tom Harrow was saying. All his peasant concentration was fixed on Franz, and a frightful look began to glitter in his eyes. He crouched there, like a huge beast waiting to spring. He listened with savage attention. But Franz did not speak to the stranger again. Once Jan lifted his fists and poised them a moment over the other's serenely unaware head, as if to crush it. Then he dropped his fists on his knees, and held them there, like weapons, waiting.

The slow but violent thoughts curled like smoke through the chambers of his mind. He breathed laboriously as he identified each one, until all his huge body was a seething living mass of hatred and murder. Terrible surprise flashed through him, like lightning. The enemy had been beside him for years, and he had given the enemy his secret. The enemy had been a friend of Tom Harrow, and was now plotting to destroy him. Jan was astounded. His mouth opened, and he gaped stupidly. He moved his head on his bull-like neck, as though strangling. His astonishment increased, as though he had seen something fabulous within the flesh of a familiar form. He was lost in the profound wonderment of his peasant simplicity.

The ponderous but killing wrath of the simple man began to rise in him, not swiftly, but like the slow piling of stones, each settling heavily into place before the next was added. He could hear the dull building in his mind, the inexorable rising. And then he mounted the wall he had built, and looked down at it upon Franz Stoessel. Franz, happily, did not know that death sat behind him, waiting.

Franz, years later, remembered, with smiling amusement, how he had sat and sweated that night, repeating desperately, over and over to himself, a sort of incantation: "When a man has decided upon a course, nothing but death should be allowed to halt him. No natural hesitations, no weaknesses, no human considerations, are to be permitted. One moment's faltering can set up a fatal habit of a lifetime of faltering. The first step is often the last." He smiled, in those later years, at a weaker and younger Franz, who could still be touched by human considerations and softer pangs. Only an old and a successful man could permit himself, with safety, to indulge in gestures of generosity and kindness and conscience. For, by then, his position was impregnable, and it did not matter that the gestures had no heart behind them, but only calculation for effect. Once the heart was involved, the man was lost.

As he sat there that night, willing himself to strength and coldness, he heard nothing of Tom's opening words and shouts. Everything blurred before him, became nothing but a vague background against which he struggled with the colossal and unmanned forces which emerged from himself in a last desperate strife. Finally, exhausted, purged of all emotion and pain, he came to the surface of reality and listened.

Tom's dark face was transfigured. His eyes flashed and sparkled, as he gestured furiously, and marched back and forth on the resounding wooden platform on which he stood. Sometimes he squatted on his haunches, to rise, to throw up his clenched fists. Sometimes his voice dropped to a murmur, became almost inaudible, thereafter to mount swiftly to a peak of passion and exhortation. The men listened, not moving, mouths open, breathing heavily. He was like a wind that moved them in waves by its own force, swaying them backwards and forwards.

"Men!" he shouted, shaking his fists, impelling his audience with his eyes, his voice, his burning dark face, his hands. "It's Us or Them! Always, it's been Us or Them! There's never been anything else in all the world, from the time that there's been more than one blasted chap on the face of the earth! Always there's been the eater, and the one that's been eaten! Always, there's been the tiger in one man, and the lamb in the other. That's the God's truth. You can read it in the Bible, for yerselves. But, are we goin' to stand by and let all the lambs, as wants peace and a little grub, to be eaten by the tigers? No! By God, no! I'm a one as believes the lambs 'as as good a right to live as the tigers. And a better right, too. Jesus Christ was a lamb, but he made the tigers run. For a little while, anyway."

He paused. His words were crude, and without the eloquence of polished orators. But what they lacked in eloquence, they gained in passion, solemnity and sincere feelings. He panted a little. The men looked at him, and waited, their faces dark and flushed with anger and understanding.

He began to speak again, and now his voice rose almost savagely, and with a wild inspiration.

"You chaps think this is just a strike, for a little more money, for a little better right to live in peace and comfort, with your women and your babbies. But it's not! By God, it's not! It's more than a strike. Every strike is more than just this. It's a blow and a fight for human rights, everywhere in the world, wherever there's a man alive, whether it's in black Russia, or Poland, or Germany, or France, or China, or England or America. Everywhere a strike is lost, even if it's just in this town, men everywhere have lost that much right to live. Everywhere a strike is won, the black man and the yellow man, the red man and the white man, have won one more fight against Them! Against the tigers.

"Remember, when you go out tomorrow, you don't just go out for your bloody selves. You go out for all chaps, everywhere. Think of it! You are involved in a world-struggle, for men that breathe everywhere! Not just for a few more pennies, to buy yourselves a little more beer, or more bread for your kids. But for your brothers in every corner of the whole blasted world!"

Incredible, ridiculous, mad words! Mystic words spoken to cattle, who could not possibly understand. This fool was exhorting dull beasts to take up the bright sword of a transcendental mission, to gird themselves for a holy Crusade, full of mysticism, myths and glory! Franz smiled deeply in himself. This fool, Harrow, believed that canaille had souls and comprehension beyond their bellies and their lusts and their brutishness. He thought he could make them see beyond their animal-flesh and their feeble appetites. He thought he could make men of dogs, and angels of oxen. He no longer seemed dangerous to Franz. Men who were dangerous were men who could speak to swine in their own language. He had now spoken beyond their understanding and their desires, and so, he had lost them. He was no longer to be feared.

Franz, still smiling contemptuously, looked about him at the faces of the listening peasants and laborers. Then, he was filled with a furious astonishment and disbelief. He looked at those dull faces and small expressionless eyes, and saw a terrible dawning comprehension and vision. It was like seeing crude images of stone, unfinished and uncouth and without humanity, suddenly awakening to flesh and passion and exaltation, slowly, to be sure, but surely awakening.

The men were utterly silent, not shuffling their feet, hardly breathing. But the dull and heavy faces had a strange and exalted light upon them, the shadow of an inner and passionate vision, beyond self—most strangely beyond self. Each simple peasant seemed suddenly in communication with a mysterious power, and touched with a mysterious fire. Every eye was an individual pool of light, wide and glistening. The thick and calloused flesh trembled with a selfless radiance. The stolid cattle saw a vision rising over the dark hills of their formless lives, and for the first time they saw beyond themselves to a world of all men, all brothers, all creation. They were part of this world. What they did and thought was of the most vital and momentous importance to it. It gave them a trembling and vehement sense of universal brotherhood, of deep love, of mission, of grandeur, of significance. It was incredible that these simple and illiterate men, involved in the deep subterranean preoccupation of beastlike individualism, could stand up as living souls and understand the vision.

So might the poor, illiterate peasants and shepherds have listened to the Sermon on the Mount, to the Man who spoke on the shores of Galilee. Like them, these beasts and cattle were aroused to love and passionate importance and sacrifice. They lost themselves, but in doing so, they gained the world. The vague and unformed souls took stature upon themselves, the stature of men, with the light of heroism transforming thick flesh and heavy hands to the very substance of the angels.

Tom Harrow felt, without analysis, without cold logic, that man must lose himself in the flood of all men, if he would be strong and invincible, if he would become fully a man. And he knew that even the most brutish beast could be aroused to this understanding, that he could be made to comprehend that everything he did affected men everywhere. In that individual sense of importance there was no selfishness, but only love and strength and grandeur.

So, this uncouth Englishman had aroused his brother-beasts to fanaticism and stern self-sacrifice. Ah, he was more dangerous than Franz had suspected! Such men were a danger to a ruthless world, set on exploitation and inexorable self-gain. He was a danger to the tigers everywhere, the tigers who had a right to devour and destroy and rend, for very reason of their tigerhood. He was the mouthpiece of the lambs, who were born only to feed the strong. He was the fool who had set out, in his puny strength, to upset the very laws of nature, to reverse the race, to undo the battle.

Franz was still incredulous, but filled with a gathering and infuriated anger. He felt himself threatened, menaced, ambushed.

Tom was still speaking. His audience was breathless, moved, stired. Franz saw clenched fists and shining eyes and exalted smiles. He was almost weeping, and feeling his emotion, they wept with him.

"So remember, lads, that tomorrow it's just the old fight between Us and Them. Between men and the tigers. We'll win! We'll win if we want to win! Nothin' is goin' to stop us but ourselves."

Franz touched the sleeve of the burly man. "It's over," he said. "You know what you have to do." And he looked at Tom Harrow with the eyes of a relentless and savage enemy, an enemy who felt himself assailed and mortally threatened.

CHAPTER 28

FRANZ STOESSEL, who knew himself completely, always freely admitted that he had little imagination beyond the expedient and the practical. Yet even he knew that in that mean and drafty hall, lighted by smoking gas jets, and filled with the odors of sweat, acid, tobacco and beer and unwashed bodies and dirty clothing, he had seen something of tremendous drama and power. He had seen the manifestation of a force that could be terrible and majestic, sublime and affrighting. He had seen the bottomless well from which all glory and terror could be dredged, invincible and resistless.

He had seen the immense grandeur of which even the lowest man could be capable. He had seen the immortality contained even in the most formless lumps of flesh. This did not seem heroic nor beautiful to him. It had seemed grotesque, and contained a threat to himself. The morality of the strong man is his own power, he believed. When the weak seized upon some dark and mysterious power which was not tangible or material, then the strong were menaced. For the strong built their houses of stone. The lightnings which the weak could invoke by invoking their inherent immortality could devastate the houses of stone, and reduce them to heaps of gravel. Franz, with a flash of insight which was deeper than any imagination he might have possessed, suddenly realized one colossal fact: When the people behold a vision, let tyrants beware.

He saw that Tom's crude phrase: "Us or Them," was only too vividly true. In himself, he believed he belonged to "Them." Tom's challenge was directed at him. He dared not let that challenge go unheeded. As he slipped as unobtrusively as possible with John Brent out of the hall, his uneasy anger increased. He was glad of this. Now he could proceed without that vague dark pain which had assailed him in the hall. He was whole again. At the doorway, the two men were joined by Collins, a larger and more competent and ruthless man than Brent. The three consulted briefly, then Brent and Collins hurried quickly down a dark street.

Jan Kozak, whose slow mind was now a slowly boiling mass of hatred and vengeance, tried to struggle through the crowd to Tom Harrow. But in spite of his brutal thrustings and surgings, he could not reach him. Tom was exhausted. He had made a previous appointment to meet Franz at a certain place. They were to walk home together, and discuss the strike called for tomorrow. By the time Jan Kozak reached the platform by literally beating a pathway through the crowds of excited, shouting and exalted men, Tom Harrow had disappeared.

The big Hungarian was filled with despair and terror. When friends plucked at his arm to stop him on his way to the door, in order to discuss Tom's speech with him, he brutally and wildly struck off the friendly hands, shouting incoherently. They could not understand him. Dully angered, they stared after him, muttering, wondering at his large black face and glittering eyes. He reached the doorway, and peered into the street. It was dark and deserted. The flickering gas lamps were haloed in fog and drizzle, the shabby warehouses on each side of the street were blank and faceless. Over the city flickered a dim scarlet mist, like a conflagration. Jan Kozak ran up the street, groaning in despair, sobbing in his deep chest. Tom Harrow and Franz Stoessel were nowhere in sight. He raced down another street. Now he was shouting. A patrolman, thinking he was drunk, tried to stop him. Jan's fist shot out and the officer rolled impotently into the gutter. Jan stood for an instant under a gaslight, and his face was mad, like that of a jungle beast's. For over half an hour he raced up one street and down another, and met no one. He had run like this when a boy in his native Hungarian forests, and the same heavy nightmare sensation now overcame him, and put lead into his feet. He sobbed aloud, his large lips blubbering, wet with foam.

A horse-car passed, rattling and swaying. Jan leapt upon the step, peered distractedly into the kerosene-lighted interior. A few nodding laborers sprawled on the wooden seats. There was no one else. Jan jumped down into the wet gutter, slipped, cracked his head against the curb, and lay unconscious for several moments, the rain dripping down upon him.

In the meantime, Tom had met Franz at the appointed place. At the sight of his friend, his long haggard face brightened with satisfaction and a touch of happy egotism. He locked his arm in Franz's, and exclaimed: "A jolly good speech, eh? Wot d'yo think of it, 'Andsome?"

"Excellent," replied Franz, with his bland smile that revealed nothing.

Tom chuckled, turned up the collar of his shabby greatcoat, pulled down his cap. The mood of exultation was strong and intoxicating in him. He hugged Franz's arm affectionately.

"I could do with a good cup of tea," he said. "Dolly'll be waitin' for us." He laughed shortly and excitedly. "Well, lad, it's the strike tomorrow! I'd like to see their faces!" he added, and now there was a growl in his voice.

Franz halted briefly. He pretended to be absorbed in sheltering a light for his pipe against the wet chill wind. "Tom," he said, "I see your point very well. But what will the strike accomplish, after all? Can you trust these men? What if they refuse to strike tomorrow?"

Tom's eyes narrowed as he studied that calm, expressionless profile in the uncertain light of a street-lamp. "They'll strike," he said, ominously. He asked, with a sudden hardness: "And you, Fritzie? You go with us?"

Franz puffed with concentration on his pipe. "Yes. I told you I would do what the others do."

Now he looked directly at Tom Harrow, his enemy. "You could go far," he said, reflectively. "If you were not such a fool."

Then the old uneasy darkness filled him again. "Tom," he said, suddenly. "Will you talk this over with me tonight? At your house? Perhaps——"

"No," said Tom, in such a quiet voice that Franz stepped back apprehensively, "there'll be no more gabbin'. And, Fritzie," he added, looking into Franz's face, "I'm holdin' you to your word."

They went on together, in silence. Wisps of mist floated along the broken wooden walks. They heard the dismal hooting of a river vessel. The thunder of a passing train shook the heavy wet air. The warehouses loomed above them, the blank windows dripping with moisture. The sky palpitated with dim scarlet.

Franz glanced behind him furtively. Two distant figures crept swiftly along in their rear, keeping close to the bolted doors of the warehouses. Franz's heart beat quickly. He seized Tom's arm and hurried him along more rapidly. The night was cold, but his forehead was damp with sudden sickening sweat.

"Tom," he said, in a muffled voice, "we'll go to your house. We've got to talk this over, I tell you!"

Tom stopped. He wrenched his arm from the grip of his friend. His eyes bored into that hard pale face, which he could barely see in the uncertain light of a distant streetlamp. And then, as he looked, his own heart skipped a beat, began to pound painfully. A sense of imminent terror and danger attacked him. His knees shook. But his voice was low and quiet when he said: "Fritzie, wot're you up to?"

The two men stood eye to eye in a thick damp silence.

Then Franz, in a last desperation, exclaimed: "Tom, you can't do this! I tell you, it's hopeless. I know. Let us talk it over, quietly, somewhere."

Tom was silent. The skin along his spine quickened, thrilled. The wet and drizzling night, the distant howl of train and vessel, the flickering lights, the empty warehouses, suddenly impinged on his senses with an unbearable sharpness. And as part of all this, he saw the open and revealed face of his deadly enemy, hard and inexorable, the blue eyes like bits of polished stone, the flat planes of cheek and chin as set as stone, the big mouth implacable and grim.

"So," said Tom, very softly, "so that's wot you are, you bloody blighter!"

He drew a deep breath, as a sick man might breathe. His whole face sickened. The sense of danger quickened in him, but he was aware of it only as a pang of illness. His whole attention was concentrated on that relentless countenance before him, and on a curious dividing pang in his chest like that of a shaft of sorrow and despondency.

"I might've known," said Tom, almost abstractedly. "Your sort—you can't be trusted. It's not just because you're a German. There's Germans back there, in the hall, as knows what I mean. They're goin' out with us. It's not Germans, or Americans, or Englishmen, or Frenchies. It's your sort against my sort. It's always been."

A faint derisive flicker passed over Franz's immobile features. Tom saw it, in spite of the dim chill light. The flicker did not anger him. It merely increased the unnamable pang in his chest, and he could not bear it.

He shivered. He pulled down his cap closer over his eyes. He still felt no anger. A complete hopelessness, a mortal sensation of loss and desolation, almost overpowered him. He had never been one to make friends readily. He had made a friend of Franz Stoessel. He had never really trusted him, but in a reserved way, he had loved him. "He's a chap as one can talk to," he had said to his wife, Dolly.

Now, it was the treachery of his friend which so assaulted him, and his grief had no place in it for anger or hatred. His little black eyes reddened, became opaque with a bitter mist. Because of this mist, he did not see the sudden averting of Franz's own eyes, the sudden twitching of his lips. He never knew that Franz had seen everything, and that for one terrible moment he could not endure himself.

The two lurking shadows approached more swiftly, behind Tom's back. Franz was no more aware of their approach than was Tom. But at the instant they reached Tom, he glanced up and saw them.

He cried: "Tom! Look out! Look out!"

But it was too late. As in a dreadful dream, Franz saw the flash of an uplifted arm, the hand holding something blunt and thick. He heard a dull and sickening thud. He heard another and another, and the sound of animal grunts. He stepped back, thrusting himself against the wet brick wall. His legs turned to jelly.

Tom did not fall immediately. He swayed, drunkenly, under the blows of the detectives. From under his cap streams of blood flowed, and between the trickles his eyes looked only at Franz, leaning helplessly against the wall, his head sunken on his chest. Then, still without a groan, he collapsed silently into the gutter, his head, bleeding profusely, half submerged in the black and racing water.

A roaring fog, lit with red stars, enveloped Franz. And with it came such a nausea that he retched. He pressed his hands against the wall to keep himself upright. His body was seized by his retching, and suddenly, he vomited helplessly. His whole being now was sternly concentrated on the effort to retain consciousness. He thought that his legs were slowly sinking into icy water, and he felt it rising to his thighs, to his groin, and finally to his heart. He did not know that his legs shot out from under him, and that he sank heavily to the sidewalk, his back supported by the wall, his head thrust forward and downward on his chest.

CHAPTER 29

FRANZ CAME swirling up through the black fog, spiralling in wide and dizzy circles. He felt himself floating impotently, and he thought: I must be out in a boat on the sea. His mind was confused. He was certain that he was rocking in his third-class bunk on the way from England, and he thought that he heard his mother's voice, close at hand, and clear and inflexible. He heard her say to his father: "We are within sight of land. At six o'clock, we shall be in New York." It was strange, he mused, that he knew New York very well, though he had surely never been there before. He remembered the low crowded sky-line, and the movement of insect tugs in curdled brown water. He remembered a morning of opaline skies, drizzling softly, and a din of hooting and churning, and many shouts. It was ridiculous to believe he had never seen New York before. His parents were absurd. He heard his mother's excited voice, urging him to rise and go up on deck, where he would get his first glimpse of the new world. "I have been in New York before," he said, clearly. His mother apparently did not hear him. She was scolding him. "A fourteen-year-old boy, and he lies in bed like a Lumpenhund!" she exclaimed.

Fourteen years old! Ridiculous. Franz laughed aloud, then

stopped abruptly. He felt very ill. He was spiralling more rapidly, and he longed for nothing but sleep. "Get up! Get up!" his mother cried. "It is late! You sleep, and there is New York!" "Sleep, sleep," he murmured.

No, he must not sleep. He must wake up and help Tom Harrow. "Tom," he called, in the swirling darkness. He called to his mother: "You must help Tom." She replied: "Are you never going to get out of bed, Dummkopf?"

He opened his eyes. The darkness still swirled in great swooping circles about him. Bemused, he could feel surprise that no morning sky-line faced him. He saw an opposite wall, running with livid cataracts of water, lighted by a yellow gas lamp. Thin red spirals danced between him and that wall, and bursting sparks. He heard the chuckling of a gutter, and again, far dismal hoots. The wall against which he leaned shook faintly in the vibrations of a passing train nearby. A hot sickness bubbled in his stomach, enhanced by the red spirals. He closed his eyes convulsively. He became conscious that his hands were slimy, cold and wet, and that he was shivering violently.

Then, like a blow on the skull, remembrance came back to him. His heart seemed to stop. Blackness threatened to overwhelm him again. He fought it off with vicious desperation. He stared blindly and savagely through the night, forcing himself to see. He saw the street clearly, now. He was all alone, soaked to the flesh, the coldness creeping along his bones. He forced himself to his knees, sobbing in his throat. He leaned against the wall, trying to quell the agony in his chest. There was no one in sight. What had they done with Tom? Ah, he had it! They were to take Tom to the nearest police station, declaring that he had attacked them in a drunken rage. It was all over. There would be no strike. Tom would be freed in a day or two, after the danger of a strike was past, and he had come to his senses.

Franz thrust himself weakly from the wall, then collapsed back against it once more. What had happened to him? Someone, two men, had struck at Tom. Franz could hear the dull murderous thuds again, and he sickened. Had they hurt him badly? No! That was impossible. All arrangements had been made that he was not to be badly hurt. But that blood! Surely, though, it had come from small surface wounds. He had to find out! He had to be sure that they had not injured Tom severely.

He shook his aching and clouded head, forced his legs to hold him up. His cap was gone. He must find it. When he bent his head, his senses swam again, weakly. Then he saw Tom

Harrow in the gutter, his head half submerged in the racing black water.

A great cry of anguish burst from him. That cry echoed back to him on the cold and watery air, reeking with night and desolation. He staggered a few steps; he fell on his knees beside his friend. With arms both numb and failing, he tugged at the flaccid shoulders, lifted Tom's head from the gutter, laid it on the sidewalk. The flaring gaslight fell on a ghastly face, on blood-and-water matted hair, on closed eyes and slack purple lips.

He caught Tom in his arms. He rested the lolling head on his chest. He was not conscious of sobbing and screaming aloud. "Tom! Mein Gott! Mein Gott!" He shook his streaming shoulders. He slapped the bruised face. He called over and over, his voice echoing dolorously in the rain and the night. The pain in his chest was a burning fire. A band of flaming steel encircled his forehead, and his throat. His cries became more clamorous, more frantic.

"Tom! Wake up! Tom, it is I, Franz! Look at me!"

But Tom did not hear him. Others did. Franz did not hear the sound of running footsteps, was not conscious of the presence of others until he felt himself roughly shaken, and heard harsh voices. He lifted his dazed and throbbing eyes. Two policemen stood over him, shouting. He blinked. He tried to speak. But he could do nothing but sob, over and over, his friend in his arms and lying across his knees.

"What happened?" demanded a policeman, his round tall helmet dripping with water. "What did you do to him?"

The other policeman was kneeling beside Tom, running his hands rapidly over him. He looked up, and said curtly: "Pretty far gone." He put his whistle to his lips and sent out a shrill and penetrating blast. The other policeman tugged at the distraught man kneeling on the sidewalk. "Better lay him down, son. Got his blood all over you. And stop yellin', for Christ's sake!"

Franz looked at his hands. They were wet with blood, Tom's blood.

"Who did it?" asked one of the men.

"I don't know," whispered Franz, staring at his hands.

They had laid Tom gently on the sidewalk. Other feet were running towards them now. Franz knelt stupidly, looking at his hands. He was conscious of nothing else. He felt, rather than saw, a dozen new faces, policemen and workmen. He felt the rain in his face, and his own convulsive shivering.

"He's comin' to," said a voice.

Franz turned his drooping eyes towards Tom. Some one was supporting the Englishman's head. Slowly, inch by inch,

Franz crept on his knees towards his friend. Tom was slowly opening his eyes. He looked about him. Some one wiped the blood that trickled from his forehead.

"That's all right," said a policeman, in a gruff voice. "Take it slow. Don't move. That's right. Who hit you?"

Tom tried to speak. A bloody foam bubbled to his lips. He tried to turn his head, and then he saw Franz's face bent over him.

The policemen, the excitedly shouting and shabby men, knew nothing of what had happened. But even they were suddenly silenced by the strangeness of the look which passed between these two, a look so intense, so held, so understanding, so dreadful, that even the most obtuse felt its frightful import. They saw a light like the glittering edge of a knife-blade appear between Tom's half-closed lids. They saw the curious convulsion of his swollen and bleeding lips. They saw the widening of his nostrils, from which thin scarlet threads were dripping. And they saw Franz's impassive face and the blueness of his mouth.

Tom gazed steadfastly at his enemy and his murderer, and Franz gazed back. Not a word passed between them that anyone could hear, but they heard their own exchanges. Their own inner voices, inaudible to others' ears, cried across a bottomless chasm to each other, echoed back from infinity, ran crying through space and darkness. And when they had done, they looked at each other in a blinding and throbbing silence, nothing else needed to be spoken, everything finished and over.

Whatever else the spirit of Tom Harrow had said to the spirit of Franz Stoessel, it had said nothing in condemnation, hatred or anger, but only in sorrow and regret. The feeble and fumbling hand which he now painfully lifted and laid on Franz's icy fingers was only a confirmation of that deep and eternal conversation.

"Dolly," he whispered.

"Yes," said Franz, very gently, and very softly. "And the children." And he held Tom's hand strongly.

Tom closed his eyes. A policeman, seeing that his life was almost spent, shook him a little. "Who hit you?"

Tom did not open his eyes. But hs lips moved. "I don't know the barstards," he said. He sighed once. His chest heaved; his head moved spasmodically. Then he was still, with the street lamp shining on his dead face, his blood forming grotesque geometric patterns over his features.

Franz sighed. He held his friend's hand. It cooled in his fingers.

And then, as though struck savagely and violently, he

started. He looked up. Over the peering heads of the crowd of men and police, he saw Jan Kozak.

CHAPTER 30

THE FACTORY superintendent, Fritz Dietrich, glided softly into Hans Schmidt's office. He glanced swiftly across the expanse of polished floor and dark rich rug to the great, shining mahogany desk, behind which Hans sat slumped and sullen in his fat pink flesh. Shirred, gray silk draperies were drawn across the high narrow windows to shut out the sudden brilliant December sun. A small fire smouldered on the hearth of a black marble fireplace, and threw thin ribbons of rosy light on the desk, on the brown walls, and caught reflections from Hans's diamond cravat pin and the diamond ring on his pudgy hand.

There were no other chairs in the room save that on which Hans sat. He did not encourage prolonged conversation, he would say. But the real reason was that some peasant belligerence and egotism in him would not allow others to sit in his presence. On the occasions of visits of important men, chairs were brought in, and immediately removed after the visit. Between two windows behind Hans was a broad low divan covered with red velvet, on which he took brief naps when tired. Sometimes he spent the night on that divan, when his home became more than usually insupportable to him. On his desk was a small gilt-framed miniature of his daughter, Ernestine. Over the divan hung a dark portrait of his wife's late father, former absentee owner of the mills. The portrait had been painted in the best Rembrandt tradition, all umber and shadow and points of light, but perpetual smoky fog and age and imperfect pigments had blurred it almost completely to one dim tint. However, the long thin face, the narrow aristocratic nose, the cold dark eyes, looked out from the heavy gold frame with supreme and icy contempt and aloofness. That face repudiated, with a startling and living disdain and delicate fastidiousness, the fat peasant seated beneath it. Sometimes susceptible visitors thought that there was affront in the lofty expression, and passionless outrage.

Often, when alone, Hans would tuck his hands under his broadcloth coat-tails and grimace malevolently up at the portrait, with a kind of sardonic triumph. He loved aristocracy, with the deep grovelling respect of the innately servile. But he also hated its superiority, and knew its contempt for him. He would teeter back and forth on his heels, grunting under his breath, glaring at the portrait, hating it, triumphing over it. He would seem to say: "It is justice. Aristocracy stares impotently from its golden frame, but the peasant always triumphs, in his flesh and his blunt life." It is no paradox to say that he realized that coarse flesh and strong brutal urging were at once inferior and superior to attenuated delicacy and civilization. Hearty animalism used its fists on aristocracy, out of envy, hatred, respect and worship. It grovelled before intellect and birth, and kicked it savagely whenever an occasion presented itself. The grovelling came not from fear, but from adoration, and the savage kicking came also from it, and out of despair. The unattainable was regarded with awe, but out of that awe came the impulse of destruction.

The dim red fire struck life and fragile vitality from the cold face of Simeon Bradhurt as Fritz Dietrich glided silently into Hans's office. Hans grunted brutally at the entrance of his superintendent. Dietrich spoke quietly, in German:

"Mein Herr, the mills remain quiet, but frightened and uncertain. The men continue to work. They whisper. But there is no sign of disorder. Burnley has arrived——"

Hans's sullen stodgy flesh was electrified. He struck the polished desk a dull and resounding blow with the flat of his hand. His tiny blue eyes were inflamed.

"Do what you want!" he shouted, viciously. "It is no concern of mine! I have had no part in this small and contemptible occasion. Involve me in no degrading discussion! Do you hear me? I am Hans Schmidt!"

Dietrich incilned his head and murmured in respectful conciliation.

"I understand that, Herr Schmidt. It is insulting to speak of the matter to you. But the laws of America often insist on involving the important as well as the unimportant. It is disgusting."

Hans breathed loudly through his short and fleshy nose. He threw himself back in his chair. He beat an infuriated tattoo on his desk with his short fat fingers. During all this, he shot malignant glances at Dietrich.

"I, Hans Schmidt, have nothing to do with a drunken brawl between my laborers," he said, his hoarse voice filled with fury and detestation. But there was something else in his eyes: fear. Out of this fear came his rage. Dietrich knew this. He smiled deprecatingly, and inclined his head again.

"I know this too well, Herr Schmidt. Nevertheless, Burnley is here. He insists that if his men, Collins and Brent, are involved in this, he will have to protect them. He also insists upon seeing you."

At this, Hans literally leapt from his chair. He leaned his fists on his desk. His head was bent like that of a charging bull's, and he regarded Dietrich with crimson and apoplectic hatred.

"You dare bring that message to me?" he screamed incredulously. "You dare bring the demand of a cheap and scurvy detective to ME?"

Dietrich coughed delicately, as though with supreme regret. "But the message involves murder, Mein Herr," he murmured. Hans could not see the gloating in the respectfully lowered eyes.

Hans struck the desk violently with his fists.

"I have had no part in it! You brought that rabble to Nazareth, not I!"

Dietrich was silent for a moment, though he smiled a little. Then he said: "You will not see Burnley, Mein Herr? It is well. I shall deal with him, myself. Nevertheless, he remains impudent. He says we delegated Stoessel to advise Brent and Collins, his men. They acted, he declares, on the express advice of Stoessel."

"Then, let Stoessel take the consequences!"

Dietrich sighed. "In that event, no doubt Stoessel will involve us. I have never trusted that Prussian. There is a saying in Saxony that a boar and a Prussian were mothered by the same sow."

Hans said nothing. He tugged open his desk and brought out a box of cigars. He thrust one in his mouth. Dietrich leapt lithely to light it from his own box of "lucifers." Hans's broad fat face was suffused, and there was a furtive expression on it. His pursy mouth was sullen.

"You empower me, Mein Herr, to deal with Burnley to the best of my ability?" asked Dietrich, with regretful softness.

"Do what you wish. But I command you not to speak my name."

Dietrich went towards the door. There, he paused. "Have you decided, Mein Herr, on what day you will grant an interview to Mr. Jules Bouchard, of Sessions Steel?"

"That smirking swine of a Frenchman!" exclaimed Hans, with a look of contempt which could not, however, conceal the furtive gleam of his eyes. "Sessions Steel affects to ignore us, as a third-rate mill, but nevertheless when a question of manganese is involved, they will graciously become aware of our existence. Let him wait a day or two. Then, we shall write him."

Dietrich bowed, and left the office. He returned to his own desk, where a small stout man with a completely bald head, a bristling mustache and hard shrewd eyes, waited for him, smoking a prodigious cigar. He wore a loud black-and-white check suit with a black waistcoat across which swung a thick gold watch-chain. On Detrich's desk he had placed his round brown derby hat and a gold-headed cane. About him there was an air of callous surety and determination, at once compact and ruthless.

"Well?" he said shortly, seeing Detrich. He made a motion of rising.

Dietrich respectfully waved him back to his chair, and then seated himself. He then became aware for the first time of two burly men lurking near the outer door. But though he became aware of them, he affected to ignore them. He made a little bony tent of his fingers and regarded Burnley with benevolence. But Burnley was accustomed to benevolence in awkward and precarious circumstances, and his shrewd gray eyes narrowed in malicious suspicion. Moreover, Dietrich's lean foxlike face, and the pale blue eyes behind their half-lenses, did not disarm him in the least.

Dietrich coughed. He smiled affectionately, and thrust a box of cigars across his desk towards the chief of the private detective bureau. Burnley stared at the cigars, and with a grunt, helped himself to a handful, which he deliberately inserted in the capacious pockets of his waistcoat. He waited.

Dietrich coughed again, and leaned back in his chair. "I have talked to Mr. Schmidt," he said, in his high Saxon voice. "He is most regretful. But at the present moment he is unable to see you, much as he might desire to. He is engaged with a number of clerks in annotating large new orders. However," added the superintendent, with smiling briskness, "he delegates me to tell you that under no circumstances would he consider ignoring the—er—present position of your agents, should the necessity arise. He would consider bearing part of the cost of the fee, at least, for excellent attorneys——"

Burnley's eyes became glittering points of light. He glanced over his shoulder at Brent and Collins. He spoke in a voice of deep sarcasm: "Now, boys, isn't that just too jim-dandy of Mr. Schmidt? He will shed a few tears for you when you get hanged. Capital, eh?"

The two men laughed shortly, in voices like menacing growls.

Burnley turned back to Dietrich, and his face was full of cold threat.

"Look here, you, there ain't going to be any 'necessity.' You're all in it, Schmidt and the rest of you. If one of my boys hangs, he won't hang alone. Understand?"

Dietrich examined his pale fingernails with rapt attention. Then he said softly: "Let us be sensible, and consider the situation. Your agents were not commissioned to any—acts of violence. That is against all the principles of the Schmidt Steel Company. However," he said, lifting his hand to interrupt a violent outburst from Burnley, "it is hardly likely that any untoward—circumstances—shall arise. We are now awaiting the return of Franz Stoessel, who gave instructions to your agents, and who is now attending the inquest. It is not possible that he will involve himself, and your agents. I understand that the unfortunate—victim—died without incriminating any one."

Burnley threw himself back in his chair and regarded Dietrich menacingly.

"We will wait for this Stoessel," he said.

Dietrich gazed through the window contemplatively, and with an air of gentle detachment. "That might be well," he murmured. The two men near the door sat down deliberately, lit cigars, and waited, their beefy hands on their spread knees. Dietrich glanced at them fleetingly. They were ugly "customers."

Dietrich returned his attention to his desk. "You will excuse me, please," he said, in his murmuring and placating voice. He began to examine a pile of papers. His air was one of regretful dismissal of the present situation. Minute after minute passed. Burnley was not intimidated. He puffed stolidly on his cigar. His men puffed. The papers on Dietrich's desk whispered. The sound of the mills penetrated into the office in a dull subterranean roar. The pallid bright sky outside appeared and disappeared in gushes of smoke.

Half an hour went by, then the door suddenly opened, and a tall, broad-shouldered young man, with hard pale lips, ghastly color and red-veined blue eyes, entered abruptly. His manner was grim and purposeful. His eyes touched Burnley and the two agents, who stirred and muttered to themselves. Dietrich glanced up, and smiled.

"Ah, Stoessel," he said, genially. "We were waiting for you. We wish to hear the results of the inquest." He smiled at Burnley. "This is Franz Stoessel. He will now tell us about the inquest."

But Franz ignored all these niceties. He came directly to Dietrich's desk. He leaned towards the superintendent and pressed his clenched fists down on the wood. He spoke only to him, and then in German.

"The inquest is over. Closed. The verdict was an attack by unknown thieves. I beat them off." He looked at Dietrich with a slight but terrible smile. "I am a hero. I did all I could to protect my friend. The police were there. They gave their evidence. They repeated Harrow's last words, that he did not know the identity of his attackers. There is a warrant out for the unknown thieves. Three warehouse watchmen were found with excellent imaginations. They saw the thieves, and described them as three or four shabbily-dressed men with caps pulled low over their eyes, carrying clubs."

Dietrich looked at Franz with a sweet expression, and breathed with relief. He turned to Burnley, who put up a short brusque hand. "Don't interpret. I know your damned language." He stared at Franz Stoessel. "Congratulations on being a hero," he said, ironically. "Or maybe you're just a smart man. Maybe you got a touchy feeling for your own neck. My boys wouldn't have hanged alone."

"No," said Franz, very quietly, and looking only at Dietrich with his swollen and diffused eyes, "we would not have hanged alone."

Dietrich, suddenly uncomfortable, roused himself to renewed benevolence. "So, it is all finished," he said lightly. "There is nothing more to say. I advise you to take your agents, all of them, out of town immediately, Mr. Burnley. Now, there is a matter of your fee——"

Burnley slapped the desk before him heavily and slowly. "My fee, yes. It was to be two thousand dollars, for last night, and for today, if any disorders came up in your mills. But, I've decided that ain't enough. I want four thousand. My boys deserve it. They did a good night's work for you bastards." He glanced over his shoulder again at Brent and Collins. "A fair price, eh, boys, for risking your necks?"

"Preposterous!" exclaimed Dietrich. Franz still stood, leaning against the desk, leaning towards him, with those fixed and glaucous eyes. Dietrich affected to ignore him.

Burnley shrugged. "On second thought," he said, "maybe you're right. Maybe it is preposterous. My boys only removed a feller that would've cost Mr. Schmidt maybe twenty-five thousand dollars. Four thousand's too cheap for the work we done. We want six. Did I say twenty thousand dollars out of Mr. Schmidt's money-bags? If there'd been a strike, it would've cost him twice as much. If there'd been a trial, and my boys here got involved, Schmidt might just as well have closed down his mills and gone out of business, if not worse. Six thousand it is, Mr. Dietrich."

Franz stirred. It seemed even to the alarmed Dietrich that that stirring cost him a prodigious effort, that the very act of pushing himself upright involved a mortal strain. Sweat appeared on his gray face, and at the corners of his grim clenched mouth. He looked at Burnley, and something in his expression made that gentleman sit up, abruptly, as though anticipating attack.

"Two thousand dollars," said Franz, in a low voice. "Two thousand dollars for a murder. That is a lot of money. Judas got only thirty pieces of silver."

Dietrich opened his mouth as if to speak, then said nothing. Out of the corner of his eye he saw that Schmidt's door was slightly open.

Burnley narrowed his eyes to an evil slit, as he sat up in his chair, regarding Franz warily.

"So!" he said. "A big talker, ain't you? What's it got to do with you, anyway? You're a kind of gandy-dancer around here, eh? Keep your mouth shut when you ain't being consulted." He turned to Dietrich insolently. "Five thousand dollars. That's my last price. Take it or leave it."

Dietrich was silent. He looked at Franz, whose exhausted and stony face had taken on its look of implacability and hatred.

"Don't try me," he said to Burnley, in that same low pent voice. "I'm reaching the place where I don't care what happens. To me, or to any one. In five minutes, the price will be one thousand. Make up your mind."

Dietrich cleared his throat deprecatingly. "The fee agreed upon was two thousand dollars, Mr. Burnley," he said. "We must adhere to the original bargain."

Brent came forward now, walking lightly on the balls of his feet, his neck and head thrust forward, his large brutal face wrinkling like that of a gorilla's. He faced Franz, laid a gripping hand on his shoulder.

"Shut up," he said, briefly, and he raised the other hand, clenched into a fist, and pressed it viciously against Franz's chin.

Franz did not move for a moment, then he struck down the fist, and wrenched himself free from the other's grip. He smiled a little, and the red veins thickened in his eyes.

"It was you, wasn't it, Brent, who hit Harrow first? I can swear to that."

Brent lifted his fist suddenly, then held it back. His lips and eyes wrinkled still more, grimacing. His stubbled cheeks became crimson. Then, very slowly, he dropped his fist. He panted slightly. But what he had seen in Franz's face terrified him. He shook his head, as though he had been struck. He looked at Burnley.

"Chief," he said, "let's take the money. I'm gettin' out of town, right now."

Burnley said nothing for several long moments. He looked from Dietrich, faintly smiling, to Franz, and then to Brent. He chewed his lower lip. He tapped his fingers on the desk. Then he stood up.

"Two thousand dollars, then, you swine," he said, holding out his hand.

Dietrich, his smile broader, shook his head. "I am sorry, Mr. Burnley. No checks. You understand, of course. But I have the money, in cash." He unlocked a drawer, and withdrew a packet of bills, which he gently laid before the chief of detectives. Then he leaned back in his chair, and smiled again, as though amused.

Burnley lifted the packet. He slapped the desk with it, slowly, significantly. Then he clapped his hard derby on his bald head. He took up his cane. He dangled it in his hand. Then he laughed shortly.

"Remember, Mr. Dietrich, the Burnley Detective Agency is always at your service." He turned to Brent and Collins. "Boys, we're licked. But our necks ain't goin' to stretch. That's something to think of."

He left, followed by his burly men. The door banged behind him.

Then it was that Franz collapsed into the chair Burnley had vacated. He stared before him, blindly. Dietrich surveyed him with a magnanimous expression.

"Stoessel, you have saved us a great deal. You have also saved us considerable money. Mr. Schmidt——"

Franz aroused himself. He jerked himself upwards in his chair, and leaned forward as if to spring. His face and his eyes were frightful. His bitten lips showed tiny beads of blood. Dietrich, aghast, pushed his chair from his desk. His eyelids, with their pale lashes, flickered in deathly alarm. But when Franz spoke, it was in his usual quiet tones.

"I have saved you nothing, Dietrich. In fact, this little affair is going to cost the Schmidt Steel Company a great deal of money. There is Tom Harrow's widow, and his three small children. It will cost the Schmidt Steel Company just five thousand dollars as a sympathy offering to Mrs. Harrow, in her great loss."

"You are mad!" gasped Dietrich.

Franz shook his head. He smiled, as though to himself. "Five thousand dollars. The Schmidt Steel Company regrets the loss of a valued foreman, and commiserates with his widow. A noble gesture."

"You are mad," repeated Dietrich, staring at him with hating contempt. "We shall not give a penny."

"Yes, you will," said Franz, nodding his head, and smiling again, that vague and dreadful smile. "You will also listen to what I have to say.

"In the first place, there is a man here who knows. How he knows, I do not know, myself. But it is certain he does. Whether he overheard some of our arrangements or not, I do not know. I think not. I think he only surmises. He is a foreman, also, one of Harrow's most devoted followers. I have only to speak to him. A strike will follow, a very disastrous strike. That is only one of the contingencies. One of the smallest."

He paused. He drew a deep slow breath, as though something were torturing him unbearably. Dietrich regarded him palely, his mouth gripped in a thin line. The crack of Schmidt's door widened. Neither saw it.

Franz lifted his hand, spread out the fingers. He bent one. "That is the first contingency. The second is more formidable. If the money is not paid to Mrs. Harrow, I may be compelled to go to the police and tell what I know——"

Dietrich laughed evilly. "And involve yourself? Remember, it was you who gave the instructions to the detectives."

"I gave instructions only to incite a brawl with Harrow. Then to drag him away to the nearest police station, where he would be held for a day or two until all danger of the strike was past. In the first place, the whole thing was illegal. If Harrow died accidentally, it was during the commission of an illegal act. And the illegal act was perpetrated by your hirelings. It was you who called them, not I. I need not enlarge just now on the consequences following an investigation."

Dietrich's thin white nostrils dilated. He looked at Franz malignantly.

"You will hang," he said, and he repeated the words, with venomous relish: "You will hang."

Franz inclined his head. "But, as Burnley said, I shall not hang alone."

Dietrich's thin white face was a slab of pallid evil.

"This is blackmail, you schweinehund," he said.

Franz shook his head with dim and smiling wonder, and again his eyes were fixed on something not in the room.

"No, it is only the price of a man's life," he said, very softly.

"And you think a stinking Englishman is worth five thousand dollars!" Dietrich flung himself back in his chair and snickered.

Franz stood up, leaned again half-way across the desk.

"He was my friend," he said. And then again, as if to himself: "He was my friend!"

"And you killed your friend," remarked Dietrich, enjoying himself. His almost colorless eyes blinked pleasantly behind their lenses.

"No," said Franz, in a dull sick voice. "I did not kill him. It was something else that killed him." He stood upright, swaying a little. He looked through the windows, and fixed his gaze on the chimneys of the great mills.

He saw the mills. Something stirred in him, the far echoing memory of Tom Harrow's voice. When they had stared so intently at each other during those last frightful moments before Tom had died, Franz had heard that voice in himself. He had heard: "There is a devil in you, Franz. God help you."

Yes, there was a devil in him, he thought. A devil that would not let go. A devil that would drive him on, even now. It was his nature. Tom had recognized that, recognized the awful truth that no man can resist himself, that he must follow his nature, even if it led him to hell. Tom, the uncouth and uneducated, Tom who had suffered, Tom who knew everything had known this also. The appalling impotence of man against himself had been known to him. At the last, he had had only compassion.

A bell sounded in Hans's office. Dietrich sprang to his feet and glided away. Franz did not notice his going. No, he thought, it is not quite true. I can go back. Even now, I can go back.

And then he knew that he could not go back. The devil in himself had him. He lacked even the desire to resist. Later, he believed that was his strength.

Dietrich returned. Franz looked at him blindly, not seeing him. Dietrich was smiling again, almost affectionately.

"Stoessel, I am pleased to tell you that I have discussed your—suggestion—with Mr. Schmidt, and, as always, he is willing to be generous. Mrs. Harrow will receive five thousand dollars from the Schmidt Steel Company. Mr. Schmidt sympathizes with Mrs. Harrow in her great sorrow——"

Franz's eyes focussed swiftly on the superintendent's feral features. He passed his hand over his lips and chin.

"The gesture," he said, "will be an excellent deterrent to a strike."

Suddenly he burst into a wild fit of laughter. He rocked on his heels. He caught the back of a chair to keep himself from falling. He threw back his head, and his shouts of laughter filled the room with a mad and mirthless sound. He shook his head; tears spurted from his eyes, as though he were overcome.

Dietrich, appalled, retreated to the windows, and plucked at the cord of the window-shade with nervous fingers.

"Verrückt!" he muttered.

CHAPTER 31

ON THE morning of the funeral of Tom Harrow, Egon Stoessel awoke, and lay silently, gazing about him with a dumb and terrified expression.

Each night when he went to bed, he prayed humbly, and with trembling, that tomorrow there would be a change. Tomorrow, he would think, despairingly, yet with a faint hope, it would be different. He would open his eyes. He would see the ashen light of morning more clearly, as it came through the windows. There would not be, first, a complete darkness, followed thereafter by a dim glimmer, then by sudden wheels of fire whirling before his vision, and then, very slowly, as the wheels faded, the emerging of the rectangular shape of the window palely gray in the dusky wall. Tomorrow, he would say to himself, he would awake, and there would be the window, reassuringly complete and sharp, without the terrifying preliminaries which had afflicted his eyes and his senses for the past few weeks.

But this morning, the wheels of fire were more vivid, more scalding to his aching eyes, and after their passing, the window did not emerge at all. Terror set his heart to rolling and plunging. He sat upright, his flannel nightshirt dampening with sudden icy sweat. There was only darkness. Perhaps, he screamed to himself through his terror, it was still night. He fumbled in the bed for Emmi. She was not there. Then he heard the sounds of her in the kitchen, and he knew, from the sounds, that the bottom door was wide open. There should, therefore, be a long streaming upwards from the kitchen lamp, lit in the early dawn. But there was no streaming. Everything was as black as the bottom of a pit at midnight.

Impelled now, by pure primitive terror, he swung his thin legs over the side of the bed. He thrust his arms out before him, and whimpering, he felt his way to the door. It was wide open. He reached downwards with a shaking and tentative foot, found the stairway. Then, giving way entirely to his terror and horror, he plunged down the stairway, hitting against the sides of the close cold walls, his feet hardly finding the stairs. He burst into the kitchen with a great cry of anguish.

"Emmi! I cannot see! I am blind!"

He stood there, in the warm and lighted kitchen, staring blindly before him, an old thin haggard man, with a wild white face and outstretched reaching arms. His nightshirt fell about his quaking knees. His gray hair stood upright on his tremulous head. His eyes, wide and staring, bulged, and his mouth was open, and now silent, but with an expression as though he were inwardly screaming, over and over. Threads of glaucous saliva stretched from one distended lip to the other.

Emmi, paralyzed, stared at him from the stove, a large wooden spoon in her hand. For several moments, she was incapable of moving. Her face became ghastly gray in hue. Her whole vision was absorbed in the sight of that figure in the doorway, reaching for her, silently shrieking, the fingers extended and clutching air, like a drowning man clutching water.

Then the spoon dropped from her hand with a clatter onto the iron stove. Egon felt her strong reassuring arms about him, and she felt his quivering rigidity and frantic clutching hands, which first seized her shoulders, then her wrists, her hands, her shoulders again.

"Nonsense," she said, loudly, keeping her thickening voice firm and calm over her own terror and agony. "It will pass in a moment. Egon, you must control yourself."

She seized his hands strongly in her own, pressing warmth into their bony coldness, trying to subdue their awful trembling. She led him to a chair near the stove. There, she chafed his hands, talked soothingly. He gasped, stared about him, his eyes bulging madly. A film was over them. Trickles of sweat rolled down his face, hung in drops from his chin. He could not speak. He could only stare, and allow her to rub his hands, and, finally, his numb and jerking feet.

"You are cold," she scolded. "You have taken a chill. That will hurt the eyes. You must control yourself."

His voice came, bubbling, incoherent. "Emmi——!"

"Be calm. In a moment, you will see again. It is nothing. It has often happened to me," she lied, steadfastly.

At this word of hope, he broke into loud dry sobbing. He drew her hands to his chest, held them there in a spasmodic grip. He tried to see her face, but there was only complete darkness. She saw him trying to see her, and the sight of those filmed distended eyes, blind and veined with scarlet threads, was almost more than she could bear. Her heart was pounding with a torturing pain. She felt the grip of his hands, holding hers in death's own strength.

"It has happened before," he said, and he spoke as though his voice wrenched itself painfully through a paralyzed throat. "I have been afraid. I thought it would pass."

"It will pass," she said, quietly. She let him hold her hands. She sat back on her heels. Her face was still and white, her pale lips parted in her effort to breathe. The stove fumed near them, sending out rays of warmth and comfort. The lamp flickered on the table, throwing a pool of light on the plates and the cutlery. A smell of coffee and new fresh bread filled the kitchen. On its shelf over the black iron sink, a clock ticked loudly.

"Be calm," said Emmi, rubbing her husband's pallid hands over and over, after she had gently released them. "In a moment, you will see."

His trembling lessened. But his blind eyes were still fixed on her face in their wild and distended and unblinking desperation.

"Emmi, Emmi!" he whimpered, over and over.

"Yes," she said, in her quiet and unshaking voice. She reached over to a chair and took her shawl which she had laid there after the fire had warmed the cold room. She put the shawl over Egon's thin bent shoulders. Over its thick gray folds, his gaunt corded throat and quaking head emerged. His look was piteous, distraught, blue with terror. He felt nothing but her reassuring presence, her strength, upon which he had leaned for so many years. He was conscious of nothing else but the courage and firmness of her hands, and her soothing words. He clung to her with a sudden convulsive movement, leaning towards her, burying his distracted face on her shoulder. She held him to her as she might have held a child, rocking a little on her heels, murmuring in his ear. After a little, he wept. She felt his tears through the thin blue cotton of her dress, and they were like drops of blood to her.

She and Egon were alone in the dark cold flat. Franz had spent the night at Tom Harrow's cottage, sitting with a few men from the mills, while Dolly, exhausted and prostrate, slept. There was no one to send for help. There was nowhere to look for strength but in herself. And she knew that always she had had to look for strength only in her own fortitude and courage.

Moment by moment she held Egon, seeing and feeling his tears, and her own face grew perceptibly older and more shrunken. Her pale blue eyes became suffused with something more poignant than tears. The bones of cheek and jaw and eye-socket sharpened under her thoughts and her almost overwhelming fear. The temples, from which her graying yellow hair was strained upwards to their knot on the top of her head, took on a bruised appearance. There was a blue and deathly shadow about her lips and wide nostrils. But never for a moment did she allow the sobbing old man in her arms to feel or guess the anguish that pervaded her, and the nausea that sent thrills of retching through her spare body. She stared over his head unblinkingly, her eyes fixed on a terrible and mournful vision, which could sicken and temporarily strike her down, but which could never overcome her.

"It will pass," she said, over and over. "Be calm. It will pass."

Finally, he became quiet in her arms. The scalding tears grew less and less. He said, brokenly: "Emmi, what shall we do, if I am blind?"

"You are not blind," she said, vigorously. "Believe it. You are not blind. But it has been very wrong, not to tell me before. Then, this could have been spared you. I have asked you to see a physician, when your glasses did not help you any longer. But you delayed. Your eyes are strained. If you will be calm, your sight will be restored."

"Yes, yes," he whispered, his shaking lips against her neck. He believed her. Emmi had never lied to him.

Again, there was silence in the kitchen. Egon's thin old body relaxed, warmed by her arms, the stove, and the shawl. She held him closer. A great and melancholy tenderness flooded her heart, her soul. It seemed to her that her flesh could not contain such a flood, that it must burst from her, and that she must cry out, and weep aloud. She had always loved Egon with a cold and jealous and protecting passion, almost savage in its possessiveness. He had been her child. Franz had never been her child. He had, first, been her equal, and then her superior. Finally, he had hated her. Suddenly, with a sad horror, she saw that she had come to hate him in turn. But the hatred, strangely, had not dissolved her understanding of what he was, nor had it destroyed her bitter love for him. Never had she felt for him this protecting passion she felt for Egon, not even when he had lain in her arms as a child. In some way she must always have known that Egon was one of the innocents of the world, covered with wounds, eternally suffering, silent and gentle and bewildered. She knew, now, that he had always suffered. She must have known, subconsciously, that he had suffered, but never had the thought risen to her conscious mind. Now, she was appalled, aghast, filled with self-reproach and corroding remorse. All these years she had failed him, though she had loved him.

Love is not enough, she cried to herself, some coldness in her vanishing forever. Love was never enough. Love was sometimes a door separating those who loved, blinding them, feeling the loved one behind the door, but always out of reach. There must be a sensitive understanding, also. She had never understood Egon, however much she had loved and protected him. He had made her impatient, because of her lack of comprehension. He had known that impatience, and had become silent, not reproachful, only mournful, and hopeless. As in a mirror, she saw his yearning for his home; she saw the scenes he saw, which had never touched her own sensibilities. She saw his nostalgia; felt its creeping sorrow in her own bones. She had sacrificed him! She had brought him to a hateful land, which he had not hated, and which had only frightened and confused him. She had brought him to a land of coldness, which had no place in it for gentleness and placidity and humble hearts and peace. She had filled his ears with its raw clangor, the sound of its machines, the clamor of its lifeless vitality, the uproar of its growth, which was only a mechanical growth, as though some monstrous mechanism had acquired the ability to extend its arms of steel and grow new rivets and new pistons, until all the world was full of its screeching and grinding, its wheels and its rods, its belts and its whistles, a Juggernaut of steel. She was certain there was no soul in this mechanism, in its scraping bedlam of noise and brutality. Egon had been caught in its glittering and bellowing turmoil, its shifting nightmare of faces, its flashes of flame, its concatenation of din, its horrible and gigantic rhythm and bloodless pulsing. He was like a moth in a jungle of pistons and belts, fluttering feebly. He was appalled by the facelessness of American life, for all his life he had seen only man and not men. The poverty of this life, its cold fever, its greedy iron heart, had broken him, and his own horror had destroyed him.

Emmi held him with new fierce tightness in her arms.

"It has been too much for you, Egon," she said. "We shall go back to the Fatherland. I was mistaken. There is no fulfilment of dreams here. I believed lies, or I believed in a thing which has already died in America. We came too early, or too late. We shall go home."

She felt him stir fitfully against her breast.

"Emmi," he whispered, "for you to go back will be a defeat."

She stared over his head grimly.

"Not to retreat, in defeat, is idiocy. Besides, what am I? Am I important? No! Not even the dreams I had were important."

Her egotism, then, received a wound from which it would never entirely recover. But her wide hard eyes looked at the wound bitterly.

"And Franz?" whispered Egon. His stirring was stronger now, as though he were daring to hope.

"Franz will go with us. Of that I am sure. He is much attached to you. He will not let you go alone."

Egon was silent. Then suddenly, as though new strength had been given him, new joy, new realization, he lifted his head, and smiled wildly. A light even came into his blind eyes.

"Home!" he cried. 'My home! My Fatherland!"

She could not bear the sight of that convulsive ecstasy.

"Home," she repeated, and could feel relief that he could not see her dry twisted lips.

He put his hands over his face and wept aloud. She let him weep. Her embittered heart was filled with a humble and astonished wonder that she had never known before what Egon had suffered in such patient and gentle silence. It frightened her, tormented her, made her feel mean and contemptible. Egon dropped his hands. Then he started violently. He looked about him, unbelieving. He looked at Emmi, and his old pale lips parted, as though intolerably surprised.

"I see!" he cried. "I see again!"

"Yes!" she exclaimed, overcome. She took his hands. "Yes! I understand, now. It was not your eyes, my Egon. It was your mind, your heart, that could no longer endure to see your life!"

They clung to each other convulsively, weeping together, heart to heart as they had never been before.

She made him return to bed, and brought him his breakfast, though he protested, his face shining, that he had never felt so well. He watched her move about the room, he allowed her to feed him. He was like a trusting and rapturous child, brought back from death.

Once he took her hand. "You are so good to me, Emmi, Liebchen," he said, and then he kissed the back of that dry bony hand, and then the callouses on its palm. She looked

down on his bent gray head, and her heart twisted savagely
He was never to go back to the office in the Mills. That, sh
had decided. There was five thousand dollars in the bank. I
was enough. She had another inspiration. Irmgard still owne
the small farm in Germany. She, Emmi, would buy that farm
Her inspiration mounted. They would all return, she an
Egon and Franz and Irmgard! Franz and Irmgard would b
married. She, Emmi, would forget herself, forget all her sill
impassioned dreams. She would live for Egon, and her grand
children. She would be an old German frau, contented on th
land.

I have lived for nothing but myself, before, she thought
clean and swept in her renunciation of self. I thought only o
myself, and believed I had some mission. I was a fool.

Yet, she was too forthright, too honest, to believe that thi
renunciation of a life of ideals and dreams was without pai
for her. A cold and passionless emptiness pervaded her; sh
was filled with a sense of barrenness and futility. She was to
strong to live happily only for others. In such a living, sh
knew, there was the soft core of weakness. The strong liv
for themselves, for that is their nature, she said to herself
If they abandon self, they have entered spiritual monasteries
in which there is nothing but bleakness and sterility, a denia
of nature.

Nevertheless, this she must do. The sacrifice was not joy
ful to her. It was gall on her lips, vinegar in her side. No
with supreme rapture did she hang herself on her own privat
cross, believing that in renunciation she had found complete
ness and peace. She found only uncompensating death.

I am stronger than Egon, she thought. I can endure suffer
ing with more fortitude. Therefore, there must be an end t
his own suffering. It is my turn.

He fell asleep out of exhaustion, not long afterwards, hold
ing her hand. She listened to the ticking of the clock, down
stairs, and aroused herself. At eleven o'clock Tom Harrow'
funeral was to take place. She had promised Mrs. Harrow
to be at the cottage at nine o'clock. It was almost eleven
Gently, she released her hand, and stood for a moment look
ing down at Egon's drawn and sleeping face. Then she lef
the dark dank bedroom, and ran swiftly downstairs. She flun
her shawl over her head and shouders, put her keys in th
pocket in her skirt.

Then she heard a tapping on the front door. They hav
sent for me, she thought. She opened the door, and was as
tonished to see Irmgard standing there, smiling, beautiful i
a green cloth dress and black velvet jacket and green bonnet
"Well, Irmgard," she said, helplessly, clutching her shawl

which was caught by the bright strong wind of the December day.

"Aunt Emmi," said the girl. Emmi moved aside, and the two women stood in the little dark hall. Irmgard smiled again, though she was disturbed by her aunt's strange white look and drawn lips. "It is my Thursday. I thought I would spend the day with you." A faint color, like a ripple, ran over her smooth cheeks.

"It is well," said Emmi, mechanically.

Irmgard was made uneasy by Emmi's expression, so taut and rigid, yet absent, as though she were engrossed deeply in thoughts not connected with the present. She gave the impression that Irmgard had not yet completely impinged herself on her awareness.

Then, Emmi, as though finally becoming cognizant of Irmgard, kissed her on the forehead. Irmgard's faint alarm sharpened at the touch of those cold and lifeless lips, preoccupied and hasty.

"Have I come at the wrong time?" she asked, quickly. "Is there something wrong?"

"No. No, child. It is just that your uncle is not well. Do not be disturbed. It is nothing with his body. It is his mind. He cannot endure, any longer."

She waited impatiently for a puzzled look to come on Irmgard's quiet face. But no such look appeared. Irmgard's green eyes widened for an instant, and then were hidden by an opaque shadow.

"What can I do?" she asked. "Shall I see him now?"

"No." Emmi paused. Her preoccupation increased. They stood in the hall, still. Emmi had not yet invited Irmgard to come into the bleak living room. Irmgard saw that a peculiar light flickered restlessly in her aunt's eyes, and she had the sensation that in some way she was concerned with it.

"I am glad you came," said Emmi, suddenly. Her face darkened a little, inimically. "It has been long since you came. I thought you had forgotten us."

Irmgard looked away. "I never forgot," she said in a low voice. "But others needed me."

Emmi gave an impatient gesture, and again Irmgard felt that she had brushed away, not her own words, but some unimportant irrelevancy. A filtered light glimmered in from the raw cold sunlight outside through the window in the door. Irmgard saw that her aunt was consumed with some inner excitement. When she spoke again, Irmgard knew that her words were not connected with this excitement.

"Do you remember that little Englishwoman to whom I introduced you some time ago, Irmgard? On the second day

you were here? Her husband was killed a day or two ago, b
thieves. Franz was with him."

Irmgard's averted lashes flew upwards, and the color lef
her cheeks.

"Franz!" she exclaimed, and her gloved hands came to
gether swiftly.

Emmi shook her head impatiently. "Franz was not hur
by them. He drove them away, but not until they had beate
poor Mr. Harrow to death."

"How terrible," murmured Irmgard. She looked down a
her locked fingers, then deliberately relaxed them.

"It is very terrible," said Emmi. "He was Franz's onl
friend. I go, now, to the funeral. The house is down the nex
street." She paused. "Will you go with me?"

Irmgard hesitated. "Would it not be better if I remaine
with Uncle Egon, while you are away."

Emmi considered. Then, she made up her mind swiftly
Egon would speak to Irmgard, and tell her joyously of th
decision to leave America. She preferred to tell Irmgard, her
self, so that there would be no confusion, no hesitation i
her plans. Her exigent mind began to operate again, wit
great rapidity.

"He is sleeping," she said. "He must be quiet. He is no
wel. I would prefer," she added, inexorably, "that you com
with me."

Then, for the first time, Irmgard realized what a traged
had taken place. This, most probably, after all, was the rea
son for Emmi's distraction and grim whiteness of lip. The
went out into the sharp and vivid coldness of the morning
Irmgard lifted her heavy green skirts from the gritty side
walk. Under them, she wore high-buttoned boots, obviousl
new, and very trim. Emmi saw them, disapprovingly. Sh
glanced quickly at the new smart bonnet, with its pale green
ness tied under Irmgard's chin. She noticed the black ki
gloves. This girl, with the pale hair lightly curled under th
rim of the bonnet, was not the awkward country Germa
maiden who had arrived in Nazareth just a short time ag
There was an air of quiet composure and sureness about he
instead of that former stiff dignity.

"You resemble, no longer, a German girl," said Emmi, a
they walked down the bleak and deserted street. "You hav
become an American."

Irmgard smiled slightly. "Are you disappointed, Au
Emmi?"

Emmi shrugged her lean shoulders under the shawl. "Suc
swift changes are spurious," she said, with her old brutalit

"They are not in character. You are a German girl, yet you wish to deceive one that you are an American."

"I am," said Irmgard, and now she was no longer smiling.

She was startled by the sudden harshness of her aunt's glance, the sudden anger in her eyes. "You talk like a fool," said Emmi, loudly. "You do not understand what you say!"

Irmgard was silent. She heard her aunt's loud breathing. Her expression was like one who feels himself threatened, and was infuriated in consequence. Emmi walked so rapidly now that Irmgard fell behind a little, trailing in her rear. There was an air of flight in Emmi's march down the street.

"There is nothing here, in America," Emmi flung over her shoulder. "Where such things as this happen, and the police find nothing."

Irmgard still did not speak. Her heels were high, and she was not accustomed to them yet. Because of her exertion, her cheeks became rosy, her lips bright red. She concentrated on her footing on the broken wooden walks. A great beer wagon, laden with kegs, and drawn by two straining gray horses, rumbled heavily past over the cobbled street. The driver stared at Irmgard impudently, and whistled. The wind caught up small whirlpools of dirt and chaff, and blew them into her face, choking her. She was suddenly greatly depressed. The poverty and drabness of Mulberry Street choked her. She glanced at the dun cottages of the poor, and the refuse-filled yards. Even the very poor in the little town near where she had lived in Germany had not existed in such bleakness, in such ugliness. There is no excuse for filth, she thought. Such an atmosphere comes from the souls of the people. Had America drawn only dead souls from Europe?

They reached Tom Harrow's little neat cottage, with the trim worn lace curtains at the windows, and the polished knocker and door knob. Irmgard was surprised to see a large silent knot of workmen on the walks before the cottage, waiting, humbly and ponderously, like stricken beasts, resigned and suffering. Irmgard saw their grimy faces, moved and contorted with efforts to retain the stolidity of their class; she saw their shabby caps and torn clothing, their dirty woolen scarves, wound tightly about their necks. They stood, not speaking, not moving, hands thrust deep within trouser pockets for protection against the cold. Their shoulders were huddled, shrunken together, their heads bent. She had seen sick cattle in drought-blasted fields in Germany with this same immobile aspect, these same expressions of bewilderment and pain, this same hopelessness. She saw grief on those drawn and dirty faces. But she also saw fear and chronic despair.

She paused for an instant, in Emmi's wake, and looked steadfastly at these men, her heart beating with indignation and anger. What had happened to these poor creatures? What years of struggle, starvation, brutality and poverty had they endured, in this country whose lighted towers illuminated the whole earth? Had they come, like Emmi, in pursuit of a dream of warmth and freedom and happiness, only to find a worse pit, a worse city, and more barren fields? They had come from Old World little villages, with their wine-taverns and their peasant laughter; they had come from meadows and mountains and great rivers, in pursuit of that dream. And they had found sterility and dust, darkness and cold, hunger and pain. They had found ugliness beyond all imagining. In the end, they had not even a dream to bequeath their children in this new land. What was America's hope for the future, in the offspring of these betrayed innocents? What hope for patriotism and fire and loyalty and love? Ah, surely it was not the dream which had betrayed them! It was a handful of greedy and rapacious men, who had thrown the fog of their evil minds and souls over the bright colors of the hopeful flag. They had made the lighted towers destructive flames, drawing the moths to destruction. The filth of the cities was the materialization of the hopelessness of the betrayed.

A hearse trundled up, the hearse of the poor, and paused before the little neat cottage. Irmgard saw the drooping melancholy plumes, the half-starved black horses, the mud-covered wheels. The driver wore a tall black hat, a black cape, and white gloves. His face was round and rosy under the hat and impudent. He tied up the horses, took out a half-smoked cigar, and lit it. He put his hands under his coat-tails, and paced about, waiting for a signal from within.

Emmi, her gray shawl over her head and shoulders, a basket of food for Mrs. Harrow and the children on her arm, had knocked on the door. A workman's wife, slatternly and snivelling, opened it, admitted the two women into a dark close interior, raw and chill. Irmgard heard the sound of muffled weeping and sniffles, and little groans. The small parlor was filled with shawled and aproned women. Near the darkened windows, a cheap coffin stood on a trestle, draped in black. There were no flowers, except a single wreath of white roses on the white shroud. Irmgard shrank back a little, not wanting to see the dead face above the shroud. Two candles, tall and thin, burnt at the head of the coffin. They, and the darkness, momentarily blinded her. When she could accustom her eyes to the scene, she saw little Mrs. Harrow sitting in a chair near the coffin, half-fainting, bitterly sobbing, supported by two murmuring, work-stained women, against a background of other women. Three little girls stood about their mother, in black dresses, their childish faces solemn, streaked with tears and flickering candlelight.

Then Irmgard's heart gave a throbbing leap. Franz Stoessel stood at the foot of the coffin, his arms folded on his chest, his head bent, his eyes fixed on the shroud. He did not look up at the entrance of his mother and cousin. He seemed absorbed in some rigid meditation of his own. Behind him, pressed into a dim corner, was the huge bulk of a workman. For some reason, after that first aching glance at Franz, Irmgard's gaze was drawn to that workman, and could not turn aside. She did not see his face; she saw only the great bulk of his half-seen form. But the candlelight, for some reason, shone on his hands. She saw that they were clenched, like rocks, like crushing weapons. A sudden fear thrilled through her, without a name, without understanding. There was something dreadful in the silence and immobility of that shadowy form with the illumined fists, like a vengeance and a waiting menace.

Hidden by the dimness, Irmgard could see the small crowded room, full of its sobbing and sniffling women, holding aprons to their faces. She could see little Dolly and her crying children. She could see a sharp pencil of light at the bottom of the drawn shades, and the wan candlelight, and the narrow black coffin. An acrid odor of cabbage pervaded the room, for some woman had been boiling that vegetable in the kitchen. It mingled with the odors of sweat and acid and burning tallow and dust which filled the air. And, silent and motionless, Franz stood at the foot of the coffin, and behind him, that menacing shadow with the enormous clenched fists.

Emmi had given the basket to one of the women, who took it into the kitchen. She went directly to Mrs. Harrow, and laid her hand on her shoulder, speechlessly. She looked at the little shivering girls, and frowned. The room was very cold. The children, in their cheap black dresses, had blue lips and white faces. Emmi turned to one of the women.

"There is a fire in the kitchen?" she asked, abruptly.

The woman removed her apron from her face, and blinked. Then she nodded, wonderingly. Emmi beckoned to the children, peremptorily. They followed her meekly into the kitchen. Irmgard could hear her moving briskly about, and scolding under her breath; she could hear the rattle of coals in the stove, then Emmi's voice, brisk and strong; thick with its Teutonic accent:

"A little hot milk for the little maids, yes? And some of this fine cake, and this good ham, and nice bread and butter. Hands to the fire, please. It is not good for children to be cold. No, never must children be cold. You will wash your hands, please, and wipe the hands not on the dresses."

Irmgard heard a smothered childish giggle. The sounds from the kitchen penetrated into that dank chamber of death, with its sobbing and dust and chill. The sounds of life breaking in on the silence of dissolution. It was good. The poor father in his coffin must have been grateful. Then, Irmgard, for the first time, saw the sleeping face, bruised and calm, lofty with sleep and forgetfulness.

It was an ugly face, crowned with ugly, thickly-curling black hair. But it had a majesty and gentleness in it which even death could not dissipate. Irmgard felt an enormous sadness, as she gazed at that face, and a sense of mystery cold with withdrawal. So absorbed was she, that she did not notice the curious furtive glances of the women, who stared at the elegance of this young woman with the green velvet bonnet, black velvet jacket and bustled green dress. There was distrust in these glances, and enmity. She was a stranger, in her fine garments, and her beauty. One or two of the women whispered together, and pointed.

Irmgard then looked again at Franz. She could see his face clearly, now, ghastly and drawn and bitterly remote. It was a face of stone. Irmgard remembered that Emmi had told her that the dead man had been the only friend of Franz.

He grieves, she thought, with a strange rush of warmth and tenderness at her heart. He grieves as I thought he could never grieve for any one. Her thoughts ran to him, calling him, offering him consolation and love. Her eyes, in the gloom, became lighted and intense, shone with vivid green fire.

As though he had felt her at last, he looked up, abruptly. Their eyes met. His expression did not change. He saw her, yet did not appear to see her. She had nothing to do with all this. She was apart from it, extraneous. She did not impinge on him at this moment. He dropped his eyes again.

A thin sharp pain struck through Irmgard's breast, and she bit her lip. Franz! she mourned. Why will you not let me comfort you? But his stony cheek and lip, the gray flat planes of his whole face, his averted eyes, repudiated her and her comfort. However, she was not too distressed. In fact, a strange sad hope dawned in her mind. He was more than she had ever thought him.

Emmi briskly entered the room, carrying a bowl of hot sweetened milk in her hands. She brushed aside the whimpering women. Irmgard could see Mrs. Harrow more clearly now a plump, pretty little woman in her black gown, her fair hair neat in spite of her prostrating grief. Her cheeks were blotched with tears. She looked at Emmi dazedly, then at the bowl. She made a feeble gesture of refusal.

"Nonsense," said Emmi, quite loudly. "Please. It is what you need."

The women regarded her with affront, outraged at this effort to revive the chief victim of this tragedy.

Dolly flung up her hands to her face, shaking her head. "He was all I had!" she cried wildly. "My Tom! He was all I had!"

"No," said Emmi, inexorably. "You have the little maids. It is not good for you to forget them. You, their mother, are all they have."

Dolly wept, distractedly, rocking backwards and forwards on her chair. She flung her hands about; the tears streamed down her fat pretty face. Her eyes were wide open, and staring, distraught. Emmi took her by the shoulder, and shook her vigorously.

"You will drink," she said. "You will not be foolish. The children are drinking good milk, and eating, too. They wait for their mother."

She put the bowl to Dolly's lips. Over its rim the blue eyes, swimming in tears, and swollen, stared up blindly at the hard lean face above her. Then, obediently, but choking, the poor little creature drank the warm and heartening fluid, gulping, sobbing, but surely drinking. The women stepped back a trifle, glowering at this expedient harshness. The poor, thought Irmgard, hate to be deprived of their suffering victim, resent any alleviation of vicarious pain. In another's torment they feel the sadistic satisfaction of the tormented.

Dolly's sobs, after she had drunk the milk, were quieter now. Emmi stood for a moment, looking down at her with pitying but grim approval.

There was a deprecating knock on the door, and the minister, a little shrivelled man in his funeral black, entered. He had white sideburns and a small white beard, but no mustache. His air was at once meek and subservient and important. He let in a short burst of winter sunlight, and then closed the door behind him. The gloom was only the more intense for that one gush of brilliance.

He came to the coffin, the women making way for him. He stared down solemnly at the dead face. He held his book in his hands. His white hair was haloed by the candlelight. Then he lifted one hand and began to pray.

CHAPTER 32

THE WOMEN enjoyed the short service, though the minister spoke as rapidly as possible. He knew his fee would be small. The dead man and his wife were strangers to him; he had never seen them in his small and poverty-stricken church, though he had seen the little girls, Mary, Pansy and Polly at Sunday school. Moreover, there was something disreputable to him in being killed by thieves at night, on the street. Christians did not die so. They died decorously in bed, surrounded by proper and weeping relatives. Moreover, though his congregation was composed of the working class, he had little sympathy with the poor. They were tiresome and dirty, complaining, and always hungry, and simmering with revolt. Revolt was un-Christian. One must be meek and submissive. These virtues were especially edifying when accompanied by a comfortable income. His parishioners had little, and only precarious incomes. It was the wisdom of God, which must not be questioned. But the less income, the more meekness was demanded.

"I am the Resurrection and the Life," he said, in a sonorous voice, "Whosoever believeth on Me shall never die."

Irmgard experienced a sense of outrage that this little hasty man, with the small and pious face, sharpened with meanness, dared to utter these grave and holy words. But she heard them only dimly. She was watching Franz, and the shadow behind him. Franz still did not move, still did not appear to be aware of what was happening about him. Dolly sobbed quietly; the women whimpered. Emmi stood beside Dolly, her hand firmly on her shoulder. She had forbidden the children to enter the room again, and their scuffling and giggles were quite audible from the kitchen. The candlelight glimmered on the faces in the parlor, on Dolly's bent head with the frivolous curls, on the shroud and the coffin, on Franz's granite face, on the minister, given a spurious sanctity by it sacred flaring and dimming. The light threw vagrant shadows on the dark-brown walls of the tiny room, on the meagre and ugly furniture of the poor, on the black blinds shutting out the sun. It lingered, as if intentionally, on the dead and majestic face of Tom Harrow. Some of the women crossed themselves furtively, their lips moving in silent prayer.

The service was concluded. The door opened again, and the women blinked in the strong raw light. This time, the door was not closed. The undertaker, in his greenish-black long coat, top hat and white gloves, entered. He carried a hammer. Dolly saw him, and the hammer, and she suddenly screamed desperately, over and over. She staggered to her feet, flung herself on the open coffin, clutched the shroud. The women burst out into loud shrieks of sympathy.

Franz, then, stirred for the first time. His hands lifted, half extended themselves to Dolly, who lay across the body of her husband. His face was contorted, his mouth opening as though he were gasping. Irmgard took an involuntary step towards him. Her nerves were trembling, and her legs seemed to bend under her. The shadow behind Franz moved a trifle, convulsively.

Emmi, then, while the minister and the undertaker stood uneasily in the background, went to the prostrate and moaning little woman, who clutched her husband with such agony. She gently lifted her.

"No, no," she murmured. "It is not good. Let the man rest. He must have peace." She drew the fair curly head to her breast; her strong lean arms enclosed the plump and trembling body. Dolly collapsed against her, sobbing with terrible cries. Emmi nodded to the undertaker, who approached the coffin.

Through the open door Irmgard saw that two cheap hacks had joined the hearse. A woman brought Dolly's bonnet and shawl, and Emmi put them on the poor woman with deft quickness. She glanced fiercely over her shoulder at the clamoring women, frenzied now in their enjoyment of agony, and drama.

"Quiet," she said, very quietly, but with such a look that immediate silence followed. "Some one bring the children, in their coats and bonnets. Please."

"What shall I do?" sobbed Dolly, leaning against Emmi. "My little lasses. They've got no father, they as had the best. It's the workhouse for me, and the little gels. The workhouse!" she repeated, on a sudden loud scream, throwing back her head to look into Emmi's face with wild distended eyes.

Then it was that Franz came to her. He took her wet and trembling hands, held them strongly. He looked down into her face, and smiled. Irmgard saw that his forehead was glistening, and wrinkled, as though with mortal pain.

"No, Dolly," he said, gently, holding the attention of the

distracted little woman, with her bonnet askew, and the tears running in rivers down her cheeks. "No, it will not be the workhouse. I have heard that the Schmidt Steel Company is going to give you five thousand dollars. Five thousand dollars, Dolly. Because they are sorry about Tom. Because he was one of their best workmen."

She stared at him, with her wild running eyes, hardly hearing him, hardly understanding.

"Five thousand dollars, Dolly," he said, again.

The women sucked in their breaths with a loud awed sound. The minister stared. The undertaker regarded the widow with sudden respect. Dolly moaned; her eyes half-closed; she swayed against Franz, and he held her. The minister came forward, all sympathy now, all holy compassion.

"My poor child," he said, resonantly, "it is God's will. We must not question it. We must be resigned. We must think of our children." He laid his hand on Dolly's quivering back, and lifted his eyes.

It was Irmgard who first saw the stirring of the shadow which had stood behind Franz. It was Irmgard who saw him approach, on huge lumbering legs. She saw his face. An involuntary cry rose to her mouth, and she put her hand over it. For the face was full of murder and hatred.

"So," said a rough, foreign voice, "so. They pay five thousand dollars for killin' my friend, eh? You tol' them so, eh?"

Franz, holding Dolly, started violently. He looked over his shoulder, and encountered the savage and inflamed eyes of Jan Kozak. Utter silence followed his words. Every one, the women, the minister, the undertaker, Emmi, Irmgard, and even the weeping Dolly, felt the presence of murder and violence in that death chamber, felt its raw flame and its horrible intensity.

Franz said nothing. His pale lip was caught between his glistening teeth. His eyes were suddenly distended with open and inhuman fear. He could not say a word, though Irmgard saw his desperate struggles to speak, the convulsive movement of his jaw.

Jan Kozak towered over him in his gigantic height.

His face was like a bull's, and it was encrimsoned, savage with blood-lust. "I was there, that night," he said, in his painfully slow and rumbling voice. "I heard you. That night, with the man. Sayin' how to kill my friend. They was not to hurt him, you said. Just stop the strike. He got killed. Maybe wasn't your fault. Maybe accident. But you did it."

There was a single loud word, sharp and repudiating. "No!" said Emmi. "No!" She stood beside her son and Dolly, pressed against by the listening, open-mouthed women. She seemed to have increased in height, so straight and rigid was her fleshless body. Her face was white, tinged with blue. Her eyes were brilliant. The shawl had slipped from her head, and it rose above it, lean and clear as cut stone. But there was also a horror in her expression.

"No," said Irmgard, softly, closing her eyes, her hands feeling out for a support which was not there. No one noticed her. Every one was thronging about that group near the coffin, Emmi, Franz, Dolly and Jan Kozak. And Franz still held Dolly in his arms.

Jan smiled, a most frightful smile. He put his hand on the shroud. Under it, he could feel the marble hand of Tom Harrow. He looked only at Franz, and his eyes were glittering.

"I hear you," he repeated. "You are liar. You are bad man. You said, 'I give a signal, when I get him alone, on the street.' I hear you. I was behin' you. All the time, you came to the meetin's to hear what we say. So you can tell the bosses. So—you help kill my frien'. And then you go to the bosses and say, 'That killin' will cost you fi' thousand dollars.' It was a good night's work, no?"

"No," said Emmi again. But no one else spoke. Dolly had lifted herself from Franz's arms. She stared blindly at Jan Kozak.

"Jan," she whimpered. "It isn't true."

Jan lifted his great hand and pointed it inexorably at Franz.

"Ask him," he said. "He stand there, and not speak. He know I tell truth. He don't dare tell lie with Tom here."

Franz stood in silence, his arms by his side, his forehead wrinkling into deep furrows. But he looked only at Dolly, whose wet and terrified eyes were fixed in sudden horror on his.

"Franz," she moaned, almost inaudibly, "it's a lie? Say it's a lie, Franz? You didn't kill my Tom?"

A heavy shudder ran over Franz's body. He felt the murderous presence of Jan Kozak behind him. His face had turned a sickly yellow tinge, and his nostrils were wide, as though he found difficulty in breathing.

Then he spoke, in a thickened voice. "No, Dolly, I didn't kill Tom. You can believe that, Dolly. This—this Kozak imagined he heard me speak to—to someone. You believe me, Dolly?"

Then, in that dank room, with the dead man in his coffin, Jan Kozak burst into loud and savage laughter. Every one started, and shrank except Emmi, who stood beside her son, her face slowly turning to the very hue of death. Jan pointed at Franz, and he laughed again, louder and more terribly.

"He is liar. He is afraid to tell the truth. He is afraid of police. I got no proof, he will say. No, I got no proof. But he know I tell the truth. He know him and me and God know the truth. And my frien'."

He turned to Franz, and looked at him. "You and me—we got to have a talk. You stole my work. You stole my frien's life. You and me—we got to talk."

But Franz held Dolly by the arms, and she still stared at him, with terror, her eyes now dry and feverish.

"It is a lie, Dolly," he said, and he shook her slightly. "You believe me, Dolly? Tom and I—we were friends. You believe me, Dolly?"

She still stared at him. Then, very slowly, her eyes filled with tears.

"I believe you, Franz," she said.

Jan laughed again, hoarsely. The minister lifted a hand to him. "My man, this is very improper. If you have something to discuss with this gentleman, you must not do it——"

But Jan turned to the coffin. He stood and stared down at the dead face, and his own became cold and hard and suffering.

"Go to sleep, my frien'," he said, in a muffled voice. "We get justice, some time. We still got God, waitin'."

Then, without another glance at those in the room, he lumbered out of the door, and disappeared.

Dolly burst into renewed tears, loud in the utter stillness of the room. She clung to Franz, sobbing over and over her belief in him. And he held her to him. He murmured, bending over her.

But Emmi stood in silence, remote, her eyes staring into the distance as at some dreadfulness, some appalling vision. She did not feel Irmgard's touch on her arm. She felt nothing. She saw nothing but that vision.

CHAPTER 33

IRMGARD FELT that she could not endure going to the cemetery with the little funeral party, of which Emmi was a member.

The bright cold December wind had fallen, and it had suddenly begun to rain. The sky was a mass of grayish purple clouds by the time Dolly Harrow was composed enough to enter one of the hacks, which Franz, himself, had hired.

She would return to the flat on Mulberry Street; she told Emmi, and remain with her uncle. Emmi hardly seemed to listen. Irmgard was frightened by her expression, so pale and expressionless was it, since that hideous scene in the little parlor. Even when Irmgard had timidly suggested returning to her uncle, Emmi spoke abstractedly, and almost with indifference:

"He is ill, as I told you. I have promised him we shall return to Germany."

"To Germany!"

"Go, child," said Emmi, impatiently, waving her away with the gesture of one tormented beyond endurance. "Listen, and say nothing to him. I must talk to you later." And without another word, she went back to Dolly.

She had given Irmgard the key to the flat, and Irmgard went away. She walked slowly, her eyes on the ground. She could think of nothing; feel nothing. When her thought touched Franz, it veered away with a shudder. But still, she would allow herself no real thought of him. Once or twice, she put her hand to her head, and said aloud: "No. No." Her fine green skirts trailed in the dirt and the mud; rain splattered on the gay bonnet. She knew nothing of this, or did not care. She felt physically sick; her head ached with an enormous pain. Her flesh was numb, and she had the sensation of being apart from it, though aware of its heaviness.

She found Egon, wrapped in a blanket, sitting before the kitchen stove. He regarded her with pleased astonishment when she entered. She saw how frail he had become, how old and ill. But his eyes were bright and contented.

"How pleasant it is to see you again, Liebchen," he said, kissing her cheek as she bent over him. He held her hand. His own was tremulous and hot. He did not reproach her for her neglect. He regarded her with pleasure and affection. She told him, quietly, that Emmi had gone to the cemetery, and for a moment his sweet lined face became sorrowful.

"It is very bad," he murmured. "I saw him once or twice, that Tom Harrow. He, too, had dreams."

Something broke and shattered in Irmgard. She cried: "It is so foolish to have dreams, to believe in anything, or any one! The world is so horrible. It is good that such a man does not live in it any longer!"

Egon gazed at her in sudden quiet astonishment. "But what should men do, if there were no one who dreamed, my child?

What little we have gained is because dreamers have lived."

Irmgard turned away, abruptly. Her eyes were full of tears, tears that burned, that drowned and suffocated. But, still, she would not let herself think. She removed her bonnet and jacket, tied one of Emmi's aprons about her slender waist. She examined the pots on the stove, and said: "There is some good soup, here. I shall heat it for you, Uncle Egon."

He watched her in silence, as she put fresh coals on the fire, shook down ashes. She lit the lamp, for the kitchen had become dark. The light shone on her masses of light smooth hair, on her young pale cheek. Egon felt some tensity in her, some held control and wretchedness. He became mournful and abstracted.

"It is hard for Franz, this death," he murmured.

Irmgard did not reply. But her hands trembled so violently that she dropped the spoon with which she was stirring the pot, and it clattered on the floor. The sound reminded Egon of something, and he said in a more resolute voice:

"It will be good, then, for him to return with us to Germany."

"Do you think he will go?" asked Irmgard, pressing her lips together in an effort to restrain herself.

Egon was startled, and a little frightened. "Surely, yes. We could not leave him, child. I could not be happy, thinking I might never see him again. I would rather remain here."

Irmgard turned to him with sudden vehemence, and exclaimed:

"Whether Franz goes or not, Uncle Egon, you must go! You are not happy here. You are miserable. You are ill. America is too much for you."

He shook his head, smiling a little, in his melancholy. "No, it is we who are not enough for America. There is something here we have not found, not understood. That is our fault. Emmi came, expecting too much, expecting golden dreams and fulfillment. That is wrong. One must not expect Heaven to be waiting; one must make Heaven, join hands with those who are making it. As for myself," and he sighed, "I was old, when I came. Much too old, child. Perhaps I was always too old. I have always loved the small, the little corner. There are no little corners in America. There is much space, too much for me."

He added, gazing steadily at the opposite dim wall: "I love communities. But America is too big for communities, for separate entities, for men who by nature must stay apart. It may be a paradox, but it is the little country which separates itself into little communities. The large country is like a sea, into which everything flows and becomes one. If it separates itself into rivers, pools, separate streams, then it is no longer a sea, it cannot exist as one. The ocean of America is vast. In it, all men become as one. It is a huge and colossal idea, but only by adhering to it, can America survive. Should it separate into communities, into smallnesses and factions, then the Idea upon which America was begotten, shall die, and there shall remain only warring and hating little States, dangerous within, and in danger from without."

Irmgard said nothing, but she listened, full of wonder that her uncle could speak so lengthily, he who had always been so silent and few of words. She saw that his thin old face had become lighted, as though reflecting a vision which he loved and reverenced, but of which he could not, however he strived, become a part.

"My poor Emmi," he said, with a sigh and a smile, "has never realized this. The hugeness of the Idea of America affronted, and repelled her, if she guessed it at all. She saw, in this wretched town, all of America. If its climate of mind or circumstance disgusted her, it was the mind or circumstance of all of this country. She tried, in her own heart, to make a community in America, not understanding that America is one, and its thousand aspects only one aspect. Coming from a continent which is finished, old and tired, she thought to find in America a continent which was also finished, but young and strong. When she sees today, she thinks it is all of the tomorrows, also. But for America, today is never tomorrow. The Idea shines like a sun over the changing aspects, the growth and the fury and the uproar which is America. Always, there is change, but the sun shines over the change. So long as Americans behold the sun, and love it, the changes mean nothing. The danger to America lies in those who, like Emmi, believe the sun is forever obscured."

"But Aunt Emmi believes that you hate America, Uncle Egon." The girl stood before him, her spoon in her hand, and some rising excitement in her face.

He shook his head. "What she believes is wrong. I—I have never been able to tell her. I do not know what it is in me today, that I talk so, and so freely, to you, my little love." He smiled at her, with gentle tenderness, and she smiled back, her heart heaving in her breast.

He shook his head again. "I do not hate America. I love the Idea. But I have come to realize that I am too small, too timid, too weak, for that Idea. It frightens me, because I am so inadequate. I love the small corner, the little fire. The wind and the open space of the mind of America is too much for me, too chilling, too vast. I must go back to my corner, and my fire, or I shall perish of cold, of loneliness, of desolation, on the wide endlessness of America. It is my fault. I have the European mind, which deals in little men, in little corners, in little walls and gardens, in small forests and thin shallow rivers."

He added, after a moment, meditatively: "I see it so clearly, now. Franz must stay in America." His face saddened. "He does not believe in the Idea. But he does understand the vastness of this country. He will never be one with the Idea. But who knows if his children will not? One must understand, not only the physical largeness of America, but the largeness of the Idea. The real American understands so."

He continued, almost in a whisper, and the light stronger on his face:

"What a glory shall be America's, if she remembers!"

"And you will return to Germany, without Franz?" Irmgard asked, after a moment.

Egon hesitated. "How can I say what my heart will speak, when the moment arrives? In talking to you, little love, my mind clarifies. I said, a time ago, that he must return with us. Now I think: What of his children? How can I suggest that he deprive them of the Idea of America? Is this not wicked?"

He added, sadly: "It is wicked. If he wishes to remain, then perhaps, I shall remain, too. I am an old man. I love my son. I understand him, and do not hate him for the understanding. Emmi does not understand, and so, she hates him. Ah, yes," he mourned, "she hates him. Yet, with the hatred, and without the understanding, she loves him. He is her only child. She will think: Perhaps if I had remained, at the last I might have helped him. I cannot take that comfort from her."

The grief of renunciation dimmed his old tired eyes, but his expression was resolute. "Perhaps," he said, after a little silence, and with some whimsicality, "I can find some little sheltered corner in America, where I can do no harm to her. After all, I am old. I shall have no other children, whom I could teach to love the little corners, so dangerous to America."

He suddenly became completely aware of Irmgard, of her strange look, trembling lips and tear-filled eyes. Alarmed, he extended his hand to her, and took her own.

"My child, what is it?"

To his increased alarm, and pain, she knelt down beside him and put her head on his shoulder. She did not sob nor exclaim. She merely knelt there, in an attitude of extreme abandonment and suffering, her arms hanging slackly at her sides. He put his old arms about her, held her closely to him. He asked no more questions. He understood this wordless anguish, this silent misery, without knowing the cause. It was enough for him that she endured some hidden agony.

He whispered: "Little love, all things pass. The sorrow of today is not even the memory of tomorrow."

"There are some things that cannot be forgotten," she replied, her mouth muffled against his shoulder. "Nor forgiven."

He sighed, and his arms pressed more tightly about her. He looked over her head, and the lids of his eyes moistened.

"The French say, Irmgard, that to understand all is to forgive all. What men do, they do by their own nature. They are impelled by mysterious forces in themselves. It is for us, who understand, to pity. If some one has injured, or hurt you, he does so because he is not strong enough to resist his own nature. Those who resist are strong, and full of understanding. Those who cannot resist are empty, victims of themselves, and they suffer greatly, knowing their weakness."

"Empty," murmured Irmgard. She lifted her head and regarded her uncle strangely. "I have said that: he is empty. But he fills his emptiness with tragedy for others."

A look of hopelessness and utter desolation settled on her young face, pinching it, making it appear cold and lifeless. Egon touched her cheek, as though his touch might bring back its faint color.

"I do not know who this 'he' is. You need not tell me now. But you must forgive, and try to understand. And who knows but what he is misunderstood, and maligned? One must have faith. One must try to believe."

She said nothing, but her mouth softened a little.

"It is true," she said, after a long silence. "One must have faith——"

"And even if the worst is true," broke in Egon, eagerly, "one must still have faith. One must still understand. The injurer is as much his own victim as you are. Surely, you can feel pity for him?"

He yearned over her, wishing he might remove sorrow and pain from this young, clear life. "I do not know how any one can have injured you, child. You, who are so without meanness and littleness, like your dear mother. You have been here so short a time. I do not ask for your confidences. That would be impudent. But suffering, it has always been said, is part of living. The suffering is worse, when inflicted by one who is loved. The blows of strangers are hard, but the hand of a loved one is harder. But one cannot destroy the loving heart, which must still have faith, and endure everything."

She was silent, but her eyes were fixed on his with a mysterious desolation. Yet, he was heartened by the knowledge that she had listened, and comprehended, and that he had given her some courage.

Then she said again: "One must have faith. Even if the faith is misplaced, then, as you have said, one must have compassion."

She rose then, completely composed, and poured his soup into a white bowl. Egon thought of her mother, Hertha, moving in the farm kitchen, pouring milk into white mugs, with morning sunlight on her hair and quiet sweet face. It was only a flash of memory, but all at once he was overwhelmed in a wave of nostalgia, in a passion for long low meadows and the cry of a thrush in the lavender evening. It seemed to him that his very soul moaned in this nostalgia, which was less a sickness for Germany than a loneliness and urging of the spirit for some mysterious land known only to it, and not to his flesh. There was a parching thirst in him for peace and twilight, for dim hills against a fading sky, for a river that ran as livid as quicksilver through dark and lonely earth. His mind felt fevered for winds heavy with the scent of harvests, for trees bending and lashing in midnight gales under an enormous white moon.

It is not the Fatherland for which I am yearning, he thought. It is for death.

He drank the soup which Irmgard gave him, and he smiled at her. But his eyes were cloudy with his somber yearning, and though he spoke to her, and she answered, he did not know what he was saying, nor what her answers were. His whole being was absorbed and washed in his thirst and his hunger. He was conscious of a weighted feeling about his heart, like remembered sorrow. And yet, with the sorrow, there was mingled a strange faint joy, as of anticipation.

At times, when he had thought of immortality, he had turned away from the thought with weariness and distress and repulsion. Was man condemned to carry himself, his laden personality, his dustiness and tiredness, throughout all eternity? His own thoughts, his own memories, would be an insupportable burden, darkening his vision, crushing down his soul. He would be like a footsore and aching traveller through gigantic landscapes, unable to see, unable to enjoy, because of the burden on his shoulders, the burden of himself. That would be hell, not the privilege of heaven. With all his consciousness; he longed only for escape, for acquiescence, for the darkening of memory. Man at the end, he thought, is sick of himself. God cannot be so cruel as to condemn him to wander eternally through consciousness, with himself as his own companion. God, too, must be weary of being. Was there some refuge in space and time where the soul could rest, could wash off the stains of memory in some pools of Lethe, and emerge, clean and shining, awakening to new adventures and brighter dreams?

He thought so, now, huddling before the stove in the kitchen on Mulberry Street. This was the reason for the strange joy, the sudden heart-lifting anticipation.

The front door opened and Emmi, wrapped in her gray shawl, appeared. The rain had beaded the shawl with sparkling drops. Between its fold, her face was no less gray. Her clenched lips were surrounded by a large bluish circle, and her eyes were dulled and appeared to be turned inward on something too terrible for speech. Nevertheless, she bent and kissed Egon briefly, inquired as to his eyes, and turned to Irmgard. When she spoke to the girl, she dropped her eyes, and her voice was dull:

"Franz has not returned?"

"No," said Irmgard, faintly. Emmi's eyes lifted and asked a question. Irmgard shook her head with a slight motion. At the mention of Franz's name, Egon said sadly:

"This is a sorrowful day for Franz. He will return soon, Emmi?"

Emmi removed her shawl, folded it carefully and precisely, and laid it away in a drawer. "I left him at the cemetery," she said, in a toneless voice. "There were some last things to be done, I believe. I brought Mrs. Harrow home."

"What is the poor creature to do now?" asked Egon, in distress.

"There—there is some money," said Emmi.

"That is good," sighed Egon.

Emmi placed a clean cloth on the table, inspected the kettle of soup, shook up the fire vigorously. She moved with greater speed than usual, as though she wished to outstrip her thoughts. "You will remain?" she asked Irmgard, in her cold, preoccupied voice, and the words were a command.

The girl sliced some bread, washed the coffee pot. Egon rubbed his hands before the warmth of the fire-box. There was no sound in the kitchen but the crackling of the coals, the clinking of tableware, and the bubbling of the soup. Then Egon, speaking gently, and with hesitation, took Emmi's apron-corner in his hand.

"My love, I have been thinking. You spoke this morning of returning to Germany. I have changed my mind."

"That is impossible," said Emmi, loudly, pausing with a fork in her hand, and looking down at him with a grim face.

Egon shook his head. "No, Liebchen. I have decided. Franz will not return with us. We should worry about him. I see now that it is not the Fatherland for which I have been longing.

It is only for peace and quietness, some pleasant corner. We can find it here." He hesitated again, and then went on, pleadingly: "Some quiet corner. In the country. We have a little money. I am tired," he added, simply. "I could endure no journey again."

Emmi was silent. She still looked down at him, and now her leaden features worked. He could not know her thoughts. But in some way he knew that some hard inflexibility in her softened, that she experienced some overpowering relief. Nevertheless, because of the rigidity of her nature, which had already set itself in the mould of self-sacrifice and renunciation, she could not readily readjust herself.

"We shall talk of this later," she said, surlily.

"I should miss you, Aunt Emmi," Irmgard remarked, looking at her aunt with pleading. "You cannot leave me here alone."

"I thought you might return with us," said Emmi, avoiding the girl's eyes.

"I? Oh, never! Never." Irmgard's voice was oddly vehement.

"I thought of buying your farm," went on Emmi, implacably. But a faint color had come back into her granite lips.

"My farm?" Irmgard was completely surprised. "Did I not tell you? It was confiscated for debts. I had only enough left to pay my passage. There is no farm now." She was silent a moment, then resumed, in a quieter voice. "And I am glad. I can never return. I cannot ever return, to anything."

Then it was that Emmi's eyes lifted and fixed themselves with peculiar intensity upon the girl's face. There was surprise in her expression, as though she were saying to herself: This is one like me! And now her manner became gentler.

"Sometimes one has to return, against one's will. For the benefit of some one very much loved."

And, sometimes, thought Irmgard, one must remain, because of some one very much loved. But she did not answer Emmi.

Egon had lived a long time with his wife, and though he could rarely enter into her emotions, or participate in her ideas, he nevertheless understood her, and was acutely sensitive to her moods and her sufferings. Now it came to him sharply that she was tormented, that despite her calm exterior, she was seething with despair and misery, that she was enduring some tragedy. He could not deceive himself that these were the result of his decision to remain in America. He was both puzzled and terrified. He kept glancing at her with his tired eyes, and when she sometimes approached him in her duties, he wanted to put out his hands to her. He saw what she was enduring in the taut line of her jaw, in the drawn flesh about her lips and eyes. They had had a little daughter, before Franz's birth, and the child had died in her infancy. Emmi had worn a look like this for many years after that death.

I am imagining, thought Egon. She is just distressed over today's events. He forced himself to believe this. There was no other explanation.

"You have done too much today, Liebchen," he said, lovingly, touching her garments as she passed him.

"Too much," she agreed, and he wondered at the bitterness in her voice.

He glanced at Irmgard, but the girl's face was averted. She was kneeling near a chest of drawers, from which she was abstracting some napkins. Egon sighed. He pressed closer to the stove, as though suddenly cold.

"Where is Franz? Should he not be here now?"

Emmi did not answer. The cords of her throat tightened. But Irmgard looked swiftly at her uncle, and with gentleness.

"He may be with Mrs. Harrow. There is so much to be done."

"More than a lifetime!" cried Emmi, suddenly, her composure breaking. She stood in the middle of the kitchen, a stark figure of tragedy, unable to control herself. Her features were contorted, and she stared before her blindly.

Egon was terribly alarmed. He half rose from his chair. Irmgard came quickly to her aunt, almost running. She took her by the arm. She forced the older woman to see her.

"Aunt Emmi," she said, very quietly. "Aunt Emmi."

Emmi stared at her, her face drawn and quivering. She made a motion as though to drag her arms from Irmgard's grip. Then she was still. Tears rose to her eyes. She began to tremble.

"Emmi!" cried Egon, forcing himself to his feet, and swaying a little. "What is it, Emmi?"

Irmgard put her arm about her aunt's shoulders. She regarded her uncle calmly. She even smiled.

"The funeral, and your illness, Uncle Egon. You must understand. She is so very tired, and upset."

Egon embraced his wife about her waist. He felt her trembling. He leaned against her and kissed her cheek. This stark and weeping woman was no longer the strong drill-sergeant, of whom he stood in awe. This was his wife, his child, his little one. A thrill of loving power came into his feeble body, and a yearning of protectiveness.

"Yes, yes, of course," he murmured, almost weeping himself. "We never spare our Emmi. We rely upon her, believing she is not flesh and blood. Forgive me, my darling."

She turned to him, and stared at him through her blinding

tears. Then she said, brokenly: "Egon." She dropped her head to his shoulder, and sobbed aloud, with hard and tearing sobs. Irmgard released her aunt, and Egon held her to him, murmuring, smoothing her hair, kissing her cheek, comforting her. He thought himself strong, sustaining her in her troubles, giving her strength. But Irmgard knew that it was not Egon who was strong, but Emmi, bearing her agony of torment in silence, preferring anything but that he know the truth. She suffered his ministrations, because she was too exhausted to resist, and because in some way she knew that he gained some virtue from them, himself. But his comforting must have been sweet to her, for all its fragility.

She allowed him to lead her to a chair. He sat beside her, rubbing her cold hands. Her chin dropped on her flat breast. She sat in silence, not moving, hardly seeming to breathe. Irmgard, knowing that she would not speak now, continued in the preparation of the meal. She listened to Egon's tender brooding voice, and her eyes smarted.

Then she was filled with fear. Would Emmi be able to control herself when Franz appeared? Would her violent anger, her grief, her pain, be too great? Almost incoherently, she suddenly spoke, in a loud clear voice:

"Aunt Emmi, Uncle Egon and I spoke very closely when we were alone. I was not feeling very well, or happy. He said it is so necessary to have faith, even when there seems no justification for it."

"Yes, yes," said Egon, eagerly, giving the girl a loving glance.

Emmi lifted her head. Her lips parted as though she would speak, and then she gasped a little, and was silent. But her eyes fixed themselves deeply on Irmgard, with a sort of mournful contemplation.

Finally, she rose, knelt before the stove, and inspected the baking bread within. Egon watched her with anxiety and affection, and occasionally he stretched out a timid hand and touched her gently, as though wishing to reassure her.

Franz did not return. They waited. Then, at last, they sat down themselves to the meal.

Will he return? thought Emmi. And the thought pinched her features, threw a dusky shadow over them. Was it possible that he might never come home, after that frightful scene in Dolly's parlor? Had he seen his mother's face, and understood her thoughts, heard her sickened accusation? Was he afraid that she would tell his father? For the first time, Emmi suddenly realized that if Franz loved any one, he loved Egon. Surely, if he thought she had told his father, he would not return!

An enormous anxiety choked her breath, and she put down her fork. But he could not believe that! Then, she saw herself clearly through Franz's eyes, saw her own ruthlessness and hardness, which she had believed was the virtue of forthrightness and honesty. He would not believe she would hold her tongue, for his father's sake. He would believe that she would revenge herself upon him, by telling Egon. She saw now that ever since her son's birth, she had been jealous of the attachment between him and his father, had resented it, had presented Franz, at times, in an unfavorable light, to Egon. Her criticisms of Franz were always loudest in Egon's presence, her voice the most bitter. Was it because she saw Franz clearly, and resented Egon's gentle tolerance and loving blindness? Or was it something more obscure, much more shameful?

Then she thought: He is bold and brazen. He knows he has only to stand before his father, and deny everything, to be believed. Egon could not encompass such wickedness, such depravity, such slyness. Then she knew that Franz would return, and her momentary shame was forgotten in her great bitterness and grief and horror. She had never said to herself: I hate my son, and all that he is. But she knew it, now.

All at once, hurry filled her. Egon must be gotten upstairs, in bed, before Franz's return. She had things to say to Franz. Egon must not hear them. A fever rose in her, as she rehearsed the devastating things she would say to Franz, out of her horror and repudiation. For never had she doubted the truth of Jan Kozak's words. Franz's own nature, which he had ruthlessly revealed at all times to his mother, with a sort of wanton shamelessness and indecency, stamped Jan's words with verity.

At moments, complete horror and terror drove away her grief and despair, and she could feel nothing but hatred and a lust for revenge.

CHAPTER 34

EGON PROTESTED that he was perfectly well, and that he wished to see his son before going to bed.

"Your eyes," said Emmi, peremptorily.

He smiled at her, with his timid gentle smile. "I fear no more for my eyes, Liebchen. I know I shall not be blind again."

"I think it best, Uncle Egon, if you go to bed," said Irmgard. The sense of hurry and danger was upon her, also, and her cheek was dryly flushed. She had begun to tremble at every sound, fearful that Franz would return before his father was safely away. She knew, now, that Emmi would not keep silence, at the sight of Franz, that her control might burst, and even before Egon her cries of accusation and loathing might not be restrained. She knew, also, that of this Emmi herself was afraid, that she did not trust herself.

Egon finally submitted to the urgings of stronger natures, and went upstairs with his old sweet resignation. Emmi put him to bed, as though he was a child. He was always my child, she thought. I have had no other. The thought made her hands tender and solicitous. She kissed him, almost with a passionate yearning, as though he were mortally threatened, and she stood between him and an appalling danger.

She went downstairs. Her legs and body felt stiff and icy cold. Irmgard was gathering up the dishes and placing them on the iron sink. She moved gracefully, her green skirts flowing about her, her loosened hair a nimbus of light about her pale cheeks. Emmi sat down heavily in her chair, and held her head on her hand. But there was no real prostration in her attitude. Rather, it was a grim and foreboding waiting.

Rain splattered against the windows, and the wind sucked air even from the room, so that the lamp flickered. Despite the warmth of the scarlet stove, there was a feeling in the room of desolation and abandonment, and a deathly chill. The women did not speak. Irmgard carried the copper teakettle to the sink, and washed the dishes, put them neatly away. Emmi did not move. Her wide stark eyes stared fixedly at the floor.

Suddenly Emmi struck the table with a dull blow of her hand.

"I cannot bear it," she said, and her voice was loud and flat. But under the loudness and that flatness, Irmgard heard the seething of unendurable anguish, and hysteria. "My son," said Emmi. And then again: "My son."

Irmgard came to her, put her hand on her aunt's shoulder. "You have not heard him, Aunt Emmi. You cannot condemn him without a hearing."

Emmi looked up, very slowly, and her wide pale eyes fixed themselves inexorably on the girl.

"You do not believe he is innocent," she said.

Irmgard glanced aside. She left her aunt and stood before the blank black window.

"There are times when one must believe," she said, very quietly. "For one's own sake."

Then, swiftly, she turned again to her aunt. Her young face was distorted with such open pain that Emmi, in spite of her own wretchedness, was startled.

"If your son were ill of an incurable and terrible disease, you would not hate him!" she cried. "If he were covered with sores, you would not shrink from him! Do you not know there are disease and sores of the spirit, too? Why do you shrink from them? Why do you not try to heal them?"

Emmi's cold lips moved in faint words: "It is too late."

"No," said Irmgard, and there was a cry in her voice.

Emmi sat upright, and gazed at the girl for a long and ringing moment. Astonishment made her mouth open, become slack. Then she exclaimed: "You love him, Irmgard!" Incredulity gave her an almost imbecile look.

Irmgard said nothing. But her white throat throbbed, and her mouth twisted, and her eyes filled with tears. Seeing this, sternness darkened Emmi's face. She clenched the hands which lay on the table, until they became fists. Rigorous waves tightened, flexed her mouth.

"Once," she said, "I dreamt of a marriage between you and my son. I knew my son. It was a wicked thing I contemplated. Somewhere, in his blood, there is a foulness. I knew it. I was a fool. I thought perhaps you might help wash away that foulness, with your own blood. I was a fool! It cannot be. I cannot allow you to pollute yourself so. You dare not have his children, and bring others in the world like him. It is a wickedness to the world."

Then, as she saw the girl's distraught expression, her voice became mournful, and more quiet.

"Your father and your mother—they were good. I knew my sister. I knew your father. They would not rest in their graves, if they knew such a marriage might take place. I forbid it. I am your mother, in this country. I am your only protector. I forbid you to marry my son, and to have his children." She added, almost inaudibly: "He would make you a foul thing, also. He would destroy you."

Irmgard pressed her trembling hands together, and looked at her aunt with her swimming but steadfast eyes.

"I love him. That is all that matters to me. He might be as you say, and you must know, being his mother. But all that is nothing. I love him. If he wants me, I must go to him. I cannot do otherwise."

There was a click at the front door. The two women stared at each other in sudden intensity. Then Irmgard cried in a low voice: "Not in here! Uncle Egon will hear you! Let us go into the other room!"

Emmi rose. They hurried into the cold and bitter darkness of the "living room," with its horsehair furniture dully gleaming in the light of the lamp which Irmgard carried. The girl shivered with mingled chill and fright. She put down the lamp, and stood near it, her palms pressed convulsively together. But Emmi waited with a murderous calm, her arms folded on her flat chest.

Franz had evidently not expected a reception committee, no matter what else he had expected, and when he entered the room, walking with a slow and hesitating step, as though he were ill or blind, he started violently when he saw the two women, his mother and his cousin.

Then, instantly, his expression became immobile and dark, and his eyes flashed with a formidable glitter as he glanced at his mother. There was no shame in that expression, no embarrassment or remorse. But in the sudden flare of his nostrils, and the tightening of his mouth, there was a cold black hatred, naked and revealed.

He ignored Irmgard, standing near the table, with the lamplight on her white cheeks and chin. He looked only at his mother.

"Whatever you have to say," he said, with slow deliberation, "I do not care to hear it. You and I have said enough to each other, for years."

Emmi quivered, as though she had been struck. But she stood, after that first quivering, unmoved and unfrightened. Only a little of what she felt appeared in the ghastly tautness of her face.

"Liar," she said. "Murderer. Thief." Her voice was quiet, even calm.

"No!" cried Irmgard, suddenly, twisting her hands together in unendurable pain. "You must not speak to each other like this! It is not possible! It is a nightmare."

For the first time, then, he turned to her, and the stony lines of his mouth softened, and the glitter of his eyes became milder.

"This is no place for you, cousin," he said, almost gently. "Will you leave?"

She began to cry, though she was silent, and did not move. He saw the tears running helplessly over her face. He bit his lip, and averted his head.

"She will stay," said Emmi, in a deadly voice. "She has told me she loves you. And I have told her that I forbid any marriage, any association with you. You are not my son. You are a foulness. You are a monster."

Then he smiled, and at that smile, Emmi quivered again, with intense suffering. Irmgard laid her hand on her arm.

"You do not mean that, Aunt Emmi," she murmured pitifully. "He is your son. You are his mother. Do not speak so. It will be such a bitter memory."

Emmi flung off the girl's hand with a violent gesture, and Irmgard knew then how false her calm had been, and how terrible were the emotions that were assaulting her.

"Perhaps you are right," said Franz, in a hypocritically meditative voice. "You are my mother. You must know all about that foulness. It must be in you, also. We are of one blood. We are the same. You must be the judge of whether Irmgard dare become your daughter."

Deathly sickness glared from Emmi's eyes. Irmgard put her hands over her face, as though she could not endure the sight of this woman and her son, facing each other with such hatred and detestation, and, she knew, suffering.

"It is not possible for me to remain in this house," Franz went on. "The time has come when we must never see each other again. We understand each other too well. Accident turned your mind to what you call noble ideals. The same mind in myself, which I inherited from you, has made me despise your hypocrisy, your willingness to blind yourself to reality. I do what I must do, just as you do what you must do. We have always been in confiict. We have always hated each other, because we could not deceive each other. Therefore, I must go."

Emmi was silent. She hardly seemed to hear. She stood rigidly before her son, with her folded arms, but in spite of this rigidity, this inexorable posture, she gave the impression of mortal disintegration and crumbling.

Irmgard dropped her hands from her face with a sudden wild gesture of despair.

"You cannot go, Franz! Your father—he is ill. He can work no more. Your mother and he have decided to leave this city, to buy a little house, a farm, where he can have peace. You cannot desert him, yet!"

Franz listened, and his expression changed to one of gravity. "My father," he said, reflectively, and his voice was even a little sad. "No, I suppose he must not know of this—conversation, and the accusations. You are right, Irmgard," he added, and his eyes smiled at her gently. "I will remain here, until he leaves."

Then he said, quickly: "His illness—what is it?"

Irmgard sighed, and the sigh seemed to come from her heart. "It is a sickness of the mind, Franz. He cannot endure his life."

Franz smiled cynically, threw his mother an evil glance. "No wonder," he said, thoughtfully. All at once, he laughed, and Irmgard was sickened at the sound. He pointed at his mother, but he looked at Irmgard.

"Let me tell you, my cousin. This woman has made my father's life a hell. In pursuit of what she would call her 'dreams,' she wrenched him from his little quiet place in the Fatherland, where he had peace. The Fatherland was too small for her, too sensible, too conservative. It had no 'freedom,' no 'ideals,' no 'hope.' But the truth was that it had no place for her ambitions, for her egotism, for her dream of self-aggrandizement and arrogance. She has never confessed it, but she wanted money——"

"That is not true!" cried Irmgard, outraged. Again, she put her hand on Emmi's iron arm. The poor woman did not move. Her eyes were fixed in a stony and deathlike look on her son's face.

Franz nodded, with smiling ferocity. "Yes, it is true, though perhaps she does not know it, herself. But she had heard that America was rich. That is the dream that drove her. Had she become rich in America, she would not be so bitter against this country, nor so full of angry condemnations. She would have forgotten her noble dreams, which were only self-deception to cover her real passion. Like myself, she wanted power and riches. I have been honest about it. She has been dishonest. That is the only difference between us. She will say that I sacrificed many things. Even my—friends," and for a moment his expression changed. Then he continued, implacably: "She sacrificed my father, who loves her. In that sacrifice, she drove him to France, and to England. She will tell you that she found 'nothing,' there, and will give you the impression that the 'dream' had died in those countries. But the real reason for her accusation is that she found no opportunity to become rich in France and England. So—we came to America. I am glad. We were both driven by the same desire. She has failed. I shall not fail."

He paused, then in a louder voice, he said "I shall not fail. There is everything here, for the taking. I shall take. I am a man, and she is only a woman. She has sacrificed much, but it is not enough. I shall sacrifice everything."

"Everything?" whispered Irmgard. "Even me?"

She half extended her hands to him, and he could hardly bear the sweetness and misery of her look. He touched her outstretched fingers lightly with his own.

"Not you, love," he said. "I do not need to sacrifice you."

For a moment they forgot the silent and suffering woman who stared so blindly before her, at her son.

"You do not believe the thing of which I am accused?" he asked, and his eyes struck into hers sharply, as though daring her to believe.

She looked at him with her level and tear-filled eyes.

"I cannot believe," she answered, simply, and her lips became whiter than ever, in her anguish.

He smiled, though well aware of the ambiguity of her words.

"It is enough for me," he answered, very gently.

He held out his hands to her, but she shrank back, in spite of herself.

"Not yet," she whispered. "Oh, not yet!"

Then he knew that she knew the truth. He smiled, as though in cynical wonderment and delight. And relief. They regarded each other intently.

From upstairs, now, came a faint murmur and a sound, then a call: "Franz. Franz?"

"It is my father," said Franz, quickly. "I shall go to him." He hesitated. He gave his mother a vicious and inimical glance. Then he left the room, and they heard him mounting the steps in the rear.

When he had gone, Emmi still stood in her stony and unmoving attitude, her small light eyes distended as though fixed in death on something so horrible that it had killed her. Irmgard, aching with wretchedness, despair and compassion, put her arms about her aunt, wordlessly.

Then, suddenly, the poor woman uttered a loud groan. Then another, and still another. Her fixed expression changed. She looked at Irmgard with blind agony. "No, no," she groaned, and Irmgard felt her trembling. She embraced the girl with desperate arms, and began to weep. They stood there together, and now there was no sound in that dank dark room, so hideous and cheerless, but that heart-broken weeping, that final collapse of a proud and assaulted spirit, which had seen too much, and too clearly, and could not endure the seeing.

And then she murmured, brokenly, and with tearing gasps, and it was a strange thing that she said:

"O God, what will the future bring him? What will become of him?"

No accusation of hatred, rage or fury was in those words, and that dying voice. Nothing but the anguished cry of a mother:

"What will become of him? What will the end be, for him?"

Irmgard did not answer. She held her aunt more closely, and stared before her, whitely.

* * *

Franz wore a humorous, if subdued smile, when he went in to his father. Egon, faintly alarmed was sitting up in bed, in his nightshirt. He had lit the lamp. When he saw Franz, he was relieved, then immediately pitiful.

"My son," he said, and held out his hand to him. Franz sat down on the edge of the bed, and regarded his father with affection. Egon studied his face, and he saw the pinched blueness of his lips, in spite of the smile.

"I am sorry, Franz," he said, simply, and his dimmed eyes became moist. "He was your friend, that poor Englishman. I suffer for you."

Franz ceased to smile. He gazed over his father's head, and his expression became tense, and a little dark.

"Yes," he said. "He was my friend. The only friend I ever had."

Then he was silent. His hand was cold in his father's. Egon felt that a stranger sat near him, no one of his blood, but some creature of strange heritage, whom he could never understand, in spite of his love.

CHAPTER 35

"THE GERMAN is never subtle," Franz had once said, with frankness and malice. "Even his cruelties are brutish."

Nevertheless, there was refinement in the torture he inflicted on his mother the next morning. He insisted on talking brightly and volubly to her, and then, when she did not answer him, but sat like carved granite at the table, he asked her questions. His father sat at her side, smiling timidly and lovingly from one to the other, and in order to preserve his ignorance of the tragic breach between mother and son, she was forced to answer Franz. She answered him in monosyllables, it is true, but answer him she did, her small pale eyes averted. It was torment to have to speak to him, but it was torment she bore without a quiver of the voice, or a gesture, or a formidable look. For Egon's sake she would bear this heroically. Franz was not inspired with pity for her, or compassion or mercy. He enjoyed this dreadful baiting. He smiled at her, his blue eyes pointed with hatred and pleasure in her misery. Egon thought him very talkative, but was pleased, if touched, at Franz's apparent effort not to afflict his parents with his private sorrow over Tom Harrow. He kept giving his son glances of understanding, gentleness and sympathy. Emmi saw these glances, and her heart was squeezed with almost unbearable suffering. A nausea of loathing for her son made her retch internally. But her hands did not shake for an instant. A less cruel and relentless nature than Franz's would have felt some shame, some remorse. He felt neither. It gave him a kind of perverse delight to see her sharp profile tense with agony. In his masochist's diversion he found some alleviation for himself.

Egon, looking less ill and beaten than usual, talked timidly of a farm he and Emmi would buy. A quiet place, he said, looking hopefully from his wife to his son. Emmi and he had always loved the country. Five thousand dollars would buy an excellent farm, and surely there must be beauty here, as well as in the Fatherland. They would live simply. Franz would help them select the farm, and it would be home to him, also.

Emmi glanced up blindly, and her pale swollen lips parted for a moment. But she said nothing.

"On the week-ends," Franz said, with an indulgent smile at his father, "I shall visit you."

"We may live far out," said Emmi, in a dull voice, in which there was no life, but only an echo.

"What does that matter?" exclaimed Franz. "I am much attached to my parents! I could not deprive myself of seeing them regularly."

Egon smiled tenderly, and with some embarrassment, but with great joy. "Yes, yes! I did not know you cared for us so, Franz! We shall then know, on your visits, that all is well with you."

"Everything," said Franz, rising and putting his hand for a moment on his father's shoulder, "will always be well with me. You see, I know what I want. That gives me a great advantage over fools."

His malignant victory over his mother sustained him for a long time, that day. His pleasure in that victory gave him serenity and sureness. He was certain, now, that he could face the problem of Jan Kozak, and conquer it. It had been a problem that had given him a sleepless night, and had driven from his mind the dim ghost of Tom Harrow.

He had the capacity to forget the past, to shut a black door upon it. In retrospection, he knew, there was weakness and hesitation. What was dead was dead. Tom Harrow left nothing in him now but a static depression upon which his thoughts and his plottings rode brilliantly as upon a dark wave. Dolly Harrow and her children were provided for: he even said to himself, cynically: "Had Tom lived to the end of his life, he could never have secured five thousand dollars." He had convinced himself that such a life as Tom's, restless, burdened and unhappy, was well exchanged for that sum of money. He even thought, with a faint smile, that Tom, in an honest moment, would agree with him.

He thought that his expediency, his implacability, his quick adjustment even to grief and remorse, were signs of strength. Like most Germans, he worshipped what he fondly considered "strength." He did not know, as Irmgard did, that in such "strength," and the worship of it, was an ignoble if subconscious confession of fundamental and complete weakness, and futility, and emptiness. And craven fear. He did not know that in accepting, and understanding all, in bearing the complete result of action and in refusing to mitigate it with sophistries, was the real strength. Real courage and strength lay in taking up burdens of action and circumstance, and developing the capacity to bear them. In memory there was no weakness, but courage. He thought himself a realist. He did not know that realists were those who faced result of self and others with equanimity and wisdom, and made the most of it. Forgetfulness, deliberate and conscious, was the mark of the coward, who dared not meditate, who dared not confront himself.

He thought his ruthlessness the feature of the strong man. He did not know that the ruthless man exhibited himself as a weakling, who must continually make exaggerated gestures to hide his weakness.

Nevertheless, when he entered the mills, walking steadily and quietly, a sick darkness assailed him when he knew that he would see Tom Harrow no more, in his usual place. He walked boldly now, through the ranks of the silent working men, and he could not help wondering, uneasily, if they had heard Jan Kozak's terrible story. A stronger man would have faced furtive glances calmly, bearing them down with a quiet eye. But he could only look ahead, forcing an expression of indomitable contempt on his face. He knew that the men looked after him with mingled fear and hatred and scorn, and this gave him a tremor which he despised, but could not throw off.

He could not keep himself from darting quick looks about for Jan Kozak. And when he did see the big Hungarian, standing squarely in his way, he could not keep down a sudden twisting in his middle, which he would not acknowledge as fear.

A thousand thoughts darted through his uneasy mind. He was assistant to the Superintendent now. He had only to discharge Jan Kozak. But there was Dietrich, the Superintendent, who hated him, and would only be too glad to listen to any story to his detriment. But, dared Dietrich discharge him, after having learned that the foul story was common knowledge? But, again, would not his discharge establish the innocence of the Schmidt Steel Company?

He had another, and a much more disquieting thought. Had Kozak told Dietrich of the theft, by Franz, of his idea for the moulds? Dietrich, if he did not discharge Franz, would seize upon that idea, and Kozak would be the rewarded, and not Franz. The first great door to his progress would then be closed forever. Dietrich would prefer to believe Jan Kozak.

His thoughts made him stop before the Hungarian, though his first plan had been to ignore him.

Jan stood before him, arm akimbo. His torso was naked to the waist, and Franz saw clearly the thick matted black hair on the other's chest, and the giant shoulders, and the immense muscles. He also saw the wrinkling hatred on the great ape-like face, and the parted lips between which wolfish teeth glistened.

"So," said Jan, "you come back, you dog. Tom is dead. But you and me, we are not dead, no? We got things to say which ain't dead. Yes?"

Franz was silent for a moment. The men nearby stopped to listen, holding shovels or hammers in their hands, and Franz had the impression that they crouched, as though to spring. He saw their faces in the fitful yellow light of the furnaces, and clearly, as in a nightmare, he saw the web-like pulleys of the cranes, and the men who leaned out from them like spiders, listening. One of the cranes was slowly moving, stealthily, and though no doubt it was only a sick illusion, it seemed to move upon Franz. The faces about him seemed to move upon him, also, silent, deadly, gleaming with hatred and murder. The booming of the mill, and the clangor, he heard, faintly, but this background only accentuated the silence and watchfulness of the men, and the yellow and scarlet light in their eyes and on their faces was like the reflection of hell on demons. The mill was a cavern of hell, also, dusky, quivering with flames, lost in drifting gloom. And before him stood the chief demon, surrounded by his servitors, and his enormous body seemed to expand like an enveloping and crushing doom.

"Out of my way," said Franz, and his voice echoed against the fog of the sounds of the mill.

The one crane crept nearer, bearing a huge ladle of molten steel, which blazed like a miniature sun. Its light burned fiercely on Jan's ferocious features, and on the dark, waiting and savage faces of the men, which seemed disembodied and malevolent masks floating in semi-darkness. A blast of heat emanated from the ladle. Franz did not see the ladle, except vaguely. He was preoccupied with Jan Kozak. And now he felt fear, abysmal and frantic.

Jan did not move at his command. He smiled. It was a frightful smile.

"You—you thief," he said. "You no steal my brains. You are liar. You give me back my brains. Or," and he doubled up his giant fists.

The face of the man, high up in the webs of the crane, peered out and down, and grinned wickedly. Inch by inch, stealthily as death, and as remorseless, the crane and the ladle moved nearer Franz. Now the fiery light enveloped him and Jan Kozak. The man was maneuvering, with dreadful and fiendish care. Some of the men, scenting peril and horror, glanced up uneasily at the crane and moved out of the path of the ladle which was apparently bound for the moulds on the other side of the mill.

"Out of my way, you fool," said Franz, again. The skin on his back was crawling, as though inspired by some mysterious awareness of danger.

A loud and maddened shout suddenly burst from the men in the background. Franz and Jan turned. The ladle was wavering, hissing with a frightful roar, and tilting. Clouds of glittering sparks rose from its molten depths, and an aura of brilliant scarlet enveloped its round black form. The crane screeched and rocked; the man on his tiny platform was working feverishly, and apparently impotently, with levers. The men rushed backwards, blindly, thrusting outward with their arms, in order to escape from the stream of crimson death which appeared imminently to flow out over them. Their shouts echoed against the gray fog of the mill, and boomed back.

Franz was in the direct path of the ladle. Now he felt its unendurable heat, and saw the seething red and gold contents, bubbling like some infernal soup. He glanced up swiftly at the crane, and the man within it. He saw his face. And then he knew that he was deliberately marked for destruction.

He could not move. His feet seemed to have been seized by subterranean hands, which held them immovable. His flesh turned to rigid ice. A ghastly sickness filled him, and a nightmare quality pervaded his whole mind and paralyzed his will to save himself. He could only stare at the seething and shaking ladle, its blazing contents roaring, hissing, sparkling, which moved upon him with such a hideous implacability. Now he could feel its searing breath through his clothing and upon his flesh. He could see the black, pock-marked exterior of the ladle, and heard, as in a dream, the creaking of the crane. For centuries, it seemed, he stood there, blasted with the heat, waiting for the rocking ladle to tilt and pour its vivid, dissolving death upon him. Sharpened by panic, his eyes saw the hell-like reflections of the molten metal on the far dim ceiling of the mill. To him, the world swam in the red shadows, and eternity rushed in on him on a black wave. And he saw himself as a static mote of consciousness, held immovable in the path of irrevocable annihilation.

The dream heavy upon him, and fatalism preventing one wild leap out of imminent peril, he heard Jan's wild shout:

"No! No! Damn fool, no!"

The darkness engulfed him. He felt himself seized violently, and flung aside like a straw. The universe was suddenly broken into chasm of crimson light, and long shooting lightnings of burning blackness, and tumultuous thunder. He did not know whether he was lying or standing, but everything rocked about him, filled with roarings, hissings, explosions, and the screams of men and demons. He felt a dull crushing blow on his head, like a hammer blow from out of whirling space. Now he too begain to whirl in long spirals, and he threshed about with his arms and legs, a swimmer in deep lightless seas. Some one, he thought vaguely, was coming to his rescue, for he felt tugging hands, lifting him above smothering waters.

Now solidity was under him again, and a great silence, broken only by dim distant hissings, and faint shouts. He opened his eyes.

He was lying on his back. His head had struck the floor with intense force after Jan had seized him and tossed him aside from the writhing and blinding path of the poured metal. Jan had saved his life. But in the very instant of tossing him into space, the metal had struck Jan's legs almost to the groin. They had dragged him away, and Franz, also. Jan was lying on a low heap of slag near the furnaces, and the men, groaning, wringing their hands, and even weeping, stood about him, their eyes fixed on his face, and refusing to see what remained of his body. The craneman knelt beside him, sobbing like a child, supporting his head on his arm.

This Franz, forcing himself dizzily to his knees saw. He saw the pool of spilled metal, a bubbling black pool now, shot through with dull threads of scarlet. It hissed along the edges. One scallop of it was dangerously close to Franz. He shrank back from it, whimpering in his chest. Then, across the pool he saw Dethloff and Dietrich, with far white faces and dumb lips.

Now he heard Jan's gasping, dwindling voice, speaking to the craneman.

"Damn fool. He not worth hangin' for, see? Now you hang, maybe. If the boys don't lie. Boys, you lie?"

"Yes. Ja. Ja! We lie!" said the men. "The ladle—it spilled. Itself. We lie. Boze no hang for bastard."

Franz scrambled to his feet, swaying. Boze, Jan's brother, had tried to kill him. He knew the temper of the men. He was not safe, even now. He thought suddenly of Jan, horribly dying, and he was overcome with terror. He looked across the thick smoking bubbling pool of the cooling metal, and saw Dethloff and Dietrich, paralyzed, but avidly listening. He found a narrow space across which he could leap, and he went to the two men.

Dietrich regarded him with a white and wicked smile. He spoke to him in their native language.

"Perhaps you had best go home for a few days, nein? A few days. We dislike killings in our mill."

Franz put his hand to his head. A long warm trickle of blood ran over his cheek.

All at once he was violently sick. Dietrich and Dethloff watched him cynically, and even with a kind of cruel interest. And then, remembering, they became frightened, and went away quickly and furtively, followed by Franz.

CHAPTER 36

FRITZ DIETRICH was exultantly triumphant. The hour for which he had waited, in which he would destroy Franz, and the danger to himself, had come. Hans Schmidt had not yet arrived at his office, and Dietrich determined that he would act swiftly. He had come to his decision during the short walk to his office followed by Franz and Dethloff. He sat down at his desk, put the tips of his fingers together, and his elbows on his desk, and smiled at Franz malevolently. Dethloff, anticipating, leaned against the window, and waited. Franz stood before Dietrich, calmly wiping the blood from his gray face. He was horribly shaken, the happy Dietrich could see, but he was disconcertingly calm, also. His shrewd mind was already aware that the Superintendent believed his hour of victory had come.

"I have arrived at the conclusion, Stoessel," said Dietrich, "that it would be best for every one concerned, and especially for the Schmidt Steel Company, if you left these premises as quietly and quickly as possible, and did not return."

Franz said nothing, but his eyes were slivers of blue ice. Having finished wiping his face, he put away his stained handkerchief. Then he stood like a soldier, at attention.

Dietrich felt encouraged by this lack of anger and absence of protest.

"We have had a hard time in the past months, to control the men. I do not think they can now long be controlled. Even you can see that. They must have heard the—story. Now they are aroused against you. When you appear as assistant to Dethloff and myself, they will discover everything. Who knows what disorders will then arise? Who knows but what one of them will again attempt your life?"

He smiled again, with delight, remembering the death that had come so closely to Franz. But Franz's livid lips merely tightened, and again he waited.

Dietrich shook his head, with sudden solemnity. "We cannot countenance a situation which might result in your permanent injury, or death. That would be inhuman."

Then, for the first time, Franz smiled himself, cunningly. He still waited.

Dietrich's eyes sharpened swiftly, and he took on a hostile expression, openly hating now.

"Moreover, we cannot forget that you cost the Schmidt Steel Company five thousand dollars for your murder of your friend."

He stood up, with a gesture of dismissal. "I can see that you are taking this matter sensibly. I have always thought you extremely intelligent. We are willing to give you one hundred dollars as an expression of our gratitude, and our regret that we can no longer employ you."

He exchanged a quick complacent glance with Dethloff, who nodded and grinned.

But Franz did not move. He folded his arms on his chest and studied Dietrich thoughtfully.

"There are a few matters which you have not considered," he said, in a quiet voice. "I will enumerate them to you, and you will then agree with me that my presence here is very necessary. In fact, you will urge me to remain."

Dietrich frowned. He lifted his hand with an authoritative gesture.

"I think we need say nothing more, Stoessel. I will give you your money at once. I do not advise you to leave through the mills. The temper of the men is bad. Exceedingly bad. You will leave through my own door."

Franz smiled. He sat on the edge of Dietrich's desk, impertinently. He rubbed his chin with a contemplative gesture. With his other hand he played with Dietrich's long quill pen, turning it over and over in his strong fingers. But his eyes were fixed ruthlessly on Dietrich's thin fox-like face.

"I must still speak. You cannot throw me out like this. If you attempt more forcible measures, I shall go to Mr. Schmidt, himself. A moment, please. You will let me speak. Then you must decide what to do."

"Prussian dog!" exclaimed Dietrich, turning crimson. He glanced at Dethloff. "You will please remove this—man, at once."

Franz glanced idly over his shoulder at the hesitant and

middle-aged Dethloff. Apparently that look was enough, for Dethloff stopped, flushing. Franz returned to the Superintendent, as though the interruption had not taken place.

"You must remember," he said softly, "that I was attacked because I had protected the interests of this company, at great personal danger to myself. I sacrificed Tom Harrow, who had done me no harm, and who was my friend. I am sorry that he died; I had not intended it so. But that is past. It is foolish to regret anything. Nevertheless, I saved this company from a disastrous strike, and immense losses. You have said so, yourself. That alone is a consideration.

"You say the men are in a state of disorder. But what does the disorder matter, if the leader is absent? There is no leader. The two who might have led them are dead. Disorder among men is the signal to the strong to strike, and subdue. The moment is ready. I can quell this disorder in less than a day, with benefit to the Schmidt Steel Company. While the men are in this condition, we can seize our advantage. Never were we in such a strong position, as now, when they are more terrified than enraged. If you give me authority, I can not only quiet the men, but force them to accept conditions beneficial to this company. I ask you to give me this opportunity."

He paused a moment. "They will accept everything. Their own anger and disorder have weakened them."

Dietrich regarded him with leaden hatred, and fear. He knew the truth of Franz's words, and he was the more frantic to get rid of him, to destroy him in the eyes of Hans Schmidt, so mysteriously concerned with him.

"You must leave," he said, trying to make his voice inexorable. "I am busy. I have nothing more to say to you."

He furtively glanced at his watch. In less than an hour, Schmidt himself would arrive. A light dew of sweat broke out on his high receding forehead.

"Go," he said.

Franz shook his head with gentle humor, understanding everything.

"I have not finished," he said, calmly.

"I do not fear these men," he went on. "The act of one of them has terrified them. Moreover, I hold the whip again. I have only to hint that Kozak's brother will be arrested, perhaps hung, if another attempt is made to injure me. Moreover, others can be implicated. The fact that one of them failed to kill me will give me a mysterious and terrifying aspect to them. They will think, in their simplicity, that their failure has demonstrated my greater strength. Such are the workings of the mind of the simple and stupid. I shall seize this advantage. I shall announce longer hours and smaller wages. They will accept in their fright and confusion."

He stood up, confronting the Superintendent easily.

"You are at liberty to refuse all my offers, all my arguments. If you do so, I warn you that real disorders shall occur in these mills, with subsequent disaster to the company. I shall call a meeting of these men. You see, I am quite calm, and ruthless. I shall tell them that Harrow's death was deliberately plotted by the detectives you hired, and that I attempted, without success, to save his life. I shall call a strike. The consequences, then, will be that I will become a hero to these men. As for the consequences to these mills, your imagination must supply the details."

Dietrich's face elongated itself until it was only a sliver of leaden-colored flesh, in which his colorless eyes gleamed like the eyes of a reptile.

"You are attempting blackmail," he said, in a low and baleful voice.

Franz laughed frankly. "Blackmail. It is a detestable word. I did not use it. You have an evil mind. I am merely telling you candidly what will happen.

"Let me go on. I have a large advantage with which to start. The fact that I was able to secure five thousand dollars for Harrow's widow can be made either an advantage to you, dispelling all nasty rumors, or it can be an advantage to me. I can tell the men that I forced you, upon learning that your hirelings killed Harrow, to pay this money to Mrs. Harrow. You can see what an advantage that will give me. However, the decision is still yours to make."

Dietrich sat down slowly, his eyes still fixed viciously upon Franz. His thin fingers beat a tattoo upon his desk. He was silent.

Franz was palely exultant.

"On second thought, I may not decide to accept your urging that I remain. I believe I shall not accept it."

Dietrich looked up swiftly, his color returning. A slight smile began to form at the corners of his thread-like lips. But Franz raised his hand gently.

"A moment please. Once I told you that I had a secret formula for preventing the breakage of moulds. It is now perfected. No one knows of this but me. I have been a loyal fool, considering giving this secret to so small a mill as this, where the advantages to me cannot be very great. Though, of course, it will be of enormous benefit to this company. But you have demonstrated to me that loyalty is not in you, that you return efforts in your behalf with enmity and ruthlessness. Why, then, should I give the mills this secret, which will bring it great prosperity, and expansion?"

Dietrich was terribly shaken. He wet his lips. His reptilian eyes shifted.

"I do not believe you have such a secret," he began, in a stifled voice.

Franz sighed lightly. "That is for you to believe. Today, I shall go to the Sessions Steel Company, in Windsor. I shall tell them of my secret. I believe they will reward me accordingly. They are well on the way to becoming the dominant steel mills of this state. My secret will not only benefit them beyond imagination, but will end in the ruin of the Schmidt Steel Company, who must discard more than twenty-five percent of the moulds."

He took his cap from his pocket and pulled it over his aching head.

"You are not discharging me. I am leaving," he said. "The consequences are yours, not mine."

Dietrich was silent. He sweated with hatred, and fear. His mind seethed and roiled. Dethloff picked his nose feverishly in the background.

None of them knew that Han Schmidt had been in his office since eight o'clock that morning, an unusual thing. None knew that he had heard everything. So, when he appeared at his door, short, fat, pink and bristling, and grunting savagely, they turned startled and discomfitted faces upon him.

But he looked only at Franz Stoessel, and his tiny porcine eyes were blazing. They could not tell whether he was only smiling, or grimacing virulently.

He held up a finger to Franz. "You will please to come in here, lumpenhund," he said, harshly. "At once."

For a moment Franz stood rigidly at attention, his heels together. Then he smiled swiftly and malignantly at Dietrich. With a slight, ironical bow, then, he walked past the stricken and paralyzed Superintendent, and respectfully entered Hans's office, closing the door significantly behind him.

Dietrich sat immobile as wax, after Franz's departure. He did not stir even when Dethloff whinnied a little with horse-like and spiteful amusement.

CHAPTER 37

HANS SCHMIDT sat under the portrait of his wife's father, and the contrast between his squat porcine pinkness and the dark spectral and austere face and torso above him was both startling and ludicrous. "Red cabbage growing under a Lombardy poplar," thought Franz, pleased at this unusual burgeoning of imagination in himself.

He was very calm and his manner towards his employer was both easy and respectful. He had quickly guessed that Hans appreciated audacity, but not familiarity, and that only the most obvious and brutal humor would please him. Subtlety would arouse his animosity, hatred and anger, for he would believe that it was tinged with superiority and ridicule. He was a peasant, this Franz knew, and he also knew that the direct, simple and coarse approach was the only one the peasant understood. But this peasant demanded exaggerated respect, also, to tickle his ego.

Hans sat, grunting in his chest, and surveyed Franz, who stood at attention, and waited. He kept Franz standing for several long moments, while his tiny and choleric blue eyes squinted under the thick and hairy brows. His deliberate glance wandered up and down Franz, as though scrutinizing him for some weakness on which he could pounce. But his manner, though truculent, was not inimical. It was cautious, and brutish, however. He continued to make vulgar sounds in his chest, and once or twice, still without taking his eyes away from Franz, he coughed frankly, and expectorated. Finally, he opened a drawer, deliberately lit his cigar, and puffed, his short fat fingers crossed on his paunch.

Franz endured the scrutiny without wincing, or showing any evidence of uneasiness. Unobtrusively, he was also subjecting Hans to scrutiny. The diamond ring on the puffy red finger fascinated him, as did the diamond horseshoe in the crimson brocaded cravat. Hans was as clean as a fat slaughtered hog, scrupulously scrubbed and scoured for market. Franz found something vulgar even in that excessive cleanliness, as though Hans had rubbed himself to the quick to rid himself of the odor of barnyard manure.

To himself, Hans thought: A swine, but a swine out of my own pen. Deitrich is right: he is a Prussian. But I need a Prussian. He would stop at nothing. But I need men now who will stop at nothing. He is more than I thought. A gentleman, and I have always hated gentlemen. But I need a gentleman. Moreover, there is my daughter. And this is a handsome dog.

He spoke aloud, in his guttural German speech, deliberately accenting the low peasant intonations as though to offend Franz:

"So! You will threaten us?"

Franz smiled. "It is I who have been threatened, Mein Herr. I only retaliate. I am wounded. Does a man take assaults without retaliation?"

Hans was silent. He scowled. His shining pink skull was wrapped in wreaths of smoke.

"You are an impudent schweinkopf," he said, at last. "You do not know your palce. You are without loyalty. There is no discipline in you. You defy your superiors. In short, you have become an American."

Again Franz smiled, then said quickly: "That is a libel I cannot tolerate. I am none of the things you have said, Mein Herr Schmidt. But am I a worm? Must I tolerate the ingratitude of your Superintendent, and his bullying, and hatred, in the name of discipline? Would I be a German if I submitted to injustice without protest?"

Hans studied the tip of his cigar. He turned it about in his fingers. His thick pink under lip thrust itself out from under his bristling mustache.

"You think Dietrich hates you?"

"He is afraid of me," replied Franz.

"Afraid of you—a laborer in the mills?" Hans lifted his brows in an attempt to look incredulous, and succeeded only in giving a wry and surly smile.

"If I were only a laborer in the mills, you would not condescend to speak to me here, as you are now speaking," said Franz, with a stiff bow.

At this, Hans burst into loud and raucous laughter. "You are a fox!" he exclaimed. "A yellow fox. A Prussian fox, for all your claim to be a Bavarian!" He laughed again. "So! Dietrich is afraid of you! Do you know why?"

"Men of small wit are afraid of men with intelligence," answered Franz, boldly. He was feeling his way with cautiousness, advancing only when Hans showed that he would tolerate an advance.

"And you say you are not disloyal, impudent, and without

discipline!" Hans was scowling again, but Franz saw that he was not as displeased as he pretended. "You can speak so of your superior! You deserve to be whipped with the knout, as they do in the Army."

Franz now decided on even a bolder move. "Herr Dietrich is a Saxon rabbit," he said. "Is it impudent of me to despise him? In America, inferior men often dictate to the superior."

Hans drew his brows thickly together, so that his eyes were malicious blue points of light under their shadow.

"And you are superior, so?"

"I am a Bavarian," replied Franz, smiling cynically to himself as he drew up his shoulders and his head in a proud and simple gesture.

Hans' brows relaxed. He grinned sneeringly. "And I repeat—you are a fox," he said, and his harsh voice was sardonic. "Do not think you deceive me. I know all your tricks. I have exercised them, myself. You will have to learn fresh ones, if you wish to dazzle me. Use them on fools."

Franz hesitated. He wondered, for a moment, if he ought to appear insulted and hurt, or whether boldness would again serve him. He decided on the boldness. He laughed a little, affected to be embarrassed. "In my position, one must try anything," he confessed. "But, as a Bavarian also, I ought to have known better."

In himself, he was amazed. Why did Hans Schmidt waste words with him, talking to him slyly, and watching him so acutely? He was, after all, only an obscure foreman, who had just been discharged. Was it the secret of the moulds? Franz frankly doubted this. Hans was so choleric, so full of the vehemence and impulsiveness of the peasant, that in moments of stress he would forget personal advantage. Gentlemen, the superior, never forgot, and so used hypocrisy. But Hans, the peasant, was no hypocrite. What, then, was his motive for all this?

Hans, as though following his thoughts, said brutally: "You are a hypocrite. You are also a liar."

Franz, wishing to test his own amazement and awakening conjecture, bowed, said gravely: "You will then permit me to leave, Mein Herr?"

Hans leaned forward, his chair creaking, and pointed his finger at the younger man: "You admit you are a hypocrite and a liar?"

Franz was now certain that there was an ulterior motive in all this, beyond the mere fact of the "secret," and a sudden cold excitement seized him.

"Who am I to contradict you, Mein Herr?" he replied, with a slight smile.

"Bah! A clever trick! A Prussian trick, answering a question with a question! You are impudent. I am sure of that. Do you think there is room for an impudent dog in my mills?"

"That is for you to answer, Mein Herr." Franz was watching him closely, and the cold excitement increased in his mind.

Hans flung himself noisily back in his chair. His fat rosy features wrinkled sullenly. His eyes were splinters of blue malevolence.

"What is your idea for the moulds?" he asked, abruptly.

Franz was not taken off his guard, as Hans expected. He made a regretful motion with his hand. "I have patented the idea, Mein Herr. Once, I thought of not patenting it at all, and only of turning it over to your Superintendent. Subsequent events, with their cynical disregard of my services to the Company, have convinced me that I must protect myself.—You will now permit me to leave?"

Hans shouted, with sudden fury, turning crimson: "I have no idea of dismissing you! Moreover, you fox, you have no idea of leaving! Let us stop this childish fencing. Let us be open. What do you want?"

But Franz had heard only the first words completely. "I have no idea of dismissing you!" Then, in truth, there was an ulterior motive! Exultation caused him to flush, to double his fists. But he kept his voice quiet, if bold, and his eyes looked into Hans's levelly.

"I want to be Superintendent of the mills."

There was a sudden yet violent silence, in which the two men stared rigidly at each other. Then Hans, with a roaring bellow, sprang to his feet so furiously that the chair toppled over. He stood before Franz, a quivering and savage lump of pink flesh, his eyes flaming, his fists clenched. Every hair on his rosy skull bristled, as did his mustache. His chest heaved. Dull sounds issued from him, as though he were choking.

The effect was a little nullified, when Franz calmly lifted and replaced the chair. Seeing this, Hans doubled his rage.

"So! You would be a Kaiser, a King of Prussia, would you! You would be my Superintendent, would you! Who are you? A yellow Prussian swine, working in my own mills! I ought to kick you out of here, and down to the street! How dare you be so impudent, you pig?"

Franz paled. Had he gone too far? If he had, then everything was lost. Nothing more could be lost by increased boldness. Moreover, his own cold anger was rising, the murderous anger of the German. This foul fat peasant, who by a whimsy in this contemptible and casteless America, had become rich and powerful, while better men had to cater to him! In Germany, he thought, fixing Hans with eyes as black and vicious as winter ice, it is I who would boot you out of my way!

Then, another thought occurred to him. Did Hans know this, know the contempt which one like Franz would feel for him in their native country? And was he merely taking a malicious pleasure in revenging himself on Franz's helplessness? Suddenly Franz was sure of it. For Hans, still roaring, had retreated a step before Franz's fixed and contemptuous eyes. Franz quickly concealed his own feelings. He made his face express pride and affront.

"I am going," he said, and there was no respect in his words. He picked up his cap and went towards the door. He was sweating a little. But he did not walk slowly. If his intuition was correct, he would be recalled. If it was wrong, he had lost nothing.

At each step he expected the stentoriously breathing Schmidt to halt him. But he did not. I have lost, he thought. He put his hand on the door-handle. He turned it. I have lost, he thought again, with a sinking sensation.

Then Hans, who had been watching him cunningly, suddenly yelled:

"Come back, you pig! How dare you leave without my permission?"

Franz halted, his hand still on the door-handle, the door a little open. He saw Dietrich beyond, smiling slyly, Dietrich who had heard Hans's roaring. Franz opened the door wider, then looked back over his shoulder.

"I shall not stay to be insulted," he said, coldly.

Hans danced a step or two in fury. "Come back!" he shouted. "I have commanded you!"

Franz shot a quick glance at Dietrich, who had stopped smiling. The two men regarded each other through the opened slit of the door. Dietrich had turned the color of old ashes. Franz closed the door softly, smiling to himself. He went back to Hans, walking reluctantly, and he faced him.

"What more is there to say, Mein Herr?" he asked.

Hans continued to breathe hoarsely, and to scowl with ferocity. Then he fumbled for his chair, and sat down. He pointed to the one extra chair in the room. "Sit down," he said, grimacing.

Now Franz knew that he had victory. He wished that he had left the door open a little. His heart began to pound with dizzy exultation. Nevertheless, he pretended more reluctance, as he took the chair indicated. He stuffed his cap in his pocket, leaned back in the chair.

"So!" said Hans, thrusting out his lips. "You will be Superintendent, eh? You, who know nothing!"

"If you mean the men, Mein Herr," said Franz, "I do not admit I know nothing. I know them only too well. However, it is true that the theories of actual management are unknown to me. That is why I am now asking you to make me assistant Superintendent to Herr Dietrich. Not merely his 'assistant,' as proposed before. Then, after I have qualified, and learned everything, I wish to be Superintendent."

He leaned forward a little, facing the speechless Schmidt.

"There is much wrong with these mills; I have made a study. They are failing. They will continue to fail, even with my patent for my moulds. I know what is wrong. Within two years, or less, I can correct these things."

He added, reflectively: "I can make these mills the greatest in the state, perhaps even in the country."

Hans glared at him incredulously. "You conceited fool! You believe that?"

He could not believe that he had actually heard Franz's words. He stared into his eyes. He began to smile, savagely, contemptuously.

And then, all at once, he knew that Franz had spoken the truth. It was incredible! It was not to be believed! It was madness, and all insanity! Yet, his shrewd intuition, which had never failed him before, shouted that it was all true! His tiny eyes opened and fixed themselves, astounded, and the jaw sagged. He was regarding a miracle. The veins in his neck and temples swelled, became congested. He felt old stirrings in himself, which he had not felt since he was a young man, when everything had seemed possible. It was a long time since he had experienced these stirrings; he had almost forgotten how they had affected him. These last years he had become static, had accepted what success he had made, had believed he could go no further. That is why I have been failing! he thought to himself, with sudden and dumfounded revelation. When a man believes he has accomplished all that there is in him to accomplish, he has failed. He is retreating. He has no more inspirations, no more visions, no more exaltations. He lives, hovering on the edge of his own grave, not because he is only tired and old, but because he has ceased to believe in miracles.

A vast and sweating excitement filled him, and now all over his body the veins were swelling, and his heart was beating as fast as it had beaten when he was young. The placid gates of resignation had opened. He heard and saw the battle once again, and now he was once more young and excited and eager! Joy flooded him. His eyes flamed, sparkled. He exuded excitement and exultation.

Yet he said, trying to speak contemptuously, trying to laugh harshly:

"It is a mad program, spoken like a fool! You are audacious to speak so to me, who have done everything. You have done nothing. You are a braggart, like all Prussians. You are a dreamer of wild dreams."

"I never dream," said Franz, quietly. "I plot."

Hans laughed uproariously. "Tell me you have plotted today!" he shouted.

"I did!" Franz stood up now, leaned his hands on the desk, and leaned across it to Hans. "I did. Not perhaps just in this way. But I lived for today, and even for the things we have said."

Hans stopped laughing, abruptly. A sneering grin still lingered on his lips. But the sneer was not in his eyes, which bored into Franz.

"I believe you," he said at last, incredulously.

He could not endure his excitement. He stood up. He had paled; his whole round flabby face was pale. He began to smile.

"It is madness," he said. "It is not to be believed. Yet, I believe you. It is done!" he added, speaking loudly, rapidly.

He walked to the window on shaking stout legs. He stood and gazed through the dusty panes, and looked at his mills. Once he had dreamt that they would be huge, encompassing, formidable—a kingdom of steel. The dream had him again. It was not too late. Suddenly he saw Ernestine's small face.

He turned quickly. Franz was still standing near the desk, white and quiet. But his eyes were blazing.

Hans came back to the desk.

"It is done, then," he said, surlily, touching his bell for Dietrich. He wet his lips. "On New Year's Eve," he continued, as the door opened and the ashen Superintendent came in, "there is a party at my home. You will be there. At eight o'clock."

He frowned at Dietrich, who hardly seemed able to walk. "Take this man out!" he bellowed. "I have heard enough foolishness this morning!"

CHAPTER 38

ONCE DECIDING upon a course of action, Emmi wasted no time in discussion, caution, and vacillating words. Like a steel weapon, she drove home to the heart of the problem. A farm must now be bought, and she did not murmur vaguely of waiting for "better weather," and "the spring," and "perhaps we ought to look at another part of the country." Her great hatred was for those weak souls who "weigh every aspect of the situation carefully," and who fear "to do things in a hurry," and who urge "consideration and judiciousness." In such inane mumblings, she saw timidity, self-distrust, suspicion and incompetence.

Now she consulted farm-agents, and drove out, during the week before Christmas, in their wagons, their buggies and carry-alls, to survey the countryside. She inspected dozens of farms. If the agents hoped to find an easy and ignorant woman, capable of being deceived into buying worthless property and blighted land, they were woefully mistaken. Emmi, in her loud uncompromising voice, asked scores of questions, poked, investigated, gave her ruthless opinion, larded with insults anent the agent's intelligence, and marched back to her conveyance through mud and early snow with an arrogant toss of her black and shabby bonnet. Her skirts would flap about her boot-tops, and sometimes she would lift them superbly above her knees as she climbed fences, investigated roofs, disparaged chicken-coops and barns. While doing this, long expanses of white-and-black striped cotton stockings would be visible, encasing strong and sturdy legs. One agent, a former New Englander, paid her a remarkable compliment. "Ma'am," he said, doffing his hat after a very unsuccessful, and, to him, a smarting day, "you are a foreigner, but you are a blood-sister to my old grandma in Vermont. There was a vixen, beggin' your pardon, but a lady who knew her own mind and didn't care who heard her express it."

"I'll not be cheated," replied Emmi, loudly and contemptuously. "We worked very hard for our money, and I shall get my money's worth."

"You mean more than your money's worth," said the agent, respectfully.

Emmi smiled sourly. "Why not?" she asked.

Under dun skies, through rainstorms and snow-storms, though wind and hail and running roads, she marched everywhere, inexhaustibly. The rim of her bonnet often sagged with wetness, her skirts and boots were muddied, her black jacket became permanently wrinkled and weather-beaten, but her strong pale face and hard little blue eyes were undaunted. She was shocked, audibly, at the sight of neglected farms and blasted land and the general incompetence of the farming people.

"In Germany," she said, "we raised ten times the wheat on a similar acre of ground, and our cattle, though lacking much pasture, were twice as fat. As for these chickens! I would not use them for soup!"

She glowered at slatternly farm-wives and their hosts of malnourished children. She scowled at dirty farm-kitchens and smoking stoves. She insulted farmers for their lack of energy.

"Such a land!" she would exclaim. "It should flow with milk and honey. But it is sown with weeds and stones and rubbish. Look at that barn! The wind and the rain come in at will. Wicked wastefulness!"

One by one, the beaten and subdued agents abandoned her. At times, she went alone, striding through the countryside, or paying a farmer to carry her short distances in creaking, springless wagons. Sometimes she sat on the hard board seats of these wagons, rigidly holding a huge black umbrella to protect her from the merciless elements. She would look about her at the brown, drenched and bleak fields, at the broken smoking chimneys, at the black hills streaming with water under the gray skies. Her expression betrayed her disdain, her manner despised the people. Then she would tramp from farm to farm, asking if any were for sale. She was shocked at the number of them which she could buy, and she would glare at the discouraged slack faces of the owners.

"A nation which has no love for land is a nation doomed," she would say, to a bewildered and gaping farmer, who found both her accent and her words incomprehensible. "In Germany," she would add, "we love the land. That is why you will find none neglected, none blighted. Look at your orchards! It is winter, but I can tell that your trees will be blackened in the spring, and have little fruit."

She discovered that the most eager desire of most of the farmers was to sell the land and "work on the railroad," or "on public works." She was puzzled by the expression "public works," which conjured up before her inner vision vistas of vast Government buildings, mighty Government highways and avenues. When she learned that it only meant factories, she snorted: "Public works! Ha!" She kept repeating the phrase over and over, with fiercer intonations of contempt each time.

One day, near Christmas, she investigated a certain gloomy worn-out farm whose owner had more spirit than those she had previously encountered. He decided he did not like this "furrin woman," with her "hoity-toity ways," and nasty tongue. When he mentioned "public works," where a "man could make a decent living without workin' every blessed minute," she lashed out at him:

"What is to become of your country, where the people abandon the land and rush into the towns? Do you not know that eventually you will have huge cities and empty land, and that in the end all Americans will be working for a handful of masters? Have you no independence, no spirit, no pride, no self-respect? No! For a handful of dollars you will sell your liberty and your soul!"

The man's long whiskered face darkened. He spat deliberately very close to Emmi.

"Us Americans got along all right till you danged furriners came a-troopin', ma'am, and if you don't like our country you kin git out."

Emmi surveyed him in profound scorn. "A silly argument! Have you no better? You have not answered my questions. You either dare not, or you do not have the intelligence to answer."

The man fired up instantly. "I don't have to take no insults from nobody, ma'am, and you don't ack like a female, nohow! Whyn't you go over to the other furriners, the Amish folks, and stay with your own kind?"

Emmi was immediately interested. "The Amish." Her manner became more conciliatory. "Who are they? I am sorry if I have offended you. I did not mean to. Tell me about these Amish."

The man was surly; then, observing that her face had become quite kind and subdued, he said, scratching his head: "Well, ma'am, they're furriners like you, though I 'spect they been here a long time. Leastways, they was here when my grandpappy bought this here land. He kind of liked 'em, but I don't. Stuck-up folks, keepin' to themselves, and havin' their own heathen church. Won't come to ours, nohow. The wimmin-folk wear silly little bonnets, and the men got long beards and funny hats. Marry among their own kind, too, like they thought our own gals and boys wasn't good enough for 'em!" Reminded thus of a long grievance, he looked at Emmi formidably. "Furriners like that ain't got no right in our country. Our parson says we're cherishing adders in our bosom."

Emmi waited patiently.

"Got the best farms in the country, too!" went on the man, irately. "Stole it right from under our noses. No wonder we got sour land. We got the leavin's. T'ain't right. Some says they're better farmers than we uns, but that's a lie. Americans are the best of everythin' in the world. We don't need no danged furriners showin' us how to farm. We're Americans, ain't we?"

"Certainly," murmured Emmi. "But perhaps they have no aversion for work."

"What's that, ma'am?" demanded the man, suspiciously, then as Emmi did not answer, he went on, fuming:

"Ridin' around in their funny wagons, and wearin' their long faces, and jabberin' in their furrin lingo! They call 'emselves 'Dutch.' But I figger they're Germans."

"Deutsch," said Emmi. She was suddenly excited.

"How does one go to their country?"

The farmer surveyed her cautiously. He noted that her clothing was no better than his "old woman's," and that she was covered with mud. But her independent air, her arrogantly held head, her firm mouth and her strong stride, had convinced him that she was no beaten and poverty-stricken creature.

He scratched his head. "Well, ma'am, I could take you there. A right smart piece. 'Bout ten miles. Wouldn't pay me for my time, and the hoss and wagon, for less'n two dollars."

"Take me at once," said Emmi, peremptorily.

She waited in the rutted roadway while he went with more alacrity than usual to hitch his horse to his springless and mud-covered farm wagon. There had been a snow, and then a thaw. The brown ruts, jagged like old broken teeth, ran with thin black water. There was a feeling almost of spring in the air, so clear and pure was it, and so filled with the odor of the soil. Emmi looked over the bronzed and empty countryside, which rose and fell in slight waves and mounds to a distant copse of barren trees. The sky was a pale and silvery dome overhead, like highly polished pewter, in which a few crows circled and floated. There was no sound, not even a stirring of wind, except for the creaking of a pump behind the gray and weather-beaten farmhouse. Emmi breathed deeply, as though cleansing her lungs. She felt invaded by shafts of limitless pellucid air, and made free by them.

The farmer drove his wagon over the ruts, and it heaved

like a small ship on choppy waves. Emmi sat upright on the narrow board seat beside the farmer, her umbrella clutched in her black-gloved hand. For a few miles the country was bleak, the houses miserable. A barking dog or two raced after them, leaping and rushing. Emmi waved her umbrella at them, which excited them the more.

Now the country was changing. Low hills glistened with red-brown tints in the distance. The land, barren now of grass, was rich and bronzed. In one field a young farmer with a long black beard was sowing winter wheat. The houses became neater, more compact, many of them of stone, and others of white-painted clapboards with green shutters and red chimneys, which smoked against the sky. The fences were higher, and sturdily made. The silos and barns were painted a vivid scarlet. The barnyards were neat, and full of fat fowl pecking in the pale bright sunlight. The children who played in the roads, and in front of the houses were plump, plainly and warmly dressed in bonnets and hoods and knitted caps and mufflers, and their cheeks were round and hard as apples. A decent, almost smug, prosperity hung over the country. A young woman in a black dress covered by a checked apron, and wearing a tiny black bonnet of peculiar shape, was pumping water from a well, and she waved in a friendly fashion at the wagon as it rumbled past.

Emmi leaned out towards her and called: "Guten Tag, Meine Frau!" And the young woman, with a pleased, surprised expression, called a similar greeting.

They passed one or two little trim white churches, uncompromising and plain. They passed a small cemetery, on the side of a low hill, and the tombstones appeared to have been scrubbed with strong soap and water. The people had planted evergreens in a fence about the cemetery, and their deep dark green gave a promise of rest and eternity to the passerby.

The farmer humped forward on his seat, scowling. "They got the best land," he muttered.

"Nonsense," said Emmi, vigorously. "They know how to farm, and to work, and they have self-respect."

"Maybe you don't think I work hard, ma'am," replied the farmer, irrately. "Work my fool head off. It's no good, with sour land. Mighty poor crops."

Emmi said nothing. She wished he would drive faster, though even at this slow pace she found the riding hard. She glanced at the silver watch pinned on her black alpaca blouse, under the black jacket. It was half-past three.

Now they approached a low white farmhouse, with the familiar red silo and barn behind it. The windows were polished like mirrors, and hung with coarse white curtains. A brass knocker gleamed in the sun on the white door. On the window-sills Emmi could see pot after pot of crimson geraniums and ivy. A small wooden sign on the brown lawn proclaimed that a farm was for sale. It was lettered both in English and German.

"Here ye be," said the farmer, surlily. He bit his pipe. "I'll wait here for you, ma'am."

Emmi climbed down with her abrupt and agile movements, and marched up the walk, which was paved with unevenly shaped terra-cotta flag-stones. She lifted the brass knocker. Somewhere, in the interior, she heard the laughter of very young children, and then a sudden startled silence as the knocker clattered in the clear and silent air. Footsteps approached the door. It opened, and a young woman, plump, smiling and very pretty, stood there. She wore a much-washed and clumsily made dress of blue cotton, covered by a frilled and stiffly starched apron. On her hair, which was soft, brown and shining, and coiled at the nape of her short white neck, was a stiff white cap, tied under her round fresh chin with long cotton streamers. Little tendrils of her hair curled tenderly about her round pink cheeks, and her eyes, vividly blue and large and innocent, like a child's, were bright and merry. Her lips were scarlet, and parted over teeth like pearls. Her bosom, firm and young, could not be hidden by dress or apron, and rose comfortably, like a pigeon's breast. From behind her there was wafted the odor of good baking bread, and boiling sauerkraut.

"Ja, please?" she murmured. Now Emmi saw that two very small girls stood on each side of their mother, clutching her skirts, and peering out shyly and avidly at the stranger. They were dressed like the young woman, in bulky, old-fashioned garments, which fell about their tiny feet. Their hair was yellow.

Emmi spoke at once, in German. She smiled as she spoke, like a wanderer who had eagerly returned home.

"You have a farm for sale, yes? I am looking for such a farm."

The young woman opened the door. "Yes, we have a farm. Not ours, gnädige Frau, but the adjoining one. You will come in, while I send for my husband?"

Her manner was simple and gracious, and her smile ingenuous and simple. Emmi stepped across the snowy door-sill, and into a large immaculate "parlor," filled with horse-hair furniture, which was covered by lace antimacassars, large round walnut tables, heaped with books and religious literature, and the floor was covered with a thick rug flowered in sprawling roses and violent green leaves. There was a large round iron stove in the center of the room, warmly radiating, its top holding a brilliantly polished copper tea-kettle, from whose spout rose a thin bluish plume of steam. The sunshine came through the high small windows, lay on rubbed wood, and streaked the flowered wall-paper with fingers of light.

"You will sit, please?" said the young woman to Emmi, who was gazing about her with nostalgic pleasure. "I am Frau Barbour," she added, and waited.

"And I am Frau Stoessel," said Emmi, her voice gentle. She spoke slowly, in order to be comprehended, because the accent and phrasing of the German in which Mrs. Barbour spoke had a quaint and unfamiliar sound. A dialect, thought Emmi, and could not place such a dialect in her own memory of Germany.

Mrs. Barbour turned to one of the staring little girls, and said in English: "You will call to Hans, in the barn, and he will bring your Papa." Her English, like her German, had a peculiar accent. "Run, now, Liza. And May, too."

Both little girls, their butter-colored braids flying behind them, ran off, giggling shyly. Emmi sat down in a low rocker near the stove. The house was filled with clean, warm, home-like odors. Mrs. Barbour put fresh coal in the stove, and the red embers shone out of its cavernous depths.

"You will have some coffee, please?" she asked timidly, with her pretty smile. "And I have baked some fresh apfel-kuchen."

"Please," said Emmi, relaxing in her chair, her umbrella and black reticule on her knees.

With a murmured apology, Mrs. Barbour went off to her kitchen. Emmi could see it through the doorway, a huge room with red-stone floor and brick walls, white-painted furniture, flowered curtains and great black range.

"It is home," thought Emmi, with subdued envy. She had never been able to create this warm and fragrant atmosphere, and she knew it. Love and happiness and gaiety lived here, gilded with faith and content. If I knew how to be simple! thought Emmi. But simplicity is not in me. I do not know why. Perhaps it is because I have always thought too much. How Egon would love this! Perhaps I can recreate it for him, and give him contentment and peace at last.

Mrs. Barbour, moving with her light young step, returned, carrying a silver tray covered by a white linen cloth, and holding a blue plate of cake, a blue cup of coffee, and sugar and thick yellow cream. She placed the tray at Emmi's elbow, moving aside a large black Bible as she did so. The cake was still warm, and rich, golden syrup ran between the slabs of apple. The coffee was excellent, and very hot. Emmi ate almost ravenously, and thought with distaste of her own flat cooking. "How delicious this is," she said. "I am no cook. I have been concerned with less valuable things."

"Ja, is that so?" murmured Mrs. Barbour, with a sympathetic glance.

"I have been concerned with the social and spiritual welfare of mankind," said Emmi, with a wry, sour smile. "I have been tormented by dreams beyond my grasping. That is very foolish. It is better to cook, and polish furniture, and have little girls with yellow hair. And perhaps a garden."

Mrs. Barbour smiled, again with sympathy, but also with bewilderment. She was not repelled by this strangely speaking woman, but the fear of the unfamiliar subdued her smile somewhat.

"God has been very good to us," she said, uncertainly, and then her smile became bright again, with simple confidence.

"And in my seeking after Him, I have completely lost Him," Emmi said. She wiped her hands on the snowy napkin, and sipped her coffee.

Mrs. Barbour was bewildered again. Her round blue eyes stared unaffectedly at Emmi, as though with wonder and surprise.

The outer door opened again, and a tall angular young man entered. He had a long pale face and a dark beard. His brown eyes were melancholy and grave and brooding, and he wore a broad-brimmed black hat of odd shape. He wiped his feet carefully on the mat near the door, then advanced into the room. His work-clothes hung on his lean frame. When he smiled at Emmi and his wife, that smile had in it a strange sweetness, which lighted his whole somber countenance.

He acknowledged his wife's introduction, with a respectful inclination of his head, and when he spoke Emmi was surprised at his quiet and perfect English, which betrayed that he was no German. Emmi had half-suspected this. He sat down deliberately as he said:

"Yes, the farm. It was left to my wife, Mrs. Stoessel, by her widowed uncle. We have a large enough farm, over two hundred acres. We do not need this. My wife," and he smiled slightly, "did not wish it to pass out of the family, but there's no one left of it, except herself. It's a very good farm, one hundred acres of good pasture, and fifteen acres of first-growth timber. It is well-stocked, also, twelve cows, four hundred chickens, fourteen hogs, four horses, and a flock of turkeys and guinea-fowl. There are farm wagons, too, and plows, and all other equipment. Johanna's uncle died in September, and the furniture is for sale, also. A young farmer is taking care of the property just now. Perhaps, if you bought the farm, you would like to keep him, if you have no sons?"

Emmi's face took on a gray tint. She compressed her mouth. But her eyes looked straight into Mr. Barbour's. "I have no sons," she said, clearly and loudly. After a moment, she added: "There is only my husband and myself."

"I must be frank with you," said Mr. Barbour. "This is Amish country. We first offered the farm for sale to our own people, but all had sufficient land. I see you are a German, and it might not be too strange to you, here. The Amish are very friendly, though reserved at first." He smiled at his pretty wife, who blushed as though at an intimate caress. Her eyes beamed upon him with adoration.

He continued: "When I first came here, after marrying Johanna, every one was friendly to me, though I was a stranger. Now, I'm one of them." His gloomy expression lightened, and the sadness left his mouth and eyes. "You will find it so, too, I'm certain."

"I shall bring you some coffee, Reginald?" asked Mrs. Barbour, starting energetically to her feet. She left the room. In a little silence, the young grave man studied Emmi. She gazed back at him, and then her heart slowly warmed. Here, she thought, is a dreamer of dreams, also. Like myself, he perhaps found them untenable. Now, he has become content. A band of unseen but living understanding radiated between them, in which no words were necessary.

Then Emmi said: "You are an American, Mr. Barbour?"

"Yes, Mrs. Stoessel. I was born in Windsor." Now his expression darkened, as though with painful memory His voice was somewhat curt and abrupt, and Emmi saw that he did not wish to continue the subject. She asked him some questions about the farm, and then the price.

"Four thousand dollars," he said. "But we ask only half down. Is that satisfactory?"

He went on: "I advise you to keep Hermann to help you. You need pay him only ten dollars a month, and his board. I can recommend him without reservation. The Amish, when employed, are good and faithful workers. Then, I'll be glad to give you any advice or assistance you need. Johanna's uncle made a profit of nearly a thousand dollars a year on the farm, which is very good."

He drank his coffee.

"Now, if you wish, I'll drive you over to see it."

He went out to hitch his horse, and Johanna, her blue eyes swimming with love and sympathy, murmured:

"He is so sad. His dear sister died a little ago, when she

had a baby. And before that, his favorite brother was killed by miners, when there was a strike."

Something unformed stirred in Emmi's memory, and her expression became somewhat severe. "Ah, Barbour. I remember, a little. It was in the papers. But was there not some question? Was it not hinted that the young man was inadvertently shot by some member of his own family?"

Johanna dropped her eyes, miserably. "Reginald believes that. But it cannot be true!" Her lashes flew up, revealing distressed blue. "It must not be believed! People cannot be so wicked."

At another time, Emmi would have been gloomily moved by such pure innocence, but she was engrossed in disentangling the skein of newspaper memories. She looked about her, with surprise. This farm was comfortable and pleasant enough, and the house was filled with love and simplicity. But certainly no luxury.

"Your husband's father—is he not very rich? Herr Ernest Barbour?"

"It is so," said Johanna. Her round placid face became uneasy. She picked up Emmi's tray, and with a murmur, left the room hastily.

Emmi mused, with interest. Did one give up wealth and luxury, for this hard toil, frugality, and austerity? How was it to be explained? Franz, with cynical delight, would have been amused at her conjectures, and would have pointed out that her thoughts justified his cruel estimate of her. Moreover, though she would have denied it, her peculiar and passionate zest for life made her more than usually curious. Unknown to herself, she was interested more in mankind than in theory. Once Franz had said that an idealist and reformer was only a sublimated busybody and gossip, with a passion for minding the business of others. Emmi never acknowledged that there might be some truth in this

In the midst of her musings, Reginald Barbour returned, a black coat over his working-clothes. He led Emmi outside, and she saw, for the first time, the odd squarish black buggy of the Amish people, boxlike and neat. She asked the chewing farmer to wait for her, and after an antagonistic stare at Reginald, he nodded curtly.

Emmi found the buggy more comfortable than the wagon. Reginald, with his whip, indicated the good points of the country to her. A little wind had risen, and it was much colder. A few flakes of snow danced in the clear dusky air. But Emmi was protected by the shining leather curtains of the buggy, and regarded the countryside tranquilly through the ising-glass windows. Through the young man's cold aloofness and reserve, she felt his shyness and intellectual goodness, his courtesy and refinement. She looked at his hands, brown, soil-stained and callous. However, the fingers were long and sensitive, and slightly tremulous. But his manner, though scrupulous, kind and repectful, forbade any prying, even of the most casual sort, and she experienced a deep respect for him.

It was evident that he was greatly concerned for the welfare of the farm which was for sale, and questioned her if she had had any experience with the land. Discovering that she had, he became more enthusiastic, and smiled at her with his sad dark eyes.

The country increased in fatness. Now Emmi saw a distant red-brick farmhouse, compact, austere yet friendly. Clumps of great bare elms were scattered on wide lawns. Behind the house she discovered the immense red barns and silos of the country, and heard the lowing of cattle waiting to be milked. The country was rolling and rich, and very calm and wide. Against the clarified darkening of the sky an umbrella of smoke was opening from the tall stone chimneys, and the air was full of the fresh astringent odor of impending snow. Despite the wintry aspect of the country, there was no bleakness or desolation here, but only promise and security.

This is my home, thought Emmi, with lofty and almost reverential excitement, even before she entered the house. A short, stout and very blond young man, with a shy grin, opened the door for them, wiping his hands on his trousers. He ducked his head respectfully at Emmi.

There was a huge long parlor here, with tall narrow windows, a mighty fireplace in which logs of apple-wood burned. Emmi was startled by the furniture, which, though severe and unornamented, was of the best mahogany, and indicated exceptional taste. The carpet, a deep wine-color, was thick and almost luxurious, and plain. Along one side of the room were bookcases, filled with morocco-bound books. One glance convinced Emmi that the world's best literature stood here, waiting for friendly and understanding hands.

Reginald saw her surprise and appreciation. "My wife's uncle was quite worldly," he said, but he spoke with a smile and a glance of softness and appreciation at the dignity and formality of the room. "It is very like the house in which I was born, only smaller," he added.

They investigated the four large bedrooms, with their canopied fourposter beds of mahogany, the beveled mirrors, the stone fireplaces, the quiet carpets. Here had lived a man with the instincts of the aristocrat, and the reserve of a prince.

I can be happy here, Emmi thought. And again: This is my home.

After they had investigated the barnyard and the gardens, Emmi said abruptly:

"I shall buy it."

Reginald was surprised at this precipitation. "But your husband—will he not want to see it, and discuss the matter with me?"

"He is ill. I make all decisions," said Emmi, with her uncompromising stare into his eyes.

They went out towards the road again, to the waiting buggy. Emmi looked back at the house, which seemed to express some silent disappointment that she was not remaining. She sighed, heavily. She looked at the west, and over the massed darkness of the thick bare trees was a clear intensity of pale green light. Never had she seen such light, so limitless, so pure, so cold. It caught at her heart as an impulse of adoration catches at the heart of a worshipper. Tears rose to her eyes. She could only stand and look, her face uplifted, a reflection of the light on her face.

On her way home, in the springless wagon, she was silent. The profundity of her emotions absorbed her. She did not feel the thick wetness of the snow on her cheeks and lips. She stared before her, her eyes remote and entranced, her heart filled with a calm yet quivering ecstasy.

CHAPTER 39

EGON WAS accustomed to Emmi's sudden loud enthusiasms, and had lovingly learned to discount most of them. However, when she told him of the farm she had purchased, she spoke in a low, almost unemotional intensity. He listened, gazing at her colorless taut face, and knew that she was inexpressibly moved.

"It is home," she said, quietly, and there were tears in her eyes.

"Home," repeated Egon. He took her hand and held its hard roughness to his cheek. He felt her trembling.

In all his life with her, he had never complained of illnesses either of his body or his soul. And so he did not tell her now that he was ill. He was like a marble bowl filled with water, which had developed a crack, and was slowly leaking away. Each morning he awakened with a slightly increased loss of strength. Each morning, it was a little more difficult to rise and go downstairs, and more difficult than all, was the necessity to smile gently and sympathetically. He felt no more, only that slow loss of vitality and life, like an oozing wound. His body seemed floating in a warm pool of lassitude. At times, it was enormously heavy to him, so that he thought of his flesh as some pressing extraneous weight from which he yearned to be free. A cup was heavy in his hand. If he rose suddenly, his breath stopped. Sometimes, lying in his bed, he felt so leaden that he wondered vaguely how the mattress and springs sustained such immense weight as his. Surely, he must sink through them to the floor, and thence into the earth. At this thought, his heart rose like a bird on wings, with a sensation of dim ecstasy. He would close his eyes, and he seemed to hear the warm murmur of grasses over him, and the sweetness of penetrating sunlight.

His whole spirit was pervaded, not with thought and pain, but with a vast unthinking peace. Sometimes, he reflected that so a tree must feel, a consciousness not involved with mobile restlessness and aching movement, but a consciousness simply absorbing light and wind and water, and opening its heart to an existence that was only pure awareness of passive joy.

When he became aware that he was dying, he did not know. He only knew that the knowledge came in on him like a gentle noiseless tide, and he felt gratitude. Sometimes he felt a yearning sadness for Emmi, and then he would think: She will not grieve, knowing my happiness, knowing that I have felt no pain or terror. He did not know that in this dreamy thought was the final sign of dissolution. He only knew that a strange comfort was in him, like a hearth-fire.

Nevertheless, he did not tell Emmi. She was bustlingly absorbed in the final details of the purchase of the farm. He would watch her, animated, quick-moving, her angular body always in motion, and his tired bright eyes would grow soft and full of love. Never had he felt so tender towards her, so understanding. He would sit in his chair by the stove in the kitchen, beaming at her, listening. He heard her plans, full-bodied and vigorous. And he was content. When he was gone, the land would sustain and comfort her. Death, in a dark industrial city, with its ugliness, dust and noise, is a desert for the bereaved, in which pain echoes back from gritty pavements, and sorrow fixes itself like a livid patina on the face of dank walls. But death in the country, on the land, was a fulfilment of life, a golden autumn, a quiet and sleeping winter, a cycle of life which cannot be deplored, but only understood. It is prelude to spring, and birth, and brilliant skies shining with promise. Emmi would know this, he was certain. He was so happy, contemplating the quiet and lofty melancholy of her coming grief, which would contain no frenzy, no anguish.

God is good, he thought, simply. These days, he was concerned absorbedly with God. God was no longer an entity vaguely fixed in far space, involved only with gigantic systems and the furious flaming and falling of limitless life. He was the sunlight, lying on window-sills, the chirp of sparrows in the snow, light on a distant roof, the first star in the endless depths of the green evening sky. He was the glance of a beloved eye, the sound of a beloved voice, the rising of wind at midnight. He was nearer than the beat of a heart, closer than an inner sigh. He was all peace, all comfort, all consolation, all happiness. Tears would fill Egon's eyes, but they were not tears of pain. They brought humility, but they also brought exaltation and tranquillity. He did not know whether he would think or know again, after death. It is enough, for me, he thought, to have lived and known Him. What a boon it was, to have been born and become aware, if only briefly, of God! The eternal darkness of death was little enough to pay for such a fleeting awareness. The trees must be aware. They had no complaint for death. In their final falling leaf was a rustling sigh of remembered rapture. In their death there was no sorrow, no moaning. It had been enough.

He did not know that Emmi gave him furtive glances of anxiety. His patient face was becoming translucent, through which a gathering light brightened day by day. Franz had accused her of unwillingness to face reality. Against the warning of her senses, to face the doom of reality which her hidden mind detected, she put up a stern barrier of denial. Egon was in no pain, he assured her. He was very happy. He smiled more than usual. He was only tired. Her desire to believe made her pounce avidly on these false evidences of returning health. I should know it, she would say stoutly to herself, if all were not well with him. But her refusal to face reality made her deny the anguish of her knowing soul, which kept thrusting burning fingers into her heart.

Now he began to long for her realization of his true condition. His efforts to appear normal, to rise when his one desire was to sleep, to smile when he wished only to close his eyes, became almost more than he could bear. If she would only understand! he would murmur humbly to himself. It would be so restful to me. But she would not realize, and for her sake he must speak cheerfully, when the very effort exhausted him. It was his last burden. He bore it achingly, but with silent courage. Sometimes, however, he was frightened. What if, at the end, she was not resigned, not quiet, not understanding? Would he not, even in his peaceful grave, become aware of her agony? What could he do, then?

He was grateful for one thing: Franz, declaring that he must get settled, had moved to a comfortable, middle-class family hotel in Nazareth. Egon knew that Franz could not be deceived. It was a comfort that he was gone. When Emmi asked him if he did not miss Franz, who was "so selfish in his new prosperity," Egon replied: "No, I am happy." As usual, she did not understand.

Once he thought: "I shall lie forever in a strange land." At first, the thought troubled and saddened him. It would be so wonderful to lie in the soil which had given him birth, to know that the sun of his home would shine on his grave, that the voices of his own people would move over him. Then he knew that the earth and all men are one, and was comforted. If strangers spoke in strange tongues as they passed his grave, their hearts spoke only a familiar language. The sun that shone in America was the sun that shone in Germany, and the winds of both mingled into one wind, just as joy and sorrow are the same, mingling together.

He wanted to remain in Nazareth until Christmas had passed, but Emmi was strangely urgent that they leave for the farm at once. She did not know that in her very urgency was the cry of her subconscious fear and knowledge. It was this subconsciousness which pleaded that Egon must not die in the dark and hideous city, with the sound of factory whistles in his ears, and his last glance fixed on the sooty wall outside his window. He must hear the whisper of clean snow, and see, for the final time, the vast expanse of sky and hill. Hope whispered to her that surely he must be well, when they had left here. She had the sensation of one fleeing with a threatened beloved from a pestilence.

On the morning they were to leave, Egon found it impossible to rise immediately. Emmi came suddenly into the bedroom on slippered feet, and discovered him gasping on the edge of his bed. Icy panic and terror clasped her heart in iron hands. "I shall call a doctor!" she cried.

Her words aroused Egon to a last supreme effort. He caught her hand in his clammy fingers. He smiled, and the smile was an agony. The doctor, at all costs, must be prevented from coming. He must not tell Emmi the words of doom and hopelessness.

"No, I am well enough," he urged, in a dwindling voice, which only his will made audible. "It is nothing. I—I rose too fast. I am not a young man," he added, with his sweet smile.

She wanted to believe. She must believe. Against the renewed evidence before her, she thrust down her knowledge. "We must leave at once," she said. Her legs shook under her, and she hurried about the final preparations with a kind of fierce terror.

If I die here, thought Egon, forcing himself through a fog of gathering darkness to dress, Emmi will never go to the farm. She will be trapped forever in this tomb of a city. She will never overcome her sorrow. But when I die in the country, my presence in the earth will hold her there, and finally bring her peace.

The van called at eight for their boxes, bags and cases. Emmi had called upon a charitable agency and asked them to take her miserable and ugly furniture, for which she would have no more need. Egon was wrapped in his overcoat, and over his head and shoulders Emmi had fastened various shawls and scarfs. Among their folds, his thin transparent face with its tender smile, was the face of an old and suffering man, patient and resigned. It was snowing and blowing savagely outside. The dark sooty walls which leaned inward on the flat were lost in swirling white gloom.

Now Emmi appeared, gloved, bonneted, and brisk. They were to go with the van to the farm. Hurry and delight had reddened Emmi's rough flat cheeks, and her pale eyes sparkled with animation. She kissed Egon's forehead briefly, tightened a knot in the scarfs.

CHAPTER 40

ON CHRISTMAS morning, Mrs. Schmidt greeted Irmgard with tears and smiles. Lying in her bed, she took the girl's hand and held it in both her hot thin palms, so dry and tremulous.

"My dear, I do not know how you have done it, but this is

the first Christmas day in many years that I have been able to regard with pleasure and peace."

"I have done nothing," said Irmgard, in her slow reflective English. "Nothing. What have I done?"

Mrs. Schmidt was smilingly silent for a moment, her ringed and feverish eyes dwelling on the girl's serene face.

"What have you done, child? I cannot set it down in black and white. I cannot say: 'This, Irmgard has done.' That would be absurd. Perhaps it's only your presence that has worked the miracle. Just you, yourself."

Irmgard smiled indulgently as she patted Mrs. Schmidt's pillows and placed the silver breakfast tray on the little table. She had drawn the heavy curtains and the blue and silver of the winter day had burst into the great fetid room like a shout of trumpets. The trees outside were coated and outlined in pure brilliant crystal, so that in their temporary death they were shining monuments to themselves. The sidewalks were sharp wet streams through plains of whiteness, and the sun, clarified and unclouded, shone with extra radiance in a sky washed clean and infinitely far. The red stone fronts of opposite houses seemed scrubbed of all grime and soot, and windows glittered.

"A beautiful day," said Irmgard. She touched the pale gold of the tea-roses which lay on the breakfast tray, and which had come from the conservatory.

Mrs. Schmidt raised an arched thin finger. "Now, my love, no preliminaries and hints about a drive! I shall really be too busy this morning. Ah, that reminds me. Do give me that red box on that chaise longue."

Irmgard brought the box, and with triumphant sly smiles Mrs. Schmidt opened it, and revealed the soft black velvet of a sealskin jacket fastened with brilliant buttons. She extended it to Irmgard, and fresh tears were in her eyes.

Speechless, Irmgard took the weighted beautiful thing and put it on over her black alpaca frock. Its warmth enfolded her like an intimate embrace. Her smooth cheeks flushed, and her green eyes danced with crystals.

"How lovely!" sighed Mrs. Schmidt from her pillows, clasping her hands. "How bewitching it makes your hair, my dear!"

Irmgard took her hand again, and kissed the dark mottled flesh. But Mrs. Schmidt stretched her neck and touched her withered lips to the girl's forehead, simply, and with true feeling.

The party, anticipated for Christmas Eve, had not been possible, for Mrs. Schmidt had had one of her heart attacks. The party was to be held New Year's Eve, instead. "So much gayer, pet," Mrs. Schmidt had apologetically pleaded to Ernestine, and the girl's disappointment had lessened.

The door opened, and Ernestine bounced into the bedroom, carrying numerous parcels, her eyes shining with gaiety. She kissed her mother, put her arm briefly about Irmgard, and sat down on the edge of the bed.

"What a glorious day!" she cried, tossing her ringlets back from her small flushed face. "I've never been so happy! Irmgard! How elegant! Mama and I picked that jacket only after long consultation and much dreary shopping. Ah, if I were only so beautiful! Do turn around and let me see the back. It fits like a glove! What a figure you have!"

There were envy and thoughtfulness as well as affection in her voice and smile. Irmgard made her feel small and insignificant and dark and unfashionable. She sat on the bed, smiling, but her eyes clouded a little.

Recovering herself, she gave her mother a round diminutive box. Mrs. Schmidt opened it and found a tiny golden bodice watch, complete with a butterfly pin of gold and yellow and blue enamel. "Now that you are becoming a gadabout, in your carriage, you really do need a new watch, Mama," said the girl, with a kiss. She insisted on pinning it on Mrs. Schmidt's padded bed jacket, and stood off to admire it.

There was Mr. Schmidt's gift to his wife (bought by Ernestine, and not even seen by her father), a box of the finest white and black kid gloves. Mrs. Schmidt fingered the supple softness of these French creations, and smiled without speaking.

There was a muff and toque of black sealskin to match the jacket, from Ernestine to Irmgard, and these too had to be put on and admired. There was an envelope from Schmidt containing two twenty-dollar gold pieces.

"Baldur will give you his gift, himself," said Ernestine.

"You have been too good," murmured Irmgard, in a strange, subdued voice. Her face was grave, and somewhat disquieted. She carried her gifts into her own bedroom, and laid them on the bed.

Yes, they were too good to her. And soon, she must tell them that she must leave them, that she was to be married. They would be happy in her happiness, but they would be saddened. She gazed before her, mournfully. And she, too, would be saddened. It would not be easy to relinquish these pathetic friends. In some mysterious way she had brought vitality and interest to them. Now, she must deprive them. She thought of this with mingled wonder and incredulity, and without egotism. I have done nothing at all, she said to herself.

She found a letter waiting for her on her commode, and

when she recognized the writing her senses swam dizzily, knowing it an answer to a note she had sent Franz a few days ago. She opened it with shaking fingers, and her eyes misted at the passionate salutation. But as she read, she became troubled.

"You must forgive me for reminding you of my former request, that your employers not know of the relationship between us. It is not expedient, as I have told you. Therefore, I cannot visit you at the Schmidt mansion, though you remark that there is a servants' sitting-room where we can be alone, and unseen.

"However, as you have a few hours to yourself, I suggest that you come to my hotel and spend them with me. I am all alone, as you know, and I had no desire to visit my parents on their distant farm at this time. There would necessarily be some confusion, and I have always detested confusion. You will accuse me of being selfish. I admit it. Only the weak are unselfish."

At this, Irmgard smiled wryly, and a little contemptuously. How afraid he is of appearing weak! she thought. But that is the essence of weakness.

She read on: "I have already ordered a dinner for us at my hotel. We can be alone, and very happy. We have much to say to each other."

Yes, thought Irmgard, a trifle grimly, we have much to say. Nevertheless, her heart began to beat with excitement. She regarded the jacket, muff and toque with bright pleasure, and leaned down to smooth them with her hands. She imagined herself confronting Franz, arrayed in this new rich finery, and color rose swiftly to her cheeks and forehead.

When she went back into the bedroom of Mrs. Schmidt for the tray, Ernestine was curled up in a chair near the window, reading a chapter of "East Lynne" to her mother. "Ah," murmured Irmgard, shaking her head slightly, "that is a dreary book for so bright a morning."

But poor Mrs. Schmidt was one of those unfortunate creatures who find an enhancement of present happiness in reading of the sorrows of others, though the emotion is not sadistic. It is as though pure pleasure is too bright for their tired eyes, and must be subdued in a soft mist to be thoroughly enjoyed. Irmgard knew this, and after her first remonstrance she allowed Ernestine to continue reading in her high fluting voice.

"Oh, the poor Isabel!" sighed Mrs. Schmidt, her eyes fondly dwelling on her daughter, who she thought resembled the fabulous heroine. "My darling, I hope you will always give your husband the benefit of your wifely doubts."

Ernestine trilled her light childish laugh, but her little face blushed deeply. "I have no husband, Mama, as yet. Perhaps I shall never have one." The book dropped on her lap, and her eyes became deeper, as though with some shy and blissful thought.

Mrs. Schmidt shook her head archly, tenderly smiling.

"But that young man from the mills, love, that you spoke about to me only yesterday, and whom your Papa is inviting for New Year's. So clever, your Papa says. He is going to be Superintendent some day, is he not?"

Irmgard was standing by the window, gazing abstractedly down at the street. But now some vague monstrous disquiet seized her. Her hand clenched on the drapery. She did not turn, but angrily wondered at the sudden horrible leaping of her heart. She heard Ernestine's shy laughing reply through the thunders in her temples:

"Oh, Mama, don't be so fanciful, and so full of plots! I do not know the young man. Possibly he is already married, or something equally dreadful."

She did not look at her mother, though the color was still high and vivid in her face. She continued: "Papa has said that he is very brilliant, and unusual, and that is why he is inviting him. Poor Mr. Dietrich is not invited this year. I hope Papa is not annoyed with him about something."

But Mrs. Schmidt was engrossed in happy dreams about her daughter. Ernestine, in attempting to escape her mother's tender regard, turned to Irmgard.

The girl was standing with her back to the blazing radiance of the window. In that shadow made by herself, Ernestine could not see her face. But she saw her tall rigidity, the tense immobility of her shoulders and head. Ernestine frowned. The resemblance to someone teased her again. Ah, she had it! It was an extraordinary resemblance to the young man, Franz Stoessel, Papa had called him! But she dared not remark on it, for fear of her mother's excited and puzzled questions as to where her daughter had seen the gentleman. It would be very embarrassing to explain.

Ernestine frowned a little. But perhaps all Germans resembled each other, as did Englishmen, and Frenchmen. It was a racial resemblance, and nothing else. Her face cleared.

"Are we going to have a marriage?" asked Irmgard, from her strange still posture from the window.

Ernestine had never found Irmgard "impertinent" at any time, and the epithet with regard to her mother's maid would never have occurred to her before. But now it did, for some peculiar and obscure reason. With a somewhat haughty expression, Ernestine picked up the book again, without answering, and her small body and pretty profile took on a cold and rather remote aspect. What an odd question for Irmgard to ask, really! She was presuming.

But Mrs. Schmidt, smiling, nodding, looked at Irmgard fondly. "Dear me, child, nothing quite so definite. I am afraid I have given you a wrong impression. It is just my silly mother's heart, and love for her little daughter. Ernestine has not even met Mr. Stoessel, and she may not even like him. I have been very fanciful, and it is inexcusable of me," and she glanced at her daughter with timid apology.

Ernestine, in a slightly louder voice, and with a little hardness, began to read again. She was too kind-hearted to be abrupt and discourteous, even to a maid who had presumed on the affection shown her. Too, it put herself in a ridiculous and pathetic light. Her voice, as she read, touched the most sentimental passages with a steely inflexibility, and the posture of her head and her cool manner suggested to Irmgard that the girl was not needed in the room just at present.

But Irmgard did not move. Mrs. Schmidt, with her invalid's sensitiveness, felt that something was amiss in this room, something dark and dangerous, if still very vague. She did not listen to Ernestine. She looked at Irmgard.

Irmgard's face was still in shadow, her fine tall figure outlined with light. Her hand still crushed the fold of drapery she held. Mrs. Schmidt saw the tense fingers, white and clenched about the knuckles. Now she caught a shadowy glimpse of Irmgard's face, deep in the shadow. Oh, surely it was impossible, and only the effect of light and shade! But Irmgard's features were large and marble-like and bitter and understanding. Her eyes stared blindly before her, as though seeing something very clearly, very terrible.

Then, abruptly, Irmgard picked up the tray and left the room, closing the door swiftly and silently behind her. After she had gone, Ernestine put down the book with an impatient and annoyed sigh.

"Really, Mama! Your remarks were inexcusable, to Irmgard. We all love Irmgard, I am sure, but after all, we must not allow her to presume on our affection. And you have made me ridiculous. Making me appear to be a disappointed old maid avidly looking for a man, any man, to marry! I am sure Irmgard must smile at me. That is intolerable! After all, she is only a servant."

But Mrs. Schmidt, though uneasily noting Ernestine's unusual color and exasperatedly sparkling eyes, was dimly troubled for another reason. She stammered, pleadingly:

"My darling, I am sure that poor Irmgard would not laugh at you. And it is very cruel to refer to her as a 'servant.' Your attitude was very harsh, and I am afraid that you have hurt her without reason. She looked quite ghastly, after your snub."

Ernestine felt a qualm, which reduced her own annoyance. "I'm sorry if I was so hard to Irmgard, Mama," she murmured.

"She speaks only out of her love for us, dear," said Mrs. Schmidt, quickly. "I am sure she meant no impertinence."

Ernestine laughed a little. "The fault was all yours, Mama, not Irmgard's. You gave her an opening, and she cannot be blamed, I see, for her remark. I am quite a nasty minx, I'm afraid."

She bounced energetically to her feet. "I shall go to her and apologize." She bent quickly and kissed her mother, and tripped lightly to the door. But Irmgard's bedroom was empty. Ernestine returned to her mother, subdued and remorseful, her kind little heart disturbed.

CHAPTER 41

IRMGARD, UPON returning to her room, sat down on her bed. She was trembling and shivering. She gazed before her stonily, and little rigors jerked her mouth, her hands.

"I quite see," she said, aloud. An appalling sickness filled her, made her relax her limbs involuntarily. She sat in silence for some moments, her eyes fixed on some hideous vision. She wallowed in the vision, tasting bitter waters, feeling some agonized disintegration all through her being.

She had missed nothing of Ernestine's color and embarrassment. It was true that Ernestine had not yet met Franz, that she might not even like him, might despise him. But Irmgard saw the whole plot, clearly, with agonized clarity. Franz would see to it that Ernestine was entranced by him. She remembered the questions he had asked her, which had seemed at the time to be only impudent curiosity. Now she saw a purpose in the questions.

"Foul swine!" she said, quite loudly.

She saw his plottings, knew that he had coldly and viciously planned for just this time. He would charm the silly little Ernestine. He had planned that. He would leave nothing undone. He had told her often that nothing would stand in his way. From the beginning, he had planned this. Ernestine might revolt him, with her flutterings and blushings and bouncings and fragility, for he hated all these things. But that would not matter. Irmgard did not believe that mere chance had been leading to this. She knew Franz too well. The mere revulsion of his flesh against this small dark woman would be insignificant. Irmgard saw him as an explosion among the Schmidts. She knew Hans well enough to know that this invitation was not a mere courtesy extended to a promising employee. Her sharp prescience told her more things than mere logic could do. Ernestine's prolonged maidenhood disturbed Hans. For her sake, if she liked Franz Stoessel, Franz's way would be swept clear to anything he desired. It was, then, necessary for him to charm and bewitch Ernestine. He would do so. He would work grimly for this very thing, as he had long plotted to do.

A wild and devastating rage swept over her, like a gale, a murderous rage. Never had she felt like this. Mingled with the rage was an overwhelming humiliation, and frenzied terror. She saw herself confronting Franz, an embodied fury. Her hand closed convulsively about the smooth cool bedpost, and the gesture was like the seizing of a weapon. Hatred filled her, and with it, a sensation of almost voluptuous impotence. This increased her rage. Her heart beat so savagely that her face turned scarlet.

Oh, the schweinehund! Her fingers tightened about the post. The weak, bragging, remorseless, vicious, malignant scoundrel! With his cold remorseless eyes, his love for himself, his cruelty and virulence! Her lips fell open, and she panted. To this creature she had given herself, with passion, madness and love! This man who saw no one but himself, this vile plotter—she had given herself to him! It was not to be borne. She moaned aloud, pressed her hand over her lips.

Suddenly she got to her feet, and began to pace up and down, panting heavily, drops of sweat standing on her forehead and on her upper lip. The sickness mounted in her, became violently physical. She caught hold of the bedpost, pushed a lock of pale bright hair from her temple. Her face was white and blazing with suppressed fury, and standing there, with the sunlight streaming through the window upon her, she looked like some avenging Valkyrie, blowing with unearthly winds, standing on red and swirling clouds.

Then all at once a frightful agony of grief and despair fell on her like a crushing wall. Her hatred and her fury whirled into a cone of smoke, disappeared. Devastating loneliness and sorrow swept up into her heart, her soul. She moaned again, and now tears fell on her cheeks. She felt in herself a deluge of icy and desolating waters, quenching all fires, all conflagrations. She felt naked, stripped, in that flood, cringing, crying out from her heart like a voice in a great storm. Loneliness, dread, longing, passion and mourning were in that cry. She could not bear it. She wept, wringing her hands, feeling her loneliness, her desolation, her anguish and pain, her complete and abandoned nakedness.

Then, she was still, thinking with chaotic turbulence. In the midst of it, as in a dark wild storm, came cold thin flashes of cruelty. She had only to go to Ernestine and say: "This man who excites you before you know him: he is my lover. I have lain in his arms. He is mine." This would be the end of herself. But it would also be the end of Franz, the end of all his long plotting, his ruthlessness, his dreams, his plans, and all his iron hopes. He was not the sort made stronger by immense reverses. This she knew. He would be ruined. Even Ernestine, the virginal, the untouched and the ignorant, could not be able to endure the sight of a man who had embraced her servant. She would be physically, as well as mentally, sickened, this woman without blood and without bowels, this creature no longer young who knew nothing of passion, violent and elemental. She, Irmgard, could understand this passion. Had Franz developed it for Ernestine, forgetting herself, forgetting his own plots and schemes, she could have forgiven him, obliterated herself, knowing what immensities and storms this passion developed in a helpless human being. But Ernestine, so fastidious, so bloodless, could not conceive of it, and its raw panting breast, its glowing eyes, its sweat and it odor, would only revolt and terrify her.

Knowing that no passion was involved in this hideous tangle, Irmgard was the more enraged, and she brooded on the vision of Ernestine's face if she were told. She brooded, smiling evilly to herself, on Franz's face, when he knew he was utterly ruined. This was revenge. It was puling and absurd to say that revenge was weak and wicked and foolish. It was the thing for which men lived, when they were assaulted without justice!

Now her hatred extended itself like a fire to include Ernestine. She had nothing to offer Franz but money. No lust, no passion, no vitality, no strength! Fragile and delicate, the leaves of her first youth already fallen from her in spite of her deceptively childish face and immature body, she was not even a woman! Irmgard had seen her sudden coldness and reserve that morning. Under that childishness and impulsive warmth, was the patrician, the aristocrat, who remembered, at the last, that a better woman was her servant!

She thought of Franz again. He was a man who had put

his hopes of harvest in one tree, alone. He was incapable, because of his lack of imagination, of planting another tree. When his one shoot was destroyed, he, himself, was completely destroyed, and would die of starvation.

And then again, like a deep and irresistible flood, came her love for this man, overwhelming, distraught. In spite of what he was, she loved him. She could not relinquish him. She began to weep again, sobbing silently, from the very deeps of her heart. He would sell himself for so cheap, so fragile, so brittle a thing! Franz, with his Viking's face and head, his strong body and health, his intelligence which was without subtlety, his charm and his tenderness, his ruthless drive and ambition!

Irmgard sat down on her bed and covered her face with her hands. He is mine, she thought. His blood is mine, his race, his language, his thought. I cannot give him up! I shall not give him up.

Some one knocked on her other door, which led into the servants' hall. She wiped her cheeks and eyes hastily, smoothed her hair and her dress, and opened the door. Gillespie stood outside, with another letter in his hand. He smiled at her and said: "Merry Christmas, Irmgard."

She responded, with deep irony: "Merry Christmas, Gillespie." He gave her the letter, and said: "Mr. Baldur would like to see you for a few moments, Irmgard, as soon as possible." He paused, and regarded her with concern: "You are ill, Irmgard?"

"No. I have a headache. That is all." She closed the door gently in his startled face.

The letter was from Emmi. Irmgard skimmed impatiently over the short tense eulogies of the farm, and Egon's marvelously increasing interest in living. Then there was a paragraph:

"There is no longer any need, my niece, of you being in service. There is a home for you with us, in this quietness and peace. I have with me a former neighbor, a Florence Tandy, to assist me, and a young man, Hermann Schultz. So, it is not self-interest which inspires me to ask you to live with me, and share in this farm, and this happiness. I want you with me. Sometimes I am afraid, when I regard Egon— I have no one of my blood, for Franz is no longer my son. I ask you to come to me. We shall be happy."

Irmgard folded the letter, put it into her drawer. The pain in her was a dull and savage aching. Then she forgot the letter. She washed her streaked face, unfastened her long silver-gold hair. She coiled it again, removed her apron, and went quietly to Baldur's rooms.

He admitted her, at her knock, and his small pale face brightened as though moonlight had fallen on it. He urged her to sit down, which she did. She sat before him, her hands in her lap. He began to speak, then paused, standing before her, and his expression changed and darkened.

"Irmgard. Is there something wrong?" He spoke in German, quickly and well, feeling himself closer to her when he did so.

"There is nothing wrong," she replied, tranquilly enough, and with a smile.

But acquaintance with pain, long and hopeless, made him recognize it when he saw it. He did not speak for some moments, only eying her anxiously, and with foreboding. He was also frightened; the shadow of pain was so familiar to him, and it was unendurable when it appeared in the eyes of someone beloved. He knew that each hour of suffering decreases a man's ability to endure another hour, and in some dim way he knew that suffering was waiting for him again, in Irmgard's suffering. Perhaps, he thought, in his fear, it is because, having once seen the face of pain, its next appearance to him was full of dread familiarity. It is the cumulative effect of memory, and the horror of anticipation colored by that memory. The man who endures an onslaught of almost unbearable agony, whether it is mental or physical, with tremendous composure and courage, is a man who has no memory of similar pain, and can face it with a certain amount of curiosity and even a sense of novelty.

I am no hero, he thought with bitterness. I cannot suffer much more. It is the man who has suffered frequently who whimpers at the approach of the whip. The hero lacks imagination or experience, or both. Fortitude is of virgin birth.

He sat down near her, so inexpressibly weighted that he could not speak, and regarded her gravely. His misshapen figure huddled in its chair, as if cold and beaten. Now over his fear rode his compassion. To hide it, for he did not wish to embarrass her, he reached towards a table and took from it a long thin white box. He smiled at her with effort.

"My Christmas present to you, Irmgard."

She took it with a murmur of thanks. He saw that her hands were shaking. She opened it. On a white bed of satin gleamed a necklace of opals, all fire, all blueness, all life, pulsing with crimson and rose and pearl.

"You told me once that you were born in October," he said, softly. Now his large blue eyes rested on her with a deep look of passion and love.

Irmgard was silent. The opals fell across her fingers. She was afraid to speak, for the tears were thickening in her throat again. Aching for her, and more frightened than ever, he stood up hastily, and went to his piano, which was always his consolation. He began to play, smiling drily at his own sentimentality, which tried, with some puerility, to express what he felt he could not say. The notes were sweet and urging, and he sickened at them. "Mooncalf," he said aloud, but the word was covered by the music. He detested himself for this childish exhibition, which only an East Lynne heroine could appreciate, and he hated himself for using the medium of noblest emotion to speak to a girl who would wrily understand, and be amused.

He swung about on the stool and sat there, smiling sourly, a ruined shape of manhood perched like a toad on a toadstool, or so he thought himself. His helpless gesture, his smile, implored her forgiveness, and begged her not to ridicule him. But she was not smiling. She looked at him steadfastly.

"I am a fool," he said, with sudden vehemence, believing that he had embarrassed her.

"Why?" she asked, quietly.

For behaving to you like some callow cheap music-hall waiter, he thought. He slipped off the stool and came back to her. She still held the opals in her hands, running them through her fingers like a rosary. Sometimes they flashed rose, and then with a glint of steely blue. He saw her thoughtful and somber expression, as though she were pre-occupied with things far from him, and he was immediately jealous as well as apprehensive.

In an abstracted voice, he said: "I am a fool, Irmgard, for thinking you might not find me repulsive." He cringed internally as he said this, but looked at her eagerly.

She lifted her eyes and regarded him gently, understanding his pride, and even his egotism, and his helplessness.

"You speak foolishly, Mr. Schmidt. But in any event, why should you care what I think of you?"

"It is important to me," he answered, very quietly.

She blushed a little, and cupped the opals in her hands. Now he was certain that something distracted her, and again he was jealous. He saw that she was biting her lip, and that if she had caught the implications in his words she was giving them no thought at all. He also saw that she was fighting some internal distress, and was not too surprised when she spoke vehemently, glancing about the great dusky room which the brilliant sunlight outside could hardly penetrate, and using one of his own words:

"But nothing is very important to you, Mr. Baldur! You have been hurt, and you hide here, sulking! I must speak plainly. I may never have the opportunity to speak to you again. There are so many things you can do, and you do not do them!"

He leaned forward a little in his chair, and frowned, flushing somewhat.

"What, for instance, Irmgard?"

She made an impatient gesture, and unheeded, the opals slipped to the floor. "You want sympathy, Mr. Baldur. Perhaps you do not realize it, and would refuse it, if offered. But to you, I know, you appear a very sympathetic figure, even heroic."

His flush deepened, and his eyes flashed angrily, with humiliation. But she was regarding him, aroused, her cheeks colored, and he thought: There is something which drives her to speak harshly, and to hurt, for she has been hurt. He replied mildly, trying to laugh:

"It is necessary for every man to have some heroic conception of himself, just as it is necessary for a nation to have that conception. That is what is wrong with America: she has no heroic vision of herself as a people. Neither have I, perhaps. And yet again, you may be right. It is possible that I regard myself as unusual, probably even heroic." He smiled bitterly. "What would you have me do?" he added.

"You are a musician. I have listened to you, often. You could give that to others, if nothing else."

He walked to a window, clasping his hands behind his deformed back. He spoke without turning:

"Why should I bother about others? What use are they to me, or I to them?" He turned back to her.

"I've lived a number of years, Irmgard. My contacts haven't been very extended. But I have learned enough about people. I have learned that very few exist who are decent, honest and kind. Because of my—condition, my whole personality has seemed to be skinless, every nerve exposed. No one has bothered to hide himself from me, thinking me irrelevant. So, I have seen and felt. And I know that humanity is the foulest, most bestial, most treacherous, indecent, false and contemptible species alive. Do you think differently?"

"No," she replied, in a low voice. "What you say is true."

He went on, rapidly: "People speak of their 'friends.' Yet, no man has a friend, though he may have innumerable acquaintances who will eat his food, sleep in his bed, exchange the time of day with him, and enjoy his money. But let him need real help, real sympathy, real kindness, and he will find himself talking to empty air. His 'friends' will do all they can to kick him lower, to lie about him, destroy him. That is the nature of men. I accept it, without reproach, though wondering sometimes, if there is a God, why He allows humanity to profane the earth. But I am no sentimentalist. I do not believe that humanity is worth the saving, or the serving. I shun it. I have been hurt too often, by looking at the faces of others, and knowing their thoughts. I know their jealousy and envy, their hatred for their kind, their lustfulness and avarice, their cruelty and brutality. I have spent my life looking for some good, and haven't found it. So, not being able to stand what I see, I shut myself in here, sick of myself, seeing in myself everything there is in others."

"And in your mother and sister, too?"

He was not offended, as Ernestine had been narrowly offended. His mouth became gloomy.

"My mother! She is pathetic. But she is a coward. She is made that way. She has done my father no good, but has made his life miserable. He would not be so bad, if she had not been a fool. In her treatment of him, she has been treacherous. Her nature forced him into this filthy mess with Matilda. Do you think he enjoys it? She is too weak to be avaricious, too engrossed with herself to be envious. Her mind is like brackish water in which not even cruelty can exist. Would you call her good because she hasn't even the bowels to be bad? It is true she is gentle and kind at times, but these are negative virtues. I am sorry for her, and I love her very much."

He paused. "And Ernestine. Given the opportunity she would be as small and malicious as all other women, and as meanly treacherous. She merely lacks the opportunity. She is sweet because she has never been bruised. She, too, is a weakling. Like my mother. Like myself."

He looked at the silent girl, who was watching him so mournfully, and he smiled again, whimsically.

"Yet, I feel that your vices are less than your positive virtues, Irmgard. You are strong and honest. You are not too kind. You are truthful with yourself. You could be cruel and harsh, and remorseless, but not unnecessarily so. There is the thing!" he exclaimed, with sudden excitement. "People are cruel and brutal, treacherous and lying, merciless and ferocious, most often without necessity! Even wild beasts kill only for food, and never for malignancy. That is why they are superior to the human race. That is why they are clean and wholesome—I think you are clean and wholesome, Irmgard. You are not poisonous, like others, and never venomous, like other women."

For the first time since coming into that room today, Irmgard smiled, almost with amusement and enjoyment.

"You know nothing about me, Mr. Baldur. And you exaggerate. Too, why should you care about others? If, as you say, the world is so hideous, why do you not give it some beauty?"

He laughed. He came back to stand near her. "I don't give a damn about the world, Irmgard. I'm no sentimentalist. Let it rot. The quicker the better. I'd like to help it rot. I'd like to be the sole survivor of a cataclysm, and watch others destroyed. I'm not revengeful, only understanding."

Despite his laughter, she knew he spoke the truth.

"The great 'bad' men of the world, the Cæsars, the Napoleons, the Richelieus, Talleyrands and Machiavellis—they knew what men were, and so they could control them. They had no sentimentality about them. They kicked, booted and killed them, and so were made heroes. The new sentimentality —democracy—is based on the inherent goodness, independence and intelligence of men, which do not exist. That is why it will be destroyed by those it tries to elevate. The halo sits too tightly on the head of the ape. We need a Napoleon, a Machiavelli, to make the people happy. Some day some true realist will be born, who will understand mankind, and know that it can be happy only when it is enslaved, and yoked. And the sentimentalists, the idealists, will be sent to gnaw their own silly fingers in a corner, abandoned by those they tried to save." He added: "America needs a Bismarck, not a Lincoln. Men speak condescendingly of a saint, and with reverence of a brute, even when they pretend to hate him."

She was silent. He said: "You do not think so?"

"Yes," she replied. "You are right. The world cannot be made a safe place for the few good men. It would make too much misery for the others."

She started to get up from her chair, and he spoke quickly: "Irmgard, just a few moments more, please. I can talk to no one but you."

She waited, but he had fallen into an uneasy silence, watching her closely. Then he said: "What is wrong, Irmgard?"

She answered: "Nothing, except that I am sorry to leave you—this house. But I must. I am going to live with my aunt, who has just bought a farm. She needs me."

He was frightened, and bereft. "No! We can't let you go. We are selfish, and you have done so much for us! You see, I'm not thinking of you at all, or your own desires. Do not leave us, Irmgard. Do not leave me!" he cried, internally.

She regarded him with great gentleness, and he saw that she was devoured by some deep wretchedness.

"I must go, Mr. Baldur. My uncle is sick. Perhaps he will die soon. My aunt needs me."

Then he said, speaking passionately, and without reserve:

"But I need you, more than any one. Irmgard, haven't you known that?"

She did not speak, but her face flushed darkly. He took one of her cold hands, and held it feverishly.

"I have nothing to give you, Liebchen, my dearest, but money which I have not even earned myself. I am insulting you by saying all this, by asking you to marry me. But, see, I have done it."

She looked up at him, at his ruined body and beautiful ruined face. Intense pity rose like brimming waters to her eyes, and profound gentleness.

"Do not speak like that! It is not true. It is a great honor ——"

She paused, and now her eyes were pale green and icy, like the sea in winter, with her sudden thoughts. What if she married this poor creature, indeed? Franz Stoessel would then find a formidable enemy in the house which he was trying to invade, an insurmountable barrier, a barricade, a high stone wall. He would find some one as remorseless and implacable as himself, ready to dispute every step with him, ready to destroy him!

She gazed thoughtfully and somberly at Baldur, felt his hot dry palms holding her hand. She studied his face, his eager look, his imploring eyes. And then, weakness or not, she could not do this thing to him. She withdrew her hand.

"It is not possible," she said, loudly, but to herself and not to him.

"Why not?" he urged. He moistened his parched lips, pressed closer to her. "I can give you very little. You can give me everything. I can't exist without the things you can give me," and he smiled wrily, yet apologetically.

She forced herself to rise, kept the pity from her eyes and voice.

"There is somebody else, Mr. Baldur—in Germany. I ought to have told you that before. Now I must go to my aunt, and wait for him."

He acknowledged to himself, then, with frantic despair, how much he had relied upon a dream he had never admitted before even to himself. He could not speak. He had suffered before, but never like this. He felt himself seized in monstrous iron teeth, which shook and rended him. Yesterday, an hour ago, when alone, if he had thought to himself: Irmgard might marry me, he would have laughed incredulously at himself for a presumptuous and egotistic fool. Yet still, he might have hoped, and in that hope found a meagre sustenance for life. He might, however, never have dared put the hope to the test, but its dream, its pale reflection, might have sustained him during all his existence. Now, having spoken, and been refused, the earth fell away from him in utter darkness, and the last spark flickered out. Always, in previous suffering, invisible hands of determination and fortitude had supported him, and his bitter cynicism, though like vinegar, had quenched a little of his tormenting thirst. Now he had nothing. He saw how treacherous the secret and unacknowledged places in him had been, how in the hidden niches of the dank wall, which shut him out of life, fragile and colorless blooms had taken root, not planted by himself, but nevertheless reaching delicate tendrils into morsels of arid soil. He bled, now, when they were torn from their precarious beds, and thrown aside. Wave after wave of black hopelessness and complete abysmal grief rolled over him. He could only stand before Irmgard, crumbling internally, and he seemed to dwindle visibly so that he appeared to be a small deformed child fatally struck and dying. The small iron core of some secret courage crystallized in him, disintegrated, blew away into dust, and he was completely undone. He was a scarecrow, stuffed with straw, fallen limply to the ground when its wooden support had been wrenched away. He could only stare emptily, but with boundless hatred, at a God who had betrayed him again.

He looked up at her, with his dulled eyes, and he saw her compassion and pain. Instantly, he was aroused to a salutary anger, even to a rage. Mortified impotence gave him a spurious courage and pride. He even smiled, shook his head slightly.

"I was a fool to ask," he said, hoarsely.

"No," she answered, in a low tone. "I shall never forget this."

Then he saw that she was suffering almost as much as he was suffering. He watched her go to the door, and he cried out internally: Do not go! I shall die if you leave me, if I never see you again! He lifted his hand and called to her urgently, his voice breaking:

"Irmgard! You will let me know where you go?"

She heard all his agony, all his love, in that cry, all the wail of his despair. She turned to him, from the doorway, and the two who were suffering so greatly looked across the space of the room at each other.

"Yes," she said. "Oh, yes. But you must tell no one else, not even your mother and your sister."

She smiled now, and he saw the pale tightness of her lips, the blue marks about her eyes, and he went to her, and took her hand again.

"You will not tell me why you are so wretched. I know it has nothing to do with me, but I would die to help you. You know that?"

His hand was hot but firm, and it gave her some courage, some strength. As on the first day she had come here, she knew she had a friend, who would always be hers. Her eyes filled slowly with burning tears.

"Yes, I know," she faltered.

She went out, leaving him standing alone in a room from which all the light seemed to have gone. He did not move. Moment after moment passed away, and he heard only the distant hollow booming in the house. He began to shiver. Then he cried out:

"O God! O God!"

CHAPTER 42

IRMGARD DRESSED herself in a wine-colored woolen frock, tight of basque, full and draped of skirt, and decorated with black jet buttons. She put on her new sealskin jacket, and toque, and picked up the new muff. About her throat she clasped Baldur's opals, and they lay on the bodice like frozen tears. She glanced at herself in her mirror. But her new splendor, her beautiful figure and shining gilt hair could not disguise the strained harshness of her face and the bitter greenness in her eyes. She might have been a younger Emmi Stoessel standing there, implacable and gaunt, filled with anger and hatred and despair. But where Emmi was incapable of much ruthlessness, Irmgard knew that she, herself, was capable of anything.

She went silently and swiftly down the servants' back hall, then, on an impulse she turned and went through an empty room, and thence into the great corridor of the second floor. She leaned over the balustrades and looked down the curving staircase into the pit of the immense house. She saw the large deserted drawing room with its core of dim fire which burned in the black marble fireplace, the vast reaches of carpet, the lurking furniture, the gloomy draperies which held out the sun. In one window stood a gigantic Christmas tree, blazing in sunlight, the one bright spot in the somber immensity, its green boughs laden with dripping foil and tall green, white and red candles, a silver star on its topmost twig. But this was the only sign of Christmas in the house. The dining-room was desolate, its silver dimly gleaming in the dusk. Heavy shadows were everywhere, and dustiness and silence. Behind Irmgard stretched the long corridor with its closed doors. She knew that in Matilda's rooms there was some warm and cosy festivity between the woman and Hans Schmidt. But there was no lightness, no gaiety, here, in this haggard mansion.

She shivered, and thrust her hands deep into her muff. She would be glad to leave this awful place, now that no affection remained here for her. She thought of Ernestine with hatred and revulsion, and Mrs. Schmidt seemed no longer pathetic to her, but only something cloying and sickly, from which she must escape.

A long rolling chord rushed like a wave down the corridor, and she lifted her head, listening. Discordant music broke upon the stony gloom of the house like a cataract of mingled lightning and water and thunder. It was like some wild and demented spirit leaping in a storm, full of defiance and despair and savage sorrow. It shrieked and groaned its impotence, its unendurable pain, its screams of torture. Boulders crashed about it, hurled by torrents; black and twisted tree-trunks swirled about it, and mountain walls fell. But through the uproar was its high shrieking voice, always discernible, sometimes madly laughing, sometimes moaning deeply. The house groaned in answer, its very dark immobility like the motionless core of a hurricane.

Irmgard put her hands over her ears, swallowing over a sharp point in her throat. She expected that every moment each shut door would burst open, disgorging frightened faces and running forms. No one, surely, could hear that unearthly and hellish clamor and thunder without hurling himself blindly away to safety. But nothing stirred. The walls did not collapse. No door opened. She stood alone in the vortex of discordant screaming sound, shadows creeping closer about her. The sun was vivid against the vast windows, but the darkness increased inside. Everything listened, and cowered, and stood in silence.

Irmgard bent her head and ran. She flung herself down the winding marble staircase. She raced for the grilled doors of the front entrance, holding up her skirts which tried to bind her legs. She ran in a nightmare of horror, pursued by the music, which was a league of scarlet demons chasing her. She felt that any moment hideous forms would spring up about her, and clutch her. She reached the door, panting. She could hardly turn the handle. She burst out into the sunshine, dishevelled, white and gasping, closing the door behind her.

The horror was still on her, and she sped down the street. But slowly the cold and dazzling air cooled her fright. The snow was soft underfoot. Children ran about with red sleds, or carried dolls and laughed in the sunshine, watched by their nursemaids. Windows glittered. Sleighs passed, tinkling with bells, and filled with rosy happy faces and furs. Cries of "Merry Christmas!" rang in the glasslike atmosphere. Trembling from head to foot, Irmgard stood still, breathing painfully, the wind blowing her hair, skeins of sparkling snow fluttering about her skirts. Her heart slowly lessened its rolling and turning. She knew now that she could never return to that house, not even for a night. In it there lived a fury. But she did not think of that fury as Baldur. He had merely given expression to it.

The horse-car she boarded was filled with happy men, women and children, carrying large bundles wrapped in red and green and white paper. Children sucked peppermint sticks. Young girls preened in the new finery of cheap plume-trimmed velvet bonnets and fur toques, and held muffs coquettishly to bright faces. Young men, self-conscious and beaming, adjusted round gray and brown bowlers surreptitiously, and fingered new cravats stuck through with gold-plated pins. Old women, in their shawls and nodding bonnets glittering with jet, smiled benignly. The car rolled merrily; the harness jingled. Even the horses had plaited ropes of tinsel about their necks and stepped higher in the shining holiday air. Strangers exchanged murmurs of "Merry Christmas." One young couple held a slaughtered goose, bloodily wrapped in paper, on their knees, and smiled in anticipation.

Slowly, in this happy normal atmosphere of noise and goodwill, Irmgard returned to equanimity. The horror and fear which had made her hurtle herself from the Schmidt mansion began to subside. As the car passed through busy streets, in which markets still stood open displaying baskets of potatoes and turnips, barrels of pickles and windows full of hanging fowl, she began to breathe more slowly. Health and peace and the short joy of the holiday were all about her. Churches were still open, and crowds streamed in and out for brief prayers, the women and children gaily dressed, the young bloods and the old men alike splendid in new coats and mufflers. Carriages lined the curbs, sunlight splintering on wheels and polished harness, and cries of greeting shot through the air like brilliant arrows.

Irmgard began to think more quietly. Franz could not go to live in that appalling house! He had never walked through those somber rooms; he had never smelt the sickly fetidness of its corridors, nor felt the crushing weight of those walls. Franz, with his health and strength, locked in those gloomy catacombs! It was not to be permitted! Slowly, as she neared the hotel where he was now living, she thought: What have we, he and I, to do with the Schmidts? He is mine, and I am his.

Now it began to seem incredible to her that she had ever entertained the grotesque thought that he had been plotting to enter that house and marry Ernestine Schmidt. She laughed silently to herself. She, too, had become infected by the disease in those rooms. Her imagination, distorted and inflamed, had conjured up fantastic visions. Hans Schmidt had invited Franz to a New Year's Eve party. That was perfectly normal. But it was far-fetched, ridiculous, to believe that anything subterranean, dark and fiendish lay in that invitation. She, Irmgard, could imagine nothing more impossible than that Franz would be able to endure Ernestine Schmidt, or would ever presume to think of an intimate relationship with her.

As her febrile dread subsided, she could think of Franz more clearly. I have built up a monster in my mind, she thought, with some compunction, and with a deep internal smile. She could remember nothing, now, but that night she had spent with him. Her cheeks turned scarlet, and her eyes clouded with mist. He loved her. She knew that. She had never doubted it. He had said that he would never let her go, even if she might want to leave him. She knew he had spoken the truth. He had not cheaply seduced her. She remembered every moment clearly and sharply. Franz was hers! No matter what else happened, they would be together. The thought of him was a hard bright gale sweeping away smoke and noxious fumes and shadows.

I have been so hysterical, she thought with mortification, remembering her dramatic scene with poor Baldur, and her passionate decision not to remain in that house for even another night. Her next meeting with Baldur would be embarrassing.

The car stopped at a corner, and she got out, followed by admiring glances. She stood before the neat four-story hotel and family rooms. It was built of clean red brick, and was very respectable and reserved. She entered a lobby full of rubber plants in huge brass jardinieres, dignified oak chairs and tables, and gas-globes. The turkey-red carpet was clean and fresh under her feet, and everywhere polished brass glittered. The great windows, draped in crimson plush, discreetly admitted the light of the December day. The usual "drummers" who infested small town hotels were absent, and all the chairs and horse-hair sofas were occupied by sober bearded gentlemen with their stout wives and children. Irmgard climbed wide carpeted stairs to the second floor, which was paved with shining white stone and covered by the same turkey-red carpet. She was pleased by this middle-class luxury, despite its intrinsic ugliness. Her heart was beating rapidly again when she knocked at a door, and waited.

Franz opened the door, smiling. Without a word he reached out his hand and drew her in. He did not close the door. "We are very respectable here," he said, raising his brows. He left the door open some twelve inches. He appeared to be taller and handsomer than ever, in his black broadcloth coat, long and full, and his gray-striped trousers. His black satin cravat was tied elegantly, and in it nestled a fine pearl pin. Irmgard, with gentle amusement, but with heightened color, saw that he had begun to grow a mustache. It was a slight but flourishing yellow line above his mouth, and made him look very distinguished. This was not the young working-man she had first seen such a short time ago. This was a burnished gentleman.

Her embarrassment and joy kept her speechless, even while he helped her remove the new jacket. She glanced about her, shyly. Franz had done himself well. He had a small but comfortable sitting-room, with a chuckling fire under a hooded fireplace of black marble. The turkey-carpet was repeated here, but the walls were gay with huge roses and bright green leaves. Large brass and china lamps stood on round mahogany tables which were covered by velvet cloths reaching to the floor, and weighted with fringe. A mahogany bookcase against one wall was full of books. A large leather sofa was heaped with pillows. The windows, draped in fringed red plush, looked out on the busy snowy streets. A far door stood open and she saw the brass bed and the huge dresser and wardrobe.

A small table with a white cloth and heavy silver had been set before the fireplace. Holding her hand, Franz led her to a chair near the fire. She lifted her eyes, and smiled at him.

"Well?" said Franz, returning her smile.

"You have accomplished much," she replied, embarrassed, but intoxicatingly happy.

"I have only begun," he said, sitting near her, and looking about him with satisfaction. His eyes came back to her, and now their somewhat bold and shallow blueness became more intense. "I have missed you," he said, in a low voice. He took her hand again, and held it tightly.

All her body seemed to expand into a widening glow of ecstasy and joy. Her lips trembled. She stammered: "You have seen the farm?"

"The farm? Oh, the farm. No, I have not seen it, yet. Have you?"

"No."

There was a silence. They had tried to cover their thoughts with banal words. Now they could not speak, only looking at each other. Then, after a long moment, Franz got up, went into his bedroom and brought out a small white box. Irmgard opened it. He stood over her as she did so, smiling. It contained a beautiful gold bracelet, elaborately chased. Irmgard's fingers shook as she tried to fasten it about her wrist. At length, with an amused murmur, Franz bent down and snapped it. His fingers lingered on her wrist, and his touch sent waves of fire through her. Then he lifted her hand to his lips, and pressed it almost fiercely against them. She closed her eyes, all her senses swimming in rosy light, her flesh aching with rapturous pain.

"Next year," he said at last, "it will be diamonds."

He still held her hand as he sat down again. Now he did not smile. He was quite pale. "My dearest," he said, and again, "My dearest."

If she had ever doubted that he loved her, all doubt was gone now. She could only look speechlessly into his eyes, her own wet, her lips faintly smiling, her breath quickening. Never had she felt such peace, such happiness, such fulfilment.

She said, faintly: "I thought you had forgotten me."

"Forgotten you?" His voice was quiet, but she heard his incredulity, his astonishment. "How could I ever forget you? Have I not said that you belong to me, that I shall never let you go?"

She drew her hand from his, and clenched it on her lap. She looked at him levelly. "But you have not said when we shall be married."

She could not believe it when he did not answer immediately. She saw that he dropped his eyes, that he made no effort to take her hand again. Slowly, the rapture faded, and a dark coldness seemed to steal through her. She shook her head a little, as though she were puzzled, and bewildered. She looked at the top of his bent head. She could not see his face. Her lips opened on an indrawn breath, and again, she was incredulous. She was imagining that he had stiffened, that he had subtly withdrawn from her.

"Franz," she began, and then stopped, choking, more and more disbelieving. She heard the throbbing of her pulses in her ears. Her hands made a futile gesture, and her eyes stared blankly.

He stood up, abruptly, and went to the window. He kept his back to her. She saw the sleek broadness of his shoulders, his thick yellow hair. She could not endure it. Shaking violently, she stood up. She forced herself to go to him, to touch him. She was not prepared for the sudden fierceness with which he seized her in his arms, nor for the savagery of his lips on hers. She struggled for a moment, then relaxed, clinging to him, trying to draw hope and reassurance from his mouth, from his arms, from his strength. The floor appeared to move under her feet; the walls, the bright window, the room, disappeared from her sight. She felt as though she were floating in space, filled with passionate hunger and mounting fever.

She was amazed, after a while, to find herself sitting in her chair again, with Franz sitting quietly near her, gripping both her hands in his. She stared in bemusement at him, her veins still running with liquid fire. He was looking at her with pale but inexorable gravity.

"We must be sensible, my darling," he was saying. (Incredible, meaningless words!) "We cannot be married yet."

Hands seemed to be gripping her throat, and she shook her head numbly. "Why not?" she asked, forcing her voice to be audible.

He hesitated. His eyes shifted a little. "I have much to do."

Then she knew, fully and devastatingly, that he had no intention of ever marrying her. What the reason was, she could not know. She moistened lips suddenly cold and parched.

"You mean," she said, very quietly, and with such false calm that he was deceived, "that you will never marry me."

She said to herself, feeling herself dying and disintegrating: What I believed this morning is true! She could not summon up her earlier rage and hatred. Complete desolation, horror and fear and grief inundated her. Stunned and incredulous, her face white and her emerald eyes dull, she could only look at him.

He pressed his lips firmly together. He seemed to be considering a decision.

"I must talk to you," he said, finally. He had expected a turbulent scene, for he had long ago known that under Irmgard's serenity there was a hard and passionate nature. He was relieved at her quietness. But there was something in her fixed eyes which made him uneasy.

He stood up again, and standing very close to her, he began to speak:

"I have come a little distance. But I have only begun. I have not even started! Some time ago I told you that I had many plans. I have accomplished one of them. But only one. The first step. Now I see the way more clearly. I must go on alone——"

"You will never marry me," she repeated, heavily.

He hesitated again, then decided to be courageous. "I can never marry you, my heart's dearest," he said, very gently. "If I married you, I would have to give up all my plans. I might retain what I have gained, but it is so little! We would degenerate into a lower middle-class family, might even sink back. In fairness to myself, and to you, I cannot marry you. I will accomplish what I have set out to do, and you will not lose by it! All my plans include you. I will give you undreamed of things— We shall always be together, no matter what else happens."

He had expected a feeble and outraged cry of wounded female virtue from her. But he was not prepared for her quiet, her increasing pallor. He was relieved. She was a sensible woman. She had understood. But something in her eyes, her expression, heightened his uneasiness. Something seemed to be kindling deep in her pupils, like a point of illuminated steel.

"Long ago," he said urgently, "I told you that I wanted money, must have money. I am on the way. Nothing means so much to me as money. Without it, I cannot live. And I cannot take you into the hell of a moneyless life. I would be a demon to you. I would begin to hate you."

She did not speak. The cold and kindling light now invaded her face, like the reflection of moonlight on snow. She kept her eyes fixed on him, and her body was rigid.

He pressed the palms of his hands together, almost convulsively.

"In another country, my dearest one, money is not of such extraordinary importance as it is in America. But in America is the true Götterdämmerung. A man is nothing without money. My mother has said this, and I have jeered at her. But it is true. A man might be the wisest, noblest, most endowed of his kind, his family and traditions impeccable and heroic—he might have the finest blood of race and breeding, and he might compose the most heroic music, or write the most beautiful of poetry. But all this is as nothing, if he has no money. America is a land where beggars ride on horseback, and princes walk in the dirt with bare feet." He smiled, trying to woo her into a smile also, but her face remained rigid. "I read that once, in the Bible. It is true of America, more than of any other country. There is nothing here, without money. A rascal, a thief, a murderer, if he is wealthy, is adored, honored and served. This land is a pot of the foulest stew! It is filled with the ingredients of the most degenerate portions of all races. It is folly to think the brew, made of thistles, weeds and snakes and poisonous leaves, can become good wine. I am here in America. That is a fact I cannot, and would not change, now. In this den of brutish thieves, I will become a thief. I despise America, and all that is in it. I cannot live here, in obscurity. Therefore, I shall become rich and powerful, and the swine will bow down before me!"

As if the pressure of his thoughts was too great to be contained in him, he began to walk up and down the room rapidly. And Irmgard saw that he was speaking openly and truthfully today as he had never spoken before, standing unashamed before her. She saw his changing expressions, his hatred and detestation and triumph. His blue Teutonic eyes blazed. He kept clenching and lifting his fists.

"I shall get what I want—money!" he exclaimed, almost shouting. "Nothing shall stop me!"

She stood up, and confronted him. "And Miss Ernestine Schmidt is the next step?" she asked, very calmly.

He stopped in his tracks abruptly, staring at her. Then, swiftly, his implacable face flooded with dusky color.

"How do you know that?" he asked, with frank brutality.

She smiled a little, over her devouring pain and despair.

"I heard her speak of her father's invitation to you. Then, I knew it all."

"You knew—" he began, then was silent. They stood face to face, regarding each other without moving. The girl was calm and composed, in appearance almost indifferent, in spite of her smile. But her eyes gazed into his with stern bright bitterness and limitless contempt. For an instant he felt shame, dwindled in his own sight. But it was only for an instant. He bit the corner of his lip, folded his arms across his chest.

"You are very astute, Irmgard," he said, trying to speak with resolute gravity. "It is true. It may sound like a wild dream, but I intend to accomplish it. You see, I do not say: 'If it is possible.' I know that one can secure anything, if the will and the belief is there. Sentimentality does not enter in this. If Miss Schmidt will have nothing of me, then I shall waste no more time. I shall leave this town. I have a patent——"

Irmgard did not speak. He was aroused to a slow anger by her fixed smile.

"You do not understand!" he exclaimed. He forced an expression of hopeless wretchedness on his face, then abandoned it as she visibly detected his hypocrisy. Then he said, with enraged sincerity: "All my life, I have wanted only money! I have seen how humiliated, how despised, how detested and oppressed were those who had no money. And those who tormented them were lesser men, more contemptible. Would you have me endure what millions endure, hopelessly, sinking down into bitterness, pain and poverty, condemned——"

"You are a coward," she said clearly, and without emotion.

"A coward," he said. He spoke almost reflectively. "Yes, perhaps you are right. But I have seen that cowards are more intelligent than the brave. And more realistic. And, at the end, more courageous. For they refuse to endure evils they can remedy."

"Even at the expense of others, Franz?"

Because he loved her so intensely, he was moved to some compassion.

"Even at the expense of others, my dearest. I am no sentimentalist. But it will not be at your expense. Nothing will change between us."

A waiter came in discreetly, carrying a huge tray filled with covered silver dishes. He laid the tray on the table. Franz waved his hand. "It is enough," he said, in English, and threw the man a coin. He waited until the waiter had left, then said, urgently, his voice sincerely breaking:

"Irmgard, you must tell me you understand."

She turned her head to him, looking at him steadfastly. "Yes. Yes. I understand so many things."

There must be some weakness in me, he thought, or I should not feel so. But he could not control his sudden sadness for her, his longing to hold her again. She must have seen this, for she stepped back quickly from him. The green of her eyes was vivid, yet cold as ice, pointed with immeasurable pain.

"There is nothing you shall not have, Liebchen. Trust me. My life with you will be something apart, something we can keep beautiful and satisfying. You shall have everything. I shall buy you a house—" Even to himself, he felt his words were cheap and inane and insulting.

He became aware that she was regarding him with something strangely like remote curiosity and thoughtfulness, in spite of her great paleness, and her unmoved dignity. He broke out: "Irmgard! I cannot be other than what I am. That is impossible for any man. But you know that I love you, and that I shall never let you go."

She stirred then. She walked without hurry into the bedroom, put on her jacket and toque. Her hands felt frozen, without life. But she calmly smoothed her hair, picked up her muff. He followed her, forgetting caution and "respectability," and closed the door.

"Do not touch me," she said, in a loud clear voice, looking at him fully. And her eyes were like the extended points of bayonets.

Now he was enraged, brutally, against this fool of a sentimental girl. His face flushed, thickened, his nostrils flared. In his temples, veins swelled and beat in purple knots.

"You are an imbecile," he said. He stepped aside from the door. "But I have said it: You belong to me. I shall never let you go."

He watched her leave the bedroom, walk slowly and firmly across the floor of the sitting-room. He saw her open the door. Now something hot and fierce exploded in him, and he followed her hastily.

"Irmgard, do not go. Do not be unreasonable. Try to understand."

He stopped, for, with her hand on the door, she turned to him, and now she spoke quickly; her eyes glowing and sparkling:

"Yes, it is true you will get what you want. You will live in that frightful house. You will sleep in Ernestine Schmidt's bed. I cannot tell you what you will think, but I know. You will understand, then. But then it will be too late. Nothing, when it is too late, can change. All your life, you will remember what I am telling you now. You will know then that you are a coward, that you are empty, that nothing you have gotten is worth anything. You will know that you are a thief, and worse. You will have your money. Perhaps it will satisfy you. In some way, I believe it will. You may be lonely, but I do not think so. You may be desperate, but—you will have your money." Her voice took on a note of incredulity. "But I do not think you will have it otherwise, even when you know!"

"Even when I know," he said, through grim pale lips.

Now the torment came back to her, overwhelming, desperate, deprived. She wanted to cry out: "Franz, do not leave me! It does not matter what you are, what you do, let me remain with you!"

Then she thought of Ernestine Schmidt. The thought was not to be endured. A horrible nausea struck at her, and her forehead suddenly glistened, and her stricken eyes wavered, fell. She felt her feet moving, felt cold air on her cheeks. She was out in the street.

She walked rapidly, stumbling, almost staggering. She had suffered before, but never with this devouring intensity, this shattering anguish, this sensation of being split apart. Tears ran down her blind face. She sobbed aloud. Passersby stared at her strangely. One or two spoke to her, but she was unconscious of this. She began to run, as though fleeing. She told herself: I am dying. She saw the deep snow now, and longed to hurl herself into it, pull its whiteness and forgetfulness over her. She saw that it was twilight now, and exhausted, paused at a windy corner. She fell against the brick wall, doubled up in physical agony. She wept, drawing slow anguished breaths.

A street lamp glittered on something on her wrist. She stopped her weeping, stared at Franz's bracelet. A fever took hold of her. She wrenched at the bracelet, struggled with it. It came loose with a loud snap. She flung it far from her, convulsively. It fell into a snow-bank, and was lost.

She became calmer now. A hansom was passing. She waved to it, climbed heavily, blindly into the seat.

Emmi had worked hard and untiringly. She lit the lamps in the sitting-room. Egon was dozing before the fire, wrapped in his shawl. The frail moonlight lay on snowy window-sills. The whole world swam in blue translucent shadows. She could see the sleeping shrouded countryside, and could hear the rising winter wind. In the kitchen, Florence Tandy was washing the dishes of the Christmas dinner: Roast goose with sauerkraut, boiled beets and potatoes, and warm cheese-cake and coffee. Florence was singing in her tight hysterical voice, and clattering loudly. The poor creature, finding peace at last. Emmi could hear Hermann pumping water in the yard. The loud creaking filled her with content.

She threw fresh coal upon the fire. Egon did not stir. He was sleeping peacefully, smiling. She bent and touched his forehead lightly with her lips.

She heard the grating of wheels. Another visitor! She had had ten that day, shy plain countryfolk, the Amish people, coming in to greet and welcome her, and wish her a happy Christmas, speaking in their quaint and anachronistic German. She hurried to the door. But it was a city cab which stood outside, and the young woman approaching her, walking with such hasty disordered steps, was clad in city finery. The moonlight fell on her strange blind face, and Emmi saw it was Irmgard. She stood and waited, in stupefaction.

Irmgard came to her, and held out her hands. "Take me in," she said, and her voice was hollow and faint. "Oh, take me in! Let me come home."

BOOK TWO

CHAPTER 1

THE COUNTRY was replete. The yellow haze of summer spread itself like radiant smoke over burnished hill and deep green valley. The first locusts were shrilling in the trees, accentuating the immense and fecund stillness. Leaf shadows fluttered over dusty roads. Field and pasture were golden or bright green, and under thick gnarled trees the cattle panted and slept. The sky was an incandescent arch, fuming with dazzling light. From the earth came the warm rich breath of fulfilled fertility, waiting for harvest. There was vitality in the radiant heat, the largeness of peace in the hot stillness.

Emmi's flower garden assaulted the eye with crimson, blue, white, pink, scarlet and purple. She had planted and nurtured hollyhocks against the white picket fence. Ivy climbed over the red walls of the house. Fowl clucked and scratched in the sandy dust of the barnyard, and young pigs grunted about their mothers in the sties. Hermann Schultz had repainted the barns and the silos, and they rose ruddy and bright, against the sky. From the kitchen came the sweet hot odor of cherry preserves, for Emmi was making jam of the last fruit. Florence Tandy, lean, curled as always, but clad in plain brown cotton and a check apron, was busily ladling the steaming sweetness into jars. Her face was dripping with sweat, and her smile was foolish. But her eyes were beaming with pride.

Emmi paused to wipe her face on her apron. Then she tasted the last batch critically. "You do not think it too sweet?" she asked, extending the wooden spoon to Florence, who sipped solemnly.

"No, Mrs. Stoessel. It is so good. I have never tasted such preserves."

Emmi stirred the great iron pot on the black range. "My husband preferred cherries," she said. Her thin flat face saddened, and her lip arched on a spasm of uncontrollable sorrow. She glanced through the windows. The long green woods hid her view of the cemetery, where Egon had lain since he had died on Christmas night. His grave was always heaped with garden flowers, which she carried to it at least twice a week. She had planted ivy, and now it was creeping over the plain white stone. A bending willow dripped its fronds over the earth, sheltering the grave tenderly. Hermann had made a bench for her, where she could sit and rest, and commune in her mind with Egon, feeling the flakes of sunlight on her head, the grass under her feet.

But the agony, after the first hour, had not been unbearable. She felt that he was at peace, that he would have chosen this place to die and to sleep. She felt that he had not gone from her at all. When she sat near his grave, he came to her. She was sure of that. She could feel his gentleness, his touch, and she could hear his voice. This was the earth he had loved. Sometimes she experienced a faint calm joy that he lay so near her home, and that, until the summer came, she could see the cemetery from her kitchen windows. What if he had died in the city, in the fog and the rain and the soot and the noise? What if he had gone to a grave in a crowded city cemetery, with factory chimneys in the distance, and the restless feet of the miserable breaking in on his rest? God had been good, at the last. He had died in his own home. Now he would never leave it. He was with her always.

Sometimes at night she broke into wild sobbing, which she stifled in her pillows. But there was healing in the day, and even in the moonlight. Egon pervaded the house, the fields, the hills, the valleys, and even the barns. She consulted him in her mind, even argued with him. Day by day, she was surer that he was with her, that he was overjoyed at the first flower, the first green thrusting of the wheat, the first budding of their own trees, the first breaking free of the winter-locked streams. "My roses bloomed today, Egon," she would say, in her garden. "Here is a crimson one, and a white. You always preferred white roses, though I think they have little odor. Can you smell them?" She was sure that he did. She felt him at her elbow, smiling. When a bush stirred, she knew that he had touched it. She was no longer deprived, and the spasms of bitter open grief came more rarely as time passed. She took her chair in the evenings under the purple shadow of the trees, and there was always an extra chair for Egon. She would dream thoughtlessly, looking over her beloved land, knowing that Egon dreamed beside her. She had only to put out her hand to touch him.

She was certain that he loved little young Mrs. Barbour, and liked Reginald Barbour deeply, as she did. She would discuss the Amish folk with him, indulgently, kindly. Sometimes when she was a trifle malicious, she heard his voice:

"Now Emmi, that is unkind." And she would laugh lightly, shamefaced.

Hermann Schultz came into the kitchen, stamping his feet free of the dust, and Emmi scolded him, and whisked away an imaginary particle of mud. He was carrying two pails of cool water from the well. He placed them on the table. Emmi indicated a platterful of fresh cookies on another table, and he gratefully thrust a few in his mouth. His fair curling hair was wet with sweat, his simple good-humored face burned black with sun.

"Hermann, will you go out into the barn, and tell Mrs. Darmstadter to come in? She has been there too long."

He stumped out, pushing extra cookies into the pockets of his faded overalls. Sunlight lay in streaks over the scrubbed stone floor. The jam steamed. Florence stirred the pot. The golden light was changing over the country, becoming deeper, more intense, as the day sloped to the sunset. Now fingers of sunlight splashed on the walls, mingled with the brighter light of fire in the stove.

Emmi went to the kitchen door and waited anxiously for Irmgard.

"It is so hot," she said, crossly, over her shoulder to Florence Tandy. "And she will work herself to exhaustion."

Florence sighed sentimentally. "It is so hard for her," she said. "So young to be widowed. And so cruel that her husband—" She blushed a little, and dropped her eyes modestly.

"The German Army has no heart," Emmi muttered. "They will not even give her a pension, because he died of some sickness, in his bed. If he had died in war, it would have been more heroic."

"And now, when she needs him so," Florence murmured, with another sigh.

Emmi said nothing. Irmgard had emerged from the barn, her apron full of eggs. She came slowly across the dusty yard, walking heavily, picking her steps among the fowl. Her hair shone in the sun. Her face was pale and wet. But she smiled when she saw Emmi.

"You will kill yourself," called the older woman, irately. But her eyes were full of anxiety. "It is not good to the child."

Irmgard was speechless with weariness and heat. She came into the kitchen and put the eggs on the wooden table. Her large tall body was swollen and heavy with fecundity. Emmi scolded her, forced her to sit down, went into the cool pantry where stood the kettle of milk she had recently brought from the spring house. Irmgard sipped the milk gratefully, while Emmi stood over her, still scolding.

"There is so much to do, Aunt Emmi," said Irmgard, with apology. Blue dents were about her colorless lips. But her expression was serene.

"Nonsense. There are two women here, besides you, and Hermann. And the neighbors help, when needed. This morning I caught you spading in the garden. And later, you insisted upon washing all these clothes. Are you trying to kill yourself?"

She pushed a damp lock of hair from Irmgard's forehead with a rough but kind hand. She put her fingers under Irmgard's chin, and forcibly lifted her head. She studied the pale, damp face severely.

"You would not have me sit in idleness, Aunt Emmi?" smiled the girl.

"There are other things. There is sewing, and mending. We need many quilts. And the baby's clothing. Do you wish your son to be born naked?"

Florence Tandy blushed deeply, at the stove, at this immodesty. But Irmgard laughed. She counted on her fingers: "I have one dozen nightgowns, one dozen fine cambric dresses, many napkins, three coats, and several bonnets. There is to be only one child, Aunt Emmi, not three."

My grandson, thought Emmi, with a sudden mysterious leaping in her chest. "I will not have my nephew dressed like a pauper," she said, severely. "Today, there came some white silk for his christening gown, and some lace. We will consult together about it. In the meantime, you will please go to your room and rest for an hour."

Irmgard climbed slowly and wearily up the wooden staircase to her room. She lay down on the narrow white bed, with its white fringed canopy. Her tired and burning eyes moved slowly over the wall-paper on which were strewn tiny roses and violets, and over the polished wooden floor with its circular rag carpet. A painted china bowl and pitcher stood on the wooden commode, which was covered with one of Emmi's stiffest and best linens, dripping with handmade lace. A low rocker stood near the muslin-curtained window. The window itself framed the distant hills, and a sliver of green valley. Sunlight swept broadly into the room, mingling with the bright wind.

But Irmgard, now that she was alone, could let her thoughts show on her face. It became dark and grim, even fierce in its impotence. She pressed her hands harshly on her body. She hated this child she carried, as she hated its father. There was no love in her, no tenderness, only a passionate resistance and repudiation. It is not to be endured, she thought. But she must endure. She must endure to the end of her life.

Always, there would be this child, looking at her with his father's eyes, speaking to her with his father's voice. She would hate him more then than she did now.

It was useless to tell herself, as Emmi had so often pleadingly told her, that the child was coming by no will of his own, that she and Franz had guiltily summoned him into a world that would never be too kind to him. Emmi had spoken no word of prudish and horrified reproach. But she had pleaded for the child. Irmgard knew that she wanted this child of her son with hidden but immense love. It was this love that so filled her voice when she spoke to the silent girl, urging consideration and tenderness. "The little one!" she would exclaim. "You must be all things to him, both father and mother and friend. He would not come if he had the choice. You have forced the choice upon him. Do not let him suffer for your folly. For it was folly to give yourself to Franz. Had it been another man, there could be excuse."

She was not appalled at the coming of a child without a legal father. Some large respect for life was in her, and she was scornful of small man-made formalities. This child was fulfilment and beauty and strength, and it was flesh of her flesh. Only that made Irmgard forgivable. The detestable fact of the child's paternity was something to be resolutely ignored. Sometimes she felt that Irmgard had betrayed this innocent by giving him such a father. Yet, had Franz not been the father, the child would not be her grandson. The Teutonic love of kin and children was strong in her.

"There was none in my family, nor in Egon's, like Franz," she would say, consideringly. "Therefore, we need not fear that such another as Franz shall be born to you."

She knew that Irmgard cried violently when alone. She gave her no unwholesome sympathy. She urged only that the girl love the child. "It will be good to have a little one here," she said. "Egon will love him, and I shall teach him to love Egon. There will be a special garden for him, and he will learn to hoe and spade. He will follow Hermann with the cows, and get the good milk. He will grow up on the land, tall and good and strong. He will be a joy to me in my old age."

But Irmgard's face would remain unmoved and white, her eyes bitter and heavy with hatred.

"There will be no army here, to take and destroy him, and beat the kind humanity from his body," Emmi would go on. "Some day, perhaps, he might find the dream in America, which is so hidden. For surely there is a dream."

She had been hopeless about the dream. But with the coming of every child, the dream surely brightened in the earth, like waiting gold. The dream which men had buried and forgotten, but which certainly waited for the use of other unborn men.

"Perhaps it will be a girl," Irmgard once taunted her, wishing her aunt to endure a little of what she was enduring.

But Emmi shook her head firmly. "No, it shall be a son. Egon has told me." She paused. "We shall call him Siegfried, after Egon's father, who was a lovely man."

Sometimes Irmgard found Emmi's wholesome and healthy acceptance of the child, and her sensible plans for it, impossible to endure. Her voice and her words dispelled the nightmare, brought Irmgard into open day. But Irmgard did not wish for open day. She wished for nightmare and ruin and death and darkness. She wished all chaos about her, to echo the chaos in her heart and mind. She wished loud voices and hatred, and reproaches and scathing condemnations. Emmi's placidity and anticipation were frightful. She grew to hate the growing child more and more intensely.

She had run to Emmi, that bright Christmas day, distraught, looking only for shelter and refuge, for a quiet place where she could hide her agony and desolation. Egon's death, that night, was a mournful diversion, and the comforting of Emmi made the girl's own grief less desperate and overwhelming. Later, when she discovered that she was bearing Franz's child, she forgot everything but her private rage and loathing, her sorrow and anguish, her impotent torture. Had Emmi expressed severity, anger and disgust, she would have found in this counter-irritant some alleviation for the rawness in herself. But Emmi, after the first outraged shock, which aroused her from her apathy of grief, took on renewed life and vigor. Irmgard suspected that in this coming child Emmi felt not only deep love and tenderness, but a new opportunity to find the dream she had dreamt all her life. This was a new page on which she would write. She upbraided Irmgard only for her indifference and unfeeling hatred for the child.

She refused to believe that Irmgard's heart and whole life were broken. Was not she, herself, Franz's mother? Had she not borne him, suffered for him, loved him? Yet, when she finally understood completely what he was, she had removed him from her flesh and her soul, and he was no longer her son. Why should Irmgard weep, Irmgard who had known him only a little while, who had lain with him briefly, who had seen him only a few short times? It was sentimentality. But out of this foolish sentimentality, by the grace and the wisdom of life and God, there would come a new spirit.

She refused to acknowledge Irmgard's humiliation and abandonment, her frustrated passion, her loneliness and pain, her terrible love from which she could not shake herself free.

She refused to believe, or know, that this love was like the fangs of a savage animal, set in the girl's flesh. When Irmgard, infrequently, burst out into wild cries of hatred for Franz, Emmi felt that this wholesome hatred would burn away any last traces of noxious passion. She did not know that the cries were the cries of anguish, longing, desolation and grief.

When Irmgard, in the ensuing months, became calmer, quieter, working vigorously, never sparing herself, and speaking rationally and even with amusement of trivial things, Emmi was satisfied. Irmgard was a sensible girl. She did not hurl herself at iron gates. She accepted everything. Emmi kept her very busy, gave her unending tasks to tire her body so that she would not think. She felt that she had succeeded. Irmgard did not speak of Franz again. His name was never mentioned in that serene house, where Emmi worked tirelessly with new-born vigor and determination. The simple Amish and a few other farmers welcomed the new tenants of this farm, and when Emmi had explained to them that this was Mrs. Darmstadter, a young widow, and her niece, recently come from Germany to escape her grief, they were all simplicity, kindliness and sympathy. Emmi could not recall when she had ever lied before, and was sometimes appalled at the facility with which the new lies came to her lips. It shook her.

Irmgard, seeing that her incoherent hatred and weeping only annoyed Emmi, who could not understand such weak "foolishness," maintained composure during the day. But when she was alone, as she was now, she abandoned herself to storms of loathing and fury, longing for revenge, and weeping. Sometimes she felt that she was being devoured by visible teeth, and torn by visible claws. She would bite her pillows, beat her head with her clenched hands, to relieve the torture of her longing for Franz, moaning for him with stifled murmurs, pleading for him against her shut lips.

She knew he had married Ernestine Schmidt on February 25th. She had read of the elaborate wedding in the *Nazareth Morning Journal,* which the farm received every morning. All that day a horrible numbness had lain over her body, like freezing ice. She had expected this, she told herself, over and over. She had known this would come. But the coming prostrated her. To the very last, she had watched the roads hourly, secretly believing that Franz would try to find her, that he would come for her. "I will never let you go," he had said, and in her heart, she had believed this. At night, she had developed a fever, which kept her bed-bound for nearly a week, and so ill that the doctor thought she might lose the new life hardly begun in her. She wished for this with a desperate ardor and new hope. But her young body was too strong to relinquish its hold. She had recovered, slowly but surely.

It was then that she had written to Baldur Schmidt, reminding him that she was now keeping her promise to let him know where she was, and urging him to remember that he had given his word that no one was to know where she was living now. Baldur wrote her joyously. He would come to see her. He had much to tell her. But, shuddering at the thought of what changes he would see in her, she wrote to him that her uncle had recently died, and that her aunt was in a very poor state, and needed only quiet. She again asked that Baldur not mention her name to his sister and mother. "I left them without word or notice, merely disappearing, and though there were extenuating reasons, I feel guilty. It is best that they never hear of me again." She knew Baldur would be puzzled at this, but she also knew that he would obey her request.

"Some day, perhaps soon, you will let me see you," he wrote to her, in his tiny script-like hand. "Your portrait hangs on the wall in my rooms. I speak to it daily. Sometimes I believe it even smiles at me. I am a very foolish poor creature."

Slowly, she began to feel comfort in the thought of that friend, as lonely and deprived as herself, and thinking of her. Some day, she thought, she might allow him to come to her, and they would walk through Emmi's beloved rose-gardens and sit on the low hill under the shadow of the woods.

In the meantime, with acknowledged selfishness, she wrote him at least once a week. She dared not ask him for news of Franz, but she professed to be eagerly anxious about Ernestine. Baldur, who had the recluse's inverted preoccupation with self, wrote only briefly about his sister. Because of his innate reserve and good taste, his remarks were casual. He spoke of Franz without emotion. "He is a great favorite of my father's. My father has shown a new interest in everything lately, and is kind even to me. I sometimes think that not only has Ernestine acquired a husband, but my father has acquired the son he always wanted." But this was the longest remark he ever made about his family. His letters were filled with love for herself, and anxiety, and tenderness. He told her all his thoughts, with the complete lack of reserve which the recluse, once having broken, can pour out inexhaustibly. He did not know that Irmgard skipped feverishly and impatiently over these long pages to find the one casual remark about his family, and Franz. For the last three letters, he had not mentioned Franz at all. He had said only that Ernestine was "blooming," and that his mother missed Irmgard excessively, and that she was ill again.

Emmi was annoyed by these letters, and secretly, in spite of her cold condemnations, she too, wished to hear about Franz.

On the morning of this hot August day there had come another letter from Baldur.

He hinted discreetly that Ernestine was not as well as she might be, that her new color had faded, and that she did not go about among the new friends she had sedulously acquired since her marriage and her reborn interest in life. "But females at this difficult period often avoid company, preferring the company of their mothers in their new anticipations." Irmgard, after some puzzling, had an annihilating shock. Then Ernestine, too, was about to bear a child of Franz's!

It was not to be borne! It was a profanation. Irmgard, as usual, had gone to her room, and her anguish, despair and uncontrolled passion tore her apart. All her hatred and loathing and grief and desolation came back to her, enhanced a thousand times. She had walked up and down her room, sobbing dryly, beating her breast with her fists, running her fingers savagely through her disheveled hair. A thousand delirious plans for revenge rushed through her mind. She would go at once to Ernestine, exhibiting her swollen body, so soon to be relieved of its living burden. She would denounce Franz to his face, before his miserable little wife! She would scream at him, and spit at him, and curse him. For two hours, while Emmi thought the girl was resting, Irmgard alternately paced and flung herself on her bed, writhing. Her hands were tangled in strands of her own hair, and her own flesh was bruised. It was only when a living pang of fire rushed through her body like a sword, and she had to give unpreoccupied and stern attention to this new anguish, that she came to her senses.

The pang left her, and she was profoundly prostrated. She fell into a sleep like a faint. Coming to see her, Emmi found her lying across her bed, her long shining hair and head hanging over the edge, her arms half on the floor, the palms upturned. She was in an attitude of abandonment, as though she had been cruelly beaten and then tossed aside to die. Emmi found the letter on the commode, and read it, shamelessly. Her face whitened under its new brownness. Slowly, she folded the letter. She did not feel that this new child was flesh of her flesh, and she had no yearning for it, as she yearned for Irmgard's child, who was not only her grandson, but the grandson of her beloved sister. It was almost as though the little one were doubly her own. But for Ernestine Schmidt's child she felt nothing but disgust.

She had gently lifted Irmgard to a more comfortable position on the bed. She could not endure, without wincing and deep passionate sorrow, the sight of that tortured and exhausted face with the bleeding lips. She had hesitated a moment, then kissed the wet forehead, on which the pale gilt hair was so tangled and damp. She had seen the sunken eyes, and she had listened to the faint catching sobs that bubbled up from the strained throat. For the first time she realized fully what love devastated this poor girl, and what agony she was still suffering.

But when the little one comes, she thought, it will be different.

She had covered the girl's feet with an afghan, and then had gone downstairs again. There, she was somewhat shorter than usual with the foolish Florence Tandy, with her endless trillings and chatter and silly remarks. She listened for sounds from upstairs.

It was noon before Irmgard came down, controlled, very pale, but slightly smiling. Her hair was smooth. Only the blue clefts about her lips and the sunken patches of purple about her eyes betrayed what she had been suffering. Irmgard worked feverishly that day.

When, later, she had gone to her room, towards sunset, she had lain on her bed. But nothing but her hatred remained, like a great scorching fire, hatred for Franz and hatred for his child. She plotted quietly, without delirium. But each of her plots she acknowledged as foolish. There was nothing she could do. It was this impotence that so humiliated her. But finally even the impotence was gone, and there remained only her hatred, like a conflagration over a dark country.

She heard Emmi calling her, much later, for the evening meal. It was still full and brilliant day, though the western hills were becoming sharp and dense against a widening glow. But she could eat nothing. The food was dry and sickening in her mouth, and she could not swallow it. She did not protest when Emmi sent her upstairs again. She did not see Emmi's long, thoughtful, anxious following gaze. She lay on her bed, staring at the bright windows with dull and empty eyes.

Suddenly, the earlier pang of the day divided her again, and she screamed aloud before she could control herself.

CHAPTER 2

EMMI CAME running up the stairs like a young girl. She found Irmgard writhing on the bed. The girl looked at her with abysmal terror, but could not speak. Emmi made a brief examination, pressing her hands on Irmgard's body.

"It has come," she said, in a voice of quiet triumph. "A little early, but not too early."

She avoided Irmgard's stark staring, and quickly undressed her. She called down the stairs to Florence Tandy in the kitchen, urging her to ask Hermann to go for the doctor after the milking was completed. "It will not be for some time," she said to Irmgard, comfortingly.

She put fresh stiff linen on the bed, pushed back the curtains so that the rising evening wind could cool the hot room. She brought cold water and sponged the girl's red and sweating face. She combed the long hair and braided it. Irmgard lay on her coarse pillows, her golden braids over her ruffled nightgown. She could see the golden and scarlet flush of the skies, and the quiet dreaming hills. Between the intervals of her pain, she could feel nothing but great exhaustion and weakness. Even the hatred was diminished. Sometimes she had only one thought: the hope of approaching death.

At twilight, the doctor came, a small fat man with a beard, a long coat, a rusty cravat and a very large hat. He examined the apathetic girl, shook his head slightly, and informed Emmi that the child would be born probably after midnight. "In the meantime," he said, shaking out some pills in his calloused palm, "she must rest." Downstairs, he expressed some anxiety for Irmgard's condition. "There is no hope, no anticipation there," he said.

"She is a widow," replied Emmi, looking at him levelly. "She has grieved over her young husband."

Irmgard fell into a dim uneasy sleep, punctuated by sharp lightning flashes of pain. Emmi sat beside her, fanning her, holding her hand. Florence Tandy's long thin figure appeared at intervals with towels and water. She would thrust her curled forehead and horse-like face into the room, and tiptoe in with elaborate caution. Emmi could hear the shrilling of crickets, the pumping of water, the lowing of the cows. A robin, in a lonely tree, sang his sweet and melancholy prophecy of rain to the curve of the young moon, which was slowly brightening in the depths of dark cobalt sky. Over the faint shadows of the sinking hills there was a last golden gleam. Everywhere the intense stillness was like the prelude to evening prayer, and the earth seemed to lift her vast widespread arms in a large and solemn gesture. From her lips rose the incense of her breath, so that all the cooling air was heavy with the scent of soil, grass, flower and ripening field.

Emmi rose and went to the window. Now she could see the tall white and red stalks of her hollyhocks pressing about her house, the lonely white curve of the road drifting into the darkening distance. She could feel the new wind on her face. She looked at the far hills, haloed with their gilded light. She could see the outline of her good red barns and her silo. Now the crickets were beginning a louder clamor to the night, so that their shrilling enhanced the enormous silence.

"And they heard the voice of the Lord God walking in the garden in the cool of the day." Ah, surely, thought Emmi, He walked then, in lonely meditation, where a mist of light lingered over the forest, which bowed and murmured in a gentle monotone, and man, having removed his pestilential presence from the afflicted earth, had hidden himself in sleep. It was easy to imagine the sound of His footsteps on the grass, His pausing under some great bending tree, His contemplation of the immensity of the heavens.

A wide still peace flowed over Emmi, so that she forgot everything but the awareness of this Presence, and everything hot and small and tormented sank into nothingness in this flood of strength and majesty. She felt that Egon stood beside her. She was afraid to turn, for fear he might retreat, but she knew that he stood at her side, watching the night with her. She experienced a large unquestioning peace and joy.

Irmgard murmured brokenly from her bed, and Emmi, remembering with satisfaction that the haying was done, with the help of kind neighbors, went back to the girl. Irmgard was awake now. She was staring darkly at her aunt. She said: "He told me he would never let me go. I believe it. He will come to me soon."

Emmi sat down and took the hot tremulous hand.

"You are brave. You must have courage," she said.

But the mingled effect of pain and drug had loosed the iron control which Irmgard for so long had imposed upon herself. She twisted her hand restlessly from Emmi's, and she panted.

"It is not to be endured, if he does not come. Why should I live? There is nothing." She spoke in hard rapid words, between her quick breathing. "All that he is, I know. But of what consequence is that? I love him. He must come to me."

Emmi was silent, but her lips pressed themselves together in bitter grimness. Over this grimness, her eyes were gentle and heavy with compassion. She did not know what to say in comfort, in consolation.

Irmgard tossed herself with rising excitement on her hot pillows.

"That foolish woman he married. She can be nothing to him, in that hideous house. He must think of me. He promised that he would never leave me. He will come soon. Then this pain will stop, and I can sleep."

Emmi, who had listened to wild crying hatred from Irmgard in the beginning, knew then that she had underestimated the passion of this poor child for Franz. She was both horrified and frightened. She could only stare in aching silence at that darkly flushed wet face and eyes brilliant with green light in the beams of the lamp.

"You must be brave," she said at last, with difficulty. "All things come to the brave."

Irmgard regarded her with intensity, and then she smiled. "Yes, yes," she cried, eagerly. "It is so." She continued, very rapidly: "I have forgotten everything else, except that I love him."

Emmi forced her to swallow two more pills. She sat beside the girl, holding her hand firmly. Still smiling, Irmgard slept again, this time more peacefully. Emmi sat outside the lamp's thin path of light, sighing over and over.

She heard the sound of wheels, muffled and soft in the thick dust of the road. The doctor, then, had returned sooner than expected. She went downstairs swiftly and silently. Florence Tandy was already at the door, smiling her usual silly smile which always seemed to be anticipating something exciting and pleasant.

But it was not the doctor's rig which had drawn up at the gate. It was a fine handsome closed carriage, drawn by two black horses and driven by a coachman. This was not the doctor who was descending. Emmi, seeing who it was, felt a sickening lurch in herself. She could not move until the man was halfway up the walk toward the house. Then she turned quickly to Florence Tandy and whispered fiercely through shaking lips:

"Go up to Mrs. Darmstadter and stay with her! Do not let her speak, nor make a sound, no matter what you must do! Do not tell her——"

Florence Tandy's gooseberry eyes widened in bewilderment. Emmi suddenly shook her. "You understand me?"

"Yes, Mrs. Stoessel," stammered the woman. She wrung her long hands impotently in her apron, still staring.

"He must not know she is here. It is very important."

The man, a tall broad young fellow, elegantly and fashionably clad, was now within earshot. He saw the two women, and recognized his mother. He smiled, and removed his high black hat. The evening wind lifted the long skirts of his coat. His pointed shoes shone in the lamplight that streamed through the open door.

Frightened, Florence ducked her head in response to the smile and the nod, and retreated. Emmi heard her stumbling up the stairs to Irmgard's room. She clenched her hands together, and tried to control the lurching of her heart, and the coldness of her terror. She did not know what to do, what to say. She said only: "Franz."

Her first impulse was to deny him admission, to close the door in his face. But she dared not do this. He might suspect what she was hiding in this house. But to bring him in, was to risk his hearing Irmgard's moaning, or her cries, when she awoke. Torn by her fears, her indecision, her anger and dread, she could only stand before him, rigid and tall in her apron.

"Mother," he said, looking up at her, as she stood on the high step. He was still smiling easily. "Are you not going to invite me in?"

Surely Irmgard, even in her sleep, must stir and awaken at the sound of that voice. But Emmi refrained from her first impulse to glance back over her shoulder. She made her voice low, cold and hard.

"Why have you come? I asked you never to come here."

She saw now that he was glancing behind her with quick darting looks. To refuse him admission would be to confirm whatever suspicions he had. She stepped aside, and abruptly gestured to him to enter. She pressed herself back against the wall, not wishing to have him touch her. She led him into the parlor, and lit a lamp. She did not sit down, and neither did he. They confronted each other in the warm lamplight in the deserted room.

She spoke again: "When I wrote you that your father had died, I asked you to refrain from ever coming to this house. I told you I never wished to see you again. You respected my wishes then. Why have you violated them now?"

He studied her. She was livid under her brownness. But she stood before him rigidly and inflexibly, her hands clenched at her sides.

"You are making much out of nothing," he said. His blue

eyes taunted her. Then, deliberately, he sat down. "It was a hot evening, and I came out into the country for a long drive. I remembered, then, that you lived near here. Surely you can forget any past quarrels. After all, I am your son."

"You are not my son!" she cried. "I have no son!"

But as she looked at him, so elegant, so burnished, so prosperous and well-fed, her treacherous heart cried out to him: Tell me that you are happy! Tell me that you have no regrets! She could hardly endure the sudden surging of all her flesh to him, and in the effort to control herself, she turned even paler. This smooth man was not Franz, surely! This man already fattening, with a silken yellow mustache hiding his long cruel upper lip, and with a gold watch-chain swinging across the black silk of his waistcoat! This easy smiling man who had done so much that was evil and despicable! She could read nothing from his smile, from his calmness, from his well-kept hands.

"You are going too far," he said, smoothly. "I thought you had forgotten that hysteria. I had forgotten it, myself. Tonight, I remembered only that my father was dead. I had long forgiven you for not telling me before he was buried. I thought you might be lonely and sorrowful, remembering how you had loved him."

But she was thinking of something else, with renewed terror. How much did he know? Oh, those foolish letters to Baldur Schmidt! Had Franz seen any of them? She replied mechanically, over the pounding of her heart:

"I have not been lonely, nor very sorrowful. I have worked hard. I have been at peace. There was no need for this visit."

She saw that Franz, still smiling, was regarding her with merciless and narrowed eyes.

"I am glad to hear that you have needed nothing, and that you are well," he said. He paused. To her heightened imagination, she thought he was listening. "Are you able to take care of this farm, with this woman, and the young farmer, alone?"

"The neighbors help me, when necessary. They are kind and good." She strained her ears for a revealing moan from upstairs, and pressed her hand violently against her breast.

She saw that he was still watching her with an almost reptilian fixity, and that he was enjoying her agitation. But his voice was very sympathetic:

"It was wrong of Irmgard to leave you alone, and not to have remained with you to help you. She is still in Berlin with that English family?"

His tone was casual, but she saw the tightening of his big body, and a sudden gleam on his face.

"Yes," she answered, steadfastly. "She is still there. When she wrote me last she said that the family might take her to England soon, for the summer. I have not heard from her since."

"Ah," he murmured. He folded his hands over the shining ebony stick he carried. He studied her with brutal calm. In all his life, he remembered, his mother had never lied at any time. He was convinced that she was not lying now. If she were, she would not be so cold, so steadfast.

"I asked her to remain with me," said Emmi, and wondered vaguely at the facility with which lies came to her lips. She even managed to inject a faint note of indignation into her words. "But she said she wished to return to Germany. She had not liked America, after all. Then she was discovered by this Englander, this Herr Wordsworth."

"And she is content? With these strangers?"

"She is content."

They looked at each other in an electric silence. Then Franz, slowly and deliberately, drew a silver case from the tail of his long broadcloth coat. From it he removed a long cigar. He lit it from a little silver box of matches. Emmi, still not sitting, clenched her hands again until the nails wounded her calloused palms. Cold drops appeared on her brow. With all her will, all her might, she willed him to leave at once. But he sat easily on the chair, and looked about him with pleasant interest.

"A good room," he remarked, generously, with a nod at the books. "This is much better than I expected."

"I am happy here," she replied, somewhat hoarsely. Was that a moan, a faint cry, from Irmgard's room? Had he heard it?"

But it appeared that he had not even heard her reply. He was regarding her with amused affection.

"I came, thinking I might offer you some help, if you need it."

She cried out, with sudden desperation: "I need nothing! I have everything. But there is no need for you to remain here! I asked you not to come. You will do me the kindness of leaving, and of forgetting that I am here!"

He assumed an expression of slight injury. "How inflexible and narrow you are, Mother. You have asked me nothing, though I wrote you that I have married Miss Ernestine Schmidt. But surely you will be interested to know that you are soon to become a grandmother?"

Emmi's long thin lips jerked. They were pale and dry. But she said nothing. However, her agitation was apparent, to his satisfaction. "I, too, am content," he said, "though the information cannot possibly interest you."

"You are content?" she asked, in spite of herself. "You are happy with that young woman? You have nothing to regret?"

"No," he said, frankly. "I regret nothing."

It was this, then, which renewed her hatred for him. She could have struck him.

She cried out, savagely: "I had hoped you were miserable! I had hoped that you were suffering, as you have made others suffer! I had wished that you might never forget that you killed your friend, and robbed another friend! I had hoped you might never sleep, remembering!"

He stood up. His smile was gone. Now his face was harsh and brutal, and revealed.

"You are still a fool, I can see. You are right. I should never have come."

He saw that she was almost hysterical, and that her small blue eyes were thick with tears. His old dislike of her returned, and he enjoyed her misery. She walked to the door and flung it open, with a violent gesture, wordless but expressive.

"I ask only one more thing of you," he said, in a loud contemptuous voice. "Tell me where Irmgard lives, that I might write her."

"That I shall never do!" she exclaimed. "You betrayed her, as you betrayed others. She does not wish to hear of you, to know of you."

He shrugged. He picked up his hat and cane. "Very well, then. It is not necessary. I shall be able to trace her in Germany, myself."

She watched him go. He stood outside and put on his hat. He went down the walk to his waiting carriage. Something soft and treacherous, moaning and deprived, ran out from her, followed him. She gripped the open door in both sweating hands, and her lips fell open, slackly. Even when he drove away, she stood there, her heart seeming to drip in her breast in slow torturous drops of blood. She listened to the last sound of the wheels and the rattle of the harness. Long after they were lost in the silence of the night, she strained her ears for them.

She knew why he had come. He had believed to the last that she was hiding Irmgard. Now he was convinced she had told the truth. He had waited, all these months, wishing to let Irmgard suffer for her "desertion" of him, and was now magnanimously prepared to let her return. Emmi did not underestimate him. But for a while, at least, she had respite.

In the meantime, surely Irmgard would recover from her infatuation and care for nothing but her child. Then she would be safe.

CHAPTER 3

WHEN IRMGARD woke, it was only an hour before midnight. She did not awaken in her earlier condition of weakness and desperation. Now life and death had her, and in her stern and sweating preoccupation with them there was no room for less elemental forces. Emmi rejoiced to see this profound struggle of the strong young body against pain and danger.

Then, at midnight, came another lull, and the exhaustion came again. She lay on her pillows, white and lax, with closed eyes. The doctor had not yet come.

Emmi never knew, in her great fear, whether it was inspiration or not which made her say loudly and triumphantly to Irmgard, through the haze of suffering and apathy that had taken her:

"That fine gnädige Frau of his! She shall not bear such a child as yours, my little one! This child shall be strong and beautiful, but hers shall be weak and worthless. This shall be your revenge!"

At first she did not know if Irmgard had heard her or not. But slowly the sunken eyes opened, brightened like far specks seen at the end of a dark tunnel, and then quickened into life. That was all, but Emmi knew that she had conquered the monstrous unseen enemy in this room.

Irmgard did not speak. Only rarely did she groan. Her expression became severe and abstracted, as though all her energies of mind and body were absorbed in giving birth. Florence Tandy, fluttering and gesticulating, came and went, sighing. Emmi sat calmly by the bed, trimmed the lamp, wiped the girl's moist face, fanned her. And hour by hour her sense of triumph increased, and her exultation.

"This is our child, Egon," she said internally. "This is the son we should have had for our old age."

Still the doctor did not come. And so it was that it was

Emmi, herself, with the blushing and horrified assistance of the old maiden, Miss Tandy, delivered the son of Irmgard and Franz. Her heart bounded almost unbearably when she had ascertained the sex of the child. She wrapped the child quickly in a blanket warmed and prepared for him, and held him in her arms. He was strong and large, with wisps of shining golden hair on his big round skull and blue eyes that opened almost at once, simply and clearly. His body was pink and firm and vigorous, and his cries loud and sharp. Then reluctantly, lingeringly, she gave him into Florence's arms, and returned to minister to Irmgard, who had fallen into a sudden prostrated sleep.

At dawn, Irmgard awoke, pale and battered on her pillows. She said at once: "My child. Where is he?"

Emmi brought him to her and laid him on her arm. For one instant only she shrank away. But the next moment she caught him fiercely to her breast and held him clenched there, tears running over her white veined cheeks.

Emmi was satisfied. The little one would not go unloved or unwanted, then, as she had secretly feared. She heard the protesting clamors of the baby, and she saw his beating hands. He was Siegfried.

"It is Siegfried," she said aloud. "He will fight a great number of dragons."

She was somewhat mystified and mortified, coloring somewhat, when Irmgard suddenly laughed, not weakly, but with strength, amusement, and enjoyment.

CHAPTER 4

INVARIABLY, WHEN Franz Stoessel came into his office, which adjoined that of his father-in-law, Hans Schmidt, he glanced quickly at his desk for a certain envelope for which he waited eagerly from week to week. The envelope now lay there, waiting for him, and he pounced on it, without removing his pearl-gray bowler and his black coat. He tossed his cane onto a chair, and standing, read the letter rapidly. It was thick and voluminous, and was from the Burnley Detective Agency's New York office.

"Carrying our inquiries further into England, with regard to the Wordsworth family, we encountered some delicate difficulties. As you mentioned that the family was undoubtedly of some influence and importance in England, otherwise they would not employ foreign nursemaids, we had discreet inquiries of the most prominent of this name. The one family we have in mind is addicted to foreign travel, but they were very reserved and haughty, according to our investigator. It seems that an *exceedingly* famous member of this family was once entangled with a Frenchwoman, with sad results, and the surviving members did not care to discuss any other entanglements. But our investigator was indefatigable, and he is now assured that no member of this family employs any woman of German birth. We therefore went down the list of Wordsworths, with the same discouraging report.

"We have reinvestigated the ship lists for the past two years very thoroughly, and find no young lady of the name given on those lists, bound for Germany. Nor does our American investigator discover that Mrs. S. receives any letters from that country, or from England. Investigation of Mrs. S., as we have written you before, shows only that she employs two women on the farm, a Miss Florence Tandy, and a German widow with one child, a boy, who is about two years old. The widow's name is Mrs. Darmstadter, whose husband is alleged to have been a German soldier.

"We regret that our investigations have so far proved unfortunate in results. However, we shall continue them. We enclose our latest bill, and await your instructions before proceeding further. We are certain it will be only a matter of time before we discover the object of our search."

Franz, with a gloomy expression, lit a match and carefully burned the letter, holding it over the empty fireplace. He sat down, and stared before him. The fools! In this time they ought to have discovered something. There were only two solutions to this: either Irmgard was still in America, or she had sailed for Germany under an assumed name. Something to nag and knock in his brain, something elusive and persistent. But he could not identify it. He wrote out a check and enclosed it in an envelope for mailing to the Burnley Agency. The nagging and knocking began again, and he frowned, playing with his watch-chain. But still it eluded him.

He ran his hand over his hair, which was no longer rough and unkempt, but smooth, burnished and longish, and even dandified. He smoothed his thick yellow mustache abstractedly. He then observed that he had a noticeable paunch, and resolved vaguely and irritably that he must do something about this at once. His beer-drinking bouts with old Hans must be curtailed. There was a long mirror over his washstand and he went to it, observing himself critically, and with returning satisfaction. When he stood thus, straight, with broad shoulders thrown back, the paunch disappeared, and there remained only the figure of a fine gentleman with ruddy cheeks and hard blue eyes. He resembled, perhaps, an army officer, perhaps just a little softened from a sojourn on his estate. But certainly not a fleshy bourgeois!

He returned to his desk, his complacency restored. He moved with vigor and alertness. After all, he was only twenty-eight, he reminded himself. He noticed another letter from another office of the Burnley Agency, and opened it quickly with one thrust of a silver paper-knife. Ah, this was better news! The letter appeared to sing with triumph.

"Our investigations of Senator A. now produce the fact that in his youth he became amorously entangled with a young octoroon girl on his father's plantation. Reports indicate that the girl bore a child, which was sold into slavery, with the probable knowledge of Senator A. The child, a boy, died at the age of ten from ill-treatment administered by his new master. Nothing indicates any interest on the part of Senator A. You may take this report as authentic."

"Ah, that is better!" exclaimed Franz, aloud, smiling. He folded the letter and put it into his pocket. He smiled about his office, exultantly.

His office, which had once been a storeroom for miscellaneous files and books, had been converted by himself into an elegant room, with heavy mahogany furniture, rich rugs, fine paintings, draperies at the windows, and a white marble fireplace. In one corner was a bust of Goethe, in pink marble. The windows looked out, it is true, on the yard of the mills, but it was not an unwelcome view.

Because of the warmness of the late spring day no fire burned in the hearth. But a fan of gilded and painted paper filled the black opening. And on his desk was a vase filled with fresh spring flowers from the Schmidt conservatory. Franz sniffed them with pleasure. He called for his clerk, and began to dictate a letter, leaning far back in his high, red-plush chair, and smiling.

"My dear Senator Trusley: I am sending you enclosed a report on Senator A. which will interest you excessively.

"This scoundrel, so exposed in this report, is the high-minded Alabama patriot who is attempting to ruin the coal operators of the North by opening what he calls the 'rich coal-fields of my native State, which will induce some measure of prosperity to my desperate and impoverished people.' It is apparent that he has in mind, not honorable competition to which we would not overly object, but mines run by negroes who still exist, in the South, in a condition of semi-slavery and oppression. Needless to say, we operators and miners and industrialists of the North would not find it possible to operate with any reasonable profit, considering the fact that our labor is white, free and well-paid. There are, of course, unscrupulous industrialists in the North, without proper regard for human rights, who would welcome this opportunity to buy coal at ridiculous rates— The mines of Alabama must be abandoned— You, as a native Pennsylvanian, could not endure to see your people impoverished, and your holdings in various industrial enterprises jeopardized."

He dictated for a short time more, then folded the newly written letter and put it with the other in his pocket. He then went into Hans's office, after a light gay tap on the door.

Hans was in consultation with Dietrich, and looked up as his son-in-law entered, scowling from the ambush of his thick white brows. But in spite of the scowl, the tiny eyes softened and gleamed.

"What do you want, charging in here like a bull?" he asked, rudely.

Franz smiled, and seated himself, ignoring Dietrich, who shot him a glance of covert hatred. He tossed the Burnley letter and the letter to Senator Trusley onto Hans's desk. "We have him!" he exclaimed.

Hans, grunting, read the two letters, slowly and carefully. Then he laid them down. He scowled again. "Blackmail!" he said. "Do we go into blackmail now, with your schemes?"

Franz laughed indulgently. "Most certainly not. Trusley is a gentleman, and a close friend of Andrews. He has only to warn him, regretfully. But we shall leave the mode of procedure in Trusley's competent hands. Well? Are you not going to congratulate me?"

Hans shifted gloomily on his seat, and fixed Franz with truculent eyes.

"I have built up this mill with these two hands," he said, and lifted fat clenched fists. "I have made iron and steel. I have done it all myself. I do not understand, nor like, these new schemes, where men plot against each other in offices. With pictures on the walls, and velvet curtains at the windows, and flowers," he added, scathingly. "Steel is steel, and mills are mills. Plottings are for rascals and diplomats."

Dietrich murmured a discreet approbation.

Franz laughed again. "But these are new times, father! It is no longer a time of mills merely competing with each other. There is finesse, now, not bludgeoning. There are politicians now, to be placated, to be induced to fight one's growing battles in Washington. There is high finance now, and not mere sweat and labor."

Hans grunted contemptuously: "You mean that industry is no longer a matter of direct control?"

"Exactly. Few seem to realize it, but America is passing through a transition. The pioneer industrial civilization, the little individual controller of a small number of workmen, are both doomed, old-fashioned, unwieldy. We are entering the first phase of capitalistic civilization, and monopoly, and manipulation."

Dietrich, who hated Franz virulently, and who plotted continually for his disfavor in the eyes of Hans, coughed gently, and said:

"Herr Schmidt has done very well, in the past, with his hard work and direct control and self-management and close contact with the industry he has built."

Franz turned a bland eye upon him. " 'In the past,' yes. But not now. Do you realize, Dietrich, that the builder of the future, the great capitalistic industrialist, will expand and become rich and powerful? He will plot more and sweat less. This is no pioneer land any longer. I see a vision of America," and he leaned back in his chair and stared mockingly and elaborately as at some splendid sight: "I see a few mighty monopolies headed by gentlemen of intelligence and craft and statesmanship, not petty little industrialists with the stench of their own insignificant mills in their nostrils. I see these gentlemen in close touch with great bankers, great railroad builders, great politicians, great statesmen. The future of America is in the hands of a few, who know how to manipulate, not merely build."

Hans grunted, rubbed cigar ashes off his satin waistcoat. He flicked a meaning and surly glance at Dietrich, looking for comfort in a bewildering world.

"A lovely idea! And I suppose that fantastic thought of yours, hiring young dreamer chemists and metallurgists, is part of the scheme? What have they done?" he asked irately. "They have taken from my tills, and buzz busily in a little hive of their own. But that is all."

"But one of these days they will discover something tremendous," urged Franz, with his charming smile. "I know this. Just as I know that the day of crucible steel is passing. There was Bessemer, with his 'fantastic thought.' Where would steel be today without Bessemer? Nowhere. We would still be making it in teaspoonfuls. We would still have puddlers patiently pushing about a tiny little red ball for hours.

Now we have Bessemer Steel. What we have not thought of yet are new ways to use steel. Replace wooden railway coaches, for instance, with steel ones. I can think of a thousand things——"

"All more foolish than the last," grunted Hans. But he eyed Franz with secret fondness. He was very tired. He no longer yearned for new worlds. But the thought that Franz could still envision these new worlds dimly excited him.

But Franz was becoming more and more excited with his idea.

"In one direction, I agree with you about actual work in the mills. We are still, in spite of moderate successes, a small mill. We must learn the necessary way to increase volume and reduce cost. We must learn mass production. Yes. But that will come with organization, integration and consolidation."

"Words!" cried Hans. "Mere words! How shall we go about this?"

"How?" murmured Dietrich, with a faint malignant smile of superiority.

But Franz was momentarily silent, still smiling into the near distance. He played with his watch-chain; he passed his hands over his thick yellow hair, which was assiduously polished by much careful brushing. Hans exchanged an irate and puzzled glance with Dietrich, then puffed out his cheeks in mingled indignation and indulgent derision of Franz.

"Your dreams, I presume, come from your fifteen-dollar-a-week dreamers?" he asked.

Franz nodded quickly and amiably. "Most certainly! They know what I want, and I have not the sufficient imagination to do it myself. They know I want money. So they bend their heads and think, and some day they will get it for me. I have the cash for their shabby pockets. They have the brains for me."

He looked at Dietrich, now, without amiability, but with opaque blandness. "I should like to speak to Herr Schmidt alone," he said politely.

Dietrich, his fox-like face darkening, looked at Hans, silently pleading that he not be dismissed. But Hans made a brusque gesture with his hand, and Dietrich, flushing, rose and left the room.

"A fox in a pen thinks the world is filled only with little chickens," remarked Franz, and got up deftly to close the door which Dietrich had purposely left open a crack. Then he returned to Hans, who sat, bulky, with whitening hair and thickening body, in his chair under the portrait of that aristocrat, his wife's father. He did not stir when Franz seated himself again, but his little eyes were full of sulky and confused sparks.

"Now," said Franz, "we shall proceed with our discussion."

CHAPTER 5

HANS WAS acutely uneasy, and even frightened. During the three years Franz had been his son-in-law, he had alternated between periods of elation, satisfaction, affection, bewilderment, anger, confusion and fury. It is true that the mills had become quite compact and had secured considerable prosperity under Franz's "imbecile schemes," and that for the first time in many years they were actually making a lot of money. The schemes were, one and all, violently and apoplectically opposed by Hans, with a tremendous amount of screamings, oaths and epithets, but each time Franz had amicably had his way. And each time they were successful, to Hans's bewilderment, and even dismay, as well as delight. Sometimes he felt himself in a grotesque new world, where old values were no longer valid, and the wildest dreams suddenly became concrete. He felt menace in the dreams, and disorientation. But, they had succeeded. He could not understand this. He was not reconciled to the new world, even when the Schmidt Mills had been dragged back from the very verge of bankruptcy. The imminence of bankruptcy seemed to him to be more reassuring and familiar than a world in which fantasies become successful realities.

He was proud of Franz. At times, he could scarcely conceal his exultation when complimented by such as Jules Bouchard of the Sessions Steel Company for securing such a progressive and imaginative son-in-law and general manager. Jules Bouchard had, himself, written a most gracious letter to this effect, and though Hans had obscenely cursed that "scheming, lying, thieving Frenchman," he carried the letter with him always, in an upper waistcoat pocket. Once he even said: "Someday the Sessions Mills will come to us with hat in hand," and beamed upon Franz with fierce affection. Too, Franz had rescued Ernestine from old virginity.

When she became pregnant, Hans was prepared, for a little while at least, to let Franz do anything he wished with his beloved mills.

Nevertheless, he was afraid of Franz, for all his affection, and prophesied ruin. "We shall go down in a great blitz of bankruptcy some day," he gloomily remarked. He was hardly placated by the growing accounts in the banks. When bank presidents in Philadelphia actually came to Nazareth to visit him, his bewilderment was greater than ever, as was also his pride, and egotism. He began to develop sick headaches, which were becoming more and more frequent. Franz's presence comforted and infuriated him. He felt his familiar world flaking away under his feet, and his hands wildly and blindly fumbling for support. Franz, in one moment, gave him support, the next lightly removed it, leaving him dangling.

He knew, by now, that when Franz came easily and smilingly into his office like this, that he had some new "scheme" under that mane of carefully tended yellow hair. His heart began to thud with apprehension, and dull terror. I have had enough, he thought to himself. My flesh is old and heavy. I cannot endure new high winds and perilous places. This time, I shall resist.

"You have a new madness," he accused Franz. "I am tired of your madnesses."

"Even though they have been successful?" asked Franz, with gentle affection, and reproachful smile.

Hans struck his fist savagely on the desk. "Ja! It is a lunatic's success! I am tired of it. What do you want? Are you never to be satisfied?"

"No," said Franz, quietly.

Hans threw up his hands in a sudden gesture of despair and fear.

"It is enough for me! Why is it not enough for you?"

"Nothing is enough for me," said Franz, and now the hard line of his jaw showed through his flesh, and his whole face took on a ruthless and rapacious look. Then, instantly, this look was gone, and he was bland and amiable again. "I ask you only to listen, father," he added.

But Hans was obsessed by his fear, and became excited. "What more can a man wish than a success which brings him comfort and security for himself and his children, and peace, and a garden? Once, when I was young, I, too, had dreams. But they were ridiculous. It is enough, when a man is old, that he has not failed."

"There is no failure except the fear of failure. No defeat except that of accepting too little, and compromising," said Franz. He regarded Hans with cold curiosity. "What is one man's success is another's failure. I have my visions. They are not only for myself, but my children. A man must remember that his children's dreams might be larger than his own. He owes them the duty of accomplishing all that he can accomplish, and showing them greater horizons. He must not build a smug pigpen and tell them that this is the world. At the end, they will know him as a liar. At the worst, they will believe him." He paused, then with merciless shrewdness, he went on: "I owe my children a duty. I intend to give them all that is in my power to give them."

Hans's fat and purplish face, with the bushy white mustaches and eyebrows, faltered, became uncertain, fearful, and confused. He thought of his two twin grandsons, Sigmund and Joseph, and his heart swelled with emotion. Perhaps Franz was right. Perhaps, he, Hans, was a doddering old man too fearful of change, too afraid of losing what he had already secured. But such a small success!

Franz, seeing his advantage, went on quickly:

"I intend that the Schmidt Steel Company shall become the greatest single company of its kind in America."

Hans was suddenly again frenzied, and again struck his desk a thudding and frantic blow. "But how? How? We are so small, even today. You are a fool!"

But Franz, triumphing, was not offended. He smiled easily.

"We will have to expand this mill. We will beg, borrow or steal the money. Take a mortgage on the mill, if necessary. Buy new machinery. I have heard of excellent new machinery, which trebles production. Sessions has patents on it. We will get permission, on a royalty basis, to use this machinery. When we are able to increase production, we will go out, secure new and larger accounts: the railroad companies, ship-building concerns, bridge companies. One of the men, in our name, is to patent his idea for steel-frame buildings. As yet, this is impracticable, but the day will come when steel will be used for this purpose. We must create a greater demand for steel products, in different forms. The possibilities are endless! We can present these ideas, upon which my metallurgists are already working, to financiers. I will go to New York, myself——!"

Hans's dusky forehead wrinkled and knotted like the forehead of an ape as he tried to follow these monstrous dreams. He was speechless. Franz's smooth voice went on, as gently flowing as thick rich cream:

"As soon as we can convince the financiers that we have a market for our products they will be only too glad to invest their money with us. Once we have opened their coffers, we will be able to buy up small competitors, bringing into their small mills our advanced methods, and they will be able to distribute our products to the localities where needed. Once we have eliminated the small and nagging competition—who knows?—we may even combine with Sessions Steel, or reach an understanding with them to divide the market, not only in America, but Canada and South America!"

"Are these your fine ideas?" demanded Hans, in a stifled voice in which he tried to inject contempt and ridicule.

Franz laughed deprecatingly, and said with great candor: "No. Not at all. For fifteen or twenty dollars a week, each, my despised metallurgists and inventors produce the most brilliant ideas! But let me go on, please.

"How we have neglected South America! Our thoughts, the thoughts of America, still turn homeward to Europe. Yet, to the south of us are the world's most stupendous virgin markets. Do you know who realizes this? The new Germany of Bismarck, of the Franco-Prussian War. Unless we are careful, within two decades Germany will have secured these markets. We must prevent her. We can prevent her, if we can convince South America that we can serve her better."

In Hans's stupefied silence (for Hans was blinking like a man forced to look directly at the dazzling noon-day sun), Franz withdrew a little black book from his pocket and elegantly thumbed through it. "For instance, large coal fields have recently been discovered around the Great Lakes. I have taken an option on them——"

"What!" roared Hans, coming violently to life. "With what?"

Franz smiled casually. "A deposit on an option, shall I say? With my own funds, saved from the very, very generous salary you have given me. I had no doubt, you observe, that you would take up the option, when you realized the tremendous advantages of owning our own coal mines, instead of buying our coal from Barbour-Bouchard, the English-French robbers and murderers!"

Hans ran a thick finger between his fat bull neck and his cravat. He appeared about to choke. He strove for sarcasm, and spoke hoarsely:

"And where will we get this money, may I ask, mein Herr?"

"I have told you. I will go to New York and see Joseph Bryan and Company, the bankers and investors. It would be useless to see Regan, who is involved with Barbour-Bouchard. But Bryan would like to cut Regan's throat. He is our man. If the worst comes to the worst, there is always a mortgage——"

"Mortgage!" screamed Hans, with real desperate fury this

time. His eyes started from his head as though he was being throttled. He leaned across the desk towards him, as if to spring. "I owe no man anything, and never shall!"

But Franz, dreaming pleasantly, tilted his chair, and went on: "Bryan will have to have some security, of course. I will tell him my plans for expansion, which are still somewhat nebulous at this moment, but will clear up eventually. We will have to form a corporation, and reorganize, and while you, father, retain control, we will give Bryan an interest in the mills, a certain number of shares."

"But this is *my* mill!" screamed Hans, the blood rushing thickly and darkly to his face. He beat his breast with his fists. "This is mine! No man shall have it, while I am alive, and no part of it! What is this mill to you? Have you given your blood and your sweat to it, as I have done? Have you built it piece by piece, with your raw hands, from a pile of rubbish, as I did? Every stone, every chimney, every furnace is mine. It belongs to me. Yet, you would dispose of it as though I were already in my grave, and rotting!"

Suddenly his face changed, worked, became grotesque and crumpled as though with dissolving and childish grief and sorrow. He was overpowered with bewilderment at the vision of a threat of something greater than himself, which was to crush him and his era of small, sweat-stained and passionately devoted little industrialists. He was appalled at the thought of sleek alien men in distant New York offices manipulating the industry which had grown out of the hands and toil and blood of men such as himself. And then he knew that these men were reaching out for such as he, with insatiable appetites, devouring. They had no love for industry, for labor, for work and personal ingenuity and individualism. He was horrified at the vision of them, elegantly clad, cold, precise, inhuman, in their velvet chairs around mahogany conference tables. He regarded them with repulsion and frantic terror, this distant implacable and powerful foe, and he felt their ominous shadow falling over him, and saw their mighty and spectral hands reaching out for all that he loved. It was unendurable. It was a lunatic's dementia coming true, but a giant dementia.

There would no longer be independence, where a man ruled his small industrial kingdom like a prince, and knew his own pride, his own courage, his own success. Hans had never loved America, but now he loved her, with a bursting passion and a new understanding, and a wild patriotism. America of strong little men like himself, proud, hard-working, planning, conquering, owing no man anything, wresting success like marble from mountains with their own hands! This was passing. He was not given to dreams and visions, this fat old peasant from Bavarian fields, but now he saw the vast Armageddon of men like himself, wrestling with dark monsters who must invariably win, and devour him. In the end, there would not be industry, but only an attenuated if voracious capitalism, which would extend like livid veins, full of poison, into all of industry owned by rugged little men. What would become of America then, caught up in a gigantic and involved web of capitalism, in which small men were bound like flies, and devoured? America had not been built by golden hands, cold, lifeless but greedy. It had been built by living hands such as his, torn, bleeding, brown, strong and indomitable. He, and his kind, had given their blood to America. But now it was all useless. Those who knew nothing of mills, of industry, of plants and machinery and men and toil and sweat, would some day control everything, regarding industry as a huge winepress, the wine of which they would drink, but would never stamp out the grapes themselves. It was horrible. It was not to be borne! The face of America would change. It would no longer be a human face, but a grimacing mask with open mouth and deadly eyes.

The dreadful majesty, terror and ghastliness of his vision stupefied him. He could only look at Franz, and whimper:

"You do not love the mills, the industry." He swallowed convulsively. "You do not love the growth by one's hands and brain and muscle. What is it you love?"

Franz had been watching him with careful curiosity. He had caught glimpses, in those old distracted eyes, of what Hans had seen. He said: "Money. Power. Profits. That is all." He smiled a little, contemptuously, understanding the grief and despair of the old man. "If we were selling bananas, it would be the same to me. The smoke of these chimneys that you love, father? It is nothing to me. It is a stench in my nostrils. It dirties my linen."

He watched Hans narrowly. He had used ruthlessness lavishly. Now, he would either fail forever, or win. It was necessary to show his cards, for time was growing short.

Hans fluttered his fingers in the air, and struggled, as though he was drowning. He cried out: "You cannot do these things! You are a dreamer, a builder of fantasies! A madman. I shall not let you take even the first step——"

And then he knew he was defeated, not by Franz, but by a legion of others like him. His hands dropped heavily to his desk. He swallowed convulsively.

"If you do not let me do this, we shall be ruined," said Franz, quietly. He leaned across the desk, and fixed the old man with his inexorable and merciless eyes. "Do you hear? Ruined. You, and I, and your grandchildren."

Hans tried for a last victory, and again he whimpered: "But, we have so little money——"

Franz rose. He was shaking internally. He had won. He had triumphed! For a moment he was dizzy. His lips opened, tightened over his teeth.

"We have enough. We still have time. Money will buy the imagination I lack to accomplish these things. The manipulator does not need brains. He can buy them. I have already bought them for fifteen or twenty dollars a week."

He stood up. He glanced at his watch, every movement easy and controlled, though he was still internally trembling.

"It is time for our noonday meal. The carriage will here any moment. Shall we go?"

Hans rose heavily to his feet. He had to grasp the edge of his desk suddenly to support himself. He leaned across the desk and regarded Franz with a long, fierce, defeated look. "How long have you been plotting these things?"

"For years," smiled Franz. "For always."

CHAPTER 6

MRS. SCHMIDT was dying. The only one in the household who did not realize this was Ernestine, and her father and husband and brother wished to spare the little dark creature this painful knowledge. "When the summer comes," she would say, anxiously, "and Mama can resume her drives, she will be so much better." They reassured her that this was so. There was more impatience and disgust in Franz's reassurance than affection. All his life he had been accustomed to women who were strong, who looked at all things with calm level eyes, who had deep courage. Hans's and Baldur's tenderness for Ernestine, and their desire to spare her pain, annoyed him. She was no child. She was a woman in her thirties, with two children. Yet her father and brother regarded her as something too frail and delicate for the harshness of life. Absurd! Sometimes he longed, brutally, to look into those wide gray eyes and say, without preliminary gentleness: "Your mother is dying. Shortly, she will be dead."

Buried in his desire was his brutality and sadism. When he contemplated saying this thing to her, he felt an obscure pleasure. She would turn deathly pale. She would tremble. She would cry out, suffering unbearably. She might even collapse. He smiled at this to himself. Even he did not know how much he hated her. He thought she merely made him impatient, and annoyed him with her vapors, light fluting voice, childishness, innocence and ingenuousness. He knew she loved him with a kind of unreasoning adoration, and fear. This, too, vaguely infuriated him, though he realized the advantages to himself. Therefore, in Hans's presence, and even in his absence, he was everything that was kind and amiable to Ernestine. Let him once abuse, or overly frighten her, and Hans would turn on him like a savage boar, and destroy him. Sometimes he contemplated the thought of Hans's death with more than just the pleasure of an heir. He would then be free to neglect Ernestine, or even to abuse her, if he desired. It was the restraint of Hans's presence which goaded him.

He had never, even at the first, liked Ernestine. She was cloying to him, unhealthy, frail of flesh, too delicate, too timid. He said to himself that she was not a woman. Somewhere in her life, her body had stopped growing. Perhaps in early adolescence. But, too, her mind and soul had stopped growing.

He had often told himself that he liked small dark women. But these women must be quick and vivacious, with naughty slanting eyes full of mischief and promise, and bodies alive and avid. There was nothing avid in Ernestine. She submitted to him in mingled fear, dread and adoration and shame. That was all. There was no passion in her, no blood, though he had soon discovered that she could, at times, be hard and a little imperious. But never to him. To him, she was all softness, tremor, anxiety, and love. If he could once arouse her to anger against him, to complaint or annoyance, he might dislike her less. But he could never so arouse her. Let him be distrait, cold or indifferent, and she literally contorted herself in a fever of anxiety to please and placate. There was no fault in him, to her. If he were annoyed, it was all her fault! She had failed him somewhere.

Hans believed that nothing but the firmest affection was between these two. This was the result of Franz's unfailing gentleness, courtesy and kindness to his wife, a habit which he had cultivated for Hans's benefit, and so strong was the force of habit, that he, most of the time, exercised it when alone with Ernestine. But he had never deceived Baldur, whom he hated virulently, and with secret fear.

He knew he did not deceive this silent, smiling and derisive cripple. Part of his hatred was because there lived another heir to what he coveted. And the rest was because Baldur revolted him, and understood him completely. He also knew that Baldur had set himself like a sentinel to guard his sister's life while she visited in the camp of the enemy. Franz knew that Baldur was aware that an enemy had come into this house, and that he must practice eternal vigilance. So long as Baldur lived, even if Hans died, there would be this indomitable sentinel, watching, guarding.

I am a prisoner, Franz would think gloomily. A prisoner to a fool of an old man, and a poisonous cripple. A prisoner in this abominable house. He almost always forgot the presence of the sick and dying old woman upstairs in her luxurious fetid rooms. When he did remember that presence, it was with loathing, almost with nausea. Sometimes he thought himself penned in a house of pestilence and dark shadows and sickening smells. And great danger. Between himself and Matilda there was a healthy and chuckling understanding. He had soon become aware that Matilda, like himself, hated and despised the occupants of this somber and hideous mansion.

He rarely thought of his sons, Sigmund and Joseph, except as stronger holds he had on Hans Schmidt, who worshipped them fatuously, and with senility. Ah, let the evil cripple gloat and watch now! he had thought, when the children had been born. Hans's terrible anxiety and fear during the months of Ernestine's pregnancy, and the sudden sinking whiteness of his old face when they were born, seemed exaggerated to Franz, who did not know the hidden terror that had haunted the old man that these children might be maimed. Everyone in the house had carefully kept from him the defect in the blood of the Bradhursts. He thought that Hans was fearing that the little ones might be girls. He still did not understand when Hans exclaimed, with breaking hysteria: "Ah, they are perfect, these darlings, these angels! You have given them good bodies and good limbs, my son! It is the German blood."

Franz supposed, indifferently, that his children resembled all others, noisy, screaming brats and nuisances. Towards the sons of his flesh he felt nothing of the ancient Teutonic fondness for children. They hardly seemed his own. They were Ernestine's. They were small, thin and dark, and whining. One, Joseph, whined the most, and was peevish, also, and selfishly demanding, though he was not yet two years old. The other, Sigmund, named after Hans's father, was quieter, and sicklier, and appeared docile except for the rare and puzzling intervals when he was suddenly violent and uncontrollable. It was soon evident that Sigmund would be the taller, and the quieter, and the more reasonable, for all the infrequent rages. Franz felt a vague dislike for this child, who had Baldur's large blue eyes in his little dark, triangular face, and strange long quietnesses. Too, Sigmund was not the favorite of either Ernestine or Hans. They preferred the noisy and petulant Joseph, who demanded everything, and was alternately impudent and mischievous, grinning or quarrelsome. Hans fondly called him "the little princeling," for he had imperious ways and contriving slynesses. He, too, had blue eyes, but they were narrow and cunning, and glittering with precocious intelligence. Sigmund was his Uncle Baldur's favorite, and during the day he would find ways to elude his nursemaid and slip into Baldur's rooms. There he would sit quietly for hours, watching Baldur paint, and listen uncomprehendingly to Baldur's long, gentle monologues.

But in some way he discerned something beneath the ironic subleties in his uncle's voice, and he would smile, strangely and mysteriously, and with a little wildness. Seeing this smile, Baldur would be taken aback for a moment, then, after a catch at his heart, he would seize the child in his arms and hug him convulsively. "We understand each other, little one!" he would exclaim, and would laugh.

When Ernestine or the nursemaid would find him, and would seek to take him away for his nap or his walk, he would burst out into screaming cries and tears, and would fight impotently but wildly. To the last, as they carried him away, he would look over his shoulder at Baldur, despairingly.

But Joseph, even in his babyhood, frankly detested Baldur. He had the gift of mimicry, and to Franz's delight, he would strut before his father and mother, limping, his tiny shoulders bent and hunched. Ernestine was not delighted. But when she heard Franz's laughter, she would smile a foolish, forgiving smile, reprimand the child halfheartedly, and send him away. "Really, Franz, you are encouraging him to be cruel," she would say, in a fond, admonishing tone, with its undertone of fear that perhaps she was offending him.

"Nonsense," Franz would say, vigorously. "He is just a clever rascal. You cannot expect children to be hypocrites."

Slowly, day by day, he was deftly loosening the threads of Ernestine's affection for her brother. Some day, he hoped, she would regard him with increasing impatience and indifference. Another danger, then, would be removed.

The children very seldom saw their grandmother. Joseph would protest noisily, when dragged to her door. But Sigmund would enter silently, and stand by her bed, gazing at her, submitting to her feverish touch and hot dry kisses. Joseph would fight her off.

From the very first, the children had no liking for each other. Sigmund would not fight his more vigorous and cunning brother. He would only cry, which Franz found contemptible. He submitted to Joseph's sly and secret bullying, in silence. He avoided his twin, and always tried to escape him. He would hide in corners, and even retreat for hours under beds and divans. He knew, small as he was, that his mother loved him dearly but was impatient with his silences and escapes. He knew that his father was indifferent to him. He knew that only in Baldur, with his music and his beautiful pictures, was his refuge and his peace. He, only, perhaps, knew the evil inherent in his twin, and it horrified and stupefied him, little and inexperienced though he was. Joseph frightened him excessively, but this was less because he was kept in a state of apprehension for fear of his twin's malice and cruelty; rather it was because of what Joseph was. The children resembled each other closely, for they were identical twins, but no one familiar with them, even slightly, ever mistook them. There was a large, serious, dreamlike and shrinking quality about Sigmund, whereas Joseph had a sly, knowing expression and an impish wrinkling of his face when he smiled.

Franz might have remained indulgently indifferent of Sigmund, continuing, all the child's life, his usual bantering and impatient way with him, had it not been for an incident, small in itself, which made Franz actively dislike his son. Only one person had been able to understand Franz, and that had been Irmgard, and only this one could so understand him and increase his original affection. But those who even vaguely approached a complete understanding aroused his self-protectiveness, his hatred, his anger. And his deep subterranean fear, and enmity. Baldur was such a one. And now, one day, little Sigmund became another.

Never, from the very beginning, had Baldur invited his brother-in-law to enter his own rooms. The door was always carefully shut, and sometimes even locked. Franz, amused, began to feel a tantalizing desire to see those rooms, and inspect them impertinently. "He must have a captive princess there," he would say to Ernestine, and burst into a laugh at the incongruous idea. Ernestine, annoyed with her brother for his discourtesy to her adored husband, wound murmur deprecatingly: "He is so shy, and reserved. Even Mama has been in there only a few times. It is his retreat."

"A toad's retreat," Franz would say, brutishly. Ernestine's sensitive heart was wounded at both this remark, and Baldur's aloofness, but characteristically, her final impatience was for Baldur, whom she hardly seemed to understand these days. From the first, Baldur's quiet, elaborate and almost ironic courtesy towards Franz offended her. She saw something mocking in his smile, and his long level look. It was soon evident, to her, that Franz felt both dislike and irritability for Baldur, and she tried to find justification, in her infatuation, for this attitude. She soon, to her own satisfaction at least, found it. Baldur seemed genial enough, it is true, and politely attentive to Fránz and even largely amiable, but, as she said to herself, "his spirit is not really in it, and it is so annoying and perplexing of Baldur." So, finally, a cool estrangement grew up between brother and sister, which was exactly what Franz desired, and had adroitly arranged. He found frequent occasion to complain with a smile to his doting little wife: "God knows, I would like to be friends with your brother. I never had a brother, and a companion would be very agreeable. What have I done to him, my love? Why does he not invite me for conversation in his room? Am I a pariah?"

Ernestine's absorbed love rushed feverishly to defend her husband against an attitude of her brother's which appeared to her to grow increasingly reserved, and even politely contemptuous. Once she said to Baldur: "What have you against Franz? He would so like to be friendly with you. Why don't you ask him into your rooms some evening? He is so hurt."

Then it was that she saw that rare pointed spark in Baldur's blue eyes, and even though he smiled humorously the spark had in it a strange menace.

"Nothing, Tina, will ever hurt him. He needs no protection. It is others who need protection from him. I shall never ask him to visit me. I must have some retreat, some shelter."

From that day on, the coolness between brother and sister became actual coldness.

Franz, however, had determined to enter those rooms some day, less from curiosity, than from a desire to annoy Baldur, and make him impotent. He plotted to force his way in, if necessary, and thus triumph over the crippled man.

One day Mrs. Schmidt had one of her prolonged sinking attacks, and Ernestine and her brother were hastily called by her nurse. Franz went with his wife to the door of her mother's room, supporting her small shaking body, and he saw Baldur hastily leaving his own apartment. Baldur took Ernestine's hand and led her into their mother's room. His own door stood partially open. Franz saw this. His eyes brightened maliciously. He waited until the door had closed behind Baldur and his sister, and after only an instant's hestitation, he went quickly and silently down the hall, and entered the mysterious apartment, chuckling a little to himself. It was his intention to allow Baldur to discover him there. It would be very amusing.

The wide quietness and austerity of the silent apartment at first disconcerted him. Then his taste was pleased. The rooms were in cold semi-dusk, and he impudently flung aside the long velvet drapes. The spring sunshine gushed in. On an easel near the immense north window was a half-finished portrait of little Sigmund The child's great blue eyes, intent and mournful, looked back at him. Only the eyes were complete; the rest of the small face was still only sketched in. But the eyes were vivid and alive, and seemed to condemn him.

"Bah," he said, aloud, and turned away, vaguely ashamed. Nevertheless, he felt some pride that Baldur was so excellent an artist. It seemed to confer distinction on himself. Then, too, the German affection for the true craftsman, the true genius, was both touched into respect and pleasure. Like most Germans, he found real aristocracy only in those who were endowed by nature with natural refinement or great talent. He began to wander about the room, studying each hung canvas or small portrait, and his pleasure grew. "I must have one or two of these for myself," he thought, and his animosity for Baldur grew into a reluctant regard. He forgot the crippled body, the polite enmity, the turning-aside, the cold derisive smile. He even forgot the understanding, or, he thought it admirable and consistent that so fine an artist as Baldur understood him.

Before he completed his circuit, however, he came upon the immense grand piano, shining in itself, and standing in its polished reflection on the bare floor. Now his face darkened somewhat. He put his hands on the white keys, and there grew up a slow distressing pain in him. It had been so long since he had played. Echoes of mighty music rushed into his mind, the music he had played, himself, and he felt a mysterious nostalgia. Only a few times had he heard Baldur play, and that was softly, behind those hateful closed doors. He said to himself: "That is really why I had wanted to enter here!" And it was partly true.

With his hands still silently and impotently on the keys, he thought, suddenly, with a strange weak sickness: What am I doing here, in this house? Am I still Franz Stoessel? What is all this to me? And the piano seemed to breathe and listen to his thoughts, understanding them. Now the pain became dark and diffused, like old remembered grief.

He stood up, and uttered a loud Teuton curse, which was partly at himself for his folly in indulging in these thoughts, and experiencing this grief. Feeling better, and smiling a little, he flicked the keys derisively with his fingers, and walked away. He began to complete his inspection of Baldur's pictures.

The spring sunlight now quickened, brightened, flooded the rooms. There was one last portrait. He came upon it, utterly unprepared. He found himself looking at Irmgard's face, close to his. For one instant he cried out, then was silent, staring, paling.

The quiet green eyes, so remote and cool and living, gazed back at him. There was a light on the golden shining hair, a finger of light in the hollow of her throat. It was not paint, this portrait. It was translucent flesh. The rosy mouth, so firm, so contemplative, so still, only faintly smiled, and now it seemed to him that there was bitterness in the corners, and memory.

The stunning shock of his recognition slowly passed, like the shock of a profound physical blow. Now through its retreating anesthesia came the familiar monstrous anguish which he thought he had conquered in this last year, the familiar twisting torment and unbearable hunger. He bent a little, like a man who feels cold steel in his bowels, and doubles up instinctively to stop the gushing blood and alleviate the agony. Now his flesh turned to aching fire, and there was a hollow in him, as if his heart had been wrenched forcibly from his body, and he still lived, bereft, dying. He put out his hand, blindly, and supported himself by the back of a tall carved chair. His eye-sockets burned, as at too close an approach to flame. His nostrils distended. He said aloud, almost with a cry: "Irmgard, Irmgard."

He thought to himself: There is nothing for me, without her. I have got to find her. Nothing shall stop me now.

The hunger increased in him, and the overwhelming sorrow. He put his hand to his head. His sense of being an alien, an intruder, in this house filled him with a slow hating rage. He did not belong here. He was still Franz Stoessel. Irmgard was still a part of him. This house would make him something he was not, removed from all vigor, all beauty, all splendor, all desire. Irmgard's face was an open door, wide to escape.

Then he heard a faint sound. He swung about. Deep in the recesses of a large velvet chair was little Sigmund. The child did not wriggle, did not move. But he regarded his father with profound gravity and quiet, as if he understood. Usually, he looked at Franz with shy fear, and retreated. But now there was no fear, only prolonged contemplation.

Franz was slightly stunned for a few moments. Then, suddenly, devastatingly, he was enraged. He could not endure those grave childish eyes, so mature, so understanding. He was filled with a savage hatred. He came to the child in three quick steps. He caught him up, and set him on the floor so abruptly that little Sigmund staggered. Then he struck the small face violently, and it was as if he struck himself.

"Little swine!" he muttered, through his teeth. "Spying on me!"

The child did not cry out, though one cheek became purplish red. He usually cried even at a slight rough word of disapproval. But now he only stared at his father, his eyes widening, repudiating the man, disdainful of him. Franz lifted his hand. He would have struck that proud little face again, had he not heard Baldur entering quickly.

Baldur's face was white and drained from the past anxiety he had been suffering for his mother. But his eyes were blue fire, blazing harshly. Franz flushed. His hand dropped to his side. He tried to smile, to speak jocularly:

"I know you don't want any one to enter here. I passed your door, and saw this impertinent little brat. I came to take him out, and gave him a slap to teach him better manners."

Baldur did not speak. He turned to Sigmund. He put his hand on the small dark head. Suddenly the little one, without a cry or a word, convulsively embraced his uncle's legs, and buried his head against Baldur's side. That gesture told Baldur everything he needed to know. He looked at Franz, with open anger and deep contempt, and his arm went about the child protectingly. He felt the trembling of the small body, the loathing, the fear. Deep within Baldur's large strained eyes the spark grew, brightened, became vivid and dangerous.

"Sigmund comes in here frequently. I am painting him." He paused. The spark quickened into a cold flame.

Franz shrugged, easily. "Then, I am at fault, it seems. I am sorry." He reached out and pulled Sigmund away from Baldur, gave him a humorous tap. "Run away, little one. It is time for your sleep."

The child literally flung himself out of the room. Baldur watched him go with a curiously sorrowful expression. His lips tightened to a pale tense line.

Franz, very uncomfortable, tried to put himself at ease. He smiled at Baldur, who did not return the smile.

"I have a bad temper," he said, disarmingly.

Baldur turned half away. "Don't brag," he said, quietly. He went to his easel, and stood there, looking down at Sigmund's face. There was dismissal in his air. Franz sensed the dismissal. He was infuriated at what he termed this impudence and gentlemanly contempt. He followed Baldur, still smiling.

"You are a great artist," he said. "You have concealed yourself."

Baldur was silent. He turned the portrait on the easel. Now he looked at Franz steadfastly.

Franz included the room with a wave of his hand. "I have been looking at your work. You have no right to hide it."

Baldur's mouth relaxed in a slight frosty smile. "Who has a right to it?" he asked.

Franz felt his disdain of him. "Every one," he said, largely. All at once he wanted this great artist to think better of him, to listen to him without that polite scorn. "I know something—of this. I am not only what you think me, an opportunist——"

"I have thought nothing of you at all," said Baldur, quietly, and with unaffected indifference.

But Franz would not be turned aside. He laughed a little. "I, too, used to play. I was once a considerable musician. When we were in Paris, my parents took me to the opera, to the museums, to the Louvre. Once I thought of painting, also." He assumed a humorous, self-deprecating air. "We Germans appreciate all art. We are a nation of artists. We love all that is beautiful, and are lavish with honors for those endowed——"

Baldur said nothing. He still regarded Franz levelly. But, despite himself, there grew in him a faint compassion for this handsome lusty man, so greedy, so rapacious, who had not yet completely murdered his inheritance and could still feel an eager wistfulness for it. He was touched by Franz's adulation, and this seemed deserving of pity. He saw, startled, that Franz, at rare moments like this, might despise himself, might have contempt for all the things he seized so ruthlessly. He felt his first kindness for his sister's husband.

"Some day," he said, "I shall ask you to play for me."

Franz was surprised at this kindliness, and almost humbly touched. "I have not played for years," he replied.

There was a little silence. Baldur was dismissing him again, he discerned, though the spark had gone from his eyes and he was smiling gently. Franz did not want to leave these rooms. They drew him, held him. In some confusion, he looked away, and once more he encountered Irmgard's portrait, watching so intently from the wall. He paled again, forgot Baldur. He lifted his hand and pointed.

"That portrait—" he said, in a stifled voice.

"Ah," murmured Baldur, and there was some annoyance in his tone. He pulled the draperies close about the windows with a quick gesture, and the great room was plunged into gloom. "It is nothing. It is a portrait of my mother's maid.

The girl, Irmgard, about whom Ernestine has told you before. She left very suddenly, without explanation, as you know. She was very beautiful."

Something in his voice struck through Franz's sick preoccupation. He swung about, and confronted the other man. For an instant there was a swift wolfish gleam of teeth against his suddenly drawn lips. "Yes," he said slowly, watching Baldur, "she was very beautiful, it seems."

But Baldur had forgotten him. He approached the portrait and stood below it, his eyes lifted with deep sadness to the painted face. He appeared to have fallen into a sorrowful and withdrawn meditation. He seemed to be speaking silently, addressing the portrait. Franz saw his sadness, his preoccupation, the look of lostness about his mouth and eye-sockets. He might have been looking at a dead face, and remembering.

Then Franz was filled with fury and outrage and animal jealousy. How dared this monster, this distorted parody of a man, look at Irmgard like this! His fists clenched, and his face swelled murderously, coloring. It was this look, this attitude, which Baldur confronted when he turned from the portrait.

He was both appalled and astonished. He watched Franz visibly relaxing. He saw him struggling to smile. His astonishment grew, and he could not prevent himself from exclaiming: "You knew her!"

It was not possible! Yet those eyes, that look, on Franz's face, so revealing!

Franz smiled with difficulty. Baldur saw the moist gleam on his forehead. "No," said Franz, deliberately. "I never saw her before."

But Baldur, more and more astonished, looked from the living face of the man to the painted face of the girl. He was incredulous. Strange that he had never noticed it before, the resemblance between these two! It was a flesh resemblance never to be denied. Baldur's brows drew together, wrinkled. Some faint memory of something Irmgard had said began to tantalize him, sharply. He could not recall it, but it remained, like a dim nagging pain. He stared closely at the portrait, as if to find the answer there. The mouth, the nose, the wide forehead, the modelling of cheek and chin, and attitude of head! They were all there. It was not to be denied. Baldur's heart began to beat quickly, with a curious sinking excitement. He turned back to Franz and studied him thoughtfully. And now he saw that the other man was coloring with guilty painfulness.

"She had much character," said Baldur, slowly, deliberately. "We missed her very much, when she left." He watched

Franz closely. He discovered, without much surprise, that Franz was also watching him as closely, with a savage eagerness.

Again, he was not too surprised when Franz said, quickly: "You know where she is? You have found her?"

Baldur did not reply for a moment. He was too engrossed by the betraying expression on Franz's face, the tenseness. Because of his disability, his sensibility, he had learned to read expressions, even the more subtle, in self-defense. He read much, now. A cool warning thrill ran through him.

He said, slowly: "No. I do not know where she is. I have not seen her since she left."

Once more, he was not astonished at the sudden darkening of Franz's eyes, the sudden misery and passionate disappointment. He watched Franz, forgetting him, move to the door, reluctantly. He saw, to the last, that Franz looked at the portrait, and that his expression was that of a hungry beast.

When he was alone, Baldur turned back to the portrait, frowning. Perhaps he was wrong. Perhaps Franz, being the healthy animal that he was, had only been lustfully hungry and aroused at this girl's beautiful cold face. But there was the resemblance. Of course, these two were both Germans. It was probably only a racial resemblance.

Baldur rubbed his forehead. Then suddenly he remembered the remark he had been trying to recall. He remembered that Irmgard had once remarked that she had, in Nazareth, an aunt, an uncle, and a cousin. She had been reticent at Baldur's polite inquiries, and had changed the subject. He remembered that she had blushed a little, uneasily. She had admitted that the cousin was a man, and that he worked somewhere in some factory. Then she had said that she was tired, and must return to Mrs. Schmidt who no doubt had awakened. The whole insignificant incident had then passed from Baldur's memory, and he had not thought of it again.

Now the blood rushed violently to his head, and his pulses roared. It was fantastic! He was too imaginative, like all recluses. He was too given to romancing, to fabricating, to dreaming! It was not possible. He was a fool.

He turned with a sudden wild resolution. Since Irmgard had left, she had steadfastly refused to see him, though she wrote him once a month, now, still, after these four years. She promised to see him some day, but was vague about the day.

He almost ran from the room, fastening on his cape, catching up his hat. He called for a carriage.

CHAPTER 7

BALDUR WAS hardly out of the little city when he became aware that he was going on a foolish and fantastic errand. He remembered, suddenly, that he had always written to Irmgard addressing her as "Mrs. Darmstadter." He had assumed that this was the name of her relatives, and that by addressing her so at the farm in that remote farming district, his letters would have a better chance with the erratic mail delivery in the rustic regions. Of course, there was a possibility that "Mrs. Darmstadter" was another relative, but he remembered distinctly that she had said she had only these three relatives in America. There was still another possibility, and this gave him some slight hope: that "Mrs. Darmstadter" was indeed Franz's mother, but that she had remarried a "Darmstadter."

Then he forgot, partially, this part of his errand, and began to feel a great quickening at the thought of seeing Irmgard again. For nearly four years, he had tried to invent an adequate excuse for invading her strict privacy, and ignoring her pleas that he not try to see her "yet." He now had this excuse, however impertinent or fantastic. Should he approach her seriously, or lightly? He became involved in the matter of the adequate approach. Then he became aware that he was sitting excitedly on the edge of the plush seat of the carriage, and that his lips were dry and his breath quick. He looked through the polished windows, and it seemed to him that the opening countryside was taking on a sharp brilliance and significance.

Unlikely many recluses, he was not fond of the country. Some delicate, or decadent, timidity in him repudiated largeness, open spaces, strangenesses and enormous winds. In such surroundings, he felt exposed, vulnerable to attack. Four close walls and shut windows and barred doors gave him the only sense of security he could know, the only safety. His nature made him a "cave-dweller," he would say to himself. In his "cave," he could deceive himself that the world was small and compact, cleared of danger. In darkness, he could hide, and be hidden from menacing eyes.

But now, because of his new excitement, he felt no strangeness, no danger, in this unfamiliar wide country. He could look at it with a detached and surprised and appreciative eye. I have missed much, he thought. He considered that here was a beauty he might paint. Heretofore, in his absorption with the faces of others, he had painted only portraits. A man paints what interests him most, he knew. His infirmity had caused him to scan other faces with anxious and suspicious interest, until every shade of thought could be discerned by him. He looked at the countryside, now, with the eye of a bemused and startled stranger.

It was late spring, and late afternoon, and a Sunday. The fields were empty of plowmen and farmers, but here and there a mute plow stood, waiting, in seas of fixed brown earth. He saw few houses, and these were buried in new masses of thick bright green trees. He saw splashes of hollyhocks against walls and white fences, and the ruddy round silos and roofs of red barns stood in light against ineffably blue skies. In the distance, drifted the pale purple smoke of far hills. And over all the country ran tides of blue, translucent shadow, clarified and cool. He passed meadows of brilliant green, in which cattle stood kneehigh in lush grass, lifting their brown and white heads in curiosity at the sound of the carriage. Long leaf-shadows fretted the dusty road, and birds sang long liquid trills in the trees. He had never seen nor heard such lofty and contented peace, untroubled and unconcerned. He wondered if the men who lived here were removed from the hot fever of living which infected the cities, or, if they too, were suffering from the miserable disease of living. When he passed the Amish cemetery, and saw the stones leaning, shining, against the sky, he felt no melancholy, but only peace. Nothing, he thought, was quite so melancholy, so somber, as city cemeteries, grimed, drooping, dirty, separated only from life by a wall or an iron fence. Even in death, in such a place, there was no escape. Not to have an escape, was what made life so intolerable. Surely, if there was a God, He would have, in His compassion, allowed man brief escapes into death, to relieve them of the monstrous prison-house of living.

He smiled whimsically to himself. Perhaps there were such escapes into death and darkness, before the torment of living must proceed again. I am getting fanciful, he thought. If I lived here, I might soon burst out into "Gloria in Excelsis Deo!"

The carriage was turning into a narrow but smooth brown road, and Baldur saw before him a snug red-brick house surrounded by white picket fences overgrown with hollyhocks. He smiled in appreciation, and his excitement grew. In a few moments, now, he would see Irmgard! It was not possible. She had become a remote, cold and lovely dream, which he had dreamed within his dark walls. She was no reality at all. Yet, reality stood waiting before him now. He could hardly contain himself. He was on the edge of his seat, gripping the folds of his cloak, long moments before the carriage stopped before a white door embellished by a shining brass knocker.

Then, though the coachman opened the carriage door, he found he could not move for weakness. He was taken by a peculiar fright. He wanted to order the coachman to turn about, and drive the carriage away, with himself huddled and hiding on the seat. He thought to himself that this was an impudent and inexcusable intrusion, that he was like an exigent man bursting into the bedroom of some strange woman. It was impertinent! But beneath this thought was his fear of seeing Irmgard again, of dissipating the bright cold dream, which, like the moon at its full, had lighted the darkness and creeping shadows of his life. Mingled with this was a powerful and mournful yearning to hear her voice again, and an aching sorrow.

The coachman stared at him curiously. He was a young man, new to this employment, and had never seen Irmgard in the Schmidt house. He wondered, with some contempt, what this miserable cripple was doing in this remote countryside, and he sensed his excitement and fear. He saw the moisture on the thin white face, and the distended sockets of the strained eyes.

Then, shaking visibly, Baldur stepped slowly and painfully from the carriage. He saw, in his confusion, that a tall bony woman had come to the door, and was standing there. He had never seen her before, but instantly, as he saw her, all his doubts vanished. She was a woman, and aging, but he saw Franz's own lineaments there, and he was sure. He was surprised, however, to see that in some way she recognized him, and that she was visibly agitated. She stepped out upon the white doorstep, and closed the door tightly behind her. She waited for him to approach, now her lips were drawn grimly together.

He removed his broad black hat, and tried to smile, as he came up the walk.

"Mrs. Darmstadter?" he murmured, politely, giving his sad parody of a bow.

The woman's lips parted hastily, as though she would deny something, then remained open, silent. Her pale eyes fixed themselves on him, inimically. Then, after a prolonged moment, she said harshly, in her strongly accented voice:

"What is it you wish? Please."

He saw that she was very frightened, and alarmed. She kept glancing at the waiting carriage. He did not know what it was that made him say quickly: "I am quite alone."

She relaxed, and her expression became less inimical. But it was no less cold and harsh.

"You wish to see some one?" she asked.

He bowed again. "I am Mr. Schmidt," and paused.

She was not surprised. She merely stared at him, still waiting, still unbending.

Then he said, boldly: "I should like to see Irmgard, if I may."

There was a prolonged silence, while they gazed at each other steadfastly. A strong look of dislike deepened on the woman's face, and with it, fear. He studied her with calm curiosity, and with his own personal dislike, because of her uncanny resemblance to Franz Stoessel. There were the same hard eyes, the same line of harsh jaw and flat but wide cheek-planes, the same look of implacability and strength. But in this woman's face, he saw that there was no craft, no cruelty, and his dislike lessened. He smiled at her encouragingly.

"Please believe me, I am her friend," he said, gently. "She must have spoken of me to you. We have corresponded frequently." He spoke in German, and the rigidity of her expression slowly relaxed. "She is not expecting me, but I have something of importance to say to her. I should not have come, but for this."

And now he saw an intense expression of anxiety appear in her eyes. She took a step towards him. He saw that she desperately wanted to ask him a question, but dared not. But her eyes searched his face hungrily, pathetically. He became quite bold now, and said, clearly: "No, there is nothing wrong with Franz."

He watched her closely, as he said this. He saw her face clear of its great pain and anxiety, and become almost flabby in its relief. He heard her draw a deep breath. Then, quite suddenly, she was angry, and her eyes flashed.

"Then, she lied to me? She told you?" Her voice was loud, unrestrained.

Baldur lifted his eyebrows. "Irmgard told me nothing," he replied, with conciliation. "It was just this morning that I guessed. I have a portrait of Irmgard, which I painted. Franz saw it for the first time this morning, and I immediately saw the resemblance between them. Also, he betrayed himself by his eagerness, and his questioning of me."

A curious change passed over the woman's face, as though her thoughts were deeply agitated and disturbed. He saw anger, contempt, longing, uncertainty, in that change. Then she recovered herself with visible effort. She said: "I think it best that you go, Herr Schmidt. If Irmgard did not ask you to come, she will be very annoyed."

"Nevertheless, I will see her," he answered in a firm hard voice, and she saw, for the first time, that the large melancholy eyes, which she had thought too feminine in their blue gentleness, had become as smooth and cold as blue stone. She was both angered and abashed by them, and looked away with anxious sullenness. Then another thought must have occurred to her, and she looked at him quickly, with real if furtive alarm.

"I cannot prevent you from seeing her, mein Herr. But I strongly advise against it. It will embarrass her, believe me. I cannot tell you why, but it is so. You will do her a great harm, and distress her. You say you are her friend. If you are, you will go at once."

Her perturbation was sincere, he discerned, and he frowned a little. However, he said: "I cannot believe that the sight of me will embarrass Irmgard. I must see her."

She was silent, regarding him piercingly. She told herself, reluctantly, that Irmgard had not exaggerated when she had told her of this man. There was no viciousness in him, though there could be a coldness and a danger. She saw that he was kind and even noble, and firmly obstinate. She sighed, shrugged.

"Then, there is nothing I can do, Herr Schmidt. You will understand, however, why I have prevented you from seeing her. You will wait here while I call her? She is in the garden."

He smiled. "No, do not call her. I will go to her myself."

He bowed politely, and started away towards the rear of the house. He heard her quick footsteps behind him, and felt her pluck his sleeve. He turned and looked inquiringly up into her face. Her features were working, and her eyes were dim.

"Forgive me," she murmured. "But I must ask you. Franz? He is happy?"

He was filled with pity, and said gently: "Franz will always have what he wants. That is his happiness."

Her pale thin mouth trembled, and her look was sharp and urgent.

"Those are only words. He is happy? Please? He loves his wife? His children? They are my grandsons——"

Baldur was much moved, and he felt a deep anger and contempt for Franz.

"My sister loves him very much, Frau Stoessel. She lives only for him. Franz—is very amiable to her. The children are healthy. But Sigmund is my favorite. A lovely child. One of these days I shall bring him to see you." He paused. "I think he is what you would have your son be."

She smiled, and he was hurt by that smile. She wrung her hands in her apron. "Sigmund," she murmured. "He is good? He is talented? He is a dear child?"

"Yes, yes," he said, and he touched the clutching fingers on his arm. "But do not think Joseph is lacking. He is a very lively child, and intelligent. You will love them both very much."

He left her then. Her pale withering face was radiant. His anger against Franz increased, until there was a throbbing pain in his temples. That foul man! That smiling handsome swine! Baldur saw that no virtue was needed to attract love. "A man may smile and smile, and be a villain," he quoted to himself. Those who were evil, selfish, cruel, brutal and greedy seemed to have some magic in them which inspired adoration, while the worthy, the pure, the good and the kind apparently attracted only enemies. There was some flaw in human nature——

He came to the rear of the house, and stood still a moment, looking at the view beyond. A valley dipped below him, rimmed in the far purple haze of hills. The trees in the valley floated in a radiant mist, crowned with misty light. He saw distant fields, green as jewels, and the pewter glint of a winding river. He heard sleepy sounds from the barnyard, the drowsy clucking of fowl. The sun was a cataract of light. He saw white fences about the garden, heavy with rambler roses. He smelled the damp fecund earth, and the exhalations of growing things. In one corner of the large garden a young woman was kneeling, and beside her knelt a child, gravely and solemnly handing her trowels and bulbs and small plants. They were murmuring together in deep confidence. Baldur saw the sunlight on her smooth pale hair, and on her large strong shoulders. The child's yellow head was like a daffodil.

It was the little boy who saw him first, and he lifted his head and turned his face to Baldur with startled shyness. Baldur halted a moment, and tightened his lips. So, he thought, that is it. I understand, now.

The child touched his mother, and Irmgard turned her head sharply. For a long moment the man and woman regarded each other in a strange prolonged silence. Baldur could see her face clearly. He saw that it was an older face, and a gentler, and somewhat worn. Those serene, cool green eyes had softened, become almost sweet and tender, and there was a shadow in them as of great old pain. The large rosy mouth he remembered had become tighter, thinner, as though compressed to restrain weeping and the sound of suffering. She was thinner, yet, as she slowly rose to her feet, he saw that the heroic and majestic lines of her body had become more pronounced, and, standing in the garden with her basket at her feet, she might have been Ceres startled in the midst of her work, and gravely displeased.

"Irmgard," said Baldur.

She came towards him, in her much-washed and voluminous blue cotton dress, and the basque tight across her high breasts, her skirt trailing on the brown wet earth. She held her head loftily, and walked without hurry or agitation. She reached him, looking down at him, and smiled. Then, simply, she gave him her earth-stained hand.

"Baldur," she replied.

He felt her hand in his, warm, strong, calloused. Her physical presence overpowered him, made him faint. She smelled of the earth, the sun, the young plants, the flowering trees, and the strong bright wind. His grip on her hand tightened, and his fingers rubbed her flesh in an instinctive hunger and ecstasy.

"You must forgive me for coming without permission," he said, his voice thick in his throat. "But I felt I must."

"I am glad you came," she replied, quietly. He still held her hand. She regarded him with serene affection, without embarrassment. The tightness of her lips relaxed, and she smiled again, as if with sudden delight. "I ought to have asked you to come before this. You are such a friend to me!"

He did not answer. His heart was beating rapidly, with mingled pain and joy. His eyes fixed themselves upon her, and he suddenly experienced a sensation of ineffable and inconsolable loss, and ancient grief. He knew now how much he had missed her, and how much more unendurable life was to be without her.

"Let us find a seat in the shade," she said, calmly, and still allowing him to hold her hand, she led him to a great elm tree at the end of the garden, which was surrounded by a wooden seat. They sat down, side by side, their hands clasped, smiling breathlessly at each other. The child slowly followed. He stood before his mother and the strange misshapen stranger. Baldur regarded him intently. Such a small round face, rosy, grave and quiet! Such level blue eyes, without embarrassment or awkwardness! It was Franz's face, become refined and true and pure. The thick curling hair, as yellow as butter, was crested with light on the large round head. The child's body was strong and tall, well-shaped, beautiful, and his bare legs and sturdy arms and hands were brown as autumn apples.

The two, man and child, stared at each other with great gravity and piercing search. Then, simultaneously, they smiled. Baldur held out his free hand, and the little boy took it, with a small laugh. He leaned against Baldur's knee. His eyes, so brilliant, so shining and blue, danced in a beam of sunlight. Baldur turned his head and asked a question of Irmgard with his eyes, and she nodded slightly. Then she said: "How did you know?"

"It was this morning," he replied. "Franz came into my rooms. He saw your portrait. Then, I discerned the resemblance between you clearly. For four years, there was something about him which tantalized me with a vague familiarity. Now, I saw. He tried to pretend he had never known you, nor seen you. But from his questioning, his agitation, I guessed the truth. He was very disturbed."

She had lost color a little, and no longer smiled. She looked at her child with a peculiar sternness. Baldur drew the child closer to him, put his arm about him. Now his own face turned pale, even cold.

"You might have trusted me, Irmgard," he said.

"Why should I have disturbed you?" she muttered, not looking at him. "She—she is your sister. Would it have made you happier?"

He was silent. He paled even more, and his expression became dark. He knew she was waiting eagerly for him to say more, but perversely, he kept his silence. Now he was conscious of an anger against her, a resentment, a sickness of jealousy and outrage.

Finally he said, his arm loosening about the child: "I was a fool. I thought you were writing to me because of friendship, and regard, for me. I might have remembered, knowing that every one is activated only by self-interest, that perhaps you might too be so activated. I might have known that you would write to me so regularly, not out of affection for me, but for some secret reason of your own. You have made a fool of me, Irmgard."

Her lips trembled. Her head dropped. "Forgive me," she whispered. Then she lifted her head and looked at him directly. She spoke very quickly: "But, even if it had not been for—him—I should have written to you! Please believe it. It is true I have been very selfish, waiting only to hear about—him. But under any other circumstances, I should have written, I should have wanted to see you!"

He saw that her eyes were filled with tears, that her mouth was shaking. He said to himself, bitterly: She is lying. She is saying this out of shame and pity. But he could not quite believe it. Nevertheless, he wanted to punish her, though he was deeply touched, and relieved. His jealousy, his heart-ache, his suffering, demanded alleviation by tormenting her.

"Why did you not ask me directly? Why did you not trust me? Why were you dishonest? You could have written me:

'Franz Stoessel is my cousin, my lover, the father of my child. I wish to know of him. I must know of him.' "

She colored deeply. "But there was your sister. She was his wife. You have troubles enough. How could I know but what you would go to him and denounce him?"

"Could you trust me that little?" he asked, quick with pain.

She sighed. "Perhaps, too, I was ashamed."

He shook his head to himself, as though with bewildered denial. "You were not ashamed," he said, coldly.

She wrung her hands together, with a gesture of wretchedness. "You do not understand!" she exclaimed. "I was ashamed that I had loved such a one! I felt degraded, debased! Surely you believe that?"

Despite himself, his expression softened, and he smiled with sudden, almost disbelieving relief, and his jealousy lessened.

"Then," he said, watching her closely, "he is nothing to you now?"

Her lips parted, and he saw how pale they were. Her profile, outlined against the bright lucidity of the sky, was stern, yet shaken. She did not answer. His original anger returned, and his original anguish. He exclaimed involuntarily:

"How can you think of him! He is everything that is detestable! Have you no pride, Irmgard!"

She wrung her hands again, but did not turn to him.

"I have told myself that, a thousand times. But it does no good. No good at all. I remember that he promised to marry me, that he said he loved me. I remember that he deserted me, and that he told me calmly that money meant the world to him, and that if he could, he would marry your sister. I remember——"

But Baldur cried out, turning a dark infuriated red: "You knew this, and you had no loyalty to us, to Ernestine, who loved you? You had no courage, no affection, which might force you to come to us and tell us the truth? You allowed Tina to marry your cousin, knowing what he was, and that he was plotting to marry her for his own advantage, no matter what it might do to her? You could not bring yourself to warn us, Irmgard?"

His voice was so harsh and loud, his manner so threatening, that the child shrank from him, and crept away to his mother's side. But she did not notice him. She was looking at this strange, malformed man with an expression the boy had never seen before.

"You have called me selfish," she said, and now there was a cold anger in her words. "Do you not realize that you are selfish? At this moment you are not thinking of me. You are thinking of your dear sister, and some imagined wrong which you believe I have done her. You think I should have humiliated myself, that I should have gone on my knees to your dear sister, and have said: 'This man you are to marry: he is the lover of your servant. He has degraded himself with me. He is not good enough for you.' "

Her eyes flashed upon him like green flame, and there was hatred in her look. She began to rise from her seat, with pride and haste. But he caught her hand, and pulled her back again. They regarded each other, breathing quick and audibly.

"You have not thought of me," she said, in a muffled voice. "You have not considered that I was wounded, heart-broken. You have not thought that my only impulse was to run away, and hide. No, you have not thought these things. You believe that I should have been more than human. Noble, self-sacrificing, thinking only of your sister. And what is your sister to me? You say she loved me." Her lips curled with bitter pain. "It was the casual love of a mistress for a dog. I refused to be her dog any longer. No, you have never thought of me." She breathed deeply, as though with difficulty. "It is you who have failed me. It is you who have disappointed me. At the last, it is your family pride, your sister, which means everything to you. I am nothing." She struggled with the huskiness in her throat. "I must ask you to go now."

Tears suddenly ran over her cheeks. He held her hand tightly, but the grip was less angry now, and less painful. He could not bear her tears. He lifted her hand to his lips, laid his cheek against it. He felt its cold trembling.

"You are right," he said, almost inaudibly. "It is I who am selfish, and brutal. I understand. I understand what you have suffered, little one."

She dragged her hand away. "No!" she cried, passionately. "How could you understand? If you had understood, you would not have said these things! You remembered, deep in your mind, that I was your sister's servant, and that I allowed my lover, who was not worthy of your sister because he was my lover, to marry her!"

"Do you think I am so base?" he exclaimed, angered again. "Did I not ask you to marry me?" But under his anger he was ashamed, knowing that there was some truth in her accusations. "The wrong to Tina was marrying her without affection, and only for the advantages she could bring him!"

The little boy, who had been closely watching his mother, pointed a stern finger at Baldur. "Go away!" he shouted. "Bad man!"

Baldur looked impatiently at the child, agitated as he was. Then he could not help smiling. He reached out his hand and pulled the little one to him. "Yes," he said, "I am a bad man.

But don't send me away." He spoke, now, in English. "Let me stay with you and your Mama. Will you let me stay?"

The child regarded him with grave hesitation. "You made my mama cry," he accused.

Irmgard, in her distraction, pulled the child away from Baldur. "Run away," she exclaimed. "This is no place for you. There is work in the garden. Go at once, Siegfried!"

The child obeyed at once, simply, without muttering. He walked away with dignity. Baldur smiled involuntarily, as he watched the child go. But Irmgard was still distraught. She said: "There is no reason for us to talk longer, Herr Schmidt. And I am very busy. If you have any regard for me, you will leave now."

Baldur did not speak for some moments. He gazed thoughtfully at the sun-soaked garden, and at the first roses on the white fences. He contemplated the dream-filled valley, floating in its mist of light, in which the trees were vague green islands. He looked at the smoke of the purple hills, drifting against the lighted heavens. A warm, earth-scented breeze touched his face, and the drowsy cackling of the fowl in the barnyard filled the quiet air. He seemed to forget the stormily breathing woman beside him. His hands lay open on the bench, and between his hunched shoulders his face took on quietness and meditation. In spite of her agitation, Irmgard slowly became impressed by his preoccupation, and as she looked at him, she was suddenly and sadly touched.

"We speak to each other angrily because we do not understand," she said, in a low voice.

"Yes," he replied, still gazing at the valley. "That is true."

He sighed, turned to her. "I forgot you were human," he said, trying to smile. "You have been a dream to me. I thought you were more than just a woman. Always, in my life, there have been no shades of color. People were either very good or completely foul. I thought—" and he stopped.

She smiled a little, drearily. "That there was no foulness in me? You were wrong. But," and now her expression became deeply moved, "I am certain there is no foulness in you."

He regarded her gravely, then suddenly laughed. "We are both innocents," he said, obscurely.

Then, as he looked at her, at her thin beautiful face, at the heroic lines of her figure, at her green and mournful eyes, his own face changed, darkened. His nostrils distended hungrily, and with pain.

"I have always loved you, Irmgard. I have always been your friend. I have always wanted you. There is nothing I would not do——"

"Yes, I know," she said, very gently.

He sighed, restlessly, and there was no softness in his look. His mood changed. He moved away from her a little.

"Before I go, there are some questions you would like to ask me." His voice became harder, even contemptuous. "Ask them. You would like to ask me if Franz is happy."

She was silent.

He laughed shortly. "I will tell you this: he hates my sister. That makes you happier, yes?"

"No!" she cried, stung. "That does not make me happy! But who could hate Miss Ernestine?"

"He does," he said, calmly, watching her. "He has always hated her. If it were not for my father, and me, protecting her, he would do wicked things to her. But one of these days, she will guess how much he hates her. Even such a gentle fool as Tina must know it some day."

She did not speak. She appeared to be on the verge of weeping openly.

"He hates everything, and every one," Baldur continued, still watching her narrowly. "He was born full of hatred. But it is an easy, smiling hatred, without bitterness, and only with amusement. There is the hatred which comes from wounds, pain and oppression. No one has ever wounded him, pained him, or oppressed him. His is a natural, and I might even say, healthy hatred, part of his very spirit. There is the hatred which poisons the hater. But he is not poisoned. He enjoys living. He is full of plots and intrigues. For all humanity, he has a vast contempt and detestation. That is why he is so dangerous. What his real stature is, only time will tell. I have discerned that he has no real greatness. But others will think him great. My father thinks so, and my father is no fool."

He paused. She still did not speak. He sighed, and went on:

"It is not necessary to be great to succeed. One needs only to deceive others. He is a genius at deception. He knows this. Only I am not deceived. I know he is a liar and a traitor, and ruthless as death. I know that he is unfaithful to my sister, and that he hates her. I thought he could love no one. I find, now, that he loves you. But even his love is mixed with his natural, easy hatred."

Irmgard looked at him quickly. He could not read her strange expression.

He said: "He hates his little son, Sigmund, who is my favorite. For his other son, Joseph, he has an indulgent affection. There is no natural emotion in him. Often I think: What has his childhood been? Who have been his parents? And then I know that the fault is in him, only. He was born that way. Many are born that way, and humanity invariably suffers. He is beyond good or evil. He operates in some distorted and violent world of his own. He will end in pettiness, or in power, depending on his ability to maintain deception." He added, slowly: "He is waiting for my father to die. My father no longer trusts him, but he is dazzled by him. My father is very unhappy lately. I do not know why. He leans heavily on Franz. But the leaning is killing him. He is no longer himself."

"Why are you telling me these things!" cried Irmgard.

"You want to know, do you not?" asked Baldur, implacably.

She did not answer. He said: "He does not know of this child?"

She came to life, in feverish alarm. "No. He does not even know where I am. He must never know."

"Why?"

She moved as if tormented. "You would not understand. I never wish to see him again."

"Even though you love him still?"

"Because of that," she whispered.

He sighed bitterly, and stood up. "I will go now." He held out his hand to her, and she took it simply. Tears began to run over her white cheeks. He pressed her hand in both of his.

"You will let me come again? Often?" He could not refrain from saying with sad tormenting: "I can bring you news of him, of course."

"Come again!" she cried, with a pang. "You need never mention him, if you will only come!"

He looked at her in a long silence, searching her eyes. "I believe you," he said at last, very gently.

He left her then. She watched him go. She had the feeling that she was watching the departure of the only friend she had in the world.

CHAPTER 8

On the night that Mrs. Schmidt died, only Hans and Baldur were in her room. Not even Matilda, who had been nursing her, was there. Ernestine, of course, had not been informed that death was imminent, and was peacefully sleeping at the side of her husband. The whole house slept in its tall dark walls and gloomy corridors. The doctor had been in at sunset, and had said that the poor woman might live a day or two longer, and that he would call in the morning. There was no immediate danger of death, he had said.

Matilda, in these last days, had exhibited much theatrical and emotional solicitude for her mistress. She had been very "devoted." She sighed loudly and audibly whenever she had an audience, and spoke sadly of her pallor, her weariness, and her anxiety. Her brisk buxom step slowed, when any one approached, to a heavy and patient movement. Hans kept urging her to rest, and then she would look at him with heroic and suffering eyes, exclaiming: "How can I rest? It is unnatural!" She would dab her eyes briefly, and with dignity, and then, with bowed head would reenter Mrs. Schmidt's chamber. She deceived no one but Ernestine and Hans. Mrs. Flaherty, the cook, made audible and ribald comments about such devotion, and the chambermaids snickered behind their hands. But Ernestine was deeply and tearfully touched at such loyalty and self-sacrifice. She forgave Matilda her onerous position in this household, and was full of remorse. Surely she had been wrong! Surely her horrible suspicions were unjustified! She would look at Franz imploringly, and he would pat her shoulder or kiss her cheek, assuring her that she had been very narrow-minded and unjust. Once, while doing this, he caught Matilda's obscenely winking eye, and winked back in return. There was no deception between these two.

Because Mrs. Schmidt appeared to be resting so easily, Matilda allowed herself to be ordered out of the room by Hans "to rest." She went to her apartments and immediately fell into a lusty and snoring sleep. She was very satisfied. When the "old hag" was safely dead, then she could take her rightful place in this household. She slept, smiling, imagining herself addressed as "Mrs. Schmidt." She had no doubt of the ultimate event.

There had been a stormy and bloody sunset this evening, which was three days before Christmas. When the sky had finally darkened, a blizzard swept down upon the city, accompanied by bellowing and furious gales. Under the streetlamps, the streets were all deserted. Heaps of snow, like dunes, piled up against curbs, about trees and walls. Their ridged whiteness glittered under the lights. In large areas, the wind swept the streets bare. The wind was almost visible, so violently did the icy air palpitate under its shocks, and the gas flickered in the lamps, like feeble candles. The great Schmidt mansion stood ponderously in the path of the gale, which was filled with ice and snow particles as harsh and choking as sand. Nothing could shake that mansion, but every tall window and every door shuddered and creaked and rattled, and smoke blew in from fireplaces.

For a time Baldur, sunk in a chair at the foot of his mother's bed, was alone. One tall white candle burned on a table near the bed, and it was sufficient only to fill the darkness with a dim and trembling lighter shadow. The walls were lost in dimness, and on the ceiling was a round pool of wavering light in which the plaster-white carvings were like a tiny bas-relief of the face of the moon. Baldur could just discern the heavy trembling of the thick draperies drawn across the windows. They moved constantly in blasts of bitter air which found their way through minute crevices. But they moved without sound. There was no sound but the wind, and in the intervals, so intense was the silence, that Baldur imagined he could hear the ghostly whisper of the flickering candle. There was nothing else visible in the room but his mother's bed, carved, high, drifting with dull crimson silk covers. From the chair where he was sitting, he could see the slight ridge her body made under the silk, and the dark blur which was her head. From time to time, he rose and looked down at the dying face on its satin pillows. He would stand there for a long time, gazing, his hand on a carved post. Sometimes he would bend down to listen to her halting breath, which came only irregularly through cracked and widely parted lips. Her eyes were bruised spots, sunk in her claylike face, and he saw the cords in her sallow neck, and the fluttering of her flat tired breast.

In her dying, for the first time in her life, there was something heroic about the poor creature, something of dignity and aloofness. It is only in tragedy, he thought, that men approach the gods. Now that his mother stood in the gateway of death, she acquired a pride she had never possessed in life. Her dim and meaningless life, so petty, so without substance, took on some mysterious significance, like a link in a long chain whose beginning and end were not visible. Her usual timid and vacillating expression had gone, to be replaced by a thin austerity and sternness. He could not grieve for her, in her new dignity, her last majestic estate. He looked at the emaciated hands on the coverlet, already folded in the lofty resignation of final peace. He hoped she would die like this, without awakening again to the degradation of life. A great blasted tree, he thought, has more awe in it, more somber wonder and grandeur, than any lush growth wild with leaves, and noisy with birds.

He knew that she would die tonight. He went slowly back to his chair, and sat unmoving, watching the blur on the pillows. Long motionless thoughts stood in his mind, dark static, yet without torment. He seemed to be standing on a vast plain under an endless night, where there were no sound, no life, no horizons. There was only eternity, solemn and immense, in which all personal being was lost. Here man could measure no time, nor could twist it into grotesque and painful patterns. He was not aware that he slept, but he awoke with a start, awakened by a faint rustling whisper.

He got to his feet, feeling numb and dazed, and approached his mother. Her eyes, like dark bottomless holes, stared at him. "Hans?" she murmured.

He bent over her and touched his lips to her cold damp forehead. "It is Baldur, Mama," he said.

Now she recognized him, and a glimmer of a smile passed over her pale lips. Her hand fluttered. He took it. It was already icy. He sighed deeply. As if his sigh stirred some suffering life in her, her hand trembled, and her expression changed.

"Baldur," she whispered. The holes which were her eyes brimmed with terrible tears. But she could say nothing else. He saw her tears, and he could not bear the seeing. He went for his father.

Hans came to his bedroom door, his white nightshirt reaching to his ankles, a white flannel night-cap with a tassel tilted rakishly on his large pink skull. He blinked and scowled stupidly at his son, for he had been sleeping heavily. Behind him, his room, glaring with sudden gaslight, was stark and bitterly cold.

"My mother is dying," said Baldur, in a low voice.

Hans continued to blink and scowl in silence, trying to understand.

"She has asked for you. Please come at once," urged Baldur. He dropped his voice even lower. "I don't think it wise to call Ernestine."

Hans said nothing. In the past few years he had grown rapidly older. There was a flaccidity and hopelessness and sullen gloom about him, which had replaced his former bellicosity and loud belligerence. He was less fat; his broad shoulders stooped wearily. Moreover, there was a bewilderment, a confusion, in his tiny blue eyes, and his mustache did not bristle any longer. He was a very old man, lost in a perplexing and frightening world, which had grown too noisy, too exigent, too big for him. His disposition, never renowned for its sweetness and gentleness, had become thinly ferocious, so that he resembled an old stricken boar attacked in a thicket where he had gone to die. At moments, his old violence flared up, but it was gone like a sudden flame is gone, swallowed in impotent smoke. Sometimes his face worked grotesquely, as though he would burst into tears. He had long periods of brooding silence, from which he would rouse himself with a dazed look, and a trembling of his eyelids.

He was no longer hateful to Baldur, who knew everything, but only pathetic. He was even more pathetic, standing there in his doorway, blinking. Baldur went into his room and brought his father his black silk dressing gown, helped him to put it on. Hans obeyed automatically, hardly aware of what he was doing. Once, in the operation, he looked at Baldur, tried to scowl, succeeded only in grimacing.

They went into Mrs. Schmidt's room together, tiptoeing in the black coldness of the hall. Hans, with slow reluctant feet, waddled to his wife's beside. But she had fallen into a light doze again. Baldur placed a chair for his father beside his own. "We must wait," he whispered. "She will soon be conscious."

Hans sat down. His short fat body collapsed in the chair. His white night-cap was tremulous in the gloom. Baldur could not guess what he was thinking. He had folded his little white fat hands on his belly. He stared unblinkingly before him, his under lip thrust out. Baldur could see the wrinkling of his pink forehead. He knew that Hans was not thinking of his wife. Still bemused by sleep, he had fallen again into one of those stolid, heavily bewildered meditations so usual these days with him. He had come into this death chamber only to resume them consciously. Once he looked at Baldur unseeingly, and Baldur was touched by that blank groping stare. He knew that his father was not aware of the coldness of the room, which the faint pink fire could not alleviate. When Baldur stirred up the fire and put fresh coal on it, Hans watched him as a very young infant watches the movements of an adult, without comprehension, without thought. He was merely a moving object to Hans, upon which his eyes fixed without consciousness. Once an expression of some subterranean pain wrinkled his thick pink features, but again, the pain did not reach his awareness.

Baldur guessed some part of the ponderous turmoil and imageless misery that had his father. But there was nothing he could say or do. His pity increased. He sat down, tried to find something he could say. But Hans's chin had fallen on his broad fat chest, and his eyes were sightless. Then Baldur saw his lids droop, and a faint snore came from between his fallen lips.

The winter gale increased in intensity. The candlelight moved vaguely about the room, touching the arm of a chair, a fold of the trembling draperies at the window. The fire rose a little. Hans had begun to mutter in his sleep.

"Gleichschaltung!" he murmured. He repeated the word, and now it was like a faint cry of despair, impotent, contemptuous, and suffering. "Nein! Nein! That is folly! I shall not have it! You are ruining me!"

Baldur, fearful that his mother would be awakened, gently shook his father's arm. Hans's eyes flew open, blankly, not seeing. His pink face was very pale, and there was a look on it of complete fright and wretchedness.

"Nein!" he repeated, very loudly. "It is all lost! You are taking from me my life! You shall not do these things! Today it must stop!" Sweat sprang out visibly upon his face, and he started up, clutching the arms of his chair. "It is wrong! You shall not do it! Too long I have been silent!"

"Father," urged Baldur, with a fearful glance at his mother.

But Hans was aware of nothing but his agony. His eyes started from his head. His lips shook. He was like a man cornered by executioners.

"There is money, you say! But what is money? Ach, I thought it much! But it is nothing now. You have pushed me away. You laugh at me. I am an old man with old ideas. I am done. You will make us all very rich. Ach, that is what you say! But it is not enough. You are taking from me my life!"

Baldur shook him again, and now comprehension came into those little wild eyes, so strained, so bloodshot, so starting. Baldur felt the hard trembling muscles on the arm he grasped, the desperate straining. Then the muscles relaxed, slackly. The old man was trying to scowl again.

"You wake me," he muttered. "Does she want me?"

"No, not yet. But you were talking too loudly in your sleep."

"Ach," said Hans, falling back in the chair. He began to pluck at the black silk of his robe. He glowered. But even the glowering was pathetic. Once he muttered again, exhaustedly: "Gleichschaltung!"

Hail rattled against the windows, and the light of the candle bowed, flared, wavered, sank into semi-darkness. Hans shivered. His hands, plucking, moved feverishly. He was groping in some fathomless despair of his own. All at once he lifted his head and fixed his eyes on Baldur, blankly. Then, slowly, to Baldur's uneasy surprise, he began to smile, cunningly, slyly. The smile became static, frozen, like the grimace on the face of a statue. Baldur was even more surprised when his father spoke thickly, haltingly:

"You do not like Franz, nein?"

Baldur sighed. "I do not think of him at all. My mother is dying."

But Hans was suddenly imbued with a febrile activity. He caught Baldur's thin wrist in his sweating fingers.

"You are my son! I see, there is a way!" He dropped Baldur's wrist. But his smile remained, cunning, lighted, infinitely crafty.

Baldur was taken aback. He could not understand. He frowned a little, sighing.

He knew only that some deep sleepless agony had his father, as formless but encompassing as universal pain. He knew that his father was lost and blind in that pain. He saw Hans slowly push himself to his feet, and move to Mrs. Schmidt's bedside. Hans gripped the bedpost. He stood motionless, looking down at the dying woman, who hardly breathed.

Then to Baldur's moved surprise, the old man suddenly began to weep.

"Fanny," he whimpered. "It is I, your Hans. Fanny."

His short fat legs wavered. He collapsed on his knees. He laid his head and his tear-wet face on the pillows beside the head of his wife. He was like a terrified child, fleeing at last to his only refuge.

His voice, his presence, awakened Mrs. Schmidt to life for the first time. She stirred, and her eyes opened. She saw her husband beside her. She smiled, as a mother smiled. Her hand moved, lifted, fluttered, laid itself gently on his cheek. She sighed once, smiled again, closed her eyes. Hans's whimpering rose higher and higher, until it was a far howl.

A few days later, after the funeral, Mrs. Schmidt's will was read.

To Ernestine, her daughter, she had left all her many jewels and personal treasures, locked safely away in bank vaults.

To her husband, there was left what he already had: the Schmidt Steel Comany, which had been her father's.

To Baldur was left two-thirds of the bonds of the Schmidt Steel Company. Now Baldur was a very wealthy man, for in one year he would be thirty-five, the date on which he would inherit the vast fortune of his grandfather, which had been left in trust for him.

CHAPTER 9

THE SHOCK of Mrs. Schmidt's will was a profound one to Franz Stoessel. He knew that she had in her possession two-thirds of the bonds of the Schmidt Steel Company. He had thought that Ernestine would inherit them. When he discovered that the will, leaving the bonds to Baldur, had been made only two months before her death, he suspected, with vicious insight, that in some way the poor creature had been influenced to do this. Could it be Baldur? He doubted it. Then, he knew that Hans had done this thing to him.

He was appalled, and infuriated. Had he been too indiscreet in forcing Hans too rapidly? He knew that Hans was inordinately proud of him, that he had deep rough affection for him. He also knew that Hans detested Baldur. What then, lay behind this? He dared not ask outright. When he tried delicate questioning, Hans displayed a subtlety and reserve which Franz did not know he possessed.

However, one day he said bluntly, with a peculiarly furtive glance at Franz: "Is it not enough for you? The bonds, you would have, ja? Why? My wife, she thought that Tina and you would have the mills some day. That is not enough for you, but you should have the bonds, ja?"

When he said this, Franz was enormously relieved. It was not the bonds so much, that had frightened him. Shortly, he began to renew the pressure on Hans, but now with more finesse and tact. This chaffed and infuriated him. He believed in riding a rising tide. The tide was rising rapidly, and now he must dally, side-step, and wait, while the tide rose higher and higher. For one of his nature, this was intolerable.

His lack of inner resources had kept him from developing a philosophy which might have sustained him in a hiatus. This was both his strength and his weakness. The strength of this lack prevented him from indulging in a patience which would have really been complacence, and forced him to continue to advance, paradoxically, while he marked time. The weakness of his lack resulted in a moody restlesness and irritation, for he found no satisfaction in anything but the advancement of his own purposes. The world, for him, possessed three dimensions only when it was colored and made solid by self-gain and triumph. When he was forced to wait, or move very slowly, the world became backless cardboard, without color or substance, an arid place of sawdust, gloom and silence. A lesser, or a greater, man, would have filled these periods with lightness, gaiety, amusement, education, travel, reading or music. But something in him shrank from music, so that he would close his doors, or leave the house, when Baldur played. The music, when he could not flee from it, produced in him a sort of thick smoldering despair and bitter hunger, which he dared not analyze. Something strange and dark and mournful stirred in him, when he could not escape, something which made Irmgard appear before him, vivid, lost, and warm. But it was even beyond Irmgard; she was only a symbol. He no longer read, not even his favorite poets. Once he picked up a volume of Shakespeare, but a few passages aroused in him such a hot tormenting fever, such a sensation of complete desolation, that he flung the book from him with a loud cry.

One night he encountered Baldur in the hallway. Baldur had been softly playing excerpts from Mozart, and had left his piano for a few moments.

"You are leaving? And just before dinner?" asked Baldur, with his invariable politeness.

Franz regarded him with open savagery just before he assumed his usual bland and charming smile.

"Yes. There is some business." And then he had gone, with a courteous inclination of his head. But Baldur looked after him reflectively, with a sensation of amused but saddened compassion. He was beginning to understand his brother-in-law more and more every day, and the understanding, while it increased his original detestation and disgust, also increased his pity and interest. Baldur, these days, had been finding life less dull. There was Irmgard, restored to him though at long intervals. There was little Sigmund. And last, but certainly not least, there was Franz. Yes, he would think, life was definitely assuming some frail excitement.

In the meantime, Franz moved with a definite, though maddeningly careful progress. In the mills, he had begun to roll steel instead of casting it. (In every move now, he respectfully consulted Hans, and deftly contrived, in most instances, to infer that the innovations were those of the old man, and not his own. Quite frequently, Hans was deceived.) Slowly, Franz began to abandon making rails by the Bessemer process. In the Bessemer method phosphorus had been the brittling agent, which caused rail-failure. By the open hearth process, the phosphorus was eliminated. Too, rails too often "crocked." The hydrogen had little time to escape. Franz began to roll rails, at the suggestion of one of his insignificant research men.

Another of his men declared that the father-to-son method of welding was unscientific. He suggested improvement which Franz cautiously put into operation without Hans's immediate knowledge.

Orders were growing enormously. When Franz had married Ernestine, a customer was content, when ordering 20 per cent carbon steel, to take 30 per cent or even 40 per cent. Franz was able to reduce this to even less than 15 per cent.

Now, at another suggestion of one of his obscure and ill-paid little research workers, Franz began to use coke for fuel, though Hans and Dietrich vehemently protested, prophesying complete failure. But it was not a failure. It was a tremendous success. The old blast furnaces were considered satisfactory if they produced fifty to one hundred tons a day. Franz was able to increase this production to as high as four hundred tons. He was able, then, to reduce the price of his steel far below the existing market rate. "The only way steel can be used for many more purposes than it is today being used for, is to make it cheaper," he said.

The iron ore deposits in Northern Michigan were now, to a satisfying extent, in the hands of the Schmidt Steel Company, this making the company, in a large measure, independent of the Pennsylvania mines owned by the Sessions Steel Company. As a result, Sessions Steel offered their iron ore at greatly reduced rates. Jules Bouchard, in person, came to Nazareth with his offers.

In the meantime, having heard that Brazil had been discovered rich in manganese ore, Franz quietly bought up options in that country, and began to import the ore, which had originally been obtained from Russia. The savings were enormous. Sessions Steel, fuming and enraged, bought the ore from Franz at his own price, which he cleverly kept considerably under the price of the Russian ore. He negotiated with the owners of freight boats, tied them up with contracts. Sessions Steel began to regard him with immense and thoughtful respect, while hating him.

In the meantime, he secretly began experimenting with structural steel. He continued his experiments with the rolling of steel instead of casting it.

The Schmidt Steel Company, now, from originally being a small tidy concern, humbly grateful for a place in the industrial sun allowed it by such concerns as Sessions Steel, began to lift its chimneys far above all others, and to turn its thoughts to the widening and ever-accelerating future. Wall Street regarded it respectfully. Andrew Carnegie spoke of it with irritation. John D. Rockefeller rubbed his chin, and said nothing, but thought a great deal. The mills in Nazareth had expanded, in less than seven years, to three times their original size, and employed ten times their first number. Franz had cleverly contrived to import his own laborers from Europe, in spite of the Alien Contract Labor Law, which Sessions, among the original sufferers from this law, loudly brought to the attention of Washington. But Franz had carefully prepared the ground in advance, among his many politician friends, among them even Nicholas Session himself, who was not above good rich bribes at the expense of his own brother's loss.

Once Jules Bouchard said to his brother, Leon, with much ruefulness, but admiration: "This German swine is an even greater rascal than I am. For a member of a race completely lacking in subtlety and real imagination, he is doing very well."

To which Leon replied: "He has replaced subtlety with the blunderbuss and the club. Who knows? Perhaps the day is coming when the club will be more effective than clever conversation."

But Jules said, reflectively: "I have talked with him. He is no fool. But he is also no genius. He uses other men's brains, while we distrust them. Perhaps that is his secret. But it is not in our character to treat respectfully the brains of others. We French are too egotistic."

Leon answered: "It may be the Germans have the secret of the future: the use of other men's wit as well as their strength."

And now Joseph Bryan, arch-enemy of the Bouchards and the Barbours, and the Sessions Steel Company, and their patron, Jay Regan, smiled smugly in his black-walnut and crimson New York office, and congratulated himself that Franz Stoessel had persuaded him to grant certain loans. "I never make a mistake in a man," he boasted, for Bryan was an Irishman and had no false modesty.

Franz Stoessel, forced to move with delicacy and caution for a little while, watched the rising tide of his life arch high above his head, and fumed.

But on the whole, it was not too bad. He was a millionaire

now. He was not satisfied. If he had all the world, he knew, he would never be satisfied. There was a thirst and a hunger in him to which he would give no recognition, but they were there, consuming.

CHAPTER 10

SINCE HER mother's death, a sick suspicion had come into Ernestine's mind that she was desperately, horribly, alone. Some invisible and intangible barrier, but a strong one, had risen between her and her father, and her brother, and her children. There was no comfort for the confused and miserable little creature even in her children. Sigmund, she discovered, was hardly her child. He was so quiet, so remote, so timid, and yet so haughty. There was Joseph, the pride of his father, but he was even less her child than Sigmund. There remained only Franz, and from the night of a certain dream, she regarded him with vague dim bewilderment, touched with fear.

She dreamt that she was in the immense and gloomy drawing-room on a cold dark night. She could see the fire faintly burning, and heard the wind at the windows. She was sewing before the fire, and long white lengths, dimly glistening, flowed from her knees onto the carpet. She sewed desperately, and with a kind of fever, for the dream had begun on a note of deathly panic. She must finish this sewing! She looked up, and the room was filled with her family: Hans, Baldur, the children, and Franz. In a far corner, endlessly watching, sat Matilda, her plump hands on her fat knees.

Suddenly the panic gripped Ernestine fiercely by the throat. She looked at her father, who sat near her, staring at the fire. She called to him. He did not answer. He appeared frail and tenuous, with pale slack cheeks and bowed head. She thought to herself: He is old. She stood up abruptly, and the shining stuff fell about her feet. She ran to her father, reached out to touch him, and saw that he had disappeared. His chair was empty. She uttered a loud cry. She turned to Baldur, and called to him. He did not look at her. She reached out to him, and then his chair was empty. Horror seized her, the black horror of a nightmare. She turned to her children, holding out her arms to them. They were playing on the carpet, in utter pale silence. She approached them, and the spot where they had been became empty. She was conscious of icy wind in the room, and she thought confusedly: The windows have been blown in!

She turned to Franz, the terror and ghastliness of the nightmare thick upon her. She ran to him, screaming, for protection. The lights became dimmer. She was in a wide empty place of complete desolation. Franz rose up to meet her, as she stumbled across a floor suddenly become a sucking marsh. Wind froze her flesh; her legs bent under her. Her arms fumbled for Franz. He was waiting for her, not moving. She came to him, ready to fling herself for protection upon his chest. Then she saw that he loomed over her, tremendous, silent, smiling. It was his smile that stopped her, for it was so gloating, so hating, so brilliant with malignance. She stood, shuddering, staring at him. He said nothing. She could see the glittering of his eyes, the fixed loathing and triumph of his smile. Her heart became iron, studded with spikes, turning over and over in her breast. She felt the complete fear of death, and something else, unnamable, but formed of terror and approaching dissolution.

He stood and looked at her, and it seemed to her that eons passed, while she stared, her flesh dissolving. She thought: He is my enemy. He has always been my enemy. He has hated me. He has driven away my father and my mother and my brother and my children, so that he can destroy me. There was no grief in this thought, but only despair and terror, and the desire for flight. But she could not move.

All at once she heard Matilda's laughter, shrill, high, inhuman. It was that sound that released the icy grip on her body. She turned. She tried to run. But everything was dark and swirling. Suddenly she felt Franz's hand on her shoulder, crushing down to the bone. She struggled. The nightmare gag on her tongue was momentarily loosened. She uttered a wild and despairing scream, such as an animal might utter. Then she woke up.

It was Franz who had awakened her, impatiently, but with an indulgent smile. He had lit a lamp, and now stood by the bedside, laughing a little. "What a dream that must have been!" he exclaimed. From her pillows she stared up at him with wild eyes, motionless, distended. He reached out to touch her reassuringly, but she shrank back from him, whimpering.

"Go away," she pleaded. "Oh, please! Go away!"

He had shrugged, and had left the room. She lay on her bed, shivering, unable to warm herself. She did not wonder where he had gone, in the middle of the night. She was not concerned. She continued to stare at the opposite wall until long after daylight. For several days thereafter, she was unusually silent, and pale and nervous, and given to sudden inexplicable gusts of weeping, which made Franz impatient. "It is your condition, my love," he would say, indulgently, for Ernestine was four months pregnant with her third child. "But you must control yourself. It is not good for the little one."

His voice, rather quick, mobile and fluent for a man of his stature and build and race, and accented, which had never failed before to soothe, reassure and charm her, now only filled her with vague, unformed misery. With all her lonely and wretched heart, she longed for his affection and tenderness. She knew she had only to implore him for them, and he would respond quickly. But it would only be falseness, she thought, involuntarily, and the thought, when she analyzed it, increased her chronic terror and misery, and appalled her. I am wronging him, my darling! she cried to herself. But she could not approach him, yet. She would not let him touch her. Desolation thickened about her daily, and her weeping increased. Was it her imagination, or did there really exist between him and that horrible Matilda a loathesome kind of rapport? And was it her imagination indeed which made her see little significant glances exchanged, little humorous nods of the head, little smiles, as though these two found the Schmidts contemptible, stupid, detestable? Did they really hate the Schmidts, Hans, Baldur, Ernestine? Never had Ernestine felt so lonely, so desperate, so terrified. She felt enemies about her, creeping in darkness, hidden behind ambushes of smiling affection and gestures of concern and solicitude.

These sensations did not decrease as the days went on. Now, when her father returned home, with his new heaviness and perturbation and his new lack of bellicosity, she would fly to him, to huddle in his arms, to cling to him speechlessly, overcome with her numb anguish. He would pet her, pat her back, ruffle her dark curls, murmur to her. But he never asked her the cause of her deep trouble. Was this because he knew, or because he was growing old and was preoccupied with his own pains? At any rate, this fat old man was not the father of her younger years, full of loud fierce laughter, shouting words, and strength. There was no comfort for her in him.

Now, in her appalling loneliness, anguish and misery, she thought of her brother, who had always loved and protected her. She saw, with remorse and dismay, how far she had alienated herself from him. Confused, she tried to understand how this had happened. But she was too ingenuous to see the malevolent hand which had pulled her away from Baldur. I have been too engrossed with my children, and my husband, she thought, reproaching herself for her neglect of this friend as well as brother.

Yet, her subconscious must have been aware of the real truth, for she found a bewildering reluctance in herself to approach Baldur, a kind of guiltiness and shame. This all increased her hunger for Baldur, a yearning for his understanding and gentleness. She would look across the long dining-room table at him with her misery, dismay and pain in her large dark eyes, but her lips were mute and stiff. She saw many things she had never seen before. She saw that though Baldur was, as always, scrupulously kind and courteous to her, that he was also cold and reserved. I have hurt him, she thought, and dimly wondered at the strength of the pang which assailed her, which even to her innocent self seemed all out of proportion to the fancied cause.

One mornng in the early fall, Baldur heard a faint tentative knock on his door. He was reading by his window, and finding pleasure in occasional glimpses of the russet and yellow trees, and the bright grass sprinkled with crisp fragments of crimson and gold. Since his reunion with Irmgard, he had become aware again of how beautiful the world was, how large, how infinitely full of thoughts and movements and winds. He was experiencing once more that rare peace, that substance-filled solitude, which comes only to the man of thought whose life is refined of grossness, expediency, and greedy ambition.

When he heard the knock, he smiled and put aside the book. That would be little Sigmund, coming for his morning conversation with his uncle. But when the door opened, it was Ernestine who stood there.

Brother and sister regarded each other in a prolonged silence, in the clarity of the morning light. Baldur was so surprised that he did not immediately invite his sister to enter, and she stood, wavering, on the threshold. He saw, suddenly, how frail and attenuated she had become, how white were her drawn cheeks, how hollow her dark eyes and colorless her lips. She was so small and delicate of body and stature that she had never seemed to age to Baldur and her father, but all at once Baldur thought: She is middle-aged. She is becoming old. She looks like my mother. Ernestine was thirty-six now, five years older than her husband. She appeared much more, standing there, hesitating, her hand on the door-jamb.

There were thin streaks of pure white through her dark girlish curls, and there were pale shadows at her thin and sunken temples. It was her expression, however, which filled Baldur with pain, so sick with chronic terror was it, so fugitive, so ill. Again, he thought of his mother.

A faint cloud passed across the autumn sun, and its dimness muffled Ernestine's expression, reduced the sharp threads of whiteness in her hair. She wore a ruffled white-silk morning peignoir, which concealed the swelling of her small thin body. Swirling and graceful as it was, it gave her a spurious girlishness and immaturity. Under its influence, Baldur called gently: "Good morning, Tina. Please come in."

He watched her narrowly as she entered the room. Her step was uncertain, as though she had been ill a long time. She did not look away from him. Her eyes fastened themselves on him with a drowning expression. She did not speak. She sat down in a chair near him, poised on its edge like a broken white bird, her hands clenched together on one little thin knee. Now the sun came out from behind its cloud, and Baldur saw her clearly again, and he thought to himself: She is sick. She is dying. She is being consumed by fear and bewilderment.

But, in spite of his alarm, and the return of his old tenderness for her, he said nothing, only waited. There was no embarrassment in him, only regret and uneasiness. She was like a loved one who had returned from a far journey a stranger. One must move cautiously. Yes, he thought, one must move cautiously, for fear of alarming this bewildered and stricken traveller. Then, all at once, he knew what had driven her to him, instinctively. His alarm grew, and with it, his compassion. He regarded her with hidden alertness, though he retained an attitude of careful ease.

Her lips, pale and parched, divided in a sigh. She tried to smile. Then her face changed abruptly, became blank yet distracted. A whimper, long-drawn, only half audible, issued from her throat.

"Baldur," she began, in a trembling voice.

"Yes, Tina?" he said, gravely, softly, still holding his book in his hands.

She smiled again, convulsively. "It is so long since you have called me 'Tina!' " she exclaimed, with a thin note of hysteria in her words.

"It is so long since you and I have talked at all," he replied, speaking carefully, and watching her acutely.

She made a swift futile gesture with her small white hands, a distraught and fumbling gesture. Again, she smiled.

"I—there have been so many things," she murmured. "So busy." She moistened her lips. Baldur said nothing.

Suddenly, her face changed again, became wild, blind. Again she whimpered. "I want my mother!" she said.

Baldur's eyes darkened. Ernestine had seemed overcome at her mother's death, but her emotion had been short-lived, and had passed quickly. That had surprised him, for mother and daughter had been very intimate and affectionate. But Ernestine, since her marriage, had appeared engrossed in a kind of bemused and happy enchantment, which had no place in it for grief of any tenacity. His understanding grew larger, deeper.

"But mother has been dead over a year," he said. "Much over a year."

Again, she made that distraught gesture, which he saw was the gesture of a person involved in intense suffering.

"It just now occurs to me—that she is dead." Her voice was faint, without resonance.

Once more there was silence. Ernestine's lips twisted, and she wet them with the tip of her tongue. Her eyes did not leave his face. What is it she wants to say? he thought. Why has she come to me, now? Will she say what she wishes to say?

She was speaking again. "I wish I had a female friend," she said. "I have only acquaintances. I wish Irmgard were here. You remember Irmgard?" Her tone was childish. Her eyes were slowly filling with childish tears.

"Yes," he said, reflectively. "I remember Irmgard."

She spoke with sudden querulousness. "I still cannot understand why she left! It was so ungrateful! And without a word to us! We had been so good to her! Only that day, Christmas, we had given her such valuable gifts, far beyond her station. She was not treated as a servant—Mama was like a mother to her. I—I was her friend. Yet, without a word! And only that little note, arriving a day or two later, after that silence in which we were so worried about her! So cold, so heartless!"

Baldur could not keep the sharpness and impatience from his voice when he answered this selfish and childish outburst:

"How do you know that, Tina? How do you know she was cold and heartless? Did it ever occur to you that she had a life of her own, and that in that life she might have had some deep trouble, some sorrow you knew nothing about? How did you know but what she was distracted, or frightened, or wretched? No, you never asked yourself this. You thought only that your convenient servant had run away, without apology or leave. She was a woman, too, and human."

"But we were her friends!" she cried, though her eyes

dropped with sullen guiltiness. "She might have told us! We might have helped her."

"Have you ever thought she had dignity, that she did not wish to impose her troubles or misfortunes upon you, Tina? That, to me, is the highest form friendship can take."

She shook her head, stubbornly. "She was all alone, except for that aunt and uncle. She had no other ties here. What misfortunes could she have had?"

Baldur said nothing. He knew now that this complaint came not very deeply from his sister, and the cause was not very important to her. There was something else. He knew that he had guessed rightly, for she now appeared restless and impatient, as though the subject annoyed and bored her, and had diverted her attention from her real misery and pain.

"I am all alone," she murmured to herself. He hardly caught the words. He did not know what to answer, but his concern for her, and his consternation, grew. She wrung her hands on her knees, and again her hunted eyes implored him, furtively. He could not endure it. He bent towards her.

"What is it, Tina? Can't you tell me?"

His voice, filled with the old solicitude, unnerved her. She kept her features rigid, but tears swam up to her lids, ran over them. Her body moved towards him, as though seeking refuge. She cried: "I don't know! I—I feel ill! Everything is so strange!" In that cry he read her overwrought terror, her grief, her confusion, her abandonment.

His first impulse was to go to her, and hold her in his arms. He could hardly resist that anguished, twisted face, those tears, that trembling. But he said to himself: Careful. If she tells me too much, she will hate me. She has come to me for the first time in years: something is terribly wrong. Has she found him out? But if I dare intimate I know this, she will really hate me, and will never come to me again. So, he regarded her calmly, judiciously, repudiating the confidence he knew would destroy the last thread between them. He knew that she was coming to him now for reassurance, not for advice after a confession.

He made his voice normal, strong and warm, even a little tenderly indulgent.

"Naturally, you feel ill. Women always do under these circumstances, don't they? They are given to fancies, I have heard. And imaginings. They are also given to strange premonitions, and fears, and dreams—"

"Dreams!" she exclaimed, moving a little towards him on her chair. Now her expression was less distracted, and had become somewhat eager. "Yes, dreams! So frightening! Nightmares." Her voice dwindled. She looked at him imploringly.

He shrugged, and smiled. "And nightmares, in your condition, take on undue importance and substance." Nevertheless, he was curious to know what her nightmare had been. He believed that nightmares came without casualness. He believed that there was some deep underlying knowledge in the soul which made it cast up the lurid shadows of terrifying dreams into the conscious mind. "Tell me your nightmare, Tina."

He was sure he had come upon the truth when she colored slightly, and dropped her eyes. "Silly," she murmured. She tried to laugh a little, and the sound pained him like the stab of a knife. This miserable, small, unprotected and frightened creature, whom he still loved so much! She looked at him now, and laughed again. "It was so absurd. It was a month ago. I—I dreamt you all disappeared, you and Papa, and the children. There was only Franz. And Matilda. I—I dreamt they were my enemies. I tried to run away. It was really very silly."

"Very silly," he echoed. But his heart had begun to beat rapidly.

She was less overwrought now. Her smile was less wild. She relaxed a little, and spoke more normally.

"I was so frightened, Baldur! You can't imagine. The influence has stayed with me all this time. I don't feel normally, towards Franz. That is so unjust, isn't it?"

"Very unjust," he said, quietly, and mechanically. He watched her closely. "And without justification, too." There was just the slightest questioning inflection in his phrasing.

"Oh, yes, without justification. He is so sweet and good to me. Always so considerate, and thoughtful. No one could have a better husband. This is being very unkind to my husband——"

"An unkindness I am sure he will forgive, under the circumstances," said Baldur. He hesitated. "Have you told him about your dream?"

"Oh no! How could I be so foolish? It would hurt him so."

Baldur was silent. He plucked at his lower lip, inscrutably. I should like to see his face if she told him, he thought, and was immediately ashamed of this very human thought.

She had begun to talk rapidly, feverishly, beating her small fists quickly on her knees as she spoke:

"I have never liked Matilda. But I—I don't mind her so much, lately. Papa—Papa does not seem to see her any more. She is just the housekeeper, which is very proper, and just as it should be. She is in her proper place, at last. So, the dream seems even more silly, doesn't it? Of course, I can see why I dreamt of her. She and Franz, they are Germans. There

—there must be a language link, don't you think so? But, he is very particular about servants keeping their place, more so than I am. But he is so kind, and indulgent, and so he doesn't say anything to Matilda about impertinences. I—I suppose I should be more strict—the mistress of the house now, since poor Mama died——"

She was very incoherent. Over the feverish stream of her voice her eyes implored him again.

"You are making something of nothing," said Baldur, calmly, clearly. "But, if you cannot endure Matilda, why don't you discharge her? As you say, father won't mind. Now. He is hardly aware of her existence. You can easily discharge her." He kept the hope out of his voice.

"Discharge Matilda?" She was incredulous, but her own hope lightened her face, subdued her hysteria momentarily. "What should I do without Matilda? I am such a silly little person. I know nothing of managing a home. I wouldn't even be competent enough to engage another housekeeper."

She laughed, and the laugh was almost normal, as her eyes pleaded with him for his affectionate indulgence.

"Nonsense," he replied, in the mood she forced upon him. "You could really be very competent, if you wished. You are just lazy."

He was almost overwhelmed with his passionate desire to go to her, to say to her: "Your dream was true. These two are your enemies. Rid yourself of this woman. Drive this man away. He cannot hurt you. If he tries, I know enough to prevent him. He will kill you, eventually. That is what he wishes. He is a monster. For all our sakes, send him away."

But he dared not say this.

She nodded her head brightly, smiling with foolish self-indulgence. "Yes," she said, almst archly. "I am really despicably lazy."

Baldur had a sudden thought. "Let Matilda go. You know that Aunt Elizabeth has offered to come to live with us. You wouldn't consider it before. She is almost an old woman now, but she is an excellent manager, and would take Matilda's place."

He knew, by the sudden flaring of relief and excitement on her face, how intense had been her dream, how intense had been her preoccupation with it, and her dread, and the sceret knowledge of her submerged soul.

"That is an excellent idea, Baldur! I shall write to her, to-day!"

She looked at him with real relief, and joy. She was the younger Tina again, released from intolerable terror.

"And, in the meantime," he said, again watching her acutely, "there are the children. You are not so alone."

The joy faded. She paled. "The children," she murmured.

"There is Sigmund," he urged, hoping against hope that he could arouse some maternal passion in her for that poor child.

But her expression had become sullen again, and resistant. "He has such a bad temper, Baldur. I don't understand the boy. And so rude to Franz, too. So distant, and difficult. He is quite beyond me. I know he hurts Franz, too, with his runnings-away, and his crying when Franz so much as comes near him."

He saw it was useless. She was forever aliented from Sigmund, because of the child's aversion for his father. He saw then how profound was her infatuation, how deathly.

"I find him a splendid character," he said, mildly, and with some listlessness.

The resistant look turned upon him then, and with it was mixed some hostility. "You indulge him, Baldur. Franz has often remarked about it. We think this has something to do with his impudence, and secretiveness."

So, thought Baldur, with hatred, he cannot leave even this little one alone. How intense must be his hatred of everybody!

He tried to turn the hostility aside with lightness. "Every one must have a favorite. Sigmund is mine. I intend to make him my heir. Tell Franz that."

"That is unjust to Joseph!" she exclaimed, flushing.

"But Joseph has you, and my father, and Franz," he could not resist saying.

"And so has Sigmund! Baldur, you are being unkind."

He was suddenly bored with her, and wished her to leave. This foolish woman, who had come to him instinctively, in her distraction! Now he had reassured her. She was herself again. The hostility she had developed for him under Franz's expert hands had returned. She was no longer his, Baldur's sister. She must really leave him alone! He put up his hand to hide, not too carefully, a polite yawn. He took up his book again. Yet, he was saddened, and felt infinitely lonely

Then he had another thought. "Franz is in Windsor for a few days, and Pittsburgh. Men dislike changes in household routine. Why don't you discharge Matilda before he returns?" He thought to himself: Why should I still be so concerned over her, and her safety, and her sanity?

She stood up with new briskness, smoothing the white silk of her robe. "Do you think that would be best? As you say, Baldur, dear, men dislike changes so. And upsetting."

"I think it would be best, indeed. If you like, I shall discharge her, saving you the disagreeable duty. Today, perhaps? Before Papa returns? After all, you are mistress of this house, and she can say nothing."

She sighed, contentedly. She came to him now and kissed him lightly on the forehead. He endured the caress, his frail muscles tensing with sad repulsion. She touched his cheek with her little smooth hand. He tried to smile.

"You are so encouraging, Baldur. You have made everything right again. I even forgive you for making Sigmund such a little wretch!" She laughed archly, and before he could speak again, she had floated from the room.

He tried to resume his calm contemplation of the autumn day. But suddenly he felt a profound revulsion, and a sickness. The book dropped from his knee to the floor.

"We live in a kind of Walpurgis Night," he said to himself. "And the one sane one among us, the only healthy one, is Franz Stoessel. Because he is elemental. Because he knows what he wants. Because he is a demon."

Sighing, he rose and pulled the bell-rope for Matilda. She entered, fat, blonde, and belligerent, disdaining an attitude of respect for this miserable cripple, so sure was she of her position. She folded her arms upon her billowing breasts, thrust out her pink and heavy under lip, cocked her head, and eyed him in impudent silence tinged with contemptuous impatience.

Baldur regarded her calmly. He had never favored this woman even with his scorn or disgust. It was paradoxically that in spite of his universal and detached compassion for all things, he had a certain aristocratic temper that hardly admitted humanity in servants and underlings, or those in obscure positions. He would never have imposed upon them, or treated them cruelly, but for him they existed only as animals existed, in a limbo beyond his kind. He spoke to them with an indifferent and impersonal kindness. But for Matilda he did not even have this kindness; he considered her unworthy of the mechanical respect he had for all useful things.

"Matilda," he said, calmly, "I am sorry to tell you that we have made certain other arrangements. Mrs. Stoessel, who is alone, and in a delicate condition, has decided that she needs the care and comfort of her nearest relative, our aunt, Mrs. Trenchard. Mrs. Trenchard has been invited to live with us here, and take charge of the household. You can see, therefore, that much as we regret this, it will be necessary for you to leave us."

Matilda's large fat face expressed blank consternation for a few moments. Then she flushed violently, and her eyes glinted evilly. She drew a deep loud breath. Her lip thrust itself outwards like a shelf, and she regarded Baldur with infuriated detestation.

"I shall ask Mr. Schmidt about this!" she exclaimed. And now she smiled with deliberate obscenity, and moved towards the door.

"A moment," said Baldur, gently, lifting his hand. His voice, though soft, arrested her, and she swung about, baring her teeth.

Baldur helped himself to a cigarette, lit it with quiet deliberation.

"Matilda," he said, "you force me to be very harsh with you, and I regret this, remembering the years you have been with us. You have had—considerable influence over Mr. Schmidt——"

At this, she grinned broadly, put her hands akimbo on her hips, tossed her head.

"O yes!" she said, in a loud slow voice. "I have been very good to Mr. Schmidt, and he will not forget!"

Baldur shook his head regretfully.

"And, we have not forgotten, Matilda." He eyed her deliberately. "There is also something else I, myself, have not forgotten, though Mrs. Stoessel is happily ignorant of the matter. I remember, for instance, that Mr. Stoessel spent an evening with you, in your apartment. It was, no doubt, a very agreeable and very innocent evening, but Mrs. Stoessel might misunderstand this. And Mr. Schmidt, also."

A deep and dusky tide flowed over Matilda's face. Her jaw fell open. She stared at Baldur with hatred and terror.

But Baldur regarded the fingernails of his right hand meditatively.

"Mr. Schmdt," he went on, "has forgotten your existence for some time, Matilda. Nevertheless, he would be considerably annoyed if I told him of that very innocent and pleasant evening. Old gentlemen are peculiar about these things." He paused. "In fact, if you should go to him, protesting about Mrs. Stoessel's decision, I should be obliged to discuss the matter with him."

"He would not believe you!" she shouted, but she glanced fearfully over her shoulder.

"Indeed he would," said Baldur, with a regretful smile. "He knows that I have never lied to him. Moreover, I might even be obliged to accuse Mr. Stoessel in Mr. Schmidt's presence, and that would make matters even more disagreeable. In the end, to restore family peace, you would have to leave, anyway. And, without the thousand dollars I am willing to give you now as a little remembrance for your years of good service. And without a character, which would hamper you in obtaining another position."

He continued, while she looked at him, distraught, at bay, and full of murderous rage:

"There is also the matter of one of my mother's diamond brooches. It has been missing since her death. Mrs. Stóessel has often wondered what became of it. Now, no doubt you know nothing about it, but the police would question you, and this, added to the fact that you would have no character references, would prevent you from finding another position."

"You are accusing me of stealing?" she demanded, now white as death, and consumed with terror. All her hatred was gone, and there was only shock remaining. Baldur felt some compunction. He had never believed for a moment that Matilda had been a thief. Nevertheless, he forced himself to be merciless. He shrugged.

"Who knows?" he murmured. "A woman who has occupied a position such as you have occupied is always open to suspicion. I fear that prospective employers might take this into consideration."

She leaned against the wall, trembling, honestly overcome and brutally shocked. Baldur rose and went to his desk. He wrote a check, handed it to the quivering woman.

"A thousand dollars," he said, softly. "It is a lot of money. You have also received considerable money from my father, and many gifts. This should enable you to go to Pittsburgh, or Philadelphia, and establish yourself. Mrs. Stoessel, I know, will be glad to give you an excellent reference."

She stared blindly at the check. Her heavy features worked. She burst into tears. Then, without another word, she fumbled for the handle of the door, opened it, and left the room, walking as if dazed.

Ruthlessness, thought Baldur, with a wry smile, has its uses, especially when dealing with the ruthless.

CHAPTER 11

ONE EVENING, just before Christmas, Hans Schmidt, old, feeble, silent and hesitating, came into the vast dim dining-room where his daughter and son were already at the table, waiting for him. He walked with a slow uncertain step, peering about him, like a man half-blind, through his spectacles, frowning with only a shadow of his old formidable glance. He fumbled for his chair with such a helpless seeking hand that Baldur, against all the memories of his father's brutality, derision and hate, rose quickly and helped him into his seat. He expected a look of repudiation and detestation, a brusque waving aside, as though Baldur had offered him pollution.

But Baldur, already beginning to shrink instinctively, and with apprehension, for these expected manifestations, was astounded to observe that his father, from his chair, looked up at him with strange and suddenly awakening eyes. Those eyes held the crippled man, and his hand remained on the back of the chair while he looked down with quick attentiveness at his father.

"You are well, my father?" he asked, in Hans's beloved German. It was not often that he spoke in this language to Hans. When alone, he loved the sound of his father's tongue. When with Hans, he loathed it, never spoke it, and even, with rare malice, used complicated English terms in order to bemuddle the old man. That was the only method in which he could employ delicate revenge for a whole lifetime of vicious enmity and persecution.

Hans did not reply. He still continued to regard Baldur with that long strange look, which his son, in spite of his usual astuteness and sharpness of perception, could not interpret.

Ernestine, who was inspecting the beef-broth with assumed criticalness, glanced up, concerned. "Papa, you are feeling better today?"

Hans, slowly and with great effort, turned his eyes away from his son and regarded her blankly. He began to blink. He had been at home, now, for nearly a week, mumbling something about his headaches, backaches, and rheumatism. But he had spent his days locked in his room, refusing medical treatment. What he did in his rooms no one knew. He appeared at meals, and sat through them, silent, hardly eating. Only when Franz entered did he come alive, and then with a watchful aliveness in which there was no affection or interest, but only the attitude of a threatened and helpless animal.

Tonight, Franz had not appeared. He had left a message in the morning that he "might" go to Windsor to see Mr. Jules Bouchard, and "might" be delayed until the next day. As he made frequent short journeys away from Nazareth, the family was accustomed to these absences.

Ernestine began to prattle with the high light nervousness which was now habitual to her.

"I shall be so glad when Aunt Elizabeth comes after Christmas," she said, trying to make conversation in the immense and hollow gloom, which was only dimly lighted by the great crystal chandeliers. "Since Matilda left, I am in such a muddle. So distressing. The servants do as they wish, serve what they wish."

"You have only to give orders to Mrs. Flaherty," said Baldur.

Ernestine raised her finely marked dark brows helplessly. "But I can see that she thinks I am incompetent," she protested. "I order goose, and chicken appears. 'Geese are not good this time of year,' she will say, without apology. It is very disturbing."

There was a little rattle of china, as Hans's thick blind hand missed the saucer with his cup. A long thin stream of coffee trailed across the white cloth. Ernestine saw this. She pressed her pale lips together in a thin line, and gave her brother a tight exasperated look. Gillespie came forward quickly, slipped a napkin under Hans's plate. The old man watched him dully; his eyes moved like those of an infant's, mechanically, without comprehension. His fat body had fallen together, pulplike, these last few months, until it was a shapeless mass. His chins hung flabbily on his chest, his cravat awry. His fat square hands trembled continuously. There was a blankness, an abstraction about him, as though he were drugged. His broadcloth, his linen, always so immaculate, now were dusty and stained and wrinkled. His fingernails were dirt-rimmed. But it was his expression that was so marked, so blank was it, so helplessly abstracted, so lightless, so thickened, so dull. Ernestine saw nothing of it. She only knew, vaguely, that her father had no vitality any longer, no fierceness, no vehemence or violence. In a way, she considered this an improvement. He was becoming a proper, "nice" old man. Besides, Papa was really growing old. Franz had so kindly expressed his concern to her. Papa, he would say, with a disturbed look, had worked too hard all his life. It was time that he should rest, remain at home with his daughter and his grandchildren. He was exhausted. There was a time when a man must retire. But, he, Franz, would be the last to suggest this to Ernestine's father, who, like many tiresome old men, believed himself indispensable. "And dear Franz so considerate, so competent, so well able to take care of dull business matters himself," Ernestine would mourn to her brother, with more than a little impatience and bewilderment. "Papa ought to realize that the mills can be in no better hands. He ought to realize that he is too old to make decisions, and he should be thankful that he has some one like Franz to assume responsibility and management." She added: "I have suggested to Franz that he speak to Papa, himself, but he is so considerate, so careful of others' feelings."

To this, Baldur had said nothing. But he remembered. He particularly remembered, tonight, after his father had given him that long strange regard, blind, yet oddly seeing. His own expression became dark and somber, and he ate silently.

Ernestine had become a pale, thin, shrewish woman, with restless eyes and a nervous, irritable manner. Everything annoyed her, except Franz, whom she adored with a slavish preoccupation. She was large with child, and her sallow skin was threaded with visible veins. Her small hands, delicate and uncertain, had become brownish in tint, and spotted. She brushed her dark curly hair severely about her head, and piled it on top, unbecomingly. She wore "wrappers" at home, of dull brown silk or deep blue, severe of line, though ruffled with lace at the throat. She imagined that she had become a competent wife and mother, and her petulant severity with the servants would have sent them packing their bags, had they not been so long in the service of the Schmidts. As it was, Mrs. Flaherty, who had assumed the position of temporary housekeeper, found it difficult to keep parlor- and chambermaids, who all complained of Ernestine's peevishness and unpredictability and irritable impatience. They disliked her, while not respecting her. Her contradictory orders, her flurries, her complaints, her disorder of mind, impressed them with her futility and lack of sense. The children's governess, Miss Hortense Whitmore, an Englishwoman, definitely despised her.

Ernestine was certain that she, herself, was a brisk competent woman, continually frustrated and beset by a family that was most unsatisfactory. There was Papa, who was so tiresome, and worse than a child himself, and becoming so feeble and obstinate. There was Baldur, locked in his rooms, shutting out poor Franz, who loved music so, and being so uncivil and sardonic with Franz during their encounters at the dining table. And worse then all, upholding that horrible little Sigmund in his tantrums and his moods, and brooding over the child as though he were persecuted and misunderstood, instead of having a Mama who really lived only for her family. Baldur was really impossible, she had concluded, angrily. Truly, it was disgusting, the way he smirked at Franz, when Franz attempted a brotherly friendliness and amiability, and tried to draw Baldur into a discussion of politics, or music, or literature. It was as though Baldur were amused by Franz, an impossible and outrageous situation! And really cruel of them all, in view of her present condition. She was so overburdened! The servants were not like the servants of her girlhood, swift, respectful, competent, obedient. They were impudent, and given to flouncing out of the house. One of them had even been guilty of slapping dear little Joseph vigorously, when he playfully bit her on the arm. Servants had no understanding of children, no tenderness. Simply animals. She had had to discharge one governess, who had soundly trounced Joseph for beating Sigmund. Children must learn to fight their own battles, she had said largely and indignantly to Franz, that night. Miss Schultz was a brute. There was actually a mark on little Joseph's cheek, where the bestial woman had struck him. And it was certainly high time that Sigmund learned to be a little man, instead of a whining little creature, who frequently flew into impotent rages. Miss Whitmore had reported that on one occasion he had taken a heavy iron figurine and had begun to attack Joseph with it when the poor child had only meant a little playful teasing. Only in Franz and Joseph did she find comfort and sustenance, she would complain.

It was a relief to her when Franz, always so considerate, packed her and the child and the governess and two maids off to Asbury Park, or the mountains, or Atlantic City in the summer. And he was so pleased by the coming of Aunt Elizabeth. She spoke of this often to Baldur, with a smiling, childlike complacency, completely forgetting that it was her brother who had suggested this originally. Franz always wanted to spare her, she would assert. She had apparently forgotten the dream her more intelligent soul had forced upwards into her conscious mind.

It was Franz, too, who agreed with her that this horrible old house was no longer a fit place for the family. The street was definitely deteriorating. Why, there was actually a Hungarian doctor in the next block, and a coarse German scientist who had been imported to teach at Nazareth's new medical college! Such an impossible boorish man, not a German like dear Franz or Papa. Possibly even a Jew! Then, the mansion itself had seemed to grow gloomier, darker and more inconvenient. Papa disliked gas so, and consequently it was rarely used in the house. He loved his smelly old oil lamps and candles. The old were so tedious and lacked progressive thoughts, and distrusted the new. When she, Ernestine, had installed a telephone, he had raged for days, and literally screamed profane remarks when its tinkle sounded through the rooms.

But Franz was so considerate, dear Franz! He had gently explained to her that it would be cruel to insist on detaching the old man from the mansion which represented to him his lifetime of work and success. (As if the "success" were not entirely of Franz's doing! But then, Franz was so modest, so dear, so good!) "He is old, and hasn't so much more time to live," he would say to Ernestine, fondly smoothing her hair, or her hand. "Let him live in peace. When he has gone, then we shall consider a fine new house in the suburbs, more in keeping with our position."

Franz, so alive, so robust, so vigorous, forced to live in these horrible dark rooms, which had begun to smell of drains and dust and mustiness. It was dreadful, but so touching, she would say to Baldur, her dark-rimmed tired eyes shining with love and infatuation. And Baldur would listen silently and coldly, thinking those secret thoughts which now so infuriated his sister. He knew that Franz did not dare insist upon abandoning this house. To do so would awaken Hans to a last frantic realization of what had happened to him. Safe in the walls he had built, he retained a last security, a last belief that he still held authority. It was a necessity for Franz to allow him to believe this, the while he daily and deftly stripped the old man of his final kingship. Wrapped in this false security, this false and pathetic faith, he was the more easily undone, the more easily betrayed. Franz was satisfied. In the mills, they knew who was master. Even Dietrich knew, and had accepted. Day by day, sinking deeper into his somber house, still desperately believing in himself, Hans was an impotent, whimpering old dog gnawing his bones, shutting his eyes whenever he could, for the sake of his own reason and his own survival.

Thinking these many things tonight, Baldur watched his

father closely. He saw that Hans barely ate anything, that Gillespie carried away his plate almost untouched. He saw that his father was literally dying, drawn into that last abstraction of the old and the beaten. He saw the blind dead glance, the fumbling hands. He heard the deep hoarse sighs. He knew that his father saw nothing, heard nothing.

The meal over, Ernestine fluttered off to the nursery to hear the children's prayers, and to be sure that Miss Whitmore had not neglected to beat an egg into Joseph's milk, and had not forgotten to flavor it, artfully, with coffee. (The dear child had such an aversion to milk, just like herself at his age!)

Baldur sat alone with his father, under the spectral light of the chandelier, which seemed like some palely illuminated stalactite in the dim hollow cave of the great room. He sipped a glass of wine, holding the fragile crystal thoughtfully in his slender fingers, and watching Hans. The old man sat sunken deeply in his immense carved chair. His bowed whitened head, round and smooth, almost hairless, was outlined sharply against the crimson velvet. He appeared to be asleep, so still was he, so motionless, so hardly breathing. His eye-glasses shone with a ghostly reflected light. For a time Baldur thought he was drowsing, and then, through the glasses, he saw the opaque fixity of his eyes, staring at the table-cloth, and the slack fallen thickness of his lips. The diamond on his hand twinkled a little, like a drowned star. But that was the only life about him.

It was this attitude, abandoned, done, lost, pathetically tragic and impotent, which stirred Baldur as no gesture, no wild crying word, no broken murmur, could have done. Had his father always been retiring, reserved, coldly quiet, his present attitude would have been acceptable as natural senility. But Hans, violent, exuberant, bellicose, degenerated into this pulpy mass of dumbly agonized flesh, was not to be borne with indifference. Baldur had not forgotten the hatred and the murderous enmity which had blighted his whole life. Yet even this memory, paradoxically, increased his compassion and his bitter understanding. Nothing had defeated Hans but Franz Stoessel. And the old man still did not know the nature of the thing which had destroyed him.

Or did he know, at last? In this Walpurgis Night of a house, in this den of monstrous things, had he come to realization? Baldur looked more closely at those fixed unblinking eyes behind the glasses. He looked more closely at the slack hand on the table-cloth.

He wanted to speak, gently, softly. But he had no words to say. Between these two was only a horrible memory, too terrible for speech, too impassable, like a chasm which could not be bridged.

Then, very slowly, as if the very lifting of his lids was at the expense of a mortal effort, Hans looked at Baldur in the shadowy dusk of the silent room, and Baldur, sitting at the other end of the table, looked back. The shining white cloth glimmered between them, with its litter of crystal and silver, only half seen in the dusk. Not even the voice of a servant could be heard, not the creak of a closing door, not a footstep. The snow fell silently outside, and even the wind was still. The fire at the far end of the room burned without sound.

"My son," said Hans, and his voice was a hoarse croak.

Something lurched and fell in Baldur, and something dim made the dim room almost dark before him. His fingers tightened on his glass. But he made no other gesture. "My son," Hans had said. He had never said it before like this, but always with derision, fury and repudiation.

"Yes, Father," replied Baldur, very quietly.

Hans sighed, and Baldur bit his lip at the sound. Hans stirred on his chair, as though his exhausted body had been stricken with a pang, which, though sharp, was not sharp enough to move that dying flesh.

And now Hans groaned, feebly. His hand on the tablecloth lifted and fell. It was not much, but it revealed to Baldur, more eloquently than a furious motion, how close to dissolution the old man was, how tormented. Baldur did not rise. He knew, subtly, that if his father saw again his misshapen body, what he had to say would never be said. Sitting on his padded chair as he was, Baldur gave an illusion of less deformity, even of some strength, for his head was so large and so heroic.

Again, Hans groaned, and the sound seemed to rise from his opening and dying heart. But his eyes had quickened to a dull fever.

"I am sick," muttered the old man, simply. "I am dying. My life, it is over."

Baldur said no quick word of negative, no conventional denial, soothing and false. He said only, very softly, in German: "What is it you wish me to do, my father?"

Now Hans had begun to breathe audibly and hoarsely, as though struggling for breath. He forced himself upright in his chair. A dark suffused flush flowed over his face, and his features became congested. Baldur could see his waistcoat throbbing and heaving. The cravat was like a twisted rope about his thick neck. He struggled for breath, for words to say the things he must say.

"That man—it is my mills—my mills they are lost. No more

the mills are mine. What can I say? The men like him—the mills, the factories, the lands, they are taking from the little men. Like me. Like your father. It eats in my heart," and slowly, poignantly, he struck his chest a slow heavy blow with his clenched fists. "I cannot say what is in my heart——"

"I know," said Baldur, gently.

Hans stared. His hand fell on the table, and the fingers unclenched. Baldur gazed at his father with infinite compassion, the while Hans's suffused tiny blue eyes gaped at him intensely. Then, very slowly, to Baldur's mournful distress, those eyes filled with acrid and most terrible tears, tears like blood seeping upward from his tortured soul.

Then Hans said heavily, ponderously: "Ja." And again, "Ja."

There was silence again. Hans averted his head, stared at the fire. Baldur saw his thick porcine profile. It was somber, sad, no longer blank, but only full of comprehension and weighted despair. It had lost its chronic brutish expression. Now it had a kind of solemn dignity in it, a tragic nobility.

He began to speak once more, almost inaudibly: "Never have I had a friend. Never have I talked to a man. There were no words. Now, in my son, I find my words." He seemed to be thinking aloud, with a sort of humble wonder and grief.

"Yes," said Baldur, very gently. "But you need not speak. I know."

Hans nodded his head, as he still stared at the fire. "It is true," he muttered.

Baldur sighed. "But you and I know, my father, that there is nothing we can do. It is not—Franz, alone. It is all America. Is it good? Is it bad? Who can tell? We cannot stop the flow of change, however we may grieve. That is not to be done."

His voice fell into the silence, as into a dark pit. Baldur thought his father had not heard, for his fixed expression did not change. And then, like a soldier proudly surrendering his sword to invincible defeat, the old man nodded slowly.

"It is true. I must understand it. But, there is my daughter. And my grandchildren. They must not suffer. You understand that, my son?"

"Yes, yes, I understand. But what can I do?"

Now the old man turned his head, and a cunning, monkey-like look wrinkled his features.

"It is for me to do," he said.

He tried to get to his feet, but fell back in his chair, panting. Baldur went to him, and held out his hand. The old man stared at him, first at his face, compassionate, gentle, smiling, comprehending everything, and then at the outstretched hand. Then, very slowly, he gave Baldur his hand. Baldur was alarmed at its coldness and dampness. But he continued to smile. Hans's features worked like those of a child who is about to burst into loud weeping. Then, without speaking, he leaned on that hand, and that arm, and forced himself to his feet.

They went up the great winding staircase together. Hans's eyes moved over the stairs, over the walls, over the stained window, as though he were seeing them for the first time, or the last. They said nothing. Hans's feet seemed numb and stumbling. It was he, not Baldur, who was now the cripple.

Baldur took him to his room. At the doorway, they halted.

"Goodnight, my father," said Baldur gravely.

Hans was silent. He regarded his son with a long strange look. And then he spoke, almost whisperingly:

"Goodnight, my son. Goodnight, my son."

CHAPTER 12

NIGHT AFTER NIGHT, listening to somber January winds, Baldur had waited for Franz Stoessel to come to him.

He knew he would come. At the dinner table, no one could have been more suave, quiet and considerate than Franz, no one more conventional and impersonal. He was gentle and courteous to his wife, amiable to the sententious and dolorous "Auntie Elizabeth," smilingly indulgent to her "impossible" children, Richard and Marcia. (Baldur knew how much iron self-control that involved, for he had long known that Franz detested the young.) With Baldur, he maintained a quiet and aloof dignity. Baldur sat, now, in his father's empty seat, though he knew that Ernestine had privately protested to Franz, with considerable indignation. In these days, Baldur had come to admire Franz, not reluctantly, but wholeheartedly, as he always admired the valorous. He knew now that Franz had a species of real valor, all the more amazing when one was aware of his real emptiness and long chronic fear. Baldur also knew that this valor, though compounded in no small part of hypocrisy, self-seeking and opportunism and falseness, nevertheless had a measure of genuine verity. It came from his blood, which, though denied for years, had in it the elements which made Emmi Stoessel inflexible, honest, and grimly shining with integrity.

Baldur, these days, was frequently overcome with fresh wonder at the complexity of the human spirit, in which all vices and viciousness could live in comparatively peaceful juxtaposition with nobilities. He was no bright-eyed enthusiast, who believed men were either good or evil. He was contemptuous of those who declared that "evil" was the result of childhood obstacles and handicaps, or perverse misunderstanding. (As well declare, he would say, that storms and earthquakes and cyclones, came not from a nature designed to be "beneficent," but from some malignant causes outside of, and in spite of, nature. The storms and earthquakes and cyclones in the human spirit were as inherent in it as were its social "goodnesses." They must be reckoned with dispassionately. It was folly to treat them as "illnesses." Men were born with them, as they were born with blue eyes or brown, with crooked noses or straight.) And so, he was not overly amazed that Franz Stoessel, the expedient, the ruthless, the cruel and the treacherous, and the fear-ridden and merciless, could display this dignified and bitter valor. He was not amazed that Franz frequently was genuinely kind and gentle. He had long ago discovered that he was truly fond of a certain boardinghouse keeper, a Mrs. Dolly Harrow, and her three young daughters, and he had come upon other occasions, believed by Franz to be secret, when he had displayed evidences of selflessness, courage and understanding. Consistency in character, thought Baldur, is found only in the novels of Charles Dickens and others of his school. The one real fact in human nature is inconsistency.

He did not feel a new respect or softness for Franz in the recognition of his valor. It did not surprise him. He did not think, foolishly: "I have underrated him. I have done him some injustice." He did not discard all his knowledge of Franz's wickednesses with the large and emotional cry of: "He is really an excellent person, whom I have wronged!" He merely accepted the valor as another one of Franz's attributes which he had not heretofore recognized. It did not increase either his respect or contempt for Franz. It only increased his comprehension, and heightened his interest.

Knowing that he would come to him, Baldur, that he must come, Baldur was, nevertheless, surprised at the long delay. He had expected the coming within two weeks of Hans's death, just after Christmas. But now it was nearly the end of

January, and Franz had not come. Baldur's interest and curiosity were enhanced. He had come to find life very exciting recently. What was delaying Franz? Baldur did not for an instant believe that it was resignation, or compromise. He knew Franz too well. In fact, only he of all who knew and had known Franz, really understood him. But still Franz did not come. He treated his brother-in-law with reserve and politeness. He never spoke of the mills. He sat at Baldur's left hand at the table, paler, thinner, less vital, perhaps, in a physical way, than usual. But what he lost in physical vitality he had regained in a vitality of spirit, which had made him grim, silent, more inexorable, more dangerous. Baldur would frequently and covertly study him, observing the new sharpness in eyes never soft at best, the new hardness of a mouth once given to easy smiles, the new deep line in the high light forehead, the new chiselling of the planes of cheek and chin and temple. Baldur knew that he was suffering. And men like Franz, when suffering, were deadly. If he could kill me, thought Baldur with amusement, he would do so. A little more courage, a little more cunning, a little less caution, and perhaps, a little less valor, and he would contrive that I should have an "accident" of some sort. But, he lacks daring.

Baldur knew that Franz had frequently been daring in his life. But it was not the daring of the true adventurer, the true reckless of spirit. There was too much of the German in him. He dared only when he had nothing to lose, and when he had a fair chance of gain. Then, he was completely ruthless. But never would he sacrifice, for one gesture of daring, what he had already secured.

Was it patience that was delaying Franz's coming? The patience of the German who never moved except when he had a fair chance of succeeding? Sometimes Baldur, with pleasant excitement, suspected that Franz was playing a cat-and-mouse game with him, that he was trying to lull him into indifference or boredom. He had come to accept this latter theory in a measure, for though Franz's voice was always grave, measured, courteous and calm with him, his eyes were like bits of polished steel. Franz was watching him. Baldur pretended that he was unaware of this. And now, he began to try to hasten Franz's coming by assuming an air of languid unawareness and forgetfulness. Was he deceiving Franz? At times he had been impressed with Franz's acuteness with regard to human nature. And then he had discovered that Franz was acute only when confronting those attributes in another with which he was familiar, having found them in himself. Attributes which he did not possess puzzled and infuriated him, rendered him helpless and confused. Had he been a Frenchman, a Latin, a Jew, an Oriental, Franz would, by delicate intuition, have been able to understand alien attributes. But Germans never understood the nature of others unlike them. That accounted for an obtuseness which puzzled, amused or alarmed other races. At the end, some day, Baldur would think, we shall have to reckon with this ominous and dangerous obtuseness. Since 1860, the world had had to reckon with it three times, to its dismay, its wounds, and its shock. What did the future hold? (Baldur, though half-German himself, never thought of himself as anything but an American, as alien to Franz as a Chinaman.)

Then, one night, Franz came.

At the dinnertable, Franz had been even paler than usual, even more silent. There was an abstraction about him, gloomy and somber. When Ernestine, in her adoration, had fluttered about him anxiously, he replied to her tremulous inquiries by saying that he was tired. He had answered her patiently and gently. His eyes, Baldur had observed, became less hard when he looked at her. Was it fondness, or exhaustion? Was he, at last, grateful for her unquestioning adoration in a world which had become somewhat too much for him? Baldur doubted that a little, though he did not discard the idea. Or was he giving, for Baldur's benefit, and subsequent softening, an exhibition of husbandly appreciation? Baldur subscribed to this theory not a little. He had noticed that Franz was less malicious with his wife since Hans's death, especially in Baldur's presence, less obscurely ridiculing, less jocose. He must be carrying this attitude over even into the privacy between husband and wife, for Ernestine no longer had that faintly lost and bewildered expression when emerging from the chambers she shared with him.

Baldur watched closely that night. Suddenly he knew that this was the night when Franz would come to him. He listened to Ernestine's urging that Franz "retire" immediately after dinner. He heard Franz agree that "that might be best." Husband and wife left the dining-room together, Ernestine, small and frail and aging, fluttering at his elbow. Baldur, smiling a little to himself, went up to his rooms.

He drew the heavy draperies across the face of the dark wet night outside. He stirred up his fire. He placed two glasses and a decanter of cognac on a little table. He opened a box of cigars, put fresh cigarettes in a silver box beside it. Then he sat down near his fire, opened a book, read and waited. The firelight fell in long fluttering shadows over the quiet austerity of the great studio. The high beamed ceiling was lost in dusk. The few chairs stood waiting, emptily. The wind mourned at the shrouded windows. Baldur did not glance at the mahogany clock which ticked on the mantel. He reckoned that it would be an hour or two before Franz came. He read quietly. Above his head hung Irmgard's portrait, and it seemed to watch and wait, also.

Baldur, thinking of this night which must come, had contemplated it with anticipatory amusement. But for some reason he was not now amused. He was only quiet. He was reading "Madame Bovary," which was one of his favorites. Nevertheless, he believed that Flaubert had touched only the surface in his analysis of the unhappy woman, and this irritated him. Absorbed, the hours went by. He aroused himself with a start. The clock chimed a soft eleven. He frowned. Had his judgment been wrong? Surely, it was too late for Franz to come now. The house was sleeping.

There was a curious quality to the slumber of the great old house, hideous as it was in a sort of formless deformity of stone and brick. It was when the mansion slept that Baldur realized with what intensity and repulsion he hated it. Then it lay like an unconscious giant, all its ugliness, its sinister outlines, its brooding darkness, revealed. No matter how high the fires were piled, how well the new central heating worked, there was a dank coldness like a vault or an underground cavern about it. Since poor Hans's death, this quality had seemed to thicken, to become dense, like a fog. Once, Baldur had heard Ernestine mention that they would soon be thinking of a new home in the suburbs, a "bright, pretty house, with flowers and grass and trees." Baldur, who knew the reason why Franz had remained while Hans was alive, knew now that again Franz did not dare to leave, because of himself, Baldur.

He stared at the fire, listening to its slow dropping of coals, louder now in the Stygian stillness, and to the ticking of the clock, dropping the moments into oblivion. Then he heard the knock at the door, subdued, but firm. It was Franz. Baldur began to smile irresistibly, then composed his features. He called gravely to enter.

Franz came in. Baldur watched him with deep curiosity. Yes, he had lost much weight. He was no longer sleek and suave, like a well-fed blond seal or well-scrubbed hog. He was no longer pink. His fine broadcloth, dark and smooth, seemed too large for him. His linen was immaculate, his cravat was tied with its old fastidiousness. Leaner, quieter, not smiling, there was a dangerous fixed quality about him, which held Baldur's attention. Those eyes were the eyes of a deadly enemy. His pale wide lips were smooth and pale, faintly glistening. He moved with sureness and quickness. He did not smile. He sat down on the opposite side of the fireplace, and the two men looked intently at each other.

"It is time for a talk between us," said Franz, in a hard voice.

Baldur inclined his head, gravely and courteously, without speaking.

Franz had expected a look of mocking or ironic surprise, a light superficial word, which was Baldur's usual manner whenever he approached him. He was somberly angered at Baldur's gravity, his polite indifference, and a cold shaft of flame sprang from his eyes to the other man's. His pale lips stretched in a grimace, and Baldur saw the sudden white gleam of teeth, like those of a savage. Dangerous, he commented again to himself, and felt a thrill of amused and contemptuous excitement. What does he expect? Does he actually believe he can frighten me with his hating looks and his murderous eyes? And yet, he felt compassion again for this man driven by himself, sometimes against his own will, sometimes against the cry of his own misery.

Franz caught his breath, and his nostrils distended. He was trying to control himself, trying to be cold and calm over his inward passion and fury.

"I have decided to take my wife and children away," he said, in a low harsh voice. "Perhaps to another city." He paused. "Perhaps to Windsor."

"Indeed," murmured Baldur, inclining his head again, thoughtfully. His expression was all brotherly interest. "The climate, they say, is very superior."

He saw the spasmodic clenching of Franz's fists, their sudden relaxing, as though at a command. His body retained its calm, but Baldur felt its iron coldness and tenseness as though Franz's flesh were his own. When Franz suddenly smiled, he felt the aching of his own facial muscles.

"You will miss Sigmund," said Franz.

There was a little silence. All compassion for him left Baldur. He felt his heart grow molten with detestation, contempt, anger, and even a small bitter fear. Deep in his large blue eyes the ominous spark grew. But he said, very quietly:

"Yes, I shall miss Sigmund. However, you must let me see him often. He is my heir, you know." He paused, then continued tranquilly, watching Franz: "The mills, of course. Everything. However, I have decided, in the event you leave, to sell the mills. Not to the Sessions Company." He shook his head, gently smiling. "No. No. To Carnegie. He has already made me a private offer through his agents."

In his mind he reverted to his father's tongue, and thought: schweinehund, I have you there!

It gave him a savage and even violent pleasure to see Franz's face, to observe his efforts to maintain a control fast slipping, to watch him use his actor's ability, so transparent now, to impress his brother-in-law. He watched the indulgent smile, in which there was no real indulgence, spread over Franz's haggard and ghastly face, already faintly glistening with moisture. He watched the blond eyebrows lift, as though in affectionate surprise. His own face, calm and pale, became grim and fixed.

"To Carnegie? But that is foolish. If you sell, you will of course sell to me." And then Baldur heard his indrawn breath, harsh and painful.

Baldur stretched out his hand calmly, took a cigarette, extended a wax taper to the fire. He lit the cigarette, and indicated the box of cigars to Franz. "Excellent," he murmured.

Franz took a cigar, and Baldur courteously lit it with his taper. He saw the trembling of Franz's fingers, and despite himself, he felt a thrill of compassion again. But, he thought, if you will play, then I will play with you. I am a better master of playing than you, my good murderous friend. You play as a German plays, not even trying to understand your adversary. For that, you will have to suffer a little.

He said, aloud: "What price?"

The cigar almost fell from Franz's fingers as he held it to his lips. Then he withdrew it. His face had come alive, and tense, and viciously relieved. He relaxed. But his hand still trembled.

"What is your price?" he countered.

Baldur stared at him with a strange expression. Then he stood up, faced the fire, standing in his complete deformed profile before Franz. In spite of his efforts, his voice shook.

"You haven't sufficient money to buy—my mills. You must understand that at once."

He turned his face to Franz, and his eyes were full of anger, sadness and contempt.

"Are you never honest? Must you always think other men are like you? Must you always lie, and expect nothing but lies from others?"

Franz did not answer. He could not look away from Baldur. But his face became congested, crimson. His temples, beneath his thick yellow hair, became knotted with purple veins. Then he stood up, suddenly. He threw his cigar into the fire. His fists clenched again. All at once his wild savagery, his rage, his hatred, his frustration and despair, boiled to the surface, and he could no longer control himself. He began to speak in a turmoil of furious gasping words, hurling them at Baldur like stones, stones flung by a vehement but distraught hand. And he spoke in German.

"What are these mills? I have made them? They are mine! Even you must admit that! All my life, it is in these mills! They were nothing. They were failing. Do you hear? Failing! I took them, and made them what they are! Your father," and his face, his voice, were terrible in their hatred, their malignancy, "your father!" He paused, and the crimson turned purplish in his swollen face; he struggled for breath. "I had every reason to believe, from what he said, from the things he did, that the mills would be left, rightfully, to me! You had no need of them. They were nothing to you. You knew nothing of them, cared less. But they were mine!" He struck himself a dull blow on the chest with his fist, and in his mad and almost insane sincerity, there was nothing melodramatic in the gesture. "It is not I who lied. It was your father! For some reason, at the last, he turned against me—" He glared at Baldur, and then was silent, his voice choking in his throat.

Baldur regarded him silently, with deep gravity. Then he said: "You are quite right. I agree with you. The mills ought to have been left to you. My father turned against you, yes. Because he was old. Because he hated and dreaded this new day of industrial development." He smiled slightly. "You see, we agree much better when you are honest, when you play no games with me, when you are yourself, instead of a controlled counterfeit gentleman, and a liar."

Franz, still choked by his fury and despair, was completely bewildered. His color paled, until he was ghastly again. He was trembling violently. He was compelled to reach out his hand and grasp the mantelpiece to support himself. And he looked at Baldur, without comprehension, and even with an idiot's look of complete blankness. Then his mouth began to twitch, and a muscle stretched and throbbed in his drawn cheek.

"Nevertheless," said Baldur, seating himself, "the mills are mine. Willed to me, out of my father's bewilderment, fear and hatred of change. Perhaps it was a revenge upon you. But it still remains that the mills belong to me. The mills you have made from your duplicity, your cleverness, your opportunism, your greed and relentlessness and exploitation of your betters. Is this fair? Logically, and as a civilized man, I am compelled to answer 'no.' It is not fair. But ironically, and I appreciate irony, it is fair. The idea gave my father the only pleasure he has had since he was unfortunate enough to have known you. Do not look at me like that. But it was a misfortune, in a way, for him, was it not? Let us be honest. You took from him everything that made his life worth living. You took his self-respect, and his vanity, for he had met in you a worse rascal than himself. And he did pride himself on his rascality!" He smiled with humor, a humor which Franz most visibly did not appreciate.

Baldur fitted his slender fingers together so that they formed a fragile tent. He smiled at them, as though they were a pattern of intense jocularity.

"I do not agree with my father, as I have said. 'Industry must go on.' But why? Do not mind me. I am given to improper reflections. I see no progress in an ever-growing industrial civilization. But that is because I have the spirit of a recluse, and men of action are always detestable to me. I am not incomprehensible?"

Again, Baldur saw the gleam of Franz's teeth, like a flash in his lead-colored face. He saw the narrowed eyes, in which something unhuman and monstrous eddied and swirled.

"You are not incomprehensible," said Franz.

But you would kill me if you dared, thought Baldur, with enjoyment. He made a large gesture, deliberately intending to inflame the other more.

"If I had my way—and who knows but what I will?—I would turn these mills back to the workers, who, speaking in fairness, really deserve them, and own them. It is they, after all, who have made it possible for you to be a rich man. Ah, but there I am becoming improper again! Men of my kind are not realists. But when I think of this, I come against another logic: in another sense, the mills really do belong to you. In fact, they belong to all of us!"

He smiled blandly, pleased, assuming an expression of childlike surprise as though he had come upon some sweet shining truth.

Franz had become as white, cold and rigid as death. Baldur, with sudden admiration, studied him. He admired the quiet voice when the other spoke:

"You have asked me to be honest. I now ask you to be honest. You are playing with me. Speak honestly. This is too serious to me."

Bladur nodded his head, and his look became stern.

"Play, then, with fools. Not with me. I know a few tricks of my own. Will you sit down?"

Franz sat down. They surveyed each other with gravity and with bitterness. And then Baldur knew that he had not been mistaken in believing that this man possessed valor. He knew, also, that those who had valor deserved a measure of respect even from enemies. For valor was not courage, which was purely a physical phenomenon, and not more to be admired than the animal strength and brutality of a wild beast, or the mane of a lion, or the audacity of a tiger. Valor frequently accompanied cowardice, fear and despair, and was admirable because it surmounted them in one supreme gesture. In his valor, Franz was not a German. He was only a man. The true German had courage, but no valor.

His thoughts finally dissolved the bitterness in Baldur's level gaze. He said, almost kindly:

"I have discovered something about you, Franz. To you, it would seem contemptible, if I explained it. I do not find it contemptible. It deserves candor and honesty, and demands dignity in my treatment of you."

Franz's eyes narrowed craftily. He smiled slightly, and because of the inexplicable stroking of his vanity, he felt an odd warmth for Baldur, and an ease. Color returned to his face. His hand had stopped its ceaseless trembling. Yet, Baldur sensed a wariness in him. He is trying to maintain the mysterious thing which has aroused my admiration, he thought, even though he does not know what it is.

"I shall not waste your time, Franz. I do not want to waste my own time. You spoke of going to Windsor. At first, I thought that was a crude lie on your part, calculated to force me to some of your terms. I do not think it is a lie, now. Tell me about it."

His vanity again stroked, Franz said candidly: "I was not lying. Since your father's death, I have been to see Jules Bouchard. He has offered to make me Vice-President of Sessions, at a very large salary. We have been having some very amiable conversations, for the past few years. He wants to use me. But I can play his game! We can have a very fine time playing games with each other! I think I would win some of them. He knows that. He would enjoy my winning, if I were clever enough. I have seriously thought of accepting his offer."

"Why?" asked Baldur, coolly.

Franz hesitated. He dropped his eyes. Should he lie? He glanced up, swiftly, furtively, to see Baldur watching him closely. The accursed, damned cripple, who saw everything! He must continue to tell the truth, and the truth was strange and unfamiliar to him.

He said: "As I have told you, I have made these mills of your father's, because I believed I would have them when he died. I can work only for myself, never for others, never for 'family.' I am not made in that way. The instinct of a German is in, and for, his family. I lack that instinct. I can think only of myself, of my own game. If I remained here, I thought, I would be working for you, for my wife, for my children. That is intolerable to me, especially when I remember that I would be, in a large way, only your hireling. That is not sufficient. I would prefer to work for a stranger, for Jules Bouchard."

He added: "Will you not sell the mills to me?"

But Baldur said: "I see. I understand." He was silent for a moment, then resumed: "The mills are nothing to me. I can sell them, of course. But not to you. Why? Because I do not want you to have them that way." He looked at Franz blandly, and Franz's jaw tightened, and again his eyes were cold and hating flame. But he said nothing.

Baldur said reflectively: "You cannot 'work' for me, because you have your pride. I understand that, too. I understand many things. I have said I care nothing for the mills. But they are my hold on you. I do not trust you, you see," he continued, smiling.

There was a long pause. Then Baldur said: "I will make you an offer. I hold the controlling interest in the Schmidt Steel Company, and I intend to keep it. That is, if you remain. If you do not remain, I shall sell them. Do not think for a moment that I shall regret this. I would prefer to be rid of them."

A spasm, as of acute and aching pain, passed over Franz's face. But he listened intently, hardly breathing.

"I hold the controlling interest," repeated Baldur. "Nevertheless, if you wish, I shall make you president of the mills. I shall be a 'silent' chairman, never interfering with you, not even if some of the things you do in the mills strike me as outrageous. I am not concerned with social justices, or what you do. I am not a reformer. I shall retain the interest, if you remain with me, solely to have a hold on you."

"Why?" asked Franz, in a low voice.

"Because of Sigmund," said Baldur, coldly.

There was still another silence. Baldur observed Franz with great intentness, reading all his dark and obscure and malignant thoughts. Then he said: "However, if you think to use me through the child, you are wasting your time. Take the child away, and I assure you that I shall forget him. I can always forget what I want to forget. But if you remain, I have my demands, also."

Franz looked at him, and said: "What are they?"

"That you leave the child to me. Listen carefully. I do not ask that you abandon the child to me, or that you live in continual fear that I shall be blackmailing you, and that if you do not please me by some treatment of him, I shall put unfair pressure on you. I could not endure such a life, for I am very lazy, very inert, and do not like unpleasantnesses. But I do ask that we have a secret between us, and that in matters I consider important, you will consult with me about him. And that, after due consideration, I have the final decision. That is all."

Franz bit his lip. His eyes studied Baldur long and deeply, under his thick blond brows drawn and knitted and knotted together. Then he said: "And the mills——"

"I shall leave my shares to Sigmund. But he shall not inherit them until you and I are both dead. He will never know of this arrangement, however."

His expression became stern and melancholy. "This is a curious pact. It is yours to accept or refuse."

Franz stood up abruptly, and walked to the windows. He flung aside the draperies, and stared out into the wailing darkness. Without glancing at him, and looking only at the sinking fire, Baldur said softly:

"You are the child's father. I ask you to treat him with a little more justice. But even if you continue as you have done, tormenting him, hating him, I shall do nothing more than to try to alleviate his misery, as I have always done. You do not care for him. That is your misfortune and his. But more your misfortune. Sometimes I believe you have tormented him, to hurt me. I must ask you not to do that again. That is the least I can ask. I do not demand, however: I believe that there is some humanity in you, some latent decency. Try to exercise it.

"Suppose, however, that you decide to leave me. You will go to Sessions. You will be hampered there. By Jules Bouchard. I have seen him only once or twice. You know more about him than I do. I ask you to reflect on him, and consider if he will be a better master than I. Or if you will go farther with him. You will not even make as much money! And you will certainly not have the freedom, the authority. Perhaps, however, that will not be so important to you as thwarting me."

Franz, not turning, said in a muffled voice: "Nothing is so important to me as doing what I have been doing, in these mills. I have never let personal considerations interfere with anything I wish to do."

Baldur looked reflectively at the fire, and said quietly: "You accept, then?"

Franz came back. He sat down slowly. Again, he was very pale. "Yes," he said, deliberately. "I would be a fool to refuse. You have offered me everything."

And then, for the first time since he had entered this room tonight, he looked at Irmgard's portrait on the wall above Baldur's head. Baldur, though he did not lift his eyes from the fire, knew that he looked, and again, he felt admiration for this man who could forget everything in his one supreme purpose, his own desire for limitless power, his own love for himself, though it was a love deeply intermingled with profound hatred.

CHAPTER 13

EACH MORNING the children came in to see their parents after their nursery breakfast. Because Franz could not endure breakfast in the chill gloomy vault of the dining-room, his own breakfast, and Ernestine's, was served in what he considered the only cheerful room in the house. After Mrs. Schmidt's death, her large chamber had been converted into a "morning-room" for Ernestine, and assisted by Baldur's suggestions, she had made it into a sunny, gaily colored and comfortable apartment, with much emphasis on yellow, coral and light-green. She had, in late years, manifested her mother's desire for darkness and heaviness and somber draperies, which Baldur, seconded by Franz, had declared to be sickly and disheartening. At times, these days, she found the sunlight a little overpowering, and the colors of the room not too flattering to her increasing sallowness and pallor, but Franz declared the room to be gay and cheerful and homelike. This was enough for her. Because he liked flowers, every vase and bowl overflowed, even in winter, with masses of soft bloom and sprays of ferns. The fire burned in a grate beneath a simple white-marble mantelpiece, over which hung a large canvas of yellow roses. (Mrs. Trenchard, that dolorous and sententious lady, declared that the room was "vulgar," and had no "elegance nor air." This however, did not discourage Franz, who said privately to his wife that there was "air and air," with different connotations.)

In this room he could be amiable, and assume, without much trouble, an aspect of paterfamilias. He could even endure his wife's company for an hour, in the midst of this warm gaiety of color. He could be indulgent to his sons, throwing them a word from behind his morning newspaper and the cloud of smoke from his cigar. In truth, he felt relaxed in this room, whether the early winter morning demanded gaslights or fire, or whether rain gushed in cataracts at the widely exposed windows.

The January winds and rain had halted in the night, but there was an iron silence, an iron gloom, about the air, the sky and the earth today. Moreover, it had become very cold, and tiny icicles had formed on the window-ledges. Ernestine, in her crimson-velvet peignoir, which was trimmed with bands of white ermine, shivered involuntarily as she sat before the fire, her feet on the brass fender. Always conscious of her seniority over her husband, and increasingly conscious of her swollen body and shrinking sallow features, she attempted a coquettish hair-dress. Her front hair was banged and frizzed in the latest mode, the back and sides swirled to a large bun on the top of her head. But because it lacked vitality and youth, there were always a number of untidy and frayed locks straggling over her thin neck, which had lost its former whiteness and innocence. Lost, too, was the former delicate shyness and the fragile, uncertain gaiety she had possessed as a young woman, qualities Hans had loved. There had once been a pathetic eagerness about her, and a sweetness, a softness. All these had been replaced, and the impulsiveness, too, by a fretful and chronic semi-invalidism, a slight but constant hysteria, a melancholy and tired uncertainty. And a feverish bewilderment, both painful and tedious to her associates. Moreover, she had developed a peevishness with every one but Franz, with whom she was always nervously fearful, solicitious, eager to please, adoring and possessive, yet servile. Her absorption in him had given her once-soft and upcurling lips a hysterical, half-parted droop, imparting to her countenance a look of blankness and instability. Her feeble health, rapidly declining, had sallowed her complexion, and had encircled her eyes with dark streaked circles. Even her eyes had lost something of their large simplicity and childlike ingenuousness, which had been replaced by a wandering and febrile stare. She looked much as her mother had looked at her age, and the resemblance was markedly increasing every day. Her voice, once high and sweet, had sharpened, developing an undertone of petulance. Because of brown spots on her small thin hands, she affected much frothing of lace at the sleeves, and many rings, which repulsed Franz, who liked simplicity and cleanness in women, or, in some women, healthy exuberance and sparkle. There was something in Ernestine which he found unhealthy and unclean, no matter her perfumes and her Pears' soap. Perhaps this was because her body, in spite of two pregnancies, remained flat and immature, and without vitality. Her shriveled flesh and bad color, her ringed eyes and fluttering hands, made him distend his nostrils as though they had encountered a fetid odor, which revolted him. At one time, during the early years of their marriage, he had sometimes liked a certain illusive delicacy in her, a certain light laugh and innocent eagerness. These had gone, leaving an aging woman full of pains and weariness behind, a woman who disgusted him with her love and her hands, which gave him, in his health and strength, a sense of personal violation.

He had not forgotten Irmgard. But the singular quality of his mind prevented him from concentrating upon her to the hurt of his ambitions and his expediency. However, she remained for him a symbol of that cleanness and freshness which he secretly loved, and which became all the more precious to him in this atmosphere of cloying adoration, dark corners, gloomy corridors and close unaired smells. When he thought of Irmgard, he seemed to see her on a high windy hill-top, silhouetted against a brilliant blue sky. He had never seen her like this, with the odors of sweet hay and pungent fields heavy about her, and sun on her hair and on her lifted profile. Yet, he was sure he had really seen it, and the memory tormented him when he was alone at night. Somewhere in his mind the clue lurked, tantalizing, yet promising a momentous revelation if he could find it. He still searched for Irmgard, but without much hope, and now, without much passion. She had become a dream to him, as she was a dream to Baldur. But the dream made his life with Ernestine all the more unbearable, and increased his hatred for his wife, and his disgust. However, his self-control, which came from his shrewd and scheming lack of imagination, made him put aside anything which might distract him and give him pain. Baldur suspected hypocrisy in Franz's blandness and amiability. But there was more than hypocrisy. There was self-protectiveness, and a real ability to make the most of the passing moment, and the passing acquaintance.

He had a curiosity about his children, half-instinctive, half-malicious, and so he endured Ernestine's cosy and maternal interviews with the little boys in the morning. He would put down his paper and smile at them indulgently and pleasantly. He would rally them, chuck them under their chins, tease them more than a little, then admonishing them with a sudden hard sternness which Sigmund found distracting, he would yawn, rise, kiss his wife on her flabby thin cheek, pat the boys on the head, and leave. For the rest of the day he never gave them a thought.

Ernestine had a headache this morning. The headaches her physician ascribed to her "delicate condition." But she remembered that she had been having them for years. She detested the thought of spectacles, which would enhance her appearance of seniority, and, fond of reading romantic and grandiloquent novels, she would squint for hours over fine close print. Thereafter, she would be exhausted and almost blind. Last night she had read until three in the morning, not putting down her book until she heard Franz's soft feline steps on the carpet in the corridor. She had hurriedly blown out her bedside lamp, pretending to sleep. Never did she reproach him for these long mysterious absences at night. Something instinctive warned her against the revelation which would bring her agony, for she had no doubt, in her subconscious mind, that Franz would take a malevolent pleasure in telling her, if she asked. But, consciously, she told herself that she pretended sleep because he would be annoyed at this threat to her health in long sleepless hours of reading.

The little boys came in, having eaten their breakfast. They were small for their nine years, but they were neat in their tight little trousers, long black stockings and buttoned boots, and dark-blue blouses with wide, braid-trimmed sailor collars. Their boots shone; their hair was brushed and smoothed until it gleamed. Joseph was slightly smaller than his twin, and quicker, and more given to quick sly grins. Sigmund walked reluctantly one step in Joseph's rear, his diminutive triangular face watchful and somewhat sullen. There was a bruise on his cheek.

Ernestine held out her arms to them with a wide dramatic gesture. "My darlings!" she fluted, in her high voice which had for some time taken on a thin tremor. She never lost the hope that her children would spring lovingly into her arms, and she would hold them to her breast, looking wide-eyed and smiling over their heads at Franz. (There was just such a picture in the novel she was now reading: "Mrs. Smitherley's Secret Loves." She was enamored of the picture she would make, but the picture never materialized. Joseph invariably sidled over to her, crab-wise, impatiently evading her arms, and letting her warm kiss touch his ducking ear. Then he would dart away, on some restless errand of exploration. Sigmund, however, would approach within a wary two feet of her, and would hang back as she would literally drag him to her knee. There he would suffer a kiss on his cheek. He did not move. He would merely grow rigid and very stiff. She would, at the last, have to push him away with a half-playful, half-impatient laugh. "Such a cold child," she would say, and in her smile was something repellent and inimical.

The same pantomime transpired this morning. Franz found it enjoyable. He knew what Ernestine wished, and what she thought, and he found her invariable frustration one of the happier moments of his morning. Consequently, his smile for his children would be genuinely amiable and amused, as if he were grateful. He found nothing pathetic in the scene. He never considered the heart-hunger behind the dramatics. He only knew that Ernestine produced this little play in order to seduce him into a fresh realization of their own intimacy as parents of these children. His satisfaction at her wistful disappointment and frustrated sickly sentimentality made him feel quite a real, if only momentary, fondness for the little boys. They were conspirators with him against the unhealthiness which was their mother.

There was a smudge of egg on Joseph's upper lip this morning, and Ernestine complainingly called him back to her. Protesting, scowling, the little fellow returned to her, struggled while she wiped off the egg with a wisp of handkerchief saturated with eau de cologne. (Always, in later years, the children were nauseated by that strong lemon odor, for it reminded them of their mother's morning-room, her damp thin hands, her aura of ill-health and forlornness.) In the meantime, Sigmund waited rigidly for his mother to comment peevishly on something in his toilette, after the more gentle ministrations offered Joseph. He was not disappointed. When Joseph darted away to his father, Ernestine critically examined Sigmund. The English governess, however, was exemplary. Nothing was wrong. Ah, yes: one dark brown lock of hair did not lie so closely to his long narrow skull as it might have done. She pulled him to her with a hard and wiry jerk, and forcibly laid down the lock. Her hand had an almost vicious strength in it as she did so.

"Such an untidy little boy," she sighed. Sigmund's large blue eyes met hers. He felt the old familiar pang, vague, insecure, half-frightened, at the expression in her eyes, pointed, cold and suspicious. It was this he saw, not the fond smile. He did not love his mother. He was even more repelled by her than Joseph, for his sensibilities were sharper and more delicate. But it frightened him that any one should dislike him so, that he, a child, should be regarded by an adult with personal animosity. His world, unstable enough as it was in this gaunt dark mansion, surrounded by servants, filled with hatred for his father and repulsion for his mother, tottered even more precariously during these cosy morning interviews.

Joseph had climbed upon Franz's knee. He was chattering loudly in his childish treble. It was no gay juvenile talk, full of babyish laughter and high spirits. It was a pack of exaggerated lies and complaints about the governess. Joseph was a born liar. He lied without provocation, and merely for dramatic effect. He lied with malice and cruelty, hoping for revenge on everything and every one. Franz listened, amused and knowing. His big strong hand held the thin little body on his knee. He smiled into Joseph's narrow sparkling eyes.

"Dirty, little, lying schwein," he said at last, indulgently. Joseph paused. He grinned. He was not offended. Franz's hand explored tentatively in one of his pockets, and Joseph waited, with eagerness. Franz produced a silver coin, which Joseph snatched, with a squeal of delight. Ernestine watched, smiling affectionately, her head on one side. "But he does lie dreadfully, Franz," she murmured.

"This is no world for an honest man," he replied. He was already bored with the child. He pushed him off his knee. He looked down at his paper. Then his eye, travelling downward, encountered the face of Sigmund, watching unblinkingly.

Franz's hand, reaching for his paper, halted in midair. He was used to these eye-encounters with his other son, but they never failed to disconcert him, and infuriate him. There was no fear in the little boy's expression at these times, only an inscrutable wideness and something too large even for conjecture. Franz frowned slightly. He had been able to quell the treacherous and unnamed thing which sometimes made him wish to reach out suddenly for the child and hold him, as one held a strange verity in the midst of chaos. He had been able to quell it, yes, but its pang remained, like a chronic sore, angering him, shaming him, depressing him. Lately, it made him want to inflict some cruelty on this helpless child, in revenge for his own pain.

"What are you staring at, you little monkey?" he asked, not smiling, his expression and his voice brutal.

Ernestine came alertly to life, and frowned severely on Sigmund.

"What a rude little boy!" she said. "Why do you not answer your Papa?"

Sigmund slowly turned and looked at her. "I was just looking at him," he said. Then he seemed to shrink, bent his head, and wandered disconsolately to the window. Franz's eye followed him, and his scowl deepened.

Ernestine, the sycophant wife, became feverishly animated. She looked after the child. "I don't know what is to become of him!" she complained, loudly. "He is so ungrateful, so impertinent. And so quiet. I have heard that quiet people are not to be trusted. I hope Sigmund is not going to hurt his Mama and his Papa when he grows up, and repay them with naughtiness for all their love and care."

Franz repressed a sudden contemptuous smile. Sigmund stood at the window, his chin on the level with the high sill. His small back was stiff and straight, pathetic and stubborn, yet very defenseless. Franz, watching him, became thoughtful. He allowed an amicable smile to spread over his broad fair face.

"Leave the child alone, Tina," he said. "You don't understand him. He is not bad. Are you, Sigmund?"

Ernestine's eyes became hollow and fixed with surprise at this unexpected championing. Bewildered, she looked from father to son. Sigmund did not turn. But the small thin shoulders trembled a little, as though they had been struck. Joseph, who had been restlessly handling his mother's bric-a-brac in the forbidden what-not, dropped a Dresden figurine on the carpet. He glanced surreptitiously at his parents. To his surprise, and gratitude, he saw that they were looking at his brother. He kicked the delicate broken figurine under the convenient leg of a sofa, and ran impishly toward Sigmund. He seized his twin by the sailor-collar, which he dexterously twisted, thus dragging Sigmund backwards.

"Joseph!" protested Ernestine, still bemused by her startled wonder. Franz rose, snatched the two children apart, and administered a sound thwack to the seat of Joseph's trousers. Joseph set up a loud howl at this unexpected attack. But Sigmund, very pale and still, merely straightened his collar, and stared.

"This is enough," said Franz, sternly, to his favorite son. "You must not hurt your brother. I am tired of it. Leave him alone." His eye sidled to Sigmund, and he tried for a friendly glance. "Why don't you thrash him, you little coward?"

"Franz!" murmured Ernestine, aghast, and increasingly bewildered.

But Sigmund looked straightly at his father. "They beat me when I do," he said, quite clearly, quite dispassionately. "And you beat me," he added, without fear.

Franz laughed suddenly. "And I shall beat you, if you don't," he said. He patted Sigmund's head. He did not meet those straight large eyes. Joseph, wailing tearlessly but stentoriously at all this infuriating treachery, halted his uproar, and stared.

Franz picked up his paper, kissed his wife, laughed again, shortly, and left the room, leaving a confused Ernestine, a snivelling Joseph, and a silent Sigmund behind.

It was all too much for Ernestine, whose headache had returned with renewed ferocity. She wanted to console Joseph, but Franz had been displeased with him, so she restrained herself, trying to eye him admonishingly. She did not look at Sigmund, whom she incontinently blamed for all this confusion and noise. She rang the bell, sank back exhaustedly in her chair, and closed her eyes.

Her maid entered. She held her handkerchief to her face, and waved helplessly at the children. "Do take them away," she implored. Long after the children had gone, she lay in her chair, shivering a little, the fire hot on her feet.

The immense gray stillness of the morning, the sterile and arid cold, penetrated into the mansion, and into this pleasant room with the fire and the gay draperies. Ernestine's febrile and confused mind began to feel itself lost in the center of a huge gaseous world, full of loneliness and fear and vague things which she refused to face. I am so tired, she whimpered to herself. And so afraid, said something sharp and involuntary in her. At this, her heart leapt like a bird in ambush at the approach of the hunter, and she sat upright in her chair, trembling. She reached a shaking hand for the bell, and pulled it violently. She began to gasp slightly, and to breathe uneasily, staring about her as though fearful of pouncing enemies. When her maid came, she asked that Mrs. Trenchard be requested to come to the morning-room. Waiting for her aunt, she was obliged to wipe away cool moisture from her brow and her upper lip.

Mrs. Trenchard came in with a hard short step, very brisk and competent. She was a little woman, with a remarkable facial resemblance to her late sister, Ernestine's mother. She was withered of flesh and face, and very dark, but she wore an expression of spinsterish determination and primness and chronic disapproval. She dressed her thin hair, black and heavily streaked with white, in a chignon. Her straight bangs, cut severely across a sallow and narrow forehead, were an absurdly childish fringe, which enhanced the sharp boniness of her nose, the straight hard line of her puckered lips, and the cold suspicion of her small black eyes. Though it was still early in the morning, she never allowed herself the luxury of casual attire. Her black bombazine dress, tight of basque, and scantily draped, was in perfect and austere order, the prime white lace at her throat fastened with an opal broach set in old gold. Everything was dry and trim and unlovely about her, and she carried herself with a sharp egotism and uncompromising agility, as though she was always alert for softness and weakness and incompetence.

"Good morning," she said, coldly. "My dear Ernestine! You are not dressed?" She knew that Ernestine never dressed before noon, but she delivered this little reproachful tirade every morning, invariably. She stood near Ernestine, and stared down at her without compassion, and even with annoyed disdain. Ernestine was afraid of her, but her coming always reassured the poor sick woman. She stammered a faint incoherent apology, and then murmured an invitation to sit down.

Mrs. Trenchard shook her head with hard vigor. "Certainly not, Ernestine. I have a lot to do, as you very well know. You look ill," she added, almost as though she felt some vindication for her attack on Ernestine's state of undress.

Ernestine's lip trembled, and she sighed. "I am ill, truly," she replied. "But Franz and the doctor say it is my condition."

Mrs. Trenchard's lips tightened. "It does you no good, my dear, to lounge before the fire all day. A little walk—exercise. Some interest in your establishment. You indulge yourself."

Nevertheless, she finally sat down on the edge of a chair, and immediately another aspect of her character manifested itself. Her face took on a look of dolorous melancholy, not compassionate, but even slightly vindictive. "Our family is known for its frail constitution. Remember your poor mother. But she would take no advice from any one. I would recommend barley water for the kidneys, and iron for the blood, and would regularly send her medical books. She ignored it all. I hope you are not so obstinate."

Ernestine touched her eyes with her handkerchief. Mrs. Trenchard settled in her chair. Her eyes and lips became even more disapproving and somber.

"You are not just to your husband, my dear girl," she said. "Gentlemen feel aversion for female illnesses. They prefer a cheerful disposition, and a light though decorous manner. Sometimes I am astonished at Franz's patience and kindness. He has an excellent character, and you are very blessed——"

"Oh, I know that!" exclaimed Ernestine, with pathetic self-reproach and eagerness. She regarded her aunt with imploring eyes.

Mrs. Trenchard shook her head. "But you do not allow him to see this. You are always ill. I do not condemn you too much, remembering our family's constitution." She cocked her head in a valorous and martyred attitude. "But Mr. Trenchard had nothing to complain of in me, though only Heaven knows how I suffered for years. There was never a morning that I did not have a fever, or a headache, or some indisposition. But I maintained a cheerful air, and did my duty to him and the children. Women must be patient martyrs, smiling over their female sufferings. You do not even try, Ernestine."

Ernestine whimpered, but said nothing.

Mrs. Trenchard, through whose sententious character ran a broad red streak of sadism, tossed her head. "Your children are undisciplined and ill-mannered," she said, accusingly, watching her crushed niece with a sharp thrill of pleasure. "I have never seen such naughty boys. Sigmund is worse than Joseph, though Joseph is very spoiled, too. Sigmund is rude and silent, and unresponsive to everything that is done for him——"

"But your own Dick is very fond of him," said Ernestine, timidly.

Mrs. Trenchard bit her lip with annoyance. "Dick is an angel, Ernestine. He finds good in every one. Your own brother is partial to Dick. Not that I consider Baldur an excellent judge of character, and considering everything, I cannot imagine why your Mama and Papa left him such an enormous fortune. It was not fair." Nevertheless, remembering Baldur's partiality for his young cousin, she smiled a little. She had a high respect for wealth, and revered it. She was an extremely wealthy woman herself, and very avaricious.

Her smile suddenly faded, and her eyes pointed with curiosity and interest, for Ernestine's thin sallow face had flushed crimson. She was sitting up in her chair, and the hand that held the handkerchief had clenched. She was extremely agitated, and her breath came short and quick in a sudden fit of hysterical anger. What else Franz and the years had made of her, they had not succeeded in making her a hypocrite.

"I can't understand Papa!" she exclaimed, thinly, incoherently. "It was very terrible! At first, I was broken-hearted, when he died. He has only been dead a little while, but I just can't feel grieved, Auntie Elizabeth. Not after his will—I can't understand it! To treat poor Franz so! It was inexcusable!"

Mrs. Trenchard, inwardly aroused, excited and pleased, pressed her lips disapprovingly together and eyed Ernestine coldly. "It is wrong to speak badly of the dead, Ernestine. Let them rest in peace. Whatever your poor Papa did, for unknown reasons, he must not be condemned for it. I agree with you that it is very puzzling. But let him rest peacefully in his grave." She paused, hitched herself a little nearer to

Ernestine, regarded her avidly. "Have you any idea, Ernestine, why he did it?" Her voice dropped into a conspirator's hush.

Ernestine's agitation increased. "How could I know? Papa always seemed so fond of Franz—I know now that he brought us together. He was so proud of him. And then, this—this horrible injustice, after all Franz has done for the mills. He has given all his life—!" She stopped abruptly, and into her dark eyes there came a hard and vicious glint. "It must have been Baldur! I've often thought it. But Baldur wasn't Papa's favorite at all. Towards the last though, poor Papa was not himself. He seemed ill, and hardly aware of anything. Baldur must have influenced him—" She halted, frightened but defiant, and glared challengingly at her aunt.

Mrs. Trenchard, thrilling, nodded mysteriously. "One never knows," she said. "One must always be prepared for the unexpected. People are so strange. But why should Baldur want the mills, and the money? He never takes any interest in anything. But there are some queer people who love money for its own sake," she added with conviction, out of her own knowledge.

Ernestine's feverish and sick excitement grew. "No one ever understood Franz but me! Such a wonderful character, Auntie Elizabeth. So forbearing and just and kind. He—he has made me so happy—no tongue can tell. I thought at first that he wouldn't be able to endure it, the way Papa treated him. He was so pale and quiet, and grew so thin, though he was always so considerate of me. Think what a blow to his pride it was when Baldur made him president of the mills—at a salary! Franz, a paid employee of the mills, when they were justly his! That shows how tolerant and broadminded he was, though I know his heart was broken! And then when I just couldn't refrain from criticizing and reproaching Baldur to him, he became very annoyed, and was stern with me. He forbade me to criticize Baldur even in the slightest. And when I complained that Baldur was spoiling Sigmund," her eyes sharpened now, with augmented vindictiveness, "he told me that I was hard on the child. My own child!" she cried, shrilly.

Mrs. Trenchard's lips pursed with uncharitable shrewdness, as she drove a blow home. "Perhaps Franz has to be—polite—to Baldur, considering that Baldur pays his salary."

Ernestine's anger now turned with thin fury upon her aunt. "Auntie, how can you say that! Franz needn't have stayed. The Sessions Steel Company offered him an enormous salary. They appreciated him. They offered him much more than Baldur offered. Franz is just loyal; that is why he is staying!"

Mrs. Trenchard had no high regard for the human species' tendency to loyalty, and merely looked knowing. This tantalizing expression enhanced Ernestine's agitation. "You don't understand Franz!" she cried, wringing her hands. "He told me only yesterday that it would have been cruel to leave Baldur in the lurch, with the mills on his hands, and all alone in this horrible house. The mills would have failed——"

"And with them, your own income," interposed Mrs. Trenchard, deftly.

Ernestine was silent. Suddenly she began to sob, putting her hands over her convulsed face. "Franz! Franz!" she cried, in a muffled voice. "Every one is so cruel to you, my darling!"

Mrs. Trenchard rose briskly. "There, there, Ernestine, you upset yourself. That is your condition, and your poor constitution. But you must learn self-control. Learn to smile when things are most disagreeable. A brave face must always be put upon things. One must never give way. One must learn to march onwards, like a soldier. That was a lesson I had to learn, myself, but I learned it, and did not flinch."

She brought Ernestine her smelling-salts, but the poor woman waved them away distractedly. She allowed herself, however, to be helped to her chaise-longue, where she collapsed. Mrs. Trenchard called her maid, gave orders for ministration. Finally Ernestine was calm. Mrs. Trenchard delivered herself of a few more sanctimonious platitudes, then remarking that after all, household management called her in spite of her own indisposition, she marched away, invigorated. Ernestine watched her leave, her eyes dull and bemused, clouded over with the opaqueness of heavy misery.

When she was alone, she broke out into fresh sobbing, then was suddenly silent. She fell into an uneasy sleep, which was penetrated with large and frightening half-visions. When she awoke, it was to pain and anguish of body and mind.

CHAPTER 14

THE AFTERNOONS, two hours before dinner, were pleasant occasions for Baldur.

He would have a big fire built in his rooms, and the curtains would be drawn against the iron twilight of the winter day. A table would be spread with a white cloth, and set with a pitcher of milk, fresh hot tea, spicy sandwiches and little cakes. Then he would wait, reading placidly, or playing softly on his piano. Shortly afterwards, there would come a knock on his door, and Richard and Marcia Trenchard, his young cousins, and Sigmund, would come in, suddenly smiling at the sight of him, waiting for them.

"I had just about given you rascals up," he would say, and they would laugh, coming eagerly towards him, and seating themselves about him, Sigmund on the hearth rug near his feet, Marcia primly on his right hand on a small stiff chair, and Richard at his left. Richard, being of a restless disposition, hardly remained in the chair for more than a few minutes at a time, and with sandwich or glass or cake in his hand, he would rush about the room, talking rapidly and incontinently, with a kind of frenzied vehemence, his eyes sparkling like those of a fanatic's.

He was seventeen years old, and tall, thin and weedy. He had a dark triangular face, with wide sharp cheekbones, delicate aquiline nose, and a vivid passionate mouth, always mobile, and sometimes too expressive of his intense emotions, which were always reflected in fierce gray eyes set deeply under heavy and frowning black brows. His hair, cut in the longish mode affected by young men of his class and age, was thick, black and curling, and had a habit of standing upright as though forced into that position by the blast of an inward flame. His wrists hung far below his white cuffs, and his hands were always in motion, angrily, passionately, or impatiently. His voice was always a subdued shout, even when he was comparatively still, and when aroused, he bellowed. His dress, despite his mother's rigid efforts, was untidy, even disorderly, his cravat having a tendency to slide under his left ear, however firmly pinned. His pantaloons were always baggy and wrinkled, his boots perpetually dusty. A wind seemed to blow about him always, so that he had an air of being surrounded by rushing gales, and whipped by them. He literally crackled with vitality and ardor and youthful violence.

His sister, Marcia, on the other hand, was quiet and still as a forest pool lying deeply under dark cool ferns. Like that pool, she had a dim sparkle and mystery. She was small, slender and fragile, and her breath hardly moved her virginal young breast. Yet, there seemed a flame in her, like her brother's, but a motionless flame, which rose sometimes to her sweet and smiling blue eyes and stood reflected there in a gentle warmth. She had no color, but her skin possessed a luminous pallor, and her young mouth was tender and pensive. Her hair was a soft rippling light brown, rolled into a chignon so glossy and so heavy that it seemed too weighted for her slender white neck. Her dress was always precise and dainty, and today she wore a gown of dark blue silk, exquisitely fitted to her tiny figure, and draped gracefully. The delicate lace at her throat was white and frothy, and in its folds, despite Mrs. Trenchard's cold disapproval, hung a simple gold "Papish" cross. Her hands were never in motion, like Richard's, but lay folded quietly in her lap. They were of the texture and delicacy of porcelain, and she wore no rings. About her was the quality of a nun, secluded, cloistered and calm. She had a nun's beauty, also, immaculate and perpetually untouched and asexual. One could never imagine her as a wife, though, paradoxically, she could be visualized as a mother.

Sigmund, nine years old now, resembled his second cousin, Richard, remarkably, if only physically. There was the same triangular face, but the eyes, though the same color, were still and contemplative and very large. He did not possess Richard's vehemence and crackling ardor; rather, he was more like Marcia in his character, nor was his hair, smooth, dark and gleaming, like Richard's. But the formation of his features, the turn of his head, his body, his sudden quick smile, betrayed the relationship between Richard and himself. And between them, despite their unlikeness of character, was a deep and silent sympathy and understanding.

The young people helped themselves to the little repast prepared for them. Richard ate ravenously, but with abstraction. He did everything ravenously, and always with that curious aloofness and impatience, as though his mind objected to anything that distracted it. Marcia sipped daintily at her milk, ate a small cake. Sigmund, who had no interest in food, pretended to eat a little, out of politeness. Baldur watched them, smiling, drinking tea. He had no particular love for young people, but he loved these three, who loved him. He gave them flattering attention, this seventeen-year-old boy, this eighteen-year-old girl, and this nine-year-old child, and the attention was not affected.

"What have you been doing today?" he asked Richard.

Richard flung his half-eaten sandwich violently on the table. "Oh, that accursed school!" he cried, loudly. "That stupid Scofield! That abominable Walters! That contemptible Blanchard! Such ninnies! Such nincompoops! Such dried-up rulers and chalk-covered fools! What do they know? Nothing!" He glared fiercely at the sandwich, snatched it up, crammed it into his mouth. Through the bread and jam he mumbled furiously: "I'll never get through school! And Ma set on Harvard for me!" He snorted, and crumbs flew from his lips in a small shower.

"You might try studying, you know," Baldur reminded him, mildly.

This infuriated Richard. "Studying what?" He choked, coughed, turned scarlet, caught his breath, and swallowed, gulping. "Latin? Greek? What for? Am I going to be a damned school-master?" Marcia murmured protestingly, and received a glare in return. "Am I going to be a school-master? No! So why should I study that rot?"

"Just to learn," said Baldur, smiling. He lifted a hand. "Now then, we've been over all that before. Learning never hurt any man."

"What have Latin and Greek got to do with living?" demanded Richard, vehemently. "And I'm interested in living. In life. Everything," and he flung his arms wide with an embracing gesture.

"You're vague," said Baldur. "I've always complained of that. I've been advising you to try to decide what you want to do. And you always say 'everything.' That means nothing. First, you wanted to be a painter, and you wangled paints and a teacher from your mother. Then you threw that away. Then you had an idea you were a composer, and you made the days and nights hideous around here with your pounding on the piano downstairs, and on mine. Until you put them both out of tune. Then you were going to be an architect, or a bridge-builder, with subsequent confusion. You abandoned everything. What is it now?"

Richard looked sheepish for exactly thirty seconds, then the flame bounded up in him again. "That was just trial and error," he said, largely. "It is just beginning to dawn on me, what I want. And it isn't learning a pack of dry dead nonsense in dusty schoolrooms. It's—it's living!" He paused, and his brows drew together in fierce concentration. "It's men. It's the substance of life. I don't know just how to go about it, but it's beginning to dawn on me, I tell you, Baldur!"

Baldur was silent, waiting and smiling. Marcia was listening gravely, and Sigmund had fixed his eyes intently on his fiery cousin. Then Richard suddenly flung himself before Baldur, on his knees, his hands clutching the arms of his cousin's chair. His dark thin face was alive, passionately working, and before that intensity Baldur ceased his smiling.

"I only know I want to go into the mills. Oh, I'm not interested in learning the confounded business! It's the men I want to know, the men who work there, sweating all hell out of themselves to make Franz rich, and all of us rich! We aren't real. But the men who work there, are, and it's their realness, and what they think, and how they live, that I want to know. Don't you understand?" he cried, and shook Baldur's chair in his thin hands, his face twisting in a dark fire.

Baldur did not answer. His expression became grave and thoughtful, and he looked reflectively at his young cousin. His sensibilities, his perceptions, were so acute that he could understand everything, even that which was alien to him. Through the eyes of others he saw strange and confused and unfamiliar worlds. He saw Richard's mind, dark, twisting, full of living turmoil, and as vitally alive as a nebula swirling into turbulent being. The sudden vision excited him, and he had the thought that he was gazing at something tremendous and full of meaning and passion and strength. But his own weakness of body, his own delicate and reticent mind, shrank away from the vision as at the touch of robust and painful fingers.

"Yes," he said, slowly, at last, "I think I understand. Why don't you, then, ask Franz to let you into the mills?"

Richard sprang to his feet, began to race up and down the room, clenching his fists and shaking them in the air. "He'll laugh at me, I tell you! He already thinks I am a fool, the damn German! Germans can only understand things that have a concrete and practical reason behind them. They can't understand things that are real, but without hard substance. But I'll ask him," he added, threateningly, suddenly pausing before Baldur, and shaking his fists in front of his chest. He breathed loudly. His eye sparkled darkly.

"I've learned something. He got around the alien contract labor law slyly enough. Now he 'lends' those poor Poles, Prussians, Bavarians and Hungarians the boat fare They pay him back, with enormous interest, when they go to work in the mills. They really never get finished paying him. There are so many extras. It's a scandal! Why doesn't the government stop him? Because he's bought too many politicians, that's why. And then when he's wrung the poor brutes dry, he throws them out, and gets more, from Europe. It's got to be stopped, the whole damn business of bringing them here——"

Baldur nodded his head. "Yes, I agree with you there, Dick. Those who come to America because they were persecuted in Europe for racial or religious reasons, those who come because they can't endure tyranny and oppression, are valuable to America. They bring with them courage and fortitude and faith, and understanding. They have seen what America is, potentially. But those who come because they were starving in their own countries, and because they think America can make them comfortable, or rich, are a great danger to us. They bring only avarice and stupidity here, and a dull brutishness. Their children will continue to be an increasing danger, for they will never understand America, and will never feel a loyalty for her, and never any affection. They are the real vandals inside the gates——"

"Yes, they will be a danger!" cried Richard, explosively. He eyed Baldur with ferocious hostility. "But not in the way you mean! The danger is in men like Franz, who bring them here. Men like Franz starve the poor wretches, make slaves out of them, brutalize them, deprive them of real humanity. Men like Franz have no moral responsibility. That is the danger! A population of creatures without manhood and strength, without the courage to fight for justice and freedom. And why? Because they've never had a chance in America to become Americans. And America can't endure with a populace of perpetual aliens. We'll all go down, I tell you! One day we'll be a nation of a ruling aristocracy of money at the head of a nation of weak dull slaves, without faith and vision. How can we endure? How can we defend ourselves from enemies with a people who have never had the opportunity to become friends?"

"How can strangers, who are different from us in blood, race and culture, become our friends?" asked Baldur, smiling with an air of reasonableness.

"But Americans aren't a race—they are a people!" shouted Richard, furiously. "We're all races, and all cultures, and all bloods! But we can have one philosophy, which will make us one people. But men like Franz destroy the philosophy right at the roots, at the very beginning. Because they exploit the newcomers, they force them to herd together, keep them isolated from America, prevent their children from becoming Americans. They build a wall about them, and never give them time or opportunity to be free. For they know that if these poor brutes were free, they wouldn't be able to make so much money, and keep it."

He halted, his face working. He flung out his arms with an angry hopelessness. "But what's the use? You don't understand."

"But you aren't very clear, yourself, Dick."

Richard beat one fist into the palm of his other hand. "I know that! That's what I'm fumbling after—to make it clear. It will come clear some day, I know. That's why I've got to get close to the men in the mills and the mines. I've got to help them get free, from such men as Franz—" His face lighted up, as though it had been struck by a vivid external illumination. "That's it! I've got to help them get free! For their sake, for the sake of America!"

He flung himself on the rug before Baldur, and seized Baldur's small thin knees. His eyes blazed. He smiled passionately. "You always help me, Baldur. You've helped me. The first step is to get into the mills——"

Baldur was silent. He looked down at the vibrating thin young body, consumed with its wild fanaticism and idealistic intolerance and superb ignorance of a hideous and devious world. And then he understood that worlds were not made, not undone, not set upon a path ablaze with fires and stars and the thunders of becoming, by such reasonable and detached men like himself, who love a cynical status quo that has made them comfortable. All the glories and the turmoils which have raised men from apehood into a precarious but shining humanity have burst out like coronas from the individual suns of such as Richard, who are without cold reason and sterile contemplation. Such reason and such contemplation are arid and dusty, the dried and crumbling bones of life, stripped of warm and pulsing flesh. But Richard, who refused to see the derisively smiling faces on the pillars of salt, looked forward eagerly, glowing with the mystic knowledge of unreason, believing in impossible dreams that tomorrow will make possible. Those who do not see the world as it is create new worlds, where fantasies of glory and beauty crystallize into white cities of light, and a vision becomes a reality.

Baldur was shaken, in spite of his icy reason, and he felt

a consuming pang of envy and melancholy. Surely to have a dream, however preposterous, but blazing with passion and beauty, was better than to live in a dusky prison of a world in which only beasts fought and fed and excreted. But I should not like to have such a dream, he thought. It would be so uncomfortable, and dangerous.

He said: "Go into the mills, then, Dick."

But Richard's mind, like a racer carrying the torch of an immortal flame, had already sped far beyond him. "What do men like Franz care about America? They hate America." His voice was low and muttering and more than a little savage. "They love only money. And because they love only money, they will destroy America, and everything that is American."

He fell into a deep and brooding silence, where he looked at his dreams. His head fell on his chest. He stared at the fire, his young profile large and fierce against the red light. With relief, Baldur abandoned him, turned his eyes smilingly on Marcia and Sigmund. The girl had listened to her brother quietly, hardly seeming to breathe. When the flame had lept in him, there had been in her eyes an answering shine and glimmer. Now she met Baldur's look seriously, and with an expression of exaltation.

"Have you spoken to your mother yet, Marcia," he asked.

She shook her head slightly. "Not yet," she answered gravely. Her mouth seemed to pale in distress, then tightened with severe resolution. "But I shall have to do so, soon. I know she won't consent." She sighed. "But that won't matter, not very much."

"You've spoken, then, to Father Brunswick?"

"Yes." Her voice was low, almost inaudible. "Yesterday. I'm eighteen. I can enter the convent without Mama's consent. I don't want to do it, but I must. I've always wanted this. There is nothing else I ever wanted."

Baldur put out his thin white hand and touched the glossy chignon. "I shall miss you, Marcia," he said, very gently. Strange that this pretty child, brought up in the cold and formal tenets of an indifferent Protestantism, should have this urgent and devouring desire to immure herself in the cloister of a foreign creed. He could well imagine Mrs. Trenchard's rage and horror and shock. But who knew the mysterious and inexplicable urgings of the human heart? Who could tell from where they came? Baldur knew that it was no romanticism, no fear of life, that impelled Marcia. Perhaps her desire came from loneliness, from an isolation of soul, from some passionate dedication with which she was born. This dedication, though cooler, more lofty, more calm and more attenuated than Richard's, was the very same. Odd that such a mother should have given birth to these children. Their father had been a dull rich little man, involved in stocks and bonds and financial manipulations, whose imagination embraced only money. Yes, it was very strange.

As if she understood his thoughts, Marcia put out her hand and laid it over her brother's. He lifted his head alertly, his eyes still clouded with his dreams. They smiled at each other, deeply, intensely, like comrades come together in an alien land. Their smile was full of love.

Sigmund had listened silently to all this, turning his head slowly from one speaker to another, as if he understood in his child's mind. He had the quality of isolation, also, and he had the defenselessness of those who live in themselves. Baldur also knew that in spite of the boy's stubbornness, pride and natural hauteur, he was too sensitive, too vulnerable. This had given him a pervading weakness. He would always be too open to attack, and before it, he would eventually disintegrate. Could he, Baldur, save him? He would try! Whether he would succeed or not, only time would tell.

"The cakes are drying up," he said, speaking very loudly, as if to shout down his thoughts, and the thoughts of the others.

Some one knocked on the door. The frightened face of old Gillespie appeared. "Mr. Schmidt, Mrs. Trenchard would like to speak to you, in Mrs. Stoessel's rooms. Mrs. Stoessel is unwell."

CHAPTER 15

"YOU'VE SENT for Franz, and the doctor?" asked Baldur, on the threshold of Ernestine's sitting-room.

"Yes, of course," snapped Mrs. Trenchard. But she was pale and disturbed, and there was a disordered look about her brisk body and face as though she had had some sort of a guilty shock. Something had apparently alarmed her, and her manner was both perturbed and hostile. "You must think me an idiot, Baldur!"

Baldur, frowning a little, followed her hard and agile step through the sitting-room into Ernestine's bedroom. Lamps had been lighted, shades drawn, and a fire lit. The room was large and comfortable and warm. Ernestine lay, supported by pillows, her emaciated face ghastly pale and covered with drops of moisture. She had been watching the door achingly, and Baldur caught her eager look, the shine of her sunken and tortured eyes before they faded, upon his appearance. "Oh, Baldur," she murmured dully, and turned her head aside.

Pained and somber, Baldur came to the bedside, took the cold and tremulous hand. Ernestine did not look at him. He felt a deep convulsion seize her body, but she made no sound. Baldur laid the hand down gently, and regarded his sister with great anxiety. Mrs. Trenchard stood on the other side of the bed, regarding her niece with a curious mingling of fear, concern and resentment. She kept tossing her head slightly, and compressing her lips, as though she were having an acrimonious argument in her mind with Ernestine. At last she said aloud, with a gloomy pride:

"The females in our family were always of a poor constitution. There is no strength there."

In spite of his anxiety for his sister, Baldur added silently to himself, with bitterness: And there is I, too! He thought of Mrs. Trenchard's brother, and his mother's, who was another such as he. He gazed at his sister, his alarm for her increasing. Between the spasms of her silent pain, her exhaustion was profound, and frightening. She kept her eyes shut. Her thick dark lashes lay on her sunken cheek; her mouth drooped. Lying like this, she appeared young again, and vulnerable, and pathetically helpless. Her hands, lying palm up on the bed, looked like the hands of one struck by some one unsuspected of cruelty and hatred. She had forgotten Baldur. Her finely cut profile, drawn with suffering, had taken on a pale dignity and aloofness. The embroidered cambric ruffles at her throat and wrists trembled faintly as though her body was still reverberating to the notes of pain. Her dark hair, released from coils and pins, lay on the white pillows in touching, gray-streaked tendrils.

Baldur's alarm suddenly quickened to the heights of panic. He bent over his sister, and said in a low and urgent voice: "Tina! Speak to me, Tina."

Her eyelids quivered, then subsided, and she sighed feebly.

But she did not look at him, nor speak. Baldur sat down, his legs quaking. "She is very ill," he said to Mrs. Trenchard.

"She lets herself go," replied his aunt. "She refuses to make an effort. One must control oneself."

He looked at her, his brows drawing together, his eyes points of blue fire under them. Mrs. Trenchard, meeting that look, quailed, fell back.

"What brought this about?" he demanded, sternly.

A dull flush crept over her cheekbones. She shook her head, avoiding his gaze. "I'm sure I don't know, Baldur. I went in to see her this morning, as usual, and she complained of feeling ill. I helped her into bed, and made her comfortable. Of course, her condition—" and she dropped her eyes decorously. "It is almost time."

Baldur said nothing. He leaned over the bed and studied Ernestine closely. Was she conscious? He did not know. She seemed fallen into a profound abstraction, some half-sleep. Her expression became more and more austere, more aloof. Her lips were folded in a stony calm.

Then, all at once, she stirred, sighed heavily. She said, not opening her eyes, and very feebly: "Baldur." Her hand moved. He caught it strongly in his own. "Yes, Tina. Yes?"

But she said nothing more, only repeating, over and over, her deep sighing. Baldur could not endure it. Her hand was cold and clammy in his, the fingers curled about his with desperate strength. He sat there, holding her hand, not moving his eyes from her.

"Is there anything I can do for you, Tina?" he whispered.

For a long moment he thought she had not heard. Then, so slow was the movement that it was hardly perceptible, her eyelids rose. She looked at him out of the fathomless deeps of her pain and anguish, and he saw only prostrated accusation there, and dying hostility.

"So unjust—to Franz," she murmured, through her livid lips.

He was shocked, and sickened. He felt her draw her cooling hand from his. He caught it again. He held it tightly. And then he knew that her accusation, her enmity, came from her own terror, which was killing her. The nightmare had her again, and would not let her go. He saw the shadows of it on her face.

At all cost, she must have peace now. He bent over her. He forced her to look at him.

"Yes," he said, in a low clear voice, "I was unjust. I was wrong. He is everything—that you think he is, Tina. Tina, my dear."

The shadow lightened on that poor face. Her lips trembled into the ghost of a smile. The hand ceased its struggling in his. She regarded him with eagerness.

"And Papa—" she whispered.

"He was wrong, Tina," he said, firmly. "And unjust, too. But he was very ill, and old. He—he did not understand Franz. He was so very old."

"Yes," she sighed, smiling almost brilliantly. She closed her eyes again. She breathed more naturally. Her hand warmed a little.

Baldur suddenly glanced up. Mrs. Trenchard was smiling, tight-lipped, cynical, knowing. Their eyes met. He hated her. In some way he knew that Tina's collapse was due to this woman. She saw the vivid blue pointing of his eyes, and shrank away.

The doctor arrived, and made his examination, very gravely. Then he and Baldur went into the sitting-room. The old man hesitated, tapping his fingers with his spectacles, and eyeing Baldur with hesitation.

"The child will be born soon, somewhat early, Mr. Schmidt." He shook his head. "Her constitution—I am not satisfied. There is a collapse there, a will to die. I don't like it."

"No, she mustn't die," said Baldur. The doctor shook his head again.

Franz arrived, concerned and pale, and Baldur stood in the background while the doctor repeated what he had said. Franz said nothing; his lips twitched, drew together. Is he acting? thought Baldur. Strange, that one could never tell about Franz. Only he, Baldur, had been able to detect, on occasion, whether the man was hypocritical or not.

"Is there a question of the mother—or the child?" asked Franz at last, in a stifled voice.

The doctor paused. "It is a question," he said. "As the husband and father, I must ask you to make a painful decision, if it occurs."

Franz averted his head. Baldur saw his strong broad shoulders, his straight strong back. What was he thinking? In his heart, he despised Ernestine, even hated her. But there had been times when Baldur had seen him look at her with real, if passing, compassion. What was streaming in his mind, now? thought Baldur, objectively. The possible release from Ernestine? The release from a cloying domestic existence in a horrible house?

Franz spoke: "If the question occurs, the mother must be saved, of course."

Baldur frowned to himself. The voice was natural, and firm

enough, but there was something else there. Was it hope? Was all this sheer hypocrisy? Was it a quiver of a calloused conscience? Irmgard had told him years ago of that scene in the parlor of the Harrow house. Franz had been guilty, but he had not been acting. His grief had been real enough, and his shame and wretchedness. He did things that brought him equal torment with the torment of those he wounded and destroyed. If he caused destruction of others, he also brought himself destruction. He perpetrated the ruin with open eyes, and suffered. But he could not refrain from the ruin.

He heard Franz say again: "She must be saved. That is all that matters." His voice, with its hard gutturals, its accent, was stronger than ever. Even he does not dare to say otherwise, thought Baldur.

He accompanied Franz into the bedroom. Franz went immediately to Tina and knelt down beside her. He took her hand. He called to her urgently. She opened her eyes and looked at him, and a well of light rose into them, and her whole face brightened as though struck by the sun. She moved towards him, and he held her in his arms. Baldur saw his profile, full of compassion, and very pale. Ernestine's head lay on his shoulder, her thin dark hand pressed against his cheek.

"O Franz," she murmured. "O Franz," and the sound was like an expiring breath.

Baldur left the room, returned to his study. The young people had gone. A servant had removed the tray and cleared the table. The fire was low. There was no sound in the great mansion, only far and muffled echoes. Baldur sat before the fire, which slowly died. It began to get cold in the large dim room. He went to a window and pulled back a curtain. It had begun to snow. An hour passed, so. No one came to his rooms, as he sat there, waiting.

One by one they had died, his mother, his father, and now his sister. Soon, there would be no one left tied to him by blood or by love in this house but Sigmund. Little Sigmund, with his fear and courage, his desperate rages, his weakness, his vulnerability and his loneliness and despair. Baldur felt his own loneliness now, like an empty gale out of eternity. He had always fought it contemptuously. Now it inundated him. The cold of the room and the cold of his heart turned his deformed flesh into ice.

Some one knocked at the door, and Mrs. Trenchard entered, with reddened eyes and twitching lips. Baldur regarded her in silence.

"Ernestine," she said, and could say nothing more.

Baldur did not speak.

"And the child?" he said, finally, after a long emptiness.

"A little girl, Baldur. Such a pretty little girl, with golden hair and blue eyes, but so very frail, like all our family." She began to weep, with hard sobs.

"It would have been better if she had died, too," said Baldur, calmly.

Mrs. Trenchard stopped her sobbing. She gazed at him with horror. She tried to speak. Then, with a choked sound she turned and went away.

It was almost midnight when Baldur went to Franz, who sat alone in the sitting-room adjoining the bedroom where Ernestine lay, now so quiet, and at peace.

A fire had been built, and was kept burning in the sitting-room. Franz sat before it, his elbow on the arm of his chair, his hand supporting his head. Baldur had entered so quietly that Franz did not hear him. Baldur saw his profile against the flickering fire. It was white and tense, and exhausted. Moreover, it expressed profound melancholy and sadness, though sorrow was absent. He looked older, absorbed, haggard.

Baldur spoke gently: "I am sorry, Franz."

Franz lifted his head, and smiled painfully. But he said nothing.

Baldur stood near him, and they both looked at the fire. Then Baldur said, very softly, almost meditatively:

"You have been a bad husband, and you are a bad father. You are a liar and a hypocrite. I know all about you, Franz. You are a swine. Quite a thorough swine." He paused. "But you brought Ernestine the only happiness she ever had. I don't think you cared whether she was happy or not. Her happiness was accidental. But it existed, whether you wanted it or didn't want it, or cared. I thank you for it."

He left him then. Franz watched him go, and his expression was inscrutable.

CHAPTER 16

BY LATE summer, the new mansion was ready for occupancy.

Franz had bought a large piece of ground near the outskirts of Nazareth, some twenty acres of gently rolling land, its highest point crowned with a circle of high pointed poplars. In the midst of this majesty he built his new house, of clean white stone with red roof and red chimneys. He hated the tall narrow red houses of his era, with their high narrow windows and gloomy box-like rooms. "It is the English tradition." he said. "They build their houses to match their climate, and their characters." He had the German's love for space, for cleanness, for light and air. The house was long, rectangular, with broad deep windows full of sunshine, and verandahs that ran all the way around the building, supported by shining white columns of stone. Ivy was started even before the rooms were finished, and by late summer had added its fresh dark green to the pellucid whiteness of the building. The rooms were huge, with light walls and ceilings, and clear polished floors. Scores of men worked feverishly on the grounds, landscaping them, filling them with flower-beds, grottoes, red-flagged walks, broad driveways, summer-houses, servants' quarters, and red stables.

Mrs. Trenchard was horrified by all this light and windswept space. "The sun will fade these expensive carpets and draperies," she protested. She was already aghast at the furnishings, chairs in blue, gold, rose and white damask, and delicate sofas in soft colors, and fragile graceful tables. She thought it all frivolous and unstable, for she had a love for heavy gloomy mahogany, dark fabrics and thick dull textures. She sniffed in outraged disapproval of the light soft carpets, the fragile chandeliers of crystal and gilt, the white winding stairways. It seemed to her that the whole air of the house was insecure and a little immoral in its lightness and color, for she had no eye for simplicity, openness and grace. She was further confirmed in this opinion when she learned that most of the furniture, the draperies, the ornaments and the rugs came from France. "Louis Fifteenth!" she complained. "It is all very disturbing, and no atmosphere for children. All this French furniture! I really do not know!"

To her daughter, she said severely: "Of course, Franz is a foreigner, and has no taste. I prefer crimson plush and wine velvets, and lace, which is proper, and rich. Whatever could have inspired him!"

Marcia replied gently: "I think it is beautiful. And so kind of him to let us furnish our apartment as we wish."

"That is one consolation," said Mrs. Trenchard, primly tossing her head.

Her own apartment was furnished with the furniture she had chosen from the Schmidt mansion. Here she could draw ponderous draperies against the sun, and revel in mighty plush sofas, leather chairs, horse-hair couches and mahogany, and line her walls with what-nots crowded with bric-a-brac. "Everything will soil in this house," she said, grimly. "Servants will be forever cleaning and scrubbing. Dark colors are wearable, economical and do not show dirt."

Marcia had furnished her bedroom with nothing but a narrow white bed, a dresser and a commode. There were no carpets on the shining floors, no draperies at the windows. It was a convent room, chaste and pure and hard. She had not yet told her mother that she was to enter the Convent of the Sacred Heart of Mary in Philadelphia after Christmas. In the meantime, she secretly took Catholic instruction from Father John Brunswick of the Nativity Church in Nazareth. She thought of nothing else. She had already withdrawn from the world. Her mother's insistence upon returning calls and visits was endured by her with silent patience and meekness. She lived alone, in quietness and unearthly peace, reading her pious books, studying, walking in the solitude of the beautiful grounds, her eyes luminous with virginal and ecstatic thoughts. Baldur often saw her slight pretty figure moving over the sun-swept grass, and he was saddened. A life of love and completeness awaited her, if she wanted it, a life full of the clamorous and adventurous world. But she did not want it. Her soul was cloistered, shut away, shining with silence. When she entered the convent, her body would follow where her spirit already lived.

It may be true, thought Baldur, that every soul is dedicated at birth to a certain life. The unhappy are those who never find their own life. Marcia has found it. That is why she is happy. Nevertheless, he was sad. All that sweet youth and grace and beauty locked away like a flower behind stone walls! How had this child, of Anglo-Saxon blood and tradition, conceived such a cool passion for an alien strange creed, born of Jerusalem and Rome in inexplicable marriage? Faith was universal, but this Church had arisen from Paganism, had incorporated in itself this Paganism and more than a touch of Hebraic ritual, and had produced a creed and a faith distinct to itself, and alien to the robust factualism of the Anglo-Saxon. Baldur's German blood dimly asserted itself, and he thought: It would be more natural for Marcia, with her English and old Teutonic heritage, if she worshipped the gay Freya, the Nordic Odin or Wotan, the Tannhäuser-Thor. These are creatures of our own blood and our own flesh and soul, creatures of our forests and earth and streams and mountains, and their birth was our birth. Was there in Marcia a Latin or Hebraic strain now suddenly come to life in her Nordic flesh?

These uneasy thoughts mingled with his real pleasure in the mansion, which Franz, suddenly demonstrating his lack of imagination, had banally called "The Poplars." Baldur was especially pleased by the fact that Franz had frequently and persistently consulted him about the house and the furnishings, and Mrs. Trenchard complained of them without knowing their source. Baldur, coming out of his solitude, had actually gone to New York to purchase the furniture, and when he saw Franz's admiration, he was absurdly gratified. "Ah, I had to fit the furnishings to the house," he said, with sincerity, for the house pleased and delighted him. He had a large apartment for himself, which he furnished simply and with elegance. He shared, with Franz, a love for space and largeness and light.

The family moved into the new home in October. At Christmas, Franz entertained a number of family friends, very quietly, in deference to the memory of Ernestine, who had been dead not quite a year. He was very popular, and had many friends, charming every one with his amiability, his elaborate courtesies, his attentive and fascinating smile, his good temper and air of Teutonic kindliness. Moreover, men as well as women admired his handsome face and figure. "Not quite a gentleman," some of the older men would say, stroking their beards with consideration. "But a man," they would add, judiciously. Manhood was beginning to be regarded as almost as valuable as gentlemanliness, and though it was a heresy, and daring, more and more people looked on the idea with tolerance. It is true that Franz was not "elegant," and would never be a "gentleman of fashion," but these things were already becoming suspect even among the city elect as savoring of Continentalism. The opening of the west, and the production thereafter of virile and sweaty men, had aroused the suspicion, even among "gentlemen," that there was emerging in America a true American type, healthy, strong, unhampered and robust. It was becoming common knowledge that even in New York, the railroad aristocracy, and the old financiers, were graciously accepting into their midst even such unlikely characters as Lillian Russell and Jim Brady, and others of slightly odorous kind. Of course, it was all very tentative, but "gentlemen" were beginning to lose some of their sanctity and almost pious repute.

Relations between Baldur and Franz grew increasingly amiable and friendly as the months after Ernestine's death passed. It was evident to Baldur that Franz sincerely regretted his wife's death, that he found the sudden absence of adoration depressing, however much he had been revolted by it during Ernestine's lifetime. Perhaps remorse was mingled with this regret, Baldur thought. At any rate, he was kinder to his children, especially to Joseph, of whom he now seemed genuinely fond. He ceased his old habit of speaking shortly and harshly to Sigmund, and he punctuated long periods of complete neglect of the child with kindliness. Sigmund had a room of his own now, near Baldur's, and seemed freer and happier than ever before. No one but Baldur truly missed Ernestine. He forgot her years of petulance and enmity against him. He remembered her only as the young Ernestine, with her shyness, fragile gaiety, and quick light eagerness. Mrs. Trenchard remained with the family. Franz disliked her secretly, but she was convenient, and he was grateful. Moreover, she found no wrong in him, and admired him, which was soothing. He pretended, at the least, a friendship for young Richard, who had entered the mills, much to Franz's puzzled amusement. Mrs. Trenchard was a rich woman, and though Franz had not yet thought of a way in which he could use her wealth, he liked to have affluent people about him as potentialities.

The little girl, Gretchen, however, was loved by every one, even the sly and cruel Joseph, and even by Franz. His German instinct for children bloomed suddenly for this child, who resembled him remarkably. He delighted in her soft golden hair, her large blue eyes, her rosy mouth, and warm baby flesh. She was dimpled, very amiable, and exceedingly pretty. There was something of Ernestine in her shyness and fragile timidity. From the first, she worshipped her father, and, flattered and pleased, he spent hours in the nursery with her, singing German lieder to her as she sat on his knee, and even tucking her into her bed. He had never demanded any religious instruction for his sons, but now he seriously discussed the matter with Mrs. Trenchard, declaring that as soon as the child was mentally and physically capable of absorbing instruction, she must have it. As a preparation, he drove his sons rigorously to Sunday School every week, and saw to it personally that they accompanied Mrs. Trenchard to the Episcopal Church in spite of their protests and sullenness. "You've been heathens long enough," he told them sternly. On Holidays, he even accompanied them himself, sitting upright, attentive and very handsome in the family pew which he had never honored with his presence before. He contributed large sums to the church, even larger sums than Ernestine and her mother had given. The minister became his devoted friend. From the very first day when Gretchen began to form words, he taught her German phrases as well as English. As the months passed, his devotion became almost fatuous. He saw himself reflected in the blue eyes so like his own, and to himself he promised that those things which he believed had destroyed his own innocence would never destroy hers.

The Schmidt Steel Company, in the meantime, was expanding enormously. Franz found comfort in this. He was increasingly engrossed in the company. Once or twice he had attempted to acquaint Baldur with certain procedures, and was relieved when Baldur laughingly refused to listen. "Do as you wish," he would say. "I care nothing about it. Once a year, I promise you, I will look over your reports. But that is all."

No one knew that young Richard Trenchard was Franz's wife's cousin. He worked in the mills as a laborer with the other men. Franz soon lost interest in the peculiar conduct of the young man. He soon forgot him. He had a vague idea that Richard wished to be a writer, and was gathering material. But so long as no one annoyed him by forcing himself into his awareness, he was grateful, and did not interfere.

The lovely new mansion had its effect on every one who lived in it. Light, beauty, space and air contributed to a more healthy atmosphere. Little Gretchen bloomed daily. Joseph was less restless. Even Sigmund took on tranquillity and a new young dignity. He and Baldur had a plot marked out for themselves, which they cultivated. They had a greenhouse to themselves, also, where they could continue their gardening.

Franz, moving among his family with amiability, tolerance and good temper, was a pleasant stranger to every one but Gretchen. Even Joseph saw less of him. He lived his life in the mills, and, after Gretchen was in bed, in another section of the city.

Every one thought less and less of Ernestine. She was connected in their minds with the dark gloom of the mansion on Mulberry Street, which lay empty and dusty for many years before it was converted into a rooming-house. Only Baldur remembered. But even with him, the ghost of Ernestine did not come into "The Poplars." She remained behind on Mulberry Street, a disconsolate and weeping shadow, mournfully searching through the echoing rooms for her lost family.

Sometimes Baldur had his carriage driven by the mansion, as though to visit his sister, and comfort her. He would look up at the tremendous windows, blank, dust-filmed and blind, and he could imagine that he saw Ernestine's pale face looking out from her bedroom window, sadly and eagerly watching for Franz, as it had done many years before. He would half lift his hand in sad greeting to her. He had the strange idea that she saw him, and waved in return, and that she was grateful and less sorrowful.

CHAPTER 17

MRS. ETHELBERTA CHISHOLM shared a handsome residence on Goddard Street with a remarkable milliner, Mlle. Le Clair (née Murphy). It was gay and baroque, this residence, of white wood, with many turrets, grilled windows, and brass-decorated doors. It had no particular style, having managed to combine the most rococo Victorianism with early Regency and American Colonial, all of which gave the house and its furnishing a slightly incoherent air, more than a little disreputable, but very amusing and light-hearted. Everything about it was very expensive and plushy, from the draperies with their gilt threads mingling with the lavish embroidery, to the thick rugs and the many high-colored vases and mirrors. Mrs. Chisholm was reputed to be a lady with a "private income," though there were serious doubts about the sources of the income. Mlle. Le Clair, of course, shared the expenses, but her share could hardly have accounted for the two polished carriages in the stables, the six sleek horses, the two coachmen, two parlor-maids, cook and butler. Too, not one of Mrs. Chisholm's gowns could have been bought for less than one hundred and fifty dollars, and her furs and gloves and reputedly silken underwear, must have cost thousands a year.

The gentlemen of fashion in Nazareth and surrounding cities and towns knew of the gaming-tables on the third floor, and the pretty gay young ladies, six of them, who occasionally visited Mrs. Chisholm and entertained guests. It was all very costly, discreet, good-tempered and entertaining, and the gentlemen kept their own counsel except when with the initiated. No man who could not give the most impeccable references, including banking references, was ever admitted. It was a closed brotherhood. It would have been cruel to call this a house of assignation, for there was nothing hushed or furtive about it, or faintly criminal. It is true that none of the ladies of Nazareth would have dreamed of inviting Mrs. Chisholm to call, but this was less because of her musky reputation than because she was so "different," and not "quite a lady." To acknowledge even among themselves that Mrs. Chisholm was outside the pale would have given the idea that their own innocence was not quite intact.

Mrs. Chisholm, herself, had fiery red hair of doubtfully natural origin, and so lustrous and beautifully dressed that it had become a kind of legend in Nazareth. She was closer to forty than to thirty, and was a "fine figure of a woman." Very tall, of commanding bust, incredibly small waist, and swelling hips, round white arms and column-like neck, she was of impressive appearance. She had a round white face under her brilliantly red tresses, and a large crimson mouth, small nose, and flaming black eyes. Her expression was knowing and robust, full of laughter and good temper and intelligence, and when she smiled, which was almost always, she displayed the most wonderful white teeth, which even malice could not report were false. Her voice was hoarse and deep and booming, like a man's, and very loud. She had a remarkably profane and careless vocabulary, and used it to amusing advantage, so that she was as renowned for her wit and bon mots as she was for her chic and virility. Forthright, vulgar, subtle and alive, she was adored by the elect who frequented her house, for she was as shrewd as she was handsome, and as genuinely sympathetic as she was avaricious. Moreover, she kept herself well informed on politics, and more than one State Senator, party "boss," and mayor, came to her for advice, which was usually sound and penetrating. She knew everything. She had a fine library of the best classics, which she actually read. Her one regret, she would say frankly, was that she had been born a woman. She was a natural politician, a natural busybody, humorous, understanding, quick-witted and blunt.

She dressed as exuberantly as possible, or perhaps it was her vital personality that made even the simplest and most modest gown spectacular. She loathed black. Her gowns were of the lightest mauve, blue, rose or violet, lavishly decorated, and made of the most expensive silks and velvets. When she swept through the large bright rooms of her house, she rustled loudly, and an aura of thick hypnotic scent blew about her. Coarse she was, unscrupulous she was known to be; yet her every word, her every flash of eye and hoarse laughter, her every movement, exhaled such health and gay turbulence that she was compellingly fascinating. She loved jewelry, and wore diamonds on bosom, ears, hair, fingers and arms at all hours, and very lavishly.

She often said that "I have the loosest tongue. I tell everything." But only the obtuse believed that she told anything at all. Nevertheless, she had a reputation of finding nothing sacred, which was a reputation she had artfully created. She had long ago abandoned a youthful effort to be beautiful, and had resigned herself to chic, wit, and dazzling toilettes, which were all the more lasting and more impressive.

She had her favorite among the gentlemen who frequented her house "for a quiet cosy evening." And her favorite was Franz Stoessel, who had never been able to deceive her, and whom she called "a great scoundrel, a perfect rascal, a brute and a most abominable liar." But she said these things with a wink, and a pleasant, cynical laugh, a deep smile, and with fondness. She would have admired him, if only for his handsomeness and his extravagant gifts of jewelry and money. But with these he gave her real excitement and a humorous affection. "I can take off my shoes with you," he would say. "Bertie, you are good for my soul."

He visited her at least twice a week, and often more. These nights were gala ones for her. She would spend hours over her toilette, trying on various gowns and gems. She not only respected him because he had paid off her mortgage. He had re-created in her a youthful passion, which she thought had long been dead from satiation.

When he came, he joined the small crowds in the gaming-rooms, sometimes playing for discreet stakes, drinking a little, smoking, wandering through the brilliant rooms ablaze with gaslight, crystal, mirrors and the splendid gowns of the young women. He was well liked by every one, and was an especial favorite of the servants. But the men of highest social position in Nazareth, and even old austere Percival Hartford himself, who was a grim reformer in public and a foul perverse old rake in Ethelberta's house, felt that the evenings were incomplete without him. His affability, his good-temper, his affectionate smile turned democratically upon expensive whore or business associate, his manner of listening with sympathetic or amused attention to every one, endeared him. "A man may smile and smile, and be a villain," Baldur would say of him. But villains who are good-natured and amiable, equable of temper, and full of tact, were better loved than any serious man bursting with virtue, Baldur had discovered. To his cynical surprise, he had also discovered that Franz had a legion of truly devoted friends, loyal and fervently blind.

Ethelberta would frequently call her carriage when Franz appeared, and they would leave the hot blazing rooms of her house, and take a short drive in the cool dark evening air. She would put her huge plumed hat carefully on her red hair, throw her ermine or sable cape over her white damp shoulders, thrust her hands into her muff, and sit beside him as her satin-black horses trotted sedately through quiet and empty residential streets. He was very fond of her. She reminded him, in her vitality and health of comely body, of Irmgard. He enjoyed her loud hoarse laugh, her licentious tongue, the sweet strong odor of her French scents, and the glint of her eyes and teeth in the gaslamps. She was never tedious nor capricious, never bad-tempered or melancholy. Her exuberance was like a wild bright wind, full of noise, bluster and exhilaration. He told her many things which he never told any one else, except Baldur. It was curious that in these two so widely different characters he found ease and no treachery. He spoke to her as though she were a man, and by the time they returned to her house, he was refreshed and heartened, laughing so hard that his large fair face was crimson and his eyes moist. Later, when the crowds had gone, and the girls had retired to their plushy and silken bedrooms with their choice of the evening, he would climb the velvet-carpeted stairs with Ethelberta to her own chamber. It was warm in that chamber, spacious, filled with velvet chairs, heavy velvet draperies, firelight, candlelight, and rich with scent. He slept in her broad silk-covered bed beside her, and he slept as peacefully as a child, his head on her soft, luxuriant breast.

Tonight he came as usual, and after a while they drove away discreetly in her carriage. It was a fresh spring evening, silent, echoing faintly, as though the wet black earth was speaking, even in the grimy city. Stars shone thickly through still empty boughs. There had been an earlier rain, and the streets glittered darkly in the street-lamps, which were reflected back from the streets as though in a black mirror. The wind was very soft and whispering, moist on the cheek. The lower windows of the tall houses were dark, but upper chambers were yellow with gaslight. Against the dim sky, to the east, was a dull rosy glimmer from the chimneys of the Schmidt Steel Company. Lying back contentedly on her leather cushions, Ethelberta idly noticed that glimmer, and she said languidly: "You are busy at the mills, I see."

She knew that something was disturbing Franz, and astutely, she guessed that it had something to do with the mills. She was not surprised when he answered in an unusually surly voice: "Not as busy as I should like, curse Jules Bouchard!"

Ethelberta touched his arm with affectionate concern, and waited. Franz stared gloomily at the back of the coachman.

"We've been delayed four weeks, now, on the last shipment of ore from our Great Lakes mines. As I told you before, Barbour-Bouchard own and control the Philadelphia and Windsor Railroad, and we have to ship over it. Before I underbid that French snake on those three important bids, everything was very amiable and reciprocal between us. Now, he's getting impossible. He expressed his regrets that our shipments have been shunted on sidetracks, and left standing for weeks. He said it was a mistake, and regrettable. Very regrettable! We've found only one-third of our coal, and, according to him, a 'search' is being conducted for the rest. We are operating at only half our capacity. Other shipments are taking a devil of a time to reach us. In less than two weeks, we'll have to shut down, perhaps, and wait for our coal. Another thing which annoys him is that we buy no more coal from Sessions and Barbour-Bouchard, but he said nothing much about that when he was trying to get me to come in with him. And our orders! We can't fill them at this rate."

"Have you talked with Mr. Baldur about this?" asked Ethelberta sympathetically.

Franz shrugged contemptuously. "He is not interested, as I have told you. He would not care particularly if we went out of business. I am the only one who cares about the mills. I have this worry, knowing that that foul Frenchman will do much worse than this, as time goes on. He is hamstringing me. All with polite smiles and his cursed 'regrets'! He knows he has me, for they own the right of way, and the railroad." He laughed without mirth. "However, that is my worry. I shall find a way. Yes, I shall find a way!" and he beat his knee with his clenched fist. Ethelberta saw his profile, brutal, boar-like, and she raised her eyebrows.

"I'm sure you will find a way," she said, comfortably, laying her gloved hand over the large hard fist. "In the meantime, don't think of it."

He grunted, thrust aside her hand. "That is woman-talk," he said. "The mills are not a bawdy house. They are things for men, those mills."

Ethelberta was silent, but not offended. She listened tranquilly to the trotting of the horses, and breathed deeply of the spring air. Franz sat forward on his seat, his teeth clenched.

"Democracy!" he muttered, with an ugly sound deep in his throat. "Dog catch dog, and let the better man be damned! Ah, there will be an end to it, some day, and those who have the right to rule shall rule!"

"Dear me!" exclaimed Ethelberta, with her deep baritone laugh. "What is all this?"

He turned to her, and did not smile. She heard his hard breathing, saw the narrowing of his eyes.

"Under a better system of government, Schmidt would be recognized for what it is, a superior company to Sessions. Schmidt would not be hampered, held back, allowed to be hamstrung, by the whims and greeds and connivings of such as Jules Bouchard! The best interests of the country would be recognized, and the better company given first choice of supplies, and the right of way, and the authority to choose the best labor and hold it. How can a nation advance if every hog has equal right at the trough, though by sheer weight of numbers the runts might crowd away the stronger and the finer? Can a people survive when superiority is penalized, because to curtail the activities of the lesser would be to injure their damned fine rights? Is the 'right' of the individual more valuable than the welfare of the whole? Yes, says democratic government, believing that noses are more important than brains!"

Ethelberta chuckled humorously. She tapped Franz on the shoulder with her muff. "I take it then, my fine-feathered friend, that you don't like our country. Well, don't like it. That's your privilege. But you might tell me why you don't show it a clean pair of heels, if it hurts you so bad?"

Franz smiled slightly, but only with his lips. "This is a newer, bigger, richer country. It gives me what I want. But it increases my appetite for more. I serve it, when I serve myself. America needs men like me. Not that I care. I take what America has to offer, and I see no necessity to thank America. What a country this could be, with its enormous resources, its wealth, if it would only rid itself of the barnyard politics of democracy!" His smile broadened. "If I have a duty to America, it is the duty to help change her form of government into something more realistic, something more rational and intelligent."

Ethelberta snorted thoughtfully. Then she eyed Franz shrewdly, and not with affection. "Easy, my buck," she said, indulgently, but with a slight hardness in her voice. "I kind of like my country. Pretty fine place, I say. Room for everybody. Even buckeroos like you, with a pistol in your pocket and larceny and hate in your heart. Maybe I ought to be mad at you. But somehow I'm not. Know why? I think America's too big for pirates and bandits like you. I think she's too sound. You'll come and go, cursing the government and the country, but it'll stay, this country of mine. You can't hurt it. Much. Depends though, on the people, on how much damage you do. But maybe they'll wake up some day, and kick you mighty hard in the pantaloons. That'll be one fine day!"

Franz suddenly laughed, his good temper returning. He pulled her to him and kissed her roughly on the lips, his hand grasping her flesh under the fur cape. They clung together in a sudden violent gust of passion. Then he released her. His voice was thick and low, when he spoke.

"But what would you do without me, Bertie, to pay off your mortgages and cover you with furs and silks and jewels?"

She leaned against him, her mouth close to his. "Damn you, I love you," she murmured. She glanced quickly at the smooth broadcloth back of the coachman, and said: "You need a wife, Franz. A good strong wench. You need a woman of your own. Why don't you marry some one?"

He smiled sardonically. "Who?"

She shrugged, drew away from him. "Not me. I'm not hinting. I wouldn't marry you. You're a pig. And I'm too smart. But there are plenty of women, not very bright, but nothing wrong with that. See here: your wife's been dead for over a year. You can marry again, with propriety. Get married. It won't come between us."

He looked away from her, and she saw the gloomy darkening of his face in the passing lamplight. He is thinking of some one, she thought, with a clench of jealousy at her heart. It isn't me. Who is it?

Franz was seeing again the wind-swept hill, and a woman against the sky, with blowing hair and upturned face. A woman who was Irmgard, yet not Irmgard.

CHAPTER 18

"So," SAID Jules Bouchard, "he will be here within the hour. I anticipate some amusing moments. Very amusing. He is a hypocrite, but a hypocrite without finesse."

His uncle, Ernest Barbour ("the Old Devil"), thoughtfully considered Jules's last words. "Finesse," he murmured. "I once saw a very bad print in my grandfather's house in England. Roman, I think. It showed a man, almost naked, and armed only with a lariat, and a light spear. He was fighting a heavily armed man with a shield and quite a good big sword. I never knew who won the fight. But I bet on the second man."

"Touché," said Jules, with a smile, and an inclination of his head. "But somewhere, in school, I read that the first man frequently won. With his finesse. I've always preferred finesse to brute force. Besides, finesse is delightful to watch. This won't be delightful. German pig! No finesse, the Germans. That's why, in the end, they'll always lose. No imagination. Only vindictiveness—the good big sword. I would bet on the spear."

"I'm relying on the spear," said Ernest, pointedly, returning Jules's smile. But his ice-pale eyes were impassive. "This time," he repeated, "I'm relying on the spear. On your finesse."

"You see, he is coming to me, not I to him, Uncle Ernest."

"The German always does," said Ernest, unconvinced, and very coldly.

Jules shrugged. "German pig," he said again.

"Nevertheless, Jules, you must remember he is now twice as rich and powerful as Sessions. That should never have happened."

It would never have happened, thought Jules, still smiling, but vicious, if I had had a free hand here. But you would never let me have the hand.

"I have always believed there is room for every one," went on Ernest. "I was mistaken. There is no room for this man in this State, with us. With another type, yes. But he is different."

A clerk came in to announce the arrival of Franz Stoessel. Jules winked at his uncle, leaned back negligently in his chair.

Franz entered, large, sleek and composed, and Jules, always appreciative of sartorial elegance, smiled with impersonal pleasure. The blond beast, he thought. His racial aversion to the German rose in him like a swift hot gorge, thin but virulent. The German character was baffling. Even the French, who understood the human race, and thus every man, found the German soul incomprehensible, bewildering. But it was not complex; it was merely unhuman. He greeted Franz, rising gracefully from behind his desk, and extending his smooth dark hand. Ernest Barbour sat in his own chair near his nephew's desk and appraised Franz with his basilisk eyes. He nodded courteously, said nothing.

Franz had not been prepared for the presence of this stocky and terrible Englishman, the munitions emperor, whose name he reverenced as he reverenced all power. He had never met him before, and his broad pale face, with the light eyes, the short flaring nose and tight wide lips, was familiar to him only through the medium of newspaper photographs. He saw that Ernest Barbour was stocky rather than well-built, with the Englishman's breadth of shoulder and hard round body. There was a stillness about him, but Franz was not deceived. This will be a greater struggle than I thought, he said to himself. If he is here, then it will be very bad.

His affable smile did not decrease in charm as he sat down in the chair which Jules offered. But his heart was beating with uncomfortable speed, and he was slightly unnerved. His German soul was shaken by the presence of formidable might which the older man represented, and he felt like a schoolboy. He took hold of himself with conscious grimness, remembering that this time he held the advantage. The advantage, he said to himself, as he accepted one of Jules's invariably excellent cigars. He forced himself to look at Jules only, after the formal introduction to Ernest Barbour. If he did not look at the latter, he would be safer, he knew. His fair skin had flushed a little. He saw that Jules observed this flushing with sardonic satisfaction, and his cold rage rose and strengthened him. The thin French snake, with his smooth dark head and elegant woman's hands! A brutish surge of contempt flowed from him suddenly, and Jules felt it with his subtlety.

They conversed pleasantly, with glances of mutual friendship and amiability. Neither wished to approach the subject which had brought Franz to Windsor. Jules had the delicate and sadistic patience of the French. He could wait. He could enjoy himself, while the blond beast grew hotter and more disconcerted. The attacker, in this instance, would not have the advantage. Franz felt, rather than saw, that the silent Ernest Barbour had begun to move impatiently in his chair, as if he, too, felt contempt for all this graceful fencing on Jules's part. Franz was suddenly surprised. Ernest Barbour was the deadliest enemy any man could have, yet Franz was conscious that a strange twisted sympathy ran between them, which gave them a mutual scorn of this light capering, as though they both watched a goat cavorting, and found the watching irritating.

I will not be pushed, thought Franz, but he said with sudden polite abruptness, looking at Jules: "I am a busy man. You are a busy man also, Mr. Bouchard. You know why I have come. I've grown tired of waiting for my ore. I do not find your explanations satisfactory."

Jules allowed his dark Jesuit face to grow concerned. "You have not received those last consignments from your mines? That is very bad."

"Very bad," said Franz, brutally. "I do not need to tell you what this means to me. I have accepted your explanations. I can accept them no longer. For, you see, I know what lies behind all this. You think you can cripple me. You cannot."

Jules raised a deprecating hand, gravely. "But this is absurd! My explanations, and my regrets, were sincere. I sent out telegrams. I had special agents searching. I am sure, in a few days——"

"I will receive this consignment. Yes." Franz regarded him with the hard blue points of his narrowed eyes. He did not smile. His face took on the heavy porcine look of an aroused boar, and his thick neck turned scarlet. He sat in his chair very quietly, but there was a tensed appearance to his body, as though he was about to charge. "But what of the next? And the next?" He forgot Ernest Barbour, sitting in such immobile silence near him, listening, always listening.

Jules spread out his hands artlessly, and Franz felt a brutelike aversion for him, and a loathing contempt. "We," murmured Jules, "wish always to serve our customers. We have many. You are the most important. We wish to serve you satisfactorily. But delays and errors occur. That cannot be helped, Mr. Stoessel. You are making much out of nothing. I can only say again that I am sorry, and that I hope it will not happen again. Aren't you making mountains out of molehills?"

Franz, aroused now, struck the shining desk before him with his clenched fist. He leaned towards Jules. "I have no time," he said, and his guttural accent thickened. "This must stop." Again, he felt that strange twisted wave of understanding flow from Ernest Barbour to him, in spite of the enmity and the inexorableness.

Jules was silent. Then he said: "I have explained. I can't understand all this excitement. You are creating an embarrassing situation, Mr. Stoessel. You refuse to accept my explanations. What can I do?" He regarded Franz with vicious aversion, though his smile was polite. Then he dropped his eyes to his cigar, as though he was embarrassed and distressed. He glanced at his uncle, with a look that said: What can one do with a beast like this, with a barbarian like this?

"I know what I can do," replied Franz, loudly, with a threat in his voice. His thick yellow hair seemed to rise slightly on his large head. There was an ugly aspect to his face, and his thick lips opened, squared. "This is no time for politeness. I know what I can do."

Jules raised his eyebrows with delicate and bewildered questioning. He said nothing.

Franz threw himself back heavily in his chair, and it creaked with his weight. His expression was ugly, menacing. He began to speak slowly, almost ponderously, fixing his hard intent eyes on the other man:

"Do not believe that Sessions can supply the steel demand of America, and that you can keep down competition, and destroy it. Do you think you can destroy, or hinder, me?" Now he smiled, with somber and open contempt. "This country is growing very fast. I am already supplying more vital industries than you are. My steel is going West; I am building up that territory. New railroads are being built. I am already supplying the major part of the steel, and intend to expand indefinitely. You do not like that, Mr. Bouchard?"

"I am only offended at your manner, Mr. Stoessel." Jules's smile was imperturbable, ingratiating, friendly.

Franz waved a large, impatient hand, as though to brush away a fly. His manner became more and more menacing, full of brute force and murderous determination.

"I came here today because I know what I can do, and I shall do it, if you compel me.

"You know that the turnover of my stock on the market is far greater than Sessions's, and not only that, but I intend to pay a dividend soon, which will raise my prestige and my credit, and will be an immense advertisement for Schmidt. Mr. Joseph Bryan, who is my friend, will like that. You will regret that very much, Mr. Bouchard. He would do anything to frustrate you and Regan."

At the mention of those names, Ernest Barbour stirred in his chair again, and Franz felt the full impact of those inexorable eyes upon him. But he did not look at the other man. Strength was rising in him, strength which would bludgeon down this capering Frenchman, who was gazing at him with ophidian quiet.

He went on, feeling the surging within him:

"Ten years ago, you might have destroyed Schmidt. Now, Schmidt is the giant. You cannot do this, Mr. Bouchard. You are resorting to petty efforts to annoy me. I don't like to be annoyed, Mr. Bouchard. I want this to stop. And I shall stop it, today. I own 10 per cent of Sessions stock. I can throw it on the market, among other things."

Jules did not answer. His expression was obscure, but under his dark skin he had paled a little.

Franz said, more quietly, but with a deadly intonation: "You can annoy, but not hurt me seriously. You are too involved in diversified interests. Barbour-Bouchard, which controls Sessions, is too involved. I specialize only in steel. I have already pushed you out of the major markets, and you know I am already supplying much of Europe and South America with fine steel, far beyond your capacity to produce."

Still, Jules did not speak. He no longer tried to disguise his hatred and his disgust for Franz. Worse, he knew that he was being beaten, and right before the eyes of his hated uncle. Out of the corner of his eye he saw Ernest's cold faint smile, and deep, impersonal enjoyment. He thought suddenly, absurdly, of the heavy man with the shield and the "good big sword." He twisted, internally. He tried to smile courteously, with delicate amusement. But Franz did not return his smile. His large fair face was murderous, savage. Jules saw the openly clenched fists, the thick flushed neck, and he had the ridiculous idea that this man would not hesitate to seize him and bludgeon him with those fists, if necessary.

"Shall I go on?" asked Franz, and added: "I understand you are trying to buy up all the tributary small lines to control the network of the State. Unless you permit my ore to go through at regular schedules and at reasonable prices, you will never go through with that enterprise,—for the reason that I have already talked with some of the small owners, and offered to band them into a corporation. I have options on their property, for the company which I am about to form. I promised them that I am not so much interested in the profits of the company as the service of the roads, and the prosperity of the State."

And now he did smile, broadly, with open cynicism. Jules was suffering real and acute pain. It was not in his nature to attack directly, but always with deviousness. He had a hatred for blunt directness, for the open assault. It offended some malevolent fastidiousness in him. His precise and involved mind was suddenly confused, and he winced a little, as though physically revolted. Open threats nauseated his sense of nicety. He loved the game for excitement and subtlety. Now there was no subtlety, only the raw smell of open battle with a sweating beast with whom direct contact was physically repugnant.

Then Ernest Barbour spoke, with careful cold smoothness: "Mr. Stoessel."

Franz turned and looked at the speaker, and stiffened himself against his treacherous respect and fear for him. He made himself appear attentive, but uncompromising. "Yes, Mr. Barbour?"

They regarded each other in a little silence, as antagonists regard each other, weighing, measuring.

"It seems to me," said Ernest, calmly, "that you are ignoring even the most fundamental ethics of business relationships. You have come in, into this establishment, breathing fire and smoke and threats. It is extraordinary, to say the least. Very extraordinary." His eyes were bland, but full, also, of a glazed ruthlessness. They reminded Franz of gooseberries, for they appeared of the same glassy roundness and color. Power was in them, but, very strangely, it was no power that Franz recognized in himself, or could understand. He heard Ernest continue: "In America, Mr. Stoessel, we don't do business this way. Not in quite this way. We don't charge into the offices of others, shouting threats. We conduct business as gentlemen, not as Prussians." And he gave his slight smile again, which disdainfully challenged Franz to feel offense. "We discuss our problems. We don't wave our fists. Do you understand me? This is very distressing——"

Franz's flaring nostrils distended so that their red membranes became sharply visible in his face, which had become extremely white. But he spoke as coldly as Ernest had spoken: "You imply I am not a gentleman, Mr. Barbour, and, inversely, you imply that Mr. Bouchard is. You seem to think that I ought to have come here and listened to lies and promises, and then gone away, with expressions of mutual regard. That is foolishness. Nothing would have come of all that. I want something to come of it. I have no time to waste. I was really more polite than Mr. Bouchard. I paid him the compliment of believing him to be as busy as I, with no more time to waste than I. Was I mistaken?"

A hypocrite, Jules has said, thought Ernest. But the worst kind, the hypocrite who is frank. What does he want out of Schmidt, which he has made? Power? I have wanted, and gotten power. It is all I ever really wanted. He wants it, too, but as a substitute for something else, which to him is really more valuable than power. What is it? Is he running into a blind alley of success, away from himself? And he felt a profound contempt for a man so effeminate, so childish, so weak, as to prefer something nebulous to something enormous. Were all Germans like this, bellowing ferociously, while they howled dismally inside? He could feel only disgust.

He said, so quietly that his monotonous voice was almost gentle: "You were not mistaken, Mr. Stoessel. We are busy men. We are here to adjust differences. But your approach was offensive. I repeat, we don't do business this way."

Then Franz knew that he was putting him on the defensive, thinking it would embarrass and rout him. He smiled grimly, though his respect for this formidable man was not lessened, but rather increased.

"You mean, Mr. Barbour, that it is my manner you resent, and not my intention? You mean you would rather I had made my threats in a more gentlemanly way?" But you mean, he thought, that I ought to have been overwhelmed by you, and have left here with nothing accomplished.

The glazed look diminished a little in Ernest's fixed eyes, and again he smiled, but this time as though with involuntary amusement. He waved his hand. "Go on, Mr. Stoessel—with your threats, if you wish."

Franz turned back to Jules, and did not see the wry pursing of Ernest's lips, as though the older man were acknowledging a real adversary.

"Mr. Bouchard, I am a busy man. I have just this to say: I am serving notice on you that I want shipments on time, or better. No more sidetracking, or fictitious losses. I don't want the trouble of the tributary lines, but if you force me to take the trouble, you will be the final loser, not I. For instance, you have almost the whole monopoly on fine steels for arms and other munitions, and I haven't wanted it—so far. I might never want it. I have enough just now. However, I have a very splendid laboratory staff, and if I set their minds to it, I shall find a better steel than yours, for this purpose."

He stood up. There was a long silence. Jules had covered the lower part of his thin face with his fine hand. He stared at the desk. Ernest tapped the fingers of one hand on the back of the other. There was a peculiar expression of surprise, and impersonal appreciation, on his face, and even the shadow of admiration.

Franz waited. Neither of the other two men looked at him, but he bowed to Ernest, ironically. He was choking with his sense of triumph.

"I have the honor to wish you good-day, Mr. Barbour," he said, and walked quickly from the room.

After the door had closed behind him, Ernest rose. He was smiling as his nephew had rarely seen him smile, with an odd jocularity.

"You ought to have offered him twice what you did. Perhaps we might have gotten him. Though I never liked these Germans," he added.

"In this instance," mused Jules, smoldering with mortification, yet perversely edified, "there was nothing we could do. Nothing. He was thoroughly prepared before he came here."

"It is a German trait," replied Ernest. He did not appear annoyed at his nephew's defeat, which was his own defeat. "Germans never move until the ground is entirely ready. Then they move rapidly. This convinces the superficial that they are audacious, while they are really only doggedly careful in advance."

He tapped his finger thoughtfully on the desk and stared at his nephew.

"He won, this time. But somehow I don't believe it has made him happy. Nothing will. Some men pursue power for its own sake. He pursues it partly because he can't help it, and partly because it is a substitute for something else. A kind of opium." He smiled meditatively. "If I were as young as he is, and had done this day's work, I'd be walking on air. He is walking on stones, I'll wager."

* * *

The hot crimson flush of triumph which Franz had experienced stimulated him for exactly an hour. And then, quite suddenly, he was violently sick.

CHAPTER 19

THE AUTUMN earth and sky lay before Emmi as she sat near Egon's grave.

The grave lay on the low rolling hill, which descended, like a series of smooth rambling terraces, to the wide valley below. The valley lay in a mist of radiance, gold and nebulous, and the mingled green and bronze of the earth shimmered softly in that calm and radiant light. In the far distance, the trees were russet, scarlet or still vividly green, glittering gently against a sky of such a dark blue serenity that she felt her heart rise on a suffocating wave of silent joy. It was near sunset. The west burned in deep bronze and golden waves, which slowly rose like a tide towards the cobalt zenith. She saw the distant hills, like great shoulders covered with copper-colored, yellow or crimson shawls. The air was warm, still, without breeze or movement. She could hear the rustling of fallen leaves, brown and saffron, along the gnarled black roots of trees, against the leaning head-stones, and across the thick long grass, but no wind seemed to stir them. They were like whispering voices, speaking of mysterious things. Long golden shadows streaked the earth, and through them, at intervals, ran a squirrel or a rabbit. And sometimes a pheasant, brilliant of plumage, scurried through the light and lost itself in the dark brown caves of the trees.

There was a wide shining silence over the earth which no spring, summer or winter could bestow, a peace of fulfilment, of beauty and prayer. The wheat-stacks stood yellow as butter in the bronzed fields. A feather of smoke rose from the red chimney of a toy white house against the side of a hill. The sky shone and the earth shimmered in colored answer. No bird voice streaked the brilliant quiet with a pencil of bright notes. Not even cattle lowed in the stillness. There was only the immense and fragrant silence, the welling of intense golden light in the west, the deepening warm blue of the eastern sky. The shadows of the tombstones lengthened on the long grass. The earth exhaled a rich odor, smoky and warm and full of mould. The sun still lay hot on Emmi's shawled shoulders, and upon her jet-dripping bonnet.

Her hands rested on her calico knees, the palms upturned, and her brown face, her attitude, her peaceful blue eyes, seemed part of the autumn landscape. Never had she felt so happy, so serene, so quiet. Her thoughts whispered gently like the leaves. At moments they swelled to large floating shadows, like the few clouds in the sky, and were suffused with the vast and luminous peace. Her eyes wandered vaguely, filled with dreams, down a long aisle of golden trees, whose far tunnel-like end opened on pellucid mist. Down that aisle would come her grandson, very soon, to walk home with her in the evening. His mother would send him, anxiously and with concerned vexation, saying to him: "Grossmutter is tired and old. She has been very ill. She ought not to have gone to the graveyard today, but she will go every day. You are a big little man now, and you must bring her home, and help her on the way. Bring her as fast as possible, for the evenings are cold, and come very soon."

She smiled vaguely to herself, with deep content. Soon she would see him, tall and strong in his arrogant young twelve years, his head gilt in the last sun, his bare legs and feet as brown as the leaves through which he would walk. He would not run to her, but would come purposefully, whistling softly to himself, and pretending sternness when he knew she saw him. He would help her rise from the stone bench, and would tuck her shawl carefully round her. He would insist that she hold his arm, and would watch her every step with frowning solicitude. The absurd sweetness and strength of the little fellow, whose head was already on the level with her eyes! Her smile deepened, and her breath caught in her throat. She was unbearably moved. Her diffused joy increased, sharpened, and she looked at the sky, her dry lips moving soundlessly as though she spoke a prayer of gratitude and humility. Her hands clasped together tightly. To control the shaking rapture of her heart, she looked again at the autumn fields, sky and hills, and content welled in upon her with enormous peace.

It was good to feel like this, fulfilled, drained, yet brimming with ecstasy. She had never known it was possible to feel like this. The turbulence, pain, grief, despair, frustration, disappointment and sadness of her life were less than the dark memory of a dream. They were like the winds and storms and rains and tempests of spring and summer, which drenched the earth, made it fecund, and at the last, brought forth the harvest. The torment of plowing and seeding in the dark, turning the iron earth stiff with frost, assaulted by the bitter winds, doubtful that the seed would root, fearful that it would rot or be lost, despairing of the summer: this she had known in her soul. She had seen the young fields flatten under hail, and laid waste. She had seen the fruit trees beaten bare of the flowers. She had seen the rivers overflow the land and drown it. She had felt in her heart that it was all hopeless, this living, this hoping, this struggling. And then the autumn had come, and the harvest lay thick and golden in the valley, and she saw at last that all the storms and the furies had nourished the soil and strengthened the roots, and the seeds she had planted had become the bread and sustenance of the soul. So knowing, the hatred and sorrow and torment of her life seemed after all, only the sowing and the rains, followed by fulfilment and peace, and the barns full of corn. All that man had known, all that had caused his weeping, and, at the end, his joy, was carried out in the cycle of the earth's growing and harvesting, its tempests and its serene rivers, its dark afternoons and its silver nights. Why was it not given me to know before? she thought, with wonder. And then she knew that she had been blind, and the story had been waiting for her own sight to see it.

There was no fear left in her. She knew now that fear is the craven egotism of the spirit. She thought of the multitudes of men who lived only in the livid reflection of it, and saw, in its deathly glow, a distorted universe filled with hatred and death, with greed and madness, and relentless enemies.

She could think of Franz, now, not with the hot misery of years ago, but with mournful understanding. He had always been afraid. Fear made men frantic, made them cruel and ferocious, striking blindly in the dark. Now, thinking of him, she was overwhelmed with sorrow. Her hands lifted a little, and she whispered: "My son." The words were like a prayer, spoken humbly and softly. Tears trembled in her eyes. She wanted to tell him. But how could one describe the colors of the earth to one who was still blind?

She looked at her hands, seeing how knotted and veined they were, how brown and hard with work. The nails were stained and bent. She smiled again. Good tools, that had served her very well. She felt a fondness for them, and a gratitude. They had helped her sow and tend the farm. She thought of the richness of her land, and then of the faces of her friends and neighbors. They had been there, those friends, when she had almost died this past summer, full of solicitude and affection, bringing homely dainties and flowers from their own gardens. One woman had brought a quilt she had made herself, and another a shawl, and one a concoction of herbs from her fields. The Amish deacons had come to pray beside her bed, their beards dark on their grave brown faces. They hoped she would live, for they loved her. (How beautiful to be loved, not merely by the few in one's household, but by many whom, earlier, she would have called "strangers"!) But they would not feel sorrowful if she died. They had learned very well the lesson of the earth, and knew that winter was only prelude to another spring, and another sowing and another harvest.

She thought of foolish old Miss Florence Tandy, pottering in the kitchen. She was fat and wrinkled now. She had forgotten the horrors of her life. They were a dream which had gone with the light of day. Just as my nightmares have gone, thought Emmi.

She thought of Irmgard, not young now, but more beautiful than ever, quiet, steadfast, always working, always serene and full of golden dignity. Had she forgotten her mournful dreams, also? Or was she still too young? Emmi could not know. But she did know that her niece was happy and content, strong and gentle. The management of the farm was in her hands now. Hermann Schultz had married, and he and his comely fat young wife lived in the farmhouse and helped Irmgard with the work. There was always laughter and singing and industry in the house, always the smell of bread baking, and new milk, and apples and spices, and flowers and the odor of scrubbed wooden floors. Emmi could see the sunlight on the kitchen windows, and the red geraniums on the sill. She could see her hollyhocks, and the sun-streaked backs of books in the "sitting-room." All those books! She had given them to Siegfried. She had taught him German, and the names of the great German poets and musicians. But she had never taught him the terrible names of German warriors. To Emmi, these names were shameful and detestable. But she had taught him the old folk-lore of the old Teutons, and she had filled his young mind with visions of Thor and Odin, of Freda and Loki. She had gone with him and Irmgard to the old gray stone church in the valley. She knew that in his young mind God did not live in a cloudy and unreal heaven, but in the earth and the sky. She had failed with Franz. But she had not failed with his son.

She came slowly out of her thoughts as one comes out of a cathedral, looking about with bemused eyes, heavy, still, with the memory of incense and holy quiet. The sun was less warm on her shoulders and her face and hands. It still glittered on the tops of far red trees. Yet, there seemed a dim shadow over all that burning color and yellow fields. Was it really turning colder, and a little darker? The night comes early now, she thought to herself. She shivered slightly, drew the shawl closer about her. She looked down the golden tunnel of trees. Siegfried would come soon. He ought to be here. In a moment she would see him, hear his whistle, see how the squirrels and the rabbits scurried out of his path into the saffron leaves.

Then, a dull premonition struck her ponderously in the breast. It is coming again, she thought, remembering the horrible twisting pain which had assaulted her heart in the summer. Irmgard was right: she ought not have climbed the hill today, for she had been unusually weak this morning. But she had wanted to come to Egon's grave, as she always came. Here, in this shining solitude she could think of him, and talk to him. All her thoughts were conversations with him, and here she felt the ecstasy of complete fulfilment.

She said aloud, simply: "Egon, I hope it will not be so bad this time." The rememberance of the pain could bring her the only real terror of her life. She could feel it creeping upon her, like a deadly enemy in ambush. She clenched her hands on her knees, fixed her eyes sternly on the tunnel of trees. Ah, it was here now, in the open, seizing her throat, throttling her. She leaned against the back of the bench, fighting for breath, holding down her whimpering. It surged over her, a tide, a drowning black wave, and she fought in it, gasping, tightening her teeth. "Egon," she whispered.

Then it had gone, completely, leaving only weakness and a great lassitude behind it. She looked about her, dazedly. A veil of milky radiance had fallen over the landscape, and the earth trembled in it, as in water. But how supernally beautiful it was, like a vision of heaven! She was filled with amazement and rapture, and deep solemnity.

She looked down the tunnel of trees. The radiant mist at the end was brighter than ever, like a glory fallen from the sky. She could hardly look at it, so dazzling was it, as though the sunset had wheeled to the east and was shining down the tunnel.

She saw a figure in the light. It was Siegfried at last. She heard her voice calling to him. But she could scarcely see him. He was only a moving outline in the light. He was coming closer. But he was not singing. He was taller, and moved slower than usual, the light brightening steadily behind him.

And then a great cry broke from her. It was not Siegfried. It was Egon. And she saw that he was smiling, and holding out his hands to her.

CHAPTER 20

FRANZ LISTENED to the wild, soft, half-mad notes leaping along the wide white corridors of the upper rooms of his house. He had left his room to listen, leaning against the closed door. The lights, in their high crystal prisms, burned dimly overhead along the corridor with its soft blue rug. The children were in bed. It was nearly eleven o'clock.

He had listened for a long time, not thinking, only his emotions, vague and dark, rising and falling like chips of wood on curling waves, without voluntary movement of their own. When the notes became minor, a somber depression made his vision opaque, so that he seemed to be watching slow dusky clouds mounting and falling very slowly and heavily. Then it seemed to him that he could hardly bear his own melancholy. When they rose in sudden wild frenzy, his heart took up the beat, his pulses clamored, and he thought that the blood which had rushed to his head would surely burst its veins. And then there would be notes of pure and ineffable sweetness, like slowly poured gold, so poignant in their sweetness that he was certain he could taste their essence on his tongue. Something of Schubert's, he thought vaguely. But Schubert had surely never been played like this before, with such loveliness and clarity, such passion and ecstasy and sorrow. The formlessness of sound became of gentle yet terrible substance, so that he had sudden flashes of vision, blinding and disturbing. A tree in the wind, a fork of lightning splitting open a black sky, a flower reflected in a pool, the bright curve of a bird's wing in purple forest shadows, a river under the moon, a precipice outlined against flame, a thin white mountain spire against a green heaven, a face, an upflung pallid hand, a cry from parted lips, a gleaming torrent, or a red rock in a violet sea. He saw them all, in blinding instants, saw them dissolve into each other in dizzying succession, so that his head began to spin.

He felt the urgent sorrow which only those who truly know music can feel. Yet, with the sorrow was a sudden simple gladness that he had not yet lost the capacity to experience emotion. The keenness was blunted to a certain extent, but the impulse was there, trying to cleave through the callouses. It was absurd, childish, to feel such gladness, and his hard realism was affronted.

He straightened himself, prepared to return to his own apartments. Yet, with his hand on the door handle, he paused. He was angrily appalled at the sudden malaise which took hold on him, the sudden overpowering weariness and loneliness. It was like the opening of a deep scar, which suddenly gushed blood. His thoughts rushed to a spinning point. He must leave the house, though he was tired. He thought of friends, and women, and was sickened. There was no place for him to go!

Then he knew for a long time that he had never really had any place to go at all! Everywhere was just an escape. From himself. He had no friends. He had no one who knew him. He could think of no one who really knew him, except Baldur, whose playing had sunken again to a sad and melancholy meditation.

He released the door handle, turned with sudden determined purpose, and went down the hall to Baldur's room. He knocked on the door. Despite himself, he could not make the knock firm and quick. It was only tentative. The music stopped instantly, and Baldur called to him to enter.

He opened the door, forced himself to smile affably. Baldur had swung himself about on his stool, and sat there, slightly surprised when he saw his brother-in-law. Gnome-like, deformed, he was like an old child perched on the stool, his light hair heavily streaked with gray, his face pale and furrowed. But his eyes were still large, blue and clear, and unswervingly level.

"Franz," he said, courteously, and smiled. "Come in. Did you knock?"

"Who else?" replied Franz. He was absurdly delighted. Baldur was not reserved, as usual. He appeared almost pleased at the intrusion. Franz came into the room, and sat down. "I heard you playing. Schubert?"

"Schubert. Yes."

There was a small abrupt silence. Baldur waited, calmly. It pleased him to give Franz the impression of polite waiting, for Franz invariably aroused him to rare thin cruelty in spite of his understanding and compassion. He liked to see the faint color of discomfort rise to the tired and haggard face.

Even the expression on that face, worn, preoccupied and exhausted, gave him pleasure, while it newly aroused his pity.

Slightly disconcerted, Franz glanced about the room, which he had seen only a few times. Its loftiness and beauty soothed him, its open space and uncluttered shining floor gave him the sense of having drawn a deep clean breath. It is what I have always tried to produce, but never could, he thought. His wandering eye rose, fixed itself on Irmgard's unchanging portrait, and the old pang, deep and aching, divided his heart. He thought he had forgotten. Now he knew he would never forget. In spite of the uselessness of any renewal of search, he could not forget. But hope had gone. Baldur saw his look, the sharp tightening of muscle which caused Franz's jaw to grow sharp and hard, as though with unexpected pain. His compassion was gone, all at once, in the poison of envy and anger.

He envied and hated Franz for his handsomeness, his whole body, his ruthless health. He hated him because Irmgard loved him. He was amazed at himself for feeling this now, for he had not felt it before. Because I thought he had forgotten, and she had forgotten, he said to himself. But neither can forget.

He became aware that Franz was regarding him curiously, and he forced himself to assume an expression of serenity. "You like Schubert?" he asked, somewhat inanely.

Franz smiled. The mastery had passed to him from Baldur. He knew this, subtly, but what he had mastered he did not know.

"Yes. But I didn't come to discuss Schubert with you." He stood up, and approached the piano. His large strong hands touched the keys. They moved awkwardly, like the uncertain hands of a blind man. He struck a note or two, finally, then another, and another. The sound was deep, hoarse and slow, discordant, yet with a strange music also. Baldur watched the hands, fascinated, saw their fumbling and their strength. The sound became deeper, more imperative, yet weary. It was no chord he recognized. He knew it came from the distorted spirit of this man, always restless and unsleeping, always wretched and rapacious. Then the slow march halted abruptly, and Franz smiled down at him sheepishly.

"I'm rusty, now," he said. "But once I could play. Not so well as you. But I could play, provided every note was before me. My mother used to say I played like a mathematician. That disgusted me, and finally I stopped playing. Music has nothing in common with mathematics. I had the emotion necessary, I think. But I couldn't seem to express it."

He went back to his chair. He looked at Baldur, and said, lifting his eyebrows humorously: "Yet, music has always seemed to me the extreme essence of living. Am I extravagant?"

Baldur shrugged, smiling gently. He ran his hand carelessly over the keys, evoking a long and brilliant ripple of sound, like a laugh, mocking, yet not really gay. He said nothing.

"Aren't you interested in knowing the progress of your company?" asked Franz. "It is nearly a year since you last asked me."

The old malice and cruelty returned to Baldur. "I'm afraid I'm not really interested," he replied, with a bland and artless look. "I know you are very—adequate. You couldn't help being. But if you were not, it wouldn't disturb me much."

He was pleased at the surly darkening of Franz's face, and felt amused at the long slow glance of contempt. But he also saw that Franz was considerably disturbed. I have said this many times before, he thought, but he never really believed me until now.

Franz waved his hand with affected indulgence. "After all, only the greater part of your fortune is invested in the Schmidt Steel Company," he said, lightly.

Baldur raised an eyebrow. "My wants are not lavish, Franz. I could subsist on much less." He might have been speaking of something inconsequential, and Franz was both aghast and outraged. But he pressed his lips together, and only the hard blue sparkling of his eyes showed his anger. He recovered himself, tried to speak with a heavy assumption of jocularity:

"I thought you might be interested in knowing of a certain encounter of mine with Jules Bouchard. And," he added, with involuntary impressiveness that Baldur found very amusing, "with Mr. Ernest Barbour, himself."

"Please tell me," said Baldur, his renewal of pity making his voice interested.

He listened carefully and politely to Franz's narrative. Subconsciously, however, he listened less to the words than to the voice, and he heard its forced triumph, its false enthusiasm, its heavy and mirthless gloating. Franz seemed a stage characterization of a successful man, who mouthed words but felt no echo of them in himself, but instead was infinitely weary of the character he delineated. When Franz had finished, Baldur said, trying to make his voice coolly admiring: "That was very clever. Indeed. But you thought out the plan well in advance, didn't you? Men who make plans are never audacious. I congratulate you on your lack of audacity."

Franz was puzzled and affronted. He stared at Baldur's

calm face, trying to understand. "What is the use of being audacious, unless one is sure?" he asked, irritably. "Only fools——"

"Plunge in where good businessmen fear to tread," interrupted Baldur, with a smile. "Yes, yes, of course. Frankly, I've always admired audacity. But I can see where one can't, and dare not, be audacious with stockholders' money. They mightn't like it. Finance, I can see, was never for me."

He added, curiously: "There was a personal, as well as business, triumph in defeating Sessions?"

"It is something to defeat Ernest Barbour," answered Franz, impatiently. Somehow, his great victory had fallen very flat in the telling. Of course, it was ridiculous that he should feel this deflation after narrating the story to Baldur. What did this aging cripple know of business, of triumphs, of victories wrenched like iron out of mountains? He saw through the small end of a telescope, where everything was made minute and insignificant. It was absurd of him, Franz, to experience this acrid sensation of disappointment. It was alarming of him, Franz, to feel all at once that the victory had been nothing at all. Like the petty triumph of children playing with stones, and quarrelling over worthlessnesses, in the shadow of a great sunlit wall. The hideous and almost physical malaise, colored darkly with despondency, fell over him again, and he thought, with real terror, that this wave had been coming with closer frequency in the last year or two. It made him feel impotent and weak, flaccid and powerless.

It was this terror which made him exclaim loudly, as a man shouts over crushing breakers: "But how could you understand? It is nothing to you that I have made Schmidt the greatest steel-making company in America! You can't know what effort was involved, what struggle, what sleeplessness and ambition——"

"And exploitation, and skulduggery, and greed, and expediency," said Baldur, goadingly.

Franz flung up his hands with a contemptuous and hopeless gesture. "Words! Sentimental, childish words!" He relapsed into German now, as he always did under stress. "The words of old maidens, who knit under trees and sip coffee! The words of a man removed from life, and living, and a world of men. They annoy me, as the prattlings of my little children annoy me. I cannot tell how you disappoint me——"

You mean, thought Baldur, you dare not tell me how well I understand you. You are afraid that I will knock down your house, which you already know in your heart is a house of cards.

He shrugged. "I have told you, Franz, that I know nothing, and care nothing, about the mills. My life seems small and petty to you. And, yours seems small and petty to me. Who is wrong? Perhaps I have teased you too much. I am sorry. I really admire you, and the work you have done. But men like me often pretend contempt for men like you. Perhaps we only envy you. Impotence always derides, and secretly envies, potency. I know all this. But in some way, I can't believe your type of potency is very valuable. Perhaps that is my rationalization. Otherwise, my life might really become too unendurable. What I have said may be only a kind of self-defense. But let me tell you now that I am frequently proud of you. You have come a long way, with nothing but your hands, and your—er—ambition, to help you."

He smiled placatingly, out of his treacherous compassion, which always destroyed, at the last moment, his own ruthless irony. He could not always bear the results of his irony, just as he could rarely refrain from voicing it.

He thought that Franz would look relieved and flattered at his words. But Franz was silent. His tired drawn face became darker, as though he were thinking. You are a weakling, thought Baldur, compassionately. You are not an Ernest Barbour. Neither of you has a conscience. But you, at least, know there is something else beyond what you have made for yourself. Ernest Barbour would contemptuously accept flattery as a tribute. You accept it suspiciously as irony.

He said: "We can't seem to arrive on common ground, can we? Let us talk of something we can both understand. How is Dick progressing at the mills?"

Franz aroused himself. "Eh? Dick. Ah, yes. I had forgotten him. I have reports that he asks a great many questions, without doing much work. But they say he is very clever, when he does work. He is friendly with the other laborers. That is all I know. Have you really any idea why that whippersnapper went into the mills? It always puzzled me."

"I think he is just hungry to learn everything he can about everything," said Baldur, vaguely. He smiled to himself. Dick was less impulsive and heedless than he thought. Even an incendiary, it seems, can learn to walk drably and quietly.

"A waster of time," said Franz, impatiently. "His mother is wealthy. That is the trouble. If he had to work by necessity, he would have some idea what he wants. You can be sure I shall never indulge my children like that."

"I am certain your children will know what they want, Franz. I'm much encouraged about Sigmund. He is much less nervous and vapory, and has learned to control himself to a great extent."

But Franz was not interested in Sigmund. He had begun to smile. "Joseph is a rascal. His teachers can do nothing with him. That is because they are stupid. They admit he's beyond them. He keeps them in a ferment. You have always thought that Sigmund had more intelligence, but Joseph is two grades ahead of him, and the schoolmaster says that he is afraid that Sigmund is more than a little dull."

"The schoolmaster is a fool," said Baldur, annoyed. "But then, most schoolmasters are. They have a certain standard, and those who are above it are suspect." He could not resist adding: "Do you think it is a mark of cleverness that Joseph is cruel and foxy, and that he has been suspected of stealing, especially from weaker children who cannot defend themselves?"

Franz waved his hand. "He took. He did not steal. There is a difference. But you would not understand that. You never liked Joseph, because he is so quick and sharp. I admit he is a pig. But it is necessary to be a pig in this world. Your degree of success is measured by your degree of piggishness. Unfortunate, perhaps, but true. I have great hopes for Joseph. He is really very subtle. You would call that slyness. But time will tell. You will have to admit I am right, eventually."

His expression changed. "But there is my little Gretchen! Do you know what the little maid said to me tonight? 'Papa is tired. Papa must go to sleep. Papa sleep with Gretchen.' " His face took on a look of sheepish softness. "The child is only a handful, but she has sharp eyes. I am tired, I confess."

Baldur watched him narrowly. "The little one needs a mother. Some kind good woman. Have you ever thought of marrying again, Franz?"

Now his expression changed somberly. "I'm finished with marrying. I have had enough. You will think that insulting to your sister. But there is no room for more than a casual woman in my life."

He stood up, restlessly. Baldur slowly turned back to his piano, as though to dismiss him. He struck a few notes. Then his hands wandered feverishly over the keys. The notes became stronger, wilder, more tempestuous, as though to shut out his thoughts. They became a wind, a sunlit storm, a torn fragment of lightning on a hill.

Franz listened, fascinated. He saw again that wind-swept hill, with the tall strong woman upon it, against the sky. Clearly now, more sharply than ever before, he saw how the wind carved her full dress against her large thigh and heroic breast, and how the sun lay golden on her lifted profile. The woman who was Irmgard, yet not Irmgard.

Now the impression was becoming vivid with clarity. A child—watching the young woman on the hill, standing below her. There were others with him—his father and mother. His mother was holding his hand. He could feel the warm hardness of her fingers. He could hear her rather harsh laugh. He clenched his fists, and panted a little, concentrating so fiercely that beads of sweat appeared on his suddenly pale face, and his eyes, fixed on Irmgard's portrait, became large and dark with the intensity of his concentration. There was an impression of strangeness in his mind, of a small white house in the valley below, which he hardly knew. A stranger's house, which he had visited. And an unfamiliar countryside, drenched with light, a harder, more turbulent and less friendly country than his own. Yes, he and his parents had been visiting that country! He was hardly five years old— And the young woman on the hill, laughing, but bemused with the wind and the sun, a young woman who had recently lifted him in his arms, and had kissed him, and called him beautiful. Who was she? It was coming clearer now. A relative, perhaps, whom he had never seen before, and had never seen since. A kind of relative— He had it! It was the sister of Irmgard's father, Emil Hoeller! She was married. There was a baby, in the little house in the valley. What was her name? Why was it so terribly important to remember her name?

The tip of his tongue touched the sweat on his upper lip. His whole body was damp. The music which Baldur was creating was like a shouting urgent voice, full of frightful sound, like a voice that cried out behind a thick wall, the words unintelligible but coming clearer. His flesh shivered; his forehead pounded with swelling blood. He closed his eyes, sternly willing himself to remember.

The name. Yes, he had it now! Darmstadter! Young Frau Darmstadter!

Suddenly, he was deathly still, and turning very cold. The clue had come to him. The Mrs. Darmstadter who helped his mother on the farm. Was it she, the stranger whom he and his parents had visited? His mind rocked; his hands reached out desperately, as though clutching in the dark. Let me see, he thought, feverishly. The report of my detectives was that this woman was young. She had a little boy. It was impossible. She would be old, now, as old as his mother. In her sixties. The baby in the house in the valley would be a man now, almost as old as himself, in his late thirties. Who, then, was this young woman with the little boy, in his mother's house, this young Mrs. Darmstadter? Another relative?

Suddenly, quite completely, quite calmly, he knew.

He had the sensation, immediately afterwards, of his blood running out of his body, and an immense weakness invading him. He was obliged to catch the edge of the piano. There was a darkness before his eyes. He was not aware that Baldur had stopped playing, and was staring with lively curiosity at his white face and lifted, fixed eyes. He did not know that Baldur was looking at the slipping hand that gripped the piano. He was a man in a trance, shaking violently.

"What is it?" exclaimed Baldur, rising from his stool. "Are you ill?"

Franz looked at him, but did not see him. Baldur heard his hard, uneven breathing. Then, to his immense surprise, Franz shook his head, numbly, turned and walked from the room, like a man walking in an overpowering dream.

CHAPTER 21

I HAD forgotten how it is, thought Franz, as he was driven rapidly through the windy autumn countryside. He had forgotten how the earth smelt, rich, warmly dark, smoke-filled, and how brilliant the light of the sky could be, bright blue and infinitely vast. He had forgotten that the world was not drab and gritty. He looked almost with wonderment at the color of the landscape, and when, through the open carriage window the wind blew in scented with leaves, he was ashamed at the sudden tightening of his heart. He passed an apple orchard. The fruit hung red and russet on the weighted, twisted boughs. Heaps of it lay in the shadow of the withered yellow leaves. He reached out and caught an apple, tasted its crisp juicy sweetness. I had forgotten how an apple tastes, ripened on the bough, he thought. Cloud shadows flung themselves over the bronzed valley, streaking the earth in long dimnesses, and leaving the tops of hills in golden incandescence. There was an immense and holy silence over the earth, broken only by the fire of distant trees, and the faint sound of the vivid blue creek over which the carriage passed on a covered bridge.

A sleepless night of emotion had so drained Franz that he could feel nothing sharply except the silence and the brilliance of the countryside. He felt himself part of it. The desolation and dissolution of late autumn had not yet blighted the air, and the earth, and so it was that he felt the sudden uplift of excitement and promise such as one feels in the spring. Irmgard was part of it, just as she was part of this silent dazzling glory of earth and sky. For one of the very few times in his life he was unbearably happy, and it was a profound and simple happiness without thought or doubt.

He became interested in the neat snug farms about him, which reminded him, in their mathematical precision, of Germany. Yes, the Amish lived here, the "Pennsylvania Dutch," old Germans who had not forgotten old German ways. For the first time in many years he felt at home, that he had returned to familiar earth and familiar voices. The few farm folk he saw were familiar also, and he called out German greetings to them, and was answered in simple and friendly return. He began to laugh silently to himself, a little sheepishly, but with abandon.

It was a ride of many miles, but he did not find it long. It was a ride to a dream, through a world of tinted warm dreams. He felt no sense of hurry, or impatient eagerness. Fulfilment waited for him, and he approached it calmly, no longer tired or wretched or confused. I have been so damned tired, he thought, not with self-pity, but with a kind of amused contempt. I have had no time to live. Yet, he knew that peace was not for him. This was only an interlude. He was struck with nostalgia. It was a pleasant nostalgia, for he knew he could never be really satisfied with peace and tranquillity.

It was burning and radiant noon when he approached his mother's farm. Now he began to feel curious about how he would be received. Emmi would try to shut the door in his face again. He remembered her terror, and now he knew that she had been afraid that he would guess that Irmgard was in the house. He felt a surge of contemptuous anger, and outrage. All these years, and she had been within fifteen miles of him! All that money poured out in a world-wide search by stupid men, and she had been almost on his doorstep! But it was he who had been stupid, after all. He ought to have guessed.

It did not occur to him that Irmgard had changed with the years. He thought of her as the nineteen-year-old girl who had run from him in the winter, more than thirteen years ago. Nor did it ocur to him that she would repudiate him again. Without actually thinking of it, he was certain that she would come to him as simply and passionately as he was going to her. Now the years were only a narrow bridge, and not a landscape full of mountains and rivers and dark places. He was a young Franz again, and it was only yesterday that Irmgard had run away. He did not think of the "little boy," of his detectives' report. He had thought of him, but had vaguely considered that the child was some orphan, some waif, when he thought at all.

He saw that the carriage was winding up a narrow rutted road. He remembered that road, slightly. He remembered the house with its red roof and its red barns and silos, and he was amusedly impressed by the air of prosperity and fatness of the farm. Mother has done well, he thought. The only thing in which she failed was myself. She would still consider me a failure.

The hollyhocks were still bright against the side of the house, and along the white fences. The trees bending over the roof were saffron, brown and crimson. A pencil of blue smoke rose against a bluer sky from the red chimneys. And then he saw a familiar landau tied up near the gate.

He uttered a short hard word, and his coachman drew up the horses. Franz leaned out of the window, and stared unbelievingly at the landau. His face turned white and tight, and he could do nothing but gape incredulously. Baldur's landau! It was not possible! He heard the thick beating of his heart, and his forehead turned scarlet with fury. He thrust open the door of his carriage, and stepped out. The ground seemed to rock under his feet. He glared murderously at the silent shining windows of the house. He could feel the thunderous murmur of his fierce blood in his ears. He approached the waiting landau, still incredulous. There was no doubt about it. The horses were black and sleek. He knew them only too well. He put his hand on the satin haunch of one of them, and the horse turned his head and looked at him with equine recognition.

"That's Mr. Schmidt's landau," said his own coachman, with disbelief. "Ain't it, Mr. Stoessel?"

Franz did not answer. He walked rapidly to the door, breathing unevenly. His hand slipped on the knocker, then he seized it and struck it loudly. Then, not waiting for an answer, he opened the door and stepped into the narrow bright hall. He stared about him. He looked into the parlor, where he saw the sunlight on rows of books. No one came to him. No one had heard him, apparently. He heard the faint murmur of voices from the parlor, and the sob of a woman, muffled and heartbreaking.

He went towards the voices, and found himself in the parlor, with its blowing white curtains and its worn, sun-splashed rug and pleasant old furniture. Near a fireplace filled with flowers he saw Baldur, sitting near Irmgard. She was weeping. He was holding her hand, and murmuring softly to her. She had covered her face with a handkerchief, and was shaking with sobs.

Franz stood in the doorway, and watched them through an ebbing and deepening mist of rage. They had not seen him yet.

"Of course, you miss her," Baldur was saying, gently. "That is to be expected, and understood. But she was happy. She was always happy here. She told me so, herself. She was old, too, remember. She died peacefully. You ought to be glad of that, my dear."

Irmgard continued to weep. "I know! I know, Baldur! I am not crying for her. I'm crying for myself. Now I have no one——"

"O yes, you have, Irmgard. You have everything." He sighed, and smiled. "And remember, you always have me."

"Yes," she murmured. She dropped her handkerchief, and Franz saw her face now, blotched and pale, the green eyes swollen with tears. It was an older face, grief-stricken, browned with wind and sun, but a woman's face, full of dignity and beauty. He forgot everything when he saw her, forgot his rage and bewilderment, forgot the strange things he had been hearing. He took a step towards her, and cried, "Irmgard!"

He saw them start violently, and as in a dream, he saw the sun strike Irmgard's suddenly lifted head with its pale gilt hair. He saw nothing else but her changing face, which showed shock, horror, numbed amazement, then complete blankness. She rose slowly to her feet, and he saw the clear open greenness of her eyes, her beloved eyes, so well-remembered now, no longer a dream, but a passionate reality. She stood before him, silent and trembling, in her faded blue calico dress, voluminous and neat with its plain white ruffle at her throat. He had not remembered that she was so tall and so straight, or so slender, or so full of dignity and pride. This was no longer a girl, stiff and quiet with awkwardness, but a woman, and he knew now that it was not remembered old passion which he felt for her, but love. And feeling this, he came to her and held out his hands to her.

She looked at his face, not his hands. Her expression became cold and withdrawn, and only the sudden blaze of her eyes disturbed the calmness of her pale drawn face. She said nothing. She showed no fear, no confusion. But her hands clasped suddenly together in a convulsive gesture.

Baldur rose slowly, flushing a little. He held the back of his chair as though to support himself. He was profoundly embarrassed and uneasy.

"Irmgard," said Franz, again, in a choked and muffled voice.

Irmgard gazed at him steadfastly, silently. The corners of her white lips quivered, and her nostrils distended a little. She thought: I feel nothing. Nothing at all. Small blue lines, like trembling threads, appeared about her mouth, and in her temples. She was dimly surprised at the coldness which seemed to spread from her heart like ice-filled veins.

Then to her terror, as she looked at him, her heart plunged, lifted, dissolved in exploding heat. This was Franz, standing before her, imploringly, smiling slightly, his eyes saying what words could not say! She felt the lurch of her body towards him, irresistibly, as steel is drawn to a magnet, and she held herself rigidly and desperately against the inexorable pull. She said to herself: This is a stranger, and I never knew him. Surely this was not Franz, this man no longer young, with the gray shadow at his temples, and the deep clefts in his forehead, about his eyes, and his mouth. She saw, acutely, that he was harder and thinner than she remembered, that his fresh robust color was gone, and replaced by a duller pallor. This was a tighter, more compact man, more attenuated, harder and grimmer, as though he had forgotten to smile impulsively and easily. He was like the hated Prussians she remembered from her childhood, and girlhood, the Prussians of the cold and merciless eyes, the harsh jutting nose, the heavy drawn lips, the stony forehead, the high skeletal cheekbones, the carved sharp chin and the icy flesh. It is not Franz, she said to herself, while all her body shook and trembled at the lie. She looked into those Prussian eyes, and she knew that it was always Franz.

"Go away!" she cried out, in her despair, and stepped back from him. She fumbled blindly for Baldur's hand, and he took it in silence, and held it tightly. But she did not look away from Franz. Her face became distorted with fear, not of him, but of herself, and her eyes overflowed in wild sorrow and rising fright.

He did not move towards her. The changed face, which was his, and yet not his, turned dark. He turned slowly and regarded Baldur with cold vindictiveness. He was terribly shaken, and his breath was audible, and harsh.

"So," he said, "you knew all the time—you Schafskopf?"

Baldur was not angered at this insult, nor intimidated by the evil look of the other man. "Yes," he said, very calmly, looking at Franz straightly.

Franz doubled his fists, and his eyes narrowed so that they were only slits of blue flame. "And you never told me."

"No," replied Baldur, and there was a quick gleam of contempt for this display of wrath on his own face. "Why should I? Why should I have betrayed Irmgard, who wanted nothing of you?" He drew Irmgard a little closer to him, with a tender and reassuring gesture, as though to protect her. "You see, I know all about you and Irmgard. You have no right in this house. You can see she doesn't want you here. You are a trespasser."

He was disdainfully amused at Franz's expression, and not in the least frightened by the red shadow of the blood-lust in his eyes. He was more concerned at Irmgard's constant trembling, and the cold sweating of the hand he held.

Franz stared at him, and his mouth opened as if he drew an incredulous breath. He had lived in the house with this man for many years. They had been as friendly as it was possible for them to be. They had understood each other. Baldur had been his friend—of that he was certain. He felt a sudden sickened pang of betrayal; he was literally aghast at this treachery, he who had always been treacherous and devious. He hated himself for the ignominious shock of grief and bewilderment which assaulted him. He was conscious of a disintegration in himself, of wounds and sufferings, and now his rage rose against himself for this shameful softness, this ache. He has always been my enemy, he thought. Fascinated, he stared at Baldur, and he saw, or imagined he saw, an aloof amusement in those pensive eyes, and in that calm and level look, an amusement not untinged by an impersonal triumph and cruel curiosity. He felt himself, in the midst of his pain and aching, a contemptible and impotent figure of a man, defeated by a cripple who had never really been his friend. In his extremity, he told himself that Baldur had waited for this time, as he himself, in a similar position, would have waited.

To his own horror and disgust, he heard himself say lamely: "I thought you were my friend!"

He did not know of the wave of compassion that struck Baldur. He only heard him say coolly: "Why should you have expected any one to be your friend—you who were never a friend to any one? It is very impudent of you, you know. Very egotistic."

Franz had wanted to kill many times before in his life, but not with this overpowering obsession, this lust and hunger and irresistible urge. But it was not because of Irmgard he felt this. It was because of Baldur's betrayal of him, his deceit in maintaining a pretense of affection and friendship upon which Franz had come to rely with enormous simplicity. Only now did he realize what trust he had had in Baldur, what ease and relaxation, what relief and pleasure. He forgot Irmgard. He forgot everything but Baldur, and he was physically prostrated by the tremendous sense of loss and desolation he was experiencing in the midst of his rage and madness. Baldur had struck at him, silently, like a thin long blade held in a friendly hand, and even in his fury he could think: Now, there is nobody, in all the world.

His fists were knotted like stones, and he said in a thick and trembling voice: "You have always hated me."

Baldur saw the pain in the protruding eyes, the blanched lined lips, and he felt the weakness of compassion and gentleness in himself.

"No," he said, very quietly. "I have really liked you, at times. There was something in you, which made me feel very sorry for you. You aren't really as bad as you would like to be. You are rather bad; in fact, you are a rascal, a mountebank, a murderer, a thief, and a monumental scoundrel. But I always suspected you hated yourself for all this, and that, had circumstances been different, you, yourself, might have been happier not to be what you are. I always knew you were miserable. True rascals are never miserable. It was your wretchedness which made me your friend. Whether you believe it or not, I am really your friend, after all." He paused. "But I am also Irmgard's friend."

Franz was silent. The sick darkness in his mind clouded his vision. He saw Baldur glance deeply at Irmgard, and he turned to the silent and shaking woman. He tried to speak, but he could say nothing.

He heard Baldur say to him: "Please go away. There is nothing for you here. Shall we go together? Now?"

But Franz did not look at him, though his pain and rage against him was like a seeping wound. He looked only at Irmgard. He began to speak, in a stifled and incoherent voice, in German:

"I have looked everywhere for you. All over the world. I never stopped looking. You knew I never would. It is my stupidity, that I did not look for you here. There has never been any peace for me, since you ran away from me. Did you think I would ever forget?"

This was the young Franz now, pleading with her, and suffering divided her like the cleavage of an ax. She saw his changed face, his tormented eyes, the uncontrollable jerking of the muscles about his mouth. She wanted to turn from him, to run away, but she could not move. Tears ran down her cheeks, touched the corners of her shaking lips.

He approached her, very slowly. But he did not touch her, though he felt her overpowering nearness, and he was wrenched by his longing.

"Irmgard," he whispered. "My darling, my dear."

She stiffened, as though with terror that he would touch her. "Go away!" she cried, hoarsely. "I cannot have you here, Franz! I did not run away from you—you left me! It is all over now. I have had some peace here. Leave me in peace. If you stay, even for a moment longer, I shall really hate you! Believe me, I shall really hate you!"

Her voice rose on a louder cry, as if she was affrighted. He saw the real anguish, the real fear, in her eyes, and he responded to it, in convulsed pain.

"Irmgard!" And then his hands dropped, despairingly. Only his eyes pleaded with her.

He felt Baldur take his arm, and he shook him off. But Baldur took hold of him again.

"Franz, you must listen to me. Irmgard has had a lot to bear. Your mother—her aunt—just recently died. She is upset. Perhaps another day——"

Franz heard the words, but it was some moments before they made an impression on his mind. Then he turned slowly and regarded Baldur with a changed look.

"My mother—she is dead?"

He heard Irmgard's renewed weeping.

"Yes," said Baldur, compassionately. "About a month ago. Irmgard wanted to tell you. But she was afraid—of this. That you would come here again. That she—that she would be disturbed. Why don't you leave her in peace? This is doing no good at all——"

Franz was motionless, staring blindly. His mother was dead. Chaotic thoughts moved numbly and painfully behind his forehead. He felt no real grief, only a heavy despondency and regret and weakness. He ran his hand through his hair. He sighed.

"I am sorry," he whispered. His head fell forward, and he regarded the floor unseeingly.

Baldur sent a swift glance at Irmgard. The woman was looking at Franz with her whole soul. She had taken a step towards him. And then when Baldur saw her eyes, he knew it was hopeless, everything he had begun to hope. He could not bear it when he saw her touch Franz timidly, and then with a sudden quickening, as if all the hunger of her heart could not be frustrated any longer.

Franz felt her touch. He put his hand over the hand on his arm. She did not shrink away from him. They looked into each other's eyes, speechlessly, but with terrible and unashamed longing, seeing only each other.

"O Franz," said Irmgard, and the words were like a heart-broken cry, weary and sorrowful, but not surrendering. And in her expression were all her long years of loneliness and grief, of desolation and despair, of yearning and hopelessness.

Franz put her hand to his mouth, and held it there. She closed her eyes. He pressed the hand to his cheek, and then again to his mouth. She was trembling visibly, but an ineffable light began to spread over her face, as if final relief from long agony had come to her.

He dropped her hand gently. "Do you want me to go, Irmgard? And if I go, shall I come back? Some day? Soon?"

Baldur, watching them, thought: It is all over for me. So, he could not help saying, out of his own bitterness and pain:

"It is not so easy as that, Franz. Things—aren't renewed so easily. There is some one else. Irmgard, why don't you tell him?"

There had been a glow on Irmgard's lips, like a renewal of life. But now it faded. She gazed at Baldur with startled despair.

"Yes," she said, dully. She stepped back from Franz, and now her eyes were bitter and cold. "There is some one else, now, Franz. Did you think it could be so simple?"

She turned from him with swift abruptness, and walked rapidly to the door. She opened it, and disappeared. Baldur and Franz were alone. Franz regarded the door with bemusement and confusion. He heard Baldur speak to him, and even then he was aware of the cold malignancy in the other's calm voice.

"You have a little reckoning to make. And then, if you are only a half a man, and have only a little decency, you will go away from here, and never come back."

A sensation of approaching dread pervaded Franz. He turned to Baldur slowly. The dread quickened, and he felt his lips become frosty and thick. His throat closed. He did not know what he expected, but in some way he knew he would be profoundly shaken when it came, and unbearably overcome.

They stood, confronting each other in silence. Baldur was smiling faintly, cruelly. He was very calm. He sat down, and rested his delicate veined hands on his knees. He appeared to fall into some malevolent meditation. All his senses acute, as a sick man dreading renewed pain becomes acute, Franz saw the pencils of light on the books on the wall, the streaks of light on the white curtains at the window, the flowered old carpet, the smooth old mahogany of the furniture. He was even conscious of the serene brown countryside shining beyond the windows, and the blazing whiteness of the picket fence about the lawns. A hideous nausea welled in him. There was a ring of fire about his forehead, and the veins in his temples began to pound sickeningly, with premonition.

The door opened again, and Irmgard entered the room, holding the hand of a tall young boy, perhaps twelve years old, or a trifle older. Franz stared at him, unbelievingly. He saw the clear fresh face, the level blue eyes, the shock of yellow hair, the broad straight young shoulders, the brown bare legs and bare brown arms. It was his own young face that confronted him, puzzled and interested, and intelligent.

Baldur stood up, disturbed now, and regretful. "Irmgard," he began, "do you think it wise? The boy— It is not fair to him."

But Irmgard looked only at Franz, whose face was graying rapidly. Her expression was grim and ruthless, and avenging. She said nothing. She knew that there was no necessity to speak. She had her revenge now. She could not resist it. She was not a soft woman, but a hard one. She dropped the boy's hand, and stepped back from him, so that Franz and his son stood alone in the middle of the old room, in a deep and humming silence.

Siegfried was interested in this strange man who stood regarding him without speaking. A sick man, apparently, from his color, and his attitude. Who was he? An elegant stranger, in black broadcloth, polished boots and white dazzling linen. Siegfried was intrigued by the diamond and black-pearl pin in the crimson cravat, and the glitter of the diamond on the man's hand. His mother had no visitors but the neighbors, and Uncle Baldur. Why was this stranger here, this large and handsome man, a city man? Siegfried had seen the elaborate carriage outside. He was much excited. The man was looking at him with such passionate intensity. The boy saw the slack and shaking mouth, the wrinkling forehead, the fixed blue eyes. Was he some relative, some magnificent blood kin, come to make life exciting for him and his mother? He was fascinated by the man's silence, and intense regard. He smiled a little. He decided that he liked the stranger, who was tall and strong and personable, and most evidently rich and cosmopolitan. Yes, he liked him. He felt response in himself, like an urge, and he was more than a trifle amused at the perturbation he seemed to have aroused in the man.

He held out his hard young hand with a straight-forward gesture. "My name is Siegfried Darmstadter," he said clearly. "Are you my uncle? Did you come from Germany?"

Franz's fixed eye travelled mechanically to the brown outthrust hand of his son. He started slightly, as if struck by an invisible blow. He moistened his parched lips. He tried to smile. His hand rose slowly, and took Siegfried's. He felt the warmth of the boy's fingers, and involuntarily, almost convulsively, his grip tightened. He looked at Siegfried's open smiling face, his own face. But he still could say nothing.

Baldur rose. He looked at Irmgard warningly, concerned now only for Siegfried. In a loud careful voice he said, still looking only at Irmgard: "Yes, Siegfried, the gentleman is from Germany, also. He is your mother's cousin. This is Mr. Franz Stoessel."

The boy was delighted. His fingers were being crushed in the man's grip, but the sensation was warm and pleasurable. More and more, each instant, he was drawn to Franz, and the warmth on his hand rose to his heart in an affectionate surge. He spoke in German, in a slow clear voice, very formal and respectful: "It is a great pleasure to know you, sir."

My son, thought Franz. My son, he said to himself, in the bright and dizzying waves of a primitive exaltation. He said this to himself as if he had no other sons, and indeed, he did not think of his dark thin boys at "The Poplars," with their undersized scrawny bodies and smooth brown hair. Even Joseph, his pet, was nothing to him now. He remembered only little Gretchen, whose coloring, and whose large simplicity of expression resembled Siegfried's. And then, after a moment or two, he saw that a firm hardness underlay the boy's evident simplicity, and that the blue eyes, rather small like his own, were quick and alive with sharp intelligence and keen awareness. Is he a hypocrite? thought Franz. No, there was no hypocrisy in this son of his. But he decided, after a long full study, that there was ruthlessness, and uncompromising determination.

Siegfried's curiosity increased as Franz's regard became more minute. He wondered, uneasily, if this elegant cousin of his found him too rustic, too boorish. He colored slightly, with mingled embarrassment and hauteur. His mother should have warned him, and then he could have put on his Sunday clothes, with the new laced boots, and the long pantaloons. He became irritatingly aware that his overalls, rolled at the knees, were stained and patched, and that his shirt, after working with Hermann in the fields, was soiled. He removed his hand, and stood in silent dignity, his mouth tight with annoyance.

"So, you are Siegfried?" asked Franz, in an abstracted voice.

"Yes, sir. What shall I call you? Mr. Stoessel, or Cousin Franz?" The questions were simple and direct, without impudence.

Franz's face colored darkly. He bit his lip. He glanced at Irmgard, and saw that she was smiling scornfully. He stammered when he spoke.

"You may call me—Uncle Franz, if you wish, Siegfried." When he said this, he felt shame, regret, embarrassment and real sadness. He added hastily: "You speak German excellently. You do not learn this in school?"

"I don't go to school," answered the boy, with pride. "My grandmother taught me. She was not really my grandmother, though I called her Grossmutter. She was my mother's aunt." He quickened with surprise. "Was she your aunt, also, Mr. Stoessel?"

Franz's color deepened. He glanced aside, evasively. He saw Baldur's cold, amused smile. He said: "No, Siegfried. She was my mother."

Siegfried was frankly amazed. "But how could that be? She had no sons!"

"Perhaps," said Baldur, in a slow, smiling voice, "she forgot."

Siegfried turned to Baldur, and regarded him with a long disdainful look.

"That is not possible, Uncle Baldur. Unless," he added, shrewdly, "she wished to forget."

And now he gazed at Franz with open speculation, implacable and frank. Thoughts raced across his blue eyes. Very quietly, thoughtfully, he began to smile.

"She wished to forget," he said.

Franz smiled painfully. "My mother and I never agreed, Siegfried. That is all. Perhaps it is difficult for you to understand."

The boy shook his head. "No. I am not a child, Uncle Franz."

There was an intense and embarrassed silence. Franz, Baldur and Irmgard looked at the boy, with his smile, and his friendly amusement. He was studying Franz with sharper and sharper interest. Had his uncle just arrived from Germany? No, this was no "greenhorn." Where did he live? What was his business? He said: "You live in Philadelphia, Uncle Franz?"

"No, Siegfried. In Nazareth."

Again, there was a silence. Siegfried, then, remembering his mother, turned to her. He was concerned at her paleness, and her tears. He went to her, and took her arm. But he looked at Franz. There was something here he could not understand. But he was intrigued, and touched, by Franz's regard of him, so yearning, so sad, so strange was it. Why didn't his mother speak? He felt the coldness of her flesh through the blue calico sleeve. Why was she so stiff and silent, so bitter and antagonistic, to this new relative? Was she angered because this relative had not forgotten old enmities, and had not come to his mother's funeral? Why had he waited to come, until Grossmutter was buried? He felt a vast contempt for petty adult antagonisms, which seemed childish and trivial to him.

"Would you like to see Grossmutter's grave, Uncle Franz?" he asked.

Franz hesitated, and while he did so, Irmgard spoke in a loud angry voice: "If Mr. Stoessel wishes to see his mother's grave, he will make that decision himself, Siegfried." She released her arm from the boy's hand, and said peremptorily: "Hermann is waiting for you. It is time, now, to milk the cows. Go at once."

Franz lifted his hand. "A moment, please. I wish to ask the boy some questions. Siegfried, would you like to go to school, some school in Philadelphia, or New York?"

Irmgard gasped. She gripped her son's shoulder, glared savagely at Franz.

"No!" she exclaimed. "He is nothing to you. He is my son. He shall remain here with me. Your interest is belated, Franz. It is too late. It was always too late." Terror sounded shrilly in her voice. She pushed the boy from her, and said again, louder, more harshly: "Go at once! You must obey me."

Siegfried hesitated. He turned pink with embarrassment at his mother's tone, and his eyes flashed. But obedience was too long in him to be challenged now. He looked at Franz, put his bare heels together, bowed formally. He turned to Baldur, and bowed in the same manner. Then with immense dignity and calm, he left the room. Franz watched him go, saw the straight tall young back and the brown sturdy legs. My son, he thought again, with a peculiar twist of his heart.

When the boy had gone, he thought rapidly, his yellow brows drawn and knotted together. His first sadness and shame were gone. He held a corner of his lip between his teeth, and stared intently at Irmgard. Baldur rose, cleared his throat, tapped Franz on the arm.

"Shall we go, Franz? This has been an exciting day—for all of us. Let us leave Irmgard in peace——"

Franz ignored him. A spark grew in his eyes.

"He is my son," he said to Irmgard. "I want him. I must have him."

She clenched her hands in her apron, and regarded him with white contempt, and a hard smile.

"You have no claim on him. And, you would not dare tell him, Franz. No, you have no claim on him, either morally, or legally. You can do nothing."

"There is nothing that money cannot do," he answered, inexorably. He met her eyes, coldly, impassively.

He is acting, thought Baldur. He wants the boy, but he wants Irmgard more. Does he actually think he can frighten her?

He said: "Stop pretending, and threatening, Franz. You see, I know what you are thinking. You know as well as I do what a legal suit to get Siegfried will mean. You wouldn't care about the publicity, and the public laughter—no, you wouldn't like it at all! You know what the newspapers could do to you. 'Steel baron sues mother of his illegitimate son for custody.' Do you think Irmgard is afraid of that? She lives here quietly, anonymously, and her neighbors never read the dirty sheets of the cities. When it was all over, the law would still leave the custody with her. And what about Siegfried? After the hue and cry had died down, he would hate you, for what you did to him and his mother." He added, meaningly: "And any future association with him would be definitely ended. He would refuse to see you. 'There is nothing that money cannot do,' you say. But you wouldn't like what you would finally get."

Franz, knowing the truth of this, knowing that Baldur knew what was really in his mind, turned upon the other with rage.

"You filthy cripple, with your cleverness! Let me tell you this: money is potent in America. I wouldn't lose. I never lose. In the end, I would win."

Baldur had turned ghastly with affront and anger. He looked Franz in the eye, and said slowly:

"You forget. Yes, you forget. I would ruin you. Lift a hand against Irmgard, or her son, and I will ruin you. You understand this?"

Franz glared at him, breathing loudly. He crouched slightly. Red light blazed in his eyes. He was like a great wild boar cornered in a dark forest.

Baldur nodded his head, smiling grimly. "Yes, Franz."

Violence turned Franz's face purple, and Irmgard, terrified, stepped to Baldur's side as if to protect him. But Baldur was not afraid. He looked at Franz with profound contempt, not showing one glimmer of his real compassion for this man he had defeated. He took Irmgard's hand.

"Don't be frightened, my dear. He is not so impulsive as he appears. He would like to kill me. But he won't even lift his hand for a light tap. Do you think that even for you, or Siegfried, or his personal satisfaction, that he would jeopardize himself, and what he has made for himself? He may threaten you, Irmgard. But that is only to frighten you, to make you do what he wants. He won't hurt himself, if by hurting you, he suffers personal injury."

But, for a moment, as he looked at Franz's suffused eyes and swollen savage face, he had his perturbed doubts. Franz was really close to murder and physical violence. Never in his life had he been so stripped of self-control. He forgot himself, and his own care for himself. He wanted to kill with a primitive lust and hatred, self-forgetting. Baldur saw the evil mad emotions race like gleams of fire across those eyes and that unhuman face. He knew that Franz could kill him with one blow of his meaty fist, and he also knew that Franz was thinking this, in the depths of his primordial fury. But Baldur was not very alarmed. He regarded Franz calmly, holding firmly to Irmgard's hand.

Then Irmgard, with a choked sick cry, covered her face with her hands, and cried again, heartbroken. Franz started in the midst of his scarlet rage and abysmal hatred. He turned his large boar's head in her direction. His face changed, the strangled color ebbed. He listened to her weeping, and he appeared to be horribly shaken. He forgot Baldur.

"Irmgard—" he muttered. He sighed. There were great wet drops on his forehead, now. He took out his white kerchief and wiped them away. He appeared distraught.

Then, slowly, he turned and went to the door. He opened it. He walked like a stricken man. Without looking back, he left the room, closing the door silently behind him. He had gone.

The silence in the room was intense, as though a storm had withdrawn. Baldur put his arm about Irmgard's shoulders.

"It is all right now, my dear," he said, gently. "He has gone."

She dropped her hands. She looked about her, white and ravished. Swiftly, an anguished and grief-stricken expression widened her eyes. She wrung her hands together.

"No!" she cried, in an agonized tone. "O no! Franz! Franz!"

She ran to the door, flung it open, her dishevelled hair falling about her face. Baldur heard her running across the hall, into the bright autumn air. He heard her crying aloud, as a woman in desperate travail and torment cries:

"Franz! Franz! Come back to me!"

Baldur had never known that there was such speed in his maimed legs. He limped and flashed through the shining hall, caught Irmgard at the door. He held her arm tightly, in grim and panting silence. She strained away from him, like a doe from the grip of a dog, her face and neck stretched outward through the door she had opened. She was beside herself, and her cries broke wildly from her lips.

"Irmgard," he said, very quietly, and it was this quietness that caught her distracted attention at last. She turned her face to him, and his heart moved at the despairing desolation of her eyes. She had begun to tremble again, and she stared at him.

"No, no, Irmgard," he said, and his voice was even quieter. "Not yet. Not yet, for your sake, and Siegfried's."

She listened, but the desolation in her eyes increased.

"Not yet," he repeated. "Perhaps, some day. But now, there will be only misery for you. For Siegfried. I know. I know what he is, even now."

She was still at last, only looking at him. He reached beyond her, and gently shut the door. She looked at it, as one looks at a grave. Then he led her back into the room. She came blindly, like a bemused child.

He began to speak again, very softly, looking piercingly into her eyes so she would understand:

"You must go again, far away, Irmgard. Because he will come back. He won't let you alone. Then, Siegfried will begin to know. That can't happen—yet. It can't happen until Franz comes to full realization. And some day, perhaps, he will."

CHAPTER 22

MANY YEARS before, on a certain night, Baldur knew that Franz would come to him. So, on this iron-gray November day, he knew that Franz would come again, as he had come over three years ago to Emmi's house, for Irmgard.

For these three years, now, Baldur had been living in this house, after Irmgard and her son had gone away, swiftly, secretly. And all this time Baldur had lived here in peace and silence, visited only by young Sigmund on the holidays, and in the summer, for even in his hatred and frustration Franz had not forgotten the power that Baldur held over him. But Baldur had known he could not live at "The Poplars" with Franz any longer.

Baldur had been expecting him for months now, sometimes watching the long twisting road to Nazareth, sometimes glancing through the window at the sound of carriage wheels. What day he would come, he was not yet sure. But this day he was sure.

How he knew, he did not know, himself. Perhaps there was something in the ash-grayness and emptiness of the silent day, which seemed suspended, motionless and hollow, in time. All his life, certain days had certain qualities for Baldur. This day was like a huge, smoke filled glass globe, hung between heaven and earth, not spinning, not trembling, but static and cold, and filled with faint gloomy echoes. The autumn gold and scarlet and bronze had gone in a last blaze of deep blue sky and golden sun, and now only the black twisted trees were left, the dull brown earth, the fog-filled windy sky, the dun hills and the dim pewter river. There was an acrid smell in the dry bitter air, a sterile smell like old ashes too long on the hearth. The far landscape had a chill and deathly beauty, in its gray and brown desolation.

A few fowl, their feathers ruffled, picked listlessly in the barnyard. The flowers were dead, their stalks waving in the arid gusts of wind. The grass, bleached and high, trembled. The white picket fence glimmered through dead vines and dead hollyhocks. Where the sun should be shining through clouds, there was only a leaden diffused circle, and long, darker-gray, shadows roamed wildly over the earth and hills. Even the red roofs were dimmed in the shifting gloom. Smoke curled up from the brick chimneys, and Baldur sat before his fire, waiting.

But there was a good warm smell of burning wood in the house, and baking apple cake, spiced with cinnamon. Hermann Schultz's fat wife sang under her breath in the kitchen. A lamp sent a yellow glow through the book-lined room where Baldur sat. At his elbow, leaning against the arm of the chair, was his cane. In these last few years he had become more lame, and increasingly infirm. He was in almost constant dull pain, which he bore in silence and in his accustomed resignation. His face had become smaller, more gaunt and shrivelled in these last years, and it was the face of suffering, proud, patient and quiet. His eyes had enlarged as his face withered, and their blue steadfastness and sparkle had increased as his chronic fever mounted. His hair was almost entirely white. But his mouth still had its old sweetness and its old irony, which was without bitterness.

He knew that he was not to live much longer. Last spring, he had felt rebellion, and sadness. But now it was autumn. Something of Emmi's lofty resignation had come to him, but without its hope and mystic exaltation. He had no longings, no desires, no beliefs, in any future existence. He had lived his life, such as it had been. It was done. Perhaps there was a kind of immortality for those that desired it. He did not desire it. He had the curious notion that one, at the end, had the choice of immortality, or eternal extinction He preferred the extinction. It had more dignity, something of grandeur, something of nobility. Man, immortal, carried his indignity, his meagreness, his littleness, into eternity, and that was ignominious. What had God, the universe, time and eternity, to do with this small blind creature, endowed with shamefulness, nakedness and whimperings and petty evils? It was embarrassing to contemplate it.

So, silently, in himself, Baldur made his curious decision not to live again. He would lie down beside Egon and Emmi Stoessel; he would shut his eyes, and give to eternity and the earth the dignity of his extinction, the last pride of his final breath. There was magnificence in knowing that one was to be part of the earth forever. Strong roots would grow through his dead flesh, and the trunk of a tree would rise from his heart. That was the only immortality which could not affront the vast splendor of time.

He thought of Franz, hot, exigent, wretched and despairing, and he was filled with his ancient pity for this man who had sought everything, and found nothing but his own face staring at him, a frustrated tired face with dead eyes. He shivered a little. How terrible to be Franz! When the winter came, he (Baldur) would lie sleeping under whiteness. But Franz would go on, staring at his own face, for many years. It was a hideous thing to remember.

He heard the crunching of carriage wheels on the gravel, and turned his head. Through the large, small-paned windows, he could see Franz's glittering carriage at the gate. He smiled deeply and sadly. He watched Franz's tall broad figure coming up the flagged walk, as it had come on that day he had found Irmgard. The sudden thought of Irmgard still had the power to twist Baldur with pain, but even the pain was numb now, like the memory of sorrow. He looked tentatively at his cane, made a motion to rise, sank back. He now had the excuse not to make even the smallest courteous effort. Pain and illness had their uses. They relieved one of polite hypocrisies.

Dry yellow leaves ran before Franz's heavy footsteps, like little animals fleeing. Baldur heard the hollow sound of the iron knocker, and he heard Hermann's wife answering the door, and the sound of her German voice in respectful inquiry. Franz replied to her in German. His voice was somewhat hoarser than Baldur remembered, and slower, and hideously tired.

Then, though he did not turn his head, he knew that Franz was in the room. He could feel that urgent heavy presence, but all at once he felt that the urgency was mechanical and forced. He said, quietly:

"Franz. Come in."

Now Franz stood at his right hand, near the door. Baldur looked up, and their eyes met. They smiled in silence, these two who had, at all times, been simultaneously the profoundest friends and the most ruthless enemies. Franz's yellow hair had coarsened into grayed streaks, and the ruddy, purple-tinged complexion, which betrayed both high blood pressure and constant psychological pressure, gave his face a weary and bloated look. His blue eyes, always small, were smaller than ever, pointed, glazed, impervious as porcelain. But Baldur saw that the porcelain appeared cracked and faded. Thickened lips advertised sensuality, avarice and brutishness, and his nose had thickened also between the broad high planes of his Prussian cheeks. It was a powerful and implacable face, and still handsome, still affable. Yet the very power and implacability had the implication of disintegration in them, as though that which had inspired and sustained them had gone.

Baldur saw all this, but he saw something more. He saw the wretchedness, uneasiness and unquenchable misery of the man, no longer hidden under the well-fed flesh as they had once been. Franz had built his "strong city," and was now locked in it, behind the "high wall of his conceit." Did he still look through the gates to see the land of far distances from which he had shut himself? Did a man ever escape from himself?

Baldur was no sentimentalist. The pious and the envious said that wealth did not bring happiness. This was folly. Nothing brought happiness to men but understanding themselves and all things as one, and as a whole. The possession of riches brought no less unhappiness than did poverty. The poor man in his tenement was no happier than the powerful man in his strong city. Many times, indeed, the poor man was much more wretched, much more frustrated. He did not even have the consolation of the powerful, that at least in one thing they had attained success. It was much less blissful to sit by a cold fire than a warm, even if the warm fire brought no lasting happiness to the heart. Sadness in a great rich room, lit with candlelight, and fortified by the knowledge of good bank accounts, was more endurable than sadness on barren land and in lightless hovels. Nor was the powerful man less virtuous than the disinherited. He, at least, was free from the misery of envy, while the disinherited must consume his life in hatred for those whom nature had endowed more lavishly with the ability to attain.

If Franz Stoessel had attained only success and power and wealth, he had attained those things which are still the most sought-after by humankind. If he had not attained happiness, but only a kind of psychic frustration and despair, he was still the object of justified envy by those who also suffered frustration and despair, and had not even the consolation of the security which power and wealth can bring. He was no happier nor less happy than all the rest of mankind, who build their own private strong cities and look through the gates with hopelessness. The powerless and the powerful have a common anguish in being born, and in striving after those things which lie outside themselves. Only in himself, thought Baldur, can man discover the true kingdom, the true freedom, the true release from fear.

It was not Franz's power which saddened Baldur. It was

because Franz knew that outside his strong city lay his true inheritance, which he had abandoned.

Franz spoke in German: "You look at me strangely," and he smiled, as though amused. "Here I am, after all this time, and you only look at me."

Baldur continued to gaze at him with his quiet eyes. "It was only yesterday," he said, absently. Only yesterday, that scene of violence and grief and hatred. Yet Franz could stand there and smile affably and wearily, as though it had happened in another life, another time. "Sit down, Franz," said Baldur. "You are getting fat," he added, with malice.

Franz laughed, and sat down. "You look the same," he said. But he knew it was a lie. However, his old amiability, and habit of pleasant hypocrisy was too strong for him. The room was too hot for him, also. Hearty living had narrowed his arteries. He gasped for air, but was too polite to allow Baldur to hear the gasp.

"I was expecting you," said Baldur, in his calm voice. "To-day."

Franz raised skeptical eyebrows. He said: "Yes. We have a lot of things to talk about, haven't we?"

Baldur was silent. He felt Franz's narrow and penetrating eyes fixed on him. He felt Franz's sustained misery and desolation, and despairing hopelessness. Finally, the hopelessness was there, the loathing of self, the weary repudiation of living, the turning aside in nausea from the things which he had made for himself.

Then he heard Franz say, in such a low voice that he could hardly hear it: "I've looked—for Irmgard. Everywhere. Only you know where she is."

"Yes," said Baldur, clearly. "I know where she is."

"She—is well? She needs nothing? She and the boy?"

"She is well. She needs nothing. Do you think I would let her want anything?"

"No. I know that." Franz's voice was strangely gentle, strangely understanding, no longer jeering and contemptuous and full of hatred.

Baldur said: "And your own family? How are they? Sigmund at school writes me hardly anything."

"Ungrateful," murmured Franz, mechanically. Baldur said nothing. Then Franz, with an exhausted effort, said: "I've kept sending you reports about the mills. You are satisfied? Everything is as you wish?"

Baldur could not help smiling. "You know I am satisfied, because I don't care."

"But you ought to know everything." Franz waited. Baldur

did not speak. Then Franz began to tell of his new expansions and successes. His voice rose strongly, but Baldur, with curiosity, heard that the strength was forced, hypocritical, though proud. He is simulating, thought Baldur. But the pride is there. It is the pride of something he has done long ago, which doesn't excite him now. Franz talked steadily for a long time, but Baldur heard only his voice, drained, forced, lifeless as steel is lifeless, though strong. Finally, it was still, and the silence in the room mounted like clouds, higher and higher.

Baldur glanced at him quickly, furtively. Franz was staring at the fire, his clasped hands between his knees. He had forgotten Baldur. He looked at the flames emptily, and Baldur saw his face, stripped, desolate, full of gloom and wretchedness.

He said: "But Franz, all that means nothing to you, does it?"

Franz still looked at the fire, and in a peculiar voice, as though speaking in a dream, he said: "No. It means nothing. It wasn't really what I always wanted. I see that now." He suddenly started, and looked at Baldur with anger, as if the other man had caught him naked. "That is nonsense," he said, with violence. "I've always gotten what I wanted——!"

"But not Irmgard," said Baldur, with relentlessness, and he smiled, as if gloating.

It was that gloating look, that triumphant look which Baldur could not disguise, which sent the flames of fury leaping into Franz's face. This miserable cripple had defeated him at the last, but never until now did he fully realize what this defeat had cost him. Never until now had he realized that it was Baldur who had stood between him and the only thing he had ever really wanted. It was Baldur who had known all the time, for years, since his marriage to Ernestine, what he really was, what a constant torment was in him. He felt stripped, exposed, humiliated and shamed forever. He had kept himself so hidden, even from himself, so chained and put away in the darkness of forgetfulness, and now this miserable creature was showing him that all the time he knew the secret place and had often looked in at it. He must have been laughing for years! Laughing because he knew that Franz had never really wanted the things he had gotten, but had taken them because he was afraid! It was the knowledge that Baldur had known always of this shameful fear that was so maddening. Baldur had known what a coward he was, that he had built his strong city to fortify himself against the world, against living, which he had not had the courage to face. You are a coward, said Baldur's eyes, as they gazed at him. The builders of strong cities are always cowards. The builders of fortresses know that they have enemies, but the enemies are always themselves.

And then, with his rage, a cold dry sickness came to Franz, like gritty sand thrown on a leaping fire. It choked the fire, but it smouldered underneath. He thought to himself: Why should I care? I am tired. Very tired.

Yet, he must always dissemble. He thought his need to dissemble came from his pride, about which he had always been conceited. But it came from his terror of nakedness and revealing candor. His hypocrisy and deceit were the thin rags behind which he hid himself, in his fear.

So now, he told himself that he must not let Baldur see how tired he was, how hopeless, how indifferent. All men became tired, their life like stale dry bread in their mouths, only their surface senses aware of living, their inner warmth withered and dead like old fruit. Emotion and ecstasy were the things of youth; they passed like storm and lightning, leaving the quiet and desolation of death behind them. Baldur must feel this, also. Franz glanced up furtively and saw Baldur watching him silently, with a peculiar expression. There was something in that look, something of compassion, and seeing it, Franz was enraged again, and ashamed.

He said, in a dwindled and stifled voice: "You have always accused me of being a hypocrite. I never realized before what a contemptible hypocrite you are!"

He had thought that Baldur would laugh lightly, and was vaguely startled that Baldur's face suddenly became grave, stern and hard, and even evil. He saw that Baldur had gripped the arms of his chair so tightly that his knuckles sprang whitely to his skin. Seeing this, some primitive ferocity leapt up in Franz. He spoke in German, rapidly, with gathering madness:

"I can see everything clearly! You always envied me. You envied me for what I was, knowing what I wanted, with the ability to get it! You envied me Irmgard, my children, Siegfried—everything! This is your revenge on me! Why aren't you brave enough to admit it, admit that you could not struggle with me face to face, but must creep up on me and strike me in the back?"

Baldur said nothing. His furrowed face shrivelled, dwindled, turned gray. But he looked at Franz directly, as though seeing something for the first time.

And again Franz spoke: "Most of all, you envied me my desire. You never really desired anything, and you hated me because you wanted nothing, and I wanted everything. You were always helpless, because you found nothing valuable——"

"—and you," said Baldur, in a strange, low tone, "you found something valuable in what you desired?"

Franz's mouth opened, and then closed, slowly, and he was silent.

"You were the worst hypocrite," said Baldur, "because you deceived yourself. Perhaps you are right: perhaps I envied your self-deception. But I can see now that you deserve the greater pity, and perhaps the greater blame."

He averted his head. "I have always been sorry for you. You see, I knew what you really wanted; I knew everything else you got, at such a cost of self-torment, self-hatred, effort and suffering, such exploitation and cruelty and remorselessness, was not what you wanted, and wasn't what you really thought was valuable. Everything else was substitution, and a despicable one at that."

Franz laughed, shortly.

"At least, I tried substitution. You didn't even have the guts for that!"

But Baldur felt no anger. He said, quietly: "You are right. But now we are here in this room, together, looking back at our lives, and ahead, to what remains of them. Who has gained the most, you or I? Who has lost the most?"

And then there was a prolonged silence in the room, and neither spoke. They understood each other. With passionate relief, they had both discarded hypocrisy and pretense, knowing that they saw each other clearly without deception.

Then Franz said, in a queer, strained voice: "I think you have gained and I have lost the most."

He was silent for a long time, then began to speak very quietly, as though thinking aloud, and feeling his way:

"I knew there was something wrong, quite a long time ago.—It all began with my mother, and her dreams. I believed her. A child always believes his parents, in the beginning. It was not until later that I knew her dreams were silly, absurd and impossible. It was her belief that men could live together in herds, in peace and contentment. It was only the 'evil ones' who made this impossible. She forgot that man is by nature a solitary beast, a hunter, a carnivore, and such a beast's nature makes him unfit for herd living. Only necessity, because of his physical weakness, has forced him into herds. His whole misery is because he has tried to reconcile nature with necessity.—There are some of us in which the solitary is more healthy, more pronounced, than in others, more primitive. We must work in the framework of the herd, but we carry out our hunting instincts, our predatory instincts, in that framework. The herd suffers—" His words became inaudible.

"But you," said Baldur, softly, "were not one of the predatory ones."

Franz looked at him, and for a moment the old hypocrisy tried to conceal his expression. Then it was gone.

"No," he said, simply, "I wasn't one of them. I thought I was. But I see now it was because I recognized the predatory instinct in men, and it frightened me. Even when I was a child, it frightened me. I might have been a little more discerning than other children, perhaps. I began to see that the human herd was not really a herd, though it had the appearance of one. It was really a wolf-pack, hunting. It hunted together, but when the hunt was over, it turned on its own members and tried to destroy them. I can't tell you how much I was frightened!"

The old, half-forgotten terror of his childhood rose up in him.

"And then, there was my poor mother, believing that the wolf-pack was really a gentle herd of sheep! I began to hate her for her foolishness, because I could feel the pack right at our heels. I knew that the weak were always destroyed by the pack; the pack waited, its tongues lolling, its eyes full of fire—I—I was afraid," he added, with moving simplicity. "I began to tell myself that I wasn't really a sheep—I was a hunter, one of the predatory ones." His voice lost the inflections of the English language, and now it was the voice of a German who had never left his native hearth.

"I believed it. I had to believe it, because I was so frightened. I saw that I had to hate, and I persuaded myself that hatred was strength. That has always been the curse of the German, his belief that hatred is strong. That is because he is afraid, and has no real defense against the packs that roam the rest of the world. He has no spiritual fortitude. He believes he must hate and destroy, all in a rapture of terrified hysteria, when all the time he is only a docile herd animal threatened by the packs. And in his hysteria there is a great danger to all the rest of the world, which won't let him munch with his herd— His very ferocity is only terror and panic."

He continued, flatly, without emotion: "I began to hate my mother when I was very young, for she seemed silly to me, and blind. I began to see how the pack had hunted her, and my father, and my uncle, Irmgard's father, and all the other poor creatures who believed that wolves were really men, and needed only a kind of St. Francis to lead them. Dozens of these poor gentle things came to our house in Germany, with shining eyes and with hot noble words in their mouths. I began to despise them. They frightened me, because I saw how defenseless they were against the packs, and I knew I had to leave them or the pack would be after me, too. I had the choice between the herd and the pack, and I chose the pack."

He sighed. He stood up and faced the fire, as if to hide his face.

"But the hunting never gave me any peace, or any satisfaction. I was driven by my fear, only.—I've met many hunters, who really liked to hunt, and found fulfillment in it. Men like Ernest Barbour, Jules Bouchard, Jay Regan and Joseph Bryan. I've envied them, and hated them. Sometimes I used to wonder if they really didn't feel like myself, when they were alone. But later, I knew they didn't. They were the true wolves; they had fulfilled themselves, and they were happy. I wasn't one of them."

He paused, and then said, suddenly, sharply: "But I would do it over again! I would have been just as miserable, with the herd! Because I would have been much more frightened——"

"And you are never frightened, now?" asked Baldur, very softly.

Franz was silent a moment. Then he said: "Yes, I am still frightened. I can't stop. I keep thinking that perhaps I haven't made myself strong enough to keep the pack off. What if there is a war, or a revolution, or a great social upheaval? What if I lose everything, then?—We've got to keep the status quo, men like me, or the pack will get us after all."

"And you don't think there are greater strengths than money, Franz?" Baldur's tone was very gentle. "Fortitudes? Faiths? Acceptances? Inner integrity?"

Franz turned his head and looked at him, and for a moment his expression was derisive. Then it changed. He shook his head in weary negation. "If there are, I don't know them. Once—I thought I did. Now it is too late." He said, suddenly: "What about you? Have you any of them?"

Baldur smiled sadly. "Every man must make his own compromise with reality. I made mine. I built a strong city, too. A graveyard, where nothing could disturb me." He added: "It was even more vulnerable than yours."

They looked at each other, as though both had called out; and now there was nothing but understanding in their eyes. Involuntarily, they held out their hands to each other, and they met, slowly, firmly, tightly, like the grasp of kinsmen on a lonely road in the heart of a strange and frightful country.

Then, as their hands still met, Baldur smiled a little, and said:

"I think Irmgard would like to come home, now. Yes, I am sure she would like to come home to you, Franz."